PENGUIN ENGLISH LIBRARY

BYRON: SELECTED PROSE

Peter Gunn was born in 1914 in Sydney, Australia,
read classics at Melbourne University. Before the
he travelled extensively in Europe. After the
during which he served in the Rifle Brigade, he
Moral Sciences at Trinity College, Cambridge.
was lecturer at the Royal Military Academy Sa
hurst, 1949–56, a post which he resigned in orde.
devote himself to writing. He now lives in Swaledale,
Yorkshire.

Mr Gunn has written several books, which include
*A Concise History of Italy, My Dearest Augusta: A
Biography of Augusta Leigh, Byron's half-sister, The
Actons* and *Napoleon's Little Pest: The Duchess of
Abrantès.*

BYRON:
SELECTED PROSE

Edited, with notes and
some biographical details,
by Peter Gunn

PENGUIN BOOKS

Penguin Books Ltd, Harmondsworth, Middlesex, England
Penguin Books, 625 Madison Avenue, New York, New York 10022, U.S.A.
Penguin Books Australia Ltd, Ringwood, Victoria, Australia
Penguin Books Canada Ltd, 2801 John Street, Markham, Ontario, Canada L3R 1B4
Penguin Books (N.Z.) Ltd, 182–190 Wairau Road, Auckland 10, New Zealand

—

This collection first published in Penguin English Library 1972
Reprinted 1982

Made and printed in Singapore by
Richard Clay (S.E.Asia) Pte Ltd
Set in Monotype Times

CONTENTS

PREFACE

THE chief source for this selection from Byron's prose has been *The Works of Lord Byron: Letters and Journals*, edited by Rowland E. Prothero (Lord Ernle) in six volumes, 1898–1901. Further, for many letters not published by Prothero – and this includes Byron's side of the fascinating and revealing correspondence with Lady Melbourne – the editor has had recourse to *Lord Byron's Correspondence*, edited by John Murray in two volumes, 1922. These two main sources have been supplemented by reference to *Byron: A Self Portrait*, edited by Peter Quennell, in two volumes, 1956. For additional matter he has consulted *The Life and Letters of Anne Isabella, Lady Noel Byron* by Ethel Coburn Mayne, 1929, and *Byron: A Biography* by Leslie A. Marchand, three volumes, 1957.

It is to be hoped that the gaps that appear in the text will be filled when the publishing house of Messrs John Murray, so intimately connected with Byron and to which every student of Byron is so deeply in debt, brings out the proposed complete edition of his works in, it is envisaged, the not so remote future. In a few gaps, where for one reason or another the editor has felt confident to supply a missing word, the addition is enclosed in square brackets.

For permission to include letters at present in copyright the editor and publishers are indebted to the executors of the late Sir John Murray, to Mr Peter Quennell, to Messrs A. P. Watt, the representatives of Professor Marchand, and above all to Mr John Grey Murray, who has also been most kind and helpful in other ways.

INTRODUCTION

WRITING in 1818, Matthew Arnold prophesied that by the turn of the year 1900 the first two names in an assessment of English poets of the preceding century would be those of Wordsworth and Byron. Time has not borne out this judgement; contemporary taste would almost universally place the poetic achievement of Keats higher than that of Byron. Nevertheless, when we survey Byron's work as a whole, the prose as well as the poetry – viewed in conjunction with his life and its crowning culmination at Missolonghi – we cannot fail to recognize that the stature of the artist and the man has grown with the years. Byron today, on a balanced evaluation, is rated among the greatest figures of his century – an estimate of his position, incidentally, made in his own day (with the perspicuity of genius) by Goethe. The impact of Byron's personality on his contemporaries was so powerful as to blind many; only some of those closest to him could perceive his virtues; and his patrician contempt of the philistines restricted him in disabusing those who saw fit only to abuse him. When he did take up his pen in his own defence, as in the spirited 'Reply to Blackwood's', party feeling and outraged morality alike saw to it that his words went largely unheeded.

The reappraisal of Byron by modern critics has reversed many of the moral strictures formerly levelled against him; in fact, in the work of Professor G. Wilson Knight it has reached a point very close to apotheosis. If much of Byron's poetry is autobiographical, yet there were forces present in its writing which necessarily obscure the more personal elements. 'In rhyme', he wrote, 'I can keep more away from facts; but the thought always runs through, through . . . yes, yes, through.' It is rather in the published occasional articles, in the remaining journals, which are a record at certain periods of his thoughts, reminiscences and day-to-day activities (the memoirs having been destroyed by too zealous well-wishers), and especially in the splendid letters addressed to his intimate friends that we seem to come into the presence of the actual man, and find there revealed the rich, generous, vehement, caustic, ironic, playful, loving – and above all else – humane nature, that was so essentially Byron's. A just appreciation of Byron, therefore, requires a knowledge of his prose works. As a letter-writer he stands very high, among the highest, so that they may be read not only for their inherent interest (the insight they give us into a remarkable personality), but also for the pleasure derived from their literary merit.

George Gordon Byron was born in London on 22nd January 1788, at 16 Holles Street, a modest but decent lodging house, which has since been demolished to make way for the Oxford Street store of Messrs John Lewis. On both sides of the family his heredity was marked by characteristics of some mental instability, which was manifested in acts of violence, in wild self-indulgence and in a total disregard of social responsibility; and the effects of these hereditary factors would not have been lessened by the peculiar circumstances of his early environment. The Byrons claimed descent from Norman followers of William the Conqueror, who rewarded their services by the grant of large estates in the Midlands. At the dissolution of the monasteries Sir John Byron acquired the Priory of Newstead in Nottinghamshire. During the Civil War the Byrons were Royalist to a man, a later Sir John being created Baron Byron of Rochdale by Charles I in 1643. The victory of the Parliamentarians cost Lord Byron his estates, and loyally he followed Charles II into exile. At the Restoration his successor, Richard, second Lord Byron, retrieved part of the family property by repurchase. In 1720 William, the fourth Lord, married as his third wife Frances Berkeley, daughter of William Lord Berkeley, of whose six children three survived: Isabella, the eldest, who married the fourth Earl of Carlisle; William, the later fifth Lord Byron; and John, who became an admiral in the Royal Navy ('Fairweather Jack'), the poet's grandfather.

It was with William, fifth Lord Byron, who succeeded to the title at the age of fourteen in 1736, that the wildness in the Byron strain first clearly showed itself. He became well known in London and in the country for his luxurious manner of living, and for his lack of principle when his will or tastes were thwarted. In London his reputation was that of a rake; but it was at Newstead, where he constructed miniature forts and 'follies' in which he held his gay parties, that there grew up the legend of the 'Wicked Lord'. In 1765 he fought a duel in a London tavern with his neighbour and kinsman, William Chaworth of Annesley Hall, who received a wound from which he died next day. Brought to trial by his peers, Lord Byron was found guilty of manslaughter, but was released from prison on some technicality of an ancient statute. Thereupon he retired to Newstead, where he lived out his embittered days, after his wife abandoned him, and his only son eloped with a cousin. His eccentricities and whims were provided for by his housekeeper 'Lady Betsy' and his servant Joe Murray, who lived on to serve his heir, George Gordon Byron, when he succeeded as the sixth Lord Byron in 1798.

The 'Wicked Lord's' errant son had died in 1776, leaving also an only son, another William, who was killed in Corsica in 1794. The title thus passed through the descendants of the 'Wicked Lord's' brother, Admiral John Byron ('Fairweather Jack'), whose eldest son, likewise named John, was George Gordon's father. Born in 1756, John Byron, who grew up a handsome, profligate spendthrift, was commissioned in the Guards, and saw some service in America. His amorous exploits on his return to London had earned him the name of 'Mad Jack', and possibly his father (no prude himself) had already seen fit to disinherit him, when at the age of twenty-two he carried off the beautiful, rich and cultivated Amelia, Lady Carmarthen, wife of the future fifth Duke of Leeds, and Baroness Conyers in her own right. A divorce followed; the couple were married in 1779, and went to live in Paris, where their sole surviving child, Augusta Mary Byron, was born in 1784. Amelia Byron died soon after Augusta's birth. His wife's income having ceased with her death, the impoverished Jack Byron returned to England to find himself an heiress, which he speedily achieved, marrying Catherine Gordon of Gight in Bath in May 1785.

The Gordons of Gight were a branch of the numerous Gordon

11

clan, the family being descended from the marriage of Annabella
Stuart, daughter of James I of Scotland, to George, the second
Earl of Huntley. The Gight Gordons were a lawless, brutal race,
whose turbulence and disrespect for authority frequently brought
them into trouble with the government. Catherine's father,
George Gordon, the twelfth laird, was suspected of suicide (as
indeed was her grandfather), and the child, whose mother had
died early, was brought up by her Duff relations. She could have
had few attractions apart from her small fortune, since she was
plain, dumpy, ill-educated, with a quick, imperious temper and
an inordinate pride. She was fascinated by her handsome husband,
with his fine presence and his Parisian elegance. But disagree-
ments were not long in coming when 'Mad Jack' began his
voracious inroads into her capital. By 1787 the Gight property
had to be sold to meet his creditors; France offered a temporary
asylum to the couple, who were joined in Paris by the little
Augusta Mary, now aged three and a half. After her return to
London and George Gordon's birth, Mrs Byron rented lodgings
and later a small flat in Aberdeen, and tried to make ends meet on
her meagre income. 'Mad Jack' paid several visits, but after
squeezing what ready money he could from a wife who still
found difficulty in denying him anything, he retired to France,
where, continuing until the last his amours with local girls ('I
have had one third of Valenciennes'), he died in poverty in 1791.
Augusta Mary Byron had been taken in by her maternal grand-
mother, Lady Holdernesse, and 'the little boy in Aberdeen', who
had suffered from birth from a deformed right foot, was left
alone with his doting, violent mother. In 1794, at the age of six
and a half, he learned that he was heir presumptive to the Byron
title and estates; and he was a ten-year-old pupil at the Aberdeen
Grammar School, when the news reached him in May 1798 that
he was now the sixth Lord Byron. Accompanied by his mother
and a maid, the young Byron journeyed south to enter into his
inheritance.

At Newstead they found a pitiable state of affairs, the result of
the 'Wicked Lord's' extravagance and gross neglect. So heavily
encumbered were the Newstead and Rochdale estates that no

money was forthcoming to meet the cost of Byron's education: a grant of £300 a year was first provided by the Duke of Portland from the Civil List, which was later increased by £500 advanced by the Court of Chancery. In August 1798 Byron went as a boarder to Dr Glennie's school at Dulwich; then in April 1801 he entered Harrow, where he remained until he went up to Trinity College, Cambridge in October 1805.

*

This selection from Byron's prose opens with a letter to his aunt, Mrs Christopher Parker, written from Newstead Abbey in November 1798, when he was ten years and ten months old. It closes with a letter from Missolonghi to his banker in Genoa, Charles F. Barry, which he wrote on 9 April 1824. In the evening of that day he returned wet through after a ride, and complained of a feverish chill, which proved to be the beginning of a fatal illness. He died at six o'clock on the evening of 19 April. In the brief quarter of a century of what might be called his literary life Byron became an inveterate, indeed a compulsive 'scribbler' – to use the term in which he referred contemptuously to himself and his need to seek relief from emotional and intellectual pressures in composition. In the present volume there has been no single, exclusive principle of selection, unless those passages which would be of the greatest interest both to the general reader and to the student of English literature be considered the criterion. Inclusion or rejection, nevertheless, has been a matter of very considerable difficulty, for the reason that Byron never wrote a dull word, and his (seemingly) most negligent remark can be singularly revealing. For the reader's convenience, the book has been divided into six chronological sections, each of which is prefaced by such biographical information as will allow him to place the selected passages in their relevant context – a procedure made necessary by the omission in places of details which in a complete edition of Byron's prose writings would be self-explanatory.

It was Goethe who drew attention to the fluency and reality of Byron's representation of things, a faculty akin, he thought, to 'improvising'. Byron was gifted with a remarkable memory, not only of the written or spoken word, but also visually. Keats, distinguishing the essential difference between Byron and himself, once wrote, 'He describes what he sees; I describe what I imagine'. Again, Matthew Arnold, in the critical introduction to his selection from the poetry, remarks on this quality of *verisimilitude* in Byron. Here all three were referring specifically to Byron's poetry; nevertheless the observations apply with equal force to his prose. Byron, in his horror of cant and his hatred of fiction ('the talent of a liar') expresses himself in his letters and journals with an unrestrained (but not unguided) loquacity, revealing in every touch the Protean personality, which Goethe among his contemporaries rightly noted, and which Swinburne was later to discover in 'the splendid and imperishable excellence which covers all his offences and outweighs all his defects: the excellence of sincerity and strength'. In a sense Byron wrote as he swam: with unfatiguing power and supple ease. He wrote, too, from an inner compulsion, the necessity to unburden himself. 'To withdraw *myself* from *myself* (oh that cursed selfishness!) has ever been my sole, my entire, my sincere motive in scribbling at all; and publishing is also the continuance of that same object, by the action it affords to the mind, which else recoils upon itself.' He wrote with intense concentration and at great speed, *calamo currente*,[1] seldom bothering to read over what he had written. To Leigh Hunt he remarked: 'I write in great haste, and I doubt, not much to the purpose; but you have it hot and hot, just as it comes, and so let it go . . .' Even his ill-fated *Memoir*, he admitted to Moore, he had 'never even re-read, nor, indeed, *read* at all what is there written'. Yet possibly it is for just the reason that it was the spontaneous unreleasing of his powerful and brilliant intelligence, the sheer relief in the extempore unburdening, that we find in everything he wrote 'a burst, and a lightness, and a glow'.

Undoubtedly the characteristic qualities which place Byron high among English prose writers are revealed more often in the correspondence than in the journals; it seems that he required the eye or ear of the recipient to bring forth the full force, variety, subtlety and perfection of diction that mark his prose style at its best. Rarely indeed does Byron's spontaneity descend, as is sometimes alleged, to the slap-dash. Latterly, when he was at Cephalonia, he disavowed any facility of composition; writing, he remarked, 'which (however difficult it may seem for one who has written so much publicly to refrain) is, and always has been, to me a task and a painful one. I could summon testimonies, were it necessary; but my handwriting is sufficient. It is that of one who thinks much, rapidly, perhaps deeply, but rarely with pleasure.' His handwriting, it may be added, was considered by the Regency courtesan Harriet Wilson to resemble rather curiously that of a 'washerwoman's laboured scrawl'. To Moore he wrote (2 January 1821):

... I feel exactly as you do about our 'art', but it comes over me in a kind of rage every now and then, like — and then, if I don't write to empty my mind, I go mad. As to that regular, uninterrupted love of writing ... I do not understand it. I feel it as a torture, which I must get rid of, but never as a pleasure. On the contrary, I think composition a great pain.

Although these remarks refer specifically to his 'art', we can sense the same compulsion in much of his prose.

It may seem, looking no deeper than the surface, something of a paradox that Byron should have found in Ruskin so staunch a champion both of his writings and of his personal qualities. And no less strange is the picture we get in *Praeterita* (I.163) of the reading habits of a Victorian middle-class family of Tory and strong evangelical principles, where *Don Juan* was read aloud to a boy of twelve. Three years later, that is, 'by the end of this year 1834,' Ruskin wrote, 'I know my Byron pretty well all through...' At that time he resolved that Byron should be his model in verse; it is now clear that Byron became also a model in prose for one of the great literary stylists of the century. Fundamentally, the qualities that drew Ruskin to Byron were moral, as he himself recognized: 'the volcanic instinct of justice', the sincerity, the humanity, the refusal to be muffled, gagged or silenced – this last, even when those who sought to restrain him were his friends and firmest admirers. In many ways no two men could have been more dissimilar (particularly in their attitude towards sex), yet the work of both is informed by the same clarity of purpose, and the same pervasive magnanimity. As an advocate Ruskin is revealing (of himself as well as of Byron):

The first thing you have to do, in reading Byron to purpose, is to remember his motto, 'Trust Byron'. You always may; and the more, that he takes some little pleasure at first in offending you. But all he says is true, nevertheless, though what worst there is of himself to tell, he insists upon at once; and what good there may be, mostly leaves you to find out. To the end of his life, he had a schoolboy's love of getting into mischief: and a general instinct for never doing anything he was bid; which extends up even as far as the Commandments themselves. But he never either recommends you to break them, or equivocates in the smallest degree about what they *are* . . .

So far Ruskin the moralist: however, we should mark well his words, when he speaks as the critic of Byron's prose and cites the celebrated passage from his letter to Tom Moore, written from Venice on 1 June 1818, after he had spent the night on the town. Byron is defending Sheridan against his detractors:

The Whigs abuse him; however, he never left them, and such blunderers deserve neither credit nor compassion. – As for his creditors, – remember, Sheridan *never had* a shilling, and was thrown, with great powers and passions, into the thick of the world, and placed upon the pinnacle of success, with no other external means to support him in his elevation. Did Fox — *pay his* debts? or did Sheridan take a subscription? Was the —'s drunkenness more excusable than his? Were his intrigues more notorious than those of all his contemporaries? and is his memory to be blasted and theirs respected? Don't let yourself be led away by clamour, but compare him with the coalitioner Fox, and the pensioner Burke, as a man of principle, and with ten hundred thousand in personal views, and with none in talent, for he beat them all *out* and *out*. Without means, without connexion, without character, (which might be false at first, and drive him mad afterwards from desperation,) he beat them all, in all he ever attempted. But, alas! poor human nature! Good night or rather, morning. It is four, and the dawn gleams over the Grand Canal, and unshadows the Rialto. [Then the characteristic postscript] Excuse errors – no time for revision . . .

16

Ruskin quotes this excerpt, and goes on:

Now, observe, that passage is noble . . . But it is more than noble, it is *perfect*: because the quantity [of thoughts] it holds is not artificially or intricately concentrated, but with the serene swiftness of a smith's hammer strokes on hot iron; and with choice of terms which, each in its place, will convey far more than they mean in the dictionary. Thus, 'however' is used instead of 'yet', because it stands for 'howsoever', or, in full, for 'yet whatever they did'. 'Thick' of society, because it means, not merely the crowd, but the 'fog' of it; 'ten hundred thousand' instead of 'a million', or 'a thousand thousand', to take the sublimity out of the number, and to make us feel that it is a number of nobodies. Then the sentence in parenthesis, 'which might be false', etc. is indeed obscure, because it is impossible to clarify it without a regular pause, and much loss of time; and the reader's sense is left to expand it for himself into 'it was, perhaps, falsely said of him at first, that he had no character', etc. Finally, the dawn 'unshadows' – lessens the shadow on – the Rialto, but does not *gleam* on that, as on the broad water.

Perhaps what most strikes the modern reader is the felicity of the verbal music of this passage of Byron's, not only in the play of consonants and vowels, in their resonances and changes, but moreover in the perfect appropriateness of the varying rhythms – as if in the onrush of his generous enthusiasm the rhythms dictated themselves. And then the exquisite closing cadences: 'Good night, or rather morning. It is four, and the dawn gleams over the Grand Canal, and unshadows the Rialto.'

Byron admired the style of the Augustans both as poets (Pope he ranked very high) and as writers of prose, but their practice of carefully polishing their letters, with an eye to a circulation among a circle beyond the recipient, was far removed from the apparently negligent haste with which he customarily 'scribbled'. The result is a gain in spontaneity, naturalness and immediacy; we are led to share imperceptibly and unreservedly the wide range of his interests, and to be witnesses to the continual shifts in the play of his feelings and emotions. By the age of sixteen he already commanded considerable resources of language, especially when roused to indignation by the intolerable treatment at the hands of his mother, or (allegedly) at those of his Harrow schoolmasters. Writing on 18 August 1804 to his half-sister Augusta, he complains of his mother,

my tormentor, whose *diabolical* disposition (pardon me for staining my paper with so harsh a word) seems to increase with age, and to acquire new force with Time. The more I see of her the more my dislike augments; nor can I so entirely conquer the appearance of it, as to prevent her from perceiving my opinion; this, so far from calming the Gale, blows it into a *hurricane*, which threatens to destroy everything, till exhausted by its own violence, it is lulled into a sullen torpor, which, after a short period, is again aroused into a fresh and renewed phrenzy, to me most terrible, and to every other Spectator astonishing . . .

Byron's eye for the exotic scene and his powers of description are apparent in the letters sent home from his tour of the Balkans, undertaken on his coming of age, and after he had taken his seat in the House of Lords. Evidence of this is the account he gave of his visit to Ali Pasha at Tepaleen, written from Prevesa on 12 November 1809.

On the 27 February 1812 Byron delivered his maiden speech before the House of Lords, a reasoned and impassioned plea for the mitigation of the severe penalties against frame-breakers embodied in the Frame-work Bill. The success of his speech brought Byron to the attention of the Whig aristocracy centred on Holland House; but it was the publication of *Childe Harold's Pilgrimage* in March that raised him to fame overnight, and made him the most sought-after man in fashionable London society. This period of Byron's life is illustrated by the magnificent series of letters to Lady Melbourne, which include those that have been interpreted as hinting at his relations with his half-sister Augusta. Of fascinating interest and particular excellence are those letters which give a detailed, minute-to-minute account of his house-party affair with Lady Frances Webster. These have been likened to Laclos's *Les Liaisons Dangereuses*, but in Byron the element of suspense is heightened by the reality, by our knowledge that the events related are actually taking place at the moment of Byron's writing (the husband at times in the room), and by our wondering and concern at what the outcome will be.

At the time of Byron's separation from his wife another,

tenderer side of his character reveals itself: the calm dignity of his reply to his father-in-law, Sir Ralph Milbanke, is followed by the pathos and patent sincerity of his fruitless appeals to the feelings of his wife.

The gloom engendered by his exile, his thoughts of Augusta, and the callous curiosity of the English abroad did not lift until he had settled in Venice in November 1816; and the reason for this lifting of spirits was his falling in love. On 17 November he gave a short but vivid sketch of his mistress to Tom Moore:

Mariana [Segati] (that is her name) is in her appearance altogether like an antelope. She has the large, black, oriental eyes, with that peculiar expression in them which is seen rarely among *Europeans* – even the Italians – and which many of the Turkish women give themselves by tinging the eyelid, – an art not known out of that country, I believe. This expression she has *naturally*, – and something more than this. In short, I cannot describe the effect of this kind of eye, – at least upon me. Her features are regular, and rather aquiline – mouth small – skin clear and soft, with a kind of hectic colour – forehead remarkably good: her hair is of the dark gloss, curl and colour of Lady J[ersey]'s: her figure is light and pretty, and she is a famous songstress – scientifically so; her natural voice (in conversation, I mean) is very sweet; and the naïveté of the Venetian dialect is always pleasing in the mouth of a woman.

Of her successor, Margarita Cogni, *La Fornarina* (the baker's wife), Byron wrote a long account to John Murray (1 August 1818), which has the form almost of a short story. Unforgettable is the picture he draws of her anguished wait for him during one of those sudden and violent Mediterranean storms:

... we were overtaken by a heavy squall, and the Gondola put in peril – hats blown away, boat filling, oar lost, tumbling sea, thunder, rain in torrents, night coming, and wind increasing. On our return, after a tight struggle, I found her on the steps of the Mocenigo palace, on the Grand Canal, with her great black eyes flashing through her tears, and the long dark hair, which was streaming drenched with rain over her brows and breast ...

Byron loved many women; but few men have observed them so closely, so minutely aware of their individuality, or described

19

them with their peculiar attributes so faithfully. Yet his suscepti-
bility to women had something of an ambivalence which puzzled
him, as he records in his intimate journal on 17 February 1814:
'There is something to me very softening in the presence of a
woman – some strange influence, even if one is not in love with
them – which I cannot at all account for, having no very high
opinion of the sex. But yet, – I always feel in better humour with
myself and everything else, if there is a woman within ken.'

Byron's letters express the whole gamut of his emotions, not
excluding the bitterness of soul which the separation had caused
in him; this remained as gall to his pride, and found utterance
in the few later letters to Lady Byron, and in his quite devilish
delight at the news of Sir Samuel Romilly's suicide. (An indica-
tion that Byron was deeply moved is the absence of ordinary
punctuation, which is replaced by angry dashes.) But in the main
his letters are characterized by good humour, even boisterous on
occasions, and marked by private expressions current among his
friends, and a plentiful scattering of Shakespearean quotations.
Of this almost schoolboy humour is the letter he wrote to Hob-
house from Venice in June 1818, ostensibly from his servant
Fletcher: 'Sir, with great grief I inform you of the death of my
late dear Master, my Lord, who died this morning at ten of the
clock of a rapid decline and a slow fever, caused by anxiety, sea-
bathing, women, and riding in the Sun against my advice . . .'
And he could be very amusing indeed, as can be seen in his
satiric letter to William Roberts, the editor of 'My Grand-
mother's Review – the British'. One striking exception to his
usual good humour is the very irritable letter to John Murray
written from Ravenna, 24 September 1821. In a word, Byron's
prose is distinguished by its variety of subject-matter and of tone:
from the moving tribute he pays to Hobhouse's friendship in the
dedication to the fourth, concluding canto of *Childe Harold*, the
deep affection so evident in his letters to Augusta, to the sincere
and natural camaraderie of his correspondence with the charm-
ing Tom Moore.

Byron's literary criticism began with a review of Wordsworth's
poems in the *Monthly Literary Recreations* for July 1807,

written while still an undergraduate – a slight enough piece, which recognized Wordsworth's strength at his best, but castigated the 'namby-pamby' of such verses as those beginning 'The cock is crowing'. A fuller expression of his views both on his favourite Pope and on other poets, including those of the 'Cockney school', is found in the excerpts from the extended (and admittedly prolix) controversy with the Rev. W. L. Bowles, the editor of Pope and the propounder of the 'Invariable Principles of Poetry', which called forth Byron's defence of Pope and his scorn for any such invariable principles and for much of contemporary verse. To Keats ('John Ketch') he failed to do justice, but after Keats's death he retracted his criticism, and even went so far as to praise the opening of 'Hyperion' by comparing it with Aeschylus.

The change that came over Byron, when he set out on his last journey to Greece, and gave himself up whole-heartedly to the conduct of military matters and the complexities of the political situation, is seen in his dispatches, his communications with the London Greek Committee and with the rival political parties among the insurgents; all he wrote is informed by a practical mastery of strategy and detail, by his profound humanity and by his insight into human motivation, this in marked contrast to the earlier letters and journals from Ravenna, which showed him irked into despondency, a prey to the boredom and restlessness of his dual role of *cavalier servente* and sceptical *Carbonaro*. Whatever we think of war – even of wars of national liberation – nothing in his life became Byron so well as his last days in Greece; nothing brought out so clearly his stature as a man of feeling and a fearless man of action. We may, or we may not, regard Byron with the judgement of Professor Wilson Knight as 'the greatest poet in the widest sense of the term since Shakespeare', yet feel nonetheless the element of truth in his pronouncement: 'I do not know where we shall look for his master in prose.'

1. THE FORMATIVE YEARS

January 1798 – July 1811

INTRODUCTION

BYRON was fortunate in having as legal adviser, and later as sympathetic mentor, the Chancery solicitor John Hanson, who was at Newstead to greet the new arrivals and to attempt to straighten out the confusion into which the estate had fallen. Mrs Byron remained in the dilapidated Abbey, while Byron went to stay with his Parkyns relations at Nottingham, where he received some academic instruction, and suffered under the ministrations of a quack practitioner named Lavender in a vain attempt to cure his lameness. Hanson, in the meanwhile, had persuaded Byron's reluctant kinsman, the Earl of Carlisle, to serve as guardian during his minority, and had secured the provision of £300 from the Civil List. In August 1799, Byron entered Dr Glennie's school at Dulwich. His holidays he spent at Hanson's hospitable house in Kensington. In the summer, on a visit to Nottingham and Newstead, he essayed his 'first dash into poetry', inspired by his beautiful cousin Margaret Parker. His earliest love had been for another cousin, Mary Duff; but these and his later love for Mary Chaworth were passionate affairs of his imagination. His introduction into sexual intimacies had been at the hands of his nurse, May Gray, at the age of nine. This was discovered by Hanson, and the girl dismissed.

At Easter 1801, Byron went to Harrow, his tutor being Henry Drury, son of the headmaster. With Drury he quarrelled violently, but in later life they became the firmest of friends. At first he was not popular at school, but his fearlessness and pugnacity won him respect. His school work was desultory, although he seems to have read widely at irregular hours. For a time he refused to return to school, absorbed in his love for Mary Chaworth – it was only his last eighteen months at Harrow as a senior that he enjoyed, and he left for Cambridge with real regret. Afterwards he recalled that 'C. P. Hunter, Curzon, Long, and Tattersall, were my principal friends. Clare, Dorset, C. S. Gordon, De Bath[e], Claridge, and John Wingfield, were my juniors and favourites, whom I spoilt by indulgence.' To this list should be added Delawarr, Wildman (who subsequently purchased Newstead) and William Harness. Newstead having been let to Lord Grey de Ruthyn, Mrs Byron had taken a small house, Burgage Manor, at Southwell, and here Byron joined in the theatricals and, though preternaturally shy, formed friendships with the Pigot family, the girl Elizabeth becoming his confidante when he was up at Cambridge. Of his half-sister Augusta, Byron had seen little (Mrs Byron not being accepted by the relatives with whom Augusta stayed after the death of her grandmother Lady Holdernesse), but from 1804 they entered into a frequent and intimate correspondence, Augusta becoming the sympathetic recipient of his lurid accounts of violent scenes with his unbalanced mother. He appears to have had some amatory experiences with the girls of Southwell, but it was not until he was (nominally) in residence in Cambridge after October 1805 that he found the opportunities that London offered to a titled young man (with money in his pockets, even if obtained from the money-lenders) to indulge his sensual appetites. Byron spent only three full terms and a short duration of two others at Trinity. In 1808 he admitted to Hanson that his debts amounted to some £12,000.

In his first period of residence at Cambridge his Harrovian friend Long was much in his company; they swam in what is still known as 'Byron's pool' at Grantchester, read Moore's poems together, and played music in the evening. However, the consuming passion of Byron's life at this period was for the chorister John Edleston, his 'Cornelian', the subject of the 'Thyrza' poems. A break with Augusta, which caused her great anguish and went for long unhealed, was caused by her informing Lord Carlisle of Byron's dealings with the money-lenders. During his absence from the university he brought out, at his own expense, a volume of verse, *Fugitive Pieces* (1806). A revision of these verses, *Poems on Various Occasions*, appeared in 1807, followed by *Hours of Idleness* (with a singularly ill-advised preface, omitted in the second edition), which was thoroughly cut up by the *Edinburgh Review*. In his wrath Byron began what was to be 'English Bards and Scotch Reviewers', where he laid about him with all the remarkable vigour and invective already at his disposal. This was published in March 1809. Just after, having attained his majority, he took his seat in the House of Lords. Lord Carlisle, who, as a relative, had not assisted Byron as he might have been expected in the formalities of proving his title, came in for some cruel lines in 'English Bards'.

In his last period at Cambridge Byron became one of a distinguished, if somewhat dissipated set. William Bankes, 'the father of all mischiefs', had gone down, as had the talented Charles Skinner Matthews; but there were still the more sober John Cam Hobhouse and Francis Hodgson, fellow of King's, and another fellow of the same college, far from sober, the dandy, wit and gamester, Scrope Berdmore Davies, an associate of Beau Brummell's, and Douglas Kinnaird (later Byron's banker and financial adviser). Most of these were of liberal tendencies and Byron joined the select Whig Club. He left Cambridge at Christmas 1807, and the University grudgingly granted his M.A. degree in the following year.

Before he returned to Newstead (Lord Grey's lease having expired) in the summer of 1808, Byron so completely explored the delights of London and Brighton as seriously to injure his health. At Newstead he gathered together a convivial set of his friends, and some handsome 'Paphian' serving-girls. In the intervals of their carousals he polished his satire, and planned a tour of the East. Hanson was pressed to raise the money, which he was unable to do, and it was a fortunate run of luck at the gaming-tables that allowed Scrope Davies to provide a loan of £4,800. With Hobhouse as companion – he had quarrelled with his father and was without money – Byron set out from Falmouth Roads on 2 July 1809 aboard the Lisbon packet on his tour of the East.

The Peninsular War was at its height, but this did not prevent the travellers from visiting Lisbon (where Byron swam the Tagus), and progressing overland through Spain to Cadiz and thence by sea to Gibraltar, where they embarked for Sardinia and Malta. In Valetta Byron felt obliged to challenge the Governor's boorish aide-de-camp, Captain Cary, who apologized; and

27

entered into what might have been a serious affair (at least on the lady's side) with the beautiful Mrs Spencer Smith, which was arrested by the sailing of the *Spider* which took them to Patras. In a vivid letter to his mother Byron described their visit to Ali Pasha, the most powerful man in those parts, who was up country in Albania. At Jannina Byron began *Childe Harold*. With an Albanian escort they passed through Missolonghi, and crossed to Patras. After visiting Delphi and Parnassus, on Christmas Day Byron and Hobhouse entered Athens, where they lodged with the widowed Mrs Tarsia Macri, the mother of three attractive daughters, one of whom, Theresa, was to be celebrated as 'The Maid of Athens'. They left Athens with regret on 4 March 1810, accepting a passage on H.M.S. *Pylades* bound for Smyrna, where they were housed for a month with the British Consul-General, before departing on the frigate *Salsette* for Constantinople. Delayed by adverse winds off Cape Sigeum, a party went ashore to visit the site of ancient Troy. It was during this enforced delay that Byron and a Mr Ekenhead, a lieutenant of marines, succeeded (on their second attempt) in emulating Leander by swimming the Hellespont (3 May 1810).

From Constantinople Byron, who had accompanied the British ambassador's party on a ceremonial visit to the Grand Signor Mahmoud II, abandoning his projected tour of Persia and India, returned to Athens on the *Salsette*, and parted company with Hobhouse who returned to England. For the best part of another year Byron remained in Greece, touring the country or staying in the Capuchin monastery at the foot of the Acropolis. He studied Italian and modern Greek (Romaic), but his leisure moments were occupied with liaisons with the young of both sexes. He wrote to Hobhouse, 'Tell M[atthews] that I have obtained above two hundred pl&optCs and am almost tired of them.' (The expression, used in Byron's Cambridge circle, has been pointed out by Professor Gilbert Highet as coming from Petronius's *Satyricon*, Loeb ed., 86, p. 170, '*coitum plenum et optabilem*' – 'the full enjoyment of sexual intercourse'.) He had finished the second canto of *Childe Harold*, 'Hints from Horace' and a satire on Lord Elgin, the despoiler of the Parthenon marbles, 'The Curse of Minerva', by the spring of 1811. On 22 April he left for Malta where Mrs Spencer Smith awaited him, but he was ill, weakened by fever, and Malta sickened him. The frigate *Volage* sailed from Valetta on 2 June bound for England, and with it Byron, depressed by the state of his finances, by the prospects of his future in England – part of this dejection, no doubt, proceeding from physical causes, since, as he wrote to Hodgson, he had been treated 'for three complaints, viz. a *Gonorrhea*, a *Tertian fever*, and the *Hemorrhoides*, all of which I literally had at once . . .' Byron landed in England at Sheerness on 14 July 1811, two years and twelve days after setting sail from Falmouth.

TO MRS PARKER   *Newstead Abbey, Nov. 8th, 1798*

Dear Madam, – My Mamma being unable to write herself desires I will let you know that the potatoes are now ready and you are welcome to them whenever you please.

She begs you will ask Mrs Parkyns if she would wish the poney to go round by Nottingham or to go home the nearest way as it is now quite well but too small to carry me.

I have sent a young Rabbit which I beg Miss Frances will accept off and which I promised to send before. My Mamma desires her best compliments to you all in which I join.

I am, Dear Aunt, yours sincerely,

                                BYRON

I hope you will excuse all blunders as it is the first letter I ever wrote.

TO HIS MOTHER   *Nottingham, 13th March, 1799*

Dear Mama, – I am very glad to hear you are well. I am so my-self, thank God; upon my word I did not expect so long a Letter from you; however I will answer it as well as I can. Mrs Parkyns and the rest are well and are much obliged to you for the present. Mr Rogers could attend me every night at a separate hour from the Miss Parkynses, and I am astonished you do not acquiesce in this Scheme which would keep me in Mind of what I have almost entirely forgot. I recommend this to you because, if some plan of this kind is not adopted, I shall be called, or rather branded with the name of a dunce, which you know I could never bear. I beg you will consider this plan seriously and I will lend it all the assistance in my power. I shall be very glad to see the Letter you talk of, and I have time just to say I hope every body is well at Newstead,

And remain, your affectionate Son,

BYRON

P.S. Pray let me know when you are to send in the Horses to go to Newstead. May desires her Duty and I also expect an answer by the miller.

TO HIS MOTHER   *Harrow-on-the-Hill, Sunday, May 1st, 1803*

My Dear Mother, – I received your Letter the other day. And am happy to hear you are well. I hope you will find Newstead in as favorable a state as you can wish. I wish you would write to Sheldrake to tell him to make haste with my shoes. I am sorry to say that Mr Henry Drury has behaved himself to me in a manner I neither *can* nor *will bear*. He has seized now an opportunity of showing his resentment towards me. To day in church I was talking to a Boy who was sitting next me; *that* perhaps was not right, but hear what followed. After Church he spoke not a word to me, but he took this Boy to his pupil room, where he abused me in a most violent manner, called me *blackguard*, said he *would* and *could* have me expelled from the School, and bade me thank his *Charity* that *prevented* him; this was the Message he sent me, to which I shall return no answer, but submit my case to *you* and those you may think *fit* to *consult*. Is this fit usage for any body! had I *stole* or behaved in the most *abominable* way to him, his language could not have been more outrageous. What must the boys think of me to hear such a Message ordered to be delivered to me by a *Master?* Better let him take away my life than ruin my *Character*. My Conscience acquits me of ever *meriting* expulsion at this School; I have been *idle* and I certainly ought

30

not to talk in church, but I have never done a mean action at this School to him or *any one*. If I had done anything so *heinous*, why should he allow me to stay at the School? Why should he himself be so *criminal* as to overlook faults which merit the *appellation* of a *blackguard*? If he had had it in his power to have me expelled, he would long ago have *done* it; as it is, he has done *worse*. If I am treated in this Manner, I will not stay at this *School*. I write you that I will not as yet appeal to Dr Drury; his son's influence is more than mine and *justice* would be *refused* me. Remember I told you, when I *left* you at *Bath*, that he would seize every means and opportunity of revenge, not for leaving him so much as the mortification he suffered, because I begged you to let me leave him. If I had been the Blackguard he talks of, why did he not of his own accord refuse to keep me as his *pupil*? You know Dr Drury's first letter, in it were these Words: 'My son and Lord Byron have had some disagreements; but I hope that his future behaviour will render a change of Tutors unnecessary.' Last time I was here but a short time, and though he endeavoured, he could find nothing to abuse me in. Among other things I forgot to tell you he said he had a great mind to expel the boy for speaking to me, and that if he ever again spoke to me he would expel him. Let him explain his meaning; he abused me, but he neither did nor can mention anything bad of me, further than what every boy else in the School has done. I fear him not; but let him explain his meaning; 'tis all I ask. I beg you will write to Dr Drury to let him know what I have said. He has behaved to me, as also Mr Evans, very kindly. If you do not take notice of this, I will leave the School myself; but I am sure *you* will not see me *ill treated*; better that I should suffer anything than this. I believe you will be tired by this time of reading my letter, but, if you love me, you will now show it. Pray write me immediately. I shall ever remain,

Your affectionate Son,

BYRON

P.S. Hargreaves Hanson desires his love to you and hopes you are very well. I am not in want of any money so will not ask you for any. God bless, bless you.

31

Burgage Manor,

TO THE HON. AUGUSTA BYRON   *March 22nd, 1804*

Although, My ever Dear Augusta, I have hitherto appeared remiss in replying to your kind and affectionate letters; yet I hope you will not attribute my neglect to a want of affection, but rather to a shyness naturally inherent in my Disposition. I will now endeavour as amply as lies in my power to repay your kindness, and for the Future I hope you will consider me not only as *a Brother* but as your warmest and most affectionate *Friend,* and if ever Circumstances should require it your *protector.* Recollect, My Dearest Sister, that you are the *nearest relation* I have in *the world both by the ties of Blood* and *affection.* If there is anything in which I can serve you, you have only to mention it; Trust to your Brother, and be assured he will never betray your confidence. When you see my Cousin and future Brother George Leigh, tell him that I already consider him as my Friend, for whoever is beloved by you, my amiable Sister, will always be equally Dear to me.

I arrived here today at 2 o'clock after a fatiguing Journey, I found my Mother perfectly well. She desires to be kindly remembered to you; as she is just now Gone out to an assembly, I have taken the first opportunity to write to you, I hope she will not return immediately; for if she was to take it into her head to peruse my epistle, there is one part of it which would produce from her a panegyric on *a friend of yours,* not at all agreeable to me, and I fancy, *not particularly delightful to you.* If you see Lord Sidney Osborne I beg you will remember me to him; I fancy he has almost forgot me by this time, for it is rather more than a year Since I had the pleasure of Seeing him. – Also remember me to poor old Murray; tell him we will see that something is to be done for him, for *while I live he shall never be abandoned In his old Age.* Write to me Soon, my Dear Augusta, And do not forget to love me, in the meantime, I remain, more than words can express, your ever sincere, affectionate

Brother and Friend,   BYRON

P.S. – Do not forget to knit the purse you promised me, Adieu my beloved Sister.

TO THE HON. AUGUSTA BYRON *Southwell, March 26th, 1804*

I received your affectionate letter, my ever Dear Sister, yesterday and I now hasten to comply with your injunction by answering it as soon as possible ...

I am as you may imagine a little dull here; not being on terms of intimacy with Lord Grey I avoid Newstead, and my resources of amusement are Books, and writing to my Augusta, which wherever I am, will always constitute my Greatest pleasure. I am not reconciled to Lord Grey, *and I never will.* He was once my *Greatest Friend*, my reasons for ceasing that Friendship are such as I cannot explain, not even to you, my Dear Sister, (although were they to be made known to any body, you would be the first,) but they will ever remain hidden in my own breast.

They are Good ones, however, for although I am *violent* I am not capricious in my *attachments*. My mother disapproves of my quarrelling with him, but if she knew the cause (which she never will know,) She would reproach me no more. He Has forfeited all *title to my esteem*, but I hold him in too much *contempt* ever *to hate him* ...

TO THE HON. AUGUSTA BYRON   *Burgage Manor,*
                                      April 2d, 1804

... You tell me that you are tired of London. I am rather surprised to hear that, for I thought the Gaieties of the Metropolis were particularly pleasing to *young ladies*. For my part I detest it; the smoke and the noise feel particularly unpleasant; but however it is preferable to this horrid place, where I am oppressed with *ennui*, and have no amusement of any kind, except the conversation of my mother, which is sometimes very *edifying*, but not always very *agreeable*. There are very few books of any kind that are either instructive or amusing, no society but old parsons and old Maids; – I shoot a Good deal; but, thank God, I have not so far lost my reason as to make shooting my only amusement. There are indeed some of my neighbours whose only pleasures consist in field sports, but in other respects they are only one degree removed from the brute creation.

These however I endeavour not to imitate, but I sincerely wish for the company of a few friends about my own age to soften the austerity of the scene. I am an absolute Hermit; in a short time my Gravity which is increased. by my solitude will qualify me for an Archbishoprick; I really begin to think that I should become a mitre amazingly well. You tell me to write to you when I have nothing better to do; I am sure writing to you, my Dear Sister, must ever form my Greatest pleasure, but especially so, at this time. Your letters and those of one of my Harrow friends form my only resources for driving away *dull care* . . .

TO THE HON. AUGUSTA BYRON
Burgage Manor,
August 18th, 1804

My Dearest Augusta, – I seize this interval of my *amiable* mother's absence this afternoon, again to inform you, or rather to desire to be informed by you, of what is going on. For my own part I can send nothing to amuse you, excepting a repetition of my complaints against my tormentor, whose *diabolical* disposition (pardon me for staining my paper with so harsh a word) seems to increase with age, and to acquire new force with Time. The more I see of her the more my dislike augments; nor can I so entirely conquer the appearance of it, as to prevent her from perceiving my opinion; this, so far from calming the Gale, blows it into a *hurricane*, which threatens to destroy everything, till exhausted by its own violence, it is lulled into a sullen torpor, which, after a short period, is again roused into fresh and renewed phrenzy, to me most terrible, and to every other Spectator astonishing. She then declares that she plainly sees I hate her, that I am leagued with her bitter enemies, viz. Yourself, L^d C[arlisle], and Mr H[anson], and, as I never Dissemble or contradict her, we are all *honoured* with a multiplicity of epithets, too *numerous*, and some of them too *gross*, to be repeated. In this society, and in this amusing and instructive manner, have I dragged out a weary fortnight, and am condemned to pass another or three weeks as happily as the former. No captive Negro, or Prisoner of war, ever looked forward to their emancipation, and return to Liberty with more Joy, and with more lingering expectation, than I do to my escape from this maternal bondage, and this accursed place, which is the region of dullness itself, and more stupid than the banks of Lethe, though it possesses contrary qualities to the river of oblivion, as the detested scenes I now witness, make me regret the happier ones already passed, and wish their restoration.

Such Augusta is the happy life I now lead, such my *amusements*. I wander about hating everything I behold, and if I remained here a few months longer, I should become, what with *envy, spleen and all uncharitableness*, a complete *misanthrope*, but notwithstanding this,

Believe me, Dearest Augusta, ever yours, etc., etc.,

BYRON

TO HIS MOTHER   [*Harrow-on-the-Hill 1804 ?*]

... If Dr Drury can bring one boy or any one else to say that I have committed a dishonourable action, and to prove it, I am content. But otherwise I am stigmatized without a cause, and I disdain and despise the malicious efforts of him and his Brother. His Brother Martin not Henry Drury (whom I will do the justice to say has never since last year interfered with me) is continually reproaching me with the narrowness of my fortune, to what end I know not; his intentions may be good, but his manner is disagreeable. I see no reason why I am to be reproached with it. I have as much money, as many clothes, and in every respect of appearance am equal if not superior to most of my school-fellows, and if my fortune is narrow it is my misfortune, not my fault. But, however, the way *to riches, to greatness* lies before me. I can, I will cut myself a path through the world or perish in the attempt. Others have begun life with nothing and ended greatly. And shall I, who have a competent if not a large fortune, remain idle? No, I will carve myself the passage to Grandeur, but never with Dishonour. These, Madam, are my intentions ...

TO THE HON. AUGUSTA BYRON   *Harrow-on-the-Hill,*
Novr., Saturday, 17th, 1804

I am glad to hear, My dear Sister, that you like Castle Howard so
well, I have no doubt what you say is true and that Lord
C[arlisle] is much more amiable than he has been represented to
me. Never having been much with him and always hearing him
reviled, it was hardly possible I should have conceived a very
great friendship for his L^dship. My mother, you inform me,
commends my *amiable disposition* and *good understanding*; if she
does this to you, it is a great deal more than I ever hear myself,
for the one or the other is always found fault with, and I am told
to copy the *excellent pattern* which I see before me in *herself*. You
have got an invitation too, you may accept it if you please, but if
you value your own comfort, and like a pleasant situation, I
advise you to avoid Southwell. – I thank you, My dear Augusta,
for your readiness to assist me, and will in some manner avail
myself of it; I do not however wish to be separated from *her*
entirely, but not to be so much with her as I hitherto have been,
for I do believe she likes me; she manifests that in many in-
stances, particularly with regard to money, which I never want,
and have as much as I desire. But her conduct is so strange, her
caprices so impossible to be complied with, her passions so out-
rageous, that the evil quite overbalances her *agreeable qualities*.
Amongst other things I forgot to mention a most *ungovernable*
appetite for Scandal, which she never can govern, and employs
most of her time abroad, in displaying the faults, and censuring
the foibles, of her acquaintance; therefore I do not wonder, that
my precious Aunt, comes in for her share of encomiums; This
however is nothing to what happens when my conduct admits of
animadversion; 'then comes the tug of war'. My whole family
from the conquest are up-braided! myself abused, and I am told
that what little accomplishments I possess either in mind or body
are derived from her and *her alone* . . .

Ever your affectionate Brother,

BYRON

TO THE HON. AUGUSTA BYRON   *Burgage Manor*
                                             April 23d. 1805

. . . I assure you upon my *honour*, jesting apart, I have never been
so *scurrilously*, and *violently* abused by any person, as by that
woman, whom I think I am to call mother, by that being who
gave me birth, to whom I ought to look up with veneration and
respect, but whom I am sorry I cannot love or admire. Within
one little hour, I have not only heard myself, but have heard my
whole family, by the father's side, *stigmatized* in terms that the
blackest malevolence would perhaps shrink from, and that too in
words you would be shocked to hear. Such, Augusta, such is my
mother; *my mother*! I disclaim her from this time, and although
I cannot help treating her with respect, I cannot reverence, as I
ought to do, that parent who by her outrageous conduct forfeits
all title to filial affection. To you, Augusta, I must look up, as my
nearest relation, to you I must confide what I cannot mention to
others, and I am sure you will pity me; but I entreat you to keep
this a secret, nor expose that unhappy failing of this woman,
which I must bear with patience. I would be very sorry to have it
discovered, as I have only one week more, for the present. In the
meantime you may write to me with the greatest safety, as she
would not open any of my letters, even from you. I entreat then
that you will favour me with an answer to this. I hope however
to have the pleasure of seeing you on the day appointed, but if you
could contrive any way that I may avoid being asked to dinner
by L^d C[arlisle] I would be obliged to you, as I hate strangers.
Adieu, my Beloved Sister,

    I remain ever yours,

                                                  BYRON

TO THE HON. AUGUSTA BYRON   [Address cut out]
                                   Tuesday, July 2d. 1805

My Dearest Augusta, – I am just returned from Cambridge,
where I have been to enter myself at Trinity College. – Thursday
is our Speechday at Harrow, and as I forgot to remind you of its

approach, previous to our first declamation, I have given you *timely* notice this time. If you intend doing me the *honour* of attending, I would recommend you not to come without a Gentleman, as I shall be too much engaged all the morning to take care of you, and I should not imagine you would admire *stalking* about by yourself. You had better be there by 12 o'clock as we begin at 1, and I should like to procure you a good place; Harrow is 11 miles from town, it will just make a *comfortable* mornings drive for you. I don't know how you are to come, but for *Godsake* bring as few women with you as possible. I would wish you to Write me an answer immediately, that I may know on Thursday morning, whether you will drive over or not, and I will arrange my other engagements accordingly. I *beg, Madam,* you may make your appearance in one of his Lordships most *dashing* carriages, as our Harrow *etiquette*, admits of nothing but the most *superb* vehicles, on our Grand *Festivals*. In the meantime, believe me, dearest Augusta,

Your affectionate Brother,

BYRON

TO THE HON. AUGUSTA BYRON *Trin. Coll.*
(*Wednesday*), *Novr. 6th, 1805*

My Dear Augusta, – As might be supposed I like a College Life extremely, especially as I have escaped the Trammels or rather *Fetters* of my domestic Tyrant Mrs Byron, who continued to plague me during my visit in July and September. I am now most pleasantly situated in *Super*excellent Rooms, flanked on one side by my Tutor, on the other by an old Fellow, both of whom are rather checks upon my *vivacity*. I am allowed 500 a year, a Servant and Horse, so Feel as independent as a German Prince who coins his own Cash, or a Cherokee Chief who coins no Cash at all, but enjoys what is more precious, Liberty. I talk in raptures of that *Goddess* because my amiable Mama was so despotic. I am afraid the Specimens I have lately given her of my Spirit, and determination to submit to no more unreasonable demands, (or the insults which follow a refusal to obey her implicitly whether right or wrong,) have given high offence, as I had a most *fiery* Letter from the *Court* at *Southwell* on Tuesday, because I would not turn off my Servant,[1] (whom I had not the least reason to distrust, and who had an excellent Character from his last Master) at her suggestion, from some caprice she had taken into her head. I sent back to the Epistle, which was couched in *elegant* terms, a severe answer, which so nettled her Ladyship, that after reading it, she returned it in a Cover without deigning a Syllable in return.

The Letter and my answer you shall behold when you next see me, that you may judge of the Comparative merits of Each. I shall let her go on in the *Heroics*, till she cools, without taking the least notice. Her Behaviour to me for the last two Years neither merits my respect, nor deserves my affection. I am comfortable here, and having one of the best allowances in College, go on Gaily, but not extravagantly. I need scarcely inform you that I am not the least obliged to Mrs B. for it, as it comes off my property, and She refused to fit out a single thing for me from her own pocket; my Furniture is paid for, and she has moreover a handsome addition made to her own income, which I do not in the least regret, as I would wish her to be happy, but by *no means* to live with me in *person*. The sweets of her society I have already drunk to the last dregs, I hope we shall meet on more affectionate Terms, or meet no more.

But why do I say *meet*? her temper precludes every idea of happiness, and therefore in future I shall avoid her *hospitable* mansion, though she has the folly to suppose She is to be mistress of my house when I come of [age.][2] I must apologize to you for the [dullness?][3] of this letter, but to tell you the [truth][4] [the effects][5] of last nights Claret have no[t gone][6] out of my head, as I supped with a large party. I suppose that Fool Hanson in his *vulgar* Idiom, by the word Jolly did not mean Fat, but *High Spirits*, for so far from increasing I have lost one pound in a fortnight as I find by being regularly weighed.

Adieu, Dearest Augusta

[Signature cut out]

TO JOHN HANSON   *Trinity College, Cambridge*
                                        Novr. 30, 1805

Sir, – After the contents of your epistle, you will probably be less surprized at my answer, than I have been at many points of yours; never was I more astonished than at the perusal, for I confess I expected very different treatment. Your *indirect* charge of Dissipation does not affect me, nor do I fear the strictest inquiry into my conduct; neither here nor at *Harrow* have I disgraced myself, the 'Metropolis' and the 'Cloisters' are alike unconscious of my Debauchery, and on the plains of *merry Sherwood* I have experienced Misery alone; in July I visited them for the last time. Mrs Byron and myself are now totally separated, injured by her, I sought refuge with Strangers, too late I see my error, for how was kindness to be expected from *others*, when denied by a *parent*? In you, Sir, I imagined I had found an Instructor; for your advice I thank you; the Hospitality of yourself and Mrs H. on many occasions I shall always gratefully remember, for I am not of opinion that even present injustice can cancel past obligations. Before I proceed, it will be necessary to say a few words concerning Mrs Byron; you hinted a probability of her appearance at Trinity; the instant I hear of her arrival I quit Cambridge, though *Rustication* or *Expulsion* be the consequence. Many a weary week of *torment* have I passed with her, nor have I forgot the insulting *Epithets* with which myself, my *Sister*, my *father* and my *Family* have been repeatedly reviled.

To return to you, Sir, though I feel obliged by your hospitality, etc., etc., in the present instance I have been completely deceived. When I came down to College, and even previous to that period I stipulated that not only my Furniture, but even my Gowns and Books, should be paid for that I might set out free from *Debt*. Now with all the *Sang Froid* of your profession you tell me, that not only I shall not be permitted to repair my rooms (which was at first agreed to) but that I shall not even be indemnified for my present expence. In one word, hear my determination. I will *never* pay for them out of my allowance, and the Disgrace will not attach to me but to *those* by whom I have been deceived.

Still, Sir, not even the Shadow of dishonour shall reflect on *my* Name, for I will see that the Bills are discharged; whether by you or not is to me indifferent, so that the men I employ are not the victims of my Imprudence or your Duplicity. I have ordered nothing extravagant; every man in College is allowed to fit up his rooms; mine are secured to me during my residence which will probably be some time, and in rendering them decent I am more praiseworthy than culpable. The money I requested was but a secondary consideration; as a *Lawyer* you were not obliged to advance it till due; as a *Friend* the request might have been complied with. When it is required at Xmas I shall expect the demand will be answered. In the course of my letter I perhaps have expressed more asperity than I intended, it is my nature to feel warmly, nor shall any consideration of interest or Fear ever deter me from giving vent to my Sentiments, when injured, whether by a Sovereign or a Subject.

I remain, etc., etc,,

BYRON

TO THE HON. AUGUSTA BYRON   *16 Piccadilly,*
                                     Decr. 27th, 1805

My Dear Augusta, – You will doubtless be surprised to see a second epistle so close upon the arrival of the first, (especially as it is not my custom) but the Business I mentioned rather mysteriously in my last compels me again to proceed. But before I disclose it, I must require the most inviolable Secrecy, for if ever I find that it has transpired, all confidence, all Friendship between us has concluded. I do not mean this exordium as a threat to induce you to comply with my request but merely (whether you accede or not) to keep it a Secret. And although your compliance would essentially oblige me, yet, believe me, my esteem will not be diminished by your Refusal; nor shall I suffer a complaint to escape. The Affair is briefly this; like all other young men just let loose, and especially one as I am, freed from the worse than bondage of my maternal home, I have been extravagant, and consequently am in want of Money. You will probably now

41

imagine that I am going to apply to you for some. No, if you would offer me thousands, I declare solemnly that I would without hesitation refuse, nor would I accept them were I in danger of Starvation. All I expect or wish is, that you will be joint Security with me for a few Hundreds a person (one of the money lending tribe) has offered to advance in case I can bring forward any collateral guarantee that he will not be a loser, the reason of this requisition is my being a Minor, and might refuse to discharge a debt contracted in my nonage. If I live till the period of my minority expires, you cannot doubt my paying, as I have property to the amount of 100 times the sum I am about to raise; if, as I think rather probably, a pistol or a Fever cuts short the thread of my existence, you will receive half the *Dross* saved since I was ten years old, and can be no great loser by discharging a debt of 7 or £800 from as many thousands. It is far from my Breast to exact any promise from you that would be detrimental, or tend to lower me in your opinion. If you suppose this leads to either of those consequences, forgive my impertinence and bury it in oblivion ... I know you will think me foolish, if not criminal; but tell me so yourself, and do not rehearse my failings to others, no, not even to that proud Grandee the Earl, who, whatever his qualities may be, is certainly not amiable, and that Chattering puppy Hanson would make still less allowance for the foibles of a Boy. I am now trying the experiment, whether a woman can retain a secret; let me not be deceived. If you have the least doubt of my integrity, or that you run too great a Risk, do not hesitate in your refusal. Adieu. I expect an answer with impatience, believe me, whether you accede or not,

[Signature cut out]

TO JOHN HANSON   *Southwell, April 2nd, 1807*

... I return you my thanks for your favorable opinion of my muse; I have lately been honoured with many very flattering literary critiques, from men of high Reputation in the Sciences, particularly Lord Woodhous[lee] and Henry Mackenzie, both *Scots* and of great Eminence as *Authors* themselves. I have received also some most favorable Testimonies from *Cambridge*. This you will *marvel* at, as indeed I did myself. Encouraged by these and several other Encomiums, I am about to publish a volume at large; this will be very different from the present; the amatory effusions (not to be wondered at from the *dissipated* Life I have led) will be cut out, and others substituted. I coincide with you in opinion that the *Poet* yields to the *orator*; but as nothing can be done in the latter capacity till the Expiration of my *Minority*, the former occupies my present attention, and both *ancients* and *moderns* have declared that the two pursuits are so nearly similar as to require in a great measure the same Talents, and he who excels in the one, would on application succeed in the other. Lyttelton, Glover, and Young (who was a celebrated Preacher and a Bard) are instances of the kind. *Sheridan* and *Fox* also; *these* are *great Names*. I may imitate, I can never equal them.

You speak of the *Charms* of Southwell; the *Place* I *abhor*. The Fact is I remain here because I can appear no where else, being *completely done* up. *Wine* and *Women* have *dished* your *humble Servant*, not a *Sou* to be *had*; all *over*; condemned to exist (I cannot say live) at this *Crater* of Dullness till my *Lease* of *Infancy* expires. To appear at Cambridge is impossible; no money even to pay my College expences ...

Adieu. Remembrance to Spouse and the Acorns.

Yours ever,

BYRON

REVIEW OF WORDSWORTH'S POEMS
(2 VOLUMES 1807)

(From *Monthly Literary Recreations* for July 1807)

THE volumes before us are by the author of Lyric Ballads, a collection which has not undeservedly met with a considerable share of public applause. The characteristics of Mr Wordsworth's muse are simple and flowing, though occasionally inharmonious verse; strong, and sometimes irresistible appeals to the feelings, with unexceptionable sentiments. Though the present work may not equal his former efforts, many of the poems possess a native elegance, natural and unaffected, totally devoid of the tinsel embellishments and abstract hyperboles of several contemporary sonneteers. The last sonnet in the first volume, p. 152, is perhaps the best, without any novelty in the sentiments, which we hope are common to every Briton at the present crisis; the force and expression is that of a genuine poet, feeling as he writes: –

> Another year! another deadly blow!
> Another mighty empire overthrown!
> And we are left, or shall be left, alone – ...

The pieces least worthy of the author are those entitled 'Moods of my own Mind'. We certainly wish these 'Moods' had been less frequent, or not permitted to occupy a place near works which only make their deformity more obvious; when Mr W. ceases to please, it is by 'abandoning' his mind to the most commonplace ideas, at the same time clothing them in language not simple, but puerile. What will any reader or auditor, out of the nursery, say to such namby-pamby as 'Lines written at the Foot of Brother's Bridge'?

> The cock is crowing
> The stream is flowing,
> The small birds twitter,
> The lake doth glitter,

The green field sleeps in the sun;
The oldest and youngest,
Are at work with the strongest;
The cattle are grazing,
Their heads never raising,
There are forty feeding like one.
Like an army defeated,
The snow hath retreated,
And now doth fare ill,
On the top of the bare hill.

'The ploughboy is whooping anon, anon,' etc., etc., is in the same exquisite measure. This appears to us neither more nor less than an imitation of such minstrelsy as soothed our cries in the cradle, with the shrill ditty of

Hey de diddle,
The cat and the fiddle:
The cow jump'd over the moon,
The little dog laugh'd to see such sport,
And the dish ran away with the spoon.

On the whole, however, with the exception of the above, and other INNOCENT odes of the same cast, we think these volumes display a genius worthy of higher pursuits, and regret that Mr W. confines his muse to such trifling subjects. We trust his motto will be in future 'Paulo majora canamus'.[7] Many, with inferior abilities, have acquired a loftier seat on Parnassus, merely by attempting strains in which Wordsworth is more qualified to excel.

TO ELIZABETH BRIDGET PIGOT *Trin. Coll. Camb.,*
July 5, 1807

Since my last letter I have determined to reside *another year* at Granta, as my rooms, etc., etc., are finished in great style, several old friends come up again, and many new acquaintances made; consequently my inclination leads me forward, and I shall return to college in October if still *alive*. My life here has been one continued routine of dissipation – out at different places every day, engaged to more dinners, etc., etc., than my *stay* would permit me to fulfil. At this moment I write with a bottle of claret in my *head* and *tears* in my *eyes*; for I have just parted with my '*Cornelian*', who spent the evening with me. As it was our last interview, I postponed my engagement to devote the hours of the *Sabbath* to friendship: – Edleston and I have separated for the present, and my mind is a chaos of hope and sorrow. To-morrow I set out for London: you will address your answer to 'Gordon's Hotel, Albemarle Street', where I *sojourn* during my visit to the metropolis.

I rejoice to hear you are interested in my *protégé*; he has been my *almost constant* associate since October, 1805, when I entered Trinity College. His *voice* first attracted my attention, his *countenance* fixed it, and his *manners* attached me to him for ever. He departs for a *mercantile house* in *town* in October, and we shall probably not meet till the expiration of my minority, when I shall leave to his decision either entering as a *partner* through my interest, or residing with me altogether. Of course he would in his present frame of mind prefer the *latter*, but he may alter his opinion previous to that period; – however, he shall have his choice. I certainly love him more than any human being, and neither time nor distance have had the least effect on my (in general) changeable disposition. In short, we shall put *Lady E. Butler* and *Miss Ponsonby* to the blush, *Pylades* and *Orestes* out of countenance, and want nothing but a catastrophe like *Nisus* and *Euryalus*, to give *Jonathan* and *David* the 'go by'. He certainly is perhaps more attached to *me* than even I am in return. During the whole of my residence at Cambridge we met every day, summer and winter, without passing *one* tiresome moment, and separated each time with increasing reluctance. I hope you will one day see us together. He is the only being I esteem, though I *like* many . . .

PREFACE TO THE FIRST EDITION OF
'HOURS OF IDLENESS'

IN submitting to the public eye the following collection, I have not only to combat the difficulties that writers of verse generally encounter, but may incur the charge of presumption for obtruding myself on the world, when, without doubt, I might be, at my age, more usefully employed.

These productions are the fruits of the lighter hours of a young man who has lately completed his nineteenth year. As they bear the internal evidence of a boyish mind, this is, perhaps, unnecessary information. Some few were written during the disadvantages of illness and depression of spirits: under the former influence, 'CHILDISH RECOLLECTIONS', in particular, were composed. This consideration, though it cannot excite the voice of praise, may at least arrest the arm of censure. A considerable portion of these poems has been privately printed, at the request and for the perusal of my friends. I am sensible that the partial and frequently injudicious admiration of a social circle is not the criterion by which poetical genius is to be estimated, yet 'to do greatly' we must 'dare greatly'; and I have hazarded my reputation and feelings in publishing this volume. I have 'passed the Rubicon', and must stand or fall by the 'cast of the die'. In the latter event I shall submit without a murmur; for, though not without solicitude for the fate of these effusions, my expectations are by no means sanguine. It is probable that I may have dared much and done little; for, in the words of Cowper, 'it is one thing to write what may please our friends, who, because they are such, are apt to be a little biassed in our favour, and another to write what may please everybody; because they who have no connexion, or even knowledge of the author, will be sure to find fault if they can.' To the truth of this, however, I do not wholly subscribe; on the contrary, I feel convinced that these trifles will not be treated with injustice. Their merit, if they possess any, will be liberally allowed; their numerous faults, on the other hand, cannot expect that favour which has been denied to others of maturer years, decided character, and far greater ability.

I have not aimed at exclusive originality, still less have I studied any particular model for imitation; some translations are given of which many are paraphrastic. In the original pieces there may appear a casual coincidence with authors whose works I have been accustomed to read; but I have not been guilty of intentional plagiarism. To produce anything entirely new, in an age so fertile in rhyme, would be a Herculean task, as every subject has already been treated to its utmost extent. Poetry, however, is not my primary vocation; to divert the dull moments of indisposition, or the monotony of a vacant hour, urged me 'to this sin': little can be expected from so unpromising a muse. My wreath, scanty as it must be, is all I shall derive from these productions; and I shall never attempt to replace its fading leaves, or pluck a single additional sprig from groves where I am, at best, an intruder. Though accustomed, in my younger days, to rove a careless mountaineer on the Highlands of Scotland, I have not, of late years, had the benefit of such pure air, or so elevated a residence, as might enable me to enter the lists with genuine bards, who have enjoyed both these advantages. But they derive considerable fame, and a few not less profit, from their productions; while I shall expiate my rashness as an interloper, certainly without the latter, and in all probability with a very slight share of the former. I leave to others 'virûm volitare per ora'.[8] I look to the few who will hear with patience, 'dulce est desipere in loco'.[9] To the former worthies I resign, without repining, the hope of immortality, and content myself with the not very magnificent prospect of ranking amongst 'the mob of gentlemen who write'; – my readers must determine whether I dare say 'with ease', or the honour of a posthumous page in 'The Catalogue of Royal and Noble Authors', – a work to which the Peerage is under infinite obligations, inasmuch as many names of considerable length, sound, and antiquity, are thereby rescued from the obscurity which unluckily overshadows several voluminous productions of their illustrious bearers.

With slight hopes, and some fears, I publish this first and last attempt. To the dictates of young ambition may be ascribed many actions more criminal and equally absurd. To a few of my own age the contents may afford amusement; I trust they will, at least, be found harmless. It is highly improbable, from my situation and pursuits hereafter, that I should ever obtrude myself a second time on the public; nor even, in the very doubtful event of present indulgence, shall I be tempted to commit a future trespass of the same nature. The opinion of Dr Johnson on the poems of a noble relation of mine,[10] 'That when a man of rank appeared in the character of an author, he deserved to have his merit handsomely allowed,' can have little weight with verbal, and still less with periodical, censors; but were it otherwise, I should be loth to avail myself of the privilege, and would rather incur the bitterest censure of anonymous criticism, than triumph in honours granted solely to a title.

TO ELIZABETH BRIDGET PIGOT *Gordon's Hotel*
July 13, 1807

... P.S. Lord Carlisle, on receiving my poems, sent, before he opened the book, a tolerably handsome letter: – I have not heard from him since. His opinions I neither know nor care about: if he is the least insolent, I shall enrol him with *Butler*[11] and the other worthies. He is in Yorkshire, poor man! and very ill! He said he had not had time to read the contents, but thought it necessary to acknowledge the receipt of the volume immediately. Perhaps the Earl '*bears no brother near the throne*', – *if so*, I will make his *sceptre* totter *in his hands*. – Adieu!

TO ELIZABETH BRIDGET PIGOT *Trinity College, Cambridge,*
October 26, 1807

My Dear Elizabeth, – Fatigued with sitting up till four in the morning for the last two days at hazard, I take up my pen to inquire how your highness and the rest of my female acquaintance at the seat of archiepiscopal grandeur go on. I know I deserved scolding for my negligence in not writing more frequently; but racing up and down the country for these last three months, how was it possible to fulfil the duties of a correspondent? Fixed at last for six months, I write, as *thin* as ever (not having gained an ounce since my reduction), and rather in better humour; – but after all, Southwell was a detestable residence. Thank St Dominica, I have done with it: I have been twice within eight miles of it, but could not prevail on myself to *suffocate* in its heavy atmosphere. This place is wretched enough – a villainous chaos of din and drunkenness, nothing but hazard and burgundy, hunting, mathematics, and Newmarket, riot and racing. Yet it is a paradise compared with the eternal dulness of Southwell. Oh! the misery of doing nothing but make *love, enemies,* and *verses* . . .

I have got a new friend, the finest in the world, a *tame bear.* When I brought him here, they asked me what I meant to do with him, and my reply was, 'he should *sit for a fellowship*'. Sherard will explain the meaning of the sentence, if it is ambiguous. This answer delighted them not. We have several parties here, and this evening a large assortment of jockeys, gamblers, boxers, authors, parsons, and poets, sup with me, – a precious mixture, but they go on well together; and for me, I am a *spice* of every thing except a jockey; by the bye, I was dismounted again the other day.

Thank your brother in my name for his treatise. I have written 214 pages of a novel – one poem of 380 lines,[12] to be published (without my name) in a few weeks, with notes, – 560 lines of Bosworth Field, and 250 lines of another poem in rhyme, besides half a dozen smaller pieces. The poem to be published is a Satire. *Apropos,* I have been praised to the skies in the *Critical Review,* and abused greatly in another publication. So much the better, they tell me, for the sale of the book: it keeps up controversy, and prevents it being forgotten. Besides, the first men of all ages have had their share, nor do the humblest escape; – so I bear it like a philosopher. It is odd two opposite critiques came out on the same day, and out of five pages of abuse, my censor only quotes *two lines* from different poems, in support of his opinion. Now, the proper way to *cut up,* is to quote long passages, and make them appear absurd, because simple allegation is no

proof. On the other hand, there are seven pages of praise, and more than *my modesty* will allow said on the subject. Adieu.
P.S. – Write, write, write!!!

TO JOHN CAM HOBHOUSE   *Dorant's, February 27th, 1808*

Dear Hobhouse, – I write to you to explain a foolish circumstance, which has arisen from some words uttered by me before Pearce and Brown[e], when I was devoured with Chagrin, and almost insane with the fumes of, not 'last night's Punch' but that evening's wine. In consequence of a misconception of something on my part, I mentioned an intention of withdrawing my name from the Whig Club. This I hear has been broached, and perhaps in a moment of Intoxication and passion such might be my idea, but *soberly* I have no such design, particularly as I could not abandon my principles, even if I renounced the society with whom I have the honour to be united in sentiments which I never will disavow. This I beg you will explain to the members as publicly as possible, but should not this be sufficient, and they think proper to erase my name, be it so. I only request that in this case they will recollect I shall become a *Tory* of *their own making*. I shall expect your answer on this point with some impatience. Now a few words on the subject of my own conduct . . .

As an author, I am cut to atoms by the E[dinburgh] Review. It is just out, and has completely demolished my little fabric of fame. This is rather scurvy treatment from a Whig Review, but politics and poetry are different things, and I am no adept in either. I therefore submit in Silence.

Scrope Davies is meandering about London, feeding upon Leg of Beef Soup, and frequenting British Forum. He has given up hazard, as also a considerable sum at the same time. Altamont is a good deal with me. Last night at the Opera Masquerade, we supped with seven whores, a *Bawd* and a *Ballet master*, in Madame Catalani's apartment behind the Scenes, (of course Catalani was *not* there). I have some thoughts of purchasing Dégrille's pupils: they would fill a glorious Haram.

I do not write often, but I like to receive letters. When therefore you are disposed to philosophize, no one standeth more in need of precepts of all sorts than

Yours very truly,

BYRON

TO JOHN CAM HOBHOUSE   *Dorant's, March 26th, 1808*

Dear Hobhouse, – I have sent Fletcher[13] to Cambridge for various purposes, and he has this *dispatch* for you. I am still living with my Dalilah, who has only two faults, unpardonable in a woman – she can read and write. Greet in my name the Bilious Birdmore. If you journey this way, I shall be glad to furnish you with Bread and Salt.

The university still chew the Cud of my degree. Please God they shall swallow it, though Inflammation be the consequence.

I am leading a quiet though debauched life.

Yours very truly,

BYRON

Newstead Abbey, Notts,
TO FRANCIS HODGSON   *Nov. 3, 1808*

... Hobhouse and your humble are still here. Hobhouse hunts, etc., and I do nothing; we dined the other day with a neighbour-ing Esquire (not Collet of Staines), and regretted your absence, as the Bouquct of Staines was scarcely to be compared to our last 'feast of reason'. You know, laughing is the sign of a rational animal; so says Dr Smollett. I think so, too, but unluckily my spirits don't always keep pace with my opinions. I had not so much scope for risibility the other day as I could have wished, for I was seated near a woman,[14] to whom, when a boy, I was as much attached as boys generally are, and more than a man should be. I knew this before I went, and was determined to be valiant, and converse with *sang froid*; but instead I forgot my valour and my nonchalance, and never opened my lips even to laugh, far less to speak, and the lady was almost as absurd as myself, which made both the object of more observation than if we had conducted ourselves with easy indifference. You will think all this great nonsense; if you had seen it, you would have thought it still more ridiculous. What fools we are! We cry for a plaything, which, like children, we are never satisfied with till we break open, though like them we cannot get rid of it by putting it in the fire . . .

Believe me, my dear Sir, yours ever sincerely,

BYRON

Newstead Abbey, Notts.,
TO JOHN HANSON   *November 18th 1808*

Dear Sir, – I am truly glad to hear your health is re-instated. As for my affairs I am sure you will do your best, and, though I should be glad to get rid of my Lancashire property for an equivalent in money, I shall not take any steps of that nature without good advice and mature consideration.

I am (as I have already told you) going abroad in the spring; for this I have many reasons. In the first place, I wish to study India and Asiatic policy and manners. I am young, tolerably vigorous, abstemious in my way of living; I have no pleasure in fashionable dissipation, and I am determined to take a wider field than is customary with travellers. If I return, my judgment will be more mature, and I shall still be young enough for politics. With regard to expence, travelling through the East is rather inconvenient than expensive: it is not like the tour of Europe, you undergo hardship, but incur little hazard of spending money. If I live here I must have my house in town, a separate house for Mrs Byron; I must keep horses, etc., etc. When I go abroad I place Mrs Byron at Newstead (there is one great expence saved), I have no horses to keep. A voyage to India will take me six months, and if I had a dozen attendants cannot cost me five hundred pounds; and you will agree with me that a like term of months in England would lead me into four times that expenditure. I have written to Government for letters and permission of the Company, so you see I am *serious*.

You honour my debts; they amount to perhaps twelve thousand pounds, and I shall require perhaps three or four thousand at setting out, with credit on a Bengal agent. This you must manage for me. If my resources are not adequate to the supply I must *sell*, but *not Newstead*. I will at least transmit that to the next Lord. My debts must be paid, if possible, in February. I shall leave my affairs to the care of *trustees*, of whom, with your acquiescence, I shall *name you* one, Mr Parker another, and two more, on whom I am not yet determined.

Pray let me hear from you soon. Remember me to Mrs Hanson, whom I hope to see on her return. Present my best respects to the young lady, and believe me, etc.,

BYRON

TO THE HON. AUGUSTA LEIGH   *Newstead Abbey, Notts.,*
Novr. 30th 1808

My Dearest Augusta, – I return you my best thanks for making me an uncle, and forgive the sex this time; but the next *must* be a nephew. You will be happy to hear my Lancashire property is likely to prove extremely valuable: indeed my pecuniary affairs are altogether far superior to my expectations or any other person's. If I would *sell*, my income would probably be six thousand per annum; but I will not part at least with Newstead, or indeed with the other, which is of a nature to increase in value yearly. I am living here *alone*, which suits my inclinations better than society of any kind. Mrs Byron I have shaken off for two years, and I shall not resume her yoke in future, I am afraid my disposition will suffer in your estimation; but I never can forgive that woman, or breathe in comfort under the same roof.

I am a very unlucky fellow, for I think I had naturally not a bad heart; but it has been so bent, twisted, and trampled on, that it has now become as hard as a Highlander's heelpiece.

I do not know that much alteration has taken place in my person, except that I am grown much thinner, and somewhat taller! I saw Col. Leigh at Brighton in July, where I should have been glad to have seen you; I only know your husband by sight, though I am acquainted with many of the Tenth. Indeed my re-

54

lations are those whom I know the least, and in most instances, I am not very anxious to improve the acquaintance. I hope you are quite recovered, I shall be in town in January to take my seat, and will call, if convenient; let me hear from you before.

[Signature cut off]

TO WILLIAM HARNESS
*8 St. James's Street,
March 18th, 1809*

... – I am glad to hear you like Cambridge: firstly, because, to know that you are happy is pleasant to one who wishes you all possible sublunary enjoyment; and, secondly, I admire the morality of the sentiment. *Alma mater* was to me *injusta noverca*;[15] and the old beldam only gave me my M.A. degree because she could not avoid it. – You know what a farce a noble Cantab. must perform.

I am going abroad, if possible, in the spring, and before I depart I am collecting the pictures of my most intimate school-fellows; I have already a few, and shall want yours, or my cabinet will be incomplete. I have employed one of the first miniature painters of the day to take them, of course, at my own expense, as I never allow my acquaintance to incur the least expenditure to gratify a whim of mine. To mention this may seem indelicate; but when I tell you a friend of ours first refused to sit, under the idea that he was to disburse on the occasion, you will see that it is necessary to state these preliminaries to prevent the recurrence of any similar mistake. I shall see you in time, and will carry you to the *limner*. It will be a tax on your patience for a week; but pray excuse it, as it is possible the resemblance may be the sole trace I shall be able to preserve of our friendship and acquaintance. Just now it seems foolish enough; but in a few years, when some of us are dead, and others are separated by inevitable circumstances, it will be a kind of satisfaction to retain in these images of the living the idea of our former selves, and, to contemplate, in the resemblances of the dead, all that remains of judgment, feeling and a host of passions. But all this will be dull enough for you, and so good night; and, to end my chapter, or rather my homily,

Believe me, my dear H., yours most affectionately.

TO EDWARD ELLICE   *Falmouth, June 25th, 1809*

... We are waiting here for a wind and other necessaries. Nothing of moment has occurred in the town save the castigation of one of the fair sex at a Cart's tail yesterday morn, whose hands had been guilty of 'picking and stealing' and whose tongue of 'evil speaking' for she stole a Cock and *damned* the corporation. She was much whipped, but exceeding impenitent. I shall say nothing of Falmouth because I know it, and you don't, a very good reason for being silent as I can say nothing in its favour, or you hear anything that would be agreeable. The Inhabitants both female and male, at least the young ones, are remarkably handsome, and how the devil they come to be so is the marvel! for the place is apparently not favourable to Beauty. The Claret is good, and Quakers [?] plentiful, so are Herrings salt and fresh. There is a port called St Mawes off the harbour, which we were nearly taken up on a suspicion of having carried by storm. It is well defended by one able-bodied man of eighty years old, six ancient demi-culverins that would exceedingly annoy anybody except an enemy, and parapet walls which would withstand at least half a dozen kicks of any given grenadier in the kingdom of France.

Adieu, believe me your obliged and sincere

BYRON

TO FRANCIS HODGSON   *Lisbon, July 16, 1809*

Thus far have we pursued our route, and seen all sorts of marvellous sights, palaces, convents, etc.; – which, being to be heard in my friend Hobhouse's forthcoming Book of Travels, I shall not anticipate by smuggling any account whatsoever to you in a private and clandestine manner. I must just observe, that the village of Cintra in Estremadura is the most beautiful, perhaps, in the world.

I am very happy here, because I loves oranges, and talks bad Latin to the monks, who understand it, as it is like their own, – and I goes into society (with my pocket-pistols), and I swims in the Tagus all across at once, and I rides on an ass or a mule, and swears Portuguese, and have got a diarrhoea and bites from the mosquitoes. But what of that? Comfort must not be expected by folks that go a pleasuring.

When the Portuguese are pertinacious, I say *Carracho*! – the great oath of the grandees, that very well supplies the place of 'Damme', – and, when dissatisfied with my neighbour, I pronounce him *Ambra di merdo*.[16] With these two phrases, and a third, *Avra bouro,* which signifieth 'Get an ass', I am universally understood to be a person of degree and a master of languages. How merrily we lives that travellers be! – if we had food and raiment. But, in sober sadness, any thing is better than England, and I am infinitely amused with my pilgrimage as far as it has gone.

To-morrow we start to ride post near 400 miles as far as Gibraltar, where we embark for Melita and Byzantium. A letter to Malta will find me, or to be forwarded, if I am absent. Pray embrace the Drury and Dwyer, and all the Ephesians you encounter. I am writing with Butler's donative pencil, which makes my bad hand worse. Excuse illegibility.

Hodgson! send me the news, and the deaths and defeats and capital crimes and the misfortunes of one's friends; and let us hear of literary matters, and the controversies and the criticisms. All this will be pleasant – *Suave mari magno,*[17] etc. Talking of that, I have been sea-sick, and sick of the sea. Adieu.

Yours faithfully, etc.

TO HIS MOTHER   *Gibraltar, August 11th, 1809*

.. Seville is a beautiful town; though the streets are narrow, they are clean. We lodged in the house of two Spanish unmarried ladies, who possess *six* houses in Seville, and gave me a curious specimen of Spanish manners. They are women of character, and the eldest a fine woman, the youngest pretty, but not so good a figure as Donna Josepha. The freedom of manner, which is general here, astonished me not a little; and in the course of further observation, I find that reserve is not the characteristic of the Spanish belles, who are, in general, very handsome, with large black eyes, and very fine forms. The eldest honoured your *unworthy* son with very particular attention, embracing him with great tenderness at parting (I was there but three days), after cutting off a lock of his hair, and presenting him with one of her own, about three feet in length, which I send, and beg you will retain till my return. Her last words were, *Adios, tu hermoso! me gusto mucho* – 'Adieu, you pretty fellow! you please me much'. She offered me a share of her apartment, which my *virtue* induced me to decline; she laughed, and said I had some English *amante* (lover), and added that she was going to be married to an officer in the Spanish Army ...

Cadiz, sweet Cadiz, is the most delightful town I ever beheld, very different from our English cities in every respect except cleanliness (and it is as clean as London), but still beautiful, and full of the finest women in Spain, the Cadiz belles being the Lancashire witches of their land. Just as I was introduced and began to like the grandees, I was forced to leave it for this cursed place; but before I return to England I will visit it again. The night before I left it, I sat in the box at the opera with Admiral Cordova's family; he is the commander whom Lord St Vincent defeated in 1797, and has an aged wife and a fine daughter, Sennorita Cordova. The girl is very pretty, in the Spanish style; in my opinion, by no means inferior to the English in charms, and certainly superior in fascination. Long black hair, dark languishing eyes, *clear* olive complexions, and forms more graceful in motion than can be conceived by an Englishman used to the drowsy, listless air of his country-women, added to the most becoming dress, and, at the same time, the most decent in the world, render a Spanish beauty irresistible.

I beg leave to observe that intrigue here is the business of life; when a woman marries she throws off all restraint, but I believe their conduct is chaste enough before. If you make a proposal, which in England will bring a box on the ear from the meekest of virgins, to a Spanish girl, she thanks you for the honour you intend her, and replies, 'Wait till I am married, and I shall be too happy'. This is literally and strictly true.

Miss Cordova and her little brother understood a little French, and, after regretting my ignorance of the Spanish, she proposed to become my preceptress in that language. I could only reply by a low bow, and express my regret that I quitted Cadiz too soon to permit me to make the progress which would doubtless attend my studies under so charming a directress. I was standing at the back of the box, which resembles our Opera boxes, (the theatre is large and finely decorated, the music admirable,) in the manner which Englishmen generally adopt, for fear of incommoding the ladies in front, when this fair Spaniard dispossessed an old woman (an aunt or a duenna) of her chair, and commanded me to be seated next herself, at a tolerable distance from her mamma. At the close of the performance I withdrew, and was lounging with a party of men in the passage, when, *en passant*, the lady turned round and called me, and I had the honour of attending her to the admiral's mansion. I have an invitation on my return to Cadiz, which I shall accept if I repass through the country on my return from Asia . . .

TO HIS MOTHER   *Malta, September 15, 1809*

Dear Mother, – Though I have a very short time to spare, being to sail immediately for Greece, I cannot avoid taking an opportunity of telling you that I am well. I have been in Malta a short time, and have found the inhabitants hospitable and pleasant.

This letter is committed to the charge of a very extraordinary woman, whom you have doubtless heard of, Mrs Spencer Smith, of whose escape the Marquis de Salvo published a narrative a few years ago. She has since been shipwrecked, and her life has been from its commencement so fertile in remarkable incidents, that in a romance they would appear improbable. She was born at Constantinople, where her father, Baron Herbert, was Austrian Ambassador; married unhappily, yet has never been impeached in point of character; excited the vengeance of Buonaparte, by a part in some conspiracy; several times risked her life; and is not yet twenty-five. She is here on her way to England, to join her husband, being obliged to leave Trieste, where she was paying a visit to her mother, by the approach of the French, and embarks soon in a ship of war. Since my arrival here, I have had scarcely any other companion. I have found her very pretty, very accomplished, and extremely eccentric. Buonaparte is even now so incensed against her, that her life would be in some danger if she were taken prisoner a second time.

You have seen Murray and Robert[18] by this time, and received my letter. Little has happened since that date. I have touched at Cagliari in Sardinia, and at Girgenti in Sicily, and embark to-morrow for Patras, from whence I proceed to Yanina, where Ali Pacha holds his court. So I shall soon be among the Mussulmans. Adieu.

Believe me, with sincerity, yours ever,

BYRON

TO CAPTAIN CARY, A.D.C.   *3 Strada di Torni (Malta),*
September 18th, 1809

Sir, – The marked insolence of your behaviour to me the first time I had the honour of meeting you at table, I should have passed over from respect to the General, had I not been informed that you have since mentioned my name in a public company with comments not to be tolerated, more particularly after the circumstance to which I allude. I have only just heard this, or I should not have postponed this letter to so late a period. As the vessel in which I am to embark must sail the first change of wind, the sooner our business is arranged the better. To-morrow morning at 6 will be the best hour, at any place you think proper, as I do not know where the officers and *gentlemen* settle these affairs in your island.

The favour of an immediate answer will oblige,

Your obedient servant,

BYRON

TO HIS MOTHER   *Prevesa, November 12, 1809*

My Dear Mother, – I have now been some time in Turkey; this place is on the coast, but I have traversed the interior of the province of Albania on a visit to the Pacha. I left Malta in the *Spider*, a brig of war, on the 21st of September, and arrived in eight days at Prevesa. I thence have been about 150 miles, as far as Tepaleen, his Highness's country palace, where I stayed three days. The name of the Pacha is *Ali*, and he is considered a man of the first abilities: he governs the whole of Albania (the ancient Illyricum), Epirus, and part of Macedonia. His son, Vely Pacha, to whom he has given me letters, governs the Morea, and has great influence in Egypt; in short, he is one of the most powerful men in the Ottoman empire. When I reached Yanina, the capital, after a journey of three days over the mountains, through a country of the most picturesque beauty, I found that Ali Pacha was with his army in Illyricum, besieging Ibrahim Pacha in the castle of Berat. He had heard that an Englishman of rank was in his dominions, and had left orders in Yanina with the commandant to provide a house, and supply me with every kind of necessary *gratis*; and, though I have been allowed to make presents to the slaves, etc., I have not been permitted to pay for a single article of household consumption.

I rode out on the vizier's horses, and saw the palaces of himself and grandsons: they are splendid, but too much ornamented with silk and gold. I then went over the mountains through Zitza, a village with a Greek monastery (where I slept on my return), in the most beautiful situation (always excepting Cintra, in Portugal) I ever beheld. In nine days I reached Tepaleen. Our journey was much prolonged by the torrents that had fallen from the mountain, and intersected the roads. I shall never forget the singular scene on entering Tepaleen at five in the afternoon, as the sun was going down. It brought to my mind (with some change of *dress*, however) Scott's description of Branksome Castle in his *Lay*, and the feudal system. The Albanians, in their dresses, (the most magnificent in the world, consisting of a long *white kilt*, gold-worked cloak, crimson velvet gold-laced jacket

61

and waistcoat, silver-mounted pistols and daggers,) the Tartars with their high caps, the Turks in their vast pelisses and turbans, the soldiers and black slaves with the horses, the former in groups in an immense large open gallery in front of the palace, the latter placed in a kind of cloister below it, two hundred steeds ready caparisoned to move in a moment, couriers entering or passing out with the despatches, the kettle-drums beating, boys calling the hour from the minaret of the mosque, altogether, with the singular appearance of the building itself, formed a new and delightful spectacle to a stranger. I was conducted to a very handsome apartment, and my health inquired after by the vizier's secretary, *à-la-mode Turque*!

The next day I was introduced to Ali Pacha. I was dressed in a full suit of staff uniform, with a very magnificent sabre, etc. The vizier received me in a large room paved with marble; a fountain was playing in the centre; the apartment was surrounded by scarlet ottomans. He received me standing, a wonderful compliment from a Mussulman, and made me sit down on his right hand. I have a Greek interpreter for general use, but a physician of Ali's named Femlario, who understands Latin, acted for me on this occasion. His first question was, why, at so early an age, I left my country? – (the Turks have no idea of travelling for amusement). He then said, the English minister, Captain Leake, had told him I was of a great family, and desired his respects to my mother; which I now, in the name of Ali Pacha, present to you. He said he was certain I was a man of birth, because I had small ears, curling hair, and little white hands, and expressed himself pleased with my appearance and garb. He told me to consider him as a father whilst I was in Turkey, and said he looked on me as his son. Indeed, he treated me like a child sending me almonds and sugared sherbet, fruit and sweetmeats, twenty times a day. He begged me to visit him often, and at night, when he was at leisure. I then, after coffee and pipes, retired for the first time. I saw him thrice afterwards. It is singular that the Turks, who have no hereditary dignities, and few great families, except the Sultans, pay so much respect to birth; for I found my pedigree more regarded than my title.

Today I saw the remains of the town of Actium, near which Antony lost the world, in a small bay, where two frigates could hardly manoeuvre: a broken wall is the sole remnant. On another part of the gulf stand the ruins of Nicopolis, built by Augustus in honour of his victory. Last night I was at a Greek marriage; but this and a thousand things more I have neither time nor *space* to describe.

His highness is sixty years old, very fat, and not tall, but with a fine face, light blue eyes, and a white beard; his manner is very kind, and at the same time he possesses that dignity which I find universal amongst the Turks. He has the appearance of anything but his real character, for he is a remorseless tyrant, guilty of the most horrible cruelties, very brave, and so good a general that they call him the Mahometan Buonaparte. Napoleon has twice offered to make him King of Epirus, but he prefers the English interest, and abhors the French, as he himself told me. He is of so much consequence, that he is much courted by both, the Albanians being the most warlike subjects of the Sultan, though Ali is only nominally dependent on the Porte; he has been a mighty warrior, but is as barbarous as he is successful, roasting rebels, etc., etc. Buonaparte sent him a snuff-box with his picture. He said the snuff-box was very well, but the picture he could excuse, as he neither liked it nor the original. His idea of judging of a man's birth from ears, hands, etc., were curious enough. To me he was, indeed, a father, giving me letters, guards, and every possible accommodation. Our next conversations were of war and travelling, politics and England. He called my Albanian soldier, who attends me, and told him to protect me at all hazard; his name is Viscillie, and, like all the Albanians, he is brave, rigidly honest, and faithful; but they are cruel, though not treacherous, and have several vices but no meannesses. They are, perhaps, the most beautiful race, in point of countenance, in the world; their women are sometimes handsome also, but they are treated like slaves, *beaten*, and, in short, complete beasts of burden; they plough, dig, and sow. I found them carrying wood, and actually repairing the highways. The men are all soldiers, and war and the chase their sole occupations.

The women are the labourers, which after all is no great hardship in so delightful a climate. Yesterday, the 11th of November, I bathed in the sea; today is so hot that I am writing in a shady room of the English consul's, with three doors wide open, no fire, or even *fireplace*, in the house, except for culinary purposes.

I am going to-morrow, with a guard of fifty men, to Patras in the Morea, and thence to Athens, where I shall winter. Two days ago I was nearly lost in a Turkish ship of war, owing to the ignorance of the captain and crew, though the storm was not violent. Fletcher yelled after his wife, the Greeks called on all the saints, the Mussulmans on Alla; the captain burst into tears and ran below deck, telling us to call on God; the sails were split, the mainyard shivered, the wind blowing fresh, the night setting in, and all our chance was to make Corfu, which is in possession of the French, or (as Fletcher pathetically termed it) 'a watery grave'. I did what I could to console Fletcher, but finding him incorrigible, wrapped myself up in my Albanian capote (an immense cloak), and lay down on deck to wait the worst. I have learnt to philosophise in my travels; and if I had not, complaint was useless. Luckily the wind abated, and only drove us on the coast of Suli, on the main land, where we landed, and proceeded, by the help of the natives, to Prevesa again; but I shall not trust Turkish sailors in future, though the Pacha had ordered one of his own galliots to take me to Patras. I am therefore going as far as Missolonghi by land, and there have only to cross a small gulf to get to Patras.

Fletcher's next epistle will be full of marvels. We were one night lost for nine hours in the mountains in a thunder-storm, and since nearly wrecked. In both cases Fletcher was sorely bewildered, from apprehensions of famine and banditti in the first, and drowning in the second instance. His eyes were a little hurt by the lightning, or crying (I don't know which), but are now recovered . . .

I could tell you I know not how many incidents that I think would amuse you, but they crowd on my mind as much as they would swell my paper, and I can neither arrange them in the one, nor put them down on the other, except in the greatest confusion.

I like the Albanians much; they are not all Turks; some tribes are Christians. But their religion makes little difference in their manner or conduct. They are esteemed the best troops in the Turkish service. I lived on my route, two days at once, and three days again, in a barrack at Salora, and never found soldiers so tolerable, though I have been in garrisons of Gibraltar and Malta, and seen Spanish, French, Sicilian, and British troops in abundance. I have had nothing stolen, and was always welcome to their provision and milk. Not a week ago an Albanian chief, (every village has its chief, who is called Primate,) after helping us out of the Turkish galley in her distress, feeding us, and lodging my suite, consisting of Fletcher, a Greek, two Athenians, a Greek priest, and my companion, Mr Hobhouse, refused any compensation but a written paper stating that I was well received; and when I pressed him to accept a few sequins, 'No', he replied; 'I wish you to love me, not to pay me'. These are his words.

It is astonishing how far money goes in this country. While I was in the capital I had nothing to pay by the vizier's order; but since, though I have generally had sixteen horses, and generally six or seven men, the expense has not been *half* as much as staying only three weeks in Malta, though Sir A. Ball, the governor, gave me a house for nothing, and I had only *one servant*. By the by, I expect Hanson to remit regularly; for I am not about to stay in this province for ever. Let him write to me at Mr Strané's, English consul, Patras. The fact is, the fertility of the plains is wonderful and specie is scarce, which makes this remarkable cheapness. I am going to Athens, to study modern Greek, which differs much from the ancient, though radically similar. I have no desire to return to England, nor shall I, unless compelled by absolute want, and Hanson's neglect; but I shall not enter into Asia for a year or two, as I have much to see in Greece, and I may perhaps cross into Africa, at least the Egyptian part. Fletcher, like all Englishmen, is very much dissatisfied, though a little reconciled to the Turks by a present of eighty piastres from the vizier, which, if you consider every thing, and the value of specie here, is nearly worth ten guineas English. He has suffered nothing but from cold, heat, and vermin, which those who lie in cottages and cross mountains in a cold country must undergo, and of which I have equally partaken with himself; but he is not valiant, and is afraid of robbers and tempests. I have no one to be remembered to in England, and wish to hear nothing from it, but that you are well, and a letter or two on business from Hanson, whom you may tell to write. I will write when I can, and beg you to believe me.

Your affectionate son,

BYRON

P.S. . . . I have been introduced to Hussein Bey, and Mahmout Pacha, both little boys, grandchildren of Ali, at Yanina; they are totally unlike our lads, have painted complexions like rouged dowagers, large black eyes, and features perfectly regular.They are the prettiest little animals I ever saw, and are broken into the court ceremonies already. The Turkish salute is a slight inclination of the head, with the hand on the heart; intimates always kiss. Mahmout is ten years old, and hopes to see me again; we are friends without understanding each other, like many other folks, though from a different cause. He has given me a letter to his father in the Morea, to whom I have also letters from Ali Pacha.

TO HENRY DRURY   *Salsette frigate,*
                                        May 3, 1810

. . . We stopped a short time in the Morea, crossed the Gulf of Lepanto, and landed at the foot of Parnassus; – saw all that Delphi retains, and so on to Thebes and Athens, at which last we remained ten weeks.

His Majesty's ship, *Pylades*, brought us to Smyrna; but not before we had topographised Attica, including, of course, Marathon and the Sunian promontory. From Smyrna to the Troad (which we visited when at anchor, for a fortnight, off the tomb of Antilochus) was our next stage; and now we are in the Dardanelles, waiting for a wind to proceed to Constantinople.

This morning I swam from *Sestos* to *Abydos*. The immediate distance is not above a mile, but the current renders it hazardous; – so much so that I doubt whether Leander's conjugal affection must not have been a little chilled in his passage to Paradise. I attempted it a week ago, and failed, – owing to the north wind, and the wonderful rapidity of the tide, – though I have been from my childhood a strong swimmer. But, this morning being calmer, I succeeded, and crossed the 'broad Hellespont' in an hour and ten minutes.

Well, my dear sir, I have left my home, and seen part of Africa and Asia, and a tolerable portion of Europe. I have been with generals and admirals, princes and pashas, governors and ungovernables, – but I have not time or paper to expatiate ...

I like the Greeks, who are plausible rascals, – with all the Turkish vices, without their courage. However, some are brave, and all are beautiful, very much resembling the busts of Alcibiades; – the women not quite so handsome. I can swear in Turkish; but, except one horrible oath, and 'pimp' and 'bread', and 'water', I have got no great vocabulary in that language. They are extremely polite to strangers of any rank, properly protected; and as I have two servants and two soldiers, we get on with great *éclat*. We have been occasionally in danger of thieves, and once of shipwreck, – but always escaped ...

On the 2d of July we have left Albion one year – *oblitus meorum obliviscendus et illis*.[19] I was sick of my own country and not much prepossessed in favour of any other; but I 'drag on my chain' without 'lengthening it at each remove.' I am like the Jolly Miller, caring for nobody, and not cared for. All countries are much the same in my eyes. I smoke, and stare at mountains, and twirl my mustachios very independently. I miss no comforts, and the musquitoes that rack the morbid frame of H[obhouse] have, luckily for me, little effect on mine, because I live more temperately.

I omitted Ephesus in my catalogue, which I visited during my sojourn at Smyrna; but the Temple has almost perished, and St Paul need not trouble himself to epistolise the present brood of Ephesians, who have converted a large church built entirely of marble into a mosque, and I don't know that the edifice looks the worse for it.

My paper is full, and my ink ebbing – good afternoon! If you address to me at Malta, the letter will be forwarded wherever I may be. H. greets you; he pines for his poetry, – at least, some tidings of it. I almost forgot to tell you that I am dying for love of three Greek girls at Athens, sisters, I lived in the same house. Teresa, Mariana, and Katinka, are the names of these divinities, – all of them under fifteen.

Your ταπεινοτατος δουλος,[20]

BYRON

TO FRANCIS HODGSON   *Salsette frigate, in the Dardanelles off Abydos, May 5, 1810*

. . . Of my return I cannot positively speak, but think it probable Hobhouse will precede me in that respect. We have been very nearly one year abroad. I should wish to gaze away another, at least, in these evergreen climates; but I fear business, law business, the worst of employments, will recall me previous to that period, if not very quickly. If so, you shall have due notice.

I hope you will find me an altered personage, – I do not mean in body, but in manner, for I begin to find out that nothing but virtue will do in this damned world. I am tolerably sick of vice, which I have tried in its agreeable varieties, and mean, on my return, to cut all my dissolute acquaintance, leave off wine and carnal company, and betake myself to politics and decorum. I am very serious and cynical, and a good deal disposed to moralise; but fortunately for you the coming homily is cut off by default of pen and defection of paper.

Good morrow! If you write, address to me at Malta, whence your letters will be forwarded. You need not remember me to any body, but believe me,

Yours with all faith,

BYRON

Constantinople, May 15, 1810

P.S. – My Dear H., – the date of my postscript 'will prate to you of my whereabouts'. We anchored between the Seven Towers and the Seraglio on the 13th, and yesterday settled ashore.The ambassador is laid up; but the secretary does the honours of the palace, and we have a general invitation to his palace. In a short time he has his leave of audience, and we accompany him in our uniforms to the Sultan, etc., and in a few days I am to visit the Captain Pacha with the commander of our frigate. I have seen enough of their Pashas already; but I wish to have a view of the Sultan, the last of the Ottoman race ...

TO HIS MOTHER   *Constantinople, June 28, 1810*

... Fletcher is a poor creature, and requires comforts that I can dispense with. He is very sick of his travels, but you must not believe his account of the country. He sighs for ale, and idleness, and a wife, and the devil knows what besides. I have not been disappointed or disgusted. I have lived with the highest and the lowest. I have been for days in a Pacha's palace, and have passed many a night in a cowhouse, and I find the people inoffensive and kind. I have also passed some time with the principal Greeks in the Morea and Livadia, and, though inferior to the Turks, they are better than the Spaniards, who, in their turn, excel the Portuguese. Of Constantinople you will find many descriptions in different travels; but Lady Mary Wortley errs strangely when she says, 'St Paul's would cut a strange figure by St Sophia's'. I have been in both, surveyed them inside and out attentively. St Sophia's is undoubtedly the most interesting from its immense antiquity, and the circumstance of all the Greek emperors, from Justinian, having been crowned there, and several murdered at the altar, besides the Turkish Sultans who attend it regularly. But it is inferior in beauty and size to some of the mosques, particularly 'Soleyman', etc., and not to be mentioned in the same page with St Paul's (I speak like a *Cockney*). However, I prefer the Gothic cathedral of Seville to St Paul's, St Sophia's, and any religious building I have ever seen.

The walls of the Seraglio are like the walls of Newstead gardens, only higher, and much in the same *order*: but the ride by the walls of the city, on the land side, is beautiful. Imagine four miles of immense triple battlements, covered with ivy, surmounted with 218 towers, and, on the other side of the road, Turkish burying-grounds (the loveliest spots on earth), full of enormous cypresses. I have seen the ruins of Athens, of Ephesus, and Delphi. I have traversed great part of Turkey, and many other parts of Europe, and some of Asia; but I never beheld a work of nature or art which yielded an impression like the prospect on each side from the Seven Towers to the end of the Golden Horn ...

It is my opinion that Mr B— ought to marry Miss R—. Our first duty is not to do evil; but, alas! that is impossible; our next is to repair it, if in our power. The girl is his equal: if she were his inferior, a sum of money and provision for the child would be some, though a poor, compensation: as it is, he should marry her. I will have no gay deceivers on my estate, and I shall not allow my tenants a privilege I do not permit myself – *that* of debauching each other's daughters. God knows, I have been guilty of many excesses; but, as I have laid down a resolution to reform, and lately kept it, I expect this Lothario to follow the example, and begin by restoring this girl to society, or, by the beard of my father! he shall hear of it. Pray take some notice of Robert [Rushton], who will miss his master; poor boy, he was very unwilling to return. I trust you are well and happy. It will be a pleasure to hear from you.

Believe me, yours very sincerely,

BYRON

P.S. – How is Joe Murray?
P.S. – I open my letter again to tell you that Fletcher having petitioned to accompany me into the Morea, I have taken him with me, contrary to the intention expressed in my letter.

TO EDWARD ELLICE   *Constantinople, July 4th, 1810*

... I am sorry to hear that my sister Mrs Leigh is annoyed at my attack on the Earl of C[arlisle],[21] though I had motives enough to justify any measures against that silly old man. Had I been aware that she would have laid it to heart, I would have cast my pen and poem both into the flames, and, in good truth (if she knew the feelings of us scribblers) no small sacrifice. But the mischief is done, Lord forgive me! This it is to have tender-hearted she-relations. If I had been lucky enough to be a bastard, I might have abused everybody to my dying-day, and *nobody never* the *worser* . . .

TO JOHN CAM HOBHOUSE   *Patras, July 29th, 1810*

Dear Hobhouse, – the same day which saw me ashore at Zea, set me forth once more upon the high seas, where I had the pleasure of seeing the frigate in the *Doldrums* by the light of sun and moon. Before daybreak I got into the Attics at Thaskalio, hence I dispatched men to Keratia for horses, and in ten hours from landing I was at Athens. There I was greeted by my Lord Sligo, and next day Messrs North, Knight, and Fazakerly paid me formal visits. Sligo has a brig with 50 men who won't work, 12 guns that refuse to go off, and sails that have cut every wind except a contrary one, and then they are as willing as may be. He is sick of the concern, but an engagement of six months prevents him from parting with this precious ark. He *would* travel with me to Corinth, though as you may suppose I was already heartily disgusted with travelling in company. He has 'en suite' a painter, a captain, a gentleman misinterpreter (who boxes with the painter), besides sundry idle English varlets. We were obliged to have twenty-nine horses in all. The captain and the *Drogueman* were left at Athens to kill bullocks for the crew, and the Marquis and the limner, with a ragged Turk by way of Tartar, and the ship's carpenter in the capacity of linguist, with two servants (one of whom had the gripes) clothed both in leather breeches (the thermometer 125°!!), followed over the hills and far away. On our route, the poor limner in these gentle latitudes was ever and anon condemned to bask for half-an-hour, that he might produce what he himself termed a 'bellissimo sketche' (pardon the orthography of the last word) of the surrounding country. You may also suppose that a man of the Marchese's kidney was not very easy in his seat. As for the *servants*, they and their *leather breeches* were equally immovable at the end of the first stage. Fletcher, too, with his usual acuteness, contrived at

71

Megara to ram his damned clumsy foot into a boiling tea-kettle. At Corinth we separated, the M[arquis] for Tripolitza, I for Patras. Thus far the ridiculous part of my narrative belongs to others, now comes my turn. At Vortitza I found my dearly-beloved Eustathius, ready to follow me not only to England, but to Terra Incognita, if so be my compass pointed that way. This was *four* days ago: at present affairs are a little changed. The next morning I found the dear soul upon horseback clothed very sparsely in Greek Garments, with those ambrosial curls hanging down his amiable back, and to my utter astonishment, and the great abomination of Fletcher, a *parasol* in his hand to save his complexion from the heat. However, in spite of the *Parasol* on we travelled very much enamoured, as it should seem till we got to Patras, where Strané received us into his new house where I now scribble. Next day he went to visit some accursed cousin and the day after we had a grand quarrel. Strané said I spoilt him. I said nothing; the child was as forward as an unbroken colt, and Strané's Janizary said I must not be surprised, for he was too *true* a *Greek* not to be disagreeable. I think I never in my life took so much pains to please any one, or succeeded so ill. I particularly avoided every thing which *could possibly give* the *least offence* in *any manner*. Somebody says, that those who try to please will please. This I know not; but I am sure that no one likes to fail in the attempt. At present he goes back to his father, though he is now become more tractable. Our *parting* was vastly pathetic, as many kisses as would have sufficed for a boarding school, and embraces enough to have ruined the character of a county in England, besides tears (not on *my* part) and expressions of 'Tenerezza'[22] to a vast amount. All this and the warmth of the weather has quite overcome me. Tomorrow I will continue. At present, 'to bed', 'to bed', 'to bed'. The youth insists on seeing me to-morrow, the issue of which interview you shall hear. I wish you a pleasant sleep.

July 30th, 1810

I hope you have slept well. I have only dozed. For this last six days I have slept little and eaten less. The heat has burnt me brown, and as for Fletcher he is a walking Cinder. My new Greek acquaintance has called thrice, and we improve vastly. In good truth, so it ought to be, for I have quite exhausted my poor powers of pleasing, which God knows are little enough, Lord help me! We are to go on to Tripolitza and Athens together. I do not know what has put him into such good humour unless it is some Sal Volatile I administered for his headache, and a green shade instead of that effeminate parasol. But so it is. We have *redintegrated* (a new *word* for you) our affections at a great rate. Now is not all this very ridiculous? Pray tell Matthews. It would do his heart good to see me travelling with my Tartar, Albanians, Buffo, Fletcher and this amiable παιδη[23] prancing by my side. Strané hath got a steed which I have bought, full of spirit, I assure you, and very handsome accoutrements. My *account* with him was as I stated on board the Salsette. Here hath just arrived the Chirugeon of the Spider from Zante, who will take this letter to Malta. I hope it will find you warm. You cannot conceive what a delightful companion you are now you are gone. Sligo has told me some things that ought to set you and me by the ears, but they shan't; and as a proof of it, I won't tell you what they are till we meet, but in the meantime I exhort you to behave well in polite society. His Lordship has been very kind, and as I crossed the Isthmus of Corinth, offered if I chose to take me to that of Darien, but I liked it not, for you have cured me of 'villainous company'.

I am about – after a Giro of the Morea – to move to Athens again, and thence I know not where; perhaps to Englonde, Malta, Sicily, Egypt, or the Low Countries. I suppose you are at Malta or Palermo. I amuse myself alone very much to my satisfaction, riding, bathing, sweating, hearing Mr Paul's musical clock, looking at his red breeches; we visit him every evening. There he is, playing at stopper with the old Cogia Bachi. When these amusements fail, there is my Greek to quarrel with, and a sopha to tumble upon. Nourse and Dacres had been at Athens scribbling all sorts of ribaldry over my old apartment, where Sligo, before my arrival, had added to your B.A. an A.S.S., and scrawled the compliments of Jackson, Deville, Miss Cameron, and '*I am very unappy Sam Jennings*'. Wallace is incarcerated, and wanted Sligo to bail him, at the 'Bell and Savage', Fleet Rules. The news are not surprising. What think you? Write to me from Malta, the Mediterranean, or Ingleterra, to care of ὁ μογόλοο Στράνε.[24]

Have you cleansed my pistols? and dined with the 'Gineral'? My compliments to the church of St John's, and peace to the ashes of Ball. How is the Skipper? I have drank his cherry-brandy, and his rum has floated over half the Morea. Plaudite et valete.[25]

Yours ever,

BYRON

TO JOHN CAM HOBHOUSE *Tripolitza, August 16th, 1810*

Dear Hobhouse, – I am on the rack of setting off for Argos amidst the usual creaking, swearing, loading and neighing of sixteen horses and as many men, serrugees included. You have probably received one letter dated Patras, and I send this at a venture. Vely Pasha received me even better than his father did, though he is to join the Sultan, and the city is full of troops and confusion, which, as he said, prevented him from paying proper attention. He has given me a very pretty horse, and a most particular invitation to meet him at Larissa, which is singular enough as he recommended a different route to Lord Sligo, who asked leave to accompany him to the Danube. I asked no such thing, but on his enquiry where I meant to go, and receiving for answer that I was about to return to Albania, for the purpose of penetrating higher up the country, he replied, 'No, you must not take that route, but go round by Larissa, where I shall remain some time, on my way. I will send to Athens, and you shall join me; we will eat and drink and go a hunting.' He said he wished all the old men (specifying under that epithet North, Forresti, and Strané,) to go to his father, but the young ones to come to him, to use his own expression, 'Vecchio con Vecchio, Giovane con Giovane'.[26] He honoured me with the appellations of his *friend* and *brother*, and hoped that we should be on good terms, not for a few days but for life. All this is very well, but he has an awkward manner of throwing his arm round one's waist, and squeezing one's hand in *public* which is a high compliment, but very much embarrasses '*ingenuous youth*'.

The first time I saw him he received me *standing*, accompanied me at my departure to the door of the audience chamber, and told me I was a παλικαρι and an εὔμορφω παιδι.[27] He asked if I did not think it very proper that as *young* men (he has a *beard* down to his middle) we should live together, with a variety of other sayings, which made Strané stare, and puzzled me in my replies. He was very facetious with Andreas and Viscillie, and recommended that my Albanians' heads should be cut off if they behaved ill. I shall write to you from Larissa, and inform you of our proceedings in that city. In the meantime I sojourn at Athens. I have sent Eustathius back to his home; he plagued my soul out with his whims, and is besides subject to *epileptic* fits (tell M[atthews] of this) which made him a perplexing companion; in *other* matters he was very tolerable, I mean as to his learning, being well versed in the Ellenics. You remember Nicolo at Athens, Lusieri's wife's brother. Give my *compliments* to *Matthews*, from whom I expect a congratulatory letter. I have a thousand anecdotes for him and you, but at present, τί να κάμω?[28] I have neither time nor space, but in the words of Dawes, 'I have things in store'. I have scribbled thus much. Where shall I send it? Why, to Malta or Paternoster Row. Hobby, you wretch, how is the Miscellany? that damned and damnable work. What has the learned world said to your Paradoxes? I hope you did not forget the importance of Monogamy. Strané has just arrived with bags of piastres, so that I must conclude by the usual phrase of

Yours etc. etc.,

BYRON

P.S. You knew young Bossari at Yanina; he is a piece of Ali Pacha's!! Well did Horace write 'Nil Admirari'.

TO JOHN CAM HOBHOUSE   *The Convent, Athens*
                                        August 23rd, 1810

My Dear Hobhouse, – Lord Sligo's unmanageable brig being
remanded to Malta, with a large quantity of vases, amounting in
value (according to the depreciation of Fauriel) to one hundred
and fifty piastres, I cannot resist the temptation of assailing you
in this third letter, which I trust will find you better than your
deserts, and no worse than my wishes can make you. I have
girated the Morea, and was presented with a very fine horse (a
stallion), and honoured with a number of squeezes and speeches
by Velly Pasha, besides a most pressing invitation to meet him at
Larissa on his way to the wars. But of these things I have written
already. I returned to Athens by Argos, where I found Lord
Sligo with a painter, who has got a fever with sketching at midday,
and a dragoman who has actually lied himself into a lockjaw. I
grieve to say the Marchese has done a number of young things,
because I believe him to be a clever, and I am sure he is a good
man. I am most auspiciously settled in the Convent, which is
more commodious than any tenement I have yet occupied, with
room for my *suite*; and it is by no means solitary, seeing there is
not only 'il Padre Abbate', but his 'schuola', consisting of six
'Ragazzi',²⁹ all my most particular allies. These gentlemen
being almost (saving Fauriel and Lusieri) my only associates, it is
but proper their character, religion, and morals, should be
described. Of this goodly company three are Catholics, and three
are Greeks, which schismatics I have already set a boxing to the
great amusement of the Father, who rejoices to see the Catholics
conquer. Their names are Barthelemi, Giuseppè, *Nicolo*, Zani,
and two anonymous, at least in my memory. Of these, Barthelemi
is a 'simplice Fanciullo',³⁰ according to the account of the
Father, whose favourite is Giuseppè, who sleeps in the lantern
of Demosthenes. We have nothing but riot from noon to
night.

The first time I mingled with these sylphs, after about two
minutes' reconnoitring, the amiable Signor Barthelemi, without
any previous notice, seated himself by me, and after observing by

way of compliment that my 'Signoria' was the 'piu bello' of his English acquaintance, saluted me on the left cheek, for which freedom being reproved by Giuseppè, who very properly informed him that I was μεγάλος, he told him I was his φίλος, and 'by his beard' he would do so again, adding, in reply to the question 'διὰ τὶ ἀσπάσετε?'[31] 'you see he laughs', as in good truth I did heartily. But my friend, as you may easily imagine, is Nicolo [Giraud], who by-the-by, is my Italian master, and we are already very philosophical. I am his 'Padrone' and his 'amico', and the Lord knows what besides. It is about two hours since, that, after informing me he was most desirous to follow *him* (that is me) over the world, he concluded by telling me it was proper for us not only to live, but 'morire insieme'.[32] The latter I hope to avoid – as much of the former as he pleases. I am awakened in the morning by those imps shouting 'Venite abasso', and the friar gravely observes it is 'bisogno bastonare'[33] everybody before the studies can possibly commence. Besides these lads, my suite, – to which I have added a Tartar and a youth to look after my two new saddle horses, – my suite, I say, are very obstreperous, and drink skinfuls of Zean wine at eight paras the olne daily. Then we have several Albanian women washing in the '*giardino*', whose hours of relaxation are spent in running pins into Fletcher's backside. '*Damnata di mi, if I have seen such a spectaculo in my way from Viterbo.*' In short, what with the *women*, and the *boys*, and the *suite*, we are very disorderly. But I am vastly happy and childish, and shall have a world of anecdotes for you and the 'citoyen'.[34]

Intrigue flourishes: the old woman, Theresa's mother, was mad enough to imagine I was going to marry the girl; but I have better amusement. Andreas is fooling with Dudu, as usual, and Mariana has made a conquest of Dervise Tahire; Vircillie, Fletcher and Sullee, my new Tartar, have each a mistress – 'Vive l'Amour'.

I am learning Italian, and this day translated an ode of Horace, 'Exegi monumentum', into that language. I chatter with everybody, good or bad, and tradute prayers out of the mass ritual; but my lessons, though very long, are sadly interrupted by scamperings, and eating fruit, and peltings and playings; and I am in fact at school again, and make as little improvement now as I did then, my time being wasted in the same way.

However, it is too good to last; I am going to make a second tour of Attica with Lusieri, who is a new ally of mine, and Nicolo goes with me at his own most pressing solicitation, 'per mare per terras'. 'Forse' you may see us in Inghilterra, but 'non so, come, etc.' For the present, good-even, Buona sera a vos signoria. Bacio le mani:[35] – August 24th, 1810.

I am about to take my daily ride to the Piraeus, where I swim for an hour despite of the heat; here hath been an Englishman ycleped Watson, who died and is buried in the Tempio of Theseus. I knew him not, but I am told that the surgeon of Lord Sligo's brig slew him with an improper potion, and a cold bath.

Lord Sligo's crew are sadly addicted to liquor. He is in some apprehension of a scrape with the Navy concerning certain mariners of the King's ships.

He himself is now at Argos with his hospital, but intends to winter in Athens. I think he will be sick of it, poor soul, he has all the indecision of your humble servant, without the relish for the ridiculous which makes my life supportable.

I wish you were here to partake of a number of waggeries, which you can hardly find in the gun-room or in Grub Street, but then you are so very crabbed and disagreeable, that when the laugh is over I rejoice in your absence. After all, I do love thee, Hobby, thou has so many good qualities, and so many bad ones, it is impossible to live with or without thee.

Nine in the Evening.

I have, as usual swum across the Piraeus, the Signor Nicolo also laved, but he makes as bad a hand in the water as L'Abbé Hyacinth at Falmouth; it is a curious thing that the Turks when they bathe wear their lower garments, as your humble servant always doth, but the Greeks not; however, questo Giovane e vergonó[36] [sic].

Lord Sligo's surgeon has assisted very materially the malignant fever now fashionable here; another man *dead* today, two men a week, like fighting Bob Acres in the country. Fauriel says he is like the surgeon whom the Venetians fitted out against the Turks, with whom they were then at war.

I have been employed the greater part of today in conjugating the verb 'ἀσπαζω'[37] (which word being Ellenic as well as Romaic may find a place in the Citoyen's Lexicon). I assure you my progress is rapid, but like Caesar 'nil actum reputans dum quid superesset agendum'. I must arrive at the pl & opti,[38] and then I will write to [Matthews?] I hope to escape the fever, at least till I finish this affair, and then it is welcome to try. I don't think without its friend the drunken Pothecary it has any chance. Take a quotation: – 'Et Lycam *nigris* oculis, nigroque *crine* decorum'.[39]

Yours and the *Sieur's* ever, B.

TO JOHN CAM HOBHOUSE   *Patras, Morea, October 4th, 1810*

My Dear Hobhouse, – I wrote to you two days ago, but the weather and my friend Strané's conversation being much the same, and my ally Nicolo in bed with a fever, I think I may as well talk to you, the rather, as you can't answer me, and excite my wrath with impertinent observations, at least for three months to come. I will try not to say the same things I have set down in my other letter of the 2nd, but I can't promise, as my poor head is still giddy with my late fever. I saw the Lady Hesther Stanhope at Athens, and do not admire 'that dangerous thing a female wit'. She told me (take her own words) that she had given you a good set-down at Malta, in some disputation about the Navy; from this, of course, I readily inferred the contrary, or in the words of an *acquaintance* of ours, that 'you had the best of it'. She evinced a similar disposition to *argufy* with me, which I avoided by either laughing or yielding. I despise the sex too much to squabble with them, and I rather wonder you should allow a woman to draw you into a contest, in which, however, I am sure you had the advantage, she abuses you so bitterly. I have seen too little of the Lady to form any decisive opinion, but I have discovered nothing different from other she-things, except a great disregard of received notions in her conversation as well as conduct. I don't know whether this will recommend her to our sex, but I am sure it won't to her own. She is going on to Constantinople. Ali Pacha is in a scrape. Ibrahim Pacha and the Pacha of Scutari have come down upon him with 20,000 Gegdes and Albanians, retaken Berat, and threaten Tepaleni. Adam Bey is dead, Vely Pacha was on his way to the Danube, but has gone off suddenly to Yanina, and all Albania is in an uproar. The mountains we crossed last year are the scene of warfare, and there is nothing but carnage and cutting of throats . . .

Athens is at present infested with English people, but they are moving, *Dio bendetto*! I am returning to pass a month or two; I think the spring will see me in England, but do not let this transpire, nor cease to urge the most dilatory of mortals, Hanson. I have some idea of purchasing the Island of Ithaca; I suppose you will add me to the Levant lunatics. I shall be glad to hear from your Signoria of your welfare, politics, and literature. Tell M[atthews] that I have obtained above two hundred pl&optCs and am almost tired of them; for the history of these he must wait my return, as after many attempts I have given up the idea of conveying information on paper. You know the monastery of Mendele; it was there I made myself a master of the first. Your last letter closes pathetically with a postscript about a nosegay; I advise you to introduce that into your next sentimental novel. I am sure I did not suspect you of any fine feelings, and I believe you were laughing, but you are welcome. *Vale*: 'I can no more', like Lord Grizzle.

Yours, Μπαίρων[40]

TO HIS MOTHER   *Athens, January 14, 1811*

. . . It is probable I may steer homewards in spring; but to enable me to do that, I must have remittances. My own funds would have lasted me very well; but I was obliged to assist a friend, who, I know, will pay me; but, in the mean time, I am out of pocket. At present, I do not care to venture a winter's voyage, even if I were otherwise tired of travelling; but I am so convinced of the advantages of looking at mankind instead of reading about them and the bitter effects of staying at home with all the narrow prejudices of an islander, that I think there should be a law amongst us, to set our young men abroad, for a term, among the few allies our wars have left us.

Here I see and have conversed with French, Italians, Germans, Danes, Greeks, Turks, Americans, etc., etc., etc.; and without losing sight of my own, I can judge of the countries and manners of others. Where I see the superiority of England (which, by the by, we are a good deal mistaken about in many things), I am pleased, and where I find her inferior, I am at least enlightened. Now, I might have stayed, smoked in your towns, or fogged in your country, a century, without being sure of this, and without acquiring any thing more useful or amusing at home. I keep no journal, nor have I any intention of scribbling my travels. I have done with authorship, and if, in my last production, I have convinced the critics or the world I was something more than they took me for, I am satisfied; nor will I hazard *that reputation* by a future effort. It is true I have some others in manuscript, but I leave them for those who come after me; and, if deemed worth publishing, they may serve to prolong my memory when I myself shall cease to remember. I have a famous Bavarian artist taking some views of Athens, etc., etc., for me. This will be better than scribbling, a disease I hope myself cured of. I hope, on my return, to lead a quiet, recluse life, but God knows and does best for us all; at least, so they say, and I have nothing to object, as, on the whole, I have no reason to complain of my lot. I am convinced, however, that men do more harm to themselves than ever the devil could do to them. I trust this will find you well, and as happy as we can be; you will, at least, be pleased to hear I am so, and

Yours ever

TO HIS MOTHER   *Volage frigate, at sea*
                                                June 25th, 1811

Dear Mother, – This letter, which will be forwarded on our arrival at Portsmouth, probably about the 4th of July, is begun about twenty-three days after our departure from Malta. I have just been two years (to a day, on the 2d of July) absent from England, and I return to it with much the same feelings which prevailed on my departure, viz. indifference; but within that apathy I certainly do not comprise yourself, as I will prove by every means in my power. You will be good enough to get my apartments ready at Newstead; but don't disturb yourself, on any account, particularly mine, nor consider me in any other light than as a visitor. I must only inform you that for a long time I have been restricted to an entire vegetable diet, neither fish nor flesh coming within my regimen; so I expect a powerful stock of potatoes, greens and biscuit; I drink no wine. I have two servants, middle-aged men, and both Greeks. It is my intention to proceed first to town, to see Mr Hanson, and thence to Newstead, on my way to Rochdale. I have only to beg you will not forget my diet, which it is very necessary for me to observe. I am well in health, as I have generally been with the exception of two agues, both of which I quickly got over.

My plans will so much depend on circumstances, that I shall not venture to lay down an opinion on the subject. My prospects are not very promising, but I suppose we shall wrestle through life like our neighbours; indeed, by Hanson's last advices, I have some apprehension of finding Newstead dismantled by Messrs Brothers, etc., and he seems determined to force me into selling it, but he will be baffled. I don't suppose I shall be much pestered with visiters; but if I am, you must receive them, for I am determined to have nobody breaking in upon my retirement: you know that I never was fond of society, and I am less so than before. I have brought you a shawl, and a quantity of attar of roses, but these I must smuggle, if possible. I trust to find my library in tolerable order . . .

2. FAME AND SOCIETY

August 1811–January 1815

INTRODUCTION

BYRON'S gloom and foreboding on his homecoming to England in July 1811 were borne out only too soon by events both personal and financial. Hanson had been unable to clarify the affairs of the Rochdale estate. Byron had not even sufficient funds to travel down to Dover to meet Hobhouse, whose father had forced him to accept a commission in the army. In London, attempting to raise money from the money-lenders, Byron handed over the manuscript of 'Hints from Horace' to a distant relation, the sycophantic R. C. Dallas, who had offered to find a publisher; but Dallas, disappointed in the satire, asked if he had written nothing more descriptive of the romantic parts where he had so recently been. Byron then presented him as an outright gift with the manuscript of *Childe Harold's Pilgrimage*, which was immediately accepted by John Murray. On 1 August he heard that his mother was seriously ill, and on the same day, after he had borrowed £40 from Hanson to travel, a further messenger arrived with the news that his mother was dead. Hardly had he arrived at Newstead than a letter from Scrope Davies informed him of the fearful death by drowning, entangled in the weeds of the Cam, of the brilliant Charles Skinner Matthews. Nor was this all: a few days later he learned of the death in Spain of one of his most cherished Harrow friends, the Hon. John Wingfield. Yet a further event occurred which touched his feelings even more deeply: a letter from Ann Edleston, written on 26 September, told him that her brother John, the Trinity chorister, had died in the preceding May. Byron found utterance for his grief in the 'Thyrza' poems and in added stanzas to *Childe Harold*: 'Thou too art gone, thou loved and lovely one!'

A challenge from Tom Moore, which had been withheld by Hodgson, for some mocking lines in 'English Bards', was settled amicably, and a meeting took place at the house of Samuel Rogers, the banker-poet, where Thomas Campbell was also present. Byron's friendship with the talented, kind-hearted and

honourable Moore was a lasting one. He and the loyal Hobhouse
were perhaps the most intimate of his friends, although Byron,
with his delight in widely different types of humanity, from the
sentimentally amorous yet pious Hodgson to the fencing-
master Angelo and the pugilists Jackson and Tom Cribb, was
quickly extending his acquaintances and acquiring new friends.
His financial position was precarious and, against his will, it was
realized that Newstead would have to be sold. On 15 January
1812, after returning to London from Newstead, where he had
experienced some trouble with his 'seraglio' of pretty serving-
girls, he occupied himself principally with politics and the publica-
tion of his poems. Byron delivered his maiden speech – a powerful
plea for leniency – on the Frame-work Bill on 27 February. On
10 March appeared *Childe Harold's Pilgrimage*, the original
edition being sold out in three days. Byron's name was on
everyone's lips; accepted by the Whig aristocracy of Holland and
Melbourne houses, he became 'overnight' (as he expressed it)
the lion of London society.

Byron's headlong, passionate affair with Lady Caroline Lamb
was not only the first of his liaisons with the most fashionable
and desirable of those Whig patricians, who in betraying their
husbands were only following the accepted mode of matrimonial
conduct; it was also the one which caused him the most trouble,
and finally an intense irritation amounting to disgust. For
Caroline recognized no bounds, and her indiscretions were re-
garded even in that tolerant society as scandalous. Early in the
season he had been observed by the intellectual and prim Anne
Isabella Milbanke, Lord Wentworth's heiress. She was niece to
Caroline Lamb's mother-in-law, the intelligent, vivacious and
still beautiful Lady Melbourne, who was acknowledged, with
Lady Holland, as the leading hostess in Whig society, and
known to be friend (if not something more) of the Prince Regent.
With Lady Melbourne Byron had no secrets; they corresponded
almost daily, and it was through the aunt that Byron, in order to
free himself of Caroline's infatuation, made a vague proposal of
marriage to 'Annabella' Milbanke. He was not dismayed by her
refusal, for he was delightfully occupied with Lady Oxford at

Eywood. A prospective buyer of Newstead, Claughton, was dilatory in paying the stipulated instalments of the purchase money; and Byron, deeply in debt, was in no mood to accept Caroline's continued threats, when he took up his abode at 4 Bennet Street, St James's in January 1813. He was sickened by his 'senatorial duties', and confessed to Augusta, who was also in her customary financial difficulties, that he planned to go abroad, but would like to meet her before he left England. 'The Giaour' appeared in June. It was at this time that Byron met the remarkable Mme de Staël at Lady Jersey's. His plan to go abroad with the Oxfords fell through, just at the moment when Augusta arrived in London to consult him about her own matrimonial troubles. (Her husband had quarrelled with the Regent, whose equerry he had been, and was without employment.)

Evidence of the nature of the relationship of Byron with his half-sister Augusta Leigh is (not unnaturally) circumstantial, the most conclusive being his self-revelatory correspondence with Lady Melbourne, who was so fully in his confidence. But further evidence is abundant of the love of Byron and Augusta for each other, and it does appear that they almost certainly consummated their love. However, there is no evidence from a credible and unbiased source to show that Elizabeth Medora Leigh, who was born on 15 April 1814, was Byron's daughter. Lady Melbourne, seeking to break the liaison with Augusta, whom she blamed, encouraged Byron in his enigmatic flirtation with Lady Frances Webster, and even appeared to approve of the desultory correspondence, which her niece Annabella Milbanke had resumed.

To relieve his obsessed mind Byron poured out his love for Augusta in 'The Bride of Abydos' and 'The Corsair', both written at high speed during his social activities in the London season. Such was the enthusiastic reception that ten thousand copies of 'The Corsair' were sold in one day. At Newstead with Augusta in the autumn of 1812, he wrote an equivocal letter (9 September) to the persistent Annabella Milbanke, who regarded it as a proposal of marriage, which she readily accepted. In October Byron left to visit the Milbanke family at Seaham in County Durham, calling on Augusta on the way. Doubts of the

Annabella marriage were uppermost in his mind, which the Seaham visit did nothing to dispel. He felt his own weakness had led him into a position in which marriage was the sole, relentless solution. Finally, accompanied by Hobhouse as his groomsman, Byron set out for Seaham and marriage on Christmas Eve, but dawdled on the way – 'Never was lover less in haste,' wrote Hobhouse in his diary, and 'bridegroom more and more *less* impatient'. On 2 January 1815, Byron married Annabella Milbanke in the drawing-room at Seaham.

TO SCROPE BERDMORE DAVIES *Newstead Abbey, August 7, 1811*

My Dearest Davies, – Some curse hangs over me and mine. My mother lies a corpse in this house; one of my best friends[1] is drowned in a ditch. What can I say, or think, or do? I received a letter from him the day before yesterday. My dear Scrope, if you can spare a moment, do come down to me – I want a friend. Matthew's last letter was written on *Friday* – on Saturday he was not. In ability, who was like Matthews? How did we all shrink before him? You do me but justice in saying, I would have risked my paltry existence to have preserved him. This very evening did I mean to write, inviting him, as I invite you, my very dear friend, to visit me. God forgive — for his apathy! What will our poor Hobhouse feel? His letters breathe but of Matthews. Come to me, Scrope, I am almost desolate – left almost alone in the world – I had but you, and H[obhouse], and M[atthews], and let me enjoy the survivors whilst I can. Poor M., in his letter of Friday, speaks of his intended contest for Cambridge, and a speedy journey to London. Write or come, but come if you can, or one or both

Yours ever.

TO JOHN CAM HOBHOUSE *Newstead Abbey, August 10th, 1811*

My Dear Hobhouse, – From Davies I had already received the death of Matthews, and from M. *a letter* dated the *day* before his *death*. In that letter he mentions you, and as it was perhaps the last he ever wrote, you will derive a poor consolation from hearing that he spoke of you with that affectionate familiarity, so much more pleasing from those we love, than the highest encomiums of the world.

My dwelling you already know is the house of mourning, and I am really so much bewildered with the different shocks I have sustained, that I can hardly reduce myself to reason by the most frivolous occupations. My poor friend, J. Wingfield, my mother, and your best friend (and surely not the worst of mine), C.S.M., have disappeared in one little month, since *my return*, and without my seeing *either*, though I have *heard* from *all*. There is to me something so incomprehensible in death, that I can neither speak nor think on the subject. Indeed, when I looked on the mass of corruption which was the being from whence I sprung, I doubted within myself whether I *was*, or she *was not*. I have lost her who gave me being, and some of those who made that being a blessing. I have neither hopes nor fears beyond the grave, yet if there is within us 'a spark of that Celestial fire', M[atthews] has already 'mingled with the gods'.

In the room where I now write (flanked by the *skulls* you have seen so often) did you and Matthews and myself pass some joyous unprofitable evenings, and here we will drink to his memory, which though it cannot reach the dead, will soothe the survivors, and to them only death can be an evil. I can neither receive nor administer consolation; time will do it for us; in the interim let me see or hear from you, if possible both. I am very lonely, and should think myself miserable were it not for a kind of hysterical merriment, which I can neither account for nor conquer; but strange as it is, I do laugh, and heartily, wondering at myself while I sustain it. I have tried reading, and boxing, and swimming, and writing, and rising early, and sitting late, and water, and wine, with a number of ineffectual remedies, and here I am, wretched, but not 'melancholy or gentleman-like'.

My dear '*Cam of the Cornish*'[2] (Matthews's last expression!!) may man or God give you the happiness which I wish rather than expect you may attain; believe me, none living are more sincerely yours than

BYRON

TO R. C. DALLAS   *Newstead Abbey, Notts.*
                                       August 12, 1811.

Peace be with the dead! Regret cannot wake them. With a sigh
to the departed, let us resume the dull business of life, in the
certainty that we also shall have our repose. Besides her who gave
me being, I have lost more than one who made that being toler-
able. – The best friend of my friend Hobhouse, Matthews, a man
of the first talents, and also not the worst of my narrow circle,
has perished miserably in the muddy waves of the Cam, always
fatal to genius: – my poor school-fellow, Wingfield, at Coimbra –
within a month; and whilst I had heard from *all three*, but not
seen *one*. Matthews wrote to me the very day before his death;
and though I feel for his fate, I am still more anxious for Hob-
house, who, I very much fear, will hardly retain his senses: his
letters to me since the event have been most incoherent. But let
this pass; we shall all one day pass along with the rest – the
world is too full of such things, and our very sorrow is selfish.

I received a letter from you, which my late occupations pre-
vented me from duly noticing. – I hope your friends and family
will long hold together. I shall be glad to hear from you on
business, on commonplace, or any thing, or nothing – but death
– I am already too familiar with the dead. It is strange that I look
on the skulls which stand beside me (I have always had *four* in
my study) without emotion, but cannot strip the features of those
I have known of their fleshly covering, even in idea, without a
hideous sensation; but the worms are less ceremonious. – Surely,
the Romans did well when they burned the dead. – I shall be
happy to hear from you, and am,

   Yours, etc.

TO THE HON. AUGUSTA LEIGH   *Newstead Abbey,*
                                       August 30th, 1811

My Dear Augusta, – The embarrassments you mention in your
last letter I never heard of before, but that disease is epidemic in
our family. Neither have I been apprised of any of the changes

at which you hint, indeed how should I? On the borders of the Black Sea, we heard only of the Russians. So you have much to tell, and all will be novelty.

I don't know what Scrope Davies meant by telling you I liked Children. I abominate the sight of them so much that I have always had the greatest respect for the character of Herod. But, as my house here is large enough for us all, we should go on very well, and I need not tell you that I long to see *you*. I really do not perceive any thing so formidable in a Journey hither of two days, but all this comes of Matrimony, you have a Nurse and all the etcæteras of a family. Well, I must marry to repair the ravages of myself and prodigal ancestry, but if I am ever so unfortunate as to be presented with an Heir, instead of a *Rattle* he shall be provided with a *Gag*.

I shall perhaps be able to accept D[avies'] invitation to Cambridge, but I fear my stay in Lancashire will be prolonged, I proceed there in the 2d week in Sep[tr] to arrange my coal concerns, and then if I can't persuade some wealthy dowdy to ennoble the dirty puddle of her mercantile Blood, – why – I shall leave England and all its clouds for the East again; I am very sick of it already. Joe [Murray?] has been getting well of a disease that would have killed a troop of horse; he promises to bear away the palm of longevity from old Parr. As you won't come, you will write; I long to hear all those unutterable things, being utterly unable to guess at any of them, unless they concern *your* relative the Thane of Carlisle, – though I had great hopes we had done with him.

I have little to add that you do not already know, and being quite alone, have no great variety of incident to gossip with; I am but rarely pestered with visiters, and the few I have I get rid of as soon as possible. I will now take leave of you in the Jargon of 1794. 'Health and *Fraternity*!'

Yours alway,

B.

TO THE HON. AUGUSTA LEIGH   *Newstead Abbey,*
                                             Sept. 2d. 1811

... As to Lady B., when I discover one rich enough to suit me and foolish enough to have me, I will give her leave to make me miserable if she can. Money is the magnet; as to Women, one is as well as another, the older the better, we have then a chance of getting her to Heaven. So, your Spouse does not like brats better than myself; now those who beget them have no right to find fault, but *I* may rail with great propriety.

My 'Satire!' – I am glad it made you laugh for Somebody told me in Greece that you was angry, and I was sorry, as you were perhaps the only person whom I did *not* want to *make angry.*

But how you will make *me laugh* I don't know, for it is a vastly *serious* subject to me I assure you; therefore take care, or I shall hitch *you* into the next Edition to make up our family party. Nothing so fretful, so despicable as a Scribbler, see what *I* am, and what a parcel of Scoundrels I have brought about my ears, and what language I have been obliged to treat them with to deal with them in their own way; – all this comes of Authorship, but now I am in for it, and shall be at war with Grubstreet, till I find some better amusement.

You will write to me your Intentions and may almost depend on my being at Cambridge in October. You say you mean to be etc. in the *Autumn*; I should be glad to know what you call this present Season, it would be Winter in every other Country which I have seen. If we meet in October we will travel in my *Vis.* and can have a cage for the children and a cart for the Nurse. Or perhaps we can forward them by the Canal. Do let us know all about it, your '*bright thought*' is a little clouded, like the Moon in this preposterous climate. Good even, Child.

Yours ever,

B.

TO FRANCIS HODGSON   *Newstead Abbey,*
                                                      Sept 3, 1811

My Dear Hodgson, – I will have nothing to do with your im-
mortality; we are miserable enough in this life, without the
absurdity of speculating upon another. If men are to live, why
die at all? and if they die, why disturb the sweet and sound sleep
that 'knows no waking'? 'Post Mortem nihil est, ipsaque Mors
nihil ... quaeris quo jaceas post obitum loco? Quo *non* Nata
jacent.'[3]

As to revealed religion, Christ came to save men; but a good
Pagan will go to heaven, and a bad Nazarene to hell; 'Argal'
(I argue like the gravedigger) why are not all men Christians? or
why are any? If mankind may be saved who never heard or
dreamt, at Timbuctoo, Otaheite, Terra Incognita, etc., of Galilee
and its Prophet, Christianity is of no avail: if they cannot be
saved without, why are not all orthodox? It is a little hard to send
a man preaching to Judaea, and leave the rest of the world –
Negers and what not – *dark* as their complexions, without a ray of
light for so many years to lead them on high; and who will
believe that God will damn men for not knowing what they were
never taught? I hope I am sincere; I was so at least on a bed of
sickness in a far-distant country, when I had neither friend, nor
comforter, nor hope, to sustain me. I looked to death as a relief
from pain, without a wish for an after-life, but a confidence that
the God who punishes in this existence had left that last asylum
for the weary.

'Ον ὁ θεός ἀγαπάει ἀποθνήσκει νέος[4]

I am no Platonist, I am nothing at all; but I would sooner be a
Paulician, Manichean, Spinozist, Gentile, Pyrrhonian, Zoroas-
trian, than one of the seventy-two villainous sects who are tearing
each other to pieces for the love of the Lord and hatred of each
other. Talk of Galileeism? Show me the effects – are you better,
wiser, kinder by your precepts? I will bring you ten Mussulmans
shall shame you in all goodwill towards men, prayer to God, and
duty to their neighbours. And is there a Talapoin, or a Bonze
who is not superior to a fox-hunting curate? But I will say no

more on this endless theme; let me live, well if possible, and die without pain. The rest is with God, who assuredly, had He *come* or *sent*, would have made Himself manifest to nations, and intelligible to all . . .

TO JOHN MURRAY   *Newstead Abbey, Notts.*
                                       Sept. 5th, 1811

Sir, – The time seems to be past when (as Dr Johnson said) a man was certain to 'hear the truth from his bookseller', for you have paid me so many compliments, that, if I was not the veriest scribbler on earth, I should feel affronted. As I accept your compliments, it is but fair I should give equal or greater credit to your objections, the more so as I believe them to be well founded. With regard to the political and metaphysical parts, I am afraid I can alter nothing; but I have high authority for my Errors in that point, for even the *Aeneid* was a *political* poem, and written for a *political* purpose; and as to my unlucky opinions on Subjects of more importance, I am too sincere in them for recantation. On Spanish affairs I have said what I saw, and every day confirms me in that notion of the result formed on the Spot; and I rather think honest John Bull is beginning to come round again to that Sobriety which Massena's retreat had begun to reel from its centre – the usual consequence of *un*usual success. So you perceive I cannot alter the Sentiments; but if there are any alterations in the structure of the versification you would wish to be made, I will tag rhymes and turn stanzas as much as you please. As for the 'Orthodox', let us hope they will buy, on purpose to abuse – you will forgive the one, if they will do the other. You are aware that any thing from my pen must expect no quarter, on many accounts; and as the present publication is of a nature very different from the former, we must not be sanguine.

You have given me no answer to my question – tell me fairly, did you show the MS. to some of your corps? – I sent an introductory stanza to Mr Dallas, that it might be forwarded to you; the poem else will open too abruptly. The Stanzas had better be

numbered in Roman characters, there is a disquisition on the
literature of the modern Greeks, and some smaller poems to
come in at the close. These are now at Newstead, but will be sent
in time. If Mr D. has lost the Stanza and note annexed to it,
write, and I will send it myself. – You tell me to add two cantos,
but I am about to visit my *Collieries* in Lancashire on the 15th
instant, which is so *unpoetical* an employment that I need say
no more.

I am, sir, your most obedient, etc, etc.,

BYRON

TO FRANCIS HODGSON   *Newstead Abbey,*
                                            Sept. 25, 1811

... I am plucking up my spirits, and have begun to gather my
little sensual comforts together. Lucy is extracted from War-
wickshire; some very bad faces have been warned off the premises,
and more promising substituted in their stead; the partridges are
plentiful, hares fairish, pheasants not quite so good, and the
Girls on the Manor — Just as I had formed a tolerable establish-
ment my travels commenced, and on my return I find all to do
over again; my former flock were all scattered; some married,
not before it was needful. As I am a great disciplinarian, I have
just issued an edict for the abolition of caps; no hair to be cut on
any pretext; stays permitted, but not too low before; full uniform
always in the evening; Lucinda to be commander – *vice* the
present, about to be wedded (*mem*, she is 35 with a flat face and a
squeaking voice), of all the makers and unmakers of beds in the
household.

My tortoises (all Athenians), my hedgehog, my mastiff and the
other live Greek, are all purely. The tortoises lay eggs, and I
have hired a hen to hatch them. I am writing notes for *my* quarto
(Murray would have it a *quarto*), and Hobhouse is writing text
for *his* quarto; if you call on Murray or Cawthorn you will hear
news of either. I have attacked De Pauw, Thornton, Lord Elgin,
Spain, Portugal, the *Edinburgh Review*, travellers, Painters,
Antiquarians, and others, so you see what a dish of Sour Crout

Controversy I shall prepare for myself. It would not answer for me to give way, now; as I was forced into bitterness at the beginning, I will go through to the last. *Væ Victis*! If I fall, I shall fall gloriously, fighting against a host.

Felicissima Notte a Voss. Signoria,[5]

B.

TO R. C. DALLAS
*Newstead Abbey,
Oct. 11, 1811*

... I have been again shocked with a *death*,[6] and have lost one very dear to me in happier times; but 'I have almost forgot the taste of grief', and 'supped full of horrors' till I have become callous, nor have I a tear left for an event which, five years ago, would have bowed down my head to the earth. It seems as though I were to experience in my youth the greatest misery of age. My friends fall around me, and I shall be left a lonely tree before I am withered. Other men can always take refuge in their families; I have no resource but my own reflections, and they present no prospect here or hereafter, except the selfish satisfaction of surviving my betters. I am indeed very wretched, and you will excuse my saying so, as you know I am not apt to cant of sensibility ...

TO FRANCIS HODGSON
*Newstead Abbey,
Oct. 13, 1811*

... I am growing *nervous* (how you will laugh!) – but it is true, – really, wretchedly, ridiculously, fine-ladically *nervous*. Your climate kills me; I can neither read, write, nor amuse myself, or any one else. My days are listless, and my nights restless; I have very seldom any society, and when I have, I run out of it. At 'this present writing', there are in the next room three *ladies*, and I have stolen away to write this grumbling letter. – I don't know that I sha'n't end with insanity, for I find a want of method in arranging my thoughts that perplexes me strangely; but this looks more like silliness than madness, as Scrope Davies would facetiously remark in his consoling manner. I must try the hartshorn of your company; and a session of Parliament would suit me well, – any thing to cure me of conjugating the accursed verb 'ennuyer' ...

TO JOHN CAM HOBHOUSE *Newstead Abbey,*
October 14th, 1811

Dear Hobhouse, – In my last I answered your queries and now I shall acquaint you with my movements, according to your former request. I have been down to Rochdale with Hanson; the property there, if I work the mines myself, will produce about £4000 pr.ann.; but to do this I must lay out at least £10,000 in etceteras, or if I chance to *let* it without incurring such expenditure, it will produce a rental of half the above sum, so we are to work the collieries ourselves, of course. Newstead is to be advanced immediately to £2100 pr.ann., so that my income might be made about £6000 pr.ann. But here comes at least £20,000 of debt, and I must mortgage for that and other expenses, so that altogether my situation is perplexing. I believe the above statement to be nearly correct, and so ends the chapter. If I chose to turn out my old bad tenants, and take monied men, they say Newstead would bear a few hundreds more from its great extent; but this I shall hardly do. It contains 3800 acres, including the Forest land, the Rochdale manor, 8256 acres of Lancashire, which are larger than ours. So there you have my territories on the earth, and in 'the waters under the earth'; but I must marry some heiress, or I shall always be involved.

Now for higher matters. My Boke is in ye press, and proceeds leisurely; I have lately been sweating notes, which I don't mean to make very voluminous, – some remarks written at Athens, and the flourish on Romaic which you have seen will constitute most of them. The essence of that '*valuable information*', as you call it, is at your service, and shall be sent in time for your purpose. I had also by accident detected in Athens a blunder of Thornton, of a ludicrous nature, in the *Turkish language*, of which I mean to make some 'pleasant mirth', in return for his abuse of the Greeks. It is the passage about Pouqueville's story of the 'Eater of Corrosive Sublimate'. By-the-bye, I rather suspect we shall be at right angles in our opinions of the Greeks; I have not quite made up my mind about them, but you I know are decisively inimical . . .

TO JOHN CAM HOBHOUSE   *King's College Ce.,*
                                        October 22nd, 1811

My dear Hobhouse, – I write from Scrope's rooms, whom I have just assisted to put to bed in a state of *outrageous* intoxication. I think I never saw him so bad before. We dined at Mr Caldwell's, of Jesus Coll., where we met Dr Clarke and others of the gown, and Scrope finished himself as usual. He has been in a similar state every evening since my arrival here a few days ago. We are to dine at Dr Clarke's on Thursday. I find he knows little of Romaic, so we shall have *that* department entirely to ourselves. I tell you this that you need not fear any competitor, particularly so formidable a one as Dr Clarke would probably have been.

I like him much, though Scrope says *we* talked so bitterly, that he (the said Scrope) lost his listeners.

I proceed hence to town, where I shall enquire after your work, which I am sorry to say stands still for '*want of copy*', to talk in technicals.

I am very low spirited on many accounts, and wine, which, however, I do not quaff as formerly, has lost its power over me. We all wish you here, and well, wherever you are, but surely better with us. If you don't soon return, Scrope and I mean to visit you in quarters.

The event I mentioned in my last[7] has had an effect on me, I am ashamed to think of. But there is no arguing on these points. I could 'have better spared a better being'. Wherever I turn, particularly in this place, the idea goes with me. I say all this at the risk of incurring your contempt; but you cannot despise me more than I do myself. I am indeed very wretched, and like all complaining persons I can't help telling you so.

The Marquis Sligo is in a great scrape about his kidnapping the seamen; I, who know him, do not think him so culpable as the Navy are determined to make him. He is a good man. I have been in Lancashire, Notts, but all places are alike; I cannot live under my present feelings; I have lost my appetite, my rest, and can neither read, write, or act in comfort. Everybody here is very polite and hospitable, my friend Scrope particularly; I wish to God he would grow sober, as I much fear no constitution can long support his excesses. If I lose him and you, what am I? Hodgson is not here, but expected soon; Newstead is my regular address. Demetrius is here, much pleased with ye place, Lord Sligo is about to send back his Arnaouts. Excuse this dirty paper, it is of Scrope's best. Good night.

Ever yours,

BYRON

TO THOMAS MOORE *Cambridge, October 27, 1811*

Sir, – Your letter followed me from Notts. to this place which will account for the delay of my reply. Your former letter I never had the honour to receive; – be assured in whatever part of the world it had found me, I should have deemed it my duty to return and answer it in person.

The advertisement you mention, I know nothing of. – At the time of your meeting with Mr Jeffrey, I had recently entered College, and remember to have heard and read a number of squibs on the occasion; and from the recollection of these I derived all my knowledge on the subject, without the slightest idea of 'giving the lie' to an address which I never beheld. When I put my name to the production, which has occasioned this correspondence, I became responsible to all whom it might concern, – to explain where it requires explanation, and, where insufficiently or too sufficiently explicit, at all events to satisfy. My situation leaves me no choice; it rests with the injured and the angry to obtain reparation in their own way.

With regard to the passage in question, *you* were certainly *not* the person towards whom I felt personally hostile. On the contrary, my whole thoughts were engrossed by one, whom I had reason to consider as my worst literary enemy, nor could I foresee that his former antagonist was about to become his

99

champion. You do not specify what you would wish to have done: I can neither retract nor apologise for a charge of falsehood which I never advanced.

In the beginning of the week, I shall be at No. 8, St James's Street. – Neither the letter nor the friend to whom you stated your intention ever made their appearance.

Your friend, Mr Rogers, or any other gentleman delegated by you, will find me most ready to adopt any conciliatory proposition which shall not compromise my own honour, – or, failing in that, to make the atonement you deem it necessary to require.

I have the honour to be, Sir,
Your most obedient humble servant,

BYRON

TO THOMAS MOORE   *8, St. James's Street,*
November 1, 1811

Sir, – As I should be very sorry to interrupt your Sunday's engagement, if Monday, or any other day of the ensuing week, would be equally convenient to yourself and friend, I will then have the honour of accepting his invitation. Of the professions of esteem with which Mr Rogers has honoured me, I cannot but feel proud, though undeserving. I should be wanting to myself, if insensible to the praise of such a man; and, should my approaching interview with him and his friend lead to any degree of intimacy with both or either, I shall regard our past correspondence as one of the happiest events of my life. I have the honour to be,

Your very sincere and obedient servant,

BYRON

TO JOHN CAM HOBHOUSE   *8, St. James's Street,*
December 9th, 1811

My dear Hobhouse, – At length I am your rival in good fortune. I, this night, saw *Robert Coates* perform Lothario at the Haymarket, the house crammed, but bribery (a bank token) procured

100

an excellent place near the stage. Before the curtain drew up, a performer (all gemmen) came forward and thus addressed the house, Ladies, etc. 'A melancholy accident has happened to the gentleman who undertook the part of Altamont –' (here a dead stop – then –) 'this accident has *happened* to his *brother*, who fell this afternoon through a *loophole* into the *London Dock*, and was taken up dead, Altamont has just entered the house, distractedly, is – now dressing!!! and will appear in five minutes!!!' Such were verbatim the words of the apologist; they were followed by a roar of laughter, and Altamont himself, who did not fall short of Coates in absurdity. Damn me, if I ever saw such a scene in my life; the play was closed in 3rd act; after Bob's demise, nobody would hear a syllable, he was interrupted several times before, and made speeches, every soul was in hysterics, and all the actors on his own model. You can't conceive how I longed for *you*; your taste for the ridiculous would have been gratified to surfeit. A farce followed in dumb-show, after Bob had been hooted from the stage, for a bawdy address he attempted to deliver between play and farce. 'Love à la mode' was damned, Coates was damned, everything was damned, and damnable. His enacting I need not describe, you have seen him at Bath. But never did you see the *others*, never did you hear the *apology*, never did you behold the 'distracted' survivor of a 'brother neck-broken through a *loop-hole* in y^e *London Docks*'. Like George Faulkner these fellows defied burlesque. Oh, Captain! eye hath not seen, ear hath not heard, nor can the heart of man conceive tonight's performance. Baron Geramb was in the stage box, and Coates in his address *nailed* the *Baron* to the infinite amusement of the audience, and the discomfiture of Geramb, who grew very wroth indeed.

I meant to write on other topics, but I must postpone, I can't think, and talk, and dream only of these buffoons. ''Tis done, 'tis numbered with the things that were, would, would it were to come' and you by my side to see it.

Heigh ho! Good-night.

Yours ever,

B.

TO WILLIAM HARNESS   *8, St. James's Street,*
                                             Dec. 15, 1811

. . . Yesterday I went with Moore to Sydenham to visit Campbell. He was not visible, so we jogged homeward merrily enough. Tomorrow I dine with Rogers, and am to hear Coleridge, who is a kind of rage at present. Last night I saw Kemble in Coriolanus; – he *was glorious*, and exerted himself wonderfully. By good luck I got an excellent place in the best part of the house, which was more than overflowing. Clare and Delawarr, who were there on the same speculation, were less fortunate. I saw them by accident, – we were not together. I wished for you, to gratify your love of Shakspeare and of fine acting to its fullest extent. Last week I saw an exhibition of a different kind in a Mr Coates, at the Haymarket, who performed Lothario in a damned and damnable manner.

I told you the fate of B[land] and H[odgson] in my last. So much for these sentimentalists, who console themselves in their stews for the loss – the never to be recovered loss – the despair of the refined attachment of a couple of drabs! You censure *my* life, Harness, – when I compare myself with these men, my elders and my betters, I really begin to conceive myself a monument of prudence – a walking statue – without feeling or failing; and yet the world in general hath given me a proud pre-eminence over them in profligacy. Yet I like the men, and, God knows, ought not to condemn their aberrations. But I own I feel provoked when they dignify all this by the name of *love* – romantic attachments for things marketable for a dollar! . . .

Dec. 16 –
. . . The circumstances you mention at the close of your letter is another proof in favour of my opinion of mankind. Such you will always find them – selfish and distrustful. I expect none. The cause of this is the state of society. In the world, every one is to stir for himself – it is useless, perhaps selfish, to expect any thing from his neighbour. But I do not think we are born of this disposition; for you find *friendship* as a schoolboy, and *love* enough before twenty . . .

TO THOMAS MOORE   *January 29, 1812.*

My Dear Moore, – I wish very much I could have seen you; I am in a state of ludicrous tribulation. —

Why do you say that I dislike your poesy? I have expressed no such opinion, either in *print* or elsewhere. In scribbling myself, it was necessary for me to find fault, and I fixed upon the trite charge of immorality, because I could discover no other, and was so perfectly qualified in the innocence of my heart, to 'pluck that mote from my neighbour's eye'.

I feel very, very much obliged by your approbation; but, at *this moment*, praise, even *your* praise, passes by me like 'the idle wind'. I meant and mean to send you a copy the moment of publication; but now I can think of nothing but damned, deceitful, – delightful woman, as Mr Liston says in the *Knight of Snowdon*.[8] Believe me, my dear Moore,

Ever yours, most affectionately,

BYRON

TO JOHN CAM HOBHOUSE   *8 St. James's Street*
                                  February 10th, 1812

... I have dismissed my Seraglio for squabbles and infidelities ...

TO FRANCIS HODGSON   *8 St. James's Street*
                                  February 16, 1812

Dear Hodgson, – I send you a proof. Last week I was very ill and confined to bed with stone in the kidney, but I am now quite recovered. The women are gone to their relatives, after many attempts to explain what was already too clear. If the stone had got into my heart instead of my kidneys, it would have been all the better. However, I have quite recovered *that* also, and only wonder at my folly in excepting my own strumpets from the general corruption, – albeit a two months' weakness is better than ten years. I have one request to make, which is, never mention a woman again in any letter to me, or even allude to the existence of the sex. I won't even read a word of the feminine gender; – it must all be *propria quae maribus*.[9]

In the spring of 1813 I shall leave England for ever. Every thing in my affairs tends to this, and my inclinations and health do not discourage it. Neither my habits nor constitution are improved by your customs or your climate. I shall find employment in making myself a good Oriental scholar. I shall retain a mansion in one of the fairest islands, and retrace, at intervals, the most interesting portions of the East. In the mean time I am adjusting my concerns, which will (when arranged) leave me with wealth sufficient even for home, but enough for a principality in Turkey. At present they are involved, but I hope, by taking some necessary but unpleasant steps, to clear every thing. Hobhouse is expected daily in London; we shall be very glad to see him; and, perhaps, you will come up and 'drink deep ere he depart', if not 'Mahomet must go to the mountain'; – but Cambridge will bring sad recollections to him, and worse to me, though for very different reasons. I believe the only human being,[10] that ever loved me in truth and entirely, was of, or belonging to, Cambridge, and, in that, no change can now take place. There is one consolation in death – where he sets his seal, the impression can neither be melted nor broken, but endureth for ever.

Yours always,

B.

P.S. – I almost rejoice when one I love dies young, for I could never bear to see them old or altered.

TO LORD HOLLAND   *8, St. James's Street,*
                                   February 25, 1812.

My Lord, – With my best thanks, I have the honour to return the Notts. letter to your Lordship. I have read it with attention, but do not think I shall venture to avail myself of its contents, as my view of the question differs in some measure from Mr Coldham's. I hope I do not wrong him, but *his* objections to the

104

bill appear to me to be founded on certain apprehensions that he and his coadjutors might be mistaken for the '*original advisers*' (to quote him) of the measure. For my own part, I consider the manufacturers as a much injured body of men, sacrificed to the views of certain individuals who have enriched themselves by those practices which have deprived the frame-workers of employment. For instance: – by the adoption of a certain kind of frame, one man performs the work of seven – six are thus thrown out of business. But it is to be observed that the work thus done is far inferior in quality, hardly marketable at home, and hurried over with a view to exportation. Surely, my Lord, however we may rejoice in any improvement in the arts which may be beneficial to mankind, we must not allow mankind to be sacrificed to improvements in mechanism. The maintenance and well-doing of the industrious poor is an object of greater consequence to the community than the enrichment of a few monopolists by any improvement in the implements of trade, which deprives the workman of his bread, and renders the labourer 'unworthy of his hire'.

My own motive for opposing the bill is founded on its palpable injustice, and its certain inefficacy. I have seen the state of these miserable men, and it is a disgrace to a civilised country. Their excesses may be condemned, but cannot be subject of wonder. The effect of the present bill would be to drive them into actual rebellion. The few words I shall venture to offer on Thursday will be founded upon these opinions formed from my own observations on the spot. By previous inquiry, I am convinced these men would have been restored to employment, and the county to tranquillity. It is, perhaps, not yet too late, and is surely worth the trial. It can never be too late to employ force in such circumstances. I believe your Lordship does not coincide with me entirely on this subject, and most cheerfully and sincerely shall I submit to your superior judgment and experience, and take some other line of argument against the bill, or be silent altogether, should you deem it more advisable. Condemning, as every one must condemn, the conduct of these wretches, I believe in the existence of grievances which call rather for pity than punishment. I have the honour to be, with great respect, my Lord, your Lordship's

Most obedient and obliged servant,

BYRON

P.S. I am a little apprehensive that your Lordship will think me too lenient towards these men, and half a *frame-breaker myself*.

DEBATE ON THE FRAME-WORK BILL,
IN THE HOUSE OF LORDS,
27 FEBRUARY 1812

THE order of the day for the second reading of this Bill being read,
Lord BYRON rose, and (for the first time) addressed their
Lordships as follows: –

My Lords, – The subject now submitted to your Lordships for
the first time, though new to the House, is by no means new to
the country. I believe it had occupied the serious thoughts of all
descriptions of persons, long before its introduction to the notice
of that legislature, whose interference alone could be of real
service. As a person in some degree connected with the suffering
county, though a stranger not only to this House in general, but
to almost every individual whose attention I presume to solicit,
I must claim some portion of your Lordships' indulgence,
whilst I offer a few observations on a question in which I confess
myself deeply interested.

To enter into any detail of the riots would be superfluous: the
House is already aware that every outrage short of actual blood-
shed has been perpetrated, and that the proprietors of the frames
obnoxious to the rioters, and all persons supposed to be con-
nected with them, have been liable to insult and violence. During
the short time I recently passed in Nottinghamshire, not twelve
hours elapsed without some fresh act of violence; and on the day
I left the county I was informed that forty frames had been
broken the preceding evening, as usual, without resistance and
without detection.

Such was then the state of that county, and such I have reason
to believe it to be at this moment. But whilst these outrages must
be admitted to exist to an alarming extent, it cannot be denied
that they have arisen from circumstances of the most unparalleled
distress: the perseverance of these miserable men in their pro-
ceedings tends to prove that nothing but absolute want could
have driven a large, and once honest and industrious, body of the

107

people, into the commission of excesses so hazardous to themselves, their families, and the community. At the time to which I allude, the town and county were burdened with large detachments of the military; the police was in motion, the magistrates assembled; yet all the movements, civil and military, had led to nothing. Not a single instance had occurred of the apprehension of any real delinquent actually taken in the fact, against whom there existed legal evidence sufficient for conviction. But the police, however useless, were by no means idle: several notorious delinquents had been detected, – men, liable to conviction, on the clearest evidence, of the capital crime of poverty; men, who had been nefariously guilty of lawfully begetting several children, whom, thanks to the times! they were unable to maintain. Considerable injury has been done to the proprietors of the improved frames. These machines were to them an advantage, inasmuch as they superseded the necessity of employing a number of workmen, who were left in consequence to starve. By the adoption of one species of frame in particular, one man performed the work of many, and the superfluous labourers were thrown out of employment. Yet it is to be observed, that the work thus executed was inferior in quality; not marketable at home, and merely hurried over with a view to exportation. It was called, in the cant of the trade, by the name of 'Spider-work'. The rejected workmen, in the blindness of their ignorance, instead of rejoicing at these improvements in arts so beneficial to mankind, conceived themselves to be sacrificed to improvements in mechanism. In the foolishness of their hearts they imagined that the maintenance and well-doing of the industrious poor were objects of greater consequence than the enrichment of a few individuals by any improvement, in the implements of trade, which threw the workmen out of employment, and rendered the labourer unworthy of his hire. And it must be confessed that although the adoption of the enlarged machinery in that state of our commerce which the country once boasted might have been beneficial to the master without being detrimental to the servant; yet, in the present situation of our manufactures, rotting in warehouses, without a prospect of exportation, with the demand for work and workmen equally diminished, frames of this description tend materially to aggravate the distress and discontent of the disappointed sufferers. But the real cause of these distresses and consequent disturbances lies deeper. When we are told that these men are leagued together not only for the destruction of their own comfort, but of their very means of subsistence, can we forget that it is the bitter policy, the destructive warfare of the last eighteen years, which has destroyed their comfort, your comfort, all men's comfort? that policy, which, originating with 'great statesman now no more', has survived the dead to become a curse on the living, unto the third and fourth generation! These men never destroyed their looms till they were become useless, worse than useless; till they were become actual impediments to their exertions in obtaining their daily bread. Can you, then, wonder that in times like these, when bankruptcy, convicted fraud, and imputed felony are found in a station not far beneath that of your Lordships, the lowest, though once most useful portion of the people, should forget their duty in their distress, and become only less guilty than one of their representatives? But while the exalted offender can find means to baffle the law, new capital punishments must be devised, new snares of death must be spread for the wretched mechanic, who is famished into guilt. These men were willing to dig, but the spade was in other hands: they were not ashamed to beg, but there was none to relieve them; their own means of subsistence were cut off, all other employments pre-occupied; and their excesses, however to be deplored and condemned, can hardly be subject of surprise.

It has been stated that the persons in the temporary possession of frames connive at their destruction; if this be proved upon inquiry, it were necessary that such material accessories to the crime should be principals in the punishment. But I did hope, that any measure proposed by his Majesty's government for your Lordships' decision, would have had conciliation for its basis; or, if that were hopeless, that some previous inquiry, some deliberation, would have been deemed requisite; not that we should have been called at once, without examination and without cause to pass sentences by wholesale, and sign death-warrants blindfold. But, admitting that these men had no cause of complaint; that the grievances of them and their employers were alike groundless; that they deserved the worst; – what inefficiency, what imbecility has been evinced in the method chosen to reduce them! Why were the military called out to be made a mockery of, if they were to be called out at all? As far as the difference of seasons would permit, they have merely parodied the summer campaign of Major Sturgeon; and, indeed, the whole proceedings, civil and military, seemed on the model of those of the mayor and corporation of Garratt. – Such marchings and countermarchings! – from Nottingham to Bullwell, from Bullwell to Banford, from Banford to Mansfield! And when at length the detachments arrived at their destination, in all 'the pride, pomp, and circumstance of glorious war', they came just in time to witness the mischief which had been done, and ascertain the escape of the perpetrators, to collect the '*spolia opima*'[11] in the fragments of broken frames, and return to their quarters amidst the derision of old women, and the hootings of children. Now, though, in a free country, it were to be wished that our military should never be too formidable, at least to ourselves, I cannot see the policy of placing them in situations where they can only be made ridiculous. As the sword is the worst argument that can be used, so should it be the last. In this instance it has been the first; but providentially as yet only in the scabbard. The present measure will, indeed, pluck it from the sheath; yet had proper meetings been held in the earlier stages of these riots, had the grievances of these men and their masters (for they also had their grievances) been fairly weighed and justly examined, I do think that means might have been devised to restore these workmen to their avocations, and tranquillity to the county. At present the county suffers from the double infliction of an idle military and a starving population. In what state of apathy have we been plunged so long, that now for the first time the House has been officially apprised of these disturbances? All this has been transacting within 130 miles of London; and yet we, 'good easy men', have 'deemed full sure our greatness was a-ripening', and have sat down to enjoy our foreign triumphs in the midst of

110

domestic calamity. But all the cities you have taken, all the armies which have retreated before your leaders, are but paltry subjects of self-congratulation, if your land divides against itself, and your dragoons and your executioners must be let loose against your fellow-citizens. – You call these men a mob, desperate, dangerous, and ignorant; and seem to think that the only way to quiet the '*Bellua multorum capitum*'[12] is to lop off a few of its superfluous heads. But even a mob may be better reduced to reason by a mixture of conciliation and firmness, than by additional irritation and redoubled penalties. Are we aware of our obligations to a mob? It is the mob that labour in your fields and serve in your houses, – that man your navy, and recruit your army, – that have enabled you to defy all the world, and can also defy you when neglect and calamity have driven them to despair! You may call the people a mob; but do not forget that a mob too often speaks the sentiments of the people. And here I must remark, with what alacrity you are accustomed to fly to the succour of your distressed allies, leaving the distressed of your own country to the care of Providence or – the parish. When the Portuguese suffered under the retreat of the French, every arm was stretched out, every hand was opened, from the rich man's largess to the widow's mite, all was bestowed, to enable them to rebuild their villages and replenish their granaries. And at this moment, when thousands of misguided but most unfortunate fellow-countrymen are struggling with the extremes of hardships and hunger, as your charity began abroad it should end at home. A much less sum, a tithe of the bounty bestowed on Portugal, even if those men (which I cannot admit without inquiry) could not have been restored to their employments, would have rendered unnecessary the tender mercies of the bayonet and the gibbet. But doubtless our friends have too many foreign claims to admit a prospect of domestic relief; though never did such objects demand it. I have traversed the seat of war in the Peninsula, I have been in some of the most oppressed provinces of Turkey; but never under the most despotic of infidel governments did I behold such squalid wretchedness as I have seen since my return in the very heart of a Christian country.

And what are your remedies? After months of inaction, and months of action worse than inactivity, at length comes forth the grand specific, the never-failing nostrum of all state physicians, from the days of Draco to the present time. After feeling the pulse and shaking the head over the patient, prescribing the usual course of warm water and bleeding, – the warm water of your mawkish police, and the lancets of your military, – these convulsions must terminate in death, the sure consummation of the prescriptions of all political Sangrados. Setting aside the palpable injustice and the certain inefficiency of the Bill, are there not capital punishments sufficient in your statutes? Is there not blood enough upon your penal code, that more must be poured forth to ascend to Heaven and testify against you? How will you carry the Bill into effect? Can you commit a whole county to their own prisons? Will you erect a gibbet in every field, and hang up men like scarecrows? or will you proceed (as you must to bring this measure into effect) by decimation? Place the county under martial law? depopulate and lay waste all around you? and restore Sherwood Forest as an acceptable gift to the crown, in its former condition of a royal chase and an asylum for outlaws? Are these the remedies for a starving and desperate populace? Will the famished wretch who has braved your bayonets be appalled by your gibbets? When death is a relief, and the only relief it appears that you will afford him, will he be dragooned into tranquillity? Will that which could not be effected by your grenadiers be accomplished by your executioners? If you proceed by the forms of law, where is your evidence? Those who have refused to impeach their accomplices when transportation only was the punishment, will hardly be tempted to witness against them when death is the penalty. With all due deference to the noble lords opposite, I think a little investigation, some previous inquiry, would induce even them to change their purpose. That most favourable state measure, so marvellously efficacious in many and recent instances, temporising, would not be without its advantages in this. When a proposal is made to emancipate or relieve, you hesitate, you deliberate for years, you temporise and tamper with the minds of men; but a death-bill must be passed off-hand, without a thought of the consequences. Sure I am, from what I have heard, and from what I have seen, that to pass the Bill under all the existing circumstances, without inquiry, without deliberation, would only be to add injustice to irritation, and barbarity to neglect. The framers of such a bill must be content to inherit the honours of that Athenian law-giver whose edicts were said to be written not in ink but in blood. But suppose it passed; suppose one of these men, as I have seen them, – meagre with famine, sullen with despair, careless of a life which your Lordships are perhaps about to value at something less than the price of a stocking-frame; – suppose this man surrounded by the children for whom he is unable to procure bread at the hazard of his existence, about to be torn for ever from a family which he lately supported in peaceful industry, and which it is not his fault that he can no longer so support; – suppose this man – and there are ten thousand such from whom you may select your victims – dragged into court, to be tried for this new offence, by this new law; still, there are two things wanting to convict and condemn him; and these are, in my opinion, twelve butchers for a jury, and a Jeffreys for a judge!

TO FRANCIS HODGSON   *8 St. James's Street,*
                                        March 5, 1812

My Dear Hodgson, – *We* are not answerable for reports of speeches in the papers; they are always given incorrectly, and on this occasion more so than usual, from the debate in the Commons on the same night. The *Morning Post* should have said *eighteen years*. However, you will find the speech, as spoken, in the Parliamentary Register, when it comes out. Lords Holland and Grenville, particularly the latter, paid me some high compliments in the course of their speeches, as you may have seen in the papers, and Lords Eldon and Harrowby answered me. I have had many marvellous eulogies repeated to me since, in person and by proxy, from divers persons *ministerial* – yea, *ministerial*! – as well as oppositionists; of them I shall only mention Sir F. Burdett. *He* says it is the best speech by a *Lord* since the '*Lord*

113

knows when', probably from a fellow-feeling in the sentiments. Lord H. tells me I shall beat them all if I persevere; and Lord G. remarked that the construction of some of my periods are very like *Burke's*!! And so much for vanity. I spoke very violent sentences with a sort of modest impudence, abused every thing and every body, put the Lord Chancellor very much out of humour; and if I may believe what I hear, have not lost any character by the experiment. As to my delivery, loud and fluent enough, perhaps a little theatrical. I could not recognise myself or any one else in the newspapers.

I hire myself unto Griffiths, and my poesy comes out on Saturday.[13] Hobhouse is here; I shall tell him to write. My stone is gone for the present, but I fear is part of my habit. We *all* talk of a visit to Cambridge.

Yours ever,

B.

TO LADY CAROLINE LAMB *Sy Evening*
[*Spring, 1812*?]

I never supposed you artful: we are all selfish, nature did that for us. But even when you attempt deceit occasionally, you cannot maintain it, which is all the better; want of success will curb the tendency. Every word you utter, every line you write, proves you to be either *sincere* or a *fool*. Now as I know you are not the one, I must believe you the other.

I never knew a woman with greater or more pleasing talents, *general* as in a woman they should be, something of everything, and too much of nothing. But these are unfortunately coupled with a total want of common conduct. For instance, the *note* to your page – do you suppose I delivered it? or did you mean that I should? I did not of course.

Then your heart, my poor Caro (what a little volcano!), that pours *lava* through your veins; and yet I cannot wish it a bit colder, to make a *marble slab* of, as you sometimes see (to understand my foolish metaphor) brought in vases, tables, etc., from Vesuvius, when hardened after an eruption. To drop my detestable tropes and figures, you know I have always thought you the cleverest, most agreeable, absurd, amiable, perplexing, dangerous, fascinating little being that lives now, or ought to have lived 2000 years ago. I won't talk to you of beauty; I am no judge. But our beauties cease to be so when near you, and therefore you have either some, or something better. And now, Caro, this nonsense is the first and last compliment (if it be such) I ever paid you. You often reproached me as wanting in that respect; but others will make up the deficiency.

Come to Lord Grey's; at least do not let me keep you away. All that you so often *say*, I *feel.* Can more be said or felt? This same prudence is tiresome enough; but one *must* maintain it, or what *can* one do to be saved? Keep to it.

[*On a covering sheet*]

If you write at all, write as usual, but do as you please. Only as I never see you – Basta![14]

TO LADY CAROLINE LAMB   *May 1st, 1812*

My Dear Lady Caroline, – I have read over the few poems of Miss Milbank [*sic*] with attention. They display fancy, feeling, and a little practice would very soon induce facility of expression. Though I have an abhorrence of Blank Verse, I like the lines on Dermody so much that I wish they were in rhyme. The lines in the Cave at Seaham have a turn of thought which I cannot sufficiently commend, and here I am at least candid as my own opinions differ upon such subjects. The first stanza is very good indeed, and the others, with a few slight alterations might be rendered equally excellent. The last are smooth and pretty. But these are all, has she no others? She certainly is a very extraordinary girl; who would imagine so much strength and variety of thought under that placid Countenance? It is not necessary for Miss M. to be an authoress, indeed I do not think publishing at all creditable either to men or women, and (though you will not believe me) very often feel ashamed of it myself; but I have no hesitation in saying that she has talents which, were it proper or requisite to indulge, would have led to distinction.

A friend of mine (fifty years old, and an author, but not *Rogers*) has just been here. As there is no name to the MSS I shewed them to him, and he was much more enthusiastic in his praises than I have been. He thinks them beautiful; I shall content myself with observing that they are better, much better, than anything of Miss M's protegee [*sic*] Blacket. You will say as much of this to Miss M. as you think proper. I say all this very sincerely. I have no desire to be better acquainted with Miss Milbank; she is too good for a fallen spirit to know, and I should like her more if she were less perfect.

Believe me, yours ever most truly,

B.

TO THOMAS MOORE   *May 20th, 1812*

On Monday, after sitting up all night, I saw Bellingham launched into eternity, and at three the same day I saw — [15] launched into the country.

I believe, in the beginning of June, I shall be down for a few days in Notts. If so, I shall beat you up *en passant* with Hobhouse who is endeavouring, like you and every body else, to keep me out of scrapes.

I meant to have written you a long letter, but I find I cannot. If any thing remarkable occurs, you will hear it from me – if good; if *bad*, there are plenty to tell it. In the mean time, do you be happy.

Ever yours, etc.

P.S. My best wishes and respects to Mrs Moore; – she is beautiful. I may say so even to you, for I was never more struck with a countenance.

TO LORD HOLLAND   *June 25th, 1812*

My Dear Lord, – I must appear very ungrateful, and have, indeed, been very negligent, but till last night I was not apprised of Lady Holland's restoration, and I shall call tomorrow to have the satisfaction, I trust, of hearing that she is well. – I hope that neither politics nor gout have assailed your Lordship since I last saw you, and that you also are 'as well as could be expected'.

The other night, at a ball, I was presented by order to our gracious Regent, who honoured me with some conversation, and professed a predilection for poetry. I confess it was a most unexpected honour, and I thought of poor Brummell's adventure, with some apprehension of a similar blunder. I have now great hope, in the event of Mr Pye's decease, of 'warbling truth at court', like Mr Mallet of indifferent memory. – Consider, one hundred marks a year! besides the wine and the disgrace; but then remorse would make me drown myself in my own butt before the year's end, or the finishing of my first dithyrambic. – So that, after all, I shall not meditate our laureate's death by pen or poison.

Will you present my best respects to Lady Holland? and believe me, hers and yours very sincerely

TO LADY MELBOURNE   [*August 12th, 1812.*]

Dear Ly M., – I trust that Lady C[aroline] has by this time reappeared or that her mother is better acquainted than I am: God knows where she is. If this be the case I hope you will favour me with a line, because in the interim my situation is by no means a *sinecure*, although I did not chuse to add to *your* perplexities this morning by joining in a *duet* with Ly. B[ess-borough]. As I am one of the principal performers in this unfortunate drama,[16] I should be glad to know what my part requires next? Mainly I am extremely uneasy on account of Ly. C. and others. As for myself, it is of little consequence. I shall bear and forbear as much as I can. But I must not shrink now from anything.
6 o'clock

Thus much I had written when I receive yours. Not a word *of* or *from* her. What is the cause of all this – I mean, the *immediate* circumstances which has led to it? I thought everything was well and quiet in the morning till the apparition of Ly. B. If I should hear from her, Ly. B. shall be informed: if *you*, pray tell me. I am

117

apprehensive for her personal safety, for her state of mind. Here I sit alone, and however I might *appear* to you, in the most painful suspense.

Ever yours,

B.

TO LADY CAROLINE LAMB   [*August, 1812*?]

My Dearest Caroline, – If tears which you saw and know I am not apt to shed, – if the agitation in which I parted from you, – agitation which you must have perceived through the *whole* of this most *nervous* affair, did not commence until the moment of leaving you approached, – if all I have said and done, and am still but too ready to say and do, have not sufficiently proved what my real feelings are, and must ever be towards you, my love, I have no other proof to offer. God knows, I wish you happy, and when I quit you, or rather you, from a sense of duty to your husband and mother, quit me, you shall acknowledge the truth of what I again promise and vow, that no other in word or deed, shall ever hold the place in my affections, which is, and shall be most sacred to you, till I am nothing. I never knew till *that moment* the *madness* of my dearest and most beloved friend; I cannot express myself; this is no time for words, but I shall have a pride, a melancholy pleasure, in suffering what you yourself can scarcely conceive, for you do not know me. I am about to go out with a heavy heart, because my appearing this evening will stop any absurd story which the event of the day might give rise to. Do you think *now* I am *cold* and *stern* and *artful*? Will even *others* think so? Will your *mother* even – that mother to whom we must indeed sacrifice much, more, much more on my part than she shall ever know or can imagine? 'Promise not to love you!' ah, Caroline, it is past promising. But I shall attribute all concessions to the proper motive, and never cease to feel all that you have already witnessed, and more than can ever be known but to my own heart, – perhaps to yours. May God protect, forgive, and bless you. Ever, and even more than ever,

Your most attached,

BYRON

118

P.S. These taunts which have driven you to this, my dearest Caroline, were it not for your mother and the kindness of your connections, is there anything on earth or heaven that would have made me so happy as to have made you mine long ago? and not less *now* than *then*, but *more* than ever at this time. You know I would with pleasure give up all here and all beyond the grave for you, and in refraining from this, must my motives be misunderstood? I care not who knows this, what use is made of it, – it is to *you* and to *you* only that they are *yourself* [*sic*]. I was and am yours freely and most entirely, to obey, to honour, love, – and fly with you when, where, and how you yourself *might* and *may* determine.

TO LADY MELBOURNE   *Cheltenham,*
                                     September 10th, 1812

Dear Lady Melbourne, – I presume you have heard and will not be sorry to hear *again*, that *they*[17] are safely deposited in Ireland, and that the sea rolls between you and *one* of your torments; the other you see is still at your elbow. Now (if you are as sincere as I sometimes almost dream) you will not regret to hear, that I wish this to end, and it certainly shall not be renewed on my part. It is not that I love another, but loving at all is quite out of my way; I am tired of being a fool, and when I look back on the waste of time, and the destruction of all my plans last winter by this last romance, I am – what I ought to have been long ago. It is true from early habit, one must make love mechanically, as one swims. I was once very fond of both, but now as I never swim, unless I tumble into the water, I don't make love till almost obliged, though I fear *that* is not the shortest way out of the troubled waves with which in such accidents we must struggle. But I will say no more on this topic, as I am not sure of my ground, and you can easily outwit me, as you always hitherto have done ...

TO LADY MELBOURNE   *Cheltenham,*
:   *September 13th, 1812*

My Dear Lady M., – The end of Lady B[essborough]'s letter
shall be the beginning of mine. 'For Heaven's sake do not lose
your hold on him'. Pray don't, *I* repeat, and assure you it is a
very firm one, 'but the yoke is easy, and the burthen is light', to
use one of my scriptural phrases.

So far from being ashamed of being governed like Lord
Delacour or any *other Lord* or *master*, I am always but too happy
to find one to regulate or misregulate me, and I am as docile as a
dromedary, and can bear almost as much. Will you undertake
me? If you are sincere (which I still a little hesitate in believing),
give me but time, let *hers* retain her in Ireland – the 'gayer' the
better. I want her just to be sufficiently gay that I may have enough
to bear me out on my own part. Grant me but till December,
and if I do not disenchant the Dulcinea and Don Quichotte,
both, then I must attack the windmills, and leave the land in quest
of adventures. In the meantime I must, and do write the greatest
absurdities to keep her 'gay', and the more so because the last
epistle informed me that 'eight guineas, a mail, and a packet
could soon bring her to London', a threat which immediately
called forth a letter worthy of the Grand Cyrus or the Duke of
York, or any other hero of Madame Scudery or Mrs Clarke.

Poor Lady B!! with her hopes and her fears. In fact it is no jest
for her, or indeed any of us. I must let you into one little secret –
her folly half did this. At the commencement she piqued that
'vanity' (which it would be the vainest thing in the world to
deny) by telling me she was certain I was not beloved, 'that I was
only led on for the sake of etc., etc.' This raised a devil between
us, which now will only be laid, I really do believe, in the *Red*
Sea; I made no answer, but determined not to *pursue*, for pursuit
it was not, but to sit still, and in a week after I was convinced –
not that [Caroline] loved me, for I do not believe in the existence
of what is called Love – but that any other man in my situation
would have believed that he was loved.

Now, my dear Lady M., you are all out as to my real sentiments ... I told you in my two last, that I did not 'like any other, etc., etc.' I deceived you and myself in saying so; there was, and is one whom I wished to marry, had not this affair intervened, or had not some occurences rather discouraged me. When our drama was 'rising' ('I'll be d—d if it falls off,' I may say with Sir Fretful), in the 5th Act, it was no time to hesitate. I had made up my mind to bear the consequences of my own folly; honour, pity, and a kind of affection all forbade me to shrink, but now if I can *honourably* be off, if *you* are not deceiving me, if she does not take some accursed step to precipitate her own inevitable fall (if not with me, with some less lucky successor) – if these impossibilities can be got over, all will be well. If not – she will travel.

As I have said so much, I may as well say all. The woman I mean is Miss Milbanke; I know nothing of her fortune, and I am told her father is ruined, but my own will, when my Rochdale arrangements are closed, be sufficient for both. My debts are not £25,000, and the deuce is in it, if with R[ochdale] and the surplus of N[ewstead], I could not contrive to be as independent as half the peerage. I know little of her, and have not the most distant reason to suppose that I am at all a favourite in that quarter. But I never saw a woman whom I *esteemed* so much. But that chance is gone, and there's an end. Now, my dear Lady M., I am completely in your power. I have not deceived you as to — [Caroline Lamb]. I hope you will not deem it vanity, when I soberly say that it would have been want of gallantry, though the acme of virtue, if I had played the Scipio on this occasion. If through your means, or any means, I can be free, or at least change my fetters, my regard and admiration would not be increased, but my gratitude would. In the meantime, it is by no means unfelt for what you have already done. To Lady B[essborough] I could not say all this, for she would with the best intentions make the most absurd use of it. What a miserable picture does her letter present of this daughter! She seems afraid to know her, and, blind herself, writes in such a manner as to open the eyes of all others ...

Yours ever most truly,

B.

P.S. Dear Lady M. – Don't think me careless. My correspondence since I was sixteen has not been of a nature to allow of any trust except to a lock and key, and I have of late been doubly guarded. The few letters of yours, and all others in case of the worst, shall be sent back or burnt. Surely after returning the one with *Mr [William] L[amb]'s message*, you will hardly suspect me of wishing to take any advantage; *that* was the only important one in behalf of my own interests. Think me bad if you please, but not *meanly* so. Lady B's under another cover accompanies this.

TO LADY MELBOURNE   *Cheltenham,*
                                           September 15th, 1812.

My Dear Lady M., – 'If I were looking in your face, entre les deux yeux', I know not whether I should find 'frankness or truth', but certainly something which looks quite as well if not better than either, and whatever it may be, I would not have it changed for any other expression; as it has defied time, no wonder it should perplex *me*. – 'Manage her!' it is impossible, and as to friendship – no – it must be broken off at once, and all I have left is to take some step which will make her hate me effectually, for she must be in extremes. What you state however is to be dreaded; besides, she presumes upon the weakness and affection of all about her, and the very confidence and kindness which would break or reclaim a good heart, merely lead her own farther from deserving them. Were this but secure, you would find yourself mistaken in me. I speak from experience; except in one solitary instance, three months have ever cured me . . .

TO LADY MELBOURNE   *Cheltenham,*
                                           September 18th, 1812.

. . . All persons in this situation are so, from having too much *heart*, or too little head, one or both. Set mine down according to your calculations. You and yours seem to me much the same as the Ottoman family to the faithful; they frequently change their rulers, but never the reigning race. I am perfectly convinced if I fell in love with a woman of Thibet, she would turn out an *emigrée cousine* of some of you.

You ask, 'Am I sure of myself?' and I answer no, but *you* are, which I take to be a much better thing. Miss M[ilbanke] I admire because she is a clever woman, an amiable woman, and of high blood, for I have still a few Norman and Scotch inherited prejudices on the last score, were I to marry. As to *love*, that is done in a week (provided the lady has a reasonable share); besides, marriage goes on better with esteem and confidence than romance, and she is quite pretty enough to be loved by her husband, without being so glaringly beautiful as to attract too many rivals. She always reminds me of 'Emma' in the modern Griselda,[18] and whomever I *may* marry, that is the woman I would wish to *have married*. It is odd enough that my acquaintance with Caroline commenced with a confidence on my part about your niece; C. herself (as I have often told her) was *then* not at all to my taste, nor I (and I may believe her) to hers, and we shall end probably as we began. However, if after all 'it is decreed on high', that, like James the fatalist, I *must* be hers, she shall be *mine* as long as it pleases her, and the circumstances under which she becomes so, will at least make me devote my life to the vain attempt of reconciling her to herself. Wretched as it would render me, she should never know it; the sentence once past, I could never restore that which she had lost, but all the reparation I could make should be made, and the cup drained to the very dregs by myself, so that its bitterness passed from her.

In the meantime, till it *is* irrevocable, I must and may fairly endeavour to extricate both from a situation which, from our total want of all but selfish consideration, has brought us to the brink of the gulf. Before I sink I will at least have a *swim* for it, though I wish with all my heart it was the Hellespont instead, or that I could cross this as easily as I did ye other. One reproach I cannot escape. Whatever happens hereafter, she will charge it on me, and so shall I, and I fear that

> The first step or error none e'er could recall,
> And the woman once fallen for ever must fall;
> Pursue to the last the career she begun,
> And be *false* unto *many*, as *faithless* to *one*.

123

Forgive one stanza of my own sad rhymes; you know I never did inflict any upon you before, nor will again . . .

I am not sorry that C. sends you extracts from my epistles. I deserve it for the passage I showed once to you, but remember that was in the *outset*, and when everything said or sung was exculpatory and innocent and what not. Moreover, recollect what absurdities a man must write to his idol, and that 'garbled extracts' prove nothing without the context; for my own part I declare that I recollect no such proposal of an *epistolary truce*, and the gambols at divers houses of entertainment with ye express, etc., tend ye rather to confirm my statement. But I cannot be sure, or answerable for all I have said or unsaid, since 'Jove' himself (some with Mrs Malaprop would read *Job*) has forgotten to 'laugh at our perjuries'. I am certain that I tremble for the trunkfuls of my contradictions, since, like a minister or a woman, she may one day exhibit them in some magazine or some quartos of villainous memories written on her 7000th love-fit.

Now, dear Lady M., my *paper* spares you.

Believe me, with great regard, Yours ever,

B.

P.S. – In your last you say you are 'surrounded by fools;' Why then 'motley's the only wear.'

> Oh that I were a fool, a motley fool;
> I am ambitious of a motley coat.

Well, will you answer, 'Thou shalt have one.'

> *Chi va piano va sano,*
> *E chi va sano va lontano.*[19]

My progress has been 'lontano', but alas! y^e 'sano' and 'piano' are past praying for.

TO LADY MELBOURNE   *September 25th, 1812.*

. . . As to Annabella, she requires time and all the cardinal virtues, and in the interim I am a little verging towards one who demands neither, and saves me besides the trouble of marrying, by being married already. She besides does not speak English, and to me nothing but Italian – a great point, for from certain coincidences the very sound of that language is music to me, and she has black eyes, and *not* a very white skin, and reminds me of many in the Archipelago I wished to forget, and makes me forget what I ought to remember, all which are against me. I only wish she did not swallow so much supper – chicken wings, sweetbreads, custards, peaches and port wine; a woman should never be seen eating or drinking, unless it be *lobster salad* and *champagne*, the only truly feminine and becoming viands. I recollect imploring one lady not to eat more than a fowl at a sitting, without effect, and I have never yet made a single proselyte to Pythagoras.

Now a word to yourself – a much more pleasing topic than any of the preceding. I have no very high opinion of your sex, but when I do see a woman superior not only to all her own but to most of ours, I worship her in proportion as I despise the rest. And when I know that men of the first judgment and the most distinguished abilities have entertained and do entertain an opinion which my own humble observation, without any great effort of discernment, has enabled me to confirm on the same subject, you will not blame me for following the example of my elders and betters, and admiring you certainly as much as you ever were admired. My only regret is that the very awkward circumstances in which we are placed prevent and will prevent the improvement of an acquaintance which I now almost regret having made, but recollect, whatever happens, that the loss of it must give me more pain than even the *precious acquisition* (and this is saying *much*) which will occasion that loss.

Ld Jersey has reinvited me to M[iddleton] for the 4th Oct., and I will be there if possible; in the meantime, whatever step you take to break off this affair has my full concurrence. But *what* you wished me to write, would be a little too indifferent; and *that* now would be an insult, and I am much more unwilling to hurt her feelings now than ever (not from the mere apprehension of a disclosure in her wrath), but I have always felt that one who has given up much has a claim upon *me* (at least – whatever she deserves from others) for every respect that she may not feel her own degradation, and this is the reason that I have not written at all lately lest some expression might be misconstrued by her. When the lady herself begins the quarrel, and adopts a new 'Cortejo',[20] then my conscience is comforted. She has not written to me for some days, which is either a very bad or very good omen.

Yrs ever,

B.

TO LADY MELBOURNE   *October 18th, 1812*

My Dear Lady M., – Of A[nnabella] I have little to add, but I do not regret what has passed; the report alluded to had hurt her feelings, and she has now regained her tranquillity by the refutation to her own satisfaction without disturbing mine. This was but fair, and was not unexpected by me; all things considered, perhaps it could not have been better. I think of her nearly as I did. The specimen you send me is more favourable to her talents than her discernment, and much *too indulgent* to the subject she has chosen; in some points the resemblance is very exact, but you have not sent me the whole (I imagine) by the abruptness of both beginning and end. I am glad that your opinion coincides with mine on the subject of her abilities and her excellent qualities; in both these points she is singularly fortunate. Still there is something of the *woman* about her; her *preferring* that the letter to you should be sent forward to me, *per essémpio* [*sic*], appears as if, though she would not encourage, she was not disgusted with being admired. I also may hazard a conjecture that an *answer* addressed to *herself* might not have been displeasing, but of this you are the best judge from actual observation. I cannot, however, see the necessity of its being forwarded, unless I was either to admire the composition, or reply to ye contents. *One* I certainly do, the other would merely lead to mutual compliments, very sincere but somewhat *tedious*.

By the bye, what two famous letters *your own* are! I never saw such traits of discernment, observation of character, knowledge of your *own sex* and sly concealment of your *knowledge* of the *foibles* of *ours*, than in these epistles; and so that I preserve you *always* as a friend, and *sometimes* as a correspondent (the oftener the better), believe me, my dear L^{dy} M., I shall regret nothing but – the week we passed at Middleton, till I can enjoy such another ...

I thank you again for your efforts with my Princess of Parallelograms, who has puzzled you more than the Hypothenuse; in her character she has not forgotten 'Mathematics', wherein I used to praise her cunning. Her proceedings are quite rectangular, or rather we are two parallel lines prolonged to infinity side by side, but never to meet. Say what you please for, or of me, and I will swear it.

Good even, my dear L^{dy} Melbourne,

Ever y^{rs} most affectionately,

B.

TO JOHN CAM HOBHOUSE   *January 17th, 1813*

... I am at Ledbury. Ly. O[xford] and famille I left at Hereford, as I hate travelling with Children unless they have gotten a Stranguary. However I wait here for her tomorrow like a dutiful Cortejo. O[xford] has been in town these ten days. Car. L. has been *forging letters* in my name and hath thereby pilfered the best picture of *me*, the Newstead Miniature!!! Murray was the imposed upon. The Devil, and Medea, and her Dragons to boot, are possessed of that little maniac. Bankes is gone or going to tourify. I gave him a few letters.

I expect and hope you will have a marvellous run and trust you have not forgotten '*monogamy* my dr. boy'. If the 'learned world are not in arms against your paradoxes' I shall despise these coster-monger days when Merit availeth not.

Excuse my buffoonery, for I write under the influence of a solitary nipporkin [?] of Grog, such as the Salsette afforded 'us youth' in the Arches [?].

Ever yrs, dr. H.,

B.

TO FRANCIS HODGSON   *February 3, 1813.*

... The 'Agnus'[21] is furious. You can have no idea of the horrible and absurd things she has said and done since (really from the best motives) I withdrew my homage. 'Great pleasure' is, certes, my object, but *'why brief,* Mr Wild?' I cannot answer for the future, but the past is pretty secure; and in it I can number the last two months as worthy of the gods in *Lucretius* ...

... The business of last summer I broke off, and now the amusement of the gentle fair is writing letters literally threatening my life, and much in the style of 'Miss Mathews' in 'Amelia', or 'Lucy' in the *'Beggar's Opera'*. Such is the reward of restoring a woman to her family, who are treating her with the greatest kindness, and with whom I am on good terms. I am still in *palatia Circes,*[22] and, being no Ulysses, cannot tell into what animal I may be converted; as you are aware of the turn of both parties, your conjectures will be very correct, I daresay, and, seriously I am very much *attached.* She has had her share of the denunciations of the brilliant Phryne, and regards them as much as I do ...

TO THE HON. AUGUSTA LEIGH   *4 Bennet Street, St. James's,*
                                  March 26th, 1813

My Dearest Augusta, – I did not answer your letter, because I could not answer as I wished, but expected that every week would bring me some tidings[23] that might enable me to reply better than by apologies. But Claughton has not, will not, and, I think, cannot pay his money, and though, luckily, it was stipulated that he should never have possession till the whole was paid, the estate is still on my hands, and your brother consequently not less embarrassed than ever. This is the truth, and is all the excuse I can offer for inability, but not unwillingness, to serve you.

I am going abroad again in June, but should wish to see you before my departure. You have perhaps heard that I have been fooling away my time with different *'regnantes'*; but what better can be expected from me? I have but one *relative,* and her I never see. I have no connections to domesticate with, and for marriage I have neither the talent nor the inclination. I cannot fortune-hunt, nor afford to marry without a fortune. My parliamentary schemes are not much to my taste – I spoke twice last Session, and was told it was well enough; but I hate the thing altogether, and have no intention to 'strut another hour' on that stage. I am thus wasting the best part of life, daily repenting and never amending.

On Sunday, I set off for a fortnight for Eywood, near Presteign, in Herefordshire – with the *Oxfords*. I see you put on a *demure* look at the name, which is very becoming and matronly in you; but you won't be sorry to hear that I am quite out of a more serious scrape with another singular personage which threatened me last year, and trouble enough I had to steer clear of it I assure you. I hope all my nieces are well, and increasing in growth and number; but I wish you were not always buried in that bleak common near Newmarket.

I am very well in health, but not happy, nor even comfortable; but I will bore you with complaints. I am a fool, and deserve all the ills I have met, or may meet with, but nevertheless very *sensibly*, dearest Augusta,

Your most affectionate brother,

BYRON.

TO LADY CAROLINE LAMB *4 Bennet St.,*
April 29th, 1813

If you still persist in your intention of meeting me in opposition to the wishes of your own friends and of mine, it must even be so. I regret it and acquiesce with reluctance. I am not ignorant of the very extraordinary language you have held not only to me but others, and your avowal of your determination to obtain what you are pleased to call 'revenge'; nor have I now to learn that an incensed woman is a dangerous enemy.

Undoubtedly, those against whom we can make no defence, whatever they say or do, must be formidable. Your words and actions have lately been tolerably portentous, and might justify

129

me in avoiding the demanded interview, more especially as I believe you to be fully capable of performing all your menaces, but as I once hazarded everything *for* you, I will not shrink *from* you. Perhaps I deserve punishment, if so, you are quite as proper a person to inflict it as any other. You say you will '*ruin* me'. I thank you, but I have done that for myself already; you say you will 'destroy me', perhaps you will only save me the trouble. It is useless to reason with you – to repeat what you already know, that I have in reality saved you from utter and impending destruction. Everyone who knows you knows this also, but they do not know – as yet – what you may and I will tell them as I now tell you, that it is in a great measure owing to this persecution; to the accursed things you have said; to the extravagances you have committed, that I again adopt the resolution of quitting this country. In your assertions you have either belied or betrayed me – take your choice; in your actions you have hurt only yourself – but is that nothing to one who wished you well? I have only one request to make, which is, not to attempt to see Lady O[xford]: on her you have no claim. You will settle as you please the arrangement of this conference. I do not leave England till June, but the sooner it is over the better. I once wished, for your own sake, Lady M. to be present – but if you are to fulfil any of your threats in word or deed we had better be alone.

Yours,

B.

TO THE HON. AUGUSTA LEIGH   *4, Bennet Street,*
                                   June 26th, 1813

My Dearest Augusta, – Let me know when you arrive, and when, and where, and how, you would like to see me – any where in short but at *dinner*. I have put off going into ye country on purpose to *waylay* you.

Ever yours,

B^N

TO THE HON. AUGUSTA LEIGH   [*June, 1813*]

My Dearest Augusta, – And if you knew *whom* I had put off beside
my journey – you would think me grown strangely fraternal.
However, I won't overwhelm you with my *own praises*.

Between one and two be it – I shall, in course, prefer seeing you
all to myself without the incumbrance of third persons, even of
your (for I won't own the relationship) fair cousin of *eleven page*
memory,[24] who, by the bye, makes one of the finest busts I have
seen in the Exhibition, or out of it. Good night!

Ever yours,

BYRON

P.S. Your writing is grown like my Attorney's, and gave me a
qualm, till I found the remedy in your signature.

TO LADY MELBOURNE   *July 1st, 1813*

... I want a *she* voucher for a ticket to the A[lmacks] Masque
tomorrow. It is for my sister, who I hope will go with me. I wish
she were not married, for (now I have no home to keep) she
would have been so good a housekeeper. Poor soul! she likes her
husband. I think her thanking you for your abetment of her
abominable marriage (*seven years* after the event!!) is the only
instance of similar gratitude upon record. However, now she is
married, I trust she will remain so.

Ever y^{rs}, dear L^y M^e,

B.

TO LADY MELBOURNE   *July 6th, 1813*

Dear L^y M, – since I wrote ye enclosed, I have heard a strange
story of C's scratching herself with glass, and I know not what
besides; of all this I was ignorant till this evening. What I did, or
said to provoke her I know not. I told her it was better to
waltz; 'because she danced well, and it would be imputed to *me*,
if she did not' – but I see nothing in this to produce cutting and

131

maiming; besides, before supper I saw her, and though she said, and did even then a foolish thing, I could not suppose her so frantic as to be in earnest. She took hold of my hand as I passed, and pressed it against some sharp instrument, and said, 'I mean to use this'. I answered, 'Against me, I presume?' and passed on with L^y R[ancliffe], trembling lest L^d. Y or L^y R. should overhear her; though not believing it possible that this was more than one of her, not uncommon, *bravadoes*, for *real feeling* does not disclose its intentions, and always shuns display. I thought little more of this, and leaving the table in search of her would have appeared more particular than proper – though, of course, had I guessed her to be serious, or had I been conscious of offending I should have done everything to pacify or prevent her. I know not what to say, or do. I am quite unaware of what I did to displease; and useless regret is all I can feel on the subject. Can she be in her senses? Yet I would rather think myself to blame – than that she were so silly without cause.

I really remained at L^y H[eathcote's] till 5, totally ignorant of all that passed. Nor do I now know where this cursed scarification took place, nor when – I mean the room – and the hour.

TO LADY MELBOURNE   *July 6th, 1813*

My Dear Lady M. – God knows what has happened, but at four in the morning L^y Ossulstone looking angry (and at that moment, ugly), delivered to me a confused kind of message from you of some scene – this is all I know, except that with laudable logic she drew the usual feminine deduction that I '*must* have behaved very ill'. If L^y C. is offended, it really must be anger at my *not* affronting her – for one of the few things I said, was a request to know her will and pleasure, if there was anything I could say, do, or not do to give her the least gratification. She walked away without answering, and after leaving me in this not very dignified situation, and showing her independence to twenty people near, I only saw her dancing and in the doorway for a moment, where she said something so very violent that I was in distress lest Ld Y. or L^y Rancliffe overheard her. I went to supper, and saw and heard no more till L^y^ Ossulstone told me your words and her own opinion, and here I am in stupid innocence and ignorance of my offence or her proceedings. If I am to be haunted with hysterics wherever I go, and whatever I do, I think she is not the only person to be pitied. I should have returned to her after her *doorway whisper*, but I could not with any kind of politeness leave L^y^ Rancliffe to drown herself in wine and water, or be suffocated in a jelly dish, without a spoon, or a hand to help her; besides if there was, and I foresaw there would be something ridiculous, surely I was better absent than present.

This is really insanity, and everybody seem inoculated with the same distemper. L^y^ W[estmoreland] says, 'You must have done something; you know between people in your situation, a word or a look goes a great way', etc. etc. So it seems indeed – but I never knew that *neither* words nor looks – in short downright, innocent, vacant, undefinable *nothing*, had the same precious power of producing this perpetual worry.

I wait to hear from you, in case I have to answer you. I trust nothing has occurred to spoil your breakfast, for which the Regent has got a fine day.

TO THOMAS MOORE *July 13th, 1813*

Your letter set me at ease; for I really thought (as I hear of your susceptibility) that I had said – I know not what – something I should have been very sorry for, had it, or I, offended you; – though I don't see how a man with a beautiful wife – *his own* children, quiet – fame – competency and friends, (I will vouch for a thousand, which is more than I will for a unit in my own behalf,) can be offended with any thing.

Do you know, Moore, I am amazingly inclined – remember I say but *inclined* – to be seriously enamoured with Lady A[delaide] F[orbes] – but this — has ruined all my prospects. However, you know her; is she *clever*, or sensible, or good-tempered? either *would* do – I scratch out the *will*. I don't ask as to her beauty – that I see; but my circumstances are mending, and were not my other prospects blackening, I would take a wife, and that should be the woman, had I a chance. I do not yet know her much, but better than I did.

I want to get away, but find difficulty in compassing a passage in the ship of war. They had better let me go; if I cannot, patriotism is the word – 'nay, and they'll mouth, I'll rant as well as they'. Now, what are you doing? – writing, we all hope, for own sakes. Remember you must edit my posthumous works, with a Life of the Author, for which I will send you Confessions, dated 'Lazaretto', Smyrna, Malta, or Palermo – one can die any where . . .

P.S. The Stael last night attacked me most furiously – said that I had 'no right to make love – that I had used — barbarously – that I had no feeling, and was totally *in*sensible to *la belle passion*, and *had* been all my life'. I am very glad to hear it, but did not know it before. Let me hear from you anon.

TO THOMAS MOORE   *July 25, 1813*

I am not well versed enough in the ways of single woman to make much matrimonial progress.

I have been dining like the dragon of Wantley[25] for this last week. My head aches with the vintage of various cellars, and my brains are muddled as their dregs . . .

The season has closed with a dandy ball; – but I have dinners with the Harrowbys, Rogers, and Frere and Mackintosh, where I shall drink your health in a silent bumper, and regret your absence till 'too much canaries' wash away my memory, or render it superfluous by a vision of you at the opposite side of the table. Canning has disbanded his party by a speech from his — – the true throne of a Tory. Conceive his turning off in a formal harangue, and bidding them think for themselves. 'I have led my ragamuffins where they are well peppered. There are but three of the 150 left alive', and they are for the *Townsend* (*query*, might not Falstaff mean the Bow Street officer?[26] I dare say Malone's posthumous edition will have it so) for life.

Since I wrote last, I have been into the country.[27] I journeyed by night – no incident, or accident, but an alarm on the part of my valet on the outside, who, in crossing Epping Forest, actually, I believe, flung down his purse before a mile-stone, with a glow-worm in the second figure of number XIX – mistaking it for a footpad and dark lantern. I can only attribute his fears to a pair of new pistols wherewith I had armed him; and he thought it necessary to display his vigilance by calling out to me whenever we passed any thing – no matter whether moving or stationary. Conceive ten miles, with a tremor every furlong . . .

TO LADY MELBOURNE   (*Bennet Street, St. James's*)
August 5th, 1813

My Dear Lady M., – My sister, who is going abroad with me, is now in town, where she returned with me from Newmarket. Under the existing circumstances of her lord's embarrassments, she could not well do otherwise, and she appears to have still less reluctance at leaving this country than even myself . . .

TO THOMAS MOORE   *Bennet Street,*
August 22, 1813

. . . P.S. – I perceive I have written a flippant and rather cold-hearted letter! let it go, however. I have said nothing, either, of the brilliant sex; but the fact is, I am at this moment in a far more serious, and entirely new, scrape than any of the last twelve months, – and that is saying a good deal. It is unlucky we can neither live with nor without these women . . .

TO LADY MELBOURNE   *August 31st, 1813*

My Dear L^y M^e, – Your kind letter is unanswerable; no one but yourself would have taken the trouble; no one but me would have been in a situation to require it. I am still in town so that it has as yet had all the effect you wish . . .

TO LADY MELBOURNE   *September 5th, 1813*

Dear Lady Melbourne, – I return you the plan of A[nnabella]'s spouse elect,[28] of which I shall say nothing because I do not understand it; though I dare say it is exactly what it ought to be. Neither do I know why I am writing this note, as I mean to call on you, unless it be to try your 'new patent pens' which delight me infinitely with their colours. I have pitched upon a yellow one to begin with. Very likely you will be out, and I must return all the annexed epistles. I would rather have seen your answer. She seems to have been spoiled – not as children usually are – but systematically Clarissa Harlowed into an awkward kind of correctness, with a dependence upon her own infallibility which will or may lead her into some egregious blunder. I don't mean the usual error of young gentlewomen, but she will find exactly what she wants, and then discover that it is much more dignified than entertaining. [*The second page of this letter has been torn off.*]

TO LADY MELBOURNE   [London], *September 8th, 1813*

My Dear L^y M^e, – I leave town to-morrow for a few days,[29] come what may; and as I am sure you would get the better of my resolution, I shall not venture to encounter you. If nothing very particular occurs, you will allow me to write as usual; if there does, you will probably hear *of*, but not *from*, me (of course) again.

Adieu! Whatever I am, whatever, and wherever I may be, believe me most truly your obliged
and faithful

B.

TO THE HON. AUGUSTA LEIGH   [*Wednesday*]
Septr 15th, 1813.

My Dear Augusta – I joined my friend Scrope about 8, and before eleven we had swallowed six bottles of his burgundy and Claret, which left him very unwell and me rather feverish; we were *tête à tête*. I remained with him next day and set off last night for London, which I reached at three in the morning. Tonight I shall leave it again, perhaps for Aston or Newstead. I have not yet determined, nor does it much matter. As you perhaps care more on the subject than I do, I will tell you when I know myself.

When my departure is arranged, and I can get this long-evaded passage, you will be able to tell me whether I am to expect a visit or not, and I can come for or meet you as you think best. If you write, address to Bennet Street,

Yours very truly,

B.

TO LADY MELBOURNE *Aston Hall, Rotherham, September 21st, 1813*

My Dear L^y M^e,– My stay at Cambridge was very short, but feeling feverish and restless in town I flew off, and here I am on a visit to my friend Webster, now married, and (according to ye Duke of Buckingham's curse) 'settled in ye country'. His bride, Lady Frances, is a pretty, pleasing woman, but in delicate health, and, I fear, going – if not gone – into a decline. Stanhope and his wife – pretty and pleasant too, but not at all consumptive – left us today, leaving only ye family, another single gentleman, and your slave. The sister, L^y Catherine, is here too, and looks very pale from a *cross* in her love for Lord Bury (Ld Alb[emarl]e's son); in short, we are a society of happy wives and unfortunate maidens. The place is very well, and quiet, and the children only scream in a low voice, so that I am not much disturbed, and shall stay a few days in tolerable repose. W[ebster] don't want sense, nor good nature, but both are occasionally obscured by his suspicions, and absurdities of all descriptions; he is passionately fond of having his wife admired, and at the same time jealous to jaundice of everything and everybody. I have hit upon the medium of praising her to him perpetually behind her back, and never looking at her before his face; as for her, I believe she is disposed to be very faithful, and I don't think anyone now here is inclined to put her to the test. W[ebster] himself is, with all his jealousy and admiration, a little tired; he has been lately at Newstead, and wants to go again. I suspected this sudden *penchant*, and soon discovered that a foolish nymph of the Abbey, about whom fortunately I care not, was the attraction. Now if I wanted to make mischief I could extract much good perplexity from a proper management of such events; but I am grown so good, or so indolent, that I shall not avail myself of so pleasant an opportunity of tormenting mine host, though he deserves it for poaching. I believe he has hitherto been unsuccessful, or rather it is too astonishing to be believed. He proposed to me, with great gravity, to carry him over there, and I replied with equal candour, that *he* might set out when he pleased, but that I should remain here to take care of his household in the interim – a proposition which I thought very much to the purpose, but which did not seem at all to his satisfaction. By way of opiate he preached me a sermon on his wife's good qualities, concluding by an assertion that in all moral and mortal qualities, she was very like 'Christ!!!' I think the Virgin Mary would have been a more appropriate typification; but it was the first comparison of the kind I ever heard, and made me laugh till he was angry, and then I got out of humour too, which pacified him, and shortened the panegyric.

Ld Petersham is coming here in a day or two, who will certainly flirt furiously with L^y F[rances], and I shall have some comic Iagoism with our little Othello. I should have no chance with his Desdemona myself, but a more lively and better dressed and formed personage might, in an innocent way, for I really believe the girl is a very good, well-disposed wife, and will do very well if she lives, and he himself don't tease her into some dislike of her lawful owner ...

TO LADY MELBOURNE   [*London*] *October 1st, 1813*

... Today I heard from my friend W[ebster] again; his *Countess* is, he says, 'inexorable'. What a lucky fellow – happy in his obstacles. In his case I should think them very pleasant; but I don't lay this down as a general proposition. All my prospect of amusement is clouded, for Petersham has sent an excuse; and there will be no one to make him jealous of but the curate and the butler – and I have no thoughts of setting up for myself. I am not exactly cut out for the lady of the mansion; but I think a stray dandy would have a chance of preferment. She evidently expects to be attacked, and seems prepared for a brilliant defence; my character as a *roué* has gone before me, and my careless and quiet behaviour astonished her so much that I believe she began to think herself ugly, or me blind – if not worse. They seemed surprised at my declining the races in particular; but for this I had good reasons; firstly: I wanted to go elsewhere; secondly: if I had gone, I must have paid some attention to some of them; which is troublesome, unless one has something in memory, or hope to induce it; and then mine host is so marvellous green-eyed that he might have included me in his calenture – which I don't deserve – and probably should not like it a bit better if I did.

I have also reasons for returning there on Sunday, with which they have nothing to do; but if C[aroline Lamb] takes a suspicious twist that way, let her – it will keep her in darkness; but I hope, however, she won't take a fit of scribbling, as she did to L^y Oxford last year – though Webster's face on the occasion would be quite a comet, and delight me infinitely more than O[xford]'s, which was comic enough.

Friday morn.– Yours arrived. I will answer on the next page.

So – L^{dy} H[olland] says I am *fattening*, and you say I talk '*nonsense*'. Well – I must fast and unfool again, if possible. But, as Curran told me last night that he had been assured upon oath by half the Court, that 'the Prince was *not* at all *corpulent*, that he was stout certainly, but by no means protuberant, or obese,' 'there's comfort yet.' As to folly, that's incurable . . .

. . . To return to the W[ebster]s. I am glad they amaze you; anything that confirms, or extends one's observations on life and character delights me, even when I don't know people – for this reason I would give the world to pass a month with Sheridan, or any lady or gentleman of the old school, and hear them talk every day, and all day of themselves, and acquaintance, and all they have heard and seen in their lives. W[ebster] seems in no present peril. I believe the woman is mercenary; and I happen to know that he can't at present bribe her. I told him that it would be known, and that he must expect reprisals – and what do you think was his answer? 'I think any woman fair game, because I can *depend* upon L^y F.'s principles – she can't go wrong, and therefore I may.' 'Then, why are you jealous of her?' 'Because – because – zounds! I am not jealous. Why the devil do you suppose I am?' I then enumerated some very gross symptoms which he had displayed, even before her face, and his servants, which he could not deny; but persisted in his determination to add to his '*bonnes fortunes*'; – it is a strange being! When I came home in 1811, he was always saying, 'B., do marry – it is the happiest', etc. The first thing he said on my arrival at A[ston] was, 'B., whatever you do, *don't marry*'; which, considering he had an unmarried sister-in-law in the house, was a very unnecessary precaution.

Every now and then he has a fit of fondness, and kisses her hand before his guests; which she receives with the most lifeless indifference, which struck me more than if she had appeared pleased, or annoyed. Her brother told me last year that she married to get rid of her family (who are ill-tempered), and had not been *out* two months; so that, to use a fox-hunting phrase, she was 'killed in covert'.

You have enough of them, and me for ye present.

Yrs. ever,

B.

TO LADY MELBOURNE   *Aston Hall, Rotherham,*
                                    October 5th, 1813

My Dear L^y M., – W. has lost his Countess, his time and his temper (I would advise anyone who finds the *last* to return it immediately; it is of no use to any but the owner). L^y F[rances] has lost Petersham, for the present at least; the other sister, as I have said before, has lost Ld Bury; and I have nobody to lose – *here*, at least – and am not very anxious to find one. Here be two friends of the family, besides your slave: a Mr Westcombe – very handsome, but silly – and a Mr Agar – frightful, but facetious. The whole party are out in carriages – a species of amusement from which I always *avert*; and, consequently, declined it to-day; it is very well with two, but not beyond a *duet*. I think, being bumped about between two or more of one's acquaintance intolerable. W[ebster] grows rather intolerable, too. He is out of humour with my *Italian* books (Dante and Alfieri, and some others as harmless as ever wrote), and requests that *sa femme* may not see them because, forsooth, it is a language which doth infinite damage!! and because I enquired after the Stanhopes, our mutual acquaintance, he *answers* me by another *question*, 'Pray, do you enquire after *my* wife of others in the same way?' so that you see my Virtue is its own reward – for never, in word or deed, did I speculate upon his spouse; nor did I ever see much in her to encourage either hope, or much fulfilment of hope, supposing I had any. She is pretty, but not surpassing – too thin, and not very animated; but good-tempered – and a something interesting enough in her manner and figure; but I never should think of her, nor anyone else, if left to my own cogitations, as I have neither the patience nor presumption to advance till met half-way. The other two pay her ten times more attention, and, of course, are more attended to. I really believe he is bilious, and suspects something extraordinary from my nonchalance; at all events, he has hit upon the wrong person. I can't help laughing to you, but he will soon make me very serious with him, and then he will come to his senses again. The oddest thing is, that he wants me to stay with him some time; which I am not much inclined to do, unless the gentleman transfers his fretfulness to someone else. I have written to you so much lately, you will be glad to be spared from any further account of the 'Blunderhead family'.

Ever y^{rs}, my dear L^y M^e,

B.

TO LADY MELBOURNE   *October 8th, 1813*

My Dear L^y M., – I have volumes, but neither time nor space. I have already trusted too deeply to hesitate now; besides, for certain reasons, you will not be sorry to hear that I am anything but what I was. Well then, to begin, and first, a word of mine host. – He has lately been talking *at*, rather than *to*, me before the party (with the exception of the women) in a tone, which as I never use it myself, I am not particularly disposed to tolerate in others. What *he* may do with impunity, it seems, but not suffer, till at last I told him that the whole of his argument involved the interesting contradiction that 'he might love where he liked, but that no one else might like what he ever thought proper to love', a doctrine which, as the learned Partridge observed, contains a 'non sequitur' from which I, for one, begged leave as a general proposition to dissent. This nearly produced a scene with me, as well as another guest, who seemed to admire my sophistry the most of the two; and it was after dinner, and debating time, might have ended in more than *wineshed*, but that the devil, for some wise purpose of his own, thought proper to restore good humour, which has not as yet been further infringed.

In these last few days I have had a good deal of conversation with an amiable person, whom (as we deal in *letters* and initials only) we will denominate *Ph*. Well, these things are dull in detail. Take it once, I have made love, and if I am to believe mere *words* (for there we have hitherto stopped), it is returned. I must tell you the place of declaration, however, a billiard room. I did not, as C. says: 'kneel in the middle of the room', but, like Corporal Trim to the Nun, 'I made a speech', which, as you might not listen to it with the same patience, I shall not transcribe. We were before on very amicable terms, and I remembered being asked an odd question, 'how a woman who liked a man could inform him of it when he did not perceive it'. I also observed that we went on with our game (of billiards) without *counting the hazards*; and supposed that, as mine certainly were not, the thoughts of the other party also were not exactly occupied by what was our ostensible pursuit. Not quite, though pretty well satisfied with my progress, I took a very imprudent step with pen and paper, in tender and tolerably turned *prose* periods (no poetry even when in earnest). Here were risks, certainly: first, how to convey, then how would it be received? It was received, however, and deposited not very far from the heart which I wished it to reach when, who should enter the room but the person who ought at that moment to have been in the Red Sea, if Satan had any civility. But *she* kept her countenance, and the paper; and I my composure as well as I could. It was a risk, and *all* had been lost by failure; but then recollect how much more I had to gain by the reception, if not declined, and how much one always hazards to obtain anything worth having. My billet prospered, it did more, it even (I am this moment interrupted by the *Marito*,[30] and write this before him, he has brought me a political pamphlet in MS. to decypher and applaud, I shall content myself with the last; oh, he is gone again), my billet produced an *answer*, a very unequivocal one too, but a little too much about virtue, and indulgence of attachment in some sort of etherial process, in which the soul is principally concerned, which I don't very well understand, being a bad metaphysician; but one generally *ends* and *begins* with platonism, and, as my proselyte is only twenty, there is time enough to materialize. I hope nevertheless this spiritual system won't last long, and at any rate must make the experiment. I remember my last case was the reverse, as Major O'Flaherty[31] recommends, 'we fought first and explained afterwards'.

This is the present state of things: much mutual profession, a good deal of melancholy, which, I am sorry to say, was remarked by 'the Moor', and as much love as could well be made, considering the time, place and circumstances.

I need not say that the folly and petulance of [Webster] has tended to all this. If a man is not contented with a pretty woman, and not only runs after any little country girl he meets with, but absolutely boasts of it; he must not be surprised if others admire that which he knows not how to value. Besides, he literally provoked, and goaded me into it, by something not unlike bullying, *indirect* to be sure, but tolerably obvious: 'he *would* do this, and he would do that', 'if any man', etc., etc., and *he* thought that every 'woman' was *his* lawful prize, nevertheless. Oons! who is this strange monopolist? It is odd enough, but on other subjects he is like other people, on this he seems infatuated. If he had been rational, and not prated of his pursuits, I should have gone on very well, as I did at Middleton. Even now, I shan't quarrel with him if I can help it; but one or two of his speeches have blackened the blood about my heart, and curdled the milk of kindness. If put to the proof, I shall behave like other people, I presume.

I have heard from A[nnabella], but her letter to me is *melancholy*, about her old friend Miss My's departure, etc., etc. I wonder who will have her at last; her letter to you is *gay* you say; that to me must have been written at the same time; the little demure nonjuror!

I wrote to C[aroline] the other day, for I was afraid she might repeat last year's epistle, and make it *circular* among my friends.

Good evening, I am now going to *billiards*.

Every y^{rs},

B.

P.S. 6 o'clock – This business is growing serious, and I think *Platonism* in some peril. There has been very nearly a scene, almost an *hysteric*, and really without cause, for I was conducting myself with (to me) very irksome decorum. Her expressions astonish me, so young and cold as she appeared. But these professions must end as usual, and *would* I think *now*, had 'l'occasion' been *not* wanting. Had anyone come in during the *tears*, and consequent consolation, all had been spoiled; we must be more cautious, or less *larmoyante*.

P.S. second, 10 o'clock. – I write to you, just escaped from claret and vocification on G–d knows what paper. My landlord is a rare gentleman. He has just proposed to me a bet that *he*, for a certain sum, 'wins any given *woman*, against any given *homme* including *all friends* present', which I declined with becoming deference to him, and the rest of the company. Is not this, at the moment, a perfect comedy? I forgot to mention that on his entrance yesterday during the letter scene, it reminded me so much of an awkward passage in 'The Way to Keep Him' between Lovemore, Sir Bashful, and my Lady, that, embarrassing as it was, I could hardly help laughing. I hear his voice in the passage; he wants me to go to a ball at Sheffield, and is talking to me as I write. Good night. I am in the act of praising his pamphlet.

I don't half like your story of *Corinne*, some day I will tell you why, if I can, but at present, good night.

TO LADY MELBOURNE   *Newstead Abbey,*
                                           October 10th, 1813

My Dear L^y M., – I write to you from the melancholy mansion
of my fathers, where I am dull as the longest deceased of my
progenitors. I have reflection on irrevocable things, and won't
now turn sentimentalist. W[ebster] alone accompanied me here
(I return tomorrow to [Aston]). He is now sitting opposite; and
between us are red and white Cham[pagn]e, Burgundy, two sorts
of Claret, and lighter vintages, the relics of my youthful cellar,
which is yet in formidable number and famous order. But I leave
the wine to him, and prefer conversing soberly with you.

Ah! if you knew what a quiet Mussulman life (except in wine)
I led here for a few years. But no matter.

Yesterday I sent you a long letter, and must recur to the same
subject which is uppermost in my thoughts. I am as much aston-
ished, but I hope not so much mistaken, as Lord Ogleby[32] at
the dénouement or rather commencement of the last week. It has
changed my views, my wishes, my hopes, my everything, and will
furnish you with additional proof of my weakness. Mine guest
(late host) has just been congratulating himself on possessing a
partner without *passion*. I don't know, and cannot yet speak with
certainty, but I never yet saw more decisive preliminary symp-
toms.

As I am apt to take people at their word, on receiving my
answer, that whatever the weakness of her heart might be, I
should never derive further proof of it than the confession,
instead of pressing the point, I told her that I was willing to be
hers on her own terms, and should never attempt to infringe upon
the conditions. I said this without pique, and believing her per-
fectly in earnest for the time; but in the midst of our mutual
professions, or, to use her own expression, 'more than mutual',
she bursts into an agony of crying, and at such a time, and in
such a place, as rendered such a scene particularly perilous to
both – her sister in the next room, and [Webster] not far off. Of
course I said and did almost everything proper on the occasion,
and fortunately we restored sunshine in time to prevent anyone

from perceiving the cloud that had darkened our horizon. She says she is convinced that my own declaration was produced solely because I perceived her previous *penchant*, which by-the-bye, as I think I said to you before, I neither perceived nor expected. I really did not suspect her of a predilection for anyone, and even now in public, with the exception of those little indirect, yet mutually understood – I don't know how and it is unnecessary to name, or describe them – her conduct is as coldly correct as her still, fair, Mrs L[amb]-like[33] aspect. She, however, managed to give me a note and to receive another, and a ring before [Webster]'s very face, and yet she is a thorough devotee, and takes prayers, morning and evening, besides being measured for a new Bible once a quarter.

The only alarming thing is that [Webster] complains of her aversion from being beneficial to population and posterity. If this is an invariable maxim, I shall lose my labour. Be this as it may, she owns to more than I ever heard from any woman within the time, and I shan't take [Webster]'s word any more for her feelings than I did for that celestial comparison, which I once mentioned. I think her eye, her change of colour, and the trembling of her hand, and above all her devotion, tell a different tale.

Good night. We return to-morrow, and now I drink your health; you are my only correspondent, and I believe friend.

Ever yours,

B.

TO LADY MELBOURNE   [*Aston*] *October 11th, 1813*
. . . .
Monday Afternoon [October 11th]

I am better to-day, but not much advanced. I began the week so well that I thought the conclusion would have been more decisive. But the topography of this house is not the most favourable. I wonder how my father[34] managed; but he had it not till L^y Carmarthen came with it too. We shall be at Newstead again, the whole party for a week, in a few days, and there the

genii of the place will be perhaps more propitious. *He* haunts me
– here he is again, and here are a party of purple stockings come
to dine. Oh, that accursed pamphlet! I have not read it; what
shall I say to the author, now in the room? Thank the stars
which I yesterday abused, he is diverted by the mirror opposite,
and is now surveying with great complacency himself – he is
gone!

Your letter has arrived, but it is evidently written before my
last three have been delivered. Adieu, for the present. I must
dress, and have got to *sheer* one of those precious curls on which
you set so high a value; and I cannot, and *would* not, play the
same pass you may laughingly remember on a similar occasion
with C. My proselyte is so young a beginner that you won't
wonder at these exchanges and mummeries. You are right, she
is 'very pretty', and not so inanimate as I imagined, and must at
least be allowed an excellent taste!!

10 o'clock

Nearly a scene (always *nearly*) at dinner. There is a Lady Sitwell,
a wit and blue; and, what is more to the purpose, a dark, tall,
fierce-looking, conversable personage. As it is usual to separate
the women at table, I was under the necessity of placing myself
between her and the sister, and was seated, and in the agonies
of conjecture whether the dish before me required carving, when
my little Platonist exclaimed, 'Ld Byron, *this* is your place.' I
stared and before I had time to reply, she repeated, looking like
C. when *gentle* (for she is very unlike that fair creature when
angry), 'Ld Byron change places with Catherine'. I did, and very
willingly, though awkwardly; but 'the Moor' (mine host)
roared out, 'B[yron], that is the most ungallant thing I ever
beheld.' Lady Catherine by way of mending matters, answered,
'Did you not hear Frances ask him?' *He* has looked like the
Board of *Green* Cloth ever since, and is now mustering wine and
spirits for a lecture to her, and a squabble with me; he had better
let it alone, for I am in a pestilent humour at this present writing,
and shall certainly disparage his eternal '*pamphlet*'.

Good even. I solicit your good wishes in all good deeds, and
your occasional remembrance.

147

TO LADY MELBOURNE   *October 13th, 1813*

My Dear L^y M., – You must pardon the quantity of my letters,
and much of the *quality* also, but I have really no other *con-
fidential* correspondent on earth, and much to say which may call
forth the advice which has so often been to me of essential
service . . .

I mentioned to you yesterday a laughable occurence at dinner.
This morning *he* burst forth with a homily upon the subject to
the *two* and myself, instead of taking us separately (like the last
of the *Horatii* with the *Curiatii*). You will easily suppose with
such odds he had the worst of it, and the satisfaction of being
laughed at into the bargain. Serious as I am – or seem, – I really
cannot frequently keep my countenance: yesterday, *before my
face*, they disputed about their apartments at N[ewstead], *she*
insisting that her sister should share her room, and he very
properly, but heinously out of place, maintaining, and proving
to his own satisfaction that none but husbands have any legal
claim to divide their spouse's pillow. You may suppose, not-
withstanding the ludicrous effect of the scene, I felt and looked a
little uncomfortable; this she must have seen – for, of course, I
said not a word – and turning round at the close of the dialogue,
she whispered, 'N'importe, this is all nothing', an ambiguous
sentence which I am puzzled to translate; but, as it was meant to
console me, I was very glad to hear it, though quite unintelligible.

As far as I can pretend to judge of her disposition and character
– I will say, of course, I am partial – she is, you know, very hand-
some, and very gentle, though sometimes decisive; fearfully
romantic, and singularly warm in her *affections*; but I should think
of a *cold* temperament, yet I have my doubts on that point, too;
accomplished (as all decently educated women are), and clever,
though her style a little too *German*; no dashing nor desperate
talker, but never – and I have watched in *mixed* conversation –
saying a silly thing (*duet dialogues* in course between young and
Platonic people must be varied with a little chequered absurdity);
good tempered (always excepting L^y O[xford], which was, out-
wardly, the *best* I ever beheld), and jealous as *myself* – the *ne*

plus ultra of green-eyed monstrosity; seldom abusing other people, but listening to it with great patience. These qualifications, with an unassuming and sweet voice, and very soft manner, constitute the *bust* (all I can yet pretend to model) of my present idol.

You, who know me and my weakness so well, will not be surprised when I say that I am totally absorbed in this passion – that I am even ready to take a *flight* if necessary, and as she says, 'We cannot part,' it is no impossible *dénouement* – though as yet *one* of us at least does not think of it. W. will probably want to cut my throat, which would not be a difficult task, for I trust I should not return the fire of a man I had injured, though I could not refuse him the pleasure of trying me as a target. But I am not sure I shall not have more work in that way. There is a friend in the house who looks a little suspicious; he can only conjecture, but if he *Iagonizes*, or finds, or makes mischief, let him look to it. To W[ebster] I am decidedly wrong, yet he almost provoked me into it – *he* loves other women; at least he follows them; *she* evidently did not love him, even before.

I came here with no plan, no intention of the kind as my former letters will prove to *you* (the only person to whom I care about proving it) and have not yet been here *ten* days – a week yesterday, on recollection: you cannot be more astonished than I am how, and why all this has happened.

All my correspondences, and every other business, are at a standstill; I have not answered A., no, nor B., nor C., nor any *initial* except your own, you will wish me to be less troublesome to *that one*, and I shall now begin to draw at longer dates upon y^r patience.

Ever yours,

B.

October 14th, 1813

But this is 'le premier pas', my dear L^y M., at least I think so, and perhaps you will be of my opinion when you consider the *age*, the *country*, and the short time since such *pas* became

149

probable; I believe little but 'l'occasion manque', and to that many things are tending. He [Webster] is a little *indirect* blusterer who neither knows what he would have, nor what he deserves. To-day at breakfast (I was too late for the scene) he attacked *both* the girls in such a manner, no one knew why, or wherefore, that one had left the room, and the other had half a mind to leave the house; this too before servants, and the other guest! On my appearance the storm blew over, but the narrative was detailed to me subsequently by one of the sufferers. You may be sure that I shall not 'consider *self*', nor create a squabble while it can be avoided; on the contrary I have been endeavouring to serve him essentially[35] (except on the *one* point, and there I was goaded into it by his own absurdities), and to extricate him from some difficulties of various descriptions. Of course all obligations are cancelled between two persons in our circumstances, but that I shall not dwell upon; of the other I shall try to make an 'affaire réglée'; if that don't succeed we shall probably go off together; but *she* only shall make me resign the hope. As for him he may convert his antlers into *powder-horns* and welcome, and such he has announced as his intention when '*any* man at *any* time, etc. etc.,' 'he would not give *him* a chance, but exterminate *him* without suffering defence.' Do you know I was fool enough to lose my temper at this circuitous specimen of Bobadil jealousy, and tell him and the other (there are a brace, lion and jackal) that *I*, not their roundabout *he*, desired no better than to put these 'epithets of war', with which their sentences were 'horribly stuffed', to the proof. This was silly and suspicious, but my liver could bear it no longer.

My poor little *Helen* tells me that there never was such a *temper* and *talents*, that the marriage was *not* one of attachment, that – in short, *my* descriptions fade before hers, all foolish fellows are alike, but this has a patent for his cap and bells.

The scene between Sir B. and Lovemore I remember, but the one I alluded to was the letter of Lovemore to L^y Constant[36] – there is no comedy after all like real life. We have progressively improved into a less spiritual species of tenderness, but the seal is not yet fixed, though the wax is preparing for the impression.

150

There *ought* to be an excellent *occasion* to-morrow; but who can command circumstances? The most we can do is to avail ourselves of them.

Publicly I have been cautious enough, and actually declined a dinner where they went, because I thought something *intelligible* might be seen or suspected. I regretted, but regret it less for I hear one of the Fosters was there, and they be cousins and gossips of our good friends the D.'s. Good-night, Do *you fear* to write to *me*? Are *these* epistles, or your answers in any peril *here*? I must remember, however, the advice of a sage personage to me while abroad – take it in their English – 'Remember, milor, that *delicaci* ensure every succès.'

Y^{rs} ever,

B.

TO LADY MELBOURNE   *Newstead Abbey,*
                                     October 17th, 1813

My Dear Lady M., – The whole party are here – and now to my narrative. But first I must tell you that I am rather unwell, owing to a folly of last night. About midnight, after deep and drowsy potations, I took it into my head to empty my *skull cup*, which holds rather better than a bottle of Claret, at *one draught*, and nearly died the death of Alexander – which I shall be content to do when I have achieved his conquests: I had just sense enough left to feel that I was not fit to join the ladies, and went to bed, where, my valet tells me, that I was first convulsed, and afterwards so motionless, that he thought, 'Good night to Marmion'. I don't know how I came to do so very silly a thing; but I believe my guests were boasting, and 'company, villainous company, hath been the spoil of me'. I detest drinking in general, and beg your pardon for this excess. I *can't* do so any more.

To my theme. You were right. I have been a little too sanguine as to the *conclusion* – but hear. One day, left entirely to ourselves, was nearly fatal – another such *victory*, and with Pyrrhus we were lost – it came to this. 'I am entirely at your *mercy*. I own it. I give myself up to you. I am not *cold* – whatever I seem to others;

151

but I know that I cannot bear the reflection hereafter. Do not imagine that these are mere words. I tell you the truth – now act as you will.' Was I wrong? I spared her. There was a something so very peculiar in her manner – a kind of mild decision – no scene – not even a struggle; but still I know not what, that convinced me that she was serious. It was not the mere '*No*,' which one has heard forty times before, and always with the same accent; but the *tone*, and the aspect – yet I sacrificed much – the hour *two* in the morning – away – the Devil whispering that it was mere *verbiage*, etc. And yet I know not whether I can regret it – she seems so very thankful for my forbearance – a proof, at least, that she was not playing merely the usual decorous reluctance, which is sometimes so tiresome on these occasions.

You ask if I am prepared to go 'all lengths.' If you mean by 'all lengths' anything including duel, or divorce? I answer *Yes*. I love her. If I did not, and much too, I should have been more selfish on the occasion before mentioned. I have offered to go away with her, and her answer, whether sincere or not, is 'that on *my account* she declines it.' In the meantime we are all as wretched as possible; he scolding on *account* of *unaccountable* melancholy; the sister very suspicious, but rather amused – the friend very suspicious too (why I know not), not at all amused – il Marito something like Lord Chesterfield in De Grammont, putting on a martial physiognomy, prating with his worthy ally; swearing at servants, sermonizing both sisters; and buying sheep; but never quitting her side now; so that we are in despair. *I* am very feverish, restless, and silent, as indeed seems to be the tacit agreement of everyone else. In short I can foresee nothing – it may end in nothing; but here are half a dozen persons very much occupied, and two, if not three, in great perplexity; and, as far as I can judge, so we must continue.

She *don't* and *won't* live with him, and they have been so far separate for a long time; therefore I have nothing to answer for on that point. Poor thing – she is either the most *artful* or *artless* of her age (20) I ever encountered. She *owns* to so much, and perpetually says, 'Rather than you should be angry,' or 'Rather than you should like anyone else, I will do whatever you please;'

'I won't speak to this, that, or the other if you dislike it,' and throws, or seems to throw, herself so entirely upon my discretion in every respect, that it disarms me quite; but I am really wretched with the perpetual conflict with myself. Her health is so very delicate; she is so thin and pale, and seems to have lost her appetite so entirely, that I doubt her living much longer. This is also her own opinion. But these fancies are common to all who are not very happy; if she were once my wife, or likely to be so, a warm climate should be the first resort, nevertheless, for her recovery.

The most perplexing – and yet I can't prevail upon myself to give it up – is the caressing system. In her it appears perfectly childish, and I do think innocent; but it really puzzles all the Scipio about me to confine myself to the laudable portion of these endearments.

What a cursed situation I have thrust myself into! Potiphar (it used to be O[xford]'s name) putting some stupid question to me the other day, I told him that I rather admired the sister, and what does he? but tell her this; and his *wife* too, who a little too hastily asked him 'if he was mad?' which put him to demonstration that a man ought not to be asked if he was mad, for relating that a friend thought his wife's sister a pretty woman. Upon this topic he held forth with great fervour for a customary period. I wish he had a quinsey . . .

Ever yrs.,

B.

P.S. – My stay is quite uncertain – a moment may overturn everything; but you shall hear – happen what may – nothing or something.

TO LADY MELBOURNE *Northampton,*
October 19th, 1813

My Dear Lady M., – [Webster] and I are thus far on our way to town – he was seized with a sudden fit of friendship, and would accompany me – or rather, finding that some business could not conveniently be done without me, he thought proper to assume ye appearance of it. He is not exactly the companion I wished to take; it is really laughable when you think of the *other* – a kind of pig in a poke. Nothing but squabbles between *them* for the last three days, and at last he rose up with a solemn and mysterious air, and spake, 'L^y Frances, you have at last rendered an explanation necessary between me and Ld. B[yron], which must take place'. I stared, and knowing that it is the custom of country gentlemen (if Farquhar is correct) to apprize their moieties of such intentions, and being also a little out of humour and conscience, I thought a crisis must ensue, and answered very quietly that 'he would find me in such a room at his leisure ready to hear, and reply'. 'Oh!' says he, 'I shall choose my own time.' I wondered that he did not choose his *own* house, too, but walked away, and waited for him. All this mighty prelude led only to what he called an explanation for *my satisfaction*, that whatever appearances were, *he* and *she* were on the very best terms, that she loved him so much, and he her, it was impossible not to disagree upon the *tender* points, and for fear a man who, etc., etc., should suppose that marriage was not the happiest of all possible estates, he had taken this resolution of never quarrelling without letting me know that he was the best husband, and most fortunate person in existence.

I told him he had fully convinced me, that it was utterly impossible people who liked each other could behave with more interesting suavity – and so on. Yesterday morning, on our going (I pass over the scene, which shook me, I assure you), 'B.,' quoth he, 'I owe to you the most unhappy moments of my life.' I begged him to tell me how, that I might either sympathize, or put him out of his pain. 'Don't you see how the poor girl *doats* on me' (he replied); 'when I quit her but for a week, as you perceive, she is absolutely overwhelmed, and you stayed so long, and I necessarily for you, that she is in a worse state than I ever saw her in before, even before we married!'

Here we are – I could not return to A[ston] unless he had asked me – it is true he did, but in such a manner as I should not accept. What will be the end, I know not. I have left everything to *her*, and would have rendered all further *plots* superfluous by the most conclusive step; but she wavered, and escaped. Perhaps so have I – at least it is as well to think so – yet it is not over.

Whatever I may feel, you know me too well to think I shall plague my friends with long faces or elegies.

My dear Lady M., Ever Yours,

B.

TO LADY MELBOURNE   *October 21st, 1813*

My Dear L^y M., – You may well be surprised, but I had more reasons than one or two. Either [Webster] had taken it into his notable head, or wished to put it into mine, aye, and worse still, into ye girls, also; that I was a pretendant to the *hand* of the sister of 'the Lady' whom I had nearly – but no matter – (to continue Archer's speech with the variation of one word) ''tis a cursed *fortnight's* piece of work, and there's an end'. This brilliant notion, besides widening ye breach between him and me, did not add to the harmony of the two females; at least my idol was not pleased with the prospect of any transfer of incense to another altar. She was so unguarded after telling me too fifty times to 'take care of Catherine,' 'that she could conceal nothing, etc., etc.,' as to give me a very unequivocal proof of her own imprudence, in a carriage – (dusk to be sure) before her face – and yet with all this, and much more, she was the most tenacious personage either from fear, or weakness, or delicate health, of G–d knows what, that with the vigilance of no less than three Arguses in addition, it was utterly impossible, save once, to be decisive – and then – tears and tremors and prayers, which I am not yet old enough to find piquant in such cases, prevented me from making her wretched. I do detest everything which is not perfectly mutual, and any subsequent reproaches (as I know by one former long ago bitter experience) would heap coals of fire upon my head. Do you remember what Rousseau says to somebody, 'If you would know that you are beloved, watch your lover when he leaves you –' to me the most pleasing moments have generally been, when there is nothing more to be required; in short, the subsequent repose without satiety – which Lewis never dreamed of in that poem of his, 'Desire and Pleasure' – when you are secure of the past, yet without regret or disappointment; of this there was no prospect with her, she had so much more dread of the d—l, than gratitude for his kindness; and I am not yet sufficiently in his good graces to indulge my own passions at the certain misery of another. Perhaps after all, I was her dupe – if so – I am the dupe also of the few good feelings I could ever boast of, but here perhaps I am my own dupe too, in attributing to a good motive what may be quite otherwise.

[Webster] is a most extraordinary person; he has just left me and a snuff-box with a flaming inscription, after squabbling with me for these last ten days! and I too, have been of some real service to *him*, which I merely mention to mark the inconsistency of human nature. I have brought off a variety of foolish trophies (foolish indeed without victory), such as epistles, and lockets, which look as if she were in earnest; but she would not go off *now*, nor render going off unnecessary. Am I not candid to own my want of success, when I might have assumed the airs of an 'aimable Vainqueur'? but that is so paltry and so common – without cause, too; and what I hear, and see every day, that I would not, even to gain the point I have missed. I assure you no one knows but you one particle of this business, and you always must know everything concerning me. It is hard if I may not have one friend. Believe me, none will ever be so valued, and none ever was so trusted, by

Yours ever,

B.

TO LADY MELBOURNE   *November 22nd, 1813*

... The occasional oddity of Ph.'s letters has amused me much. The simplicity of her cunning, and her exquisite reasons. She vindicates her treachery to [Webster] thus; after condemning deceit in general, and hers in particular, she says: 'but then remember it is to deceive "un marito", and to prevent all the unpleasant consequences, etc. etc.'; and she says this in perfect persuasion that she has a full conception of the 'fitness of things', and the 'beauty of virtue', and 'the social compact', as Philosopher Square has it. Again, she desires me to write to *him kindly*, for she believes he cares for nobody but *me*! Besides, she will then hear *of* when she can't hear *from* me. Is not all this a comedy? Next to Ld. Ossulstone's *voucher* for her discretion, it has enlivened my ethical studies on the human mind beyond 50 volumes. How admirably we accommodate our reasons to our wishes!

She concludes by denominating that respectable man *Argus*, a very irreverent appellation. If we can both hold out till spring, perhaps he may have occasion for his optics. After all 'it is to deceive un marito'. Does not this expression convey to you the strongest mixture of right and wrong? A really guilty person could not have used it, or rather they would, *but* in different words. I find she has not the *but*, and that makes much difference if you consider it. The experienced would have said it is '*only* deceiving him', thinking of themselves. She makes a *merit* of it on his account and mine . . .

Ever yrs.

B.

I must quote to you correctly – 'How easily mankind are deceived. *May he be always deceived*! and, I, alas, am the base instrument of deception; but in this instance *concealment* is not a *crime*, for it preserves the peace of "d'un marito": the contrary would,' etc. I have been arguing on wrong premises; but no matter the *marked* lines are quite as good.

TO LADY MELBOURNE   *Monday Even.* [*Nov. 1813*]

A 'person of the least consequence'! You wrong yourself there, my dear L^{dy} M. – and so far she is right – you know very well, and so do I, that you can make me do whatever you please without reluctance – I am sure there exists no one to whom I feel half so much obliged – and for whom (gratitude apart) I entertain a greater regard. With regard to her, I certainly love – and in that case it has always been my lot to be entirely at the disposal of 'la regnante'; their caprices I cannot reason upon – and only obey

157

them. In favour of my acquaintance with you there is however a special clause, and nothing shall make me cancel it, I promise you ...

TO THOMAS MOORE   *November 30, 1813*

... All convulsions end with me in rhyme; and to solace my midnights, I have scribbled another Turkish story[37] – not a Fragment – which you will receive soon after this. It does not trench upon your kingdom in the least, and if it did, you would soon reduce me to my proper boundaries. You will think, and justly, that I run some risk of losing the little I have gained in fame, by this further experiment on public patience; but I have really ceased to care on that head. I have written this, and published it, for the sake of the *employment*, to wring my thoughts from reality, and take refuge in 'imaginings', however 'horrible'; and, as to success! those who succeed will console me for a failure – excepting yourself and one or two more, whom luckily I love too well to wish one leaf of their laurels a tint yellower. This is the work of a week, and will be the reading of an hour to you, or even less, – and, so, let it go —

P.S. – Ward and I *talk* of going to Holland. I want to see how a Dutch canal looks after the Bosphorus. Pray respond.

JOURNAL: 14 NOVEMBER 1813 – 19 APRIL 1814

IF this had been begun ten years ago, and faithfully kept!!! – heigho! there are too many things I wish never to have remembered, as it is. Well, – I have had my share of what are called the pleasures of this life, and have seen more of the European and Asiatic world than I have made a good use of. They say 'Virtue is its own reward', – it certainly should be paid well for its trouble. At five-and-twenty, when the better part of life is over, one should be *something*; – and what am I? nothing but five-and-twenty – and the odd months. What have I seen? the same man all over the world, – ay, and woman too. Give *me* a Mussulman who never asks questions, and a she of the same race who saves one the trouble of putting them. But for this same plague – yellow fever – and Newstead delay, I should have been by this time a second time close to the Euxine. If I can overcome the last, I don't so much mind your pestilence; and, at any rate, the spring shall see me there, – provided I neither marry myself, nor unmarry any one else in the interval. I wish one was – I don't know what I wish. It is odd I never set myself seriously to wishing without attaining it – and repenting. I begin to believe with the good old Magi, that one should only pray for the nation, and not for the individual; – but, on my principle, this would not be very patriotic.

No more reflections, – Let me see – last night I finished 'Zuleika',[38] my second Turkish Tale. I believe the composition of it kept me alive – for it was written to drive my thoughts from the recollection of –

Dear sacred name, rest ever unreveal'd.[39]

At least, even here, my hand would tremble to write it. This afternoon I have burnt the scenes of my commenced comedy. I have some idea of expectorating a romance, or rather a tale in prose; – but what romance could equal the events –

> quaeque ipse . . . . vidi,
> Et quorum pars magna fui.[40]

. . . I have declined presenting the Debtors' Petition, being sick of parliamentary mummeries. I have spoken thrice; but I doubt my ever becoming an orator. My first was liked; the second and third – I don't know whether they succeeded or not. I have never yet set to it *con amore*; – one must have some excuse to one's self for laziness, or inability, or both, and this is mine. 'Company, villanous company, hath been the spoil of me'; – and then, I 'have drunk medicines', not to make me love others, but certainly enough to hate myself.

Two nights ago I saw the tigers sup at Exeter 'Change. Except Veli Pacha's lion in the Morea, – who followed the Arab keeper like a dog, – the fondness of the hyæna for her keeper amused me most. Such a conversazione! – There was a 'hippopotamus', like Lord Liverpool in the face; and the 'Ursine Sloth' had the very voice and manner of my valet – but the tiger talked too much. The elephant took and gave me my money again – took off my hat – opened a door – *trunked* a whip – and behaved so well, that I wish he was my butler. The handsomest animal on earth is one of the panthers; but the poor antelopes were dead. I should hate to see one *here*: – the sight of the *camel* made me pine again for Asia Minor. '*Oh quando te aspiciam*?'

November 16

Went last night with Lewis to see the first of *Antony and Cleopatra*. It was admirably got up, and well acted – a salad of Shakspeare and Dryden. Cleopatra strikes me as the epitome of her sex – fond, lively, sad, tender, teasing, humble, haughty, beautiful, the devil! – coquettish to the last, as well with the 'asp' as with Antony. After doing all she can to persuade him that – but why do they abuse him for cutting off poltroon Cicero's head? Did not Tully tell Brutus it was a pity to have spared Antony? and did he not speak the Philippics? and are not '*words things*'? and such '*words*' very pestilent '*things*' too? If he had had a hundred heads, they deserved (from Antony) a rostrum (his was stuck up there) apiece – though, after all he might as well have pardoned him, for the credit of the thing. But to resume – Cleopatra, after securing him, says 'yet go – it is your interest', etc. – how like the sex! and the questions about Octavia – it is woman all over.

Today received Lord Jersey's invitation to Middleton – to travel sixty miles to meet Madame De Stael! I once travelled three thousand to get among silent people; and this same lady writes octavos, and *talks* folios. I have read her books – like most of them, and delight in the last; so I won't hear of it, as well as read.

Read Burns to-day. What would he have been, if a patrician? We should have had more polish – less force – just as much verse, but no immortality – a divorce and a duel or two, the which had he survived, as his potations must have been less spirit-uous, he might have lived as long as Sheridan, and outlived as much as poor Brinsley. What a wreck is that man! and all from bad pilotage; for no one had ever better gales, though now and then a little too squally. Poor dear Sherry! I shall never forget the day he and Rogers and Moore and I passed together; when *he* talked, and *we* listened, without one yawn, from six till one in the morning . . .

Nov. 17

No letter from —; but I must not complain. The respectable Job says, 'Why should a *living man* complain?' I really don't know, except it be that a *dead man* can't; and he, the said patriarch, *did* complain, nevertheless, till his friends were tired and his wife recommended that pious prologue, 'Curse – and die'; the only time, I suppose, when but little relief is to be found in swearing. I have had a most kind letter from Lord Holland on '*The Bride of Abydos*', which he likes, and so does Lady H. This is very good-natured in both, from whom I don't deserve any quarter. Yet I *did* think, at the time, that my cause of emnity proceeded from Holland House, and am glad I was wrong, and wish I had not been in such a hurry with that confounded satire, of which I would suppress even the memory; – but people, now they can't get it, make a fuss, I verily believe, out of contradiction.

George Ellis and Murray have been talking something about

Scott and me, George *pro Scoto*, – and very right too. If they
want to depose him, I only wish they would not set me up as a
competitor. Even if I had my choice, I would rather be the Earl
of Warwick than all the *kings* he ever made! Jeffrey and Gifford
I take to be the monarch-makers in poetry and prose. The *British
Critic*, in their Rokeby Review, have pre-supposed a comparison
which I am sure my friends never thought of, and W. Scott's
subjects are injudicious in descending to. I like the man – and
admire his works to what Mr Braham calls *Entusymusy*. All such
stuff can only vex him, and do me no good. Many hate his
politics – (I hate all politics); and, here, a man's politics are like
the Greek *soul* – an εἴδωλον,[41] besides God knows what *other
soul*; but their estimate of the two generally go together. . .

Another short note from Jersey, inviting Rogers and me on the
23d. I must see my agent to-night. I wonder when that Newstead
business will be finished. It cost me more than words to part with
it – and to *have* parted with it! What matters it what I do? or
what becomes of me? – but let me remember Job's saying, and
console myself with being 'a living man'.

I wish I could settle to reading again, – my life is monotonous,
and yet desultory. I take up books, and fling them down again.
I began a comedy, and burnt it because the scene ran into *reality*
– a novel; – for the same reason. In rhyme, I can keep more away
from facts; but the thought always runs through, through . . .
yes, yes, through. I have had a letter from Lady Melbourne – the
best friend I ever had in my life, and the cleverest of women.

Not a word from [Lady F. W. Webster]. Have they set out
from — or has my last precious epistle fallen into the lion's jaws?
If so – and this silence looks suspicious – I must clap my 'musty
morion' and 'hold out my iron'. I am out of practice – but I won't
begin again at Manton's now. Besides, I would not return his shot. I
was once a famous wafer-splitter; but then the bullies of society
made it necessary. Ever since I began to feel that I had a bad
cause to support, I have left off the exercise.

What strange tidings from that Anakim of anarchy – Buon-
aparte! Ever since I defended my bust of him at Harrow against
the rascally time-servers, when the war broke out in 1803, he has

been a *Héros de Roman* of mine – on the Continent; I don't want
him here. But I don't like those same flights – leaving of armies,
etc. etc. I am sure when I fought for his bust at school, I did not
think he would run away from himself. But I should not wonder
if he banged them yet. To be beat by men would be something;
but by three stupid, legitimate-old-dynasty boobies of regular-
bred sovereigns – O-hone-a-rie! – O-hone-a-rie! It must be, as
Cobbett says, his marriage with the thick-headed *Autrichienne*
brood. He had better have kept to her who was kept by Barras.
I never knew any good come of your young wife, and legal
espousals, to any but your 'sober-blooded boy' who 'eats fish'
and drinketh 'no sack'. Had he not the whole opera? all Paris?
all France? But a mistress is just as perplexing – that, is, *one* – two
or more are manageable by division.

I have begun, or had begun, a song, and flung it into the fire.
It was in remembrance of Mary Duff, my first of flames, before
most people begin to burn. I wonder what the devil is the matter
with me! I can do nothing, and – fortunately there is nothing to
do. It has lately been in my power to make two persons[42] (and
their connections) comfortable, *pro tempore*, and one happy, *ex
tempore*, – I rejoice in the last particularly, as it is an excellent
man. I wish there had been more inconvenience and less gratifica-
tion to my self-love in it, for then there had been more merit. We
are all selfish – and I believe, ye gods of Epicurus! I believe in
Rochefoucault about *men*, and in Lucretius (not Busby's transla-
tion) about yourselves. Your bard has made you very *nonchalant*
and blest; but as he has excused *us* from damnation, I don't envy
you your blessedness *much* – a little, to be sure. I remember last
year, [Lady Oxford] said to me, at [Eywood], 'Have we not passed
our last month like the gods of Lucretius?' And so we had. She
is an adept in the text of the original (which I like too); and when
that booby Busby sent his translating prospectus, she subscribed.
But, the devil prompting him to add a specimen, she transmitted
him a subsequent answer, saying, that 'after perusing it, her
conscience would not permit her to allow her name to remain on
the list of subscribblers'. Last night, at Lord H[olland]'s . . . I was
trying to recollect a quotation (as I think) of Stael's, from some

Teutonic sophist about architecture. 'Architecture', says this Macoronico Tedescho, 'reminds me of frozen music'.[43] It is somewhere – but where? – the demon of perplexity must know and won't tell. I asked M[ackintosh?], and he said it was not in her; but Puységur said it must be *hers*, it was so *like*. H. laughed as he does at all '*De l'Allemagne*' – in which, however, I think he goes a little too far. B., I hear, contemns it too. But there are fine passages; and, after all, what is a work – any – or every work – but a desert with fountains, and, perhaps, a grove or two, every day's journey? To be sure, in Madame, what we often mistake, and 'pant for', as the 'cooling stream', turns out to be the '*mirage*' (criticè *verbiage*); but we do, at last, get to something like the temple of Jove Ammon, and then the waste we have passed is only remembered to gladden the contrast . . .

Mr Murray has offered me one thousand guineas for *The Giaour* and *The Bride of Abydos*. I won't – it is too much, though I am strongly tempted, merely for the *say* of it. No bad price for a fortnight's (a week each) what? – the gods know – it was intended to be called poetry.

I have dined regularly to-day, for the first time since Sunday last – this being Sabbath, too. All the rest, tea and dry biscuits – six *per diem*. I wish to God I had not dined now! – It kills me with heaviness, stupor, and horrible dreams; and yet it was but a pint of Bucellas, and fish. Meat I never touch, – nor much vegetable diet. I wish I were in the country, to take exercise, – instead of being obliged to *cool* by abstinence, in lieu of it. I should not so much mind a little accession of flesh, – my bones can well bear it. But the worst is, the devil always came with it, – till I starved him out, – and I will *not* be the slave of *any* appetite. If I do err, it shall be my heart, at least, that heralds the way. Oh, my head – how it aches? – the horrors of digestion! I wonder how Buonaparte's dinner agrees with him? . . . My head! I believe it was given me to ache with. Good even.

Nov. 22, 1813

'Orange Boven!'[44] So the bees have expelled the bear that broke open their hive. Well, – if we are to have new De Witts and

De Ruyters, God speed the little republic ... No matter, – the bluff burghers, puffing freedom out of their short tobacco-pipes, might be worth seeing; though I prefer a cigar or a hooka, with the rose-leaf mixed with the milder herb of the Levant. I don't know what liberty means, – never having seen it, – but wealth is power all over the world; and as a shilling performs the duty of a pound (besides sun and sky and beauty for nothing) in the East, – *that* is the country. How I envy Herodes Atticus! – more than Pomponius.[45] And yet a little tumult, now and then, is an agreeable quickener of sensation; such as a revolution, a battle, or an *aventure* of any lively description: I think I rather would have been Bonneval, Ripperda, Alberoni, Hayreddin, or Horuc Barbarossa, or even Wortley Montague[46] than Mahomet himself.

Rogers will be in town soon? – the 23d is fixed for our Middleton visit. Shall I go? umph! – In this island, where one can't ride out without overtaking the sea, it don't much matter where one goes.

I remember the effect of the *first Edinburgh Review* on me. I heard of it six weeks before, – read it the day of its denunciation, – dined and drank three bottles of claret, (with S. B. Davies, I think,) neither ate nor slept the less, but, nevertheless, was not easy till I had vented my wrath and my rhyme, in the same pages, against every thing and every body. Like George in the *Vicar of Wakefield*, 'the fate of my paradoxes' would allow me to perceive no merit in another. I remembered only the maxim of my boxing-master, which, in my youth, was found useful in all general riots, – 'Whoever is not for you is against you – *mill* away right and left,' and so I did; – like Ishmael, my hand was against all men, and all men's anent me. I did wonder, to be sure, at my own success –

And marvels so much wit is all his own,

as Hobhouse sarcastically says of somebody (not unlikely myself, as we are old friends); – but were it to come over again, I would *not*. I have since redde the cause of my couplets, and it is not adequate to the effect. C — told me that it was believed I alluded to poor Lord Carlisle's nervous disorder in one of the lines. I

thank Heaven I did not know it – and would not, could not, if
I had. I must naturally be the last person to be pointed on defects
or maladies.

Rogers is silent, and, it is said, severe. When he does talk, he
talks well; and, on all subjects of taste, his delicacy of expression
is pure as his poetry. If you enter his house – his drawing-room –
his library – you of yourself say, this is not the dwelling of a
common mind. There is not a gem, a coin, a book thrown aside
a chimney-piece, his sofa, his table, that does not bespeak an
almost fastidious elegance in the possessor. But this very delicacy
must be the misery of his existence. Oh the jarrings his disposition
must have encountered through life!

Southey, I have not seen much of. His appearance is *Epic*;
and he is the only existing entire man of letters. All the others
have some pursuit annexed to their authorship. His manners are
mild, but not those of a man of the world, and his talents of the
first order. His prose is perfect. Of his poetry there are various
opinions: there is, perhaps, too much of it for the present
generation; posterity will probably select. He has *passages* equal
to any thing. At present, he has *a party*, but no *public* – except
for his prose writings. The life of Nelson is beautiful . . .

Moore has a peculiarity of talent, or rather talents, – poetry,
music, voice, all his own; and an expression in each, which never
was, nor will be, possessed by another. But he is capable of still
higher flights in poetry. By the by, what humour, what – every
thing, in the '*Post-Bag*'! There is nothing Moore may not do, if
he will but seriously set about it. In society, he is gentlemanly,
gentle, and, altogether, more pleasing than any individual with
whom I am acquainted. For his honour, principle, and indepen-
dence, his conduct to — speaks 'trumpet-tongued'. He has but
one fault – and that one I daily regret – he is not *here*.

November 23

Ward – I like Ward. By Mahomet! I begin to think I like every
body; – a disposition not to be encouraged; – a sort of social
gluttony that swallows every thing set before it. But I like Ward.

He is *piquant*; and, in my opinion, will stand *very* high in the House, and every where else, if he applies *regularly*. By the by, I dine with him tomorrow, which may have some influence on my opinion. It is as well not to trust one's gratitude *after* dinner. I have heard many a host libelled by his guests, with his burgundy yet reeking on their rascally lips . . .

Came home unwell and went to bed, – not so sleepy as might be desirable.

Tuesday morning

I awoke from a dream! – well! and have not others dreamed? – Such a dream! – but she did not overtake me. I wish the dead would rest, however. Ugh! how my blood chilled, – and I could not wake – and – heigho!

> Shadows tonight
> Have struck more terror to the soul of Richard,
> Than could the substance of ten thousand —s,
> Arm'd all in proof, and led by shallow —.

I do not like this dream, – I hate its 'foregone conclusion'. And am I to be shaken by shadows? Ay, when they remind us of – no matter – but, if I dream thus again, I will try whether *all* sleep has the like visions. Since I rose, I've been in considerable bodily pain also; but it is gone, and now, like Lord Ogleby,[47] I am wound up for the day.

A note from Mountnorris – I dine with Ward; – Canning is to be there, Frere and Sharpe, perhaps Gifford. I am to be one of the 'five' (or rather six), as Lady — said a little sneeringly yesterday. They are all good to meet, particularly Canning, and – Ward, when he likes. I wish I may be well enough to listen to these intellectuals.

No letters to-day; – so much the better, – there are no answers. I must not dream again; – it spoils even reality. I will go out of doors, and see what the fog will do for me. Jackson has been here: the boxing world much as usual; – but the club increases. I shall dine at Crib's to-morrow. I like energy – even animal energy – of all kinds; and I have need of both mental and corporeal. I have not dined out, nor, indeed, *at* all, lately: have heard no music – have seen nobody. Now for a *plunge* – high life and low life. *Amant* alterna *Camœnœ!*[48]

I have burnt my *Roman* – as I did the first scenes and sketch of my comedy – and, for aught I see, the pleasure of burning is quite as great as that of printing. These two last would not have done. I ran into *realities* more than ever; and some would have been recognised and others guessed at.

Redde the *Ruminator* – a collection of Essays, by a strange, but able, old man (Sir Egerton Brydges), and a half-wild young one, author of a poem on the Highlands, called *Childe Alarique*. The word 'sensibility' (always my aversion) occurs a thousand times in these Essays; and, it seems, is to be an excuse for all kinds of discontent. This young man can know nothing of life; and, if he cherishes the disposition which runs through his papers, will become useless, and, perhaps, not even a poet, after all, which he seems determined to be. God help him! no one should be a rhymer who could be any thing better. And this is what annoys one, to see Scott and Moore, and Campbell and Rogers, who might well have all been agents and leaders, now mere spectators. For, though they may have other ostensible avocations, these last are reduced to a secondary consideration. —, too, frittering away his time among dowagers and unmarried girls. If it advanced any *serious* affair, it were some excuse; but, with the unmarried, that is a hazardous speculation, and tiresome enough, too; and, with the veterans, it is not much worth trying, unless, perhaps, one in a thousand.

If I had any views in this country, they would probably be parliamentary. But I have no ambition; at least, if any, it would be *aut Cœsar aut nihil.*[49] My hopes are limited to the arrangement of my affairs, and settling either in Italy or the East (rather the last), and drinking deep of the languages and literature of both. Past events have unnerved me; and all I can now do is to make life an amusement, and look on while others play. After all, even the highest game of crowns and sceptres, what is it? *Vide* Napoleon's last twelvemonth. It has completely upset my system

of fatalism. I thought, if crushed, he would have fallen, when
fractus illabitur orbis,[50] and not have been pared away to gradual
insignificance; that all this was not a mere *jeu* of the gods, but
a prelude to greater changes and mightier events. But men never
advance beyond a certain point; and here we are, retrograding,
to the dull, stupid old system, – balance of Europe – poising
straws upon kings' noses, instead of wringing them off! Give me
a republic, or a despotism of one, rather than the mixed govern-
ment of one, two, three. A republic! – look in the history of the
Earth – Rome, Greece, Venice, France, Holland, America, our
short (eheu!) Commonwealth, and compare it with what they
did under masters. The Asiatics are not qualified to be republicans,
but they have the liberty of demolishing despots, which is the
next thing to it. To be the first man – not the Dictator – not the
Sylla, but the Washington or the Aristides – the leader in talent
and truth – is next to the Divinity! Franklin, Penn, and, next to
these, either Brutus or Cassius – even Mirabeau – or St Just.
I shall never be any thing, or rather always be nothing. The most
I can hope is, that some will say, 'He might, perhaps, if he would'.

12, midnight

... Ward talks of going to Holland, and we have partly discussed
an *ensemble* expedition. It must be in ten days, if at all, if we wish
to be in at the Revolution. And why not? —[51] is distant, and will
be at —, still more distant, till spring. No one else, except
Augusta, cares for me; no ties – no trammels – *andiamo dunque
– se torniamo, bene – se non, ch'importa?*[52] Old William of Orange
talked of dying in 'the last ditch' of his dingy country. It is lucky
I can swim, or I suppose I should not well weather the first. But
let us see. I have heard hyænas and jackalls in the ruins of Asia;
and bull-frogs in the marshes; besides wolves and angry Mussul-
mans. Now, I should like to listen to the shout of a free Dutch-
man.

Alla! Viva! For ever! Hourra! Huzza! – which is the most
rational or musical of these cries? 'Orange Boven', according to
the *Morning Post*.

Wednesday, 24

No dreams last night of the dead, nor the living; so – I am 'firm as the marble, founded as the rock', till the next earthquake.

Ward's dinner went off well. There was not a disagreeable person there – unless *I* offended any body, which I am sure I could not by contradiction, for I said little, and opposed nothing. Sharpe (a man of elegant mind, and who has lived much with the best – Fox, Horne Tooke, Windham, Fitzpatrick, and all the agitators of other times and tongues,) told us the particulars of his last interview with Windham, a few days before the fatal operation which sent 'that gallant spirit to aspire the skies'. Windham, – the first in one department of oratory and talent, whose only fault was his refinement beyond the intellect of half his hearers, – Windham, half his life an active participator in the events of the earth, and one of those who governed nations, – *he* regretted, – and dwelt much on that regret, that 'he had not entirely devoted himself to literature and science!!!' His mind certainly would have carried him to eminence there, as elsewhere; – but I cannot comprehend what debility of that mind could suggest such a wish. I, who have heard him, cannot regret any thing but that I shall never hear him again. What! would he have been a plodder? a metaphysician? – perhaps a rhymer? a scribbler? Such an exchange must have been suggested by illness. But he is gone, and Time 'shall not look upon his like again'.

I am tremendously in arrear with my letters, – except to —, and to her my thoughts overpower me: – my words never compass them. To Lady Melbourne I write with most pleasure – and her answers, so sensible, so *tactique* – I never met with half her talent. If she had been a few years younger, what a fool she would have made of me, had she thought it worth her while, – and I should have lost a valuable and most agreeable *friend*. Mem. – a mistress never is nor can be a friend. While you agree, you are lovers; and, when it is over, any thing but friends.

I have not answered W. Scott's last letter, – but I will. I regret to hear from others, that he has lately been unfortunate in pecuniary involvements. He is undoubtedly the Monarch of Parnassus, and the most *English* of bards. I should place Rogers next in the living list (I value him more as the last of the *best* school) – Moore and Campbell both *third* – Southey and Wordsworth and Coleridge – the rest, οἱ πολλοι[53] – thus, – There is a triangular *Gradus ad Parnassum*! – the names are too numerous for the base of the triangle. Poor Thurlow has gone wild about the poetry of Queen Bess's reign – *c'est dommage*. I have ranked the names upon my triangle more upon what I believe popular opinion, than any decided opinion of my own. For, to me, some of Moore's last *Erin* sparks – 'As a beam o'er the face of the waters' – 'When he who adores thee' – 'Oh blame not' – and 'Oh breathe not his name' – are worth all the Epics that ever were composed.

Rogers thinks the *Quarterly* will attack me next. Let them. I have been 'peppered so highly' in my time, *both* ways, that it must be cayenne or aloes to make me taste. I can sincerely say, that I am not very much alive *now* to criticism. But – in tracing this – I rather believe that it proceeds from my not attaching that importance to authorship which many do, and which, when young, I did also. 'One gets tired of every thing, my angel', says Valmont.[54] The 'angels' are the only things of which I am not a little sick – but I do think the preference of *writers* to *agents* – the mighty stir made about scribbling and scribes, by themselves and others – a sign of effeminacy, degeneracy, and weakness. Who would write, who had any thing better to do? 'Action – action – action' – said Demosthenes: 'Action*s* – action*s*', I say, and not writing, – least of all, rhyme. Look at the querulous and monotonous lives of the 'genus'; – except Cervantes, Tasso, Dante, Ariosto, Kleist (who were brave and active citizens), Aeschylus, Sophocles, and some other of the antiques also – what a worthless, idle brood it is!

12, Mezza Notte

Just returned from dinner with Jackson (the Emperor of Pugilism) and another of the select, at Crib's, the champion's. I drank more than I like, and have brought away some three bottles of very fair claret – for I have no headach. We had Tom Crib up after dinner; – very facetious, though somewhat prolix. He don't like his situation – wants to fight again – pray Pollux (or Castor, if he was the *miller*) he may! Tom has been a sailor – a coal-heaver – and some other genteel profession, before he took to the cestus. Tom has been in action at sea, and is now only three-and-thirty. A great man! has a wife and a mistress, and conversations well – bating some sad omissions and misapplications of the aspirate. Tom is an old friend of mine; I have seen some of his best battles in my nonage. He is now a publican, and, I fear, a sinner; for Mrs Crib is on alimony and Tom's daughter lives with the champion. *This* Tom told me, – Tom, having an opinion of my morals, passed her off as a legal spouse. Talking of her, he said, 'she was the truest of women' – from which I immediately inferred she could *not* be his wife, and so it turned out.

These panegyrics don't belong to matrimony; – for, if 'true', a man don't think it necessary to say so; and if not, the less he says the better. Crib is the only man except —[55], I ever heard harangue upon his wife's virtue; and I listened to both with great credence and patience, and stuffed my handkerchief into my mouth, when I found yawning irresistible – By the by, I am yawning now – so, good night to thee. – Νωαίρων[56]

Thursday, November 26

... I have been thinking lately a good deal of Mary Duff. How very odd that I should have been so utterly, devotedly fond of that girl, at an age when I could neither feel passion, nor know the meaning of the word. And the effect! My mother used always to rally me about this childish amour; and, at last, many years after, when I was sixteen, she told me one day, 'Oh, Byron, I have had a letter from Edinburgh, from Miss Abercromby, and your old sweetheart Mary Duff is married to a Mr Co^e.' And what was my answer? I really cannot explain or account for my feelings at that moment; but they nearly threw me into convulsions, and alarmed my mother so much, that after I grew better, she generally avoided the subject – to *me* – and contented herself with telling it to all her acquaintance. Now, what could this be? I had never seen her since her mother's *faux pas* at Aberdeen had been the cause of her removal to her grandmother's at Banff; we were both the merest children. I had and have been attached fifty times since that period; yet I recollect all we said to each other, all our caresses, her features, my restlessness, sleeplessness, my tormenting my mother's maid to write for me to her, which she at last did, to quiet me. Poor Nancy thought I was wild, and, as I could not write for myself, became my secretary. I remember, too, our walks, and the happiness of sitting by Mary, in the children's apartment, at their house not far from the Plain-stanes at Aberdeen, while her lesser sister Helen played with the doll, and we sat gravely making love, in our way.

How the deuce did all this occur so early? where could it originate? I certainly had no sexual ideas for years afterwards; and yet my misery, my love for that girl were so violent, that I sometimes doubt if I have ever been really attached since. Be that as it may, hearing of her marriage several years after was like a thunder-stroke – it nearly choked me – to the horror of my mother and the astonishment and almost incredulity of every body. And it is a phenomenon in my existence (for I was not eight years old) which has puzzled, and will puzzle me to the latest hour of it; and lately, I know not why, the *recollection* (*not* the attachment) has recurred as forcibly as ever. I wonder if she can have the least remembrance of it or me? or remember pitying her sister Helen for not having an admirer too? How very pretty is the perfect image of her in my memory – her brown, dark hair, and hazel eyes; her very dress! I should be quite grieved to see *her now*; the reality, however beautiful, would destroy, or at least confuse, the features of the lovely Peri which then existed in her, and still lives in my imagination, at the distance of more than sixteen years. I am now twenty five and odd months . . .

Next to the beginning, the conclusion has often occupied my reflections, in the way of investigation. That the facts are thus, others know as well as I, and my memory yet tells me so, in more than a whisper. But, the more I reflect, the more I am bewildered to assign any cause for this precocity of affection . . .

– I have been pondering on the miseries of separation, that – oh how seldom we see those we love! yet we live ages in moments, *when met.*The only thing that consoles me during absence is the reflection that no mental or personal estrangement, from ennui or disagreement, can take place; and when people meet here-after, even though many changes may have taken place, in the mean time, still, unless they are *tired* of each other, they are ready to reunite, and do not blame each other for the circumstances that severed them.

[. . .]

Tuesday, 30th

Two days missed in my log-book; – *hiatus haud deflendus.*[57] They were as little worth recollection as the rest; and, luckily, laziness or society prevented me from *notching* them.

Sunday, I dined with the Lord Holland in St James Square . . . Holland's society is very good; you always see some one or other in it worth knowing. Stuffed myself with sturgeon, and exceeded in champagne and wine in general, but not to confusion of head. When I *do* dine, I gorge like an Arab or a Boa snake, on fish and vegetables, but no meat. I am always better, however, on my tea and biscuit than any other regimen, and even *that* sparingly . . .

Today (Tuesday) a very pretty billet from M. la Baronne de Stael Holstein. She is pleased to be much pleased with my mention of her and her last work in my notes. I spoke as I thought. Her works are my delight, and so is she herself, for – half an hour. I don't like her politics – at least, her *having changed* them; had she been *qualis ab incepto,*[58] it were nothing. But she is a woman by herself, and has done more than all the rest of them together, intellectually; – she ought to have been a man. She *flatters* me very prettily in her note; – but I *know* it. The reason that adulation is not displeasing is, that, though untrue, it shows one to be of consequence enough, in one way or other, to induce people to lie, to make us their friend: – that is their concern . . .

Yesterday, a very pretty letter from Annabella, which I

answered. What an odd situation and friendship is ours! – without one spark of love on either side, and produced by circumstances which in general lead to coldness on one side, and aversion on the other. She is a very superior woman, and very little spoiled, which is strange in an heiress – a girl of twenty – a peeress that is to be, in her own right – an only child, and a *savante*, who has always had her own way. She is a poetess, a mathematician, a metaphysician, and yet, withal, very kind, generous, and gentle, with very little pretension. Any other head would be turned with half her acquisitions, and a tenth of her advantages.

Wednesday, December 1, 1813

To-day responded to La Baronne de Stael Holstein, and sent to Leigh Hunt (an acquisition to my acquaintance – through Moore – of last summer) a copy of the two Turkish tales. Hunt is an extraordinary character, and not exactly of the present age. He reminds me more of the Pym and Hampden times – much talent, great independence of spirit, and an austere, yet not repulsive, aspect. If he goes on *qualis ab incepto*, I know few men who will deserve more praise or obtain it. I must go and see him again;[59] – the rapid succession of adventure, since last summer, added to some serious uneasiness and business, have interrupted our acquaintance; but he is a man worth knowing; and though, for his own sake, I wish him out of prison, I like to study character in such situations. He has been unshaken, and will continue so. I don't think him deeply versed in life; – he is the bigot of virtue (not religion), and enamoured of the beauty of that 'empty name', as the last breath of Brutus pronounced, and every day proves it. He is, perhaps, a little opinionated, as all men who are the *centre* of *circles*, wide or narrow – the Sir Oracles, in whose name two or three are gathered together – must be, and as even Johnson was; but, withal, a valuable man, and less vain than success and even the consciousness of preferring 'the right to the expedient' might excuse . . .

I shall soon be six-and-twenty (January 22d, 1814). Is there any thing in the future that can possibly console us for not being always *twenty-five*?

> Oh Gioventu!
> Oh Primavera! gioventu del' anno.
> Oh Gioventu! primavera della vita.[60]

Sunday, December 5

... Galt called. – Mem. – to ask some one to speak to Raymond in favour of his play. We are old fellow-travellers, and, with all his eccentricities, he has much strong sense, experience of the world, and is, as far as I have seen, a good-natured philosophical fellow. I showed him Sligo's letter on the reports of the Turkish girl's *aventure* at Athens soon after it happened. He and Lord Holland, Lewis, and Moore, and Rogers, and Lady Melbourne have seen it. Murray has a copy. I thought it had been *unknown*, and wish it were; but Sligo arrived only some days after, and the *rumours* are the subject of his letter. That I shall preserve, – *it is as well*. Lewis and Galt were both *horrified*; and L. wondered I did not introduce the situation into 'The Giaour'. He *may* wonder; – he might wonder more at that production's being written at all. But to describe the *feelings* of *that situation* were impossible – it is *icy* even to recollect them.

The Bride of Abydos was published on Thurdsay the second of December; but how it is liked or disliked, I know not. Whether it succeeds or not is no fault of the public, against whom I can have no complaint. But I am much more indebted to the tale than I can ever be to the most partial reader; as it wrung my thoughts from reality to imagination – from selfish regrets to vivid recollections – and recalled me to a country replete with the *brightest* and *darkest*, but always most *lively* colours of my memory ...

Morning, two o'clock

Went to Lord H.'s – party numerous – *mi*lady in perfect good humour, and consequently *perfect*.

... Asked for Wednesday to dine and meet the Stael – asked particularly, I believe, out of mischief to see the first interview after the *note*, with which Corinne professes herself to be so much taken. I don't much like it; she always talks of *my*self or *her*self, and I am not (except in soliloquy, as now,) much enamoured of either subject – especially one's works. What the devil shall I say about *De l'Allemagne*? I like it prodigiously; but unless I can twist my admiration into some fantastical expression, she won't believe me; and I know, by experience, I shall be overwhelmed with fine things about rhyme, etc. etc. The lover, Mr [Rocca], was there tonight, and C— said 'it was the only proof *he* had seen of her good taste'. Monsieur L'Amant is remarkably handsome; but I don't think more so than her book . . .

Monday, Dec. 6

. . . This journal is a relief. When I am tired – as I generally am – out comes this, and down goes every thing. But I can't read it over; and God knows what contradictions it may contain. If I am sincere with myself (but I fear one lies more to one's self than to any one else), every page should confute, refute, and utterly abjure its predecessor . . .

Redde a good deal, but desultorily. My head is crammed with the most useless lumber. It is odd that when I do read, I can only bear the chicken broth of – *any thing* but Novels. It is many a year since I looked into one, (though they are sometimes ordered, by way of experiment, but never taken,) till I looked yesterday at the worst parts of the *Monk*.[61] These descriptions ought to have been written by Tiberius at Caprea – they are forced – the *philtered* ideas of a jaded voluptuary. It is to me inconceivable how they could have been composed by a man of only twenty – his age when he wrote them. They have no nature – all the sour cream of cantharides. I should have suspected Buffon of writing them on the death-bed of his detestable dotage. I have never redde this edition, and merely looked at them from curiosity and recollection of the noise they made, and the name they had left to Lewis. But they could do no harm, except —. . .

I am so far obliged to this Journal, that it preserves me from verse, – at least from keeping it. I have just thrown a poem into the fire (which it has relighted to my great comfort), and have smoked out of my head the plan of another. I wish I could as easily get rid of thinking, or, at least, the confusion of thought.

Tuesday December 7

Went to bed, and slept dreamlessly, but not refreshingly. Awoke, and up an hour before being called; but dawdled three hours in dressing. When one subtracts from life infancy (which is vegetation), – sleep, eating, and swilling – buttoning and unbuttoning – how much remains of downright existence? The summer of a dormouse . . .

This morning, a very pretty billet from the Stael about meeting her at Ld. H.'s to-morrow. She has written, I dare say, twenty such this morning to different people, all equally flattering to each. So much the better for her and those who believe all she wishes them, or they wish to believe. She has been pleased to be pleased with my slight eulogy in the note annexed to *The Bride*. This is to be accounted for in several ways, – firstly, all women like all, or any, praise; secondly, this was unexpected, because I have never courted her; and, thirdly, as Scrub[62] says, those who have been all their lives regularly praised, by regular critics, like a little variety, and are glad when any one goes out of his way to say a civil thing; and, fourthly, she is a very good-natured creature, which is the best reason, after all, and, perhaps, the only one . . .

Went out – came home – this, that, and the other – and 'all is vanity, saith the preacher', and so say I, as part of his congregation. Talking of vanity, whose praise do I prefer? Why, Mrs Inchbald's, and that of the Americans. The first, because her *Simple Story* and *Nature and Art* are, to me, *true* to their *titles*; and, consequently, her short note to Rogers about *The Giaour* delighted me more than any thing, except the *Edinburgh Review*. I like the Americans, because *I* happened to be in *Asia*, while the *English Bards and Scotch Reviewers* were redde in *America*. If I could have had a speech against the *Slave Trade in Africa*, and an epitaph on a dog in *Europe* (i.e. in the *Morning Post*), my *vertex sublimis*[63] would certainly have displaced stars enough to overthrow the Newtonian system.

178

Friday, December 10, 1813

I am *ennuyé* beyond my usual tense of that yawning verb, which I am always conjugating; and I don't find that society much mends the matter. I am too lazy to shoot myself – and it would annoy Augusta, and perhaps —; but it would be a good thing for George [Byron?], on the other side, and no bad one for me; but I won't be tempted.

I have had the kindest letter from Moore. I *do* think that man is the best-hearted, the only *hearted* being I ever encountered; and, then, his talents are equal to his feelings.

Dined on Wednesday at Lord H[olland]'s – the Staffords, Staels, Cowpers, Ossulstones, Melbournes, Mackintoshes, etc., etc. – and was introduced to the Marquis and Marchioness of Stafford, – an unexpected event. My quarrel with Lord Carlisle (their or his brother-in-law) having rendered it improper, I suppose, brought it about. But, if it was to happen at all, I wonder it did not occur before. She is handsome, and must have been beautiful – and her manners are *princessly*.

The Stael was at the other end of the table, and less loquacious than heretofore. We are now very good friends; though she asked Lady Melbourne whether I had really any *bonhommie*. She might as well have asked that question before she told C[aroline] L[amb?] '*c'est un démon*'.True enough, but rather premature, for *she* could not have found it out, and so – she wants me to dine there next Sunday.

Monday, December 13, 1813

... Allen (Lord Holland's Allen – the best informed and one of the ablest men I know – a perfect Magliabecchi – a devourer, a *Helluo* of books, and an observer of men,) has lent me a quantity of Burns's unpublished and never-to-be-published Letters. They are full of oaths and obscene songs. What an antithetical mind! – tenderness, roughness – delicacy, coarseness – sentiment, sensuality – soaring and grovelling, dirt and deity – all mixed up in that one compound of inspired clay!

It seems strange; a true voluptury will never abandon his mind to the grossness of reality. It is by exalting the earthly, the material, the *physique* of our pleasures, by veiling these ideas, by forgetting them altogether, or, at least, never naming them hardly to one's self, that we alone can prevent them from disgusting.

December 14, 15, 16

Much done, but nothing to record. It is quite enough to set down my thoughts, – my actions will rarely bear retrospection.

December 17, 18

Lord Holland told me a curious piece of sentimentality in Sheridan. The other night we were all delivering our respective and various opinions on him and other *hommes marquans*, and mine was this: – 'Whatever Sheridan has done or chosen to do has been, *par excellence*, always the *best* of its kind. He has written the *best* comedy (*School for Scandal*), the *best* drama (in my mind, far before that St Giles's lampoon, the *Beggar's Opera*), the best farce (the *Critic* – it is only too good for a farce), and the best Address (Monologue on Garrick), and, to crown all, delivered the very best Oration (the famous Begum Speech) ever conceived or heard in this country.' Somebody told S. this the next day, and on hearing it he burst into tears!

Poor Brinsley! if they were tears of pleasure, I would rather have said these few, but most sincere, words than have written the Iliad or made his own celebrated Philippic. Nay, his own comedy never gratified me more than to hear that he had derived a moment's gratification from any praise of mine, humble as it must appear to 'my elders and my betters'.

Went to my box at Covent Garden to-night; and my delicacy felt a little shocked at seeing S—'s mistress (who, to my certain knowledge, was actually educated, from her birth, for her profession) sitting with her mother, 'a three-piled b—d, b—d – Major to the army', in a private box opposite. I felt rather indignant; but, casting my eyes round the house, in the next box to me, and the next, and the next, were the most distinguished

180

old and young Babylonians of quality; – so I burst out a laughing. It was really odd; Lady — *divorced* – Lady — and her daughter, Lady —, both *divorceable* – Mrs —, in the next the *like*, and still nearer —! What an assemblage to *me*, who know all their histories. It was as if the house had been divided between your public and your *understood* courtesans; – but the intriguantes much outnumbered the regular mercenaries. On the other side were only Pauline and *her* mother, and next box to her, three of inferior note. Now, where lay the difference between *her* and *mamma*, and Lady — and daughter? except that the two last may enter Carleton and any *other house*, and the two first are limited to the opera and b— house. How I do delight in observing life as it really is! – and myself, after all, the worst of any. But no matter – I must avoid egotism, which, just now, would be no vanity ...

Redde some Italian, and wrote two Sonnets on —. I never wrote but one sonnet before, and that was not in earnest, and many years ago, as an exercise – and I will never write another. They are the most puling, petrifying, stupidly platonic compositions. I detest the Petrarch so much, that I would not be the man even to have obtained his Laura, which the metaphysical, whining dotard never could.

January 16, 1814

... I am getting rather into admiration of [Lady Catherine Annesley] the youngest sister of [Lady Frances Webster]. A wife would be my salvation. I am sure the wives of my acquaintances have hitherto done me little good. Catherine is beautiful, but very young, and, I think a fool. But I have not seen enough to judge; besides, I hate an *esprit* in petticoats. That she won't love me is very probable, nor shall I love her. But, on my system, and the modern system in general, that don't signify. The business (if it came to business) would probably be arranged between papa and me. She would have her own way; I am good-humoured to women, and docile; and, if I did not fall in love with her, which I should try to prevent, we should be a very comfortable couple. As to conduct, *that* she must look to. But *if* I love, I shall be jealous; – and for that reason I will not be in love. Though, after all, I doubt my temper, and fear I should not be so patient as becomes the *bienséance* of a married man in my station. Divorce ruins the poor *femme*, and damages are a paltry compensation. I do fear my temper would lead me into some of our oriental tricks of vengeance, or, at any rate, into a summary appeal to the court of twelve paces. So 'I'll none on't', but e'en remain single and solitary; – though I should like to have somebody now and then to yawn with one ...

As for me, by the blessing of indifference, I have simplified my politics into an utter detestation of all existing governments; and, as it is the shortest and most agreeable and summary feeling imaginable, the first moment of an universal republic would convert me into an advocate for single and uncontradicted despotism. The fact is, riches are power, and poverty is slavery all over the earth, and one sort of establishment is no better nor worse for a *people* than another. I shall adhere to my party, because it would not be honourable to act otherwise; but, as to *opinions*, I don't think politics *worth* an *opinion*. *Conduct* is another thing: – if you begin with a party, go on with them. I have no consistency, except in politics; and *that* probably arises from my indifference on the subject altogether.

Feb. 18

Better than a month since I last journalised: – most of it out of London and at Notts., but a busy one and a pleasant, at least three weeks of it.[64] On my return, I find all the newspapers in hysterics, and town in an uproar, on the avowal and republication of two stanzas on Princess Charlotte's weeping at Regency's speech to Lauderdale in 1812. They are daily at it still; – some of the abuse good, all of it hearty. They talk of a motion in our House upon it – be it so ...

Hobhouse is returned to England. He is my best friend, the most lively, and a man of the most sterling talents extant.

The Corsair has been conceived, written, published, etc., since I last took up this journal. They tell me it has great success; – it was written *con amore*, and much from *existence*. Murray is

182

satisfied with its progress; and if the public are equally so with
the perusal, there's an end of the matter.

Nine o'clock

... Saw Rogers, and had a note from Lady Melbourne, who says,
it is said I am 'much out of spirits'. I wonder if I really am or not?
I have certainly enough of 'that perilous stuff which weighs upon
the heart', and it is better they should believe it to be the result of
these attacks than of the real cause; but – ay, ay, always *but*, to
the end of the chapter.

Hobhouse has told me ten thousand anecdotes of Napoleon,
all good and true. My friend H. is the most entertaining of com-
panions, and a fine fellow to boot.

Redde a little – wrote notes and letters, and am alone, which
Locke says is bad company. 'Be not solitary, be not idle.' – Um!
– the idleness is troublesome; but I can't see so much to regret in
the solitude. The more I see of men, the less I like them. If I
could but say so of women too, all would be well. Why can't I?
I am now six-and-twenty; my passions have had enough to cool
them; my affections more than enough to wither them, – and
yet – always *yet* and *but* – 'Excellent well, you are a fishmonger –
get thee to a nunnery'. 'They fool me to the top of my bent.'

Midnight

... The greater the equality, the more impartially evil is distri-
buted, and becomes lighter by the division among so many –
therefore, a Republic! ...

I wonder how the deuce any body could make such a world;
for what purpose dandies, for instance, were ordained – and
kings – and fellows of colleges – and women of 'a certain age' –
and many men of any age – and myself, most of all! ...

Is there any thing beyond? – *who* knows? *He* that can't tell.
Who tells that there *is*? He who don't know. And when shall he
know? perhaps, when he don't expect, and generally when he
don't wish it. In this last respect, however, all are not alike;
it depends a good deal upon education, – something upon nerves
and habits – but most upon digestion.

Saturday, Feb. 19

Just returned from seeing Kean in Richard. By Jove, he is a soul!
Life – nature – truth without exaggeration or diminution.
Kemble's Hamlet is perfect; but Hamlet is not Nature. Richard
is a man; and Kean is Richard. Now to my own concerns . . .

February 20

Got up and tore out two leaves of this Journal – I don't know
why. Hodgson just called and gone. He has much *bonhommie*
with his other good qualities, and more talent than he has yet
had credit for beyond his circle . . .

To write so as to bring home to the heart, the heart must have
been tried, – but, perhaps, ceased to be so. While you are under
the influence of passions, you only feel, but cannot describe them,
– any more than, when in action, you could turn round and tell
the story to your next neighbour! When all is over, – all, all, and
irrevocable, – trust to memory – she is then but too faithful . . .

Sunday, February 27

Here I am, alone, instead of dining at Lord H[olland]'s, where I
was asked, – but not inclined to go any where. Hobhouse says
I am growing a *loup garou*, – a solitary hobgoblin. True; – 'I am
myself alone'. The last week has been passed in reading – seeing
plays – now and then visitors – sometimes yawning and some-
times sighing, but no writing, – save of letters. If I could always
read, I should never feel the want of society. Do I regret it? –
um! – 'Man delights not me', and only one woman – at a time.

There is something to me very softening in the presence of a
woman, – some strange influence, even if one is not in love with
them – which I cannot at all account for, having no very high
opinion of the sex. But yet, – I always feel in better humour with
myself and everything else, if there is a woman within ken. Even
Mrs Mule, my firelighter, – the most ancient and withered of her
kind, – and (except to myself) not the best-tempered – always
makes me laugh, – no difficult task when I am 'i' the vein'.

Heigho! I would I were in mine island! – I am not well; and yet I look in good health. At times I fear, 'I am not in my perfect mind'; – and yet my heart and head have stood many a crash, and what should ail them now? They prey upon themselves, and I am sick – sick – 'Prithee, undo this button – why should a cat, a rat, a dog have life – and *thou* no life at all?' Six-and-twenty years, as they call them, why, I might and should have been a Pasha by this time. 'I 'gin to be a-weary of the sun.' . . .

March 10, Thor's Day

On Tuesday dined with Rogers, – Mackintosh, Sheridan, Sharpe, – much talk, and good, – all, except my own little prattlement. Much of old times – Horne Tooke – the Trials – evidence of Sheridan, and anecdotes of those times, when *I* alas! was an infant. If I had been a man, I would have made an English Lord Edward Fitzgerald.

Set down Sheridan at Brookes's, – where, by the by, he could not have well set down himself, as he and I were the only drinkers. Sherry means to stand for Westminster, as Cochrane (the stock-jobbing hoaxer) must vacate. Brougham is a candidate. I fear for poor dear Sherry. Both have talents of the highest order, but the youngster has *yet* a character. We shall see, if he lives to Sherry's age, how he will pass over the redhot ploughshares of public life. I don't know why, but I hate to see the *old* ones lose; particularly Sheridan, notwithstanding all his *méchanceté* . . .

. . . He [Hobhouse] told me an odd report, – that *I* am the actual Conrad, the veritable Corsair, and that part of my travels are supposed to have passed in *privacy*.[65] Um! – people sometimes hit near the truth; but never the whole truth. H. don't know what I was about the year after he left the Levant; nor does any one – nor — nor — nor — however, it is a lie – but, 'I doubt the equivocation of the fiend that lies like truth!' . . .

Tuesday, March 15

. . . Redde a satire on myself, called 'Anti-Byron', and told Murray to publish it if he liked. The object of the author is to prove me an atheist and a systematic conspirator against law and government. Some of the verse is good; the prose I don't quite understand. He asserts that my 'deleterious works' have had 'an effect upon civil society, which requires', etc., etc., etc., and his own poetry. It is a lengthy poem, and a long preface, with an harmonious title-page. Like the fly in the fable, I seem to have got upon a wheel which makes much dust; but, unlike the said fly, I do not take it all for my own raising.

A letter from *Bella*, which I answered. I shall be in love with her again if I don't take care.

I shall begin a more regular system of reading soon.

Thursday, March 17

I have been sparring with Jackson for exercise this morning; and mean to continue and renew my acquaintance with the muffles. My chest, and arms, and wind are in very good plight, and I am not in flesh. I used to be a hard hitter, and my arms are very long for my height (5 feet 8½ inches). At any rate, exercise is good, and this the severest of all; fencing and the broadsword never fatigued me half so much.

Redde the *Quarrels of Authors* (another sort of *sparring*) – a new work, by that most entertaining and researching writer, Israeli. They seem to be an irritable set, and I wish myself well out of it. 'I'll not march through Coventry with them, that's flat.' What the devil had I to do with scribbling? It is too late to inquire, and all regret is useless. But, an it were to do again, – I should write again, I suppose. Such is human nature, at least my share of it; though I shall think better of myself, if I have sense to stop now. If I have a wife, and that wife has a son – by any body – I will bring up mine heir in the most anti-poetical way – make him a lawyer, or a pirate, or – any thing. But, if he writes too, I shall be sure he is none of mine, and cut him off with a Bank token ...

Sunday, March 20

Redde the *Edinburgh*, 44, just come out. In the beginning of the article on Edgeworth's *Patronage*, I have gotten a high compliment,

I perceive. Whether this is creditable to me, I know not; but it does honour to the editor, because he once abused me. Many a man will retract praise; none but a high-spirited mind will revoke its censure, or *can* praise the man it has once attacked. I have often, since my return to England, heard Jeffrey most highly commended by those who know him for things independent of his talents. I admire him for *this* – not because he has *praised me* (I have been so praised elsewhere and abused, alternately, that mere habit has rendered me as indifferent to both as a man at twenty-six can be to any thing), but because he is, perhaps, the *only man* who, under the relations in which he and I stand, or stood, with regard to each other, would have had the liberality to act thus; none but a great soul dared hazard it. The height on which he stands has not made him giddy; – a little scribbler would have gone on cavilling to the end of the chapter. As to the justice of his panegyric, that is matter of taste. There are plenty to question it, and glad, too, of the opportunity . . .

The last bird I ever fired at was an *eaglet*, on the shore of the Gulf of Lepanto, near Vostitza. It was only wounded, and I tried to save it, the eye was so bright; but it pined, and died in a few days; and I never did since, and never will, attempt the death of another bird. I wonder what put these two things into my head just now? I have been reading Sismondi, and there is nothing there that could induce the recollection . . .

Tuesday, March 22

Last night, *party* at Lansdowne House. To-night, *party* at Lady Charlotte Greville's – deplorable waste of time, and something of temper. Nothing imparted – nothing acquired – talking without ideas: – if any thing like *thought* in my mind, it was not on the subjects on which we were gabbling. Heigho! – and in this way half London pass what is called life. To-morrow there is Lady Heathcote's – shall I go? yes – to punish myself for not having a pursuit . . .

Albany, March 28

This night got into my new apartments, rented of Lord Althorpe, on a lease of seven years. Spacious, and room for my books and

187

sabres. *In* the *house*, too, another advantage. The last few days, or whole week, have been very abstemious, regular in exercise, and yet very *un*well.

Yesterday, dined *tête-à-tête* at the Cocoa with Scrope Davies – sat from six till midnight – drank between us one bottle of champagne and six of claret, neither of which wines ever affect me. Offered to take Scrope home in my carriage; but he was tipsy and pious, and I was obliged to leave him on his knees praying to I know not what purpose or pagod. No headach, nor sickness, that night nor to-day. Got up, if anything, earlier than usual – sparred with Jackson *ad sudorem*,[66] and have been much better in health than for many days. I have heard nothing more from Scrope. Yesterday paid him four thousand eight hundred pounds, a debt of some standing, and which I wished to have paid before. My mind is much relieved by the removal of that *debit*.

Augusta wants me to make it up with Carlisle. I have refused *every* body else, but I can't deny her any thing; – so I must e'en do it, though I had as lief 'drink up Eisel – eat a crocodile'. Let me see – Ward, the Hollands, the Lambs, Rogers, etc., etc., – every body more or less, have been trying for the last two years to accommodate this *couplet* quarrel, to no purpose. I shall laugh if Augusta succeeds . . .

April 8

Out of town six days.[67] On my return, found my poor little pagod, Napoleon, pushed off his pedestal; – the thieves are in Paris. It is his own fault. Like Milo, he would rend the oak; but it closed again, wedged his hands, and now the beasts – lion, bear, down to the dirtiest jackal – may all tear him. That Muscovite winter *wedged* his arms; ever since, he has fought with his feet and teeth. The last may still leave their marks; and 'I guess now' (as the Yankees say) that he will yet play them a pass. He is in their rear – between them and their homes. Query – will they ever reach them?

Saturday, April 9, 1814

I mark this day!

Napoleon Buonaparte has abdicated the throne of the world. 'Excellent well'. Methinks Sylla did better; for he revenged and resigned in the height of his sway, red with the slaughter of his foes – the finest instance of glorious contempt of the rascals upon record. Dioclesian did well too – Amurath not amiss, had he become aught except a dervise – Charles the Fifth but so so – but Napoleon, worst of all. What! wait till they were in his capital, and then talk of his readiness to give up what is already gone!! 'What whining monk art thou – what holy cheat?' 'Sdeath! – Dionysius at Corinth was yet a king to this. The 'Isle of Elba' to retire to! – Well – if it had been Caprea, I should have marvelled less. 'I see men's minds are but a parcel of their fortunes.' I am utterly bewildered and confounded.

I don't know – but I think *I*, even *I* (an insect compared with this creature), have set my life on casts not a millionth part of this man's. But, after all, a crown may not be worth dying for. Yet, to outlive *Lodi* for this!! Oh that Juvenal or Johnson could rise from the dead! *Expende – quot libras in duce summo invenies?*[68] I knew they were light in the balance of mortality; but I thought their living dust weighed more *carats*. Alas! this imperial diamond hath a flaw in it, and is now hardly fit to stick in a glazier's pencil: – the pen of the historian won't rate it worth a ducat.

Psha! 'something too much of this'. But I won't give him up even now; though all his admirers have, 'like the thanes, fallen from him'.

April 10

I do not know that I am happiest when alone; but this I am sure of, that I never am long in the society even of *her* I love, (God knows too well, and the devil probably too) without a yearning for the company of my lamp and my utterly confused and tumbled-over library. Even in the day, I send away my carriage oftener than I use or abuse it. *Per esempio,* – I have not stirred out of these rooms for these four days past; but I have sparred for exercise (windows open) with Jackson an hour daily, to attenuate and keep up the ethereal part of me. The more violent the fatigue, the better my spirits for the rest of the day; and then, my evenings have that calm nothingness of languor, which I most delight in. To-day I have boxed an hour – written an ode to Napoleon Buonaparte – copied it – eaten six biscuits – drunk four bottles of soda water – redde away the rest of my time – besides giving poor [Webster?] a world of advice about this mistress of his, who is plaguing him into a phthisic and intolerable tediousness. I am a pretty fellow truly to lecture about 'the sect'. No matter, my counsels are all thrown away.

April 19, 1814

There is ice at both poles, north and south – all extremes are the same – misery belongs to the highest and the lowest only, to the emperor and the beggar, when unsixpenced and unthroned. There is, to be sure, a damned insipid medium – an equinoctial line – no one knows where, except upon maps and measurements.

> And all our *yesterdays* have lighted fools
> The way to dusty death.

I will keep no further journal of that same hesternal torchlight; and, to prevent me from returning, like a dog, to the vomit of memory, I tear out the remaining leaves of this volume, and write, in *Ipecacuanha*, – 'that the Bourbons are restored!!' – 'Hang up philosophy.' To be sure, I have long despised myself and man, but I never spat in the face of my species before – 'O fool! I shall go mad.'

January 8th, 1814

TO LADY MELBOURNE

My Dear L^y M^e, – I have had too much in my head to write; but don't think my silence capricious.

C. is quite out – in ye first place *she*[69] was not under the same roof, but first with my old friends the H[arrowby]'s in B[erkele]y Square, and afterwards at her friends the V[illiers]'s nearer me. The separation and the express are utterly false, and without even a shadow of foundation; so you see her spies are ill paid, or badly informed. But if she had been in ye same house, it is less singular than C.'s *coming* to it; the house was a very decent house, till that illustrious person thought proper to render it otherwise.

As to Me de Staël, I never go near her; her books are very delightful, but in society I see nothing but a plain woman forcing one to listen, and look at her, with her pen behind her ear, and her mouth full of ink – so much for her.

Now for a confidence – my old love of all loves – Mrs [Chaworth Musters] (whom somebody told you knew nothing about me) has written to me *twice* – no *love*, but she wants to see me; and though it will be a melancholy interview, I shall go; we have hardly met, and never been on any intimate terms since her marriage. *He* has been playing the Devil with all kinds of vulgar mistresses; and behaving ill enough, in every respect. I enclose you the *last*, which pray return immediately with your *opinion*, whether I *ought* to see her, or not – you see she is unhappy; she was a spoilt heiress; but has seen little or nothing of the world – very pretty, and once simple in character, and clever, but with no peculiar accomplishments, but endeared to me by a thousand childish, and singular recollections – you know her estate joined mine; and we were as children very much together; but no matter; *this* was a love match, they are *separated*.

I have heard from Ph.[70] who seems embarrassed with constancy. Her *date* is the *Grampian* hills, to be sure. With that latitude, and her precious *époux*, it must be a shuddering kind of existence.

C. may do as she pleases, thanks to your good-nature, rather than my merits, or prudence; there is little to dread from her love, and I forgive her hatred . . . Adieu, ever y^rs Pray write and believe

Most affect^y y^rs,

B.

TO LADY MELBOURNE   *January 13th, 1814*

My Dear L^y M^e, – I do not see how you could well have said less, and that I am not angry may be proved by my saying a word more on ye subject.

You are quite mistaken, however, as to *her*,[71] and it must be from some misrepresentation of mine, that you throw the blame so completely on the side least deserving, and least able to bear it. I dare say I made the best of my own story, as one always does from natural selfishness without intending it, but it was not her fault, but my own *folly* (give it what name may suit it better) and her weakness, for the intentions of both were very different, and for some time adhered to, and when not, it was entirely my own – in short, I know no name for my conduct. Pray do not speak so harshly of her to me – the cause of all ...

What a fool I am – I have been interrupted by a visitor who is just gone, and have been laughing this half hour at a thousand absurdities, as if I had nothing serious to think about.

Yrs ever,

B.

P.S. ... I wish I were married, and don't care about beauty, nor *subsequent* virtue – nor much about fortune. I have made up my mind to share the decorations of my betters – but I should like – let me see – liveliness, gentleness, cleanliness, and something of comeliness – and *my own* first born. Was ever man more moderate? what do you think of my 'Bachelor's wife?' What a letter have I written!

TO LADY MELBOURNE   *January 16th, 1814*

... I still mean to set off to-morrow,[72] unless this snow adds so much to the impracticability of the roads as to render it useless. I don't mind anything but delay; and I might as well be in London as at a sordid inn, waiting for a thaw, or the subsiding of a flood and the clearing of snow. I wonder what *your* answer will be on *Ph.'s letter*. I am growing rather partial to her younger sister; who is very pretty, but fearfully young – and I think a *fool*. A wife, you say, would be my salvation. Now I could have but one motive for marrying into that family – and even *that* might possibly only produce a scene, and spoil everything; but at all events it would in some degree be a *revenge*, and in the very face of your compliment (*ironical*, I believe) on the want of *selfishness*, I must say that

192

I never can quite get over the '*not*' of last summer – no – though it were to become 'yea' to-morrow.

I do believe that to marry would be my wisest step – but whom? I might manage *this* easily with 'le Père', but I don't admire the connection – and I have not committed myself by any attentions hitherto. But all wives would be much the same. I have no *heart* to spare and expect none in return; but, as Moore says, 'A pretty wife is something for the fastidious vanity of a roué to *retire* upon'. And mine might do as she pleased, so that she had a fair temper, and a *quiet* way of conducting herself, leaving me the same liberty of conscience. What I want is a companion – a friend rather than a sentimentalist. I have seen enough of love matches – and of all matches – to make up my mind to the common lot of happy couples. The only misery would be if I fell in love afterwards – which is not unlikely, for habit has a strange power over my affections. In that case I should be jealous, and then you do not know what a devil any bad passion makes me. I should very likely *do* all that C. *threatens* in her paroxysms; and I have more reasons than you are aware of, for mistrusting myself on this point.

Heigho! Good night.

Ever y^{rs} most truly,

B.

P.S. – The enclosed was written last night, and I am just setting off. You shall hear from Newstead – if one ever gets there in a coach really as large as the cabin of a '74', and, I believe, meant for the Atlantic instead of the Continent ...

TO LADY MELBOURNE   [*Undated*]
(Fragment)

... prospect. I never shall. One of my great inducements to that brilliant negociation with the Princess of Parallelograms, was the vision of our *family party*, and the quantity of domestic lectures I should faithfully detail, without mutual comments thereupon.

You seem to think I am in some scrape at present by my unequal spirits. Perhaps I am, but you shan't be shocked, so you shan't. I won't draw further upon you for sympathy. You will be in town so soon, and I have scribbled so much, that you will be glad to see a letter shorter than usual.

I wish you would *lengthen* yours.

Ever my dear L^y M^e,

B.

TO LADY MELBOURNE   *February 11th, 1814*

My Dear Lady M., – On my arrival in town on Wednesday, I found myself in what the learned call a dilemma, and the vulgar a scrape.[73] Such a clash of paragraphs, and a conflict of newspapers, lampoons of all descriptions, some good, and all hearty, the Regent (as reported) wroth; Ld Carlisle in a fury; the *Morning Post* in hysterics; and the *Courier* in convulsions of criticism and contention. To complete the farce, the Morning Papers this day announce the intention of some zealous Rosencrantz or Guildenstern to 'play upon this pipe' in our house of hereditaries. This last seems a little too ludicrous to be true, but, even if so – and nothing is too ridiculous for some of them to attempt – all the motions, censures, sayings, doings and ordinances of that august body, shall never make me even endeavour to explain, or soften a syllable of the twenty words which have excited, *what* I really do not yet exactly know, as the accounts are contradictory, but be it what it may, 'as the wine is tapped it shall be drunk to the lees'. I *have not* and shall *not* answer, and although the consequences may be, for aught I know to the contrary, exclusion from society, and all sorts of disagreeables, the 'Demon whom I still have served, has not yet cowed my better part of man'; and whatever I may, and have, or shall feel, I have that within me, that bounds against opposition. I have *quick feelings*, and not very *good nerves*; but somehow they have more than once served me pretty well, when I most wanted them, and may again. At any rate I shall try.

Did you ever know anything like this? At a time when peace and war, and Emperors and Napoleons, and the destinies of the things they have made of mankind, are trembling in the balance, the Government Gazettes can devote half their attention and columns, day after day, to 8 *lines*, written two years ago and now *republished only* (by an individual), and suggest them for the consideration of Parliament, probably about the same period with the treaty of peace.

I really begin to think myself a most important personage; what would poor Pope have given to have brought down this upon his 'epistle to Augustus'?

I think you must allow, considering all things, public and private, that mine has been an odd destiny. But I prate, and will spare you . . .

TO LADY MELBOURNE   *February 21st. 1814*

My Dear Lady M., – I am not 'forbidden' by —,[74] though it is very odd that like everyone she seemed more assured (and not very well pleased) of your influence than any other; but I suppose, being pretty certain of her own power – always said, 'do as you please, and go where you like' – and I really know no reason for my not having been where I ought, unless it was to punish myself – or – I really do not know why exactly. You will easily suppose that, twined as she is round my heart in every possible manner, dearest and deepest in my hope and my memory, still I am not easy. It is this – if anything – my own. In short, I cannot write about it. Still I have not lost all self-command. For instance, I could at this moment be where I have been, where I would rather be than anywhere else, and yet from some motive or other – but certainly not indifference – I am here, and here I will remain; but it costs me some struggles.

It is the misery of my situation, to see it as you see it, and to *feel* it as I feel it, on *her* account, and that of others. As for myself, it is of much less, and may soon be of no consequence. But I will drop ye subject . . .

TO THOMAS MOORE   *March 3, 1814*

My Dear Friend, – I have a great mind to tell you that I *am* 'uncomfortable', if only to make you come to town; where no one ever more delighted in seeing you, nor is there any one to whom I would sooner turn for consolation in my most vapourish moments. The truth is, I have 'no lack of argument' to ponder upon of the most gloomy description, but that arises from *other* causes. Some day or other, when we are *veterans*, I may tell you a tale of present and past times; and it is not from want of confidence that I do not now, – but – but – always a *but* to the end of the chapter.

There is nothing, however, upon the *spot* either to love or hate; – but I certainly have subjects for both at no very great distance, and am besides embarrassed between *three* whom I know, and one (whose name, at least) I do not know. All this would be very well if I had no heart; but, unluckily, I have found that there is such a thing still about me, though in no very good repair, and, also, that it has a habit of attaching itself to *one* whether I will or no. *Divide et impera*,[75] I begin to think, will only do for politics.

How proceeds the poem? Do not neglect it, and I have no fears. I need not say to you that your fame is dear to me, – I really might say *dearer* than my own; for I have lately begun to think my things have been strangely over-rated; and, at any rate, whether or not, I have done with them for ever. I may say to you what I would not say to every body, that the last two were written, *The Bride* in four, and *The Corsair* in ten days, – which I take to be a most humiliating confession, as it proves my own want of judgment in publishing, and the public's in reading things, which cannot have stamina for permanent attention. 'So much for Buckingham' ...

TO LADY MELBOURNE   *April 8th, 1814*

I have been out of town since Saturday, and only returned last night from my visit to Augusta ...

I left all my relations – at least my niece and her mamma – very well. L[eigh] was in Yorkshire; and I regret not having seen him of course very much. My intention was to have joined a party at Cambridge; but somehow I overstaid my time, and the inclination to visit the University went off, and here I am alone, and not overpleased with being so.

You don't think the '*Q*[*uarterly*] *R*[*eview*] so very compli-
mentary'; most people do. I have no great opinion on the subject,
and (except in the *E*[*dinburg*]*h* am not much interested in any
criticisms, favourable or otherwise. I have had my day, have done
with all that stuff; and must try something new – politics – or
rebellion – or Methodism – or gaming. Of the two last I have
serious thoughts, as one can't travel till we see how long Paris is
to be the quarter of the Allies. I can't help suspecting that my
little Pagod will play them some trick still. If Wellington, or one
hero had beaten another, it would be nothing; but to be worried
by brutes, and conquered by recruiting sergeants – why there is
not a *character* amongst them.

Ever yrs. most affect[ly],

B.

TO THOMAS MOORE   *2 Albany, April 9, 1814*

... No more rhyme for – or rather, *from* – me. I have taken my
leave of that stage, and henceforth will mountebank it no longer.
I have had my day, and there's an end. The utmost I expect, or
even wish, is to have it said in the *Biographia Britannica*, that
I might perhaps have been a poet, had I gone on and amended.
My great comfort is, that the temporary celebrity I have wrung
from the world has been in the very teeth of all opinions and
prejudices. I have flattered no ruling powers; I have never
concealed a single thought that tempted me. They can't say I
have truckled to the times, nor to popular topics, (as Johnson, or
somebody, said of Cleveland,) and whatever I have gained has
been at the expenditure of as much *personal* favour as possible;
for I do believe never was a bard more unpopular, *quoad homo*,[76]
than myself. And now I have done; *ludite nunc alios*.[77] Everybody
may be damned, as they seem fond of it, and resolve to stickle
lustily for endless brimstone ...

TO LADY MELBOURNE   *April 25th, 1814*

... Oh! but it is 'worth while', I can't tell you why, and it is *not*
an '*Ape*', and if it is, that must be my fault; however, I will
positively reform. You must however allow that it is utterly

impossible I can ever be half so well-liked elsewhere, and I have been all my life trying to make someone love me, and never got the sort that I preferred before. But positively she and I will grow good and all that, and so we are *now* and shall be these three weeks and more too ...

You will be sorry to hear that I have got a physician just in time for an old complaint, 'troublesome, but not dangerous', like Lord Stair and L^y Stair's, of which I am promised an eventual removal. It is very odd; he is a staid grave man, and puts so many questions to me about *my mind*, and the state of it, that I begin to think he half suspects my senses. He asked me how I felt 'when anything weighed upon my mind?' and I answered him by a question, why he should suppose that anything did? I was laughing and sitting quietly in my chair the whole time of his visits, and yet he thinks me horribly restless and irritable, and talks about my having lived *excessively* 'out of all compass' some time or other; which has no more to do with the malady he had to deal with than I have with the Wisdom of Solomon ...

TO LADY MELBOURNE   *April 29th, 1814*

... I don't know what to say or do about going.[78] Sometimes I wish it, at other times I think it foolish, as assuredly my design will be imputed to a motive, which, by the bye, if once fairly there, is very likely to come into my head, and *failing*, to put me into no very good humour with myself. I am not now in love with her; but I can't at all foresee that I should not be so, if it came 'a warm June' (as Falstaff observes), and, seriously, I do admire her as a very superior woman, a little encumbered with Virtue, though perhaps your opinion and mine, from the laughing turn of 'our philosophy', may be less exalted upon her merits than that of the more zealous, though in fact less benevolent advocates, of charity schools and Lying-in Hospitals.

By the close of her note you will perceive that she has been 'frowning' occasionally, and has written some pretty lines upon it to a friend (he or she is not said). As for rhyme I am naturally no fair judge, and can like it no better than a grocer does figs.

I am quite irresolute and undecided. If I were sure of *myself* (not of her) I would go; but I am not, and never can be, and what is still worse, I have no judgement and less common sense than an infant. This is *not affected* humility; with *you* I have no affectation; with the world I have a part to play; to be diffident there, is to wear a drag-chain, and luckily I do so thoroughly despise half the people in it, that my insolence is almost natural . . .

TO LADY MELBOURNE   *April 30th, 1814*

My Dear Lady M^e, – *You* – or rather *I* – have done *my A*[79] much injustice. The expression which you recollect as objectionable meant only 'loving' in the *senseless* sense of that wide word, and it must be some selfish stupidity of mine in telling my own story, but really and truly – as I hope mercy and happiness for her – by that God who made me for my own misery, and not much for the good of others, *she* was not to blame, one thousandth part in comparison. She was not aware of her own peril till it was too late, and I can only account for her subsequent 'abandon' by an observation which I think is not unjust, that women are much more *attached* than men if they are treated with anything like fairness or tenderness.

As for *your* A, I don't know what to make of her. I enclose her last but one, and *my* A's last but one, from which you may form your own conclusions on *both*. I think you will allow *mine* to be a very extraordinary person in point of *talent*, but I won't say more, only do not allow your good nature to lean to my side of *this* question; on all others I shall be glad to avail myself of your partiality . . .

Your niece has committed herself perhaps, but it can be of no consequence; if I pursued and succeeded in that quarter, of course I must give up all other pursuits, and the fact is that my wife, if she had common sense, would have more power over me than any other whatsoever, for my heart alights on the nearest *perch* – if it is withdrawn it goes God knows where – but one must like something.

Ever yrs.,

B.

TO LADY MELBOURNE   *April–May 1st, 1814*

My Dear Lady M°, – She says 'if la tante'; neither did she
imagine nor did I assert that you did have an opinion of what
Philosopher Square calls 'the fitness of things'.

You are very kind in allowing us the few merits we can claim;
she surely is very clever, and not only so but in some things of
good judgement: her expressions about A° are exactly your *own*,
and these most certainly without being aware of the coincidence,
and excepting our one *tremendous* fault.⁸⁰ I know her to be in
point of temper and goodness of heart almost unequalled; now
grant me this, that she is in truth a very *loveable* woman and I will
try and not love any longer. If you don't believe me, ask those
who know her *better*. I say *better*, for a man in love is blind as
that deity.

You yourself soften a little in the P.S., and say the letters 'make
you melancholy'. It is indeed a very triste and extraordinary
business, and what is to become of us I know not, and I won't
think just now.

Did you observe that she says '*if* la tante approved she should'?
She is little aware how much 'la tante' has to *dis*approve, but you
perceive that, without intending it, she pays me a compliment by
supposing you to be my friend and a sincere one, whose *approval*
could alter even *her* opinions.

To-morrow I am asked to Lady Jersey's in the evening, and on
Wednesday again, Tuesday I go to Kean and dine after the play
with Lord Rancliffe, and on Friday there is Mrs Hope's: we shall
clash at some of them.

What on earth can plague you? I won't ask, but am very sorry
for it, it is very hard that one who feels so much for others should
suffer pain herself. God bless you. Good night.

Ever yours most truly,

                                                                 B.

... P.S. *ad*. – It indeed puzzles me to account for —:⁸¹ it is true
she married a fool, but she *would* have him; they agreed, and agree
very well, and I never heard a complaint, but many vindications,

of him. As for me, brought up as I was, and sent into the world as I was, both physically and morally, nothing better could be expected, and it is odd that I always had a foreboding and I remember when a child reading the Roman history about a *marriage* I will tell you of when we meet, asking ma mère why I should not marry X.

Since writing this I have received ye enclosed. I will not trouble you with another, but *this* will, I think, enable you to appreciate *her* better. She seems very triste, and I need hardly add that the reflection does not enliven me.

TO LADY MELBOURNE   *May 28th, 1814*

Dear Lady M^e, – I have just received a wrathful epistle from C[aroline] demanding letters, pictures, and all kinds of gifts which I never requested, and am ready to resign as soon as they can be gathered together; at the same signal it might be as well for her to restore *my* letters, as everybody has read them by this time, and they can no longer be of use to herself and her five hundred sympathizing friends. She also complains of some barbarous usage, of which I know nothing, except that I was told of an *inroad* which occurred when I was fortunately out; and am not at all disposed to regret the circumstance of my absence, either for her sake or my own. I am also menaced in her letter with immediate *marriage*, of which I am equally unconscious; at least I have not proposed to anybody, and if anyone has to me I have quite forgotten it ...

TO LADY MELBOURNE   *June 10th, 1814*

... All you can say is exceeding true; but who ever said, or supposed that you were not shocked, and all that ? You *have* done everything in your power; and more than any other person breathing would have done for *me*, to make me act rationally; but there is an old saying (excuse the Latin, which I won't quote, but translate), 'Whom the gods wish to destroy they first madden'. I am as mad as C. on a different topic, and in a different way; for I never break out into scenes, but am not a whit more in my senses. I will, however, not persuade *her* into any *fugitive* piece of absurdity, but more I cannot promise. I love no one else (in a proper manner), and, whatever you may imagine, I cannot, or at least do not, put myself in the way of – let me see – Annabella is the most prudish and correct person I know, so I refer you to the last emphatic substantive, in her last letter to you.

There is that little Lady R. tells me that C. has taken a sudden fancy to *her* – what can that be for? C. has also taken some offence at Lady G. Sloane's frigid appearance; and supposes that Augusta, who never troubles her head about her, has said something or other on my authority – *this* I remember is in C.'s last letter – one of her twaddling questions I presume – she seems puzzled about me, and not at all near the truth. The Devil, who ought to be civil on such occasions, will probably keep her from it still; if he should not, I must invent some flirtation, to lead her from approaching it.

I am sorry to hear of your *tristesse*, and conceive that I have at last guessed or perceived the real cause; it won't trouble you long; besides, what is it or anything else compared with our melodrame? *Take* comfort, you very often give it.

Ever y^{rs},

B.

TO SAMUEL ROGERS   *Tuesday*

My Dear Rogers, – Sheridan was yesterday, at first, too sober to remember your invitation, but in the dregs of the third bottle he fished up his memory, and found that he had a party at home. I left and leave any other day to him and you, save Monday, and some yet undefined dinner at Burdett's. Do you go to-night to Lord Eardley's, and if you do, shall I call for you (anywhere)? it will give me great pleasure.

Ever yours entire,

B.

P.S. – The Staël out-talked Whitbread, overwhelmed his spouse, was *ironed* by Sheridan, confounded Sir Humphry, and utterly perplexed your slave. The rest (great names in the Red-book, nevertheless,) were mere segments of the circle. Ma'mselle danced a Russ saraband with great vigour, grace and expression.

TO LADY MELBOURNE   *June 26th, 1814*

My Dear Ly M^e. – To continue the conversation which Lord C^r has broken off by falling asleep (and his wife by keeping awake) I know nothing of C's last night adventures; to prove it there is her letter which I have not read through, nor answered nor written these two months, and then only by *desire* to keep her quiet.

You talked to me about keeping her out. It is impossible; she comes at all times, at any time, and the moment the door is open in she walks. I can't throw her out of the window: as to getting rid of her, that is rational and probable, but *I* will not receive her.

The Bessboroughs may take her if they please – or any steps they please; I have no hesitation in saying that I have made up my mind as to the alternative, and would sooner, much sooner, be with the dead in purgatory, than with her, *Caroline* (I put the name at length as I am not jesting), upon earth. She may hunt me down – it is the power of any mad or bad woman to do so by any man – but *snare* me she shall not: torment me she may; how am I to bar myself from her! I am already almost a prisoner; she has no shame, no feeling, no one estimable or redeemable quality. These are strong words, but I know what I am writing; they will avail nothing but to convince you of my own determination. My first object in such a dilemma would be to take —[82] with me; that might fail, so much the better, but even if it did – I would lose a hundred souls rather than be bound to C. If there is one human being whom I do utterly *detest* and *abhor* it is she, and, all things considered, I feel to myself justified in so doing. She has been an adder in my path ever since my return to this country; she has often belied and sometimes betrayed me; she has crossed me everywhere; she has watched and worried and *guessed*[83] and been a curse to me and mine.

You may show *her* this if you please – or to anyone you please;

if these were the last words I were to write upon earth I would not revoke one letter except to make it more legible.

Ever yours most sincerely,

BYRON.

TO THOMAS MOORE   *Hastings, August 3, 1814*

By the time this reaches your dwelling, I shall (God wot) be in town again probably. I have been here renewing my acquaintance with my old friend Ocean;[84] and I find his bosom as pleasant a pillow for an hour in the morning as his daughters of Paphos could be in the twilight. I have been swimming and eating turbot, and smuggling neat brandies and silk handkerchiefs, – and listening to my friend Hodgson's raptures about a pretty wife-elect of his – and walking on cliffs, and tumbling down hills and making the most of the *dolce far-niente* for the last fortnight. I met a son of Lord Erskine's, who says he has been married a year, and is the 'happiest of men'; and I have met the aforesaid H., who is also the 'happiest of men'; so, it is worth while being here, if only to witness the superlative felicity of these foxes, who have cut off their tails, and would persuade the rest to part with their brushes to keep them in countenance . . .

TO MISS ANNE ISABELLA MILBANKE[85] *September 9th [?], 1814*

. . . There is something I wish to say; and as I may not see you for some – perhaps for a long time – I will endeavour to say it at once. A few weeks ago you asked me a question which I answered. I have now one to propose – to which, if improper, I need not add that your declining to reply to it will be sufficient reproof. It is this. Are the 'objections' to which you alluded insuperable? or is there any line or change of conduct which could possibly remove them? I am well aware that all such changes are more easy in theory than practice; but at the same time there are few things I would not attempt to obtain your good opinion. At all events I would willingly know the worst. Still I neither wish you to promise or pledge yourself to anything; but merely to learn a *possibility* which would not leave you the less a free agent.

When I believed you attached, I had nothing to urge – indeed I have little now, except that having heard from yourself that your affections are not engaged, my importunities may appear not quite so selfish, however unsuccessful. It is not without a struggle that I address you once more on this subject; yet I am not consistent – for it was to avoid troubling you upon it that I finally determined to remain an absent friend rather than become a tiresome guest. If I offend it is better at a distance.

With the rest of my sentiments you are already acquainted. If I do not repeat them it is to avoid – or at least not increase – your displeasure . . .

TO JOHN CAM HOBHOUSE   *Newstead Abbey,*
                                        September 13th, 1814

My Dear Hobhouse – Claughton has relinquished his purchase, and twenty-five thousand pounds out of twenty-eight ditto, paid on account, and I am Abbot again – it is all signed, sealed and *re*delivered . . .

But now for other matters: – if a circumstance (which may happen but is as unlikely to happen as Johanna Southcote establishing herself as the real Mrs Trinity) does not occur – I have thoughts of going direct and directly to Italy – if so, will you come with me?

I want your opinion first, your advice afterwards, and your company always: – I am pretty well in funds, having better than £4,000 at Hoare's – a note of Murray for £700 (the price of *Larry*) at a year's date last month, and the Newstead Michaelmas will give me from a thousand to 15 – if not 1800 more. I believe it is raised to between 3 and 4,000, but then there is land upon *hand* (which of course payeth no rent for the present, and be damned to it); altogether I should have somewhere about £5,000 tangible, which I am not at all disposed to spend at home. Now I would wish to set apart £3000 for the tour, do you *think* that would enable me to see all *Italy* in a gentlemanly way? with as few servants and luggage (except my aperients) as we can help. And will you come with me? You are the only man with whom I could

travel an hour except an 'ἰατρός';[86] in short you know, my dear
H—, that with all my bad qualities (and d—d bad they are to
be sure) I like you better than anybody – and we have travelled
together before, and been old friends, and all that, and we have
a thorough fellow-feeling, and contempt for all things of the
sublunary sort – and so do let us go and call the 'Pantheon a
cockpit', like the learned Smelfungus ...

TO LADY MELBOURNE   *Newstead Abbey,*
                                     Sunday September 18th, 1814

My Dear Lady M^e, – Miss Milbanke has accepted me; and her
answer was accompanied by a very kind letter from your brother.
May I hope for your consent, too? Without it I should be un-
happy, even were it not for many reasons important in other
points of view; and with it I shall have nothing to require, except
your good wishes now, and your friendship always.

I lose no time in telling you how things are at present. Many
circumstances may doubtless occur in this, as in other cases, to
prevent its completion, but I will hope otherwise, I shall be in
town by Thursday, and beg one line to Albany, to say you will
see me at your own day, hour, and place.

In course I mean to reform most thoroughly, and become 'a
good man and true', in all the various senses of these respective
and respectable appellations. Seriously, I will endeavour to make
your niece happy; not by 'my deserts, but what I will deserve'.
Of my deportment you may reasonably doubt; of her merits you
can have none. I need not say that this must be a *secret*. Do let
me find a few words from you in Albany, and believe me ever

   Most affec^{tly} y^{rs},

                                                         B.

TO LADY MELBOURNE   *October 7th 1814*

My Dear Ly Me, –
   ... X[87] is the least selfish person in the world; you, of course,
will never believe that either of us can have any right feeling.
I won't deny this as far as regards me, but you don't know what

a being she is; her only error has been my fault entirely, and for this I can plead no excuse, except passion, which is none . . .

TO MISS MILBANKE   *14 Octr 1814*
[fragment]

I have not seen the paragraph you mention; but it cannot speak more humbly of me in the comparison than I think. This is one of the lesser evils to which notoriety and a carelessness of fame, – in the only good sense of the word, – has rendered me liable, – a carelessness which I do not now feel since I have obtained something worth caring for. The truth is that could I have foreseen that your life was to be linked to mine, – had I even possessed a distinct hope however distant, – I would have been a different and better being. As it is, I have sometimes doubts, even if I should not disappoint the future nor act hereafter unworthily of you, whether the past ought not to make you still regret me – even that portion of it with which you are not unacquainted.

I did not believe such a woman existed – at least for me, – and I sometimes fear I ought to wish that she had not. I must turn from the subject.

My love, do forgive me if I have written in a spirit that renders you uncomfortable. I cannot embody my feelings in words. I have nothing to desire – nothing I would see altered in *you* – but so much in myself. I can conceive no misery equal to mine, if I failed in making you happy, – and yet how can I hope to do justice to those merits from whose praise there is not a dissentient voice?

TO JOHN CAM HOBHOUSE   *October 17th, 1814*

My Dear Hobhouse, – If I have not answered your very kind letter immediately, do not impute it to neglect. I have expected you would be in town or near it, and waited to thank you in person. Believe me, no change of time or circumstance short of insanity can make any difference in my feelings, and I hope, in my conduct towards you. I have known you too long, and tried you too deeply; a new mistress is nothing to an old friend, the latter can't be replaced in this world, nor, I very much fear, in the next, and neither in this nor the other could I meet with one so deserving of my respect and regard. Well, H. – I am engaged, and we wait only for settlements 'and all that' to be married. My intended, it seems, has liked me very well for a long time, which, I am sure, her encouragement gave me no reason to suspect; but so it is, according to her account. The circumstances which led to the renewal of my proposal I will acquaint you with when we meet, if you think such material concerns worth your enquiry. Hanson is going down next week to Durham, to confabulate with Sir R.'s agents on the score of temporalities, and I suppose I must soon follow to my sire-in-law's that is to be. I confess that the character of wooer in this regular way does not sit easy upon me, I wish I could wake some morning, and find myself fairly married. I do hate (out of Turkey) all fuss, and bustle, and ceremony so much; and one can't be married, according to what I hear, without *some*. I wish, whenever this same form is muttered over us, that you could make it convenient to be present. I will give you due notice: – if you would but take a wife and be coupled then also, like people electrified in company through the same chain, it would be still further comfort.

Good even.

Ever yours most truly,

B.

TO LADY MELBOURNE   *Seaham,*
                                     November 4th, 1814

My Dear Lady M^e, – I have been here these two days; but waited to observe before I imparted to you – 'my confidential counsel', as Master Hoar would say – my remarks.

Your brother pleases me much. To be sure his stories are long; but I believe he has told most of them, and he is to my mind the perfect gentleman; but I don't like Lady M[ilbanke] at all. I can't tell why, for we don't differ, but so it is; she seems to be everything here, which is all very well; and I am, and mean to be, very comfortable, and dutiful, but nevertheless I wish she and mine aunt could change places, as far as regards me and mine. A[nnabella]'s meeting and mine made a kind of scene; though there was no acting, nor even speaking, but the pantomime was very expressive. She seems to have more feeling than we imagined; but is the most *silent* woman I ever encountered; which perplexes me extremely. I like them to talk, because then they *think* less. Much cogitation will not be in my favour; besides, I can form my judgments better, since, unless the countenance is flexible, it is difficult to steer by mere looks. I am studying her, but can't boast of my progress in getting at her disposition; and if the conversation is to be all on one side I fear committing myself; and those who only listen, must have their thoughts so much about them as to seize any weak point at once. However, the die is cast; neither party can recede; the lawyers are here – mine and all – and I presume, the parchment once scribbled, I shall become Lord Annabella.

I can't yet tell whether we are to be happy or not. I have every disposition to do her all possible justice, but I fear she won't govern me; and if she don't it will not do at all; but perhaps she may mend of that fault. I have always thought – first, that she did not like me at all; and next, that her supposed after-liking was *imagination*. This last I conceive that my presence would – perhaps has removed – if so, I shall soon discover it, but mean to take it with great philosophy, and to behave attentively and well, though I never could love but that which *loves*; and this I must say for myself, that my attachment always increases in due proportion to the return it meets with, and never changes in the presence of its object; to be sure, like Mrs Damer, I have 'an opinion of absence'.

Pray write. I think you need not fear that the *answer* to *this* will run any of the risks you apprehend. It will be a great comfort to me, in all events, to call you aunt, and to know that you are sure of my being

Ever y^{rs},

B.

3. MARRIAGE AND EXILE

January 1815 – November 1816

INTRODUCTION

BYRON, feeling that he had been betrayed by the woman he loved most (Augusta), by the artifices of the apparently guileless Annabella, even by Lady Melbourne – but most of all by his own vacillations and weakness, found marriage from the first an intolerable tie. After a depressing honeymoon he carried off Annabella (with conscious or unconscious perversity) on a visit to Augusta at Six Mile Bottom, where his drinking, his sexual innuendoes, and his overt preference for Augusta, drove the two women to despair. No sooner had the couple settled in No. 13 Piccadilly Terrace than the duns came down on him. Expectations from the Wentworth estate on Lord Wentworth's death had come to nothing. Although he was the owner of property worth more than a hundred thousand pounds, the assets could not be realized, and the bailiffs entered the house. Byron's behaviour became one of frenzy, brought on by his sense of the hopelessness of his position, and increased by his recourse to brandy, laudanum and a regimen of starving, followed by gorging, which he attempted to mitigate by overdoses of magnesia. Appointed to the committee of Drury Lane, he took his duties seriously, seeking new talent and even approaching Coleridge for a play; but occupied himself between times with 'transient pieces'. Annabella, seriously disturbed by his threats, called on Augusta, who arrived in Piccadilly on 15 November, but her presence only added to Byron's demented cruelty towards both women. A child, Augusta Ada, was born on 10 December 1815. Even after the birth of his daughter, Byron's violence and rages increased, especially against his wife, whom Augusta vainly tried to protect from his worst excesses. Medical opinion was sought as to his sanity, but the doctors could find no evidence of lunacy.

He had continually talked of breaking up the Piccadilly establishment and of going abroad. Finally he arranged for Annabella and the child to leave for her parents' house (the Milbankes had changed their name to Noel in accordance with a provision of Lord Wentworth's will) at Kirkby Mallory in Leicestershire, and they departed on 15 January 1816. Byron never saw his wife and child again. A legal separation followed, instigated by the Noels, but no specific charges were ever preferred as to the reason for the break; wild stories, however, were afloat in London, particularly that of incest, and Augusta was cut by Mrs George Lamb at Lady Jersey's reception. Byron possibly exaggerated the obloquy to which he attributed his 'exile'. His friends stood behind him, particularly Hobhouse, Scrope Davies, the Kinnairds, Sir Francis Burdett, Sam Rogers; Miss Mercer Elphinstone and Lady Jersey ostentatiously showed their kindness towards him. And so in a more intimate way did Claire Clairmont, who brought Mary Godwin to meet him. Byron left London for Ostend in the company of Dr Polidori and his servants on 23 April; the bailiffs entered the Piccadilly house immediately afterwards.

After a leisurely journey through the Low Countries (Byron taking the opportunity to visit the field of Waterloo) and up the Rhine, they reached Geneva in early June, where the Villa Diodati on the shores of the Lake Geneva was rented, and Byron and his establishment settled in. Claire Clairmont had anticipated his arrival, and with her and Mary Godwin Byron first met Shelley in whose company he spent much time in the months that followed, sailing on the lake and talking far into the night, until the Shelleys returned to England, taking with them the reluctant Claire, already heavy with Byron's child. (Clara Allegra was born in Bath on 12 January 1817.) At Coppet Mme de Staël frequently entertained Byron, who, though mocking her, enjoyed her company. Hobhouse and Scrope Davies arrived from England and enlivened him with their cynical realism; but thoughts of Augusta lay heavy on his mind. A trip with Hobhouse over the Bernese Oberland set his imagination on the composition of *Manfred*. He had already continued *Childe Harold* and written the touching verses to Augusta. On 5 October Byron and Hobhouse left the Villa Diodati for Venice, *via* Milan, where they entered and enjoyed Milanese society for some little while. Proceeding by way of Verona and Vicenza, they hurried on to reach Venice on 10 November 1816. Byron was immediately delighted with the city, its squares, narrow streets and canals, and set himself up in an apartment over a draper's shop in the narrow alley known as the Frezzeria, just off the Piazza San Marco. On 5 December Hobhouse left with his brother and sister on a tour of Italy. For Byron the Venetian interlude had begun.

TO LADY MELBOURNE   *Halnaby, January 3rd, 1815*

My Dearest Aunt, – We were married yesterday at ten upon ye clock, so there's an end of that matter, and the beginning of many others. Bell has gone through all the ceremonies with great fortitude, and I am much as usual, and your dutiful nephew. All those who are disposed to make presents may as well send them forthwith, and pray let them be handsome, and we wait your congrats besides, as I am sure your benediction is very essential to all our undertakings.

Lady M[ilbanke] was a little hysterical, and fine-feeling; and the kneeling was rather tedious, and the cushions hard; but upon the whole it did vastly well. The drawing-room at Seaham was the scene of our conjunction, and then we set off, according to approved custom, to be shut up by ourselves.

You would think we had been married these fifty years. Bell is fast asleep on a corner of the sopha, and I am keeping myself awake with this epistle – she desires her love, and mine you have had ever since we were acquainted. Pray, how many of our new relations (at least, of mine) mean to own us? I reckon upon George[1] and you, and Lord M[elbourne] and the Countess and Count of the Holy Roman Empire;[2] as for *Caro*[3] and Caro George,[4] and *William*,[5] I don't know what to think, do you?

I shall write to you again anon; at present, receive this as an apology for that silence of which you were kind enough to complain; and believe me ever most affectionately thine,

BYRON.

P.S. I enclose you an order for the box; it was not at liberty before. The week after next will be mine, and so on alternately.

I have lent it, for the present week only, to another person; the next is yours.

TO THOMAS MOORE   *January 19, 1815.*

. . . So, you want to know about milady and me? But let me not, as Roderick Random says, 'profane the chaste mysteries of Hymen' – damn the word, I had nearly spelt it with a small *h*. I like Bell as well as you do (or did, you villain!) Bessy – and that is (or was) saying a great deal . . .

TO THOMAS MOORE   *Seaham, Stockton-on-Tees,*
                                   February 2, 1815

. . . Since I wrote last, I have been transferred to my father-in-law's, with my lady and my lady's maid, etc., etc., etc., and the treacle-moon is over, and I am awake, and find myself married. My spouse and I agree to – and in – admiration. Swift says 'no *wise* man ever married'; but, for a fool, I think it the most ambrosial of all possible future states. I still think one ought to marry upon *lease*; but am very sure I should renew mine at the expiration, though next term were for ninety and nine years.

I wish you would respond, for I am here *oblitusque meorum obliviscendus et illis.*[6] Pray tell me what is going on in the way of intriguery, and how the w—s and rogues of the upper Beggar's Opera go on – or rather go off – in or after marriage; or who are going to break any particular commandment. Upon this dreary coast, we have nothing but county meetings and shipwrecks; and I have this day dined upon fish, which probably dined upon the crews of several colliers lost in the late gales. But I saw the sea once more in all the glories of surf and foam, – almost equal to the Bay of Biscay, and the interesting white squalls and short seas of Archipelago memory.

My papa, Sir Ralpho, hath recently made a speech at a Durham tax-meeting; and not only at Durham, but here, several times, since after dinner. He is now, I believe, speaking it to himself (I left him in the middle) over various decanters, which can neither interrupt him nor fall asleep, – as might possibly have been the case with some of his audience.

Ever thine,

B.

I must go to tea – damn tea. I wish it was Kinnaird's brandy, and with you to lecture me about it.

TO LADY MELBOURNE   *Seaham,*
February 2nd, 1815

... The *moon* is over; but Bell and I are as lunatic as heretofore; she does as she likes, and don't bore me, and we may win the Dunmow flitch of bacon for anything I know. Mamma and Sir Ralph are also very good, but I wish the last would not speak his speech at the Durham meeting above once a week after its first delivery.

I won't betray you, if you will only write me something worth betraying. I suppose your 'C[orbeau] noir' is X,[7] but if X were a raven, or a griffin, I must still take omens from her flight.

I can't help loving her, though I have quite enough at home to prevent me from loving anyone essentially for some time to come ...

TO S. T. COLERIDGE   *13 Terrace, Piccadilly,*
October 18th, 1815

Dear Sir, – Your letter I have just received. I will willingly do whatever you direct about the volumes in question – the sooner the better; it shall not be for want of endeavour on my part, as a negotiator with the 'Trade' (to talk technically) that you are not enabled to do yourself justice. Last spring I saw Wr. Scott. He repeated to me a considerable portion of an unpublished poem[8] of yours – the wildest and finest I ever heard in that kind of composition. The title he did not mention, but I think the heroine's name was Geraldine. At all events, the 'toothless mastiff bitch' and the 'witch Lady', the description of the hall, the lamp suspended from the image, and more particularly of the girl herself as she went forth in the evening – all took a hold on my imagination which I never shall wish to shake off. I mention this, not for the sake of boring you with compliments, but as a prelude to the hope that this poem is or is to be in the volumes you are now about to publish. I do not know that even 'Love' or the 'Antient Mariner' are so impressive – and to me there are few things in our tongue beyond these two productions.

Wr. Scott is a staunch and sturdy admirer of yours, and with a just appreciation of your capacity deplored to me the want of inclination and exertion which prevented you from giving full scope to your mind. I will answer your question as to the 'Beggar's Bush' tomorrow or next day. I shall see Rae and Dibdin (the acting Mrs) tonight for that purpose.

Oh – your tragedy – I do not wish to hurry you, but I am indeed very anxious to have it under consideration. It is a field in which there are none living to contend against you and in which I should take a pride and pleasure in seeing you compared with the dead. I say this *not* disinterestedly, but as a *Committeeman*.[9] We have nothing even tolerable, except a tragedy of Sotheby's, which shall not interfere with yours when ready. You can have no idea what trash there is in the four hundred *fallow* dramas now lying on the shelves of D[rury] L[ane]. I never thought so highly of good writers as lately, since I have had an opportunity of comparing them with the bad.

Ever yours truly,

BYRON.

TO LEIGH HUNT   *13 Terrace, Piccadilly,*
                                 September–October 30, 1815

My Dear Hunt, – Many thanks for your books, of which you already know my opinion. Their external splendour should not disturb you as inappropriate – they have still more within than without. I take leave to differ with you on Wordsworth, as freely as I once agreed with you; at that time I gave him credit for a promise, which is unfulfilled. I still think his capacity warrants all you say of *it* only, but that his performances since *Lyrical*

Ballads are miserably inadequate to the ability which lurks within him: there is undoubtedly much natural talent spilt over the *Excursion*; but it is rain upon rocks – where it stands and stag-nates, or rain upon sands – where it falls without fertilizing. Who can understand him? Let those who do, make him intelligible. Jacob Behmen, Swedenborg, and Joanna Southcote, are mere types of this arch-apostle of mystery and mysticism. But I have done, – no, I have not done, for I have two petty, and perhaps unworthy objections in small matters to make to him, which, with his pretensions to accurate observation, and fury against Pope's false translation of 'the Moonlight scene in Homer', I wonder he should have fallen into; – these be they: – He says of Greece in the body of his book – that it is a land of

> *Rivers, fertile plains*, and *sounding* shores,
> Under a cope of *variegated* sky.

The rivers are dry half the year, the plains are barren, and the shores *still* and *tideless* as the Mediterranean can make them; the sky is any thing but variegated, being for months and months but 'darkly, deeply beautifully blue'. – The next is in his notes, where he talks of our 'Monuments crowded together in the busy, etc., of a large town', as compared with the 'still seclusion of a Turkish cemetery in some *remote* place'. This is pure stuff; for *one* monu-ment in our churchyards there are *ten* in the Turkish, and so crowded, that you cannot walk between them; that is, divided merely by a path or road; and as to '*remote* places', men never take the trouble in a barbarous country, to carry their dead very far; they must have lived near to where they were buried. There are no cemeteries in 'remote places', except such as have the cypress and the tombstone still left, where the olive and the habitation of the living have perished . . .

These things I was struck with, as coming peculiarly in my own way; and in both of these he is wrong; yet I should have noticed neither, but for his attack on Pope for a like blunder, and a peevish affectation about him of despising a popularity which he will never obtain. I write in great haste, and I doubt, *not* much to the purpose; but you have it hot and hot, just as it comes, and so let it go. By-the-way, both he and you go too far against Pope's 'So when the moon', etc.; it is no translation, I know; but it is not such false description as asserted. I have read it on the spot; there is a burst, and a lightness, and a glow about the night in the Troad, which makes the 'planets vivid', and the 'pole glowing'. The moon is – at least the sky is, clearness itself; and I know no more appropriate expression for the expansion of such a heaven – o'er the scene – the plain – the sky – Ida – the Hellespont – Simois – Scamander – and the Isles – than that of a 'flood of glory'. I am getting horribly lengthy, and must stop; to the whole of your letter 'I say ditto to Mr Burke', as the Bristol candidate cried by way of electioneering harangue. You need not speak of morbid feelings and vexations to me; I have plenty; but I must blame partly the times, and chiefly myself; but let us forget them. *I* shall be very apt to do so when I see you next. Will you come to the theatre and see our new management? You shall cut it up to your heart's content, root and branch, afterwards, if you like; but come and see it! If not, I must come and see you.

Ever yours, very truly and affectionately,

BYRON.

P.S. – Not a word from Moore for these two months. Pray let me have the rest of *Rimini*. You have two excellent points in that poem – originality and Italianism. I will back you as a bard against half the fellows on whom you have thrown away much good criticism and eulogy; but don't let your bookseller publish in *quarto*; it is the worst size possible for circulation. I say this on bibliopolical authority.

Again, your ever,

B.

TO THOMAS MOORE *Terrace, Piccadilly,*
October 31, 1815

I have not been able to ascertain precisely the time of duration of the stock market; but I believe it is a good time for selling out, and I hope so. First, because I shall see you; and next, because

I shall receive certain monies on behalf of Lady B., the which will materially conduce to my comfort, – I wanting (as the duns say) 'to make up a sum'.

Yesterday, I dined out with a large-ish party, where were Sheridan and Colman, Harry Harris of C[ovent] G[arden], and his brother, Sir Gilbert Heathcote, Douglas Kinnaird, and others, of note and notoriety. Like other parties of the kind, it was first silent, then talky, then argumentative, then disputatious, then unintelligible, then altogethery, then inarticulate, and then drunk. When we had reached the last step of this glorious ladder, it was difficult to get down again without stumbling; and, to crown all, Kinnaird and I had to conduct Sheridan down a damned cork-screw staircase, which had certainly been constructed before the discovery of fermented liquors, and to which no legs, however crooked, could possibly accommodate themselves. We deposited him safe at home, where his man, evidently used to the business, waited to receive him in the hall.

Both he and Colman were, as usual, very good; but I carried away much wine, and the wine had previously carried away my memory – so that all was hiccup and happiness for the last hour or so, and I am not impregnated with any of the conversation. Perhaps you heard of a late answer of Sheridan to the watchman who found him bereft of that 'divine particle of air', called reason, —. He, the watchman, who found Sherry in the street, fuddled and bewildered, and almost insensible, 'Who are *you*, sir?' – no answer. 'What's your name?' – a hiccup. 'What's your name?' – Answer, in a slow, deliberate, and impassive tone – 'Wilberforce!!!' Is not that Sherry all over? – and, to my mind, excellent. Poor fellow, his very dregs are better than the 'first sprightly runnings' of others.

My paper is full, and I have a grievous head-ach.

P.S. Lady B. is in full progress. Next month will bring to light (with the aid of 'Juno Lucina, *fer opem*' or rather *opes*,[10] for the last are most wanted,) the tenth wonder of the world – Gil Blas being the eighth, and he (my son's father) the ninth.

TO SIR RALPH NOEL   *February 2, 1816*

Sir, – I have received your letter.[11] To the vague and general charge contained in it I must naturally be at a loss how to answer it – I shall therefore confine myself to the tangible fact which you are pleased to alledge as one of the motives for your present proposition. Lady Byron received no dismissal from my house in the sense you have attached to the word. She left London by medical advice. She parted from me in apparent and, on my part, real harmony, though at that particular time, rather against my inclination, for I begged her to remain with the intention of myself accompanying her: when some business necessary to be arranged prevented my departure.

It is true that previous to this period I had suggested to her the expediency of a temporary residence with her parents. My reason for this was very simple and shortly stated, viz. the embarrassment of my circumstances, and my inability to maintain our present establishment. The truth of what is thus stated may be easily ascertained by reference to Lady B. – who is truth itself. If she denies it, I abide by that denial.

My intention of going abroad originated in the same painful motive and was postponed from a regard to her supposed feelings on that subject. During the last year I have had to contend with distress without and disease within. Upon the former I have little to say – except that I have endeavoured to remove it by every sacrifice in my power; and the latter I should not mention if I had not professional authority for saying that the disorder that I have to combat, without much impairing my apparent health, is such as to induce a morbid irritability of temper, which without recurring ·to external causes may have rendered me little less disagreeable to others than I am to myself. I am, however, ignorant of any particular ill-treatment which your daughter has encountered. She may have seen me gloomy, and at times violent; but she knows the causes too well to attribute such inequalities of disposition to herself, or even to me, if all things be fairly considered. And now, Sir, not for your satisfaction – for I owe you none – but for my own, and in justice to Lady Byron, it is my duty to say that there is no part of her conduct, character, temper, talents or disposition, which could in my opinion have been changed for the better. Neither in word or deed, nor (as far as thought can be dived into) thought, can I bring to my recollection a fault on her part, or hardly even a failing. She has ever appeared to me as one of the most amiable of human beings, and nearer to perfection than I had conceived could belong to humanity in its present state of existence. Having said thus much, though more in words, less in substance, than I wished to express, I come to the point – on which subject I must for a few days decline giving a decisive answer. I will not, however, detain you longer than I can help, and as it is of some importance to your family as well as to mine, and a step which cannot be recalled when taken, you will not attribute my pause to any wish to inflict farther pain on you or yours – although there are parts of your letter which, I must be permitted to say, arrogate a right which you do not now possess; for the present at least, your daughter is my wife; she is the mother of my child; and till I have her express sanction of your proceedings, I shall take leave to doubt the propriety of your interference. This will be soon ascertained, and when it is, I will submit to you my determination, which will depend very materially on hers.

I have the honour to be,
Your most obed. and very humble servt,

BYRON.

TO LADY BYRON   *February 5, 1816*

Dearest Bell, – No answer from you yet; but perhaps it is as well; only do recollect that all is at stake, the present, the future, and even the colouring of the past. My errors, or by whatever harsher name you choose to call them, you know; but I loved you, and will not part from you without your express and expressed refusal to return to, or receive me. Only say the word that you are still mine in your heart, and

'Kate, I will buckler thee against a million.'

Ever, dearest, yours most, etc.,

B.

223

TO LADY BYRON   *February 8, 1816*

All I can say seems useless – and all I could say might be no less unavailing – yet I still cling to the wreck of my hopes, before they sink for ever. Were you, then, *never* happy with me? Did you never at any time or times express yourself so? Have no marks of affection of the warmest and most reciprocal attachment passed between us? or did in fact hardly a day go down without some such on one side, and generally on both? Do not mistake me: I have not denied my state of mind – but you know its causes – and were those deviations from calmness never followed by acknowledgements and repentance? Was not the last that recurred more particularly so? and had I not – had we not the days before and on the day we parted – every reason to believe that we loved each other? that we were to meet again? Were not your letters kind? Had I not acknowledged to you all my faults and follies – and assured you that some had not and could not be repeated? I do not require these questions to be answered to me, but to your own heart. The day before I received your father's letter I had fixed a day for rejoining you. If I did not write lately, Augusta did; and as you had been my proxy in correspondence with her, so did I imagine she might be the same from me to you.

Upon your letter to me this day I surely may remark that its expressions imply a treatment which I am incapable of inflicting, and you of imputing to me, if aware of their latitude, and the extent of the inference to be drawn from them. This is not just, but I have no reproaches nor the wish to find cause for them. Will you see me? – when and where you please – in whose presence you please. The interview shall pledge you to nothing, and I will say and do nothing to agitate either. It is torture to correspond thus, and there are things to be settled and said which cannot be written.

You say it is my disposition to deem what I have worthless. Did I deem *you* so? Did I ever so express myself to you, or of you to others? You are much changed within these twenty days or you would never have thus poisoned your own better feelings and trampled on mine.

Ever your most truly and affectly.

TO LADY BYRON   *February 15, 1816*

I know not what to say, every step taken appears to bear you farther from me, and to widen 'the great gulf between thee and me'. If it cannot be crossed I will perish in its depth ...

I have invited your return; it has been refused. I have requested to know with what I am charged; it is refused. Is this mercy or justice? We shall see. And now, Bell, dearest Bell, whatever may be the event of this calamitous difference, whether you are returned to or torn from me, I can only say in the truth of affliction, and without hope, motive, or end in again saying what I have lately but vainly repeated, that I love you, bad or good, mad or rational, miserable or content, I love you, and shall do, to the dregs of my memory and existence. If I can feel thus for you now under every possible aggravation and exasperating circumstance that can corrode the heart and inflame the brain, perhaps you may one day know, or think at least, that I was not all you have persuaded yourself to believe me; but that nothing, nothing can touch me farther.

I have hitherto avoided naming my child, but this was a feeling you never doubted in me. I must ask of its welfare. I have heard of its beauty and playfulness, and I request, not from you, but through any other channel – Augusta, if you please, – some occasional news of its wellbeing.

I am, yours, etc.,

                                                    B.

TO THOMAS MOORE   *February 29, 1816.*

I have not answered your letter for a time; and, at present, the reply to part of it might extend to such a length, that I shall delay it till it can be made in person, and then I will shorten it as much as I can.

In the mean time, I am at war 'with all the world and his wife'; or rather, 'all the world and *my* wife' are at war with me, and have not yet crushed me, – whatever they *may* do. I don't know that in the course of a hair-breadth existence I was ever, at home or abroad, in a situation so completely uprooting of present pleasure, or rational hope for the future, as this same. I say this, because I think so, and feel it. But I shall not sink under it the more for that mode of considering the question – I have made up my mind.

By the way, however, you must not believe all you hear on the subject; and don't attempt to defend me. If you succeeded in that, it would be a mortal, or an immortal, offence – who can bear refutation? I have but a very short answer for those whom it concerns; and all the activity of myself and some vigorous friends have not yet fixed on any tangible ground or personage, on which or with whom I can discuss matters, in a summary way, with a fair pretext; – though I nearly had *nailed one* yesterday, but he evaded by – what was judged by others – a satisfactory explanation. I speak of *circulators* – against whom I have no enmity, though I must act according to the common code of usage, when I hit upon those of the serious order . . .

In all this business, I am the sorriest for Sir Ralph. He and I are equally punished, though *magis pares quam similes*[12] in our affliction. Yet it is hard for both to suffer for the fault of one, and so it is – I shall be separated from my wife; he will retain his.

Ever, etc.

TO LADY BYRON *March 4, 1816*

I know of no offence, not merely from man to wife, nor of one human being to another, but of any being almost to God Himself, which we are not taught to believe would be expiated by the repeated atonement which I have offered even for the *unknown* faults (for to me, till stated, they are unknown to any extent which can justify such persevering rejections) I may have been supposed to commit, or can have committed, against you. But since all hope is over, and instead of the duties of a wife and the mother of my child, I am to encounter accusation and implacability, I have nothing more to say, but shall act according to circumstances, though not even injury can alter the love with which (though I shall do my best to repel attack) I must ever be yours,

B.

I am told that you say *you* drew up the proposal of separation; if so, I regret I hear it; it appeared to me to be a kind of appeal to the supposed mercenary feelings of the person to whom it was made – 'if you part with, etc., you will gain *so much now*, and so much at the death of', etc., a matter of pounds, shillings, and pence! No allusion to my child; a hard, dry, attorney's paper. Oh, Bell! to see you thus stifling and destroying all feeling, all affections, all duties (for they are your first duties, those of a wife and a mother), is far more bitter than any possible consequences to me.

TO LADY BYRON   [*April, 1816*]

More last words – not many – and such as you will attend to; answer I do not expect, nor does it import; but you will at least hear me. – I have just parted from Augusta, almost the last being whom you have left me to part with.

Wherever I may go, – and I am going far, – you and I can never meet in this world, nor in the next. Let this content or atone. — If any accident occurs to me, be kind to Augusta; if she is then also nothing – to her children. You know that some time ago I made my will in her favour and her children, because any child of ours was provided for by other and better means. This could not be prejudice to you, for we had not then differed, and even now is useless during your life by the terms of our settlements. Therefore, – be kind to her, for never has she acted or spoken towards you but as your friend. And recollect, that, though it may be an advantage to you to have lost a husband, it is sorrow to her to have the waters now, or the earth hereafter, between her and her brother. It may occur to your memory that you formerly promised me this much. I repeat it – for deep resentments have but *half* recollections. Do not deem this promise cancell'd, for it was not a vow . . .

TO THE HON. AUGUSTA LEIGH   *Bruxelles,*
                              [*Wednesday,*] *May 1st, 1816*

My Heart, – We are detained here for some petty carriage repairs, having come out of our way to the Rhine on purpose, after passing through Ghent, Antwerp, and Mechlin. I have written to you twice, – once from Ostend, and again from Ghent. I hope most truly that you will receive my letters, not as important in themselves, but because you wish it, and so do I. It would be difficult for me to write anything amusing; this country has been so frequently described, and has so little for description, though a good deal for observation, that I know not what to say of it, and one don't like talking only of oneself . . .

As the low Countries did not make part of my plan (except as a route), I feel a little anxious to get out of them. Level roads don't suit me, as thou knowest; it must be up hill or down, and then I am more *au fait*. Imagine to yourself a succession of avenues with a Dutch Spire at the end of each, and you see the road; an accompaniment of highly cultivated farms on each side, intersected with small canals or ditches, and sprinkled with very neat and clean cottages, a village every two miles, – and you see the country; not a rise from Ostend to Antwerp – a molehill would make the inhabitants think that the Alps had come here on a visit; it is a perpetuity of plain and an eternity of *pavement* (on the *road*), but it is a country of great apparent comfort, and of singular though *tame* beauty, and, were it not out of my way, I should like to survey it less cursorily. The towns are wonderfully fine. The approach to Brussels is beautiful, and there is a fine palace to the right in coming.

TO JOHN CAM HOBHOUSE   *Bruxelles, May 1st, 1816*

. . . At Antwerp we pictured – churched – and steepled again, but the principal street and *bason* pleased me most – poor dear Buonaparte!!! and the foundries, etc., etc. As for Rubens, I was glad to see his tomb on account of that ridiculous description (in Smollett's P. Pickle) of Pallet's absurdity at his monument – but as for his works, and his superb 'tableaux', he seems to me (who by the way know nothing of the matter) the most glaring – flaring – staring – harlotry imposter that ever passed a trick upon the senses of mankind, – it is not nature – it is not art – with the exception of some linen (which hangs over the cross in one of his pictures) which, to do it justice, looked like a very handsome table-cloth – I never saw such an assemblage of florid nightmares as his canvas contains; his portraits seem clothed in pulpit cushions ...

TO JOHN CAM HOBHOUSE   *Evian, June 23rd, 1816*

... I have taken a very pretty little villa in a vineyard, with the Alps behind, and Mount Jura and the lake before – it is called Diodati, from the name of the proprietor, who is a descendant of the critical and illustrissimi Diodati's and has an agreeable house, which he lets at a reasonable rate per season or annum as suits the lessee. When you come out don't go to an inn, not even to Secheron; but come on to headquarters, where I have rooms ready for you and Scrope, and all 'appliances and means to boot' ... At the present writing I am on my way on a water-tour round the Lake Leman, and am thus far proceeded in a pretty open boat which I bought and navigate – it is an English one, and was brought lately from Bordeaux. I am on shore for the night, and have just had a row with the Syndic of this town, who wanted my passports, which I left at Diodati, not thinking they could be wanted, except in grande route – but it seems this is Savoy, and the dominion of his Cagliari Majesty whom we saw at his own Opera in his own city, in 1809; however, by dint of references to Geneva, and other corroborations – together with being in a very ill-humour – truth has prevailed, wonderful to relate, and they actually take one's word for a fact, although it is credible and indubitable.

To-morrow we go to Meillerei, and Clarens, and Vevey, with Rousseau in hand, to see his scenery, according to his delineation in his Héloïse, now before me; the views have hitherto been very fine, but, I should conceive, less so than those of the remainder of the lake.

All your letters (that is *two*) have arrived – thanks, and greetings: – What – and who – and the devil is 'Glenarvon'?[13] I know nothing – nor ever heard of such a person; ...

TO JOHN MURRAY   *Ouchy, near Lausanne,*
                                  June 27, 1816

Dear Sir, – I am thus far (kept by stress of weather) on my way
back to Diodati (near Geneva) from a voyage in my boat round
the Lake; and I enclose you a sprig of *Gibbon's Acacia* and some
rose-leaves from his garden, which, with part of his house, I have
just seen. You will find honorable mention, in his *Life*, made
of this 'Acacia', when he walked out on the night of concluding
his history. The garden and *summerhouse*, where he composed,
are neglected, and the last utterly decayed; but they still show it
as his 'Cabinet', and seem perfectly aware of his memory . . .

I have traversed all Rousseau's ground, with the *Héloïse* before
me; and am struck, to a degree, with the force and accuracy of
his descriptions and the beauty of their reality. Meillerie, Clarens,
and Vevay [*sic*], and the Château de Chillon, are places of which
I shall say little, because all I could say must fall short of the
impressions they stamp.

Three days ago, we were most nearly wrecked in a Squall off
Meillerie, and driven to shore. I ran no risk, being so near the
rocks, and a good swimmer; but our party were wet, and in-
commoded a good deal, the wind was strong enough to blow
down some trees, as we found at landing, however, all is righted
and right, and we are thus far on return . . .

I shall be glad to hear you are well, and have received for me
certain helms and swords, sent from Waterloo, which I rode over
with pain and pleasure.

I have finished a third canto of *Childe Harold* (consisting of
one hundred and seventeen stanzas), longer than either of the two
former, and in some parts, it may be, better; but of course on that
I cannot determine. I shall send it by the first safe-looking
opportunity.

Ever very truly yours,

                                                        B.

TO THE HON. AUGUSTA LEIGH   *Diodati, Geneva,*
                                               Septr 8th, 1816

My Dearest Augusta, – By two opportunities of private convey-
ance, I have sent answers to your letter, delivered by Mr
H[obhouse]. S[crope Davies] is on his return to England and may
possibly arrive before this. He is charged with a few packets of
seals, necklaces, balls, etc. and I know not what, formed of
Chrystals, Agates and other stones – *all of* and *from Mont Blanc,*
bought by me on and from the Spot, expressly for you to divide
among yourself and the children – including also your niece Ada,
for whom I selected a ball (of Granite – a *soft* substance by the
way – but the only one there) wherewithal to roll and play, when
she is old enough, and mischievous enough and moreover a
Chrystal necklace, and anything else you may like to add for her –
the Love! The rest are for you, and the Nursery – but particularly
Georgiana, who has sent me a very nice letter. I hope Scrope
will carry them all safely, as he promised. There are seals and all
kinds of fooleries. Pray like them, for they come from a very
curious place (nothing like it hardly in all I ever saw) – to say
nothing of the giver.

And so – Lady B. has been 'kind to you', you tell me – 'very
kind' – Umph – it is as well she should be kind to some of us –
and I am glad she has the heart and the discernment to be still
your friend – you was ever so to her. I heard the other day that
she was very unwell. I was shocked enough, and sorry enough,
God knows – but never mind. H[obhouse] tells me, however, that
she is *not* ill, that she *had* been indisposed, but is better and well to
do. This is a relief. As for me, I am in good health and fair, though
unequal, spirits. But, for all that, she – or rather the separation –
has broken my heart: I feel as if an Elephant had trodden on it.
I am convinced I shall never get over it, but I try. I had enough
before I ever knew her, and more than enough. But time and
agitation had done something for me. But this last wreck has
affected me very differently. If it were *acutely,* it would not signify.
But it is not that, – I breathe lead.

While the storm lasted and you were all piping and comforting me with condemnation in Piccadilly, it was bad enough, and violent enough. But it's worse now; I have neither strength nor spirits, nor inclination to carry me through anything which will clear my brain or lighten my heart. I mean to cross the Alps at the end of this month, and go – God knows where – by Dalmatia, up to the Arnauts again, if nothing better can be done. I have still a world before me – this – or the next.

H[obhouse] has told me all the strange stories in circulation of me and mine – *Not* true. I have been in some danger on the lake (near Meillerie), but nothing to speak of; and, as to all these 'mistresses', Lord help me – I have had but one.[14] Now don't scold; but what could I do? – a foolish girl, in spite of all I could say or do, would come after me, or rather went before – for I found her here – and I have had all the plague possible to persuade her to go back again; but at last she went. Now, dearest, I do most truly tell thee, that I could not help this, that I did all I could to prevent it, and have at last put an end to it. I was not in love, nor have any love left for any; but I could not exactly play the Stoic with a woman, who had scrambled eight hundred miles to unphilosophize me. Besides, I had been regaled of late with so many 'two courses and a *desert*' (Alas!) of aversion, that I was fain to take a little love (if pressed particularly) by way of novelty. And now you know all that I know of the matter, and it's over. Pray write. I have heard nothing since your last, at least a month or five weeks ago. I go out very little, except into the *air*, and on journeys, and on the water, and to Cop[p]et, where Me de Stael has been particularly kind and friendly towards me, and (I hear) fought battles without number in my very indifferent cause. It has (they say) made quite as much noise on this as the other side of *La Manche*. Heaven knows why – but I seem destined to set people by the ears.

Don't hate me, but believe me, ever yours most affectionately,

BYRON.

TO THE HON. AUGUSTA LEIGH   *Ouchy, Sept 17, 1816*

. . . I have recently broken through my resolution of not speaking
to you of Lady B — but do not on that account name her to me.
It is a relief – a partial relief to me to talk of her sometimes to
you – but it would be none to hear of her. *Of* her you are to judge
for yourself, but do not altogether forget that she has destroyed
your brother. Whatever my faults might or may have been – *She* –
was not the person marked out by providence to be their avenger.
One day or another her conduct will recoil on her own head;
not through *me*, for my feelings towards her are not those of
Vengeance, but – mark – if she does not end miserably *tot ou tard.*
She may think – talk – or act as she will, and by any process of
cold reasoning and a jargon of 'duty and acting for the best' etc.,
etc., impose upon her own feelings and those of others for a time –
but woe unto her – the wretchedness she has brought upon the
man to whom she has been everything evil [except in one respect
(*effaced*)] will flow back into its fountain. I may thank the strength
of my constitution that has enabled me to bear all this, but those
who bear the longest and the most do not suffer the least. I do
not think a human being could endure more mental torture than
that woman has directly and indirectly inflicted upon me – within
the present year.

She has (for a time at least) separated me from my child – and
from you – but I turn from the subject for the present . . .

I still hope to be able to see you next Spring, perhaps you and
one or two of the children could be spared some time next year
for a little tour *here* or in France with me of a month or two.
I think I could make it pleasing to you, and it should be no expense
to L. or to yourself. Pray think of this hint. You have no idea
how very beautiful great part of this country is – and *women* and
children traverse it with ease and expedition. I would return from
any distance at any time to see you, and come to England for you;
and when you consider the chances against our – but I won't
relapse into the dismals and anticipate long absences –

The great obstacle would be that you are so admirably yoked --
and necessary as a housekeeper – and a letter writer – and a

place-hunter to that very helpless gentleman your Cousin, that I suppose the usual self-love of an elderly person would interfere between you and any scheme of recreation or relaxation, for however short a period.

What a fool was I to marry – and *you* not very wise – my dear – we might have lived so single and so happy – as old maids and bachelors; I shall never find any one like you – nor you (vain as it may seem) like me. We are just formed to pass our lives together, and therefore – we – at least – I – am by a crowd of circumstances removed from the only being who could ever have loved me, or whom I can unmixedly feel attached to.

Had you been a Nun – and I a Monk – that we might have talked through a grate instead of across the sea – no matter – my voice and my heart are

ever thine –

B.

A JOURNAL

Yesterday September 17th 1816 – I set out (with H[obhouse]) on an excursion of some days to the Mountains. I shall keep a short journal of each day's progress for my Sister Augusta.

Septr 17th

Rose at five; left Diodati about seven, in one of the country carriages (a Charaban), our servants on horseback; weather very fine; the Lake calm and clear; Mont Blanc and the Aiguille of Argentières both very distinct; the borders of the Lake beautiful. Reached Lausanne before Sunset; stopped and slept at Ouchy . . .

Septr. 18th

. . . Arrived the second time (1st time was by water) at Clarens, beautiful Clarens! Went to Chillon through Scenery worthy of I know not whom; went over the Castle of Chillon again. On our return met an English party in a carriage; a lady in it fast asleep! – fast asleep in the most anti-narcotic spot in the world – excellent! I remember, at Chamouni, in the very eyes of Mont Blanc, hearing another woman, English also, exclaim to her party 'did you ever see any thing more *rural*?' – as if it was Highgate, or Hampstead, or Brompton, or Hayes, – '*Rural!*' quotha! – Rocks, pines, torrents, Glaciers, Clouds, and Summits of eternal snow far above them – and '*Rural!*' I did not know the thus exclaiming fair one, but she was a very good kind of a woman.

After a slight and short dinner, we visited the Chateau de Clarens; an English woman has rented it recently (it was not let when I saw it first): the roses are gone with their Summer; the family out, but the servants desired us to walk over the interior of the mansion. Saw on the table of the saloon Blair's sermons and somebody else's (I forget who's) sermons, and a set of noisy children. Saw all worth seeing, and then descended to the 'Bosquet de Julie', etc. etc.; our Guide full of *Rousseau*, whom he is eternally confounding with *St Preux*, and mixing the man and the book. On the steps of a cottage in the village, I saw a young paysan*ne*, beautiful as Julie herself. Went again as far as Chillon to revisit the little torrent from the hill behind it. Sunset reflected in the lake. Have to get up at 5 tomorrow to cross the mountains on horseback – carriage to be sent round; lodged at my old Cottage – hospitable and comfortable; tired with a longish ride on the Colt, and the subsequent jolting of the Charaban, and my scramble in the hot sun. Shall go to bed, thinking of you, dearest Augusta . . .

Sept^r *19*th

Rose at five: order the carriage round. Crossed the mountains to Montbovon on horseback, and on Mules, and, by dint of scrambling, on foot also; the whole route beautiful as a Dream, and now to me almost as indistinct. I am so tired; for though healthy, I have not the strength I possessed but a few years ago. At Mont Davant we breakfasted; afterwards, on a steep ascent dismounted, tumbled down, and cut a finger open; the baggage also got loose and fell down a ravine, till stopped by a large tree: swore; recovered baggage: horse tired and dropping; mounted Mule. At the approach of the summit of Dent Jamant dismounted again with H. and all the party. Arrived at a lake in the very nipple of the bosom of the Mountain; left our quadrupeds with a Shepherd, and ascended further; came to some snow in patches, upon which my forehead's perspiration fell like rain, making the same dints as in a sieve: the chill of the wind and the snow turned me giddy, but I scrambled on and upwards. H. went to the highest *pinnacle*; I did not, but paused within a few yards (at an opening of the Cliff). In coming down, the Guide tumbled three times; I fell a laughing, and tumbled too – the descent luckily soft, though steep and slippery: H. also fell, but nobody hurt. The whole of the Mountain superb. A Shepherd on a very steep and high cliff playing upon his *pipe*; very different from *Arcadia*, (where I saw the pastors with a long Musquet instead of a Crook, and pistols in their Girdles). Our Swiss Shepherd's pipe was sweet, and his tune agreeable. Saw a cow strayed; am told that they often break their necks on and over the crags. Descended to Montbovon; pretty scraggy village, with a wild river and a wooden bridge. H. went to fish – caught one. Our carriage not come; our horses, mules, etc., knocked up; ourselves fatigued; but so much the better – I shall sleep.

The view from the highest points of today's journey comprized on one side the greatest part of Lake Leman; on the other, the valleys and mountains of the Canton of Fribourg, and an immense plain, with the Lakes of Neuchâtel and Morat, and all which the borders of these and of the Lake of Geneva inherit; we had both sides of the Jura before us in one point of view, with Alps in plenty. In passing a ravine, the Guide recommended strenuously a quickening of pace, as the Stones fall with great rapidity and occasional damage: the advice is excellent, but, like most good advice, impracticable, the road being so rough in this precise point, that neither mules, nor mankind, nor horses, can make any violent progress. Passed without any fractures or menace thereof.

The music of the Cows' bells (for their wealth, like the Patriarchs', is cattle) in the pastures, (which reach to a height far above any mountains in Britain), and the Shepherds' shouting to us from crag to crag, and playing on their reeds where the steeps appeared almost inaccessible, with the surrounding scenery, realized all that I have ever heard or imagined of a pastoral existence: much more so than Greece or Asia Minor, for there we are a little too much of the sabre and musquet order; and if there is a Crook in one hand, you are sure to see a gun in the other: – but this was pure and unmixed – solitary, savage, and patriarchal: the effect I cannot describe. As we went, they played the 'Ranz des Vaches' and other airs, by way of farewell. I have lately repeopled my mind with Nature ...

Septr 21st

Off early. The valley of Simmenthal as before. Entrance to the plain of Thoun very narrow; high rocks, wooded to the top; river;

new mountains, with fine Glaciers. Lake of Thoun; extensive plain with a girdle of Alps. Walked down to the Chateau de Schadau; view along the lake; crossed the river in a boat rowed by women; *women* went right for the first time in my recollection. Thoun a very pretty town. The whole day's journey Alpine and proud.

Septr 22nd

Left Thoun in a boat, which carried us the length of the lake in three hours. The lake small; but the banks fine: rocks down to the water's edge. Landed at Neuhause; passed Interlachen; entered upon a range of scenes beyond all description or previous conception. Passed a rock; inscription – 2 brothers – one murdered the other; just the place for it. After a variety of windings came to an enormous rock. Girl with fruit – very pretty; blue eyes, good teeth, very fair: long but good features – reminded me rather of F^y. Bought some of her pears, and patted her upon the cheek: the expression of her face very mild, but good, and not at all coquettish. Arrived at the foot of the Mountain (the Yung frau, i.e., the Maiden); Glaciers; torrents; one of these torrents *nine hundred feet* in height of visible descent. Lodge at the Curate's. Set out to see the Valley; heard an Avalanche fall, like thunder; saw Glacier – enormous. Storm came on, thunder, lightning, hail; all in perfection, and beautiful. I was on horseback; Guide wanted to carry my cane; I was going to give it to him, when I recollected that it was a Swordstick, and I thought the lightning might be attracted towards him; kept it myself; a good deal encumbered with it, and my cloak, as it was too heavy for a whip, and the horse was stupid, and stood still with every other peal. Got in, not very wet; the Cloak being staunch. H. wet through; H. took refuge in cottage; sent man, umbrella, and cloak (from the Curate's when I arrived) after him. Swiss Curate's house very good indeed, – much better than most English Vicarages. It is immediately opposite the torrent I spoke of. The torrent is in shape curving over the rock, like the *tail* of a white horse streaming in the wind, such as it might be conceived would be that of the '*pale* horse' on which *Death* is mounted in the Apocalypse. It is neither mist nor water, but a something between both; it's immense height (nine hundred feet) gives it a wave, a curve, a spreading here, a condensation there, wonderful and indescribable. I think, upon the whole, that this day has been better than any of this present excursion.

Sept. 23^d

Before ascending the mountain, went to the torrent (7 in the morning) again; The Sun upon it forming a *rainbow* of the lower part of all colours, but principally purple and gold; the bow moving as you move; I never saw any thing like this; it is only in the Sunshine. Ascended the Wengen Mountain; at noon reached a valley on the summit; left the horses, took off my coat, and went to the summit; 7000 feet (English feet) above the level of the *sea*, and about 5000 above the valley we left in the morning. On one side, our view comprized the *Yung frau*, with all her glaciers; then the *Dent d'Argent*, shining like truth; then the *little Giant* (the Kleiner Eigher); and the great Giant (the Grosser Eigher), and last, not least, the Wetterhorn. The height of Jungfrau is 13,000 feet above the sea, 11,000 above the valley; she is the highest of this range. Heard the Avalanches falling every five minutes nearly – as if God was pelting the Devil down from Heaven with snow balls. From where we stood, on the *Wengen* Alp, we had all these in view on one side; on the other the clouds rose from the opposite valley, curling up perpendicular precipices like the foam of the Ocean of Hell, during a Springtide – it was white, and sulphury, and immeasurably deep in appearance. The side we ascended was (of course) not of so precipitous a nature; but on arriving at the summit, we looked down the other side upon a boiling sea of cloud, dashing against the crags on which we stood (these crags on one side quite perpendicular). Staid a quarter of an hour; began to descend; quite clear from cloud on that side of the mountain. In passing the masses of snow, I made a snowball and pelted H. with it.

Got down to our horses again; eat something; remounted; heard the Avalanches still; came to a morass; H. dismounted;

H. got over well; I tried to pass my horse over; the horse sunk up [to] the chin, and of course he and I were in the mud together; bemired all over, but not hurt; laughed, and rode on. Arrived at the Grindenwald; dined, mounted again, and rode to the higher Glacier – twilight, but distinct – very fine Glacier, like a *frozen hurricane*. Starlight, beautiful, but a devil of a path! Never mind, got safe in; a little lightning; but the whole of the day as fine in point of weather as the day on which Paradise was made. Passed *whole woods of withered pines, all withered*; trunks stripped and barkless, branches lifeless; done by a single winter, – their appearance reminded me of my family.

Sept 24ᵗʰ

Set out at seven; up at five. Passed the black Glacier, the Mountain Wetterhorn on the right; crossed the Scheideck mountain; came to the *Rose* Glacier, said to be the largest and finest in Switzerland. *I* think the Bossons Glacier at Chamouni as fine; H. does not. Came to the Reichenback waterfall, two hundred feet high; halted to rest the horses. Arrived in the valley of Oberhasli; rain came on; drenched a little; only 4 hours' rain, however, in 8 days. Came to Lake of Brientz, then to town of Brientz; changed. H. hurt his head against door. In the evening, four Swiss Peasant Girls of Oberhasli came and sang airs of their country; two of the voices beautiful – the tunes also; they sing too that *Tyrolese air* and song which you love, Augusta, because I love it – and I love, because you love it; they are still singing. Dearest, you do not know how I should have liked this, were you with me. The airs are so wild and original, and at the same time of great sweetness. The singing is over: but below stairs I hear the notes of a Fiddle, which bode no good to my night's rest. The *Lard* help us – I shall go down and see the dancing.

Septr 25ᵗʰ

The whole town of Brientz were apparently gathered together in the rooms below; pretty music and excellent Waltzing; none but peasants; the dancing much better than in England; the English can't Waltz, never could, nor ever will. One man with his pipe in his mouth, but danced as well as the others; some other dances in pairs and in fours, and very good. I went to bed, but the revelry continued below late and early. Brientz but a village. Rose early. Embarked on the Lake of Brientz, rowed by the women in a long boat (one very young and very pretty – seated myself by her, and began to row also); presently we put to shore, and another woman jumped in. It seems it is the custom here for the boats to be *manned by women*: for of five men and three women in our bark, all the women took an oar, and but one man.

Got to Interlachen in three hours; pretty lake, not so large as that of Thoun. Dined at Interlachen. Girl gave me some flowers, and made me a speech in German, of which I know nothing: I do not know whether the speech was pretty, but as the woman was, I hope so. Saw another – very pretty too, and tall, which I prefer: I hate short women, for more reasons than one. Re-embarked on the Lake of Thoun; fell asleep part of the way: sent our horses round; found people on the shore, blowing up a rock with gunpowder: they blew it up near our boat, only telling us a minute before; – mere stupidity, but they might have broke our noddles. Got to Thoun in the Evening: the weather has been tolerable the whole day; but as the wild part of our tour is finished, it don't matter to us: in all the desirable part, we have been most lucky in warmth and clearness of Atmosphere, for which 'Praise we the Lord!!' . . .

[. . .]

Sept. 29th

In the weather for this tour (of 13 days), I have been very fortunate – fortunate in a companion (Mr H^e) – fortunate in our prospects, and exempt from even the little petty accidents and delays which often render journeys in a less wild country disappointing. I was disposed to be pleased. I am a lover of Nature and an admirer of Beauty. I can bear fatigue and welcome privation, and have seen some of the noblest views in the world. But in all this – the recollections of bitterness, and more especially of recent and more home desolation, which must accompany me through life, have preyed upon me here; and neither the music of the Shepherd, the crashing of the Avalanche, nor the torrent, the mountain, the Glacier, the Forest, nor the Cloud, have for one moment lightened the weight upon my heart, nor enabled me to lose my own wretched identity in the majesty, and the power, and the Glory, around, above, and beneath me.

I am past reproaches; and there is a time for all things. I am past the wish of vengeance, and I know of none like for what I have suffered; but the hour will come, when what I feel must be felt, – and the – but enough.

To you, dearest Augusta, I send, and *for* you I have kept this record of what I have seen and felt. Love me as you are beloved by me.

TO THE HON. AUGUSTA LEIGH   *Diodati,*
                                                      October 1st, 1816

My Dearest Augusta, – Two days ago I sent you in three letter-covers a journal of a mountain-excursion lately made by me and Mr H. in the Bernese Alps. I kept it on purpose for you thinking it might amuse you. Since my return here I have heard by an indirect Channel that Lady B. is better, or well. It is also said that she has some intention of passing the winter on the Continent. Upon this subject I want a word or two, and as you are – I understand – on terms of acquaintance with her again you will be the properest channel of communication from me to her. It regards my child. It is far from my intention now or at any future period (without misconduct on her part which I should be grieved to anticipate), to attempt to withdraw my child from its mother. I think it would be harsh; and though it is a very deep privation to me to be withdrawn from the contemplation and company of my little girl, still I would not purchase even this so very dearly; but I must strongly protest against my daughter's leaving England, to be taken over the Continent at so early a time of life and subjected to many avoidable risks of health and comfort; more especially in so unsettled a state as we know the greater part of Europe to be in at this moment. I do not choose that my girl should be educated like Lord Yarmouth's son (or run the chance of it which a war would produce), and I make it my personal and particular request to Lady Byron that – in the event of her quitting England – the child should be left in the care of proper persons. I have no objection to its remaining with Lady Noel and Sir Ralph, (who would naturally be fond of it), but my distress of mind would be very much augmented if my daughter quitted England without my consent or approbation. I beg that you will lose no time in making this known to Lady B. and I hope you will say something to enforce my request, I have no wish to trouble her more than can be helped. My whole hope – and prospect of a quiet evening (if I reach it), are wrapt up in that little creature – Ada – and you must forgive my anxiety in all which regards her even to minuteness. My journal will have told you all my recent wanderings. I am very well though I had a little accident yesterday. Being in my boat in the evening the pole of the mainsail slipped in veering round, and struck me on a nerve of one of my legs so violently as to make me faint away. Mr H^e and cold water brought me to myself, but there was no damage done – no bone hurt – and I have now no pain whatever. Some nerve or tendon was jarred – for a moment and that was all. To-day I dine at Coppet; the Jerseys are I believe to be there. Believe me ever and truly my own dearest Sis. most affectionately and entirely yours

B.

FRAGMENT OF BYRON'S
UNFINISHED NOVEL

June 17, 1816.

In the year 17–, having for some time determined on a journey through countries not hitherto much frequented by travellers, I set out, accompanied by a friend, whom I shall designate by the name of Augustus Darvell. He was a few years my elder, and a man of considerable fortune and ancient family: advantages which an extensive capacity prevented him alike from undervaluing or overrating. Some peculiar circumstances in his private history had rendered him to me an object of attention, of interest, and even of regard, which neither the reserve of his manners, nor occasional indications of an unquietude at times nearly approaching to alienation of mind, could extinguish.

I was yet young in life, which I had begun early; but my intimacy with him was of a recent date: we had been educated at the same schools and university; but his progress through these had preceded mine, and he had been deeply initiated into what is called the world, while I was yet in my novitiate. While thus engaged, I heard much both of his past and present life; and, although in these accounts there were many and irreconcilable contradictions, I could still gather from the whole that he was a being of no common order, and one who, whatever pains he might take to avoid remark, would still be remarkable. I had cultivated his acquaintance subsequently, and endeavoured to obtain his friendship, but this last appeared to be unattainable; whatever affections he might have possessed seemed now, some to have been extinguished, and others to be concentred: that his feelings were acute, I had sufficient opportunities of observing; for, although he could control, he could not altogether disguise them: still he had a power of giving to one passion the appearance of another, in such a manner that it was difficult to define the nature of what was working within him; and the expressions of

244

his features would vary so rapidly, though slightly, that it was useless to trace them to their sources. It was evident that he was a prey to some cureless disquiet; but whether it arose from ambition, love, remorse, grief, from one or all of these, or merely from a morbid temperament akin to disease, I could not discover; there were circumstances alleged which might have justified the application to each of these causes; but, as I have before said, these were so contradictory and contradicted, that none could be fixed upon with accuracy. Where there is mystery, it is generally supposed that there must also be evil: I know not how this may be, but in him there certainly was the one, though I could not ascertain the extent of the other – and felt loth, as far as regarded himself, to believe in its existence ...

TO THE HON. AUGUSTA LEIGH   *Milan Oct' 15, 1816*

My Dearest Augusta, – I have been at Churches, Theatres, libraries, and picture galleries. The Cathedral is noble, the theatre grand, the library excellent, and the galleries I know nothing about – except as far as liking one picture out of a thousand. What has delighted me most is a manuscript collection (preserved in the Ambrosian library), of original love-letters and verses of Lucretia de Borgia and Cardinal Bembo; and a lock of her hair – so long – and fair and beautiful – and the letters so pretty and so loving that it makes one wretched not to have been born sooner to have at least seen her. And pray what do you think is one of her *signatures*? – why this + a Cross – which she says 'is to stand for her name etc.' Is not this amusing?[15] I suppose you know that she was a famous beauty, and famous for the use she made of it; and that she was the love of this same Cardinal Bembo (besides a story about her papa Pope Alexander and her brother Caesar Borgia – which some people don't believe – and others do), and that after all she ended with being Duchess of Ferrara, and an excellent mother and wife also; so good as to be quite an example. All this may or may not be, but the hair and the letters are so beautiful that I have done nothing but pore over them, and have made the librarian promise me a copy of some of them; and I

mean to get some of the hair if I can. The verses are Spanish –
the letters Italian – some signed – others with a cross – but all
in her own hand-writing.

I am so hurried, and so sleepy, but so anxious to send you even
a few lines my dearest Augusta, that you will forgive me troubling
you so often; and I shall write again soon; but I have sent you
so much lately, that you will have too many perhaps. *A thousand
loves* to *you* from *me* – which is very generous for I only ask *one*
in return

Ever dearest thine

B.

TO THE HON. AUGUSTA LEIGH   *Oct 28ᵗʰ, 1816*

My Dearest Augusta, – Two days ago I wrote you the enclosed
but the arrival of your letter of the 12ᵗʰ has revived me a little,
so pray forgive the apparent '*humeur*' of the other, which I do
not tear up – from lazyness – and the hurry of the post as I have
hardly time to write another at present.

I really do not and cannot understand all the mysteries and
alarms in your letters and more particularly in the last. All I know
is – that no human power short of destruction – shall prevent me
from seeing you when – where – and how – I may please –
according to time and circumstances; that you are the only
comfort (except the remote possibility of my daughter's being so)
left me in prospect in existence, and that I can bear the rest – so
that you remain; but anything which is to divide us would drive
me quite out of my senses; Miss Milbanke appears in all respects
to have been formed for my destruction; I have thus far – as you
know – regarded her without feelings of personal bitterness
towards her, but if directly or indirectly – but why do I say this? –
You know she is the cause of all – whether intentionally or not is
little to the purpose – You surely do not mean to say that if I
come to England in Spring, that you and I shall not meet? If so
I will never return to it – though I must for many reasons –
business etc., etc. – But I quit this topic for the present.

My health is good, but I have now and then fits of giddiness,
and deafness, which makes me think like Swift – that I shall be

like him and the *withered* tree he saw – which occasioned the reflection and 'die at top' first. My hair is growing grey, and *not* thicker; and my teeth are sometimes *looseish* though still white and sound. Would not one think I was sixty instead of not quite nine and twenty? To talk thus – Never mind – either this must end – or I must end – but I repeat it again and again – *that woman* has destroyed me.

Milan has been made agreeable by much attention and kindness from many of the natives; but the whole tone of Italian society is so different from yours in England; that I have not time to describe it, tho' I am not sure that I do not prefer it. Direct as usual to Geneva – hope the best – and love me the most – as I must ever love you.

B.

TO THOMAS MOORE   *Verona, November 6, 1816*

... The state of morals in these parts is in some sort lax. A mother and son were pointed out at the theatre, as being pronounced by the Milanese world to be of the Theban dynasty – but this was all. The narrator (one of the first men in Milan) seemed to be most sufficiently scandalised by the taste or the tie. All society in Milan is carried on at the opera: they have private boxes, where they play at cards, or talk, or any thing else; but (except at the Cassino) there are no open houses, or balls, etc., etc. ...

The peasant girls have all very fine dark eyes, and many of them are beautiful. There are also two dead bodies in fine preservation – one Saint Carlo Boromeo, at Milan; the other not a saint, but a chief, named Visconti, at Monza – both of which appeared very agreeable. In one of the Boromean isles (the Isola bella), there is a large laurel – the largest known – on which Buonaparte, staying there just before the battle of Marengo, carved with his knife the word 'Battaglia'. I saw the letters, now half worn out and partly erased.

Excuse this tedious letter. To be tiresome is the privilege of old age and absence; I avail myself of the latter, and the former I have anticipated. If I do not speak to you of my own affairs, it is not from want of confidence, but to spare you and myself. My day is over – what then? – I have had it. To be sure, I have shortened it; and if I had done as much by this letter, it would have been as well. But you will forgive that, if not the other faults of

Yours ever and most affectionately,

B.

4. THE VENETIAN INTERLUDE

November 1816 – December 1819

INTRODUCTION

BYRON's sojourn in Venice, and his numerous liaisons with women of every class, caused much scandal in England, where reports were retailed by travellers, not always with accuracy, though true enough in the main. But, in spite of (or, perhaps, because of the release given by) his sexual promiscuity, the Venetian interlude was a period in which his literary creativity was at its most productive. He completed *Manfred*, wrote the 'Lament of Tasso', the fourth (and last) canto of *Childe Harold*, the satiric 'Beppo', the ode on Venice, and several cantos of *Don Juan*, as well as composing a number of lyrics, including the exquisite 'So we'll go no more a roving'; meanwhile he worked on his memoirs, which he presented to Moore (these were subsequently destroyed), and continued the voluminous correspondence, only a part of which can be included here. To his friends he made no secret of his affairs, sending back salacious reports of his intrigues, with humorous details of the vagaries, wilfulness and wildness of his two principal mistresses – Marianna Segati, the wife of his land-lord in the Frezzeria, and her successor Margarita Cogni (the baker's wife), who installed herself as his housekeeper, when he had settled in the Palazzo Mocenigo on the Grand Canal and had rented a summer villa at La Mira on the Brenta. Of the latter, *La Fornarina*, Byron wrote: '. . . in a few evenings we arranged our affairs, and for two years, in the course of which I had more women than I can count or recount, she was the only one who preserved over me an ascendancy which was often disputed, and never impaired.'

Newstead Abbey was sold to his old Harrovian friend Major Wildman in December 1817; thenceforth, having the banker Douglas Kinnaird and Hobhouse as his financial advisers, with powers of attorney, his income was assured; moreover, he had relinquished his former pride, and, in fact, was demanding large sums from John Murray, the publisher, for his works, which continued to attract a wide public – this in spite of the increasing

251

prudery of the age, which professed to be shocked by the 'immorality' and 'blasphemy' of *Don Juan*. In Venice he kept his horses on the Lido or at La Mira, was visited by his English friends and attended the receptions, particularly the salons of the Countess Albrizzi and, later, of the Countess Benzoni. Through Shelley as intermediary – for he would not even reply to the pathetic appeals of Claire Clairmont – his illegitimate daughter was brought to Italy, and put in the care of the Hoppners (the British Consul in Venice and his Swiss wife). Shelley, on a visit to Venice, found a deterioration in Byron's appearance, and was shocked by his avowed profligacy; but he was charmed by his conversation and convinced of his intellectual superiority, which found expression in his poem 'Julian and Maddalo'.

It was in April 1819, that Byron met at the salon of Countess Benzoni the nineteen-year-old Countess Teresa Guiccioli. He had, in fact, been introduced a year previously at a reception of the Countess Albrizzi's, when she was on her honeymoon with Count Alessandro Guiccioli, a rich Romagnuole landowner, nearly forty years her senior. The first meeting had left no impression on either, but now the mutual attraction was spontaneous, and on her side 'irresistible'; within two days they had consummated a love which was to be, in Byron's case, his last and most constant 'attachment'. Byron was not disposed to play the role of 'cavalier servente', and Teresa openly flouted the conventions in showing her love for him. Ten days after their meeting Teresa was obliged to leave Venice to accompany her husband on visits to his estates. Byron found himself in a quandary; he was almost against his will in love; and with his customary indecision found relief in an affair with a certain Angelina, and in pouring out his deepest affection for Augusta in a searing love-letter (17 May 1819). Hearing of Teresa's illness, he set off for Ravenna, where his presence, though complicated by his relations with Count Guiccioli, effected Teresa's recovery. The Count having business in Bologna, Byron followed and, with Allegra, was installed at the Count's apparently complaisant invitation in the Guiccioli palazzo.

The Count was as inscrutable as he was unpredictable; but

Teresa, on doctor's advice, was allowed to travel with Byron to Venice and La Mira. Teresa was delighted to be alone in Byron's company; but the latter, as indecisive as ever, and suspecting that the liaison would not last, had vague plans of emigrating to South America, or even of returning to England. Byron was ill with a tertian fever, tended by Teresa at the Palazzo Mocenigo, when Count Guiccioli arrived and was also put up as Byron's guest at the palazzo. Intervention by Teresa's father, Count Ruggerio Gamba Ghiselli, did nothing to ease matters which had already come to a head, and a violent quarrel ensued between Teresa and her husband, the latter demanding that she return with him to Ravenna, without Byron. Finally, with the added persuasion of Byron, she acceded to the Count's demands, but once back in Ravenna she fell so seriously ill that the Gambas called for Byron, and on Christmas Eve 1819, he reached Ravenna, henceforth held as the acknowledged 'cavalier servente' of the Countess Teresa. As he wrote: 'Love has gained the victory'.

TO THOMAS MOORE   *Venice, November 17, 1816.*

I wrote to you from Verona the other day in my progress hither, which letter I hope you will receive. Some three years ago, or it may be more, I recollect your telling me that you had received a letter from our friend Sam, dated 'On board his gondola'. *My* gondola is, at present, waiting for me on the canal; but I prefer writing to you in the house, it being autumn – and rather an English autumn than otherwise. It is my intention to remain at Venice during the winter, probably, as it has always been (next to the East) the greenest island of my imagination. It has not disappointed me; though its evident decay would, perhaps, have that effect upon others. But I have been familiar with ruins too long to dislike desolation. Besides, I have fallen in love, which, next to falling into the canal, (which would be of no use, as I can swim), is the best or the worst thing I could do. I have got some extremely good apartments in the house of a 'Merchant of Venice', who is a good deal occupied with business and has a wife in her twenty-second year. Marianna [Segati] (that is her name)

253

is in her appearance altogether like an antelope. She has the large, black, oriental eyes, with that peculiar expression in them which is seen rarely among *Europeans* – even the Italians – and which many of the Turkish women give themselves by tinging the eyelid, – an art not known out of that country, I believe. This expression she has *naturally*, – and something more than this. In short, I cannot describe the effect of this kind of eye, – at least upon me. Her features are regular, and rather aquiline – mouth small – skin clear and soft, with a kind of hectic colour – forehead remarkably good; her hair is of dark gloss, curl, and colour of Lady J[ersey]'s: her figure is light and pretty, and she is a famous songstress – scientifically so; her natural voice (in conversation, I mean) is very sweet; and the naïveté of the Venetian dialect is always pleasing in the mouth of a woman . . .

December 5

Since my former dates, I do not know that I have much to add on the subject, and, luckily, nothing to take away. . .

Of Venice I shall say little. You must have seen many descriptions; and they are most of them like. It is a poetical place; and classical, to us, from Shakespeare and Otway. I have not yet sinned against it in verse, nor do I know that I shall do so, having been tuneless since I crossed the Alps, and feeling, as yet, no renewal of the *estro*. By the way, I suppose you have seen *Glenarvon*. Madame de Stael lent it me to read from Cop[p]et last autumn. It seems to me, that if the authoress had written the *truth*, and nothing but the truth – the whole truth – the romance would not only have been more *romantic*, but more entertaining. As for the likeness, the picture can't be good – I did not sit long enough. When you have leisure, let me hear from and of you, believing me,

Ever and truly yours most affectionately,

B.

TO THE HON. AUGUSTA LEIGH   *Venice, Decr 18th, 1816*

My Dearest Augusta, – I have received one letter dated 19th Novr I think (or rather earlier by a week or two perhaps), since my arrival in Venice, where it is my intention to remain probably till the Spring. The place pleases me. I have found some pleasing society – and the *romance* of the situation – and it's extraordinary appearance – together with all the associations we are accustomed to connect with Venice, have always had a charm for me, even before I arrived here; and I have not been disappointed in what I have seen.

I go every morning to the Armenian Convent (of *friars not Nuns* – my child) to study the language, I mean the *Armenian* language, (for as you perhaps know – I am versed in the Italian which I speak with fluency rather than accuracy), and if you ask me my reason for studying this out of the way language – I can only answer that it is Oriental and difficult, and employs me – which are – as you know my Eastern and difficult way of thinking – reasons sufficient. Then I have fallen in love with a very pretty Venetian of two and twenty, with great black eyes. She is married – and so am I – which is very much to the purpose. We have formed and sworn an eternal attachment, which has already lasted a lunar month, and I am more in love than ever, and so is the lady – at least she says so. She does not plague me (which is a wonder) and I verily believe we are one of the happiest – unlawful couples on this side of the Alps. She is very handsome, very Italian or rather Venetian, with something more of the Oriental cast of countenance; accomplished and musical after the manner of her nation. Her spouse is a very good kind of man who occupies himself elsewhere, and thus the world goes on here as elsewhere. This adventure came very opportunely to console me, for I was beginning to be 'like Sam Jennings very *unappy*' but at present – at least for a month past – I have been very tranquil, very loving, and have not so much embarrassed myself with the tortures of the last two years and that virtuous monster Miss Milbanke, who had nearly driven me out of my senses.

Hobhouse is gone to Rome with his brother and sister – but

returns here in February: you will easily suppose that I was not disposed to stir from my present position.

I have not heard recently from England and wonder if Murray has published the po's sent to him; and I want to know if you don't think them very fine and all that – Goosey my love – don't they make you 'put finger in eye'?

You can have no idea of my thorough wretchedness from the day of my parting from you till nearly a month ago though I struggled against it with some strength. At present I am better – thank Heaven above – and woman beneath – and I will be a very good boy. Pray remember me to the babes, and tell me of little *Da* – who by the way – is a year old and a few days over.

My love to you all and to Aunt *Sophy:*[1] pray tell *her* in particular that I have consoled myself; and tell Hodgson that his prophecy is accomplished. He said – you remember – I should be in love with an Italian – so I am. –

ever dearest yrs.

B.

P.S. – I forgot to tell you – that the *Demoiselle*[2] – who returned to England from Geneva – went there to produce a new baby B., who is now about to make his appearance. You wanted to hear some adventures – there are enough I think for one epistle . . .

TO THE HON. AUGUSTA LEIGH *Venice, Decr 19th 1816*

My Dearest Augusta, – I wrote to you a few days ago. Your letter of the 1st is arrived, and you have '*a hope*' for me, it seems: what 'hope', child? my dearest Sis. I remember a methodist preacher who, on perceiving a profane grin on the faces of part of his congregation, exclaimed 'no *hopes* for *them* as *laughs*'. And thus it is with us: we laugh too much for hopes, and so even let them go. I am sick of sorrow, and must even content myself as well as I can: so here goes – I won't be woeful again if I can help it. My letter to my moral Clytemnestra required no answer, and I would rather have none. I was wretched enough when I wrote it, and had been so for many a long day and month: at present I am less so, for reasons explained in my late letter (a few days ago); and as I never pretend to be what I am not, you may tell her if you please that I am recovering, and the reason also if you like it. I do not agree with you about Ada: there was *equivocation* in the answer, and it shall be settled one way or the other. I wrote to Hanson to take proper steps to prevent such a removal of my daughter, and even the probability of it. You do not know the woman so well as I do, or you would perceive in her *very negative answer* that she *does intend* to take Ada with her, if she should go abroad. I have heard of Murray's squabble with one of his brethren, who is an impudent imposter, and should be trounced.

You do not say whether the *true po's* are out: I hope you like them.

You are right in saying that I like Venice: it is very much what you would imagine it, but I have no time just now for description. The Carnival is to begin in a week, and with it the mummery of masking.

I have not been out a great deal, but quite as much as I like. I am going out this evening in my *cloak* and *Gondola* – there are two nice Mrs Radcliffe words for you. And then there is the place of St Mark, and conversaziones, and various fooleries, besides many *nau*:[3] indeed, every body is *nau*, so much so, that a lady with only *one lover* is not reckoned to have overstepped the modesty of marriage – that being a regular thing. Some have two, three, and so on to twenty, beyond which they don't account; but they generally begin by one. The husbands of course belong to any body's wives – but their own ...

That amatory appendage called by us a lover is here denominated variously – sometimes an 'Amoroso' (which is the same thing) and sometimes a Cavaliere Servente – which I need not tell you is a serving Cavalier. I told my fair one, at setting out that as to the love and the Cavaliership I was quite of accord but as to the *servitude* it would not suit me at all; so I begged to hear no more about it. You may easily suppose I should not at all shine in the ceremonious department – so little so that, instead of handing the Lady as in duty bound into the Gondola,

I as nearly as possible conveyed her into the Canal, and this at midnight. To be sure it was as dark as possible – but if you could have seen the gravity with which I was committing her to the waves, thinking all the time of something or other not to the purpose. I always forget that the streets are canals, and was going to walk her over the water, if the servants and the Gondoliers had not awakened me.

So much for love and all that. The music here is famous, and there will be a whole tribe of singers and dancers during the Carnival, besides the usual theatres.

The Society here is something like our own, except that the women sit in a semicircle at one end of the room, and the men stand at the other. . . .

Ever, dearest, yours,

B.

TO THOMAS MOORE   *Venice, December 24, 1816*

I have taken a fit of writing to you, which portends postage – once from Verona – once from Venice, and again from Venice – *thrice* that is. For this you may thank yourself; for I heard that you complained of my silence – so, here goes for garrulity . . .

My flame (my *Donna* whom I spoke of in my former epistle, my Marianna) is still my Marianna, and I her – what she pleases. She is by far the prettiest woman I have seen here, and the most loveable I have met with any where – as well as one of the most singular. I believe I told you the rise and progress of our *liaison* in my former letter. Lest that should not have reached you, I will merely repeat, that she is a Venetian, two-and-twenty years old, married to a merchant well to do in the world, and that she has great black oriental eyes, and all the qualities which her eyes promise. Whether being in love with her has steeled me or not, I do not know; but I have not seen many other women who seem pretty. The nobility, in particular, are a sad-looking race – the gentry rather better. And now, what art *thou* doing?

What are you doing now,
Oh Thomas Moore? . . .

258

Are you not near the Luddites? By the Lord! if there's a row, but I'll be among ye! How go on the weavers – the breakers of frames – the Lutherans of politics – the reformers?

> As the Liberty lads o'er the sea
> Bought their freedom, and cheaply, with blood,
>   So we, boys, we
>   Will *die* fighting, or *live* free,
> And down with all kings but King Ludd! . . .

There's an amiable *chanson* for you – all impromptu. I have written it principally to shock your neighbour — [Hodgson?], who is all clergy and loyalty – mirth and innocence – milk and water . . .

When does your poem of poems come out? I hear that the *Edinburgh Review* has cut up Coleridge's *Christabel*, and declared against me for praising it. I praised it, firstly, because I thought well of it; secondly, because Coleridge was in great distress, and after doing what little I could for him in essentials, I thought that the public avowal of my good opinion might help him further, at least with the book-sellers. I am very sorry that Jeffrey has attacked him, because, poor fellow, it will hurt him in mind and pocket. As for me, he's welcome – I shall never think less of Jeffrey for any thing he may say against me or mine in future . . .

I suppose Murray has sent you, or will send (for I do not know whether they are out or no) the poem, or poesies, of mine, of last summer. By the mass! they are sublime – *Ganion Coheriza*[4] – gainsay who dares! Pray, let me hear from you, and of you, and, at least, let me know that you have received these three letters. Direct right *here, poste restante.*

Ever and ever, etc . . .

TO JOHN MURRAY   *Venice, Dec. 27, 1816*

. . . As the news of Venice must be very interesting to you, I will regale you with it.

Yesterday being the feast of St Stephen, every mouth was put in motion. There was nothing but fiddling and playing on the virginals, and all kinds of conceits and divertisements, on every canal of this aquatic city. I dined with the Countess Albrizzi and a Paduan and Venetian party, and afterwards went to the opera, at the Fenice theatre (which opens for the Carnival on that day), – the finest, by the way, I have ever seen; it beats *our* theatres hollow in beauty and scenery, and those of Milan and Brescia bow before it. The opera and its Syrens were much like all other operas and women, but the subject of the said opera was something edifying; it turned – the plot and conduct thereof – upon a fact narrated by Livy of a hundred and fifty married ladies having *poisoned* a hundred and fifty husbands in the good old times. The bachelors of Rome believed this extraordinary mortality to be merely the common effect of matrimony or a pestilence; but the surviving Benedicts, being all seized with the cholic, examined into the matter, and found that 'their possets had been drugged'; the consequence of which was much scandal and several suits at law. This is really and truly the subject of the Musical piece at the Fenice; and you can't conceive what pretty things are sung and recitativoed about the *horrenda strage*.[5] The conclusion was a lady's head about to be chopped off by a Lictor, but (I am sorry to say) he left it on, and she got up and sung a trio with the two Consuls, the Senate in the back-ground being chorus. The ballet was distinguished by nothing remarkable, except that the principal she-dancer went into convulsions because she was not applauded on her first appearance; and the manager came forward to ask if there was 'ever a physician in the theatre'. There was a Greek one in my box, whom I wished very much to volunteer his services, being sure that in this case these would have been the last convulsions which would have troubled the *Ballerina*; but he would not. The crowd was enormous; and in coming out, having a lady under my arm, I was obliged, in making way, almost to 'beat a Venetian and traduce the state', being compelled to regale a person with an English punch in the guts, which sent him as far back as the squeeze and the passage would admit. He did not ask for another; but, with great signs of disapprobation and dismay, appealed to his compatriots, who laughed at him . . .

And now, if you don't write, I don't know what I won't say or do, nor what I will: send me some news – good news.

Yours very truly, etc., etc., etc.

B.

TO JOHN MURRAY   *Venice, Jan. 2, 1817*

... To-day is the 2d of January. On this day 3 years ago *The Corsair's* publication is dated, I think, in my letter to Moore. On this day *two* years I married – 'Whom the Lord loveth he chasteneth – blessed be the name of the Lord'. – I sha'n't forget the day in a hurry; and will take care to keep the Anniversary before the Evening is over. It is odd enough that I this day received a letter from you announcing the publication of *Cd. Hd.*, etc., etc., on the day of the date of *The Corsair*; and that I also received one from my Sister, written on the 10th of Decr., my daughter's birth-day (and relative chiefly to my daughter), and arriving on the day of the date of my marriage, this present 2d of January, the month of my birth, – and various other Astrologous matters, which I have no time to enumerate.

By the way, you might as well write to Hentsch, my Genevese banker, and enquire whether the *two packets* consigned to his care were or were not delivered to Mr St Aubyn, or if they are still in his keeping. One contains papers, letters, and all the original MS. of your 3^d canto, as first conceived; and the other, some bones from the field of Morat. Many thanks for your news, and the good spirits in which your letter is written ...

The general state of morals here is much the same as in the Doges' time; a woman is virtuous (according to the code) who limits herself to her husband and one lover; those who have two, three, or more, are a little *wild*; but it is only those who are indiscriminately diffuse, and form a low connection, such as the Princess of Wales with her courier, (who, by the way, is made a knight of Malta,) who are considered as over-stepping the modesty of marriage. In Venice, the Nobility have a trick of marrying with dancers or singers: and, truth to say, the women of their own order are by no means handsome; but the general race – the

261

women of the 2ᵈ and other orders, the wives of the Advocates, merchants, and proprietors, and untitled gentry, are mostly *bel' sangue*,[6] and it is with these that the more amatory connections are usually formed: there are also instances of stupendous constancy. I know a woman of fifty who never had but one lover, who dying early, she became devout, renouncing all but her husband: she piques herself, as may be presumed, upon this miraculous fidelity, talking of it occasionally with a species of misplaced morality, which is rather amusing. There is no convincing a woman here, that she is in the smallest degree deviating from the rule of right or the fitness of things, in having an *Amoroso*:[7] the great sin seems to lie in concealing it, or in having more than one; that is, unless such an extension of the prerogative is understood and approved of by the prior claimant.

In my case, I do not know that I had any predecessor, and am pretty sure that there is no participator; and am inclined to think, from the youth of the party, and from the frank undisguised way in which every body avows everything in this part of the world, when there is anything to avow, as well as from some other circumstances, such as the marriage being recent, etc., etc., that this is the *premier pas*: it does not much signify . . .

I have not done a stitch of poetry since I left Switzerland, and have not, at present, the *estro*[8] upon me: the truth is, that you are *afraid* of having a 4ᵗʰ canto *before* September, and of another copyright; but I have at present no thought of resuming that poem nor of beginning any other. If I write, I think of trying prose; but I dread introducing living people, or applications which might be made to living people: perhaps one day or other, I may attempt some work of fancy in prose, descriptive of Italian manners and of human passions; but at present I am preoccupied. As for poesy, mine is the *dream* of my sleeping Passions; when they are awake, I cannot speak their language, only in their Somnambulism, and just now they are not dormant.

Yours, ever and truly,

B.

TO THOMAS MOORE   *Venice, January 28, 1817*

... I am truly sorry to hear of your father's misfortune[9] – cruel at any time, but doubly cruel in advanced life. However, you will, at least, have the satisfaction of doing your part by him, and, depend upon it, it will not be in vain. Fortune, to be sure, is a female, but not such a b— as the rest (always excepting your wife and my sister from such sweeping terms); for she generally has some justice in the long run. I have no spite against her, though between her and Nemesis I have had some sore gauntlets to run – but then I have done my best to deserve no better. But to *you*, she is a good deal in arrear, and she will come round – mind if she don't: you have the vigour of life, of independence, of talent, spirit, and character all with you. What you can do for yourself, you have done and will do; and surely there are some others in the world who would not be sorry to be of use, if you would allow them to be useful or at least attempt it.

I think of being in England in the spring. If there is a row, by the sceptre of King Ludd, but I'll be there; and if there is none, and only a continuance of 'this meek, piping time of peace', I will take a cottage a hundred yards to the south of your abode, and become your neighbour; and we will compose such canticles, and hold such dialogues, as shall be the terror of the *Times* (including the newspaper of that name), and the wonder, and honour, and praise, of the *Morning Chronicle* and posterity.

I rejoice to hear of your forthcoming in February – though I tremble for the 'magnificence', which you attribute to the new *Childe Harold*. I am glad you like it; it is a fine indistinct piece of poetical desolation, and my favourite. I was half mad during the time of its composition, between metaphysics, mountains, lakes, love unextinguishable, thoughts unutterable, and the nightmare of my own delinquencies. I should, many a good day, have blown my brains out, but for the recollection that it would have given pleasure to my mother-in-law; and, even *then*, if I could have been certain to haunt her – but I won't dwell upon these trifling family matters.

Venice is in the *estro* of her carnival, and I have been up these

263

last two nights at the ridotto[10] and the opera, and all that kind of thing. Now for an adventure. A few days ago a gondolier brought me a billet without a subscription, intimating a wish on the part of the writer to meet me either in gondola or at the island of San Lazaro, or at a third rendezvous, indicated in the note. 'I know the country's disposition well' – in Venice 'they do let Heaven see those tricks they dare not show', etc., etc.; so, for all response, I said that neither of the three places suited me; but that I would either be at home at ten at night *alone*, or be at the ridotto at midnight, where the writer might meet me masked. At ten o'clock I was at home and alone (Marianna was gone with her husband to a conversazione),[11] when the door of my apartment opened, and in walked a well-looking and (for an Italian) *bionda* girl of about nineteen, who informed me that she was married to the brother of my *amorosa*, and wished to have some conversation with me. I made a decent reply, and we had some talk in Italian and Romaic (her mother being a Greek of Corfu), when lo! in a very few minutes, in marches, to my very great astonishment, Marianna Segati, *in propriâ personâ*, and after making a most polite courtesy to her sister-in-law and to me, without a single word seizes her said sister-in-law by the hair, and bestows upon her some sixteen slaps, which would have made your ear ache only to hear their echo. I need not describe the screaming which ensued. The luckless visitor took flight. I seized Marianna, who, after several vain efforts to get away in pursuit of the enemy, fairly went into fits in my arms; and, in spite of reasoning, eau de Cologne, vinegar, half a pint of water, and God knows what other waters beside, continued so till past midnight.

After damning my servants for letting people in without apprizing me, I found that Marianna in the morning had seen her sister-in-law's gondolier on the stairs, and, suspecting that his apparition boded her no good, had either returned of her own accord, or been followed by her maids or some other spy of her people to the conversazione, from whence she returned to perpetrate this piece of pugilism. I have seen fits before, and also some small scenery of the same genus in and out of our island:

but this was not all. After about an hour, in comes – who? why, Signor Segati, her lord and husband, and finds me with his wife fainting upon the sofa, and all the apparatus of confusion, dishevelled hair, hats, handkerchiefs, salts, smelling-bottles – and the lady as pale as ashes, without sense or motion. His first question was, 'What is all this?' The lady could not reply – so I did. I told him the explanation was the easiest thing in the world; but in the mean time it would be as well to recover his wife – at least, her senses. This came about in due time of suspiration and respiration.

You need not be alarmed – jealousy is not the order of the day in Venice, and daggers are out of fashion; while duels, on love matters, are unknown – at least, with the husbands. But, for all this, it was an awkward affair; and though he must have known that I made love to Marianna, yet I believe he was not, till that evening, aware of the extent to which it had gone. It is very well known that almost all the married women have a lover; but it is usual to keep up the forms, as in other nations. I did not, therefore, know what the devil to say. I could not out with the truth, out of regard to her, and I did not choose to lie for my sake; – besides, the thing told itself. I thought the best way would be to let her explain it as she chose (a woman being never at a loss – the devil always sticks by them) – only determining to protect and carry her off, in case of any ferocity on the part of the Signor. I saw that he was quite calm. She went to bed, and next day – how they settled it, I know not, but settle it they did. Well – then I had to explain to Marianna about this never-to-be-sufficiently-confounded sister-in-law; which I did by swearing innocence, eternal constancy, etc., etc . . . But the sister-in-law, very much discomposed with being treated in such wise, has (not having her own shame before her eyes) told the affair to half Venice, and the servants (who were summoned by the fight and the fainting) to the other half. But, here, nobody minds such trifles, except to be amused by them. I don't know whether you will be so, but I have scrawled a long letter out of these follies.

Believe me ever, etc.

TO THOMAS MOORE   *Venice, February 28, 1817*

You will, perhaps, complain as much of the frequency of my letters now, as you were wont to do of their rarity. I think this is the fourth within as many moons. I feel anxious to hear from you, even more than usual, because your last indicated that you were unwell. At present, I am on the invalid regimen myself. The Carnival – that is, the latter part of it, and sitting up late o'nights, had knocked me up a little. But it is over, – and it is now Lent, with all its abstinence and sacred music.

The mumming closed with a masked ball at the Fenice, where I went, as also to most of the ridottos, etc., etc.; and, though I did not dissipate much upon the whole, yet I find 'the sword wearing out the scabbard', though I have but just turned the corner of twenty-nine.

> So we'll go no more a roving
>   So late into the night,
> Though the heart be still as loving,
>   And the moon be still as bright...

... If I live ten years longer, you will see, however, that it is not over with me – I don't mean in literature, for that is nothing; and it may seem odd enough to say, I do not think it my vocation. But you will see that I shall do something or other – the times and fortune permitting – that, 'like the cosmogony, or creation of the world, will puzzle the philosophers of all ages'. But I doubt whether my constitution will hold out. I have, at intervals, ex*orc*ised it most devilishly ...

Pray let me hear from you, at your time and leisure, believing me ever and truly and affectionately, etc.

TO LADY BYRON[12]   *Venice, March 5ᵗʰ 1817.*

... Throughout the whole of this unhappy business, I have done my best to avoid the bitterness, which, however, is yet among us; and it would be as well if even you at times recollected, that the man who has been sacrificed in fame, in feelings, in every thing, to the convenience of your family, was he whom you once loved, and who – whatever you may imagine to the contrary – loved you. If you conceive that I could be actuated by revenge against you, you are mistaken: I am not humble enough to be vindictive. Irritated I may have been, and may be – is it a wonder? But upon such irritation, beyond its momentary expression, I have not acted, from the hour that you quitted me to that in which I am made aware that our daughter is to be made the entail of our discussion, the inheritor of our bitterness. If you think to reconcile yourself to yourself by accumulating harshness against me, you are again mistaken: you are not happy, nor even tranquil, nor will you ever be so, even to the moderate degree which is permitted to general humanity. For myself I have a confidence in my Fortune, which will yet bear me through. ταὐτόματον ἡμῶν κάλλιον βουλεύεται.[13] The reverses which have occurred, were what I should have expected; and, in considering you and yours merely as the instruments of my more recent adversity, it would be difficult for me to blame you, did not every thing appear to intimate a deliberate intention of as wilful malice on your part as could be well digested into a system. However, time and Nemesis will do that, which I could not, even were it in my power remote or immediate. You will smile at this piece of prophecy – do so, but recollect it: it is justified by all human experience. No one was ever even the involuntary cause of great evils to others, without a requital: I have paid and am paying for mine – so will you.

TO THOMAS MOORE   *Venice, March 25, 1817*

... I have not the least idea where I am going, nor what I am to do. I wished to have gone to Rome; but at present it is pestilent with English, – a parcel of staring boobies, who go about gaping and wishing to be at once cheap and magnificent. A man is a fool who travels now in France or Italy, till this tribe of wretches is swept home again. In two or three years the first rush will be over, and the Continent will be roomy and agreeable.

I stayed at Venice chiefly because it is not one of their 'dens of thieves'; and here they but pause and pass. In Switzerland it was really noxious. Luckily, I was early, and had got the prettiest place on all the Lake before they were quickened into motion with the rest of the reptiles. But they crossed me every where. I met a family of children and old women half-way up the Wengen Alp (by the Jungfrau) upon mules, some of them too old and others too young to be the least aware of what they saw ...

I have now written to you at least six letters, or letter*ets*, and all I have received in return is a note about the length you used to write from Bury Street to St James's Street, when we used to dine with Rogers, and talk laxly, and go to parties, and hear poor Sheridan now and then. Do you remember one night he was so tipsy, that I was forced to put his cocked hat on for him, – for he could not, – and I let him down at Brookes's, much as he must since have been let down into his grave. Heigh ho! I wish I was drunk – but I have nothing but this damned barley-water before me ...

The Italian ethics are the most singular ever met with. The perversion, not only of action, but of reasoning, is singular in the women. It is not that they do not consider the thing itself as wrong, and very wrong, but *love* (the *sentiment* of love) is not merely an excuse for it, but makes it an *actual virtue*, provided it is disinterested, and not a *caprice*, and is confined to one object. They have awful notions of constancy; for I have seen some ancient figures of eighty pointed out as *Amorosi* of forty, fifty, and sixty years' standing. I can't say I have ever seen a husband and wife so coupled.

Ever, etc.

P.S. – Marianna, to whom I have just translated what I have written on our subject to you, says – 'If you loved me thoroughly, you would not make so many fine reflections, which are only good *forbisi i scarpi*', – that is, 'to clean shoes withal', – a Venetian proverb of appreciation, which is applicable to reasoning of all kinds.

TO JOHN MURRAY   *Venice, April 2, 1817*

... I am aware of what you say of Otway; and am a very great admirer of his, – all except of that maudlin bitch of chaste lewdness and blubbering curiosity, Belvidera,[14] whom I utterly despise, abhor, and detest; but the story of Marino Falieri is different, and, I think, so much finer, that I wish Otway had taken it instead: the head conspiring against the body for refusal of redress for a real injury, – jealousy – treason, with the more fixed and inveterate passions (mixed with policy) of an old or elderly man – the devil himself could not have a finer subject, and he is your only tragic dramatist.

Voltaire has asked *why* no woman has ever written even a tolerable tragedy? 'Ah (said the Patriarch) the composition of a tragedy requires —.' If this be true, Lord knows what Joanna Baillie does; I suppose she borrows them.

There is still, in the Doge's Palace, the black veil painted over Falieri's picture, and the staircase whereon he was first crowned Doge, and subsequently decapitated. This was the thing that most struck my imagination in Venice – more than the Rialto, which I visited for the sake of Shylock; and more, too, than Schiller's '*Armenian*', a novel which took a great hold of me when a boy. It is also called the 'Ghost Seer', and I never walked down St Mark's by moonlight without thinking of it, and '*at nine o'clock he died*!' – But I hate things *all fiction*; and therefore the *Merchant* and *Othello* have no great associations for me: but *Pierre* has. There should always be some foundation of fact for the most airy fabric, and pure invention is but the talent of a liar ...

You talk of 'marriage'; – ever since my own funeral, the word makes me giddy, and throws me into a cold sweat. Pray, don't repeat it.

Tell me that Walter Scott is better; I would not have him ill for the world. I suppose it was by sympathy that I had my fever at the same time. I joy in the success of your *Quarterly*; but I must still stick by the *Edinburgh*. Jeffrey has done so by me, I must say, through everything, and this is more than I deserved from him ...

There have been two articles in the Venice papers, one a Review of C. Lamb's *Glenarvon* (whom may it please the beneficent Giver of all Good to damn in the next world! as she has damned herself in this) with the account of her scratching attempt at *Canicide* (at Lady Heathcote's), and the other a Review of *Childe Harold*, in which it proclaims me the most rebellious, and contumacious admirer of Buonaparte now surviving in Europe. Both these articles are translations from the Literary Gazette of German Jena. I forgot to mention them at the time; they are some weeks old. They actually mentioned Caro: Lamb and her *mother's* name at full length. I have conserved these papers as curiosities . . .

Yours ever,

B.

TO THE HON. AUGUSTA LEIGH   *Rome, May 10ᵗʰ 1817*

My Dearest Augusta, – . . . I am very well, quite recovered, and as is always the case after all illness – particularly fever – got large, ruddy, and robustous to a degree which would please you – and shock me. I have been on horseback several hours a day for this last ten days, besides now and then on my journey; proof positive of high health, and curiosity, and exercise. Love me – and don't be afraid – I mean of my sickness. I get well, and shall always get so, and have luck enough still to beat most things; and whether I win or not – depend upon it – I will fight to the last.

Will you tell my wife 'mine excellent Wife' that she is brewing a Cataract for herself and me in these foolish equivocations about *Ada*, – a job for lawyers – and more hatred for every body, for which – (God knows), there is no occasion. She is surrounded by people who detest me – Brougham the lawyer – who never forgave me for saying that Mʳˢ Gᵉ Lamb was a damned fool (by the way I did not then know he was in love with her) in 1814, and for a former savage note in my foolish satire, all which is good reason for *him* – but not for *Lady Bⁿ*; besides her mother – etc etc etc – so that what I may say or you may say is of no great use – however – *say it*. If she supposes that I want to hate or

270

plague her (however wroth circumstances at times may make me in words and in temporary gusts or disgusts of feeling), she is quite out – I have no such wish – and never had, and if she imagines that I now wish to become united to her again she is still more out. *I never will.* I *would* to the end of the *year* succeeding our separation – (expired nearly a month ago, *Legal reckoning*), according to a resolution I had taken thereupon – but the day and the hour is gone by – and it is irrevocable. But all this is no reason for further misery and quarrel; Give me but a *fair share* of my daughter – the half – my natural right and authority, and I am content; otherwise I come to England, and 'law and claw before they get it', all which will vex and out live Sir R. and L^y N. besides making Mrs Clermont bilious – and plaguing Bell herself, which I really by the great God! wish to avoid. Now pray see her and say so – it may do good – and if not – she and I are but what we are, and God knows that is wretched enough – at least to me.

Of Rome I say nothing – you can read the Guide-book – which is very accurate.

I found here an old letter of yours dated November 1816 – to which the best answer I can make – is none. You are sadly timid my child, but so you all shewed yourselves when you could have been useful – particularly [George Byron?] but never mind. I shall not forget *him*, though I do not rejoice in any ill which befalls him. Is the fool's spawn a *son* or a *daughter*? you say one – and others another; so Sykes works him – *let him* – I shall live to see him and W[ilmot?] destroyed, and more than them – and then – but let all that pass for the present.

yrs. ever

B.

P.S. Hobhouse is here. I travelled from V[enice] *quite alone* so do not fuss about women etc – I am not so rash as I have been.

TO JOHN MURRAY   *Venice, May 30, 1817*

... From Florence I sent you a poem on Tasso, and from Rome the new third act of *Manfred*, and by Dr Polidori two pictures for my sister. I left Rome, and made a rapid journey home. You will continue to direct here as usual. Mr Hobhouse is gone to Naples; I should have run down there too for a week, but for the quantity of English whom I heard of there. I prefer hating them at a distance; unless an earthquake, or a good real eruption of Vesuvius, were insured to reconcile me to their vicinity.

I know no other situation except Hell which I should feel inclined to participate with them – as a race, always excepting several individuals. There were few of them in Rome, and I believe none whom you know, except that old Blue-*bore* Sotheby, who will give a fine account of Italy, in which he will be greatly assisted by his total ignorance of Italian, and yet this is the translator of Tasso.

The day before I left Rome I saw three robbers guillotined. The ceremony – including the *masqued* priests; the half-naked executioners; the bandaged criminals; the black Christ and his banner; the scaffold; the soldiery; the slow procession, and the quick rattle and heavy fall of the axe; the splash of the blood, and the ghastliness of the exposed heads – is altogether more impressive than the vulgar and ungentlemanly dirty 'new drop', and dog-like agony of infliction upon the sufferers of the English sentence. Two of these men behaved calmly enough, but the first of the three died with great terror and reluctance, which was very horrible. He would not lie down; then his neck was too large for the aperture, and the priest was obliged to drown his exclamations by still louder exhortations. The head was off before the eye could trace the blow; but from an attempt to draw back the head, notwithstanding it was held forward by the hair, the first head was cut off close to the ears: the other two were taken off more cleanly. It is better than the oriental way, and (I should think) than the axe of our ancestors. The pain seems little; and yet the effect to the spectator, and the preparation to the criminal, are very striking and chilling. The first turned me quite hot and thirsty, and made me shake so that I could hardly hold the opera-glass (I was close, but determined to see, as one should, see every thing, once, with attention); the second and third (which shows how dreadfully soon things grow indifferent),

I am ashamed to say, had no effect on me as a horror, though I would have saved them if I could . . .

Yours ever truly,

B.

TO THE HON. AUGUSTA LEIGH   *Venice, June 3ᵈ 1817*

Dearest Augusta – I returned home a few days ago from Rome but wrote to you on the road; at Florence I believe, or Bologna. The last city you know – or do not know – is celebrated for the production of Popes – Cardinals – painters – and sausages – besides a female professor of anatomy,[15] who has left there many models of the art in waxwork, some of them not the most decent. – I have received all your letters I believe, which are full of woes, as usual, megrims and mysteries; but my sympathies remain in suspense, for, for the life of me I can't make out whether your disorder is a broken heart or the earache – or whether it is *you* that have been ill or the children – or what your melancholy and mysterious apprehensions tend to, or refer to, whether to Caroline Lamb's novels – Mʳˢ Clermont's evidence – Lady Byron's magnanimity[16] – or any other piece of imposture; I know nothing of what you are in the doldrums about at present. I should think all that could affect *you* must have been over long ago; and as for me – leave me to take care of myself. I may be ill or well – in high or low spirits – in quick or obtuse state of feelings – like any body else, but I can battle my way through; better than your exquisite piece of helplessness G[eorge] L[eigh], or that other poor creature George Byron, who will be finely helped up in a year or two with his new state of life – I should like to know what they would do in my situation, or in any situation. I wish well to your George, who is the best of the two a devilish deal – but as for the other I shan't forget him in a hurry, and if I ever forgive or allow an opportunity to escape of evincing my sense of his conduct (and of more than his) on a certain occasion – write me down – what you will, but do not suppose me asleep. 'Let them look to their bond' – sooner or later time and Nemesis will give me the ascendant – and then 'let them look to their bond'. I do not of course allude only to that poor wretch, but to all – to the 3^d and 4th generation of these accursed Amalekites and the woman who has been the stumbling block of my —

June 4th 1817

I left off yesterday at the stumbling block of my Midianite marriage – but having received your letter of the 20th May I will be in good humour for the rest of this letter. I had hoped you would like the miniatures, at least one of them, which is in pretty good health; the other is thin enough to be sure – and so was I – and in the ebb of a fever when I sate for it. By the 'man of fashion' I suppose you mean that poor piece of affectation and imitation Wilmot – another disgrace to me and mine – that fellow. I regret not having shot him, which the persuasions of others – and circumstances which at that time would have rendered combats presumptions against my cause – prevented. I wish you well of your indispositions which I hope are slight, or I should lose my senses.

Yours ever very and truly,

B.

TO THOMAS MOORE   *La Mira, Venice, July 10, 1817*

... Do you remember Thurlow's poem to Sam – '*When* Rogers'; and that damned supper at Rancliffe's that ought to have been a *dinner*? 'Ah, Master Shallow, we have heard the chimes at midnight'. But,

> My boat is on the shore,
>   And my bark is on the sea;
> But, before I go, Tom Moore,
>   Here's a double health to thee! ...

This should have been written fifteen moons ago – the first stanza was. I am just come out from an hour's swim in the Adriatic; and I write to you with a black-eyed Venetian girl before me, reading Boccaccio ...

Last week I had a row on the road (I came up to Venice from my casino,[17] a few miles on the Paduan road, this blessed day, to bathe) with a fellow in a carriage, who was impudent to my horse. I gave him a swingeing box on the ear, which sent him to the police, who dismissed his complaint. Witnesses had seen the transaction. He first shouted, in an unseemly way, to frighten my palfry. I wheeled round, rode up to the window, and asked him what he meant. He grinned, and said some foolery, which produced him an immediate slap in the face, to his utter discomfiture. Much blasphemy ensued, and some menace, which I stopped by dismounting and opening the carriage door, and intimating an intention of mending the road with his immediate remains, if he did not hold his tongue. He held it.

Monk Lewis is here – 'how pleasant!' He is a very good fellow, and very much yours. So is Sam – so is every body – and amongst the number,

Yours ever,

B.

P.S. – What think you of *Manfred*? ...

TO JOHN MURRAY   *September 15, 1817*

... The other day I wrote to convey my proposition with regard to the 4th and concluding canto. I have gone over and extended it to one hundred and fifty stanzas, which is almost as long as the first two were originally, and longer by itself than any of the smaller poems except *The Corsair*. Mr Hobhouse has made some very valuable and accurate notes of considerable length, and you may be sure I will do for the text all that I can to finish with decency. I look upon *Childe Harold* as my best; and as I begun, I think of concluding with it. But I make no resolutions on that head, as I broke my former intention with regard to *The Corsair*. However, I fear that I shall never do better; and yet, not being thirty years of age, for some moons to come, one ought to be progressive as far as Intellect goes for many a good year. But I have had a devilish deal of wear and tear of mind and body in my time, besides having published too often and much already.

275

God grant me some judgement! to do what may be most fitting in that and every thing else, for I doubt my own exceedingly ...

With regard to poetry in general, I am convinced, the more I think of it, that he[18] and *all* of us – Scott, Southey, Wordsworth, Moore, Cambell, I, – are all in the wrong, one as much as another; that we are upon a wrong revolutionary poetical system, or systems, not worth a damn in itself, and from which none but Rogers and Crabbe are free; and that the present and next generations will finally be of this opinion. I am the more confirmed in this by having lately gone over some of our classics, particularly *Pope*, whom I tried in this way – I took Moore's poems and my own and some others, and went over them side by side with Pope's, and I was really astonished (I ought not to have been so) and mortified at the ineffable distance in point of sense, harmony, effect, and even *Imagination*, passion, and *Invention*, between the little Queen Anne's man, and us of the Lower Empire. Depend upon it, it is all Horace then, and Claudian now, among us; and if I had to begin again, I would model myself accordingly. Crabbe's the man, but he has got a coarse and impracticable subject, and Rogers, the Grandfather of living Poetry, is retired upon half-pay, (I don't mean as a Banker), –

> Since pretty Miss Jaqueline,
> With her nose aquiline,

and has done enough, unless he were to do as he did formerly...

TO THE HON. DOUGLAS KINNAIRD *Venice, November 19, 1817*

Dear Douglas, – Inferring that you are by this time in England again, I assail you on the old subject; to tell you that since your departure I have never heard from the Hansons, from which I infer that Newstead is not likely to be sold, and that I am one degree further in the latitude of hell.

Except a fooling and perplexing passage in a letter of Mrs Leigh's, I have not heard one word more upon the subject at all, and as her way of putting the most common things is more like a riddle than anything else, I can only say that I am farther than ever from understanding her – or it – or Hanson – or anything or anybody; and unless you take compassion upon me, and give me a little common sense, I shall remain in the ignorance and anxiety of the last two months upon the same topic.

If you see Augusta give my love to her, and tell her that I do not write because I really and truly do not understand one single word of her letters. To answer them is out of the question, I don't say it out of ill-nature, but whatever be the subject, there is so much paraphrase, parenthesis, initials, dashes, hints – and what Lord Ogleby calls 'Mr Sterling's damned crinkum crankum', that, sunburn me! if I know what the meaning or no meaning is, and am obliged to study Armenian as a relief . . .

Yours ever and truly,

B.

Byron's Dedication of *Childe Harold's Pilgrimage*.
TO JOHN HOBHOUSE, ESQ., A.M., F.R.S., &C.&C.&C.
Venice, January 2, 1818.

MY DEAR HOBHOUSE,
After an interval of eight years between the composition of the first and last cantos of Childe Harold, the conclusion of the poem is about to be submitted to the public. In parting with so old a friend, it is not extraordinary that I should recur to one still older and better, – to one who has beheld the birth and death of the other, and to whom I am far more indebted for the social advantages of an enlightened friendship, than – though not ungrateful – I can, or could be, to Childe Harold, for any public favour reflected through the poem on the poet, – to one, whom I have known long and accompanied far, whom I have found wakeful over my sickness and kind in my sorrow, glad in my prosperity and firm in my adversity, true in counsel and trusty in peril, – to a friend often tried and never found wanting; – to yourself.

In so doing, I recur from fiction to truth; and in dedicating to you in its complete, or at least concluded state, a poetical work which is the longest, the most thoughtful and comprehensive of my compositions, I wish to do honour to myself by the record of many years' intimacy with a man of learning, of talent, of steadiness, and of honour. It is not for minds like ours to give or to receive flattery; yet the praises of sincerity have ever been permitted to the voice of friendship; and it is not for you, nor even for others, but to relieve a heart which has not elsewhere, or lately, been so much accustomed to the encounter of good-will as to withstand the shock firmly, that I thus attempt to commemorate your good qualities, or rather the advantages which I have derived from their exertion. Even the recurrence of the date of this letter, the anniversary of the most unfortunate day of my past existence,[19] but which cannot poison my future while I retain the resource of your friendship, and of my own faculties, will henceforth have a more agreeable recollection for both, inasmuch as it will remind us of this my attempt to thank you for an indefatigable regard, such as few men have experienced, and no one could experience without thinking better of his species and of himself . . .

. Wishing you, my dear Hobhouse, a safe and agreeable return to that country whose real welfare can be dearer to none than to yourself, I dedicate to you this poem in its completed state; and repeat once more how truly I am ever

Your obliged and affectionate friend,

BYRON

TO JOHN MURRAY   *Venice, January 27, 1818*

. . . It is the height of the Carnival, and I am in the *estrum* and agonies of a new intrigue with I don't exactly know whom or what, except that she is insatiate of love, and won't take money, and has light hair and blue eyes, which are not common here, and that I met her at the Masque, and that when her mask is off, I am as wise as ever. I shall make what I can of the remainder of my youth, and confess, that like Augustus, I would rather die *standing*.

B.

TO THOMAS MOORE   *Venice, February 2, 1818*

... Your domestic calamity[20] is very grievous, and I feel with
you as much as I *dare* feel at all. Throughout life, your loss must
be my loss, and your gain my gain; and though my heart may
ebb, there will always be a drop for you among the dregs. I know
how to feel with you, because (selfishness being always the
substratum of our damnable clay) I am quite wrapt up in my own
children. Besides my little legitimate, I have made unto myself
an *il*-legitimate since (to say nothing of one before), and I look
forward to one of these as the pillar of my old age, supposing
that I ever reach – which I hope I never shall – that desolating
period. I have a great love for my little Ada, though perhaps she
may torture me like — ...

TO JOHN MURRAY   *Venice, Feb. 20, 1818*

... What you tell me of Rogers in your last letter is like him;
but he had best let *us*, that is one of us, if not both, alone. He
cannot say that I have not been a sincere and a warm friend to
him, till the black drop of his liver oozed through, too palpably
to be overlooked. Now, if I once catch him at any of his jugglery
with me or mine, let him look to it, for, if I spare him then,
write me down a good-natured gentleman; and the more that I
have been deceived, – the more that I once relied upon him, – I
don't mean his petty friendship (what is that to me?), but his
good will, which I really tried to obtain, thinking him at first a
good fellow, – the more will I pay off the balance; and so, if he
values his quiet, let him look to it; in three months I could re-
store him to the Catacombs ...

Yours,

B.

TO THOMAS MOORE   *Venice, March 16, 1818*

My Dear Tom, – ... The other day I was telling a girl, 'You must
not come to-morrow, because Margueritta [Cogni] is coming at

such a time', – (they are both about five feet ten inches high, with great black eyes and fine figures – fit to breed gladiators from – and I had some difficulty to prevent a battle upon a rencontre once before) – 'unless you promise to be friends, and' – the answer was an interruption, by a declaration of war against the other, which she said would be a *Guerra di Candia*.[21] Is it not odd, that the lower order of Venetians should still allude proverbially to that famous contest, so glorious and so fatal to the Republic?

. . . Have you ever seen – I forget what or whom – no matter. They tell me Lady Melbourne is very unwell. I shall be so sorry. She was my greatest *friend*, of the feminine gender: – when I say 'friend', I mean *not* mistress, for that's the antipode. Tell me all about you and everybody – how Sam is – how you like your neighbours, the Marquis and Marchesa, etc., etc.

Ever, etc.

TO JOHN MURRAY   *April 23, 1818*

Dear Sir, – The time is past in which I could feel for the dead, – or I should feel for the death of Lady Melbourne, the best, and kindest, and ablest female I ever knew – old or young. But 'I have supped full of horrors', and events of this kind leave only a kind of numbness worse than pain, – like a violent blow on the elbow, or on the head. There is one link the less between England and myself . . .

If your literary matters prosper, let me know. If *Beppo* pleases, you shall have more in a year or two in the same mood. And so 'Good morrow to you, good Master Lieutenant'.

Yours,

                                                             B.

TO JOHN CAM HOBHOUSE[22]   *Venice, June, 1818*

Sir, – With great grief I inform you of the death of my late dear Master, my Lord, who died this morning at ten of the Clock of a rapid decline and slow fever, caused by anxiety, sea-bathing, women, and riding in the Sun against my advice.

He is a dreadful loss to every body, mostly to me, who have lost a master and a place, – also, I hope you, Sir, will give me a charakter.

I saved in his service as you know several hundred pounds. God knows how, for I don't, nor my late master neither; and if my wage was not always paid to the day, still it was or is to be paid sometime and somehow. You, Sir, who are his executioner won't see a poor Servant wronged of his little all.

My dear Master had several phisicians and a Priest: he died a Papish, but is to be buried among the Jews in the Jewish burying ground; for my part I don't see why – he could not abide them when living nor any other people, hating whores who asked him for money.

He suffered his illness with great patience, except that when in extremity he twice damned his friends and said they were selfish rascals – you, Sir, particularly and Mr Kinnaird, who had never answered his letters nor complied with his repeated requests. He also said he hoped that your new tragedy would be damned – God forgive him – I hope that my master won't be damned like the tragedy.

His nine whores are already provided for, and the other servants; but what is to become of me? I have got his Cloathes and Carriages, and Cash, and everything; but the Consul quite against law has clapt his seal and taken an inventary and swears that *he* must account for my Lord's heirs – who they are, I don't know – but they ought to consider poor Servants and above all his Vally de Sham.

My Lord never grudged me perquisites – my wage was the least I got by him; and if I did keep the Countess (she is, or ought to be, a Countess, although she is upon the town) Marietta Monetta Piretta, after passing my word to you and my Lord that I would not never no more – still he was an indulgent master, and only said I was a damned fool, and swore and forgot it again. What could I do? she said as how she should die, or kill herself if I did not go with her, and so I did – and kept her out of my

Lord's washing and ironing – and nobody can deny that, although the charge was high, the linen was well got up.

Hope you are well, Sir – am, with tears in my eyes,

Yours faithfoolly to command,

Wm FLETCHER

P.S. – If you know any Gentleman in want of a Wally – hope for a charakter. I saw your late Swiss Servant in the Galleys at Leghorn for robbing an Inn – he produced your recommendation at his trial.

TO THOMAS MOORE *Palazzo Mocenigo, Grande Canal, Venice, June 1, 1818*

... Hunt's letter is probably the exact piece of vulgar cox-combry you might expect from his situation. He is a good man, with some poetical elements in his chaos; but spoilt by the Christ-Church Hospital and a Sunday newspaper, – to say nothing of the Surrey gaol, which conceited him into a martyr. But he is a good man. When I saw *Rimini* in MS., I told him that I deemed it good poetry at bottom, disfigured only by a strange style. His answer was, that his style was a system, or *upon system*, or some such cant; and, when a man talks of system, this case is hopeless; so I said no more to him, and very little to any one else.

He believes his trash of vulgar phrases tortured into compound barbarisms to be *old* English; and we may say of it as Aimwell says of Captain Gibbet's regiment,[23] when the Captain calls it an 'old corps', – 'the *oldest* in Europe, if I may judge by your uniform'. He sent out his *Foliage* by Percy Shelley ..., and, of all the ineffable Centaurs that were ever begotten by Self-love upon a Night-mare, I think 'this monstrous Sagittary' the most prodigious. *He* (Leigh H.) is an honest charlatan, who has persuaded himself into a belief of his own impostures, and talks Punch in pure simplicity of heart, taking himself (as poor Fitzgerald said of *him*self in the *Morning Post*) for *Vates*[24] in both senses, or nonsenses, of the word. Did you look at the

282

translations of his own which he prefers to Pope and Cowper, and says so? – Did you read his skimble-skamble about Wordsworth being at the head of his own *profession*, in the *eyes* of *those* who followed it? I thought that the poetry was an *art*, or an *attribute*, and not a *profession*; – but be it one, is that — at the head of *your* profession in *your* eyes? I'll be curst if he is of *mine*, or ever shall be. He is the only one of us (but of us he is not) whose coronation I would oppose. Let them take Scott, Campbell, Crabbe, or you, or me, or any of the living, and throne him; – but not this new Jacob Behmen, this — whose pride might have kept him true, even had his principles turned as perverted as his *soi-disant* poetry.

But Leigh Hunt is a good man, and a good father – see his Odes to all the Masters Hunt; – a good husband – see his Sonnet to Mrs Hunt; – a good friend – see his Epistles to different people; – and a great coxcomb and a very vulgar person in every thing about him. But that's not his fault, but of circumstances . . .

I do not know any good model for a life of Sheridan but that of *Savage*.[25] Recollect, however, that the life of such a man may be made far more amusing than if he had been a Wilberforce; – and this without offending the living, or insulting the dead. The Whigs abuse him; however, he never left them, and such blunderers deserve neither credit nor compassion. – As for his creditors, – remember, Sheridan *never had* a shilling, and was thrown, with great powers and passions into the thick of the world, and placed upon the pinnacle of success, with no other external means to support him in his elevation. Did Fox — *pay his* debts? – or did Sheridan take a subscription? Was the —'s drunkenness more excusable than his? Were his intrigues more notorious than those of all his contemporaries? and is his memory to be blasted, and theirs respected? Don't let yourself be led away by clamour, but compare him with the coalitioner Fox, and the pensioner Burke, as a man of principle, and with ten hundred thousand in personal views, and with none in talent, for he beat them all *out* and *out*. Without means, without connexion, without character, (which might be false at first, and make him mad afterwards from desperation,) he beat them all, in all he ever attempted. But alas, poor human nature! Good night or rather, morning. It is four, and the dawn gleams over the Grand Canal, and unshadows the Rialto. I must to bed; up all night – but as George Philpot[26] says, 'it's life, though, damme it's life!'

Ever yours,

B.

Excuse errors – not time for revision. The post goes out at noon, and I shan't be up then . . .

TO THE HON. DOUGLAS KINNAIRD   *Venice, July 15th, 1818*

Dear Douglas, – . . . Murray's letters and the credits are come, laud we the Gods! If I did not know of old, Wildman[27] to be a Man of honour, and Spooney[28] a damned tortoise in all his proceeds, I should suspect foul play in this delay of the man and papers; now that your politics are a little subsided, for God his sake, row the man of law, spur him, kick him on the Crickle, do something, any thing, you are my power of Attorney, and I thereby empower you to use it and abuse Hanson, till the fellow says or does something as a gentleman should do . . .

I have lately had a long swim (beating an Italian all to bubbles) of more than four miles, from Lido to the other end of the Grand Canal, that is the part which enters from Mestri. I won by a good three quarters of a mile, but as many quarters of an hour, knocking the Chevalier[29] up, and coming in myself quite fresh; the fellow had swum the Beresina in the Bonaparte Campaign, and thought of coping with 'our Youth', but it would not do.

Give my love to Scrope and the rest of us ragmuffins, and believe me yours ever and truly,

BYRON

Pray look very sharp after Spooney; I have my suspicions, my suspicions, Sir, my Suspicions.

TO THOMAS MOORE   *Venice, September 19, 1818*

... I suppose you are a violent admirer of England by your staying so long in it. For my own part, I have passed, between the age of one-and-twenty and thirty, half the intervenient years out of it without regretting any thing, except that I ever returned to it at all, and the gloomy prospect before me of business and parentage obliging me, one day, to return to it again, – at least for the transaction of affairs, the signing of papers, and inspecting of children.

I have here my natural daughter, by name Allegra, – a pretty little girl enough, and reckoned like papa. Her mamma is English, – but it is a long story, and – there's an end. She is about twenty months old ...

I have finished the first canto (a long one, of about 180 octaves) of a poem in the style and manner of *Beppo*, encouraged by the good success of the same. It is called *Don Juan*, and is meant to be a little quietly facetious upon everything. But I doubt whether it is not – at least, as far as it has yet gone – too free for these very modest days. However, I shall try the experiment, anonymously; and if it don't take, it will be discontinued. It is dedicated to Southey in good, simple, savage verse, upon the Laureat's politics, and the way he got them. But the bore of copying it out is intolerable; and if I had an amanuensis he would be of use, as my writing is so difficult to decipher ... I wish you good night, with a Venetian benediction, '*Benedetto te, e la terra che ti fara!*' – 'May you be blessed, and the *earth* which you will *make!*' – is it not pretty? You would think it still prettier if you had heard it, as I did two hours ago, from the lips of a Venetian girl, with large black eyes, a face like Faustina's, and the figure of a Juno – tall and as energetic as a Pythoness, with eyes flashing, and her dark hair streaming in the moonlight – one of those women who may be made any thing. I am sure if I put a poniard into the hand of this one, she would plunge it where I told her – and into *me*, if I offended her. I like this kind of animal, and I am sure that I should have preferred Medea to any woman that breathed. You may wonder that I don't in that case ... I could have forgiven the dagger or the bowl, – any thing, but the deliberate desolation piled upon me, when I stood alone upon my hearth, with my household gods shivered around me. — Do you suppose I have forgotten it? It has comparatively swallowed up in me every other feeling, and I am only a spectator upon earth, till a tenfold opportunity offers. It may come yet. There are others more to be blamed than —, and it is on these that my eyes are fixed unceasingly. . .

TO THE HON. AUGUSTA LEIGH   *Venice, Sep^tr 21st 1818*

Dearest Augusta, –

. . . If the Queen dies you are no more a Maid of Honour – is it not so? Allegra is well, but her mother (whom the Devil confound) came prancing the other day over the Appennines – to see her *child*; which threw my Venetian loves (who are none of the quietest) into great combustion; and I was in a pucker till I got her to the Euganean hills, where she and the child now are, for the present. I declined seeing her for fear that the consequence might be an addition to the family; she is to have the child a month with her and then to return herself to Lucca, or Naples, where she was with her relatives (she is English you know), and to send Allegra to Venice again. I lent her my house at Este for her maternal holidays. As troubles don't come single, here is another confusion. The chaste wife of a baker – having quarrelled with her tyrannical husband – has run away *to* me (God knows without being invited), and resists all the tears and penitence and beg-pardons of her disconsolate Lord, and the threats of the police, and the priest of the parish besides; and swears she won't give up her unlawful love (myself), for any body, or any thing. I assure you I have begged her in all possible ways too to go back to her husband, promising her all kinds of eternal fidelity into the bargain, but she only flies into a fury; and as she is a very tall and formidable Girl of three and twenty, with the large black eyes and handsome face of a pretty fiend, a correspondent figure and a carriage as haughty as a Princess – with the violent passions and capacities for mischief of an Italian when they are roused – I am a little embarrassed with my unexpected acquisition. However she keeps my household in rare order, and has already frightened the learned Fletcher out of his remnants of wits more than once; we have turned her into a housekeeper. As the morals of this place are very lax, all the women commend her and say she has done right – especially her own relations. You need not be alarmed – I know how to manage her – and can deal with anything but a cold blooded animal such as Miss Milbanke. The worst is that she won't let a woman come into the house, unless she is old and frightful as possible; and has sent so many to the right about that my former female acquaintances are equally frightened and angry. She is extremely fond of the child, and is very cheerful and good-natured, when not jealous; but Othello himself was a fool to her in that respect. Her soubriquet in her family was *la Mora* from her colour, as she is very dark (though clear of complexion), which literally means *the Moor* so that I have 'the Moor of Venice' in propria persona as part of my household. She has been here this month. I had known her (and fifty others) more than a year, but did not anticipate this escapade, which was the fault of her booby husband's treatment – who now runs about repenting and roaring like a bull calf. I told him to take her in the devil's name, but she would not stir; and made him a long speech in the Venetian dialect which was more entertaining to anybody than to him to whom it was addressed. You see Goose – that there is no quiet in this world – so be a good woman – and repent of y^r sins.

TO LADY BYRON   *Venice, Novr 18th 1818*

Sir Samuel Romilly has cut his throat for the loss of his wife. It is now exactly three years since he became, in the face of his compact (by a retainer – previous, and I believe, general), the advocate of the measures and the Approver of the proceedings, which deprived me of mine. I would not exactly, like Mr Thwackum, when Philosopher Square bit his own tongue – 'saddle him with a Judgement';[30] but

>   This even-handed Justice
> Commends the ingredients of our poisoned Chalice
> To our own lips.

This Man little thought, when he was lacerating my heart according to law, while he was poisoning my life at its sources, aiding and abetting in the blighting, branding, and exile that was to be the result of his counsels in their indirect effects, that in less than thirty-six moons – in the pride of his triumph as the highest candidate for the representation of the Sister-City of the mightiest of Capitals – in the fullness of his professional career – in the greenness of a healthy old age – in the radiance of fame, and the complacency of self-earned riches – that a domestic affliction would lay him in the earth, with the meanest of male-factors, in a cross-road with the stake in his body. if the verdict of insanity did not redeem his ashes from the sentence of the laws he had lived upon by interpreting or misinterpreting, and died in violating.

This man had eight children, lately deprived of their mother: could he not live? Perhaps, previous to his annihilation, he felt a portion of what he contributed his legal mite to make me feel; but I have lived – lived to see him a Sexagenary Suicide.

It was not in vain that I invoked Nemesis in the midnight of Rome from the awfullest of her ruins.

Fare you well.

B.

TO JOHN CAM HOBHOUSE AND   *Venice, January 19th, 1819*
THE HON. DOUGLAS KINNAIRD

Dear H. and Dear K., – I approve and sanction all your legal proceedings with regard to my affairs, and can only repeat my thanks and approbation. If you put off the payments of debts 'till *after* Lady Noel's death', it is well; if till *after* her damnation, better, for that will last for ever; yet I hope not; for her sake as well as the creditors I am willing to believe in purgatory.

With regard to the Poeshie, I will have no 'cutting and slash-ing', as Perry calls it; you may omit the stanzas on Castlereagh,

indeed it is better, and the two '*Bobs*' at the end of the 3rd
stanza of the dedication, which will leave 'high' and 'a-dry'
good rhymes without any '*double* (or single) entendre', but no
more. I appeal, not 'to Philip fasting', but to Alexander drunk;
I appeal to Murray at his ledger, to the people, in short, Don
Juan shall be an entire horse, or none. If the objection be to the
indecency, the Age which applauds the 'Bath Guide', and
Little's poems, and reads Fielding and Smollett still, may bear
with that. If to the poetry, I will take my chance. I will not give
away to all the cant of Christendom. I have been cloyed with
applause, and sickened with abuse; at present I care for little
but the copy-right; I have imbibed a great love for money, let
me have it; if Murray loses this time, he won't the next; he will
be cautious, and I shall learn the decline of his customers by his
epistolary indications. But in no case will I submit to have the
poem mutilated. There is another Canto written, but not copied,
in two hundred and odd Stanzas, if this succeeds; as to the
prudery of the present day, what is it? Are we more moral than
when Prior wrote? Is there anything in 'Don Juan' so strong as
in Ariosto, or Voltaire, or Chaucer? . . .

So Lauderdale has been telling a story! I suppose this is my
reward for presenting him at the Countess Benzoni's and show-
ing him what attention I could. Which 'piece' does he mean?
Since last year I have run the gauntlet. Is it the Tarruscelli – the
Da Mosto – the Spinola – the Lotti – the Mizzato – the Eleanora
– the Carlotta – the Giulietta – the Aloisi – the Gambieri – the
Eleanora da Bezzi (who was the King of Naples' Gioachino's
mistress – at least one of them) – the Theresina of Mazzurati –
the Glettenheim and her sister – the Luigia and her mother –
the Fornaretta – the Santa – the Caligara – the Portiera Vedova
– the Bolognese figurante – the Tintora and her sister – cum
multis aliis:[31] Some of them are countesses and some of them
cobbler's wives, some noble, some middling, some low, and all
whores. Which does the damned old 'Ladro and porco fottuto'
mean?[32] Since *he* tells a story about me, I will tell one about
him. When he landed at the *Custom House* from Corfu, he called
for '*Post horses, directly*'. He was told that there were no horses

except mine nearer than Lido, unless he wished for the four bronze coursers of St Mark, which *were at his service*.

I am, yours ever,

B.

... P.S. – Whatever brain-money you get on my account from Murray, pray remit me. I will never consent to pay away what I *earn*. That is *mine*, and what I get by my brains I will spend on *my* b—ks, as long as I have a tester or a [testicle] remaining. I shall not live long, and for that reason I must live while I can. So let him disburse, and me receive. 'For the night cometh'. If I had but had twenty thousand a year I should not have been living now. But all men are not born with a silver or gold spoon in their mouths. My balance also – my balance – and a copyright. I have another Canto, too, ready; and then there will be my half year in June. Recollect I care for nothing but 'monies'.

TO THE HON. DOUGLAS KINNAIRD *Venice, January 27th, 1819*

My Dear Douglas, – I have received a very clever letter from Hobhouse against the publication of 'Don Juan', in which I understand you have acquiesced (you be damned). I acquiesce too, but reluctantly ...

I say, that as for fame and all that, it is for such persons as Fortune chooses – and so is money. And so on account of this damned prudery, and the reviews, and an outcry, and posterity, a gentleman who has 'a proper regard for his fee' is to be curtailed of his '*darics*' (I am reading about Greece and Persia). This comes of consulting friends. I will see all damned before I consult you again. What do you mean now by giving advice when you are asked for it? ...

Yours ever,

B.

P.S. Give my love to Frere, and tell him he is right, but I will never forgive him, or any of you.

TO JOHN CAM HOBHOUSE   *Venice, April 6th, 1819*

My Dear Hobhouse, – I have not derived from the Scriptures of Rochefoucault that consolation which I expected 'in the misfortunes of our best friends' . . .

I have sent my second Canto; but I will have no gelding. Murray has my order of the day. Douglas Kinnaird with more than usual politeness writes me vivaciously that Hanson or I willed the *three per cent*, instead of the five – as if I could prefer *three* to *five* per cent! – death and fiends! – and then *he* lifts up his leg against the publication of Don Juan. 'Et tu *Brute*' (*the e mute* recollect). I shall certainly hitch our dear friend into some d—d story or other, 'my dear, Mr Sneer – Mr Sneer – my dear'. I must write again in a few days, it being now past four in the morning; it is Passion week, and rather dull. I am dull too, for I have fallen in love with a Romagnola Countess from Ravenna,[33] who is nineteen years old, and has a Count of fifty – whom she seems disposed to qualify, the first year of marriage being just over. I knew her a little last year at her starting, but they always wait a year, at least generally. I met her first at the Albrizzi's, and this spring at the Benzona's – and I have hopes, sir, – hopes, but she wants me to come to Ravenna, and then to Bologna. Now this would be all very well for certainties; but for mere hopes; if she should plant me, and I should make a 'fiasco', never could I show my face on the Piazza. It is nothing that money can do, for the Conte is awfully rich, and would be so even in England, – but he is fifty and odd; has had two wives and children before this his third (a pretty fair-haired girl last year out of a convent; now making her second tour of the Venetian Conversazioni) and does not seem so jealous this year as he did last – when he stuck close to her side – even at the Governor's.

She is pretty, but has no tact; answers aloud, when she should whisper – talks of age to old ladies who want to pass for young; and this blessed night horrified a correct company at the Benzona's, by calling out to me '*mio Byron*' in an audible key, during a dead silence of pause in the other prattlers, who stared and whispered their respective *serventi*. One of her preliminaries is that I must never leave Italy. I have no desire to leave it, but I should not like to be frittered down into a regular Cicisbeo. What shall I do? I am in love, and tired of promiscuous concubinage, and have now an opportunity of settling for life.

Yours,

B.

TO THE HON. DOUGLAS KINNAIRD *Venice, April 24th, 1819*

Dear Douglas, –

> When that the Captain came for to know it
> He very much applauded what she had done

and I only want to command 'of the gallant Thunder Bomb' to make you my 'first Lieutenant'. I meant 'five thousand pounds' and never intend to have so much meaning again. In short, I refer you Gentlemen to my original letter of instructions which, by the blessing of God, seems to bear as many constructions as a Delphic Oracle; I say I refer you to that when you are at a loss how to avoid paying my money away; I hate paying and you are quite right to encourage me. As to Hanson & *Son*, I make no distinctions – it would be a sort of blasphemy – I should as soon think of untwisting the Trinity. What do they mean by separate bills? With regard to the Rochdale suit – and the 'large discretion' or Indiscretion of 'a thousand pounds' – what could I do? I want to gain my suit; but I will be guided by you. If you think 'pounds Scottish' will do better, let me know – I am docile. Pray what could make Farebrother say that Seventeen thousand pounds had been hidden for the undisputed part of Rochdale manor? It may be so, but I never heard of it before, not even from Spooney. If anybody bids, take it, and send it to me by post; but don't pay away to those low people of tradesmen. They may survive Lady Noel, or me, and get it from the executors and heirs. But I don't approve of any living liquidations – a damned deal too much has been paid already – the fact is that the villains owe me money – and not I to them ...

Yours ever,

B.

TO THE COUNTESS GUICCIOLI[34]   *Venice, 25th April, 1819*

My Love, – I hope you have received my letter of the 22nd, addressed to the person in Ravenna of whom you told me, before leaving Venice. You scold me for not having written to you in the country – but – how could I? My sweetest treasure, you gave me no other address but that of Ravenna. If you knew how great is the love I feel for you, you would not believe me capable of forgetting you for a single instant; you must become better acquainted with me. Perhaps one day you will know that, although I do not deserve you, I do indeed love you.

You want to know whom I most enjoy seeing, since you have gone away? who makes me tremble and feel – not what you alone can arouse in my soul – but something like it? Well, I will tell you – it is the *old porter* whom Fanny[35] used to send with your notes when you were in Venice, and who now brings your letters – still dear, but not so dear as those which brought the hope of seeing you that same day at the usual time. My Teresa, where are you? Everything here reminds me of you, everything is the same, but you are not here and I still am. In separation the one who goes away suffers less than the one who stays behind. The distraction of the journey, the change of scene, the landscape, the movement, perhaps even the separation, distracts the mind and lightens the heart. But the One who stays behind is surrounded by the same things, tomorrow as yesterday, while only that is lacking which made me forget that a tomorrow would ever come. When I go to the Conversazione I give myself up to tedium, too happy to suffer ennui, rather than grief. I see the same faces – hear the same voices – but no longer dare to look towards the sofa where I shall not see *you* any more, but instead some old crone who might be Calumny personified. I hear, without the slightest emotion, the opening of that door which I used to watch with so much anxiety when I was there before you, hoping to see you come in. I will not speak of *much dearer* places still, for *there* I shall not go – unless you return; I have no other pleasure than thinking of you, but I do not see how I could see again the places where we have been together – especially those most consecrated to our love – without dying of grief.

Fanny is now in Treviso, and God knows when I shall have any more letters from you; but meanwhile I have received three; you must by now have arrived in Ravenna – I long to hear of your arrival; my fate depends upon your decision. Fanny will be back in a few days; but tomorrow I shall send her a note by a friend's hand to ask her not to forget to send me your news, if she receives any letters before returning to Venice.

My Treasure, my life has become most monotonous and sad; neither books, nor music, nor *horses* (rare things in Venice – but you know that mine are at the Lido), nor dogs, give me any pleasure; the society of women does not attract me; I won't speak of the society of men, for that I have always despised. For some years I have been trying systematically to avoid strong passions, having suffered too much from the tyranny of Love. *Never to feel* admiration – and to enjoy myself without giving too much importance to the enjoyment in itself – to feel indifference toward human affairs – contempt for many – but hatred for none, this was the basis of my philosophy. I did not mean to love any more, nor did I hope to receive Love. You have put to flight all my resolutions; now I am all yours; I will become what you wish – perhaps happy in your love, but never at peace again. You should not have re-awakened my heart, for (at least in my own country) my love has been fatal to those I love – and to myself. But these reflections come too late. You have been mine – and whatever the outcome – I am, and eternally shall be, entirely yours. I kiss you a thousand and a thousand times – but –

> Che giova a te, cor mio, l'esser amato?
> Che giova a me l'aver si caro amante?
> Perchè crudo destino –
> Ne disunisci tu s' Amor ne stringe?[36]

Love me – as always your tender and faithful,

B.

TO JOHN MURRAY   *Venice, May 15, 1819*

Dear Sir, – I have received and return by this post, under another Cover, the first proof of *Don Juan*. Before the Second can arrive, it is probable that I may have left Venice, and the length of my absence is so uncertain, that you had better proceed to the publication without boring me with more proofs. I send by last post an addition – and a new copy of 'Julia's Letter' . . .

Mr Hobhouse is at it again about indelicacy. There is *no indelicacy*; if he wants *that*, let him read Swift, his great Idol; but his Imagination must be a dunghill, with a Viper's nest in the middle, to engender such a supposition about this poem. For my part, I think you are all crazed . . . Request him not 'to put me in a phrenzy', as Sir Anthony Absolute says, 'though he was not the indulgent father that I am' . . .[37]

The story of Shelley's agitation is true.[38] I can't tell what seized him, for he don't want courage. He was once with me in a gale of Wind, in a small boat, right under the rocks between Meillerie and St Gingo. We were five in the boat – a servant, two boatmen, and ourselves. The sail was mismanaged, and the boat was filling fast. He can't swim. I stripped off my coat – made him strip off his and take hold of an oar, telling him that I thought (being myself an expert swimmer) I could save him, if he would not struggle when I took hold of him – unless we got smashed against the rocks, which were high and sharp, with an awkward surf on them at that minute. We were then about a hundred yards from shore, and the boat in peril. He answered me with the greatest coolness, that 'he had no notion of being saved, and that I would have enough to do to save myself, and begged not to trouble me'. Luckily, the boat righted, and, baling, we got round a point into St Gingo, where the inhabitants came down and embraced the boatmen on their escape, the Wind having been high enough to tear up some huge trees from the Alps above us, as we saw next day.

And yet the same Shelley, who was as cool as it was possible to be in such circumstances, (of which I am no judge myself, as the chance of swimming naturally gives self possession when near shore), certainly had the fit of phantasy which Polidori describes though *not exactly* as he describes it.

The story of the agreement to write the Ghost-books is true but the ladies are *not* sisters. One is Godwin's daughter by Mary

Wolstonecraft, and the other the *present* Mrs Godwin's daughter by a former husband. So much for Scoundrel Southey's story of 'incest'; neither was there *any promiscuous intercourse* whatever. Both are an invention of that execrable villain Southey, whom I will term so as publicly as he deserves. Mary Godwin (now Mrs Shelley) wrote *Frankenstein*, which you have reviewed, thinking it Shelley's. Methinks it is a wonderful work for a girl of nineteen, – *not* nineteen, indeed at that time . . .

I am yours very truly,

B.

TO THE HON. AUGUSTA LEIGH (?)[39] *Venice*
[*Monday*], *May 17ᵗʰ 1819*

My Dearest Love, – I have been negligent in not writing, but what can I say? Three years absence – and the total change of scene and habit make such a difference – that we have now nothing in common but our affections and our relationship. –

But I have never ceased nor can cease to feel for a moment that perfect and boundless attachment which bound and binds me to you – which renders me utterly incapable of *real* love for any other human being – for what could they be to me after *you*? My own — we may have been wrong – but I repent of nothing except that cursed marriage – and your refusing to continue to love me as you had loved me – I can neither forget nor *quite forgive* you for that precious piece of reformation. – but I can never be other than I have been – and whenever I love anything it is because it reminds me in some way or other of yourself – for instance I not long ago attached myself to a Venetian for no earthly reason (although a pretty woman) but because she was called — and she often remarked (without knowing the reason how fond I was of the name. – It is heart-breaking to think of our long Separation – and I am sure more than punishment enough for all our sins – Dante is more humane in his 'Hell' for he places his unfortunate lovers (Francesca of Rimini and Paolo whose case fell a good deal short of *ours* – though sufficiently naughty) in company – and though they suffer – it is at least together. – If ever I return to England – it will be to see you – and recollect that in all time – and place – and feelings – I have never ceased to be the same to you in heart – Circumstances may have ruffled my manner – and hardened my spirit – you may have seen me harsh and exasperated with all things around me; grieved and tortured with *your new resolution*, – and the soon after persecution of that infamous fiend who drove me from my Country and conspired against my life – by endeavouring to deprive me of all that could render it precious – but remember that even then *you* were the sole object that cost me a tear? and *what tears*! do you remember *our* parting? I have not spirits now to write to you upon other subjects – I am well in health – and have no cause of grief but the reflection that we are not together – When you write to me speak to me of yourself – and say that you love me – never mind commonplace people and topics – which can be in no degree interesting – to me who see nothing in England but the country which holds *you* – or around it but the sea which divides us. – They say absence destroys weak passions – and confirms strong ones – Alas! *mine* for you is the union of all passions and of all affections – Has strengthened itself but will destroy me – I do not speak of *physical* destruction – for I have endured and can endure much – but of the annihilation of all thoughts, feelings or hopes – which have not more or less reference to you and to *our recollections* –

Ever dearest. [Signature erased]

TO JOHN MURRAY   *Venice, May 18, 1819*

. . . I wrote to you in haste and at past two in the morning having besides had an accident. In going, about an hour and a half ago, to a rendezvous with a Venetian girl (unmarried and the daughter of one of their nobles), I tumbled into the Grand Canal, and, not choosing to miss my appointment by the delays of changing, I have been perched in a balcony with my wet clothes on ever since, till this minute that on my return I have slipped into my dressing-gown. My foot slipped in getting into my Gondola to set out (owing to the cursed slippery steps of their palaces), and in I flounced like a Carp, and went dripping like a Triton to my Sea nymph and had to scramble up to a grated window: –

> Fenced with iron within and without
> Lest the lover get in or the Lady get out.

She is a very dear friend of mine, and I have undergone some trouble on her account, for last winter the truculent tyrant her flinty-hearted father, having been informed by an infernal German, Countess Vorsperg (their next neighbour), of our meetings, they sent a priest to me, and a Commissary of police, and they locked the Girl up, and gave her prayers and bread and water, and our connection was cut off for some time; but the father hath lately been laid up, and the brother is at Milan, and the mother falls asleep, and the Servants are naturally on the wrong side of the question, and there is no Moon at Midnight just now, so that we have lately been able to recommence; the fair one is eighteen; her name, Angelina; the family name, of course, I don't tell you.

She proposed to me to divorce my mathematical wife, and I told her that in England we can't divorce except for *female* infidelity. 'And pray, (said she), how do you know what she may have been doing these last three years?' I answered that I could not tell, but that the state of Cuckoldom was not quite so flourishing in Great Britain as with us here. 'But', she said, 'can't you get rid of her?' 'Not more than is done already (I answered): You would not have me *poison her*?' Would you believe it? She made me *no answer*. Is not that a true and odd national trait? It spoke more than a thousand words, and yet this is a little, pretty, sweet-tempered, quiet feminine being as ever you saw, but the Passions of a Sunny Soil are paramount to all other considerations. An unmarried Girl naturally wishes to be married: if she can marry and love at the same time it is well, but at any rate she must love. I am not sure that my pretty paramour was herself fully aware of the inference to be drawn from her dead Silence, but even the unconsciousness of the latent idea was striking to an observer of the Passions; and I never strike out a thought of another's or of my own without trying to trace it to its Source . . .

Yours ever,

B.

TO JOHN MURRAY   *Bologna, June 7, 1819*

. . . I have been picture-gazing this morning at the famous Domenichino and Guido, both of which are superlative. I afterwards went to the beautiful cimetry of Bologna, beyond the walls, and found, besides the superb Burial-ground, an original of a *Custode*, who reminded me of the grave-digger in Hamlet. He has a collection of Capuchins' skulls, labelled on the forehead, and taking down one of them, said, 'This was Brother Desidero Berro, who died at forty – one of my best friends . . . He was the merriest, cleverest fellow I ever knew . . . He walked so actively that you might have taken him for a dancer – he joked – he laughed – oh! he was such a Frate as I never saw before, nor ever shall again.'

' . . Some of the epitaphs at Ferrara pleased me more than the more splendid monuments of Bologna; for instance: –

> *Martini Luigi*
> *Implora pace.*
>
> *Lucrezia Picini*
> *Implora eterna quiete.*[40]

Can any thing be more full of pathos? Those few words say all that can be said or sought: the dead had had enough of life; all they wanted was rest, and this they '*implore*'. There is all the helplessness, and humble hope, and deathlike prayer, that can arise from the grave – '*implora pace*'. I hope, whoever may survive me, and shall see me put in the foreigners' burying-ground at the Lido, within the fortress by the Adriatic, will see those two words, and no more, put over me. I trust they won't think of 'pickling, and bringing me home to Clod or Blunderbuss Hall'. I am sure my bones would not rest in an English grave, or my clay mix with the earth of that country. I believe the thought would drive me mad on my deathbed, could I suppose that any of my friends would be base enough to convey my carcase back to your soil. I would not even feed your worms, if I could help it . . .

I never hear any thing of Ada, the little Electra of my Mycenae; the moral Clytemnestra is not very communicative of her tidings, but there will come a day of reckoning, even if I should not live to see it . . .

TO RICHARD BELGRAVE HOPPNER *Ravenna, June 20th 1819*

. . . My letters were useful as far as I employed them; and I like both the place and people, though I don't trouble the latter more that I can help. *She* manages very well, though the *local* is inconvenient (no *bolts* and be d—d to them) and we run great risks (were it not at sleeping hours – after dinner) and *no* place but the great Saloon of his own palace. So that if I come away with a Stiletto in my gizzard some fine afternoon, I shall not be astonished.

I can't make *him* out at all – he visits me frequently, and takes me out (like Whittington, the Lord Mayor) in a coach and *six* horses. The fact appears to be, that he is completely *governed* by her – for that matter, so am I. The people here don't know what to make of us, as he had the character of jealousy with all his wives – this is the third. He is the richest of the Ravennese, by their own account, but is not popular among them.

By the aid of a Priest, a Chambermaid, a young Negro-boy, and a female friend, we are enabled to carry on our unlawful loves, as far as they can well go, though generally with some peril, especially as the female friend and priest are at present out of town for some days, so that some of the precautions devolve upon the Maid and Negro . . .

You are but a shabby fellow not to have written before – and I am,

Truly yours,

B.

TO THE HON. AUGUSTA LEIGH   *Ravenna, July 26th, 1819*

My Dearest Augusta, – I am at too great a distance to scold you, but I *will* ask you whether *your* letter of the *1st* July *is an answer* to the letter I wrote you before I quitted Venice? What? is it come to *this*? Have you no memory? or no heart? You *had* both – and I *have* both – at least for *you*.

I write this presuming that you received *that* letter. Is it that you fear? Do not be afraid of the past; the world has its own affairs without thinking of *ours* and you may write safely ...

I do not like at all this pain in your side and always think of your mother's constitution. You must always be to me the first consideration in the world. Shall I come to *you*? Or would a warm climate do you good? If so say the word, and I will provide you and your family (including that precious luggage your husband) with the means of making an agreeable journey. You need not fear about *me*. I am much altered and should be little trouble to you, nor would I give you more of my company than you like. I confess after three and a half – and *such years*! and *such a year* as preceded those three years! – it would be a relief to me to see you again, and if it would be so to you I will come to you. Pray answer me, and recollect that I will do as you like in everything, even to returning to England, which is not the pleasantest of residences were *you* out of it.

I write from Ravenna. I came here on account of a Countess Guiccioli, a girl of twenty married to a very rich old man of sixty about a year ago. With her last winter I had a *liaison* according to the good old Italian custom. She miscarried in May and sent for me here, and here I have been these two months. She is pretty, a great coquette, extremely vain, excessively affected, clever enough, without the smallest principle, with a good deal of imagination and some passion. She had set her heart on carrying me off from Venice out of vanity, and succeeded, and having made herself the subject of general conversation has greatly contributed to her recovery. Her husband is one of the richest nobles of Ravenna, threescore years of age. This is his third wife. You may suppose what *esteem* I entertain for *her*. Perhaps it is about equal on both sides. I have my saddle-horses here and there is good riding in the forest. With these, and my carriage which is here also, and the sea, and my books, and the lady, the time passes. I am very fond of riding and always *was out* of England. But I hate your Hyde Park, and your turnpike roads, and must have forests, downs, or deserts to expatiate in. I detest *knowing* the road one is to go, and being interrupted by your damned finger-posts, or a blackguard roaring for twopence at a turnpike.

I send you a sonnet which this faithful lady had made for the nuptials of one of her relations in which she swears the most *alarming constancy* to her husband. Is not this good? You may suppose my *face* when she shewed it to me. I could not help laughing – one of *our* laughs. All this is very absurd, but you see that I have good morals at bottom.

She is an equestrian too, but a bore in her rides, for she can't guide her horse and he runs after mine, and tries to bite him, and then she begins screaming in a high hat and sky-blue riding habit, making a most absurd figure, and embarrassing me and both our grooms, who have the devil's own work to keep her from tumbling, or having her clothes torn off by the trees and thickets of the pine forest. I fell a little in love with her intimate friend, a certain Geltruda (*that is Gertrude*)[41] who is very young and seems very well disposed to be perfidious; but alas! *her* husband is jealous, and the G. also detected me in an illicit squeezing of hands, the consequence of which was that the friend was whisked off to Bologna for a few days, and since her return I have never been able to see her but twice, with a dragon of a mother in law and a barbarian husband by her side, besides my own dear precious *Amica*, who hates all flirting but her own. But I have a priest who befriends me and the Gertrude says a good deal with her great black eyes, so that perhaps . . . but alas! I mean to give up these things altogether. I have now given you some account of my present state. The guidebook will tell you about Ravenna. I can't tell how long or short may be my stay. Write to me – love me – as ever

Yours most affectly

B.

P.S. – *This* affair is *not* in the least expensive, being all in the wealthy line, but troublesome, for the lady is imperious, and exigeante. However there are hopes that we may quarrel. When we do you shall hear.

TO JOHN CAM HOBHOUSE   *Ravenna, July 30th, 1819*

... I have been here these two months, and hitherto all hath *gone on well*, with the usual *excerpta* of some 'gelosie',[42] which are the fault of the climate, and of the conjunction of two such capricious people as the Guiccioli and the Inglese, but here hath been no stabbing nor drugging of possets. The last person assassinated here was the Commissary of Police, three months ago; they *kilt* him from an alley one evening, but he is recovering from the slugs with which they sprinkled him, from an 'Archibugia' that shot him round a corner, like the Irishman's gun. He and Manzoni, who was stabbed dead going to the theatre at Forli, not long before, are the only recent instances. But it is the custom of the country, and not much worse than duelling, where one undertakes, at a certain personal risk of a more open nature, to get rid of a disagreeable person, who is injurious or inconvenient, and if such people become insupportable, what is to be done? It is give and take, like everything else – you run the same risk, and they run the same risk; it has the same object with duelling, but adopts a different means. As to the trash about *honour*, that is all stuff; a man offends, you want to kill him, this is amiable and natural, but *how*? The natural mode is obvious, but the artificial varies according to education.

I am taking the generous side of the question, seeing I am much more exposed here to become the patient than the agent of such an experiment. I know but one man[43] whom I should be tempted to put to rest, and he is not an Italian nor in Italy, therefore I trust that he won't pass through Romagna during my sojourn, *because* 'gin he did, there is no saying what the fashionable facilities might induce a vindictive gentleman to meditate; besides, there are injuries where the balance is so greatly against the offender, that you are not to risk life against his (excepting always the law, which is originally a convention), but to trample as [you] would on any other venomous animal . . .

TO JOHN MURRAY   *Ravenna, August 1, 1819*

. . . You have bought Harlow's drawings of Margarita and me rather dear methinks; but since you desire the story of Margarita Cogni, you shall be told it, though it may be lengthy.

Her face is of the fine Venetian cast of the old Time, and her figure, though perhaps too tall, not less fine – taken altogether in the national dress.

In the summer of 1817, Hobhouse and myself were sauntering on horseback along the Brenta one evening, when, amongst a group of peasants, we remarked two girls as the prettiest we had seen for some time. About this period, there had been great distress in the country, and I had a little relieved some of the people. Generosity makes a great figure at very little cost in Venetian livres, and mine had probably been exaggerated – as an Englishman's. Whether they remarked us looking at them or no, I know not; but one of them called out to me in Venetian 'Why do not you, who relieve others, think of us also?' I turned round and answered her – '*Cara, tu sei troppo bella e giovane per aver' bisogno del soccorso mio*'.[44] She answered, 'If you saw my hut and my food, you would not say so'. All this passed half jestingly, and I saw no more of her for some days.

A few evenings after, we met with these two girls again, and they addressed us more seriously, assuring us of the truth of their statement. They were cousins; Margarita married, the other single. As I doubted still of the circumstances, I took the business up in a different light, and made an appointment with them for the next evening. Hobhouse had taken a fancy to the single lady, who was much shorter in stature, but a very pretty girl also. They came attended by a third woman, who was cursedly in the way, and Hobhouse's charmer took fright (I don't mean at Hobhouse, but at not being married – for here no woman will do anything under adultery), and flew off; and mine made some bother – at the propositions, and wished to consider of them. I told her, 'if you really are in want, I will relieve you without any conditions whatever, and you may make love with me or no just as you please – *that* shall make no difference; but if you are not in absolute necessity, this is naturally a rendezvous, and I presumed that you understood this when you made the appointment'. She said that she had no objection to make love with me, as she was married, and all married women did it; but that her husband (a baker) was somewhat ferocious, and would do her a mischief. In short, in a few evenings we arranged our affairs, and for two years, in the course of which I had more women that I can count or recount, she was the only one who preserved over me an ascendancy which was often disputed, and never impaired. As she herself used to say publicly, 'It don't matter, he may have five hundred; but he will always come back to me'.

The reasons of this were, firstly, her person – very dark, tall, the Venetian face, very fine black eyes – and certain other qualities which need not be mentioned. She was two and twenty years old, and, never having had children, had not spoilt her figure, nor anything else – which is, I assure you, a great desideration in a hot climate where they grow relaxed and doughy, and flumpity a short time after breeding. She was, besides, a thorough Venetian in her dialect, in her thoughts, in her countenance, in every thing, with all their naïveté and Pantaloon humour. Besides, she could neither read nor write, and could not plague me with letters, – except twice that she paid sixpence to a public scribe, under the piazza, to make a letter for her, upon some occasion, when I was ill and could not see her. In other respects she was somewhat fierce and *prepotente*, that is, overbearing, and used to walk in whenever it suited her, with no very great regard to time, place, nor persons; and if she found any women in her way, she knocked them down.

When I first knew her, I was in *relazione* (*liaison*) with la Signora Segati, who was silly enough one evening at Dolo, accompanied by some of her female friends, to threaten her; for the Gossips of the Villeggiatura[45] had already found out, by the neighing of my horse one evening, that I used to 'ride late in the

night' to meet the Fornarina.[46] Margarita threw back her veil
(*fazziolo*), and replied in very explicit Venetian, ' *You* are *not* his
wife; *I* am *not* his wife: *you* are his *Donna*, and *I* am his *Donna*:
your husband is a cuckold, and *mine* is another. For the rest,
what *right* have you to reproach me? if he prefers what is mine
to what is yours, is it my fault? if you wish to secure him, tie him
to your petticoat-string; but do not think to speak to me without
a reply, because you happen to be richer than I am.' Having
delivered this pretty piece of eloquence (which I translate as it
was related to me by a bye-stander), she went on her way,
leaving a numerous audience with Madame Segati, to ponder
at her leisure on the dialogue between them.

When I came to Venice for the Winter, she followed. I never
had any regular *liaison* with her, but whenever she came I never
allowed any other connection to interfere with her; and as she
found herself out to be a favourite, she came pretty often. But
she had inordinate Self-love, and was not tolerant of other women,
except of the Segati, who was, as she said, my regular *Amica*, so
that I, being at that time somewhat promiscuous, there was
great confusion and demolition of head-dresses and handker-
chiefs; and sometimes my servants, in 'redding the fray' between
her and other feminine persons, received more knocks than
acknowledgements for their peaceful endeavours. At the
Cavalchina, the masqued ball on the last night of the Carnival,
where all the World goes, she snatched off the mask of Madame
Contarini, a lady noble by birth, and decent in conduct, for no
other reason, but because she happened to be leaning on my arm.
You may suppose what a cursed noise this made; but this is only
one of her pranks.

At last she quarrelled with her husband, and one evening ran
away to my house. I told her this would not do: she said she
would lie in the street, but not go back to him; that he beat her
(the gentle tigress), spent her money, and scandalously neglected
his Oven. As it was Midnight I let her stay, and next day there
was no moving her at all. Her husband came, roaring and crying,
and entreating her to come back: – *not* she! He then applied to
the Police, and they applied to me: I told them and her husband

to *take* her; I did not want her; she had come, and I could not fling her out of the window; but they might conduct her through that or the door if they chose it. She went before the Commissary, but was obliged to return with that *becco ettico* ('consumptive cuckold'), as she called the poor man, who had a Ptisick. In a few days she ran away again. After a precious piece of work, she fixed herself in my house, really and truly without my consent, but, owing to my indolence, and not being able to keep my countenance; for if I began in a rage, she always finished by making me laugh with some Venetian pantaloonery or another; and the Gipsy knew this well enough, as well as her other powers of persuasion, and exerted them with the usual tact and success of all She-things – high and low, they are all alike for that.

Madame Benzone also took her under her protection, and then her head turned. She was always in extremes, either crying or laughing, and so fierce when angered, that she was the terror of men, women, and children – for she had the strength of an Amazon, with the temper of Medea. She was a fine animal, but quite untameable. *I* was the only person that could at all keep her in any order, and when she saw me really angry (which they tell me is rather a savage sight), she subsided. But she had a thousand fooleries: in her *fazziolo*, the dress of the lower orders, she looked beautiful; but, alas! she longed for a hat and feathers, and all I could say or do (and I said much) could not prevent this travestie. I put the first into the fire; but I got tired of burning them, before she did of buying them, so that she made herself a figure – for they did not at all become her.

Then she would have her gowns with a *tail* – like a lady, forsooth: nothing would serve her but '*l'abito colla coua*', or *cua*, (that is the Venetian for '*la Coda*', the tail or train,) and as her cursed pronunciation of the word made me laugh, there was an end of all controversy, and she dragged this diabolical tail after her every where.

In the meantime, she beat the women and stopped my letters. I found her one day pondering over one: she used to try to find out by their shape whether they were feminine or no; and she used to lament her ignorance, and actually studied her Alphabet, on purpose (as she declared) to open all letters addressed to me and read their contents.

I must not omit to do justice to her housekeeping qualities: after she came into my house as *donna di governo*,[47] the expences were reduced to less than half, and every body did their duty better – the apartments were kept in order, and every thing and every body else, except herself.

That she had a sufficient regard for me in her wild way, I had many reasons to believe. I will mention one. In the autumn, one day, going to the Lido with my Gondoliers, we were overtaken by a heavy Squall, and the Gondola put in peril – hats blown away, boat filling, oar lost, tumbling sea, thunder, rain in torrents, night coming, and wind encreasing. On our return, after a tight struggle, I found her on the open steps of the Mocenigo palace, on the Grand Canal, with her great black eyes flashing through her tears, and the long dark hair, which was streaming drenched with rain over her brows and breast. She was perfectly exposed to the storm; and the wind blowing her hair and dress about her thin figure, and the lightning flashing round her, with the waves rolling at her feet, made her look like Medea alighted from her chariot, or the Sibyl of the tempest that was rolling around her, the only living thing within hail at that moment except ourselves. On seeing me safe, she did not wait to greet me, as might be expected, but calling out to me – *Ah! can' della Madonna, e esto il tempo per andar' al' Lido*? (Ah! Dog of the Virgin, is this a time to go to Lido?) ran into the house, and solaced herself with scolding the boatmen for not foreseeing the '*temporale*'.[48] I was told by the servants that she had only been prevented from coming in a boat to look after me, by the refusal of all the Gondoliers of the Canal to put out into the harbour in such a moment: and that then she sat down on the steps in all the thickest of the Squall, and would neither be removed nor comforted. Her joy at seeing me again was moderately mixed with ferocity, and gave me the idea of a tigress over her recovered Cubs.

But her reign drew near a close. She became quite ungovernable some months after; and a concurrence of complaints, some true,

and many false – 'a favourite has no friend' – determined me to
part with her ...

I forgot to mention that she was very devout, and would cross
herself if she heard the prayer-time strike – sometimes when
that ceremony did not appear to be much in unison with what
she was then about.

She was quick in reply; as, for instance – One day when she
had made me very angry with beating somebody or other, I
called her a *Cow* (*Cow*, in Italian, is a sad affront and tantamount
to the feminine of dog in English). I called her '*Vacca*'. She
turned round, curtesied, and answered, '*Vacca tua, 'Celenza*'
(i.e. *Eccelenza*). '*Your* Cow, please your Excellency.' In short,
she was, as I said before, a very fine Animal, of considerable
beauty and energy, with many good and several amusing quali-
ties, but wild as a witch and fierce as a demon. She used to boast
publicly of her ascendancy over me, contrasting it with that of
other women, and assigning for it sundry reasons, physical and
moral, which did more credit to her person than her modesty.
True it was, that they all tried to get her away, and no one
succeeded till her own absurdity helped them. Whenever there
was a competition, and sometimes one would be shut in one room
and one in another to prevent battle, she had generally the
preference.

Yours very truly and affectionately,

B.

TO JOHN MURRAY   *Bologna, August 12, 1819*

... You are right, Gifford is right, Crabbe is right, Hobhouse
is right – you are all right, and I am all wrong; but do, pray, let
me have that pleasure. Cut me up root and branch; quarter me
in the *Quarterly*; send round my *disjecti membra poetae*,⁴⁹ like
those of the Levite's Concubine; make me, if you will, a spectacle
to men and angels; but don't ask me to alter, for I can't: – I am
obstinate and lazy – and there's the truth.

But, nevertheless, I will answer your friend C[ohen], who
objects to the quick succession of fun and gravity, as if in that

case the gravity did not (in intention, at least) heighten the fun. His metaphor is, that 'we are never scorched and drenched at the same time'. Blessings on his experience! Ask him these questions about 'scorching and drenching'. Did he never play at Cricket, or walk a mile in hot weather? Did he never spill a dish of tea over his testicles in handing the cup to his charmer, to the great shame of his nankeen breeches? Did he never swim in the sea at Noonday with the Sun in his eyes and on his head, which all the foam of Ocean could not cool? Did he never draw his foot out of a tub of too hot water, damning his eyes and his valet's? Did he never inject for a Gonorrhea? or make water through an ulcerated Urethra? Was he ever in a Turkish bath, that marble paradise of sherbet and Sodomy? Was he ever in a cauldron of boiling oil, like St John? or in the sulphureous waves of hell? (where he ought to be for his 'scorching and drenching at the same time'). Did he never tumble into a river or lake, fishing, and sit in his wet cloathes in the boat, or on the bank, afterwards 'scorched and drenched', like a true sportsman? 'Oh for breath to utter!' – but make him my compliments; he is a clever fellow for all that – a very clever fellow.

You ask me for the plan of Donny Johnny: I *have* no plan – I *had* no plan; but I had or have materials; though if, like Tony Lumpkin, I am 'to be snubbed so when I am in spirits', the poem will be naught, and the poet turn serious again. If it don't take, I will leave it off where it is, with all due respect to the Public; but if continued, it must be in my own way. You might as well make Hamlet (or Diggory) 'act mad' in a strait waistcoat as trammel my buffoonery, if I am to be a buffoon: their gestures and my thoughts would only be pitiably absurd and ludicrously constrained. Why, Man the Soul of such writing is its licence; at least the *liberty* of that *licence*, if one likes – *not* that one should abuse it: it is like trial by Jury and Peerage and the Habeas Corpus – a very fine thing, but chiefly in the *reversion*; because no one wishes to be tried for the mere pleasure of proving his possession of the privilege.

But a truce with these reflections. You are too earnest and eager about a work never intended to be serious. Do you suppose that I could have any intention but to giggle and make giggle? – a playful satire, with as little poetry as could be helped, was what I meant: and as to the indecency, do, pray, read in Boswell what *Johnson*, the sullen moralist, says of *Prior* and Paulo Purgante ...

TO JOHN CAM HOBHOUSE   *Bologna, August 20th, 1819*

... My time has been passed viciously and agreeably; at thirty-one so few years, months, days remain, that 'Carpe diem' is not enough. I have been obliged to crop even the seconds, for who can trust *to-morrow*? – *to-morrow* quotha? to-hour, to-*minute*. I can not repent me (I try very often) so much of anything I have done, as of anything I have left undone. Alas! I have been but idle, and have the prospect of an early decay, without having seized every available instant of our pleasurable years. This is a bitter thought, and it will be difficult for me ever to recover [from] the despondency into which this idea naturally throws onc. Philosophy would be in vain   let us try action.

Would that the Dougal of Bishop's Castle[50] would find a purchaser for Rochdale.

I would embark (with Fletcher as a breeding beast of burthen) and possess myself of the pinnacle of the Andes, or a spacious plain of unbounded extent in an eligible earthquake situation ...

TO JOHN CAM HOBHOUSE   *Bologna, August 23rd, 1819*

My Dear Hobhouse, – I have received a letter from Murray containing the 'British Review's' eleventh article. Had you any conception of a man's tumbling into such a trap as Roberts has done? Why it is precisely what he was wished to do. I have enclosed an epistle for publication with a queer signature (to Murray, who should keep the anonymous still about D. Juan) in answer to Roberts, which pray approve if you can. It is written in an evening and morning in haste, with ill-health and worse nerves. I am so bilious, that I nearly lose my head, and so nervous that I cry for nothing; at least to-day I burst into tears, all alone by myself, over a cistern of gold-fishes, which are not pathetic animals. I can assure you it is not Mr Roberts, or any of his crew that can affect me; but I have been excited and agitated, and exhausted mentally and bodily all this summer, till I really sometimes begin to think not only 'that I shall die at top first', but that the moment is not very remote. I have had no particular cause of griefs, except the usual accompaniments of all unlawful passions ...

But I feel – and I feel it bitterly – that a man should not consume his life at the side and on the bosom of a woman, and a stranger; that even the recompense, and it is much, is not enough, and that this Cicisbean existence is to be condemned. But I have neither the strength of mind to break my chain, nor the insensibility which would deaden its weight. I cannot tell what will become of me – to leave, or to be left would at present drive me quite out of my senses; and yet to what have I conducted myself? I have, luckily, or unluckily, no ambition left; it would be better if I had, it would at least awake me; whereas at present I merely start in my sleep ...

'MY GRANDMOTHER'S REVIEW'
TO THE EDITOR OF THE BRITISH REVIEW

[*Bologna, August, 1819*]

My Dear Roberts, – As a believer in the Church of England – to say nothing of the State – I have been an occasional reader and great admirer of, though not a subscriber to, your *Review*, which is rather expensive. But I do not know that any part of its contents ever gave me much surprise till the eleventh article of your twenty-seventh number made its appearance. You have there most manfully refuted a calumnious accusation of bribery and corruption, the credence of which in the public mind might not only have damaged your reputation as a Clergyman and an editor, but, what would have been still worse, have injured the circulation of your journal; which, I regret to hear, is not so extensive as the 'purity (as you well observe) of its', etc., etc., and the present taste for propriety, would induce us to expect. The charge itself is of a solemn nature, and, although in verse, is couched in terms of such circumstantial gravity, as to induce a belief little short of that generally accorded to the thirty-nine articles, to which you so generally subscribed on taking your degrees. It is a charge the most revolting to the heart of man, from its frequent occurrence; to the mind of a Statesman, from its occasional truth; and to the soul of an editor, from its moral impossibility. You are charged then in the last line of one octave stanza, and the whole eight lines of the next, viz. 209th and 210th of the first canto of that 'pestilent poem', *Don Juan*, with receiving, and still more foolishly acknowledging the receipt of, certain monies, to eulogize the unknown author, who by this account must be known to you, if to nobody else. An impeachment of this nature, so seriously made, there is but one way of refuting; and it is my firm persuasion, that whether you did or did not (and *I* believe that you did not) receive the said monies, of which I wish that he had specified the sum, you are quite right in denying all knowledge of the transaction. If charges of this nefarious description are to go forth, sanctioned by all the solemnity of circumstance, and guaranteed by the veracity of verse (as Counsellor Philips would say), what is to become of readers hitherto implicitly confident in the not less veracious prose of our critical journals? what is to become of the reviews? And if the reviews fail, what is to become of the editors? It is common cause, and you have done well to sound the alarm. I myself, in my humble sphere, will be one of your echoes. In the words of the tragedian Liston, 'I love a row,' and you seem justly determined to make one.

It is barely possible, certainly improbable, that the writer might have been in jest; but this only aggravates his crime. A joke, the proverb says, 'breaks no bones'; but it may break a bookseller, or it may be the cause of bones being broken. The jest is but a bad one at the best for the author, and might have been a still worse one for you, if your copious contradiction did not certify to all whom it may concern your own indignant innocence, and the immaculate purity of the *British Review*. I do not doubt your word, my dear Roberts, yet I cannot help wishing that in a case of such vital importance, it had assumed the more substantial shape of an affidavit sworn before the Lord Mayor, Atkins, who readily receives any deposition, and doubtless would have brought it in some way as evidence of the designs of the reformers to set fire to London, at the same time that he himself meditates the same good office towards the river Thames.

I am sure, my dear fellow, that you will take these observations of mine in good part; they are written in a spirit of friendship not less pure than your own editorial integrity. I have always admired you; and not knowing any shape which friendship and admiration can assume more agreeable and useful than that of good advice, I shall continue my lucubrations, mixed with here and there a monitory hint as to what I conceive to be the line you should pursue, in case you should ever again be assailed with bribes, or accused of taking them. By the way, you don't say much about the poem, except that it is 'flagitious.' This is a pity – you should have cut it up; because, to say the truth, in not doing so, you somewhat assist any notions which the malignant might entertain on the score of the anonymous asseveration which has made you so angry.

You say, no bookseller 'was willing to take upon himself the publication, though most of them disgrace themselves by selling it.' Now, my dear friend, though we all know that those fellows will do any thing for money, methinks the disgrace is more with the purchasers; and some such, doubtless, there are, for there can be no very extensive selling (as you will perceive by that of the *British Review*) without buying. You then add, 'what can the critic say?' I am sure I don't know; at present he says very little, and that not much to the purpose. Then comes, 'for praise, as far as regards the *poetry*, *many* passages might be exhibited; for condemnation, as far as regards the morality, all.' Now, my dear good Roberts, I feel for you and for your reputation; my heart bleeds for both; and I do ask you, whether or not such language does not come positively under the description of 'the pull collusive', for which see Sheridan's farce of *The Critic* (by the way, a little more facetious than your own farce under the same title) towards the close of scene second, act the first.

The poem is, it seems, sold as the work of Lord Byron; but you feel yourself 'at liberty to suppose it was not Lord B.'s composition'. Why did you ever suppose that it was? I approve of your indignation – I applaud it – I feel as angry as you can; but perhaps your virtuous wrath carries you a little too far, when you say that 'no misdemeanour, not even that of sending into the world obscene and blasphemous poetry, the product of studious lewdness and laboured impiety, appears to you in so detestable a light as the acceptance of a present by the editor of a review, as the condition of praising an author'. The devil it don't! Think a little. This is being critical overmuch. In point of Gentile benevolence or Christian charity, it were surely less criminal to praise for a bribe, than to abuse a fellow-creature for nothing; and as to the assertion of the comparative innocence of blasphemy and obscenity, confronted with an editor's 'acceptance of a present', I shall merely observe, that as an editor you say very well, but as a Christian divine, I would not recommend you to transpose this sentence into a sermon.

And yet you say, 'the miserable man (for miserable he is, as having a soul of which he cannot get rid)' – But here I must pause again, and inquire what is the meaning of this parenthesis. We have heard of people of 'little soul', or of 'no soul at all', but never till now of 'the misery of having a soul of which we cannot get rid'; a misery under which you are possibly no great sufferer, having got rid apparently of some of the intellectual part of your own when you penned this pretty piece of eloquence.

But to continue. You call upon Lord Byron, always supposing him *not* the author, to disclaim 'with all gentlemanly haste', etc., etc. I am told that Lord B. is in a foreign country, some thousand miles off it may be; so that it will be difficult for him to hurry to your wishes. In the mean time, perhaps you yourself have set an example of more haste than gentility; but 'the more haste the worse speed'.

Let us now look at the charge itself, my dear Roberts, which appears to me to be in some degree not quite explicitly worded:

'I bribed my *Grandmother*'s Review, the British.'

I recollect hearing, soon after the publication, this subject discussed at the tea-table of Mr S. the poet, who expressed himself, I remember, a good deal surprised that you had never reviewed his epic poem of *Saul*, nor any of his six tragedies, of which, in one instance, the bad taste of the pit, and in all the rest, the barbarous repugnance of the principal actors, prevented the performance. Mrs and the Misses S. being in a corner of the room perusing the proof sheets of Mr S.'s poems in Italy or on Italy, as he says, (I wish, by the by, Mrs S. would make the tea a little stronger,) the male part of the *conversazione* were at liberty to make a few observations on the poem and passage in question, and there was a difference of opinion. Some thought the allusion was to the *British Critic*; others, that by the expression, 'my Grandmother's Review', it was intimated that 'my grandmother' was not the reader of the review, but actually the writer; thereby insinuating, my dear Roberts, that you were an old woman; because, as people often say, 'Jeffrey's Review', 'Gifford's Review', in lieu of *Edinburgh* and *Quarterly*; so 'my Grandmother's Review' and Roberts', might be also synonymous. Now, whatever colour this insinuation might derive from the circumstance of your wearing a gown, as well as from your time of life, your general style, and various passages of your writings, – I will take upon myself to exculpate you from all suspicion of the kind, and assert, without calling Mrs Roberts in testimony, that if ever you should be chosen Pope, you will pass through all the previous ceremonies with as much credit as any pontiff since the parturition of Joan. It is very unfair to judge of sex from writings, particularly from those of the *British Review*. We are all liable to be deceived; and it is an indisputable fact, that many of the best articles in your journal, which were attributed to a veteran female, were actually written by you yourself; and yet to this day there are people who could never find out the difference. But let us return to the more immediate question.

I agree with you that it is impossible Lord Byron should be the author, not only because as a British peer, and a British poet, it would be impracticable for him to have recourse to such facetious fiction, but for some other reasons which you have omitted to state. In the first place, his lordship has no grandmother. Now the author, – and we may believe him in this – doth expressly state that the *British* is his 'Grandmother's Review'; and if, as I think I have distinctly proved, this was not a mere figurative allusion to your supposed intellectual age and sex, my dear friend, it follows, whether you be she or no, that there is such an elderly lady still extant. And I can the more readily credit this, having a sexagenary aunt of my own, who perused you constantly, till unfortunately falling asleep over the leading article of your last number, her spectacles fell off and were broken against the fender, after a faithful service of fifteen years, and she has never been able to fit her eyes since; so that I have been forced to read you aloud to her; and this is in fact the way in which I became acquainted with the subject of my present letter and thus determined to become your public correspondent.

In the next place, Lord B.'s destiny seems in some sort like that of Hercules of old, who became the author of all unappropriated prodigies. Lord B. has been supposed the author of the *Vampire*, of a *Pilgrimage to Jerusalem*, *To the Dead Sea*, of *Death*

upon the Pale Horse, of odes to *Lavalette*, to *Saint Helena*, to the
Land of the Gaul, and to a sucking child. Now he turned out to
have written none of these things. Besides, you say he knows in
what a spirit of, etc., you criticise – Are you sure he knows all
this? that he has read you like my poor dear aunt? They tell me
he is a queer sort of a man; and I would not be too sure, if I were
you, either of what he has read or what he has written. I thought
his style had been the serious and terrible. As to his sending you
money, this is the first time that ever I heard of his paying his
reviewers in *that coin*; I thought it was rather in *their own*, to
judge from some of his earlier productions. Besides, though he
may not be profuse in his expenditure, I should conjecture that
his reviewer's bill is not so long as his tailor's.

Shall I give you what I think a prudent opinion. I don't mean
to insinuate, God forbid! but if, by any accident, there should
have been such a correspondence between you and the unknown
author, whoever he may be, send him back his money: I dare say
he will be very glad to have it again: it can't be much, considering
the value of the article and the circulation of the journal; and you
are too modest to rate your praise beyond its real worth. – Don't
be angry, – I know you won't, – at this appraisement of your
powers of eulogy; for on the other hand, my dear fellow, depend
upon it your abuse is worth, not its own weight – that's a feather, –
but *your* weight in gold. So don't spare it: if he has bargained
for *that*, give it handsomely, and depend upon your doing him a
friendly office.

But I only speak in case of possibility; for, as I said before,
I cannot believe in the first instance, that you would receive a
bribe to praise any person whatever; and still less can I believe
that your praise could ever produce such an offer. You are a good
creature, my dear Roberts, and a clever fellow; else I could
almost suspect that you had fallen into the very trap set for you
in verse by this anonymous Wag, who will certainly be but too
happy to see you saving him the trouble of making you ridiculous.
The fact is, that the solemnity of your eleventh article does make
you look a little more absurd than you ever yet looked, in all
probability, and at the same time does no good; for if any body

believed before in the octave stanzas, they will believe still, and you will find it not less difficult to prove your negative, than the learned Partridge found it to demonstrate his not being dead, to the satisfaction of the readers of almanacks.

What the motives of this writer may have been for (as you magnificently translate his quizzing you) 'stating, with the particularity which belongs to fact, the forgery of a groundless fiction', (do pray, my dear R. talk a little less 'in King Cambyses' vein',) I cannot pretend to say; perhaps to laugh at you, but that is no reason for your benevolently making all the world laugh also. I approve of your being angry; I tell you I am angry too; but you should not have shown it so outrageously. Your solemn 'if somebody personating the Editor of the,' etc., etc., 'has received from Lord B. or from any other person', reminds me of Charley Incledon's usual exordium when people came into the tavern to hear him sing without paying their share of the reckoning – 'If a maun, or *ony* maun, or *ony other* maun', etc., etc., you have both the same redundant eloquence. But why should you think any body would personate you? No body would dream of such a prank who ever read your compositions, and perhaps not many who have heard your conversation. But I have been inoculated with a little of your prolixity. The fact is, my dear Roberts, that somebody has tried to make a fool of you, and what he did not succeed in doing, you have done for him and for yourself.

With regard to the poem itself, or the author, whom I cannot find out, (can you?) I have nothing to say: my business is with you. I am sure that you will, upon second thoughts, be really obliged to me for the intention of this letter, however far short my expressions may have fallen of the sincere good will, admiration, and thorough esteem, with which I am ever, my dear Roberts,

Most truly yours,   WORTLEY CLUTTERBUCK

Sept. 4th, 1819
Little Pidlington.

P.S. My letter is too long to revise, and the post is going. I forget whether or not I asked you the meaning of your last words, though not dying speech and confession let us hope, 'the forgery of a groundless fiction'. Now, as all forgery is fiction, and all fiction a kind of forgery, is not this tautological? The sentence would have ended more strongly with 'forgery'; only – it hath an awful Bank of England sound, and would have ended like an indictment, besides sparing you several words, and conferring a meaning upon the remainder. But this is mere verbal criticism. Good bye – once more yours truly,

W.C.

P.S. 2d. – Is it true that the Saints make up the losses of the review? – It is very handsome in them to be at so great an expense – Pray pardon my taking up so much of your time from the bar, and from your clients, who I hear are about the same number with the readers of your journal. *Twice* more yours,

W.C.

TO JOHN MURRAY   *Bologna, August 24, 1819*

Dear Sir, – I wrote to you last post, enclosing a buffooning letter for publication, addressed to the buffoon Roberts, who has thought proper to tie a cannister to his own tail. It was written off hand, and in the midst of circumstances not very favourable to facetiousness, so that there may, perhaps, be more bitterness than enough for that sort of small acid punch. You will tell me.

Keep the *anonymous*, in every case: it helps what fun there may be; but if the matter grows serious about *Don Juan,* and you feel *yourself* in a scrape, or *me* either, *own that I am the author. I* will never *shrink* . . .

TO THE COUNTESS GUICCIOLI   *Bologna, August 25, 1819*

My Dear Teresa, – I have read this book[51] in your garden; – my love, you were absent, or else I could not have read it. It is a favourite book of yours, and the writer was a friend of mine. You will not understand these English words, and *others* will not understand them – which is the reason I have not scrawled them in Italian. But you will recognise the handwriting of him who passionately loved you, and you will divine that, over a book which was yours, he could only think of love. In that word, beautiful in all languages, but most so in yours – *Amor mio* – is comprised my existence here and hereafter. I feel I exist here, and I fear that I shall exist hereafter, – to *what* purpose you will decide; my destiny rests with you, and you are a woman, seventeen years of age, and two out of a convent. I wish that you had stayed there, with all my heart, – or, at least, that I had never met you in your married state.

But all this is too late. I love you, and you love me, – at least, you *say so*, and *act* as if you *did* so, which last is a great consolation in all events. But *I* more than love you, and cannot cease to love you.

Think of me, sometimes, when the Alps and the ocean divide us, – but they never will, unless you *wish* it.

BYRON

TO JOHN CAM HOBHOUSE   *Venice, Oct. 3rd, 1819*

... I assure you that I am very *serious* in the idea,[52] and that the notion has been about me for a long time, as you will see by the worn state of the advertisement. I should go there with my natural daughter, Allegra, – now nearly three years old, and with me here, – and pitch my tent for good and all.

I am not tired of Italy, but a man must be a Cicisbeo and a Singer in duets, and a connoisseur of Operas – or nothing – here. I have made some progress in all these accomplishments, but I can't say that I don't feel the degradation. Better be an unskilful Planter, an awkward settler, – better be a hunter, or anything, than a flatterer of fiddlers, and fan carrier of a woman. I like women – God he knows – but the more their system here developes upon me, the worse it seems, after Turkey too; here the *polygamy* is all on the female side. I have been an intriguer, a husband, a whoremonger, and now I am a Cavalier Servente – by the holy! it is a strange sensation. After having belonged in my own and other countries to the intriguing, the married, and the keeping parts of the town, – to be sure an honest arrangement is the best, and I have had that too, and have – but they expect it to be for *life*, thereby, I presume, excluding longevity. But let us be serious, if possible.

You must not talk to me of England, that is out of the question. I had a house and lands, and a wife and child, and a name there – once – but all these things are transmuted or sequestered. Of the last, and best, ten years of my life, nearly six have been passed out of it. I feel no love for the soil after the treatment I received before leaving it for the last time, but I do not hate it enough to wish to take a part in its calamities, as on either side harm must be done before good can accrue; revolutions are not to be made with rosewater. My taste for revolution is abated, with my other passions.

Yet I want a country, and a home, and – if possible – a free one. I am not yet thirty-two years of age. I might still be a decent Citizen, and found a house, and a family as good – or better – than the former. I could at all events occupy myself rationally, my hopes are not high, nor my ambition extensive, and when tens of thousands of our countrymen are colonizing (like the Greeks of old in Sicily and Italy) from so many causes, does my notion seem visionary or irrational? There is no freedom in Europe – that's certain; it is besides a worn out portion of the globe . . .

TO THE HON. DOUGLAS KINNAIRD   *Venice, Octr 26, 1819*

. . . As to 'Don Juan', confess, confess – you dog and be candid – that it is the sublime of *that there* sort of writing – it may be bawdy but is it not good English? It may be profligate but is it not *life*, is it not *the thing*? Could any man have written it who has not lived in the world? – and [t]ooled in a post-chaise? – in a hackney coach? – in a gondola? – against a wall? – in a court carriage? – in a vis a vis? – on a table? – and under it? I have written about a hundred stanzas of a third Canto, but it is a damned modest – the outcry has frighted me. I have such projects for the Don but the Cant is so much stronger than the [Cunt] nowadays, that the benefit of experience in a man who had well weighed the worth of both monosyllables must be lost to despairing posterity. After all what stuff this outcry is – Lalla Rookh and Little are more dangerous than my burlesque poem can be. Moore has been here, we got tipsy together and were very amicable; he is gone to Rome. I put my life (in M.S.) into his hands (not for publication), you or anybody else may see it at his return. It only comes up to 1816. He is a noble fellow and looks quite fresh and poetical, nine years (the age of a poem's education) my senior. He looks younger. This comes from marriage and being settled in the country. I want to go to South America – I have written to Hobhouse all about it . . .

TO RICHARD BELGRAVE HOPPNER   *October 29, 1819*

My Dear Hoppner, – The Ferrara Story[53] is of a piece with all the rest of the Venetian manufacture; you may judge. I only changed horses there since I wrote to you after my visit in June last. '*Convent*' – and '*carry off*' quotha! – and '*girl*' – I should like to know *who* has been carried off – except poor dear *me*. I have been more ravished myself than any body since the Trojan war . . .

Count G[uiccioli] comes to Venice next week and I am requested to consign his wife to him, which shall be done – with all her linen.

What you say of the long evenings at the Mira, or Venice, reminds me of what *Curran* said to Moore – 'so – I hear – you have married a pretty woman – and a very good creature too – an excellent creature – pray – um – *how do you pass your evenings*?' it is a devil of a question that, and perhaps as easy to answer with a wife as with a mistress; but surely they are longer than the nights. I am all for morality now, and shall confine myself henceforward to the strictest adultery, which you will please to recollect is all that that virtuous wife of mine has left me . . .

5. CAVALIER SERVENTE

December 1819–July 1823

INTRODUCTION

THE motives for Count Guiccioli's complaisance in Byron's liaison with his wife are obscure; in character he was devious, impenetrable, enigmatic, and his political past was compromised. He sought (vainly) a British Vice-Consulate in Ravenna through means of Byron's English connections. He now let to Byron the upper floor of the Palazzo Guiccioli, but the relations between the two men quickly soured and finally turned to open hostility. Byron, ever open on his sexual affairs, wrote that the Count had caught him with Teresa '*quasi* in the fact'. In Ravenna Byron was extremely popular, particularly with the common people and such aristocratic families as the Gambas who were liberal in their politics and opposed to clerical government, especially when backed by Austrian arms. With young Count Pietro Gamba, Teresa's brother, he became fast friends. Count Guiccioli's enmity (he set spies to watch Byron's movements and broke open his wife's desk for incriminating evidence) was met by the support of the Gambas and their aristocratic relatives. Byron, who had joined one of the sects (the *Mericani*) of the secret society known as the *Carbonari*, who were attempting to liberalize Italian politics, was already held suspect by the ecclesiastical authorities and their police. Meanwhile, Guiccioli's relentless treatment of his (equally unrelenting) wife led the old Count Gamba to petition the Pope for a legal separation, which was granted on 4 July 1820, on condition that Teresa entered a convent or returned under the parental roof. Byron remained, with his equivocal presence, in the Palazzo Guiccioli, but found a country house at Filetto near by the Casa Gamba, so that he did manage intermittently to see Teresa, who subsequently returned openly to her father's house in Ravenna.

Through all these domestic difficulties and political unrest Byron continued to write. By the early spring of 1820 he had sent off to Murray two further cantos of *Don Juan* (III and IV), a translation of Pulci's 'Morgante Maggiore', the 'Prophecy of

Dante', a translation of the Francesca da Rimini Episode from Dante, and the 'Observations upon an Article in *Blackwood's Magazine*'. During the separation proceedings he was at work on his Venetian play *Marino Faliero*, which he completed; and by the end of the year he had finished a fifth canto of *Don Juan*.

In the winter and spring of 1821 it was seen that Metternich's policy at the Congress of Powers at Laibach – that of maintaining the status quo in Italy by force of Austrian arms – was only too successful in curbing the aspirations of the constitutionalists, and the inevitable reaction followed. Among the thousands of liberals exiled was the whole of the Gamba family. There is evidence that in enforcing this decree against the Gambas the ecclesiastical authorities in the Romagna aimed also at the removal of Byron, who was only too well known for his political sympathies and active help to the Carbonari. In this action the Cardinal-Legate felt sure that Byron would follow Teresa, who was bound to remain with her father. During those anxious winter months, awaiting the rising that never came, Byron began a journal, wrote his 'Letter to John Murray on the Rev. W. L. Bowles', composed *Sardanapalus* and *The Two Foscari* and started on *Cain*. (On 1 March he had placed Allegra in the Capuchin convent of Bagnacavallo, a short way from Ravenna on the Bologna road.) A visit from Shelley persuaded Byron to leave Ravenna for Pisa, where the former undertook to find houses for the Gambas and also for Byron – securing for the latter the ancient Palazzo Lanfranchi on the banks of the Arno. Among the procrastinations and delays of the move to Pisa, Byron found time to write 'The Blues', to finish *Cain*, to compose 'The Irish Avatar' and begin 'The Vision of Judgment' (an attack on Southey) and his 'Detached Thoughts'.

At Pisa, comfortably installed in his palazzo, with its walled orange garden, Byron collected about him a set of mainly male companions, of whom Shelley was the leading light, but which also included the Gambas, Williams, Medwin, Trelawny, Taafe and a Captain Hay. Byron paid visits to Teresa and Mary Shelley, and these two women, who became friends, would accompany the men in their carriage, when they rode out each day for pistol practice in the countryside. The Austrian police, particularly one Torelli, watched their every movement. Shelley, with his usual impetuous generosity, had invited the impecunious Leigh Hunts (a family which included the ill-disposed Marianne Hunt and her brood of six uninhibited children – a 'Hottentot *Kraal*', Byron called them) to Pisa, hoping that he would edit, together with Byron and himself, a paper to be named *The Liberal*. The Hunts were to be put up on the ground floor of the Palazzo Lanfranchi. Shelley and Williams had planned, and encouraged Byron, urged on also by Trelawny and his friend Captain Daniel Roberts, to have yachts built for them in Genova. The death of Lady Noel on 28 January brought a proportion of the returns from the Wentworth estates to Byron, whose income, together with his literary earnings, now came to something between £6,000 and £8,000 a year, and Hunt thought that he had a right to call on Byron's purse, as he had on Shelley's. A fracas with an Italian trooper named Masi brought the presence of Byron and his friends again to the notice of the authorities. On the 20 April 1822 Allegra died at Bagnacavallo, and Byron was apprised of the news two days later. Shelley's boat, the *Don Juan* arrived at Lerici on 12 May, but it was another month before Byron's cutter, which he had provocatively called after the Colombian patriot, the *Bolivar*, arrived at Leghorn. Immediately the authorities put difficulties in the way of her mooring, sailing, etc.

On 20 June Shelley heard of the Hunts' arrival at Genoa; they came on to Montenero near Leghorn, where Byron had taken the Villa Dupuy. There they witnessed another fracas between Pietro Gamba and one of his servants, which was to result in the Gambas' expulsion from Tuscany. Back in Pisa, awaiting news of an appeal for an extension of sojourn for the Gambas and a temporary asylum for them at Lucca, Byron settled the Hunts in their apartments and promised his 'Vision of Judgment' for the new journal. Then on 8 July Shelley and Williams were lost when their yacht sank in a squall off La Spezia. Henceforth help for the widowed Mary Shelley and Jane Williams, and provision for the improvident Hunts, fell entirely on Byron. Hunt's manner with Byron was most unfortunate, alternating between facetious attempts at a 'manly equality' and the necessity of making financial demands in a semi-jocular but thoroughly false estimate of his own position and prospects. Byron's contributions to the first number of *The Liberal* (his connection with the Hunt brothers being highly disapproved of by Hobhouse, Kinnaird and Moore) were 'The Vision of Judgment', the most amusing 'A Letter to the Editor of "My Grandmother's Review"', and 'Epigrams on Lord Castlereagh'.

The Gambas had removed from Lucca to Genoa and taken a large villa, the Casa Saluzzo at Albaro, overlooking the city and bay, for Byron and themselves. Byron, as unsettled as usual in his plans – whether to go to Greece, where a war of liberation from Turkish rule had broken out, or to emigrate to South America – finally followed Teresa and her family to Genoa, which he reached in October 1822. A separate house in the same suburb of Albaro had been taken for the Hunts and Mary Shelley. Jane Williams returned to England. Byron continued with his writing – 'The Island' and 'The Age of Bronze' followed, and by March 1823 he had finished and sent off the fifteenth canto of *Don Juan*, which despite the hubbub of friends and foes alike, he knew to be his masterpiece. At the Casa Saluzzo Byron was visited by the Blessingtons and Count Alfred d'Orsay; and Lady Blessington has left us a somewhat highly coloured account of her meetings with Byron in *Conversations of Lord Byron with the Countess of Blessington* (1834) and *The Idler in Italy* (1839). But more and more Byron's thoughts were turning to some warlike action in Greece, supported in this by the enthusiasm for liberty of Count Pietro Gamba. If Byron's passion for Teresa had abated with the years his sincere attachment to her, who had given up so much for him, had not diminished, and the thought of the grief his departure would occasion her added to his perplexities. However, to a letter from John Bowring (secretary of the Greek Committee in London, formed to assist the Greek war liberation) asking for his active participation, he replied on 12 May 1823, freely offering his services in the Greek cause. The die was cast. He hired for the voyage to Greece an

English brig, the *Hercules*. Leaving a distraught Teresa, Byron, accompanied by Pietro Gamba, Trelawny and his most trustworthy servants, as well as a young Italian physician Dr Francesco Bruno, with ample stores of powder, medical supplies and ready cash, finally departed from Genoa on 18 July 1823.

TO LADY BYRON   [*Ravenna, December 31st 1819*]

You will perhaps say *why* write my life?[1] – Alas! I say so too – but they who have traduced it – and blasted it – and branded me – should know – that it is they – and not I – are the cause – It is no great pleasure to have lived – and less to live over again the details of existence – but the last becomes sometimes a necessity and even a duty.

If you choose to see this you may – if you do not – you have at least had the option.

TO JOHN MURRAY   *Ravenna, February 21, 1820*

... I see the good old King[2] is gone to his place: one can't help being sorry, though blindness, and age, and insanity, are supposed to be drawbacks on human felicity; but I am not at all sure that the latter, at least, might not render him happier than any of his subjects.

I have no thoughts of coming to the Coronation, though I should like to see it, and though I have a right to be a puppet in it; but my division with Lady Byron, which has drawn an equinoctial line between me and mine in all other things, will operate in this also to prevent my being in the same procession ...

By the king's death Mr H[obhouse],[3] I hear, will stand for Westminster: I shall be glad to hear of his standing any where except in the pillory, which, from the company he must have lately kept (I always except Burdett, and Douglas K., and the genteel part of the reformers), was perhaps to be apprehended, I was really glad to hear it was for libel instead of larceny; for, though impossible in his own person, he might have been taken up by mistake for another at a meeting. All reflections on his

present case and place are so *Nugatory*, that it would be useless
to pursue the subject further. I am out of all patience to see my
friends sacrifice themselves for a pack of blackguards, who
disgust one with their Cause, although I have always been a
friend to and a Voter for reform. If Hunt had addressed the
language to me which he did to Mr H. last election, I would not
have descended to call out such a miscreant who won't fight; but
have passed my sword-stick through his body, like a dog's, and
then thrown myself on my Peers, who would, I hope, have weighed
the provocation: at any rate, it would have been as public a
Service as Walworth's chastisement of Wat. Tyler. If we must have
a tyrant, let him at least be a gentleman who has been bred to the
business, and let us fall by the axe and not by the butcher's
cleaver.

No one can be more sick of, or indifferent to, politics than I
am, if they let me alone, but if the time comes when a part must
be taken one way or the other, I shall pause before I lend myself
to the views of such ruffians, although I cannot but approve of a
Constitutional amelioration of long abuses.

Lord George Gordon, and Wilkes, and Burdett, and Horne
Tooke, were all men of education and courteous deportment; so
is Hobhouse; but as for these others, I am convinced that Robes-
pierre was a Child, and Marat a Quaker in comparison of what
they would be, could they throttle their way to power.

Yours ever,

B.

TO JOHN CAM HOBHOUSE   *Ravenna, March 3rd, 1820*

... So Scrope is gone[4] – down-*diddled* – as Doug. K. writes it,
the said Doug. being like the man who, when he lost a friend,
went to the Saint James's Coffee House and took a new one; but
to you and me the loss of Scrope is irreparable; we could have
better spared not only a 'better man', but the 'best of men'.
Gone to Bruges where he will get tipsy with Dutch beer and shoot
himself the first foggy morning. Brummell at Calais; Scrope at
Bruges, Buonaparte at St Helena, you in your new apartments,

and I at Ravenna, only think! so many great men! There has been nothing like it since Themistocles at Magnesia, and Marius at Carthage.

But times change, and they are luckiest who get over their first rounds at the beginning of the battle ...

I shall let 'dearest duck' waddle alone at the Coronation; a ceremony which I should like to see, and have a right to act Punch in; but the crown itself would not bribe me to return to England, unless business or actual urgency required it. I was very near coming, but that was because I had been very much 'agitato' with some circumstances of a domestic description, here in Italy, and not from any love to the tight little Island ...

TO JOHN CAM HOBHOUSE   *Ravenna, March 29th, 1820*

... I suppose I shall soon see your speeches again, and your determination 'not to be saddled with wooden shoes as the Gazetteer says', but do pray get into Parliament, and out of the company of all these fellows, except Burdett and Douglas Kinnaird, and don't be so very violent. I doubt that Thistlewood will be a great help to the ministers in all the elections, but especially in the Westminster. What a set of desperate fools these Utican conspirators seem to have been. As if in London, after the disarming acts, or indeed at any time, a secret could have been kept among thirty or forty. And if they had killed poor Harrowby – in whose house I have been five hundred times, at dinners and parties; his wife is one of 'the Exquisites' – and t'other fellows, what end would it have answered? 'They understand these things better in France', as Yorick says, but really, if these sort of awkward butchers are to get the upper hand, *I* for one will declare *off*. I have always been (*before* you were, as you well know) a well-wisher to, and voter for reform in parliament; but 'such fellows as these, who will never go to the gallows with any credit', such infamous scoundrels as Hunt and Cobbett, in short, the whole gang (always excepting you, B. and D.) disgust, and make one doubt of the virtue of any principle or politics which can be embraced by similar ragamuffins. I know that revolutions are not to be made with rose water, but though some blood may, and must be shed on such occasions, there is no reason it should be *clotted*; in short, the Radicals seem to be no better than Jack Cade or Wat Tyler, and to be dealt with accordingly.

... You will see that I have taken up the *Pope* question (in prose) with a high hand, and *you* (when you can spare yourself from *Party* to Mankind) must help me. You know how often, under the Mira elms, and by the Adriatic on the Lido, we have discussed that question, and lamented the villainous cant which at present would decry him. It is my intention to give battle to the blackguards and try if the 'little Nightingale' can't be heard again.

SOME OBSERVATIONS UPON AN
ARTICLE IN BLACKWOOD'S MAGAZINE
NO. XXIX., AUGUST, 1819

Ravenna, March 15, 1820

'The life of a writer' has been said, by Pope, I believe, to be '*a warfare upon earth*'. As far as my own experience has gone, I have nothing to say against the proposition; and, like the rest, having once plunged into this state of hostility, must, however reluctantly, carry it on. An article has appeared in a periodical work, entitled 'Remarks on *Don Juan*', which has been so full of this spirit, on the part of the writer, as to require some observations on mine.

In the first place, I am not aware by what right the writer assumes this work, which is anonymous, to be my production. He will answer, that there is internal evidence; that is to say, that there are passages which appear to be written in my name, or in my manner. But might not this have been done on purpose by another? He will say, why not then deny it? To this I could answer, that of all the things attributed to me within the last five years, – Pilgrimages to Jerusalem, Deaths upon Pale Horses, Odes to the Land of the Gaul, Adieus to England, Songs to Madame La Valette, Odes to St Helena, Vampires, and what not, – of which, God knows, I never composed nor read a syllable beyond their titles in advertisements, – I never thought it worth while to disavow any, except *one* which came linked with an account of my 'residence in the isle of Mitylene,' where I never resided, and appeared to be carrying the amusement of those persons, who think my name can be of any use to them, a little too far.

I should hardly, therefore, if I did not take the trouble to disavow these things published in my name, and yet not mine, go out of my way to deny an anonymous work; which might appear an act of supererogation. With regard to *Don Juan*, I neither deny nor admit it to be mine – every body may form their own opinion; but, if there be any who now, or in the progress of that poem, if it is to be continued, feel, or should feel themselves so aggrieved as to require a more explicit answer, privately and personally, they shall have it.

I have never shrunk from the responsibility of what I have written, and have more than once incurred obloquy by neglecting to disavow what was attributed to my pen without foundation.

The greater part, however, of the 'Remarks on *Don Juan*' contain but little on the work itself, which receives an extraordinary portion of praise as a composition. With the exception of some quotations, and a few incidental remarks, the rest of the article is neither more nor less than a personal attack upon the imputed author. It is not the first in the same publication: for I recollect to have read, some time ago, similar remarks upon *Beppo* (said to have been written by a celebrated northern preacher); in which the conclusion drawn was, that 'Childe Harold, Byron, and the Count in *Beppo*, were one and the same person'; thereby making me turn out to be, as Mrs Malaprop says, '*like Cerberus, three gentlemen at once*'. That article was signed 'Presbyter Anglicanus'; which, I presume, being interpreted, means Scotch Presbyterian. I must here observe, and it is at once ludicrous and vexatious to be compelled so frequently to repeat the same thing, – that my case, as an author, is peculiarly hard, in being everlastingly taken, or mistaken for my own protagonist. It is unjust and particular. I never heard that my friend Moore was set down for a fire-worshipper on account of his Guebre; that Scott was identified with Roderick Dhu, or with Balfour of Burley; or that, notwithstanding all the magicians in *Thalaba*, any body has ever taken Mr Southey for a conjuror; whereas I have had some difficulty in extricating me even from Manfred, who, as Mr Southey slily observes in one of his articles in the *Quarterly*, 'met the devil on the Jungfrau, and bullied him': and I answer Mr Southey, who has apparently, in his poetical life, not been so successful against the great enemy, that, in this, Manfred exactly followed the sacred precept, – 'Resist the devil, and he will flee from you.' – I shall have more

336

to say on the subject of this person – not the devil, but his most humble servant Mr Southey – before I conclude; but, for the present, I must return to the article in the *Edinburgh Magazine*.

In the course of this article, amidst some extraordinary observations, there occur the following words: – 'It appears, in short, as if this miserable man, having exhausted *every species* of sensual gratification, – having drained the cup of sin even to its bitterest dregs, were resolved to show us that he is no longer a human being even in his frailties, – but a cool, unconcerned fiend, laughing with a detestable glee over the whole of the better and worse elements of which human life is composed.' In another place there appears, 'the lurking-place of his selfish and polluted exile'. – 'By my troth, these be bitter words!' – With regard to the first sentence, I shall content myself with observing, that it appears to have been composed for Sardanapalus, Tiberius, the Regent Duke of Orleans, or Louis XV.; and that I have copied it with as much indifference as I would a passage from Suetonius, or from any of the private memoirs of the regency, conceiving it to be amply refuted by the terms in which it is expressed, and to be utterly inapplicable to any private individual. On the words, 'lurking-place', and 'selfish and polluted exile', I have something more to say. – How far the capital city of a government, which survived the vicissitudes of thirteen hundred years, and might still have existed but for the treachery of Buonaparte, and the iniquity of his imitators, – a city which was the emporium of Europe when London and Edinburgh were dens of barbarians, – may be termed a 'lurking-place', I leave to those who have seen or heard of Venice to decide. How far my exile may have been 'polluted', it is not for me to say, because the word is a wide one, and, with some of its branches, may chance to over-shadow the actions of most men; but that it has been '*selfish*' I deny. If, to the extent of my means and my power, and my in-formation of their calamities, to have assisted many miserable beings reduced by the decay of the place of their birth, and their consequent loss of substance – if to have never rejected an application which appeared founded on truth – if to have expended in this manner sums far out of proportion to my fortune, there and elsewhere, be selfish, then have I been selfish. To have done such things I do not deem much; but it is hard indeed to be compelled to recapitulate them in my own defence, by such accusations as that before me, like a panel before a jury calling testimonies to his character, or a soldier recording his services to obtain his discharge. If the person who has made the charge of 'selfishness' wishes to inform himself further on the subject, he may acquire, not what he would wish to find, but what will silence and shame him, by applying to the Consul-General of our nation, resident in the place, who will be in the case either to confirm or deny what I have asserted.

I neither make, nor have ever made, pretensions to sanctity of demeanour, nor regularity of conduct; but my means have been expended principally on my own gratification, neither now nor heretofore, neither in England nor out of it; and it wants but a word from me, if I thought that word decent or necessary, to call forth the most willing witnesses, and at once witnesses and proofs, in England itself, to show that there are those who have derived not the mere temporary relief of a wretched boon, but the means which led them to immediate happiness and ultimate independence, by my want of that very *selfishness*, as grossly as falsely now imputed to my conduct.

Had I been a selfish man – had I been a grasping man – had I been, in the worldly sense of the word even a *prudent* man, – I should not be where I now am; I should not have taken the step which was the first that led to the events which have sunk and swoln a gulf between me and mine; but in this respect the truth will one day be made known: in the mean time, as Durande says, in the Cave of Montesinos, 'Patience, and shuffle the cards'.

I bitterly feel the ostentation of this statement, the first of the kind I have ever made: I feel the degradation of being compelled to make it; but I also feel its *truth*, and I trust to feel it on my death-bed, should it be my lot to die there. I am not less sensible of the egotism of all this: but, alas! who have made me thus egotistical in my own defence, if not they, who, by perversely persisting in referring fiction to truth, and tracing poetry to life, and regarding characters of imagination as creatures of existence, have made me personally responsible for almost every poetical delineation which fancy and a particular bias of thought, may have tended to produce?

The writer continues: 'Those who are acquainted, *as who is not?* with the *main* incidents of the private life of Lord B.,' etc. Assuredly, whoever may be acquainted with these 'main incidents,' the writer of the 'Remarks on *Don Juan*' is not, or he would use a very different language. That which I believe he alludes to as a 'main incident,' happened to be a very subordinate one, and the natural and almost inevitable consequence of events and circumstances long prior to the period at which it occurred. It is the last drop which makes the cup run over, and mine was already full. – But, to return to this man's charge: he accuses Lord B. of 'an elaborate satire on the character and manners of his wife'. From what part of *Don Juan* the writer has inferred this he himself best knows. As far as I recollect of the female characters in that production, there is but one who is depicted in ridiculous colours, or that could be interpreted as a satire upon any body. But here my poetical sins are again visited upon me, supposing that the poem be mine. If I depict a corsair, a misanthrope, a libertine, a chief of insurgents, or an infidel, he is set down to the author; and if, in a poem by no means ascertained to be my production, there appears a disagreeable, casuistical, and by no means respectable female pedant, it is set down for my wife. Is there any resemblance? If there be, it is in those who make it. I can see none. In my writings I have rarely described any character under a fictitious name: those of whom I have spoken have had their own – in many cases a stronger satire in itself than any which could be appended to it. But of real circumstances I have availed myself plentifully, both in the serious and ludicrous – they are to poetry what landscapes are to the painter; but my *figures* are not portraits. It may even have happened, that I have seized on some events that have occurred under my own observation, or in my own family, as I would paint a view from my grounds, did it harmonise with my picture; but I never would introduce the likenesses of its living members, unless their features could be made as favourable to themselves as to the effect; which, in the above instance, would be extremely difficult.

My learned brother proceeds to observe, that 'it is in vain for Lord B. to attempt in any way to justify his own behaviour in that affair; and now that he has so *openly* and *audaciously* invited enquiry and reproach, we do not see any good reason why he should not be plainly told so by the voice of his country-men.' How far the 'openness' of an anonymous poem, and the 'audacity' of an imaginary character, which the writer supposes to be meant for Lady B., may be deemed to merit this formidable denunciation from their 'most sweet voices', I neither know nor care; but when he tells me that I cannot 'in any way *justify* my own behaviour in that affair,' I acquiese because no man can '*justify*' himself until he knows of what he is accused; and I have never had – and, God knows, my whole desire has ever been to obtain it – any specific charge, in a tangible shape, submitted to me by the adversary, nor by others, unless the atrocities of public rumour and the mysterious silence of the lady's legal advisers may be deemed such. But is not the writer content with what has been already said and done? Has not 'the general voice of his countrymen' long ago pronounced upon the subject – sentence without trial, and condemnation without a charge? Have I not been exiled by ostracism, except that the shells which proscribed me were anonymous? Is the writer ignorant of the public opinion and the public conduct upon that occasion? If he is, I am not: the public will forget both, long before I shall cease to remember either.

The man who is exiled by a faction has the consolation of thinking that he is a martyr; he is upheld by hope and the dignity of his cause, real or imaginary: he who withdraws from the pressure of debt may indulge in the thought that time and prudence will retrieve his circumstances: he who is condemned by the law, has a term to his banishment, or a dream of its abbreviation; or, it may be, the knowledge or the belief of some injustice of the law, or of its administration in his own particular; but he who is outlawed by general opinion, without the interven-tion of hostile politics, illegal judgment, or embarrassed circumstances, whether he be innocent or guilty, must undergo all the bitterness of exile, without hope, without pride, without alleviation. This case was mine. Upon what grounds the public founded their opinion, I am not aware; but it was general, and it was decisive. Of me or of mine they knew little, except that I had written what is called poetry, was a nobleman, had married, became a father, and was involved in differences with my wife and her relatives, no one knew why, because the persons complaining refused to state their grievances. The fashionable world was divided into parties, mine consisting of a very small minority: the reasonable world was naturally on the stronger side, which happened to be the lady's, as was most proper and polite. The press was active and scurrilous; and such was the rage of the day, that the unfortunate publication of two copies of verses, rather complimentary than otherwise to the subjects of both, was tortured into a species of crime, or constructive petty treason. I was accused of every monstrous vice by public rumour and private rancour: my name, which had been a knightly or a noble one since my fathers helped to conquer the kingdom for William the Norman, was tainted. I felt that, if what was whispered, and muttered, and murmured, was true, I was unfit for England; if false, England was unfit for me. I withdrew: but this was not enough. In other countries, in Switzerland, in the shadow of the Alps, and by the blue depth of the lakes, I was pursued and breathed upon by the same blight. I crossed the mountains, but it was the same; so I went a little farther, and settled myself by the waves of the Adriatic, like the stag at bay, who betakes him to the waters.

If I may judge by the statements of the few friends who gathered round me, the outcry of the period to which I allude was beyond all precedent, all parallel, even in those cases where political motives have sharpened slander and doubled enmity. I was advised not to go to the theatres, lest I should be hissed, nor to my duty in parliament, lest I should be insulted by the way; even on the day of my departure, my most intimate friend told me afterwards, that he was under apprehensions of violence from the people who might be assembled at the door of the carriage. However, I was not deterred by these counsels from seeing Kean in his best characters, nor from voting according to my principles; and with regard to the third and last apprehensions of my friends, I could not share in them, not being made acquainted with their extent, till some time after I had crossed the Channel. Even if I had been so, I am not of a nature to be much affected by men's anger, though I may feel hurt by their aversion. Against all individual outrage, I could protect or redress myself; and against that of a crowd, I should probably have been enabled to defend myself, with the assistance of others, as has been done cn similar occasions.

I retired from the country, perceiving that I was the object of general obloquy; I did not indeed imagine, like Jean Jacques Rousseau, that all mankind was in a conspiracy against me, though I had perhaps as good grounds for such a chimera as ever he had: but I perceived that I had to a great extent become personally obnoxious in England, perhaps through my own fault, but the fact was indisputable; the public in general would hardly have been so much excited against a more popular character, without at least an accusation or a charge of some kind actually expressed or substantiated, for I can hardly conceive that the common and every-day occurrence of a separation between man and wife could in itself produce so great a ferment. I shall say nothing of the usual complaints of 'being prejudiced', 'condemned unheard', 'unfairness', 'partiality', and so forth, the usual changes rung by parties who have had, or are to have, a trial; but I was a little surprised to find myself condemned without being favoured with the act of accusation, and to perceive in the absence of this portentous charge or charges, whatever it or they were to be, that every possible or impossible crime was rumoured to supply its place, and taken for granted. This could only occur in the case of a person very much disliked, and I knew no remedy, having already used to their extent whatever little powers I might possess of pleasing in society. I had no party in fashion, though I was afterwards told that there was one – but it was not of my formation, nor did I then know of its existence – none in literature; and in politics I had voted with the Whigs, with precisely that importance which a Whig vote possesses in these Tory days, and with such personal acquaintance with the leaders in both houses as the society in which I lived sanctioned, but without claim or expectation of any thing like friendship from any one, except a few young men of my own age and standing, and a few others more advanced in life, which last it had been my fortune to serve in circumstances of difficulty. This was, in fact, to stand alone: and I recollect, some time after, Madame de Stael said to me in Switzerland, 'You should not have warred with the world – it will not do – it is too strong always for any individual: I myself once tried it in early life, but it will not do.' I perfectly acquiesce in the truth of this remark; but the world has done me the honour to begin the war; and, assuredly, if peace is only to be obtained by courting and paying tribute to it, I am not qualified to obtain its countenance. I thought, in the words of Campbell,

> Then wed thee to an exiled lot,
> And if the world hath loved thee not,
> Its absence may be borne.

I recollect, however, that, having been much hurt by Romilly's conduct, (he, having a general retainer for me, had acted as adviser to the adversary, alleging, on being reminded of his retainer, that he had forgotten it, as his clerk had so many,) I observed that some of those who were now eagerly laying the axe to my roof-tree, might see their own shaken, and feel a portion of what they had inflicted, – His fell, and crushed him.

I have heard of, and believe, that there are human beings so constituted as to be insensible to injuries; but I believe that the best mode to avoid taking vengeance is to get out of the way of temptation. I hope that I may never have the opportunity, for I am not quite sure that I could resist it, having derived from my mother something of the 'perfervidum ingenium Scotorum'. I have not sought, and shall not seek it, and perhaps it may never come in my path. I do not in this allude to the party who might be right or wrong; but to many who made her cause the pretext of their own bitterness. She, indeed, must have long avenged me in her own feelings; for whatever her reasons may have been (and she never adduced them to me at least), she probably neither contemplated nor conceived to what she became the means of conducting the father of her child, and the husband of her choice.

So much for 'the general voice of his countrymen:' I will now speak of some in particular.

In the beginning of the year 1817, an article appeared in the *Quarterly Review*,[6] written, I believe, by Walter Scott, doing great honour to him, and no disgrace to me, though both poetically and personally more than sufficiently favourable to the work and the author of whom it treated. It was written at a time when a selfish man would not, and a timid one dared not, have said a word in favour of either; it was written by one to whom temporary public opinion had elevated me to the rank of a rival – a proud distinction, and unmerited; but which has not prevented me from feeling as a friend, nor him from more than corresponding to that sentiment. The article in question was written upon the Third Canto of *Childe Harold*; and after many observations, which it would as ill become me to repeat as to forget, concluded with 'a hope that I might yet return to England.' How this expression was received in England itself I am not acquainted, but it gave great offence at Rome to the respectable ten or twenty thousand English travellers then and there assembled. I did not visit Rome till some time after, so that I had no opportunity of knowing the fact; but I was informed, long afterwards, that the greatest indignation had been manifested in the enlightened Anglo-circle of that year, which happened to comprise within it – amidst a considerable leaven of Welbeck street and Devonshire Place, broken loose upon their travels – several really well born and well-bred families, who did not the less participate in the feeling of the hour. '*Why* should he return to England?' was the general exclamation – I answer *why*? It is a question I have occasionally asked myself, and I never yet could give it a satisfactory reply. I had then no thoughts of returning, and if I have any now, they are of business, and not of pleasure. Amidst the ties that have been dashed to pieces, there are links yet entire, though the chain itself be broken. There are duties, and connections, which may one day require my presence – and I am a father. I have still some friends whom I wish to meet again, and it may be an enemy. These things, and those minuter details of business, which time accumulates during absence, in every man's affairs and property, may, and probably will, recall me to England; but I shall return with the same feelings with which I left it, in respect to itself, though altered with regard to individuals, as I have been more or less informed of their conduct since my departure; for it was only a considerable time after it that I was made acquainted with the real facts and full extent of some of their proceedings and language. My friends, like other friends, from conciliatory motives, withheld from me much that they could, and some things which they *should* have unfolded; however, that which is deferred is not lost – but it has been no fault of mine that it has been deferred at all.

I have alluded to what is said to have passed at Rome merely to show that the sentiment which I have described was not confined to the English in England, and as forming part of my answer to the reproach cast upon what has been called my 'selfish exile,' and my 'voluntary exile.' 'Voluntary' it has been; for who would dwell among a people entertaining strong hostility against him? How far it has been 'selfish' has been already explained.

I have now arrived at a passage describing me as having vented my 'spleen against the lofty-minded and virtuous men', men 'whose virtues few indeed can equal'; meaning, I humbly presume, the notorious triumvirate known by the name of 'Lake Poets' in their aggregate capacity, and by Southey, Wordsworth, and Coleridge, when taken singly. I wish to say a word or two upon the virtues of one of those persons, public and private, for reasons which will soon appear.

When I left England in April, 1816, ill in mind, in body, and in circumstances, I took up my residence at Coligny, by the lake of Geneva. The sole companion of my journey was a young physician,[7] who had to make his way in the world, and having seen very little of it, was naturally and laudably desirous of seeing more society than suited my present habits or my past experience. I therefore presented him to those gentlemen of Geneva for whom I had letters of introduction; and having thus seen him in a situation to make his own way, retired for my own part entirely from society, with the exception of one English family, living at about a quarter of a mile's distance from Diodati, and with the further exception of some occasional intercourse with Coppet at the wish of Madame de Staël. The English family to which I allude consisted of two ladies, a gentleman and his son, a boy of a year old.[8]

One of '*these lofty-minded and virtuous men*', in the words of the *Edinburgh Magazine*, made, I understand, about this time, or soon after, a tour in Switzerland. On his return to England, he circulated – and for any thing I know, invented – a report, that the gentleman to whom I have alluded and myself were living in promiscuous intercourse with two sisters, 'having formed a league of incest' (I quote the words as they were stated to me), and indulged himself on the natural comments upon such a conjunction, which are said to have been repeated publicly, with great complacency, by *another* of that poetical fraternity, of whom I shall say only, that even had the story been true, *he* should not have repeated it, as far as it regarded myself, except in sorrow. The tale itself requires but a word in answer – the ladies were *not* sisters, nor in any degree connected, except by the second marriage of their respective parents, a widower with a widow, both being the off-spring of former marriages; neither of them were, in 1816, nineteen years old. 'Promiscuous intercourse' could hardly have disgusted the great patron of pantisocracy, (does Mr Southey remember such a scheme?) but there was none.

How far this man, who, as author of *Wat Tyler*, has been maintained by the Lord Chancellor guilty of a treasonable and blasphemous libel, and denounced in the House of Commons, by the upright and able member for Norwich, as a 'rancorous renegado', be fit for sitting as a judge upon others, let others judge. He has said that for this expression 'he brands William Smith on the forehead as a calumniator', and that 'the mark will outlast his epitaph'. How long William Smith's epitaph will last,

and in what words it will be written, I know not, but William
Smith's words form the epitaph itself of Robert Southey. He has
written *Wat Tyler*, and taken the office of poet laureate – he has,
in the *Life of Henry Kirke White*, denominated reviewing 'the
ungentle craft', and has become a reviewer – he was one of the
projectors of a scheme, called 'pantisocracy', for having all
things, including women, in common, (*query*, common women?)
and he sets up as a moralist – he denounced the battle of Blenheim,
and he praised the battle of Waterloo – he loved Mary Wolstone-
craft, and he tried to blast the character of her daughter (one of
the young females mentioned) – he wrote treason, and serves the
king – he was the butt of the *Antijacobin*, and he is the prop of the
Quarterly Review; licking the hands that smote him, eating the
bread of his enemies, and internally writhing beneath his own
contempt, – he would fain conceal, under anonymous bluster,
and a vain endeavour to obtain the esteem of others, after having
for ever lost his own, his leprous sense of his own degradation.
What is there in such a man to 'envy?' Who ever envied the
envious? Is it his birth, his name, his fame, or his virtues, that
I am to 'envy?' I was born of the aristocracy, which he abhorred;
and am sprung, by my mother, from the kings who preceded those
whom he has hired himself to sing. It cannot, then, be his birth.
As a poet, I have, for the past eight years, had nothing to
apprehend from a competition; and for the future, 'that life to
come in every poet's creed', it is open to all. I will only remind
Mr Southey, in the words of a critic,[9] who, if still living, would
have annihilated Southey's literary existence now and hereafter,
as the sworn foe of charlatans and imposters, from Macpherson
downwards, that 'those dreams were Settle's once and Ogilby's';
and for my own part, I assure him, that whenever he and his sect
are remembered, I shall be proud to be 'forgot'. That he is not
content with his success as a poet may reasonably be believed – he
has been the nine-pin of reviews; the *Edinburgh* knocked him
down, and the *Quarterly* set him up; the government found him
useful in the periodical line, and made a point of recommending
his works to purchasers, so that he is occasionally bought, (I
mean his books, as well as the author,) and may be found on the

same shelf, if not the table, of most of the gentlemen employed in the different offices. With regard to his private virtues, I know nothing – of his principles, I have heard enough. As far as having been, to the best of my power, benevolent to others, I do not fear the comparison; and for the errors of the passions, was Mr Southey *always* so tranquil and stainless? Did he *never* covet his neighbour's wife? Did he never calumniate his neighbour's wife's daughter, the offspring of her he coveted? So much for the apostle of pantisocracy.

Of the 'lofty-minded, virtuous' Wordsworth, one anecdote will suffice to speak his sincerity. In a conversation with Mr — upon poetry, he concluded with, 'After all, I would not give five shillings for all that Southey has ever written.' Perhaps this calculation might rather show his esteem for five shillings than his low estimate of Dr Southey; but considering that when he was in his need, and Southey had a shilling, Wordsworth is said to have had generally a sixpence out of it, it has an awkward sound in the way of valuation. This anecdote was told me by persons who, if quoted by name, would prove that its genealogy is poetical as well as true. I can give my authority for this; and am ready to adduce it also for Mr Southey's circulation of the falsehood before mentioned.

Of Coleridge, I shall say nothing – *why*, he may divine.[10]

I have said more of these people than I intended in this place, being somewhat stirred by the remarks which induced me to commence upon the topic. I see nothing in these men as poets, or as individuals – little in their talents, and less in their characters, to prevent honest men from expressing for them considerable contempt, in prose or rhyme, as it may happen. Mr Southey has the *Quarterly* for his field of rejoinder, and Mr Wordsworth his postscripts to *Lyrical Ballads*, where the two great instances of the sublime are taken from himself and Milton. 'Over her own sweet voice the stock-dove broods'; that is to say, she has the pleasure of listening to herself, in common with Mr Wordsworth upon most of his public appearances. 'What divinity doth hedge' these persons, that we should respect them? Is it Apollo? Are they not of those who called Dryden's *Ode* 'a drunken song?'

who have discovered that Gray's *Elegy* is full of faults, (see Coleridge's *Life*, vol. i. *note*, for Wordsworth's kindness in pointing this out to him,) and have published what is allowed to be the very worst prose that ever was written, to prove that Pope was no poet, and that William Wordsworth is?

In other points, are they respectable, or respected? Is it on the open avowal of apostasy, on the patronage of government, that their claim is founded? Who is there who esteems those parricides of their own principles? They are, in fact, well aware that the reward of their change has been any thing but honour. The times have preserved a respect for political consistency, and, even though changeable, honour the unchanged. Look at Moore: it will be long ere Southey meets with such a triumph in London as Moore met with in Dublin, even if the government subscribe for it, and set the money down to secret service. It was not less to the man than to the poet, to the tempted but unshaken patriot, to the not opulent but incorruptible fellow citizen, that the warm-hearted Irish paid the proudest of tributes. Mr Southey may applaud himself to the world, but he has his own heartiest contempt; and the fury with which he foams against all who stand in the phalanx which he forsook, is, as William Smith described it, 'the rancour of the renegado,' the bad language of the prostitute who stands at the corner of the street, and showers her slang upon all, except those who may have bestowed upon her her 'little shilling' ...

TO RICHARD BELGRAVE HOPPNER *Ravenna, April 22nd 1820*

... About Allegra, I can only say to Claire – that I so totally disapprove of the mode of Children's treatment in their family, that I should look upon the Child as going into a hospital. Is it not so? Have they *reared* one? Her health here has hitherto been *excellent*, and her temper not bad; she is sometimes vain and obstinate, but always clean and cheerful, and as, in a year or two, I shall either send her to England, or put her in a Convent for education, these defects will be remedied as far as they can in human nature. But the Child shall not quit me again to perish of Starvation, and green fruit, or be taught to believe that there is no Deity. Whenever there is convenience of vicinity and access, her Mother can always have her with her; otherwise no. It was so stipulated from the beginning.

The Girl is not so well off as with you, but far better than with them; the fact is she is spoilt, being a great favourite with every body on account of the fairness of her skin, which shines among their dusky children like the milky way, but there is no comparison of her situation now, and that under Elise, or with them. She has grown considerably, is very clean, and lively. She has plenty of air and exercise at home, and she goes out daily with Me Guiccioli in her carriage to the Corso.

The paper is finished and so must the letter be.

Yours ever,

B.

TO JOHN MURRAY   *Ravenna, May 20th, 1820*

Dear Murray, – ... Excuse haste: if you knew what I have on hand, you would.

In the first place, *your packets*; then a letter from Kinnaird on the most urgent business: another from Moore, about a communication to Lady B[yron] of importance; a fourth from the mother of Allegra; and, fifthly, the Contessa G[uiccioli] is on the eve of being divorced on account of our having been taken together *quasi* in the fact, and, what is worse, that she did not *deny* it: but the Italian public are on our side, particularly the women, – and the men also, because they say that *he* had no business to take the business up now after a year of toleration. The law is against him, because he slept with his wife after her admission. All her relations (who are numerous, high in rank, and powerful) are furious *against him* for his conduct, and his not wishing to be cuckolded at *three*score, when everyone else is at ONE. I am warned to be on my guard, as he is very capable of employing *Sicarii*[11] – this is in Latin as well as in Italian, so you can understand it; but I have arms, and don't mind them, thinking that I can pepper his ragamuffins if they don't come unawares, and that, if they do, one may as well end that way as another; and it would besides serve you as an advertisement: – ...

TO THOMAS MOORE   *Ravenna, July 13, 1820*

To remove or increase your Irish anxiety about my being 'in a wisp', I answer your letter forthwith; premising that, as I am a '*Will* of the wisp', I may chance to flit out of it. But, first, a word on the Memoir; – I have no objection, nay, I would rather that *one* correct copy was taken and deposited in honourable hands, in case of accidents happening to the original; for you know that I have none, and have never even *re*-read, nor, indeed, *read* at all what is there written; I only know that I wrote it with the fullest intention to be 'faithful and true' in my narrative, but *not* impartial – no, by the Lord! I can't pretend to be that, while I feel. But I wish to give every body concerned the opportunity to contradict or correct me.

I have no objection to any proper person seeing what is there written – seeing it was written, like every thing else, for the purpose of being read, however much many writings may fail in arriving at that object.

With regard to 'the wisp', the Pope has pronounced *their separation.*[12] The decree came yesterday from Babylon, – it was *she* and *her friends* who demanded it, on the grounds of her husband's (the noble Count Cavalier's) extraordinary usage. *He* opposed it with all his might because of the alimony, which has been assigned, with all her goods, chattels, carriage, etc., to be restored by him. In Italy they can't divorce. He insisted on her giving me up, and he would forgive every thing, – even the adultery, which he swears that he can prove by 'famous witnesses'. But, in this country, the very courts hold such proofs in abhorrence, the Italians being as much more delicate in public than the English, as they are more passionate in private.

The friends and relatives, who are numerous and powerful, reply to him – ' *You*, yourself, are either fool or knave, – fool, if you did not see the consequences of the approximation of these two young persons, – knave, if you connive at it. Take your choice, – but don't break out (after twelve months of the closest intimacy, under your own eyes and positive sanction) with a scandal, which can only make you ridiculous and her unhappy.'

He swore that he thought our intercourse was purely amicable, and that *I* was more partial to him than to her, till melancholy testimony proved the contrary. To this they answer, that 'Will of *this* wisp' was not an unknown person, and that '*clamosa Fama*'[13] had not proclaimed the purity of my morals; – that *her* brother, a year ago, wrote from Rome to warn him that his wife would infallibly be led astray by this *ignis fatuus*,[14] unless he took proper measures, all of which he neglected to take, etc., etc.

Now he says that he encouraged my return to Ravenna, to see '*in quanti piedi di acqua siamo*',[15] and he has found enough to drown him in. In short,

> Ce ne fut pas le tout; sa femme se plaignit –
> Procès – La parenté se joint en excuse et dit
> Que du Docteur venoit tout le mauvais ménage;
> Que cet homme étoit fou, que sa femme étoit sage.
> On fit casser le mariage.

It is best to let the women alone, in the way of conflict, for they are sure to win against the field. She returns to her father's house, and I can only see her under great restrictions – such is the custom of the country. The relations behave very well: – I offered any settlement, but they refused to accept it, and swear she *shan't* live with G[uiccioli] (as he has tried to prove her faithless), but that he shall maintain her; and, in fact, a judgment to this effect came yesterday. I am, of course, in an awkward situation enough . . .

TO JOHN MURRAY   *Ravenna, July 22nd 1820*

Dear Murray, – The tragedy is finished, but when it will be copied is more than can be reckoned upon. We are here upon the eve of evolutions and revolutions. Naples is revolutionized, and the ferment is among the Romagnuoles, by far the bravest and most original of the present Italians, though still half savage. Buonaparte said the troops from Romagna were the best of his Italic corps, and I believe it. The Neapolitans are not worth a curse, and will be beaten if it comes to fighting: the rest of Italy, I think, might stand. The Cardinal is at his wits' end; it is true that he had not far to go. Some papal towns on the Neapolitan frontier have already revolted. Here there are as yet but the sparks of the volcano; but the ground is hot, and the air sultry. Three assassinations last week here and at Faenza – an anti-liberal priest, a factor, and a trooper last night, – I heard the pistol-shot that brought him down within a short distance of my own door. There had been quarrels between the troops and people of some duration: this is the third soldier wounded within the last month. There is a great commotion in people's minds, which will lead to nobody knows what – a row probably. There are secret Societies all over the country as in Germany, who cut off those obnoxious to them, like the Free tribunals, be they high or low; and then it becomes impossible to discover or punish the assassins – their measures are taken so well . . .

TO THE HON. AUGUSTA LEIGH   *Ravenna, August 19th 1820*

My Dearest Augusta, – I always loved you better than any earthly existence, and I always shall unless I go mad. And if I did *not* so love you – still I would not persecute or oppress any one wittingly – especially for debts, of which I know the *agony by experience*. Of Colonel Leigh's bond, I really have forgotten all particulars, except that it was *not* of *my wishing*. And I never would nor ever will be *pressed* into the *Gang of his creditors*. I would *not take the money* if he had it. You may judge if I would dun him having it not —

Whatever measure I can take for his extrication will be taken. Only tell me how – for I am ignorant, and far away. *Who does* and *who can* accuse *you* of 'interested views'? I think people must have gone into Bedlam such things appear to me so very incomprehensible. Pray explain –

Yours ever and truly

BYRON

TO RICHARD BELGRAVE HOPPNER *Ravenna, Septr. 10th 1820*

... I regret that you have such a bad opinion of Shiloh;[16] you used to have a good one. Surely he has talent and honour, but is crazy against religion and morality. His tragedy is sad work; but the subject renders it so. His *Islam* had much poetry. You seem lately to have got some notion against him.

Clare writes me the most insolent letters about Allegra; see what a man gets by taking care of natural children! Were it not for the poor little child's sake, I am almost tempted to send her back to her atheistical mother, but that would be too bad; you cannot conceive the excess of her insolence, and I know not why, for I have been at great care and expense, – taking a house in the country on purpose for her. She has *two* maids and every possible attention. If Clare thinks that she shall ever interfere with the child's morals or education, she mistakes; she never shall. The girl shall be a Christian and a married woman, if possible. As to seeing her, she may see her – under proper restrictions; but she is not to throw every thing into confusion with her Bedlam behaviour. To express it delicately, I think Madame Clare is a damned bitch. What think you?

Yours ever and truly,

BN.

TO THE HON. DOUGLAS KINNAIRD *Ravenna,*
September 17th, 1820

Dear Douglas, – I got your letter – why, man! what are ye aboot? What makes you so careful of your paper? Is it for the sake of contrast? This is the Paper Age. The Golden, the Silver and the Iron ages are long since past, the two former *never to return*! We are now happily arrived at the *Age of Rags*. The *He*-mans and *She*-mans of our literature are as plenty as blackberries as we of the North say. They have made a *litter*ature of literature, which at this moment is more extensively spread; but 'tis grown shallow, it seems, in proportion to its diffusion. Our age is in everything an affected age, and where affection prevails the *fair* sex – or rather the *blue* are always strongly tinctured with it. A little learning may be swelled to an enormous size by artifice. Madam de Stael, I grant, is a clever woman; but all the other *madams* are no Staels. The philosophical petticoats of our times surpass even those of the age of Elizabeth who pretended to cultivate an acquaintance with the classics. Roger Asham tells us that, going to wait on Lady Jane Grey at her father's house in Leicestershire, he found her reading Plato's works in the Greek, while the rest of the family were hunting in the park. Possibly the lady had no objection to be interrupted in her studies – *she* was *hunting* for applause. I shall be at them one of these days – there is nothing like ridicule, the only weapon that the English climate cannot rust ...

TO RICHARD BELGRAVE HOPPNER   *Ravenna, 8 bre. 1⁰· 1820*

... The Shiloh story is true no doubt,[17] though Elise is but a sort of *Queen's evidence*. You remember how eager she was to return to them, and then she goes away and abuses them. Of the facts, however, there can be little doubt; it is just like them. You may be sure that I keep your counsel.

What you say of the Queen's affair[18] is very just and true; but the event seems not very easy to anticipate.

I enclose an epistle from Shiloh.

Yours ever and truly,

BYRON

TO JOHN MURRAY   *Ravenna, 9ᵇʳᵉ4⁰, 1820*

... P.S. – There will be shortly '*the Devil to pay*' *here*; and, as there is no saying that I may not form an *Item in his bill*, I shall not now write at greater length: *you* have not *answered* my late letters; and you have acted foolishly, as you will find out some day.

P.S. – I have read part of the *Quarterly* just arrived: Mr Bowles shall be answered; he is not *quite* correct in his statement about E[nglish] B[ards] and S[cotch] R[eviewers]. They support Pope,

I see, in the *Quarterly*. Let them continue to do so: it is a Sin, and a Shame, and a *damnation* to think that Pope!! should require it – but he does. Those miserable mountebanks of the day, the poets, disgrace themselves and deny God, in running down Pope, the most *faultless* of Poets, and almost of men.

The *Edinburgh* praises Jack Keats or Ketch, or whatever his names are: why, his is the Onanism of Poetry – something like the pleasure an Italian fiddler extracted out of being suspended daily by a Street Walker in Drury Lane. This went on for some weeks: at last the Girl went to get a pint of Gin – met another, chatted too long, and Cornelli was *hanged outright before she returned*. Such like is the trash they praise, and such will be the end of the *outstretched* poesy of this miserable Self-polluter of the human mind.

W. Scott's *Monastery* just arrived: many thanks for that Grand Desideratum of the last six months ...

TO JOHN MURRAY   R[avenn]a, 9bre 9°, 1820

... Hobhouse writes me a facetious letter about my *indolence* and love of Slumber. It becomes him: he is in active life; he writes pamphlets against Canning, to which he does not put his name; he gets into Newgate and into Parliament – both honourable places of refuge; and he 'greatly daring dines' at all the taverns (why don't he set up a *tap* room at once), and then writes to quiz my laziness.

Why, I do like one or two vices, to be sure; but I can back a horse and fire a pistol 'without winking or blinking' like Major Sturgeon; I have fed at times for two months together on *sheer biscuit and water* (without metaphor); I can get over seventy or eighty miles a day *riding* post upon [?] of all sorts, and *swim five* at a Stretch, taking a *piece* before and after, as at Venice, in 1818, or at least I *could do*, and have done it ONCE, and I never was ten minutes in my life over a *solitary* dinner.

Now, my friend Hobhouse, when we were wayfaring men, used to complain grievously of hard beds and sharp insects, while I slept like a top, and to awaken me with his swearing at them: he used to damn his dinners daily, both quality and cookery and quantity, and reproach me for a sort of 'brutal' indifference, as he called it, to these particulars; and now he writes me facetious sneerings because I *do not* get up early in a morning, when there is no occasion – if there were, *he* knows that I was always *out* of bed before him, though it is true that my ablutions detained me longer in dressing than his noble contempt of that 'oriental scrupulosity' permitted.

Then he is still sore about '*the ballad*' – he!! why, he lampooned me at Brighton, in 1808, about Jackson the boxer and bold Webster, etc.: in 1809, he turned the death of my friend E^d *Long* into ridicule and rhyme, because his name was susceptible of a *pun*; and, although he saw that I was distressed at it, before I left England in 1816, he wrote rhymes upon *D. Kinnaird, you*, and *myself*; and at Venice he parodied the lines 'Though the day of my destiny's over' in a comfortable quizzing way: and now he harps on my ballad about his election! Pray tell him all this, for I will have no underhand work with my 'old Cronies'. If he can deny the facts, let him. I maintain that he is more *carnivorously* and *carnally sensual* than I am, though I am bad enough too for that matter; but not in eating and haranguing at the Crown and Anchor, where I never was but twice – and those were at 'Whore's Hops' when I was a younker in my teens; and Egad, I think them the most respectable meetings of the two. But he is a little wroth that I would not come over to the *Queen's* trial: *lazy*, quotha! it is so true that he should be ashamed of asserting it. He counsels me not to 'get into a Scrape'; but, as Beau Clincher says, 'How melancholy are Newgate reflections!' To be sure, his advice is worth following; for experience teacheth: he has been in a dozen within these last two years. *I pronounce me the more temperate of the two* . . .

Mr Keats, whose poetry you enquire after, appears to me what I have already said: such writing is a sort of mental masturbation – f-gg-g his *Imagination*. I don't mean he is *indecent*, but viciously soliciting his own ideas into a state, which is neither poetry nor any thing else but a Bedlam vision produced by raw pork and opium . . .

357

TO THE HON. DOUGLAS KINNAIRD *Ravenna, 9bre 22nd, 1820*

... The affairs of this part of Italy are simplifying; the liberals have delayed till it is too late for them to do any thing to the purpose. If the scoundrels of Troppau decide on a massacre (as is probable) the Barbarians will march in by one frontier, and the Neapolitans by the other. They have *both asked* permission of his Holiness so to do, which is equivalent to asking a man's permission to give him a kick on the a-se; if he grants it, it is a sign he can't return it.

The worst of all is, that this devoted country will become, for the six thousandth time, since God made man in his own image, the seat of war. I recollect Spain in 1809, and the Morea and part of Greece in 1810–11, when Veli Pacha was on his way to combat the Russians (the Turkish armies make their *own country* like an enemy's on a march), and a small stretch also of my own county of Nottingham under the Luddites, when we were burning the frames, and sometimes the manufactories, so that I have a tolerable idea of what may ensue. Here all is suspicion and terrorism, bullying, arming, and disarming; the priests scared, the people gloomy, and the merchants *buying* up corn to *supply the armies*. I am so pleased with the last piece of Italic patriotism, that I have underlined it for your remark; it is just as if our Hampshire farmers should prepare magazines for any two continental scoundrels, who could land and fight it out in New Forest.

I come in for my share of the *vigorous* system of the day. They have taken it into their heads that I am popular (which no one ever was in Italy but an opera singer, or ever will be till the resurrection of Romulus), and are trying by all kinds of petty vexations to disgust and make me retire. This I should hardly believe, it seems so absurd, if some of their priests did not avow it. They try to fix squabbles upon my servants, to involve me in scrapes (no difficult matter), and lastly they (the governing party) menace to shut Madame Guiccioli up in a *convent*. The last piece of policy springs from two motives; the one because her *family* are suspected of liberal principles, and the second because mine (although I do not preach them) are known, and were known when it was far less reputable to be a friend to liberty than it is now ...

P.S. – The police at present is under the Germans, or rather the Austrians, who do not merit the name of Germans, who open all letters it is supposed. I have no objection, so that they see how I hate and utterly despise and detest those *Hun brutes*, and all they can do in their temporary wickedness, for Time and Opinion, and the vengeance of a roused-up people will at length manure Italy with their carcases, it may not be for one year, or two, or ten, but it *will* be, and so that it *could be* sooner, I know not what a man ought *not* to do, but their antagonists are no great shakes. The Spaniards are the boys after all.

TO JOHN MURRAY   *Ravenna, D^{ecr} 9th 1820*

Dear Murray, – I intended to have written to you at some length by this post, but as the Military Commandant is now lying dead in my house, on Fletcher's bed, I have other things to think of.

He was shot at 8 o'clock this evening about two hundred paces from our door. I was putting on my great coat to pay a visit to the Countess G., when I heard a shot, and on going into the hall, found all my servants on the balcony exclaiming that 'a Man was murdered'. As it is the custom here to let people fight it through, they wanted to hinder me from going out; but I ran down into the Street: Tita, the bravest of them, followed me; and we made our way to the Commandant, who was lying on his back, with five wounds, of which three in the body – one in the heart. There were about him Diego, his Adjutant, crying like a Child; a priest howling; a surgeon who dared not touch him; two or three confused and frightened soldiers; one or two of the boldest of the mob; and the Street dark as pitch, with the people flying in all directions. As Diego could only cry and wring his hands, and the Priest could only pray, and nobody seemed able or willing to do anything except exclaim, shake and stare, I made my servant and one of the mob take up the body; sent off Diego crying to the Cardinal, the Soldiers for the Guard;

and had the Commandant conveyed up Stairs to my own quarters. But he was quite gone. I made the surgeon examine him, and examined him myself. He had bled inwardly, and very little external blood was apparent. One of the slugs had gone quite through – all but the skin: I felt it myself. Two more shots in the body, one in a finger, and another in the arm. His face not at all disfigured: he seems asleep, but is growing livid. The assassin has not been taken; but the gun was found – a gun filed down to half the barrel.

He said nothing but *O Dio!* and *O Gesu* two or three times. The house was filled at last with soldiers, officers, police and military; but they are clearing away – all but the sentinels, and the body is to be removed tomorrow. It seems that, if I had not had him taken into my house, he might have lain in the Streets till morning; as here nobody meddles with such things, for fear of the consequences – either of public suspicion, or private revenge on the part of the slayers. They may do as they please: I shall never be deterred from a duty of humanity by all the assassins of Italy, and that is a wide word.

He was a brave officer, but an unpopular man. The whole town is in confusion.

You may judge better of things here by this detail, than by anything which I could add on the Subject: communicate this letter to Hobhouse and Douglas K^d, and believe me

Yours ever truly,

B.

P.S. – The poor Man's wife is not yet aware of his death: they are to break it to her in the morning.

The Lieutenant, who is watching the body, is smoking with the greatest *sangfroid*: a strange people.

TO LADY BYRON   *Ravenna, [Thursday], 10bre 28th*
                                                      1820

I acknowledge your note which is on the whole satisfactory – the style a little harsh – but that was to be expected – it would have been too great a peace-offering after nearly five years – to have been gracious in the manner, as well as in the matter. – Yet you might have been so – for communications between *us* – are like 'Dialogues of the Dead' – or 'letters between this world and the next'. You have alluded to the '*past*' and I to the future. – As to Augusta – she knows as little of my request, as of your answer – Whatever She is or may have been – *you* have never had reason to complain of her – on the contrary – you are not aware of the obligations under which you have been to her. – Her life and mine – and yours and mine – were two things perfectly distinct from each other – when one ceased the other began – and now both are closed.

You must be aware of the reasons of my bequest in favour of Augusta and her Children which are the restrictions I am under by the Settlement, which death would make yours – at least the available portion.

Yours

BYRON

P.S. – Excuse haste – I have scribbled in great quickness, – and do not attribute it to ill-humour – but to matters which are on hand – and which must be attended to – I am really obliged by your attention to my request ... You could not have sent me any thing half so acceptable but I have *burnt* your note that you may be under no restraint but your internal feeling. – It is a comfort to me *now* – beyond all comforts; that A – and her children will be thought of – after I am nothing; but five years ago – it would have been something more – why did you *then keep silence*? I told you that I was going *long* – and going *far* (not so *far* as I intended – for I meant to have gone to Turkey and am not sure that I shall not finish with it – but *longer* than I meant to have made of existence – at least at that time –) and two words about her or hers would have been to me – like vengeance or freedom to an Italian – i.e. the 'Ne plus ultra' of gratifications – She and two others were the only thing I ever really loved – I may say it now – for we are young no longer. –

TO THOMAS MOORE   *Ravenna, January 2, 1821*

... I feel exactly as you do about our 'art', but it comes over me in a kind of rage every now and then, like —, and then, if I don't write to empty my mind, I go mad. As to that regular, uninterrupted love of writing, which you describe in your friend, I do not understand it. I feel it as a torture, which I must get rid of, but never as a pleasure. On the contrary, I think composition a great pain.

EXTRACTS FROM A DIARY JANUARY 4–
FEBRUARY 27 1821

Ravenna, January 4, 1821

... I was out of spirits – read the papers, thought what *fame* was, on reading, in a case of murder, that 'Mr Wych, grocer, at Tunbridge, sold some bacon, flour, cheese, and, it is believed, some plums, to some gipsy woman accused. He had on his counter (I quote faithfully) a *book*, the Life of *Pamela*, which he was *tearing* for *waste* paper, etc., etc. In the cheese was found, etc., and a *leaf* of *Pamela wrapt round the bacon.*' What would Richardson, the vainest and luckiest of *living* authors (*i.e.* while alive) – he who, with Aaron Hill, used to prophesy and chuckle over the presumed fall of Fielding (the *prose* Homer of human nature) and of Pope, (the most beautiful of poets) – what would he have said, could he have traced his pages from their place on the French prince's toilets (see Boswell's Johnson) to the grocer's counter and the gipsy-murderess's bacon!!!

What would he have said? What can any body say, save what Solomon said long before us? After all, it is but passing from one counter to another, from the bookseller's to the other tradesman's – grocer or pastry-cook. For my part, I have met with most poetry upon trunks; so that I am apt to consider the trunk-maker as the sexton of authorship.

Wrote five letters in about half an hour, short and savage, to all my rascally correspondents. Carriage came. Heard the news of three murders at Faenza and Forli – a carabinier, a smuggler, and an attorney – all last night. The two first in a quarrel, the latter by premeditation ...

Carriage at 8 or so – went to visit La Contessa G[uiccioli] – found her playing on the piano-forte – talked till ten, when the Count, her father, and the no less Count, her brother, came in from the theatre. Play, they said, Alfieri's *Fileppo* – well received.

Two days ago the King of Naples passed through Bologna on his way to congress. My servant Luigi brought the news. I had sent him to Bologna for a lamp. How will it end? Time will show . . .

January 5, 1821

Rose late – dull and drooping – the weather dripping and dense. Snow on the ground, and sirocco above in the sky, like yesterday. Roads up to the horse's belly, so that riding (at least for pleasure) is not very feasible. Read the conclusion, for the fiftieth time (I have read all W. Scott's novels at least fifty times), of the third series of *Tales of my Landlord* – grand work – Scotch Fielding, as well as great English poet – wonderful man! I long to get drunk with him . . .

Hear the carriage – order pistols and great coat, as usual – necessary articles. Weather cold – carriage open, and inhabitants somewhat savage – rather treacherous and highly inflamed by politics. Fine fellows, though, – good materials for a nation. Out of chaos God made a world, and out of high passions comes a people.

Clock strikes – going out to make love. Somewhat perilous, but not disagreeable . . .

11 o' the clock and nine minutes. Visited La Contessa G[uiccioli] *nata* G[amba] G[hiselli] . . . At 9 came in her brother, Il Conte Pietro – at 10, her father, Conte Ruggiero.

Talked of various modes of warfare – of the Hungarian and Highland modes of broad-sword exercise, in both whereof I was once a moderate 'master of fence'. Settled that the R. will break out on the 7th or 8th of March, in which appointment I should trust, had it not been settled that it was to have broken out in October, 1820. But those Bolognese shirked the Romagnuoles.

'It is all one to Ranger.' One must not be particular, but take rebellion when it lies in the way. Come home – read the *Ten Thousand* again, and will go to bed . . .

January 6, 1821

Mist – thaw – slop – rain. No stirring out on horseback. Read Spence's *Anecdotes*. Pope a fine fellow – always thought him so.

Corrected blunders in *nine* apophthegms of Bacon – all historical – and read Mitford's *Greece*. Wrote an epigram. Turned to a passage in Guinguené – ditto in Lord Holland's *Lope de Vega.* Wrote a note on *Don Juan.*

At eight went out to visit. Heard a little music – like music . . .

Thought of the state of women under the ancient Greeks – convenient enough. Present state a remnant of the barbarism of the chivalric and feudal ages – artificial and unnatural. They ought to mind home – and be well fed and clothed – but not mixed in society. Well educated, too, in religion – but to read neither poetry nor politics – nothing but books of piety and cookery. Music – drawing – dancing – also a little gardening and ploughing now and then. I have seen them mending the roads in Epirus with good success. Why not, as well as haymaking and milking?

Came home, and read Mitford again, and played with my mastiff – gave him his supper. Made another reading to the epigram, but the turn the same. To-night at the theatre, there being a prince on his throne in the last scene of the comedy, – the audience laughed, and asked him for a *Constitution.* This shows the state of the public mind here, as well as the assassinations. It won't do. There must be an universal republic, – and there ought to be . . .

What is the reason that I have been, all my lifetime, more or less *ennuyé*? and that, if any thing, I am rather less so now than I was at twenty, as far as my recollection serves? I do not know how to answer this, but presume that it is constitutional, – as well as the waking in low spirits, which I have invariably done for many years. Temperance and exercise, which I have practised at times, and for a long time together vigorously and violently, made little or no difference. Violent passions did; – when under their immediate influence – it is odd, but – I was in agitated, but *not* in depressed, spirits.

A dose of salts has the effect of a temporary inebriation, like light champagne, upon me. But wine and spirits make me sullen and savage to ferocity – silent, however, and retiring, and not quarrelsome, if not spoken to. Swimming also raises my spirits,

– but in general they are low, and get daily lower. That is *hopeless*; for I do not think I am so much *ennuyé* as I was at nineteen. The proof is, that then I must game, or drink, or be in motion of some kind, or I was miserable. At present, I can mope in quietness; and like being alone better than any company – except the lady's whom I serve. But I feel a something, which makes me think that, if I ever reach near to old age, like Swift, 'I shall die at top' first. Only I do not dread idiotism or madness so much as he did. On the contrary, I think some quieter stages of both must be preferable to much of what men think the possession of their senses.

January 7, 1821, Sunday

Still rain – mist – snow – drizzle – and all the incalculable combinations of a climate where heat and cold struggle for mastery . . .

The Count Pietro G[amba] took me aside to say that the Patriots have had notice from Forli (twenty miles off) that tonight the government and its party mean to strike a stroke – that the Cardinal here has had orders to make several arrests immediately, and that, in consequence, the Liberals are arming, and have posted patroles in the streets, to sound the alarm and give notice to fight for it.

He asked me 'what should be done?' I answered, 'Fight for it, rather than be taken in detail'; and offered, if any of them are in immediate apprehension of arrest, to receive them in my house (which is defensible), and to defend them, with my servants and themselves (we have arms and ammunition), as long as we can, – or to try to get them away under cloud of night. On going home, I offered him the pistols which I had about me – but he refused, but said he would come off to me in case of accidents.

It wants half an hour of midnight, and rains; – as Gibbet[19] says, 'a fine night for their enterprise – dark as hell, and blows like the devil'. If the row don't happen *now* it must soon. I thought that their system of shooting people would soon produce a re-action – and now it seems coming. I will do what I can in the way of combat, though a little out of exercise. The cause is a good one . . .

Expect to hear the drum and the musquetry momently (for they swear to resist, and are right,) – but I hear nothing, as yet, save the plash of the rain and the gusts of wind at intervals. Don't like to go to bed, because I hate to be waked, and would rather sit up for the row, if there is to be one.

Mended the fire – have got the arms – and a book or two, which I shall turn over. I know little of their numbers, but think the Carbonari strong enough to beat the troops, even here. With twenty men this house might be defended for twenty-four hours against any force to be brought against it, *now* in this place, for the same time; and, in such a time, the country would have notice, and would rise, – if ever they *will* rise, of which there is some doubt. In the mean time, I may as well read as do any thing else, being alone.

January 8, 1821, Monday

Rose, and found Count P. G. in my apartments. Sent away the servant. Told me that, according to the best information, the Government had not issued orders for the arrests apprehended; that the attack in Forli had not taken place (as expected) by the *Sanfedisti* – the opponents of the *Carbonari* or Liberals – and that, as yet, they are still in apprehension only. Asked me for some arms of a better sort, which I gave him. Settled that, in case of a row, the Liberals were to assemble *here* (with me), and that he had given the word to Vincenzo G[allina?] and others of the *Chiefs* for that purpose. He himself and father are going to the chase in the forest; but V.G. is to come to me, and an express to be sent off to him, P.G., if any thing occurs. Concerted operations. They are to seize – but no matter.

I advised them to attack in detail, and in different parties, in different *places* (though at the *same* time), so as to divide the attention of the troops, who, though few, yet being disciplined, would beat any body of people (not trained) in a regular fight – unless dispersed in small parties, and distracted with different assaults. Offered to let them assemble here if they choose. It is a strongish post – narrow street, commanded from within – and tenable walls ...

At eight went to Teresa, Countess G. At nine and a half came in Il Conte R. and Count P.G. Talked of a certain proclamation lately issued. Count R.G. had been with — (the —),[20] to sound him about the arrests. He, —, is a *trimmer*, and deals, at present, his cards with both hands. If he don't mind, they'll be full. — pretends (*I* doubt him – *they* don't, – we shall see) that there is no such order, and seems staggered by the immense exertions of the Neapolitans, and the fierce spirit of the Liberals here. The truth is, that — cares for little but his place (which is a good one), and wishes to play pretty with both parties. He has changed his mind thirty times these last three moons, to my knowledge, for he corresponds with me. But he is not a bloody fellow – only an avaricious one.

It seems that, just at this moment (as Lydia Languish says), 'there will be no elopement after all'. I wish that I had known as much last night – or, rather, this morning – I should have gone to bed two hours earlier. And yet I ought not to complain; for, though it is a sirocco, and heavy rain, I have not *yawned* for these two days . . .

I wonder what figure these Italians will make in a regular row. I sometimes think that, like the Irishman's gun (somebody had sold him a crooked one), they will only do for 'shooting round a corner'; at least, this sort of shooting has been the late tenor of their exploits. And yet there are materials in this people, and a noble energy, if well directed. But who is to direct them? No matter. Out of such times heroes spring. Difficulties are the hot-beds of high spirits, and Freedom the mother of the few virtues incident to human nature.

Tuesday, January 9, 1821

. . . Dined. Read Johnson's *Vanity of Human Wishes*, – all the examples and mode of giving them sublime, as well as the latter part, with the exception of an occasional couplet. I do not so much admire the opening . . . But 'tis a grand poem – and *so true*! true as the 10th of Juvenal himself. The lapse of ages *changes* all things – time – language – the earth – the bounds of the sea – the stars of the sky, and every thing 'about, around,

368

and underneath' man, *except man himself*, who has always been, and always will be, an unlucky rascal. The infinite variety of lives conduct but to death, and the infinity of wishes lead but to disappointment. All the discoveries which have yet been made have multiplied little but existence. An extirpated disease is succeeded by some new pestilence; and a discovered world has brought little to the old one, except the p[ox?] first and freedom afterwards – the *latter* a fine thing, particularly as they gave it to Europe in exchange for slavery. But it is doubtful whether 'the Sovereigns' would not think the *first* the best present of the two to their subjects.

At eight went out – heard some news. They say the King of Naples has declared by couriers from Florence, to the *Powers* (as they call now those wretches with crowns), that his Constitution was compulsive, etc., etc., and that the Austrian barbarians are placed again on *war* pay, and will march. Let them – 'they come like sacrifices in their trim', the hounds of hell! Let it still be a hope to see their bones piled like those of the human dogs at Morat, in Switzerland, which I have seen.

Heard some music. At nine the usual visitors – news, *war*, or rumours of war. Consulted with P.G., etc., etc. They mean to *insurrect* here, and are to honour me with a call thereupon. I shall not fall back; though I don't think them in force or heart sufficient to make much of it. But, *onward*! – it is now the time to act, and what signifies *self*, if a single spark of that which would be worthy of the past can be bequeathed unquenchedly to the future? It is not one man, nor a million, but the *spirit* of liberty which must be spread . . .

January 10, 1821

Day fine – rained only in the morning. Looked over accounts. Read Campbell's *Poets* – marked errors of Tom (the author) for correction. Dined – went out – music – Tyrolese air, with variations. Sustained the cause of the original simple air against the variations of the Italian school.

Politics somewhat tempestuous, and cloudier daily. Tomorrow

being foreign post-day, probably something more will be known.
Came home – read . . .

Midnight

I have been turning over different *Lives* of the Poets. I rarely read
their works, unless an occasional flight over the classical ones,
Pope, Dryden, Johnson, Gray, and those who approach them
nearest (I leave the rant of the rest to the *cant* of the day), and –
I had made several reflections, but I feel sleepy, and may as well
go to bed.

January 11, 1821

Read the letters. Corrected the tragedy and the *Hints from
Horace*. Dined, and got into better spirits. Went out – returned . . .
Alli.[21] writes to me that the Pope, and Duke of Tuscany, and
King of Sardinia, have also been called to Congress; but the
Pope will only deal there by proxy. So the interests of millions
are in the hands of about twenty coxcombs, at a place called
Leibach!

I should almost regret that my own affairs went well, when
those of nations are in peril. If the interests of mankind could be
essentially bettered (particularly of these oppressed Italians), I
should not so much mind my own 'sma peculiar'. God grant us
all better times, or more philosophy! . . .

January 12, 1821

The weather still so humid and impracticable, that London, in
its most oppressive fogs, were a summer-bower to this mist and
sirocco, which has now lasted (but with one day's interval),
chequered with snow or heavy rain only, since the 30th of Decem-
ber, 1820. It is so far lucky that I have a literary turn; – but it is
very tiresome not to be able to stir out, in comfort, on any horse
but Pegasus, for so many days. The roads are even worse than
the weather, by the long splashing, and the heavy soil, and the
growth of the waters . . .

Scott is certainly the most wonderful writer of the day. His novels are a new literature in themselves, and his poetry as good as any – if not better (only on an erroneous system) – and only ceased to be so popular, because the vulgar learned were tired of hearing 'Aristides called the Just', and Scott the Best, and ostracised him.

I like him, too, for his manliness of character, for the extreme pleasantness of his conversation, and his good-nature towards myself, personally. May he prosper! – for he deserves it. I know no reading to which I fall with such alacrity as a work of W. Scott's ...

How strange are my thoughts! – The reading of the song of Milton, 'Sabrina fair' has brought back upon me – I know not how or why – the happiest, perhaps, days of my life (always excepting, here and there, a Harrow holiday in the two latter summers of my stay there) when living at Cambridge with Edward Noel Long, afterwards of the Guards ... The description of Sabrina's seat reminds me of our rival feats in *diving*. Though Cam's is not a very translucent wave, it was fourteen feet deep, where we used to dive for, and pick up – having thrown them in on purpose – plates, eggs, and even shillings. I remember, in particular, there was the stump of a tree (at least ten or twelve feet deep) in the bed of the river, in a spot where we bathed most commonly, round which I used to cling, and 'wonder how the devil I came there'.

Our evenings we passed in music (he was musical, and played on more than one instrument, flute and violoncello), in which I was audience; and I think that our chief beverage was soda-water. In the day we rode, bathed, and lounged, reading occasionally. I remember our buying, with vast alacrity, Moore's new quarto (in 1806), and reading it together in the evenings.

We only passed the summer together; – Long had gone into the Guards during the year I passed in Notts, away from college. *His* friendship, and a violent, though *pure*, love and passion[22] – which held me at the same period – were the then romance of the most romantic period of my life ...

Midnight

I like, however, their women [the Germans'] (I was once *so desperately* in love with a German woman, Constance,)²³ and all that I have read, translated, of their writings, and all that I have seen on the Rhine of their country and people – all, except the Austrians, whom I abhor, loathe, and – I cannot find words for my hate of them, and should be sorry to find deeds correspondent to my hate; for I abhor cruelty more than I abhor the Austrians – except on an impulse, and then I am savage – but not deliberately so . . .

January 13, 1821, Saturday

Sketched the outline and Drams. Pers. of an intended tragedy of Sardanapalus, which I have for some time meditated . . .

Dined – news come – the *Powers* mean to war with the peoples. The intelligence seems positive – let it be so – they will be beaten in the end. The king-times are fast finishing. There will be blood shed like water, and tears like mist; but the peoples will conquer in the end. I shall not live to see it, but I foresee it.

I carried Teresa the Italian translation of Grillparzer's *Sappho*, which she promised to read. She quarrelled with me, because I said that love was *not the loftiest* theme for true tragedy; and, having the advantage of her native language, and natural female eloquence, she overcame my fewer arguments. I believe she was right. I must put more love into *Sardanapalus* than I intended. I speak, of course, *if* the times will allow me leisure. That *if* will hardly be a peace-maker.

January 14, 1821

Turned over Seneca's tragedies. Wrote the opening lines of the intended tragedy of *Sardanapalus*. Rode out some miles into the forest. Misty and rainy. Returned – dined – wrote some more of my tragedy . . .

The effect of all wines and spirits upon me is, however, strange. *It settles*, but it makes me gloomy – gloomy at the very moment of their effect, and not gay hardly ever. But it composes for a time, though sullenly.

January 15, 1821

Weather fine. Received visit. Rode out into the forest – fired pistols. Returned home – dined – dipped into a volume of Mitford's *Greece* – wrote part of a scene of *Sardanapalus*. Went out – heard some music – heard some politics. More ministers from the other Italian powers gone to Congress. War seems certain – in that case, it will be a savage one. Talked over various important matters with one of the initiated. At ten and half returned home . . .

The only pleasure of fame is that it paves the way to pleasure; and the more intellectual our pleasure, the better for the pleasure and for us too. It was, however, agreeable to have heard our fame before dinner, and girl's harp after.

January 16, 1821

Read – rode – fired pistols – returned – dined – wrote – visited – heard music – talked nonsense – and went home.

Wrote part of a Tragedy – advanced in Act 1st with 'all deliberate speed'. Bought a blanket. The weather is still muggy as a London May – mist, mizzle, the air replete with Scotticisms, which, though fine in the descriptions of Ossian, are somewhat tiresome in real, prosaic perspective. Politics still mysterious.

January 19, 1821

Rode. Winter's wind somewhat more unkind than ingratitude itself, though Shakespeare says otherwise. At least, I am so much more accustomed to meet with ingratitude than the north wind, that I thought the latter the sharper of the two. I had met with both in the course of the twenty-four hours, so I could judge.

Thought of a plan of education for my daughter Allegra, who ought to begin soon with her studies. Wrote a letter – afterwards a postscript. Rather in low spirits – certainly hippish – liver touched – will take a dose of salts . . .

January 21, 1821

Fine, clear, frosty day – that is to say, an Italian frost, for their winters hardly get beyond snow; for which reason nobody knows how to skate (or skait) – a Dutch and English accomplishment. Rode out, as usual, and fired pistols. Good shooting – broke four common, and rather small, bottles, in four shots, at fourteen paces, with a common pair of pistols and indifferent powder. Almost as good *wafering* or shooting – considering the difference of powder and pistol – as when, in 1809, 1810, 1811, 1812, 1813, 1814, it was my luck to split walking-sticks, wafers, half-crowns, shillings, and even the *eye* of a walking-stick, at twelve paces, with a single bullet – and all by *eye* and calculation; for my hand is not steady, and apt to change with the very weather . . .

Tomorrow is my birth-day – that is to say, at twelve o' the clock, midnight, *i.e.* in twelve minutes, I shall have completed thirty and three years of age!!! – and I go to my bed with a heaviness of heart at having lived so long, and to so little purpose.

It is three minutes past twelve. – ' 'Tis the middle of the night by the castle clock', and I am now thirty-three!

> Eheu, fugaces, Posthume, Posthume,
> Labuntur anni;[24] –

but I don't regret them so much for what I have done, as for what I *might* have done.

> Through life's road, so dim and dirty,
> I have dragged to three-and-thirty.
> What have these years left to me?
> Nothing – except thirty-three.

January 22, 1821

1821.

Here lies
interred in the Eternity
of the Past,
from whence there is no
Resurrection

for the Days – Whatever there may be
for the Dust –
the Thirty-Third Year
of an ill-spent Life,
Which, after
a lingering disease of many months
sunk into a lethargy,
and expired,
January 22nd, 1821, A.D.
Leaving a successor
Inconsolable
for the very loss which
occasioned its
Existence.

January 23, 1821

Fine day. Read – rode – fired pistols, and returned. Dined – read. Went out at eight – made the usual visit. Heard of nothing but war, – 'the cry is still, They come'. The Carbonari seem to have no plan – nothing fixed among themselves, how, when, or what to do. In that case, they will make nothing of this project, so often postponed, and never put in action.

Came home, and gave some necessary orders, in case of circumstances requiring a change of place. I shall act according to what may seem proper, when I hear decidedly what the Barbarians mean to do. At present, they are building a bridge of boats over the Po, which looks very warlike. A few days will probably show. I think of retiring towards Ancona, nearer the northern frontier,[25] that is to say, if Teresa and her father are obliged to retire, which is most likely, as all the family are Liberals. If not, I shall stay. But my movements will depend upon the lady's wishes – for myself, it is much the same.

I am somewhat puzzled what to do with my little daughter, and my effects, which are of some quantity and value, – and neither of them do in the seat of war, where I think of going. But there is an elderly lady who will take charge of *her*, and T[eresa] says that the Marchese C. will undertake to hold the chattels in safe keeping. Half the city are getting their affairs in

marching trim. A pretty Carnival! The blackguards might as
well have waited till Lent.

January 24, 1821

Returned – met some masques in the Corso – *Vive la bagatelle*!
– the Germans are on the Po, the Barbarians at the gate, and
their masters in council at Leybach (or whatever the eructation
of the sound may syllable into a human pronunciation), and lo!
they dance and sing and make merry, 'for tomorrow they may
die'. Who can say that the Arlequins are not right? Like the
Lady Baussiere, and my old friend Burton – I 'rode on'.

Dined – (damn this pen!) – beef tough – there is no beef in
Italy worth a curse; unless a man could eat an old ox with the
hide on, singed in the sun.

The principal persons in the events which may occur in a few
days are gone out on a *shooting party*. If it were like a '*highland
hunting*', a pretext of the chase for a grand re-union of counsel-
lors and chiefs, it would be all very well. But it is nothing more
or less than a real snivelling, popping, small-shot, water-hen
waste of powder, ammunition, and shot, for their own special
amusement: a rare set of fellows for 'a man to risk his neck with',
as 'Marishall Wells' says in the *Black Dwarf*.

If they gather, – 'whilk is to be doubted', – they will not muster
a thousand men. The reason of this is, that the populace are not
interested, – only the higher and middle orders. I wish that the
peasantry *were*; they are a fine savage race of two-legged leopards.
But the Bolognese won't – the Romagnuoles can't without them.
Or, if they try – what then? They will try, and man can do no more
– and, if he *would* but try his utmost, much might be done. The
Dutch, for instance, against the Spaniards – *then* the tyrants of
Europe, since, the slaves, and lately, the freedmen.

The year 1820 was not a fortunate one for the individual me,
whatever it may be for the nations. I lost a lawsuit, after two
decisions in my favour. The project of lending money on an
Irish mortgage was finally rejected by my wife's trustee after a
year's hope and trouble. The Rochdale lawsuit had endured

fifteen years, and always prospered till I married; since which, ever thing has gone wrong – with me at least.

In the same year, 1820, the Countess T[eresa] G[uiccioli] *nata* G[amba] G[hiselli], in despite of all I said and did to prevent it, *would* separate from her husband, Il Cavalier Commendatore G[uiccioli] etc., etc., etc., and all on the account of 'P.P. clerk of this parish'.[26] The other little petty vexations of the year – overturns in carriages – the murder of people before one's door, and dying in one's beds – the cramp in swimming – colics – indigestions and bilious attacks, etc., etc., etc. –

> Many small articles make up a sum,
> And hey ho for Caleb Quotem, oh![27]

January 25, 1821

... It has been said that the immortality of the soul is a *grand peut-être* – but still it is a *grand* one. Every body clings to it – the stupidest, and dullest, and wickedest of human bipeds is still persuaded that he is immortal.

January 26, 1821

Fine day – a few mares' tails portending change, but the sky clear, upon the whole. Rode – fired pistols – good shooting. Coming back, met an old man. Charity – purchased a shilling's worth of salvation. If that was to be bought, I have given more to my fellow-creatures in this life – sometimes for *vice*, but, if not more *often*, at least more *considerably*, for virtue – than I now possess. I never in my life gave a mistress so much as I have sometimes given a poor man in honest distress; but no matter. The scoundrels who have all along persecuted me (with the help of — who has crowned their efforts) will triumph; and, when justice is done to me, it will be when this hand that writes is as cold as the hearts which have stung me.

Returning, on the bridge near the mill, met an old woman. I asked her age – she said '*Tre croci*'. I asked my groom (though myself a decent Italian) what the devil *her* three crosses meant. He said, ninety years, and that she had five years more to boot!!

I repeated the same three times – not to mistake – ninety-five years!!! – and she was yet rather active – *heard* my question, for she answered it – *saw* me, for she advanced towards me; and did not appear at all decrepit, though certainly touched with years. Told her to come to-morrow, and will examine her myself. I love phenomena. If she *is* ninety-five years old, she must recollect the Cardinal Alberoni, who was legate here . . .

Went out – found T. as usual – music. The gentlemen, who make revolutions and are gone on a shooting, are not yet returned. They don't return till Sunday – that is to say, they have been out for five days, buffooning, while the interests of a whole country are at stake, and even they themselves compromised.

It is a difficult part to play amongst such a set of assassins and blockheads – but, when the scum is skimmed off, or has boiled over, good may come of it. If this country could but be freed, what would be too great for the accomplishment of that desire? for the extinction of that Sigh of Ages? Let us hope. They have hoped these thousand years. The very revolvement of the chances may bring it – it is upon the dice.

If the Neapolitans have but a single Massaniello amongst them, they will beat the bloody butchers of the crown and sabre. Holland, in worse circumstances, beat the Spains and Philips; America beat the English; Greece beat Xerxes; and France beat Europe, till she took a tyrant; South America beats her old vultures out of their nest; and, if these men are but firm in themselves, there is nothing to shake them from without.

January 28, 1821

. . . Letters from Venice. It appears that the Austrian brutes have seized my three or four pounds of English powder. The scoundrels! – I hope to pay them in *ball* for that powder. Rode out till twilight.

Pondered the subjects of four tragedies to be written (life and circumstances permitting), to wit, Sardanapalus, already begun; Cain, a metaphysical subject, something in the style of Manfred, but in five *acts*; perhaps, with the chorus; Francesca of Rimini,

378

in five acts; and I am not sure that I would not try Tiberius. I think that I could extract a something, of *my* tragic, at least, out of the gloomy sequestration and old age of the tyrant – and even out of his sojourn at Caprea – by softening the *details*, and exhibiting the despair which must have led to those very vicious pleasures. For none but a powerful and gloomy mind overthrown would have had recourse to such solitary horrors, – being also, at the same time, *old*, and the master of the world.

Memoranda

What is Poetry? – The feeling of a Former world and Future.

Thought Second

Why, at the very height of desire and human pleasure, – worldly, social, amorous, ambitious, or even avaricious, – does there mingle a certain sense of doubt and sorrow – a fear of what is to come – a doubt of what *is* – a retrospect to the past, leading to a prognostication of the future? (The best of Prophets of the future is the Past.) Why is this, or these? – I know not, except that on a pinnacle we are most susceptible of giddiness, and that we never fear falling except from a precipice – the higher, the more awful, and the more sublime; and, therefore, I am not sure that Fear is not a pleasurable sensation; at least, *Hope* is; and *what Hope* is there without a deep leaven of Fear? and what sensation is so delightful as Hope? and, if it were not for Hope, where would the Future be? – in hell. It is useless to say *where* the Present is, for most of us know; and as for the Past, *what* predominates in memory? – *Hope baffled*. Ergo, in all human affairs, it is Hope – Hope – Hope. I allow sixteen minutes, though I never counted them, to any given or supposed possession. From whatever place we commence, we know where it all must end. And yet, what good is there in knowing it? It does not make men better or wiser. During the greatest horrors of the greatest plagues, (Athens and Florence, for example – see Thucydides and Machiavelli,) men were more cruel and profligate

than ever. It is all a mystery. I feel most things, but I know nothing
except

_____

_____

_____28

Past Midnight. One o' the clock

I have been reading Frederick Schlegel (brother to the other of
the name) till now, and I can make out nothing. He evidently
shows a great power of words, but there is nothing to be taken
hold of. He is like Hazlitt, in English, who *talks pimples* – a red
and white corruption rising up (in little imitation of mountains
upon maps,) but containing nothing, and discharging nothing,
except their own humours . . .

January 29, 1821

Yesterday, the woman of ninety-five years of age, was with me.
She said her eldest son (if now alive) would have been seventy.
She is thin – short, but active – hears, and sees, and talks in-
cessantly. Several teeth left – all in the lower jaw, and single
front teeth. She is very deeply wrinkled, and has a sort of
scattered grey beard over her chin, at least as long as my musta-
chios. Her head, in fact, resembles the drawing in crayons of
Pope the poet's mother, which is in some editions of his works.

I forgot to ask her if she remembered Alberoni (legate here),
but will ask her next time. Gave her a louis – ordered her a new
suit of clothes, and put her upon a weekly pension. Till now, she
had worked at gathering wood and pine-nuts in the forest –
pretty work at ninety-five years old! She had a dozen children,
of whom some are alive. Her name is Maria Montanari.

Met a company of the sect (a kind of Liberal Club) called the
Americani in the forest, all armed, and singing, with all their
might, in Romagnuole – '*Sem* tutti soldat' per la liberta' ('we
are all soldiers for liberty'). They cheered me as I passed – I
returned their salute, and rode on. This may show the spirit of
Italy at present.

They say that the Piedmontese have at length arisen – *ça ira*! . . .

One o'clock

I have found out, however, where the German is right – it is about the *Vicar of Wakefield*. 'Of all romances in miniature (and, perhaps, this is the best shape in which Romance can appear) the *Vicar of Wakefield* is, I think, the most exquisite'. He *thinks*! he might be sure. But it is very well for a Schlegel. I feel sleepy, and may as well get me to bed. To-morrow there will be fine weather ...

January 30, 1812

... Something must be up in Piedmont – all the letters and papers are stopped. Nobody knows anything, and the Germans are concentrating near Mantua. Of the decision of Leybach nothing is known. This state of things cannot last long. The ferment in men's minds at present cannot be conceived without seeing it.

January 31, 1821

For several days I have not written anything except a few answers to letters. In momentary expectation of an explosion of some kind, it is not easy to settle down to the desk for the higher kinds of composition. I *could* do it, to be sure, for, last summer, I wrote my drama[29] in the very bustle of Madame la Contessa G[uiccioli]'s divorce, and all its process of accompaniments. At the same time, I also had the news of the loss of an important lawsuit in England. But these were only private and personal business; the present is of a different nature.

I suppose it is this, but have some suspicion that it may be laziness, which prevents me from writing; especially as Rochefoucalt says that 'laziness often masters them all' – speaking of the *passions*. If this were true, it could hardly be said that 'idleness is the root of all evil', since this is supposed to spring from the passions only: *ergo*, that which masters all the passions (laziness, to wit) would in so much be a good. Who knows?

Midnight

I have been reading Grimm's *Correspondence*. He repeats frequently, in speaking of a poet, or a man of genius in any department, even in music, (Grétry, for instance,) that he must have *une ame qui se tourmente, un esprit violent*. How far this may be true, I know not; but if it were, I should be a poet '*per excellenza*'; for I have always had *une ame*, which not only tormented itself but every body else in contact with it; and an *esprit violent*, which has almost left me without any *esprit* at all. As to defining what a poet *should* be, it is not worth while, for what are *they* worth? what have they done? ...

February 2, 1821

I have been considering what can be the reason why I always wake, at a certain hour in the morning, and always in very bad spirits – I may say, in actual despair and despondency, in all respects – even of that which pleased me over night. In about an hour or two, this goes off, and I compose either to sleep again, or, at least, to quiet. In England, five years ago, I had the same kind of hypochondria, but accompanied with so violent a thirst that I have drank as many as fifteen bottles of soda-water in one night, after going to bed, and been still thirsty – calculating, however, some lost from the bursting out and effervescence and overflowing of the soda-water, in drawing the corks, or striking off the necks of the bottles from mere thirsty impatience. At present, I have *not* the thirst; but the depression of spirits is no less violent.

... In England, Le Man (the apothecary) cured me of the thirst in three days, and it had lasted as many years. I suppose that it is all hypochondria.

What I feel most growing upon me are laziness, and a disrelish more powerful than indifference. If I rouse, it is into fury. I presume that I shall end (if not earlier by accident, or some such termination), like Swift – 'dying at top'. I confess I do not contemplate this with so much horror as he apparently did for some years before it happened. But Swift had hardly *begun life* at the very period (thirty-three) when I feel quite an *old sort* of feel.

Oh! there is an organ playing in the street – a waltz, too! I must leave off to listen. They are playing a waltz which I have heard ten thousand times at the balls in London, between 1812 and 1815. Music is a strange thing.

February 5, 1821

At last, 'the kiln's in a low'. The Germans are ordered to march, and Italy is, for the ten thousandth time to become a field of battle. Last night the news came.

This afternoon – Count P.G. came to me to consult upon divers matters. We rode out together. They have sent off to the C. for orders. To-morrow the decision ought to arrive, and then something will be done. Returned – dined – read – went out – talked over matters. Made a purchase of some arms for the new enrolled Americani, who are all on tiptoe to march. Gave order for some *harness* and portmanteaus necessary for the horses.

Read some of Bowles's dispute about Pope, with all the replies and rejoinders. Perceive that my name has been lugged into the controversy, but have not time to state what I know of the subject. On some 'piping day of peace' it is probable that I may resume it.

February 9, 1821

Before dinner wrote a little; also, before I rode out, Count P.G. called upon me, to let me know the result of the meeting of the Ci.[30] at F. and at B. —[31] returned late last night. Every thing was combined under the idea that the Barbarians would pass the Po on the 15th inst. Instead of this, from some previous information or otherwise, they have hastened their march and actually passed two days ago; so that all that can be done at present in Romagna is, to stand on the alert and wait for the advance of the Neapolitans. Every thing was ready, and the Neapolitans had sent on their own instructions and intentions, all calculated for the *tenth* and *eleventh*, on which days a general rising was to take place, under the supposition that the Barbarians could not advance before the 15th.

As it is, they have but fifty or sixty thousand troops, a number with which they might as well attempt to conquer the world as secure Italy in its present state. The artillery marches *last*, and alone, and there is an idea of an attempt to cut part of them off. All this will much depend upon the first steps of the Neapolitans. *Here*, the public spirit is excellent, provided it be kept up. This will be seen by the event.

It is probable that Italy will be delivered from the Barbarians if the Neapolitans will but stand firm, and are united among themselves. *Here* they appear so.

February 10, 1821

Day passed as usual – nothing new. Barbarians still in march – not well equipped, and, of course, not well received on their route. There is some talk of a commotion at Paris.

Rode out between four and six – finished my letter to Murray on Bowles's pamphlets – added postscript.

February 11, 1821

... Heard a heavy firing of cannon towards Comacchio – the Barbarians rejoicing for their principal pig's birthday, which is to-morrow – or Saint day – I forget which. Received a ticket for the first ball to-morrow. Shall not go to the first, but intend going to the second, as also to the Veglioni.[32]

February 13, 1821

... Politics are quite misty for the present. The Barbarians still upon their march. It is not easy to divine what the Italians will now do.

Was elected yesterday *Socio*[33] of the Carnival Ball Society. This is the fifth carnival that I have passed. In the four former, I racketed a good deal. In the present, I have been as sober as Lady Grace herself.

384

February 14, 1821

Much as usual. Wrote, before riding out, part of a scene of *Sardanapalus*. The first act nearly finished. The rest of the day and evening as before – partly without, in conversazione – partly at home.
[. . .]

February 16, 1821

Last night Il Conte P.G. sent a man with a bag full of bayonets, some muskets, and some hundreds of cartridges to my house, without apprizing me, though I had seen him not half an hour before. About ten days ago, when there was to be a rising here, the Liberals and my brethren C[arbonar]¹ asked me to purchase some arms for a certain few of our ragamuffins. I did so immediately, and ordered ammunition, etc., and they were armed accordingly. Well – the rising is prevented by the Barbarians marching a week sooner than appointed; and an *order* is issued, and in force, by the Government, 'that all persons having arms concealed, etc., etc., shall be liable to, etc., etc.' – and what do my friends, the patriots, do two days afterwards? Why, they throw back upon my hands, and into my house, these very arms (without a word of warning previously) with which I had furnished them at their own request, and at my own peril and expense.

It was lucky that Lega was at home to receive them. If any of the servants had (except Tita and F. and Lega) they would have betrayed it immediately. In the mean time, if they are denounced or discovered, I shall be in a scrape . . .

February 18, 1821

The news are that the Neapolitans have broken a bridge, and slain four pontifical carabiniers, whilk carabiniers wished to oppose. Besides the disrespect to neutrality, it is a pity that the first blood shed in this German quarrel should be Italian. However, the war seems begun in good earnest: for, if the Neapolitans kill the Pope's carabiniers, they will not be more delicate towards the Barbarians. If it be even so, in a short time

385

'there will be news o' thae craws', as Mrs Alison Wilson says of Jenny Blane's 'unco cockernony' in the *Tales of my Landlord* . . .

To-day I have had no communication with my Carbonari cronies; but, in the mean time, my lower apartments are full of their bayonets, fusils, cartridges, and what not. I suppose that they consider me as a depot, to be sacrificed, in case of accidents. It is no great matter, supposing that Italy could be liberated, who or what is sacrificed. It is a grand object – the very *poetry* of politics. Only think – a free Italy!!! Why, there has been nothing like it since the days of Augustus. I reckon the times of Caesar (Julius) free; because the commotions left every body a side to take, and the parties were pretty equal at the set out. But, afterwards, it was all praetorian and legionary business – and since! – we shall see, or, at least, some will see, what card will turn up. It is best to hope, even of the hopeless. The Dutch did more than these fellows have to do, in the Seventy Years' War.

February 19, 1821

Came home *solus* – very high wind – lightning – moonshine – solitary stragglers muffled in cloaks – women in masks – white houses – clouds hurrying over the sky, like spilt milk blown out of the pail – altogether very poetical. It is still blowing hard – the tiles flying, and the house rocking – rain splashing – lightning flashing – quite a fine Swiss Alpine evening, and the sea roaring in the distance.

Visited – conversazione. All the women frightened by the squall: they *won't* go to the masquerade because it lightens – the pious reason!

Still blowing away. A.[34] has sent me some news to-day. The war approaches nearer and nearer. Oh those scoundrel sovereigns! Let us but see them beaten – let the Neapolitans but have the pluck of the Dutch of old, or the Spaniards of now, or of the German Protestants, the Scotch Presbyterians, the Swiss under Tell, or the Greeks under Themistocles – *all* small and solitary nations (except the Spaniards and German Lutherans), and there is yet a resurrection for Italy, and a hope for the world.

February 20, 1821

The news of the day are, that the Neapolitans are full of energy. The public spirit *here* is certainly well kept up. The *Americani* (a patriotic society here, an under branch of the *Carbonari*) give a dinner in *the Forest* in a few days, and have invited me, as one of the C^i. It is to be in *the Forest* of Boccacio's and Dryden's 'Huntsman's Ghost'; and, even if I had not the same political feelings, (to say nothing of my old convivial turn, which every now and then revives), I would go as a poet, or, at least, as a lover of poetry. I shall expect to see the spectre of 'Ostasio degli Onesti'[35] (Dryden has turned him into Guido Cavalcanti – an essentially different person, as may be found in Dante) come 'thundering for his prey in the midst of the festival'. At any rate, whether he does or no, I will get as tipsy and patriotic as possible.

Within these few days I have read, but not written.

February 21, 1821

As usual, rode – visited, etc. Business begins to thicken. The Pope has printed a declaration against the patriots, who, he says, meditate a rising. The consequence of all this will be, that, in a fortnight, the whole country will be up. The proclamation is not yet published, but printed, ready for distribution. —[36] sent me a copy privately – a sign that he does not know what to think. When he wants to be well with the patriots, he sends to me some civil message or other.

For my own part, it seems to me, that nothing but the most decided success of the Barbarians can prevent a general and immediate rise of the whole nation.

February 23, 1821

Almost ditto with yesterday – rode, etc. – visited – wrote nothing – read Roman History.

Had a curious letter from a fellow, who informs me that the Barbarians are ill-disposed towards me. He is probably a spy, or

an imposter. But be it so, even as he says. They cannot bestow
their hostility on one who loathes and execrates them more than
I do, or who will oppose their views with more zeal, when the
opportunity offers.

February 24, 1821

Rode, etc., as usual. The secret intelligence arrived this morning
from the frontier to the C^i. is as bad as possible. The *plan* has
missed – the Chiefs are betrayed, military, as well as civil – and
the Neapolitans not only have *not* moved, but have declared to
the P[apal] government, and to the Barbarians, that they know
nothing of the matter!!!

Thus the world goes; and thus the Italians are always lost for
lack of union among themselves. What is to be done *here*,
between the two fires, and cut off from the N[eapolita?]n
frontier, is not decided. My opinion was, – better to rise than be
taken in detail; but how it will be settled now, I cannot tell.
Messengers are despatched to the delegates of the other cities to
learn their resolutions.

I always had an idea that it would be *bungled*; but was willing
to hope, and am so still. Whatever I can do by money, means, or
person, I will venture freely for their freedom; and have so
repeated to them (some of the Chiefs here) half an hour ago. I
have two thousand five hundred scudi, better than five hundred
pounds, in the house, which I offered to begin with.

February 25, 1821

Came home – my head aches – plenty of news, but too tiresome
to set down. I have neither read not written, nor thought, but led
a purely animal life all day. I mean to try to write a page or two
before I go to bed. But, as Squire Sullen[37] says, 'My head aches
consumedly: Scrub, bring me a dram!' Drank some Imola wine,
and some punch!

Log-Book Continued

February 27, 1821

I have been a day without continuing the log, because I could not find a blank book. At length I recollected this.

Rode, etc. – wrote down an additional stanza for the 5th canto of D[on] J[uan] which I had composed in bed this morning. Visited *l'Amica* . . .

The old woman whom I relieved in the forest (she is ninety-four years of age) brought me two bunches of violets. *Nam vita gaudet mortua floribus.*[38] I was much pleased with the present. An English woman would have presented a pair of worsted stockings, at least, in the month of February. Both excellent things; but the former are more elegant . . .

Last night I suffered horribly – from an indigestion, I believe . . . At last I fell into a dreary sleep. Woke, and was ill all day, till I had galloped a few miles. Query – was it the cockles, or what I took to correct them, that caused the commotion? I think both. I remarked in my illness the complete inertion, inaction, and destruction of my chief mental faculties. I tried to rouse them, and yet could not – and this is the *Soul*!!! I should believe that it was married to the body, if they did not sympathise so much with each other. If the one rose, when the other fell, it would be a sign that they longed for the natural state of divorce. But as it is, they seem to draw together like post-horses.

Let us hope the best – it is the grand possession.

LETTER TO [JOHN MURRAY], ESQRE, ON THE REV. W. L. BOWLES'S STRICTURES ON THE LIFE AND WRITINGS OF POPE.
[Published in March, 1821]

'I'll play at *Bowls* with the Sun and Moon.' – *Old Song*. 'My mither's auld, Sir, and she has rather forgotten hersel in speaking to my Leddy, that canna weel bide to be contradickit (as I ken naebody likes it, if they could help themsels).' – *Tales of My Landlord: Old Mortality*, p. 163, vol. 2nd.

Ravenna, February 7th, 1821

Dear Sir, – In the different pamphlets which you have had the goodness to send me, on the Pope and Bowles controversy, I perceive that my name is occasionally introduced by both parties. Mr Bowles refers more than once to what he is pleased to consider 'a remarkable circumstance,' not only in his letter to Mr Campbell, but in his reply to the *Quarterly*. The *Quarterly* also and Mr Gilchrist have conferred on me the dangerous honour of a quotation; and Mr Bowles indirectly makes a kind of appeal to me personally, by saying, 'Lord B., *if he remembers* the circumstance, will *witness*' – (*witness* IN ITALICS, an ominous character for a testimony at present) . . . Of Mr Bowles's 'good humour' I have a full and not ungrateful recollection; as also of his gentlemanly manners and agreeable conversation. I speak of the *whole*, and not of particulars; for whether he did or did not use the precise words printed in the pamphlet, I cannot say, nor could he with accuracy. Of 'the tone of seriousness' I certainly recollect nothing; on the contrary, I thought Mr B. rather disposed to treat the subject lightly; for he said (I have no objection to be contradicted if incorrect), that some of his good-natured friends had come to him and exclaimed, 'Eh! Bowles! how came you to make the Woods of Madeira?' etc., etc.; and that he had been at some pains and pulling down of the poem to convince them that he had never made 'the Woods' do anything of the kind. He was right, and *I was wrong*, and have been wrong still up to this acknowledgment; for I ought to have looked twice before I wrote that which involved an inaccuracy capable of giving pain. The fact was, that, although I had certainly before read *The Spirit of Discovery*, I took the quotation from the review. But the mistake was mine, and not the *review's*, which quoted the passage correctly enough, I believe. I blundered – God knows how – into attributing the tremors of the lovers to the 'Woods of Madeira', by which they were surrounded. And I hereby do fully and freely declare and asseverate, that the Woods did *not* tremble to a kiss, and that the Lovers did. I quote from memory –

<blockquote>
A kiss
Stole on the listening silence, etc., etc.
They [the lovers] trembled, even as if the Power, etc.
</blockquote>

And if I had been aware that this declaration would have been in the smallest degree satisfactory to Mr B., I should not have waited nine years to make it, notwithstanding that *English Bards, and Scotch Reviewers* had been suppressed some time previously to my meeting him at Mr Roger's ...

I must now, however, say a word or two about Pope, of whom you have my opinion more at large in the unpublished letter *on* or *to* (for I forget which) the Editor of *Blackwood's Edinburgh Magazine*; – and here I doubt that Mr Bowles will not approve of my Sentiments.

Although I regret having published *English Bards, and Scotch Reviewers*, the part which I regret the least is that which regards Mr B. with reference to Pope. Whilst I was writing that publication, in 1807 and 1808, Mr Hobhouse was desirous that I should express our mutual opinion of Pope, and of Mr B.'s edition of his works. As I had completed my outline, and felt lazy, I requested that *he* would do so. He did it. His fourteen lines on Bowles's Pope are in the first edition of *English Bards, and Scotch Reviewers*; and are quite as severe and much more poetical than my own in the Second. On reprinting the work, as

I put my name to it, I omitted Mr Hobhouse's lines, and replaced
them with my own, by which the work gained less than Mr
Bowles. I have stated this in the preface to the 2ᵈ edition. It is
many years since I have read that poem; but the *Quarterly
Review*, Mr Octavius Gilchrist, and Mr Bowles himself, have been
so obliging as to refresh my memory, and that of the public. I
am grieved to say, that in reading over those lines, I repent of
their having so far fallen short of what I meant to express upon
the subject of B.'s edition of *Pope's Works*. Mr B. says, that 'Ld.
B. *knows* he does *not* deserve this character.' I know no such thing.
I have met Mr B. occasionally, in the best Society in London; he
appeared to me an amiable, well-informed, and extremely able
man. I desire nothing better than to dine in company with such
a mannered man every day in the week; but of 'his character' I
know nothing personally; I can only speak to his manners, and
these have my warmest approbation. But I never judge from
manners, for I once had my pocket picked by the civilest gentle-
man I ever met with; and one of the mildest persons I ever saw
was Ali Pacha. Of Mr B.'s 'character' I will not do him the
injustice to judge from the Edition of Pope, if he prepared it
heedlessly; nor the *justice*, should it be otherwise, because I
would neither become a literary executioner nor a personal one.
Mr Bowles the individual, and Mr. Bowles the editor, appear the
two most opposite things imaginable.

And he himself one — antithesis.

I won't say 'vile', because it is harsh; nor 'mistaken', because it
has two syllables too many: but every one must fill up the blank
as he pleases.

What I saw of Mr B. increased my surprise and regret that he
should ever have lent his talents to such a task. If he had been a
fool, there would have been some excuse for him; if he had been
a needy or a bad man, his conduct would have been intelligible:
but he is the opposite of all these; and thinking and feeling as I
do of Pope, to me the whole thing is unaccountable. However, I
must call things by their right names. I cannot call his edition of
Pope a 'candid work'; and I still think that there is an affectation

of that quality not only in those volumes, but in the pamphlets lately published.

Why *yet* he doth *deny* his prisoners.

Mr B. says that he 'has seen passages in his letters to Martha Blount which were never published by me, and I *hope never will* be by others; which are so *gross* as to imply the *grossest* licentiousness.' Is this fair play? It may, or it may not be that such passages exist; and that Pope, who was not a Monk, although a Catholic, may have occasionally sinned in word and deed with woman in his youth: but is this a sufficient ground for such a sweeping denunciation? Where is the unmarried Englishman of a certain rank of life, who (provided he has not taken orders) has not to reproach himself between the ages of sixteen and thirty with far more licentiousness than has ever yet been traced to Pope? Pope lived in the public eye from his youth upwards; he had all the dunces of his own time for his enemies, and, I am sorry to say, some, who have not the apology of dullness for detraction, since his death; and yet to what do all their accumulated hints and charges amount? – to an equivocal *liaison* with Martha Blount, which might arise as much from his infirmities as from his passions; to a hopeless flirtation with Lady Mary W. Montagu; to a story of Cibber's; and to two or three coarse passages in his works. *Who* could come forth clearer from an invidious inquest on a life of fifty-six years? Why are we to be officiously reminded of such passages in his letters, provided that they exist? Is Mr B. aware to what such rummaging among 'letters' and 'stories' might lead? I have myself seen a collection of letters of another eminent, nay, pre-eminent, deceased poet,[39] so abominably gross, and elaborately coarse, that I do not believe that they could be paralleled in our language. What is more strange is, that some of these are couched as *postscripts* to his serious and sentimental letters, to which are tacked either a piece of prose, or some verses, of the most hyperbolical indecency. He himself says, that if 'obscenity' (using a much coarser word) 'be the Sin against the Holy Ghost, he must certainly not be saved.' These letters are in existence, and have been seen by many besides myself; but would his *editor* have been 'candid' in even alluding to them? Nothing would have even provoked *me*, an indifferent spectator, to allude to them, but this further attempt at the depreciation of Pope.

What should we say to an editor of Addison, who cited the following passage from Walpole's letters to George Montagu? 'Dr Young has published a new book, etc. Mr Addison sent for the young Earl of Warwick, as he was dying, to show him in what peace a Christian could die; unluckily he died of *brandy*: nothing makes a Christian die in peace like being maudlin! but don't say this in Gath where you are.' Suppose the editor introduced it with this preface, 'One circumstance is mentioned by Horace Walpole, which, if true, was indeed *flagitious*. Walpole informs Montagu that Addison sent for the young Earl of Warwick, when dying, to show him in what peace a Christian could die; but unluckily he died drunk,' etc., etc. Now, although there might occur on the subsequent, or on the same page, a faint show of disbelief, seasoned with the expression of 'the *same candour*' (the *same* exactly as throughout the book), I should say that this editor was either foolish or false to his trust; such a story ought not to have been admitted, except for one brief mark of crushing indignation, unless it were *completely proved*. Why the words '*if true?*' that '*if*' is not a peacemaker. Why talk of 'Cibber's testimony' to his licentiousness? To what does this amount? that Pope, when very young, was *once* decoyed by some noblemen and the player to a house of carnal recreation. Mr Bowles was not always a clergyman; and when he was a very young man, was he never seduced into as much? If I were in the humour for story-telling, and relating little anecdotes, I could tell a much better story of Mr B. than Cibber's, upon much better authority, viz. that of Mr B. himself. It was not related by *him* in my presence, but in that of a third person, whom Mr B. names oftener than once in the course of his replies.[40] This gentleman related it to me as a humorous and witty anecdote; and so it was, whatever its other characteristics might be. But should I, for a youthful frolic, brand Mr B. with a 'libertine sort of love', or with 'licentiousness'? Is he the less now a pious or a good man, for not having always been a priest? No such thing; I am willing to believe him a good man, almost as good a man as Pope, but no better.

The truth is, that in these days the grand '*primum mobile*'[41] of England is *cant*; cant political, cant poetical, cant religious, cant moral; but always *cant*, multiplied through all the varieties of life. It is the fashion, and while it lasts will be too powerful for those who can only exist by taking the tone of the time. I say *cant*, because it is a thing of words, without the smallest influence upon human actions; the English being no wiser, no better, and much poorer, and more divided amongst themselves, as well as far less moral, than they were before the prevalence of this verbal decorum. This hysterical horror of poor Pope's not very well ascertained, and never fully proved amours (for even Cibber owns that he prevented the somewhat perilous adventure in which Pope was embarking), sounds very virtuous in a controversial pamphlet: but all men of the world who know what life is, or at least what it was to them in their youth, must laugh at such a ludicrous foundation of the charge of 'a libertine sort of love'; while the more serious will look upon those who bring forward such charges upon an isolated fact as fanatics or hypocrites, perhaps both. The two are sometimes compounded in a happy mixture.

Mr Octavius Gilchrist speaks rather irreverently of a 'second tumbler of *hot* white-wine negus'. What does he mean? Is there any harm in negus? or is it the worse for being *hot*? or does Mr B. drink negus? I had a better opinion of him. I hoped that whatever wine he drank was neat; or, at least, that, like the Ordinary in Jonathan Wild, 'he preferred *punch*, the rather as there was nothing against it in Scripture'. I should be really sorry to believe that Mr B. was fond of negus; it is such a 'candid' liquor, so like a wishy-washy compromise between the passion for wine and the propriety of water. But different writers have divers tastes. Judge Blackstone composed his *Commentaries* (he was a poet too in his youth) with a bottle of port before him. Addison's conversation was not good for much till he had taken a similar dose. Perhaps the prescription of these

two great men was not inferior to the very different one of a soi-
disant poet of this day, who, after wandering amongst the hills,
returns, goes to bed, and dictates his verses, being fed by a
bystander with bread and butter during the operation.

I now come to Mr B.'s 'invariable principles of poetry'.
These Mr Bowles and some of his correspondents pronounce 'un-
answerable'; and they are 'unanswered', at least by Campbell,
who seems to have been astounded by the title: The Sultan of the
time being offered to ally himself to a King of France because
'he hated the word League'; which proves that the Padishaw
(*not Pacha*) understood French. Mr Campbell has no need of my
alliance, nor shall I presume to offer it; but I do hate that word
'invariable'. What is there of *human*, be it poetry, philosophy,
wit, wisdom, science, power, glory, mind, matter, life, or death,
which is '*invariable*'? Of course I put things divine out of the
question. Of all arrogant baptisms of a book, this title to a
pamphlet appears the most complacently conceited. It is Mr
Campbell's part to answer the contents of this performance, and
especially to vindicate his own 'Ship', which Mr B. most trium-
phantly proclaims to have struck to his very first fire.

> Quoth he there was a *Ship*;
> Now let me go, thou grey-haired loon,
> Or my staff shall make thee skip.

It is no affair of mine; but having once begun, (certainly not by
my own wish, but called upon by the frequent recurrence to my
name in the pamphlets,) I am like an Irishman in a 'row', 'any
body's customer'. I shall therefore say a word or two on the
'Ship'.

Mr B. asserts that Campbell's 'Ship of the Line' derives all its
poetry, not from '*art*', but from '*Nature*'. 'Take away the waves,
the winds, the sun, etc., etc., etc., *one* will become a stripe of
blue bunting; and the other a piece of coarse canvas on three
tall poles.' Very true; take away the 'waves', 'the winds', and
there will be no ship at all, not only for poetical, but for any
other purpose; and take away 'the sun', and we must read Mr
B.'s pamphlet by candlelight. But the 'poetry' of the 'Ship' does

not depend on the 'waves', etc.; on the contrary, the 'Ship of the line' confers its own poetry upon the waters, and heightens *theirs*. I do not deny, that the 'waves and winds', and above all 'the sun', are highly poetical; we know it to our cost, by the many descriptions of them in verse: but if the waves bore only the foam upon their bosoms, if the winds wafted only the sea-weed to the shore, if the sun shone neither upon pyramids, nor fleets, nor fortresses, would its beams be equally poetical? I think not: the poetry is at least reciprocal. Take away 'the Ship of the Line' 'swinging round' the 'calm water', and the calm water becomes a somewhat monotonous thing to look at, particularly if not transparently *clear*; witness the thousands who pass by without looking on it at all. What was it attracted the thousands to the launch? They might have seen the poetical 'calm water' at Wapping, or in the 'London Dock,' or in the Paddington Canal, or in a horse-pond, or in a slop-basin, or in any other vase. They might have heard the poetical winds howling through the chinks of a pig-stye, or the garret window; they might have seen the sun shining on a footman's livery, or on a brass warming pan; but could the 'calm water', or the 'wind', or the 'sun', make all, or any of these 'poetical'? I think not. Mr B. admits 'the Ship' to be poetical, but only from those accessaries: now if they *confer* poetry so as to make one thing poetical, they would make other things poetical; the more so, as Mr B. calls a 'ship of the line' without them, – that is to say, its 'masts and sails and streamers', – 'blue bunting', and 'coarse canvas', and 'tall poles'. So they are; and porcelain is clay, and man is dust, and flesh is grass, and yet the two latter at least are the subjects of much poesy.

Did Mr B. ever gaze upon the sea? I presume that he has, at least upon a sea-piece. Did any painter ever paint the sea *only*, without the addition of a ship, boat, wreck, or some such adjunct? Is the sea itself a more attractive, a more moral, a more poetical object, with or without a vessel, breaking its vast but fatiguing monotony? Is a storm more poetical without a ship? or, in the poem of *The Shipwreck*,[42] is it the storm or the ship which most interests? both *much* undoubtedly; but without the vessel, what should we care for the tempest? It would sink into mere descriptive poetry, which in itself was never esteemed a high order of that art.

I look upon myself as entitled to talk of naval matters, at least to poets: – with the exception of Walter Scott, Moore, and Southey, perhaps, who have been voyagers, I have *swum* more miles than all the rest of them together now living ever *sailed*, and have lived for months and months on shipboard; and, during the whole period of my life abroad, have scarcely ever passed a month out of sight of the Ocean: besides being brought up from two years till ten on the brink of it. I recollect, when anchored off Cape Sigeum in 1810, in an English frigate, a violent squall coming on at sunset, so violent as to make us imagine that the ship would part cable, or drive from her anchorage. Mr H[obhouse] and myself, and some officers, had been up the Dardanelles to Abydos, and were just returned in time. The aspect of a storm in the Archipelago is as poetical as need be, the sea being particularly short, dashing, and dangerous, and the navigation intricate and broken by the isles and currents. Cape Sigeum, the tumuli of the Troad, Lemnos, Tenedos, all added to the associations of the time. But what seemed the most '*poetical*' of all at the moment, were the numbers (about two hundred) of Greek and Turkish craft, which were obliged to 'cut and run' before the wind, from their unsafe anchorage, some for Tenedos, some for other isles, some for the Main, and some it might be for Eternity. The sight of these little scudding vessels, darting over the foam in the twilight, now appearing and now disappearing between the waves in the cloud of night, with their peculiarly *white* sails, (the Levant sails not being of '*coarse canvas*,' but of white cotton,) skimming along as quickly, but less safely than the sea-mew which hovered over them; their evident distress, their reduction to fluttering specks in the distance, their crowded succession, their *littleness*, as contending with the giant element, which made our stout 44's *teak* timbers (she was built in India) creak again; their aspect and their motion, all struck me as something far more 'poetical' than the mere broad, brawling, shipless sea, and the sullen winds, could possibly have been without them.

The Euxine is a noble sea to look upon, and the port of

Constantinople the most beautiful of harbours; and yet I cannot but think that the twenty sail of the line, some of one hundred and forty guns, rendered it more 'poetical' by day in the sun, and by night perhaps still more; for the Turks illuminate their vessels of war in a manner the most picturesque, and yet all this is *artificial*. As for the Euxine, I stood upon the Symplegades – I stood by the broken altar still exposed to the winds upon one of them – I felt all the '*poetry*' of the situation, as I repeated the first lines of Medea; but would not that 'poetry' have been heightened by the *Argo*? It was so even by the appearance of any merchant vessel arriving from Odessa. But Mr B. says, 'Why bring your ship off the stocks?' for no reason that I know, except that ships are built to be launched. The water, etc., undoubtedly HEIGHTENS the poetical associations, but it does not *make* them; and the ship amply repays the obligation: they aid each other; the water is more poetical with the ship – the ship less so without the water. But even a ship laid up in dock is a grand and a poetical sight. Even an old boat, keel upwards, wrecked upon the barren sand, is a 'poetical' object, (and Wordsworth, who made a poem about a washing-tub and a blind boy, may tell you so as well as I,) whilst a long extent of sand and unbroken water, without the boat, would be as like dull prose as any pamphlet lately published ...

The beautiful but barren Hymettus, – the whole coast of Attica, her hills and mountains, Pentelicus, Anchesmus, Philopappus, etc., etc. – are in themselves poetical, and would be so if the name of Athens, of Athenians, and her very ruins, were swept from the earth. But am I to be told that the 'Nature' of Attica would be *more* poetical without the 'Art' of the Acropolis? of the Temple of Theseus? and of the still all Greek and glorious monuments of her exquisitely artificial genius? Ask the traveller what strikes him as most poetical, the Parthenon, or the rock on which it stands? The COLUMNS of Cape Colonna, or the Cape itself? The rocks at the foot of it, or the recollection that Falconer's *ship* was bulged upon them? There are a thousand rocks and capes far more picturesque than those of the Acropolis and Cape Sunium in themselves; what are they to a thousand scenes in the wilder parts of Greece, of Asia Minor, Switzerland, or even of Cintra in Portugal, or to many scenes of Italy, and the Sierras of Spain? But it is the '*art*', the columns, the temples, the wrecked vessel, which give them their antique and their modern poetry, and not the spots themselves. Without them, the *spots* of earth would be unnoticed and unknown: buried, like Babylon and Nineveh, in indistinct confusion, without poetry, as without existence; but to whatever spot of earth these ruins were transported, if they were *capable* of transportation, like the obelisk, and the sphinx, and the Memnon's head, *there* they would still exist in the perfection of their beauty, and in the pride of their poetry. I opposed, and will ever oppose, the robbery of ruins from Athens, to instruct the English in sculpture (who are as capable of sculpture as the Egyptians are of skating); but why did I do so? The *ruins* are as poetical in Piccadilly as they were in the Parthenon; but the Parthenon and its rock are less so without them. Such is the Poetry of art.

There can be nothing more poetical in its aspect than the city of Venice; does this depend upon the sea, or the canals? –

> The dirt and sea-weed whence proud Venice rose?

Is it the canal which runs between the palace and the prison, or the 'Bridge of Sighs', which connects them, that render it poetical? Is it the 'Canal Grande', or Rialto which arches it, the churches which tower over it, the palaces which line, and the gondolas which glide over the waters, that render this city more poetical than Rome itself? Mr B. will say, perhaps, that the Rialto is but marble, the palaces and churches only stone, and the gondolas a 'coarse' black cloth, thrown over some planks of carved wood, with a shining bit of fantastically formed iron at the prow, '*without*' the water. And I tell him that without these, the water would be nothing but a clay-coloured ditch; and whoever says the contrary, deserves to be at the bottom of that, where Pope's heroes are embraced by the mud nymphs. There would be nothing to make the Canal of Venice more poetical than that of Paddington, were it not for the artificial adjuncts above mentioned, although it is a perfectly natural canal, formed by the sea, and the innumerable islands which constitute the site of this extraordinary city . . .

Mr B. then proceeds to press Homer into his service, in answer to a remark of Mr Campbell's, that 'Homer was a great describer of works of art.' Mr B. contends that all his great power, even in this, depends upon their connection with nature. The 'shield of Achilles derives its poetical interest from the subjects described on it.' And from what does the *spear* of Achilles derive its interest? and the helmet and the mail worn by Patroclus, and the celestial armour, and the very brazen greaves of the well-booted Greeks? Is it solely from the legs, and the back, and the breast, and the human body, which they enclose? In that case, it would have been more poetical to have made them fight naked; and Gulley and Gregson, as being nearer to a state of nature, are more poetical boxing in a pair of drawers than Hector and Achilles in radiant armour, and with heroic weapons.

Instead of the clash of helmets, and the rushing of chariots, and the whizzing of spears, and the glancing of swords, and the cleaving of shields, and the piercing of breast-plates, why not represent the Greeks and Trojans like two savage tribes, tugging and tearing, and kicking and biting, and gnashing, foaming, grinning, and gouging, in all the poetry of martial nature, unincumbered with gross, prosaic, artificial arms; an equal superfluity to the natural warrior and his natural poet? Is there any thing unpoetical in Ulysses striking the horses of Rhesus with *his bow* (having forgotten his thong), or would Mr B. have had him kick them with his foot, or smack them with his hand, as being more unsophisticated?

Nature, exactly, simply, barely, Nature, will make no great artist of any kind, and least of all a poet – the most artificial, perhaps, of all artists in his very essence. With regard to natural imagery, the poets are obliged to take some of their best illustrations from *art*. You say that a 'fountain is as clear or clearer than glass,' to express its beauty: –

O fons Bandusiae, splendidior vitro![43]

In the speech of Mark Antony, the body of Caesar is displayed, but so also is his *mantle*: —

You all do know this *mantle*, etc.

Look! in this place ran Cassius' *dagger* through.

If the poet had said that Cassius had run his *fist* through the rent of the mantle, it would have had more of Mr Bowles's 'nature' to help it; but the artificial *dagger* is more poetical than any natural *hand* without it. In the sublime of sacred poetry, 'Who is this that cometh from Edom? with *dyed garments* from Bozrah?' would 'the comer' be poetical without his '*dyed garments*'? which strike and startle the spectator, and identify the approaching object.

... Mr Bowles makes the chief part of a ship's poesy depend upon the '*wind*': then why is a ship under sail more poetical than a hog in a high wind? The hog is all nature, the ship is all art, 'coarse canvas', 'blue bunting', and 'tall poles'; both are violently acted upon by the wind, tossed here and there, to and fro, and yet nothing but excess of hunger could make me look upon the pig as the more poetical of the two, and then only in the shape of a griskin.

Will Mr Bowles tell us that the poetry of an aqueduct consists in the *water* which it conveys? Let him look on that of Justinian, on those of Rome, Constantinople, Lisbon, and Elvas, or even at the remains of that in Attica.

We are asked, 'What makes the venerable towers of Westminster Abbey more poetical, as objects, than the tower for the manufactory of patent shot, surrounded by the same scenery?' I will answer – the *architecture*. Turn Westminster Abbey or Saint Paul's into a powder magazine, their poetry, as objects, remains the same; the Parthenon was actually converted into one by the Turks, during Morosini's Venetian siege, and part of it destroyed in consequence. Cromwell's dragoons stabled their steeds in Worcester cathedral; was it less poetical as an object than before? Ask a foreigner on his approach to London, what strikes him as the most poetical of the towers before him: he will point out Saint Paul's and Westminster Abbey, without, perhaps, knowing the names or associations of either, and pass over the 'tower for patent shot', – not that, for any thing he knows to the contrary, it might not be the mausoleum of a monarch, or a Waterloo column, or a Trafalgar monument, but because its architecture is obviously inferior.

To the question, 'Whether the description of a game of cards be as poetical, supposing the execution of the artists equal, as a description of a walk in a forest?' it may be answered, that the *materials* are certainly not equal; but that 'the *artist*', who has rendered the 'game of cards poetical', is *by far the greater* of the two. But all this 'ordering' of poets is purely arbitrary on the part of Mr. B. There may or may not be, in fact, different 'orders' of poetry, but the poet is always ranked according to his execution, and not according to his branch of the art.

Tragedy is one of the highest presumed orders. Hughes has written a tragedy,[44] and a very successful one; Fenton another;[45] and Pope none. Did any man, however, – will even Mr B. himself, – rank Hughes and Fenton as poets above *Pope*? ... If Mr B. will contend for classifications of this kind, let him recollect that descriptive poetry has been ranked as among the lowest branches of the art, and description as a mere ornament, but which should never form 'the subject' of a poem. The Italians, with the most poetical language, and the most fastidious taste in Europe, possess now five *great* poets, they say, Dante, Petrarch, Ariosto, Tasso, and, lastly, Alfieri; and whom do they esteem one of the highest of these, and some of them the very highest? Petrarch, the *sonneteer*: it is true that some of his Canzoni are *not less* esteemed, but *not* more; who ever dreams of his Latin *Africa*?

Were Petrarch to be ranked according to the 'order' of his compositions, where would the best of sonnets place him? with Dante and the other? no; but, as I have before said, the poet who *executes* best is the highest, whatever his department, and will ever be so rated in the world's esteem.

In my mind, the highest of all poetry is ethical poetry, as the highest of all earthly objects must be moral truth. Religion does not make a part of my subject; it is something beyond human powers, and has failed in all human hands except Milton's and Dante's, and even Dante's powers are involved in his delineation of human passions, though in supernatural circumstances. What made Socrates the greatest of men? His moral truth – his ethics. What proved Jesus Christ the Son of God hardly less than his miracles? His moral precepts. And if ethics have made a philosopher the first of men, and have not been disdained as an adjunct to his Gospel by the Deity himself, are we to be told that ethical poetry, or didactic poetry, or by whatever name you term it, whose object is to make men better and wiser, is not the *very first order* of poetry; and are we to be told this too by one of the priesthood? It requires more mind, more wisdom, more power, than all the 'forests' that ever were 'walked for their description', and all the epics that ever were founded upon fields of battle. The Georgics are indisputably, and, I believe, *undisputedly*, even a finer poem than the Æneid. Virgil knew this; he did not order *them* to be burnt.

The proper study of mankind is man.

It is the fashion of the day to lay great stress upon what they call 'imagination' and 'invention', the two commonest of qualities: an Irish peasant with a little whisky in his head will imagine and invent more than would furnish forth a modern poem ...

Mr Bowles compares, when and where he can, Pope with Cowper* – (the same Cowper whom in his edition of Pope he laughs at for his attachment to an old woman, Mrs Unwin; search and you will find it; I remember the passage, though not the page); in particular he requotes Cowper's Dutch delineation of a wood, drawn up, like a seedsman's catalogue, with an affected imitation of Milton's style, as burlesque as the *Splendid Shilling*.

---

* [Byron's note] ... Away, then, with this cant about nature, and 'invariable principles of poetry!' A great artist will make a block of stone as sublime as a mountain, and a good poet can imbue a pack of cards with more poetry than inhabits the forests of America. It is the business and the proof of a poet to give the lie to the proverb, and sometimes to '*make a silken purse out of a sow's ear*,' and to conclude with another homely proverb, 'a good workman will not find fault with his tools'.

These two writers, for Cowper is no poet, come into comparison in one great work, the translation of Homer. Now, with all the great, and manifest, and manifold, and reproved, and acknowledged, and uncontroverted faults of Pope's translation, and all the scholarship, and pains, and time, and trouble, and blank verse of the other, who can ever read Cowper? and who will ever lay down Pope, unless for the original? Pope's was 'not Homer, it was Spondanus'; but Cowper's is not Homer either, it is not even Cowper. As a child I first read Pope's Homer with a rapture which no subsequent work could ever afford, and children are not the worst judges of their own language. As a boy I read Homer in the original, as we have all done, some of us by force, and a few by favour; under which description I come is nothing to the purpose, it is enough that I read him. As a man I have tried to read Cowper's version, and I found it impossible. Has any human reader ever succeeded?

And now that we have heard the Catholic reproached with envy, duplicity, licentiousness, avarice – what was the Calvinist? He attempted the most atrocious of crimes in the Christian code, viz. suicide – and why? because he was to be examined whether he was fit for an office which he seems to wish to have made a sinecure. His connection with Mrs Unwin was pure enough, for the old lady was devout, and he was deranged; but why then is the infirm and then elderly Pope to be reproved for his connection with Martha Blount? Cowper was the almoner of Mrs Throgmorton; but Pope's charities were his own, and they were noble and extensive, far beyond his future's warrant. Pope was the tolerant yet steady adherent of the most bigoted of sects; and Cowper the most bigoted and despondent sectary that ever anticipated damnation to himself or others. Is this harsh? I know it is, and I do not assert it as my opinion of Cowper *personally*, but to *show what might* be said, with just as great an appearance of truth and candour, as all the odium which has been accumulated upon Pope in similar speculations. Cowper was a good man, and lived at a fortunate time for his works.

Mr B., apparently not relying entirely upon his own arguments, has, in person or by proxy, brought forward the names of Southey and Moore. Mr Southey 'agrees entirely with Mr B. in his *invariable* principles of poetry'. The least that Mr B. can do in return is to approve the 'invariable principles of Mr Southey'. I should have thought that the word 'invariable' might have stuck in Southey's throat, like Macbeth's 'Amen!' I am sure it did in mine, and I am not the least consistent of the two, at least as a voter. Moore (*et tu, Brute!*) also approves, and Mr I. Scott. There is a letter also of two lines from a gentleman in asterisks, who, it seems, is a poet of 'the highest rank': – who *can* this be? not my friend Sir Walter, surely. Campbell it can't be; Rogers it won't be.

'You have *hit the nail in* the head, and **** [Pope?] *on* the head also.

'I *remain*, yours affectionately,

'(Four *Asterisks*).'

And in asterisks let him remain. Whoever this person may be, he deserves, for such a judgement of Midas, that 'the nail' which Mr B. has 'hit *in* the head,' should be driven through his own ears; I am sure that they are long enough.

The attempt of the poetical populace of the present day to obtain an ostracism against Pope is as easily accounted for as the Athenian's shell against Aristides; they are tired of hearing him always called 'the Just'. They are also fighting for life; for, if he maintains his station, they will reach their own – by falling. They have raised a mosque by the side of a Grecian temple of the purest architecture; and, more barbarous than the barbarians from whose practice I have borrowed the figure, they are not contented with their own grotesque edifice, unless they destroy the prior, and purely beautiful fabric which preceded, and which shames them and theirs for ever and ever. I shall be told that amongst those I *have* been (or it may be still *am*) conspicuous – true, and I am ashamed of it. I *have* been amongst the builders of this Babel, attended by a confusion of tongues, but *never* amongst the envious destroyers of the classic temple of our predecessor. I have loved and honoured the fame and name of that illustrious and unrivalled man, far more than my own paltry renown, and the trashy jingle of the crowd of 'Schools' and upstarts, who pretend to rival, or even surpass him. Sooner than a single leaf should be torn from his laurel, it were better that all which these men, and that I, as one of their set, have ever written, should

> Line trunks, clothe spice, or, fluttering in a row,
> Befringe the rails of Bedlam, or Soho![46]

There are those who will believe this, and those who will not. You, sir, know how far I am sincere, and whether my opinion, not only in the short work intended for publication, and in private letters which can never be published, has or has not been the same. I look upon this as the declining age of English poetry; no regard for others, no selfish feeling, can prevent me from seeing this, and expressing the truth. There can be no worse sign for the taste of the times than the depreciation of Pope. It would be better to receive for proof Mr Cobbett's rough but strong attack upon Shakespeare and Milton, than to allow this smooth and 'candid' undermining of the reputation of the most *perfect* of our poets, and the purest of our moralists. Of his power in the *passions*, in description, in the mock heroic, I leave others to descant. I take him on his strong ground as an *ethical* poet; in the former, none excel; in the mock heroic and the ethical, none equal him; and, in my mind, the latter is the highest of all poetry, because it does that in *verse*, which the greatest of men have wished to accomplish in prose. If the essence of poetry must be a *lie*, throw it to the dogs, or banish it from your republic, as Plato would have done. He who can reconcile poetry with truth and wisdom, is the only true '*poet*' in its real sense, 'the *maker*', 'the *creator*', – why must this mean the 'liar', the 'feigner', the 'tale-teller'? A man may make and create better things than these.

I shall not presume to say that Pope is as high a poet as Shakespeare and Milton, though his enemy, Warton, places him immediately under them. I would no more say this than I would assert in the mosque (once Saint Sophia's), that Socrates was a greater man than Mahomet. But if I say that he is very near them, it is no more than has been asserted of Burns, who is supposed

> To rival all but Shakespeare's name below.

I say nothing against this opinion. But of what '*order*', according to the poetical aristocracy, are Burns's poems? There are his *opus magnum*, 'Tam O'Shanter', a *tale*; the Cotter's Saturday Night, a descriptive sketch; some others in the same style: the rest are songs. So much for the *rank* of his *productions*; the *rank* of *Burns* is the very first of his art. Of Pope I have expressed my opinion elsewhere, as also of the effect which the present attempts at poetry have had upon our literature. If any great national or natural convulsion could or should overwhelm your country in such sort as to sweep Great Britain from the kingdoms of the earth, and leave only that, after all, the most living of human things, a *dead language*, to be studied and read, and imitated by the wise of future and far generations, upon foreign shores; if your literature should become the learning of mankind, divested of party cabals, temporary fashions, and national pride and prejudice; – an Englishman, anxious that the posterity of strangers should know that there had been such a thing as a British Epic and Tragedy, might wish for the preservation of Shakespeare and Milton; but the surviving World would snatch Pope from the wreck, and let the rest sink with the people. He is the moral poet of all civilization; and as such, let us hope that he will one day be the national poet of mankind. He is the only poet that never shocks; the only poet whose *faultlessness* has been made his reproach. Cast your eye over his productions; consider their extent, and contemplate their variety: – pastoral, passion, mock heroic, translation, satire, ethics – all excellent, and often perfect. If his great charm be his *melody*, how comes it that foreigners adore him even in their diluted translations? But I have made this letter too long. Give my compliments to Mr Bowles.

Yours ever very truly,

BYRON.

To John Murray, Esq.
Post Scriptum. –

... But there is something a little more serious in Mr Bowles's declaration, that he '*would* have spoken' of his [Pope's] 'noble generosity to the outcast Richard Savage', and other instances of a compassionate and generous heart, '*had they occurred to his recollection when he wrote.*' What! is it come to this? Does Mr B. sit down to write a minute and laboured life and edition of a great poet? Does he anatomize his character, moral and poetical? Does he sneer at his feelings, and doubt of his sincerity? Does he unfold his vanity and duplicity? and then omit the good qualities which might, in part, have 'covered this multitude of sins'? and then plead that 'they did not occur to his recollection'? Is this the frame of mind and of memory with which the illustrious dead are to be approached? If Mr Bowles, who must have had access to all the means of refreshing his memory, did not recollect these facts, he is unfit for his task; but if he *did* recollect and omit them, I know not what he is fit for, but I know what would be fit for him. Is the plea of 'not recollecting' such prominent facts to be admitted? Mr. B has been at a public school, and, as I have been publicly educated also, I can sympathise with his predilection. When we were in the third form even, had we pleaded on the Monday morning that we had not brought up the Saturday's exercise, because 'we had forgotten it', what would have been the reply? And is an excuse, which would not be pardoned to a schoolboy, to pass current in a matter which so nearly concerns the fame of the first poet of his age, if not of his country? If Mr B. so readily forgets the virtues of others, why complain so grievously that others have a better memory for his own faults? They are but the faults of an author; while the virtues he omitted from his catalogue are essential to the justice due to a man ...

Note Second, on the lines on Lady M. W. Montague.

In my opinion Pope has been more reproached for this couplet[47] than is justifiable. It is harsh but partly true, for '*libelled by her Hate*' he was, and with regard to the supposed consequences of '*her Love*' he may be regarded as sufficiently punished in not having been permitted to make the experiment. He would probably have run the risk with considerable courage. The coarseness of the line is not greater than that of two lines

which are easily to be found in the great Moralist, Johnson's
'London'; the one detailing an accomplishment of a 'fasting
Frenchman' and the other on the 'Monarch's air' of Balbus. I
forbear to quote the lines of Johnson in all their extension,
because as a young lady of Trumpington used to say of the
Gownsmen (when I was at College and she was approached with
too little respect) – they are so 'curse undiliket'.

Lady Mary appears to have been at least as much to blame as
Pope. Some of her reflections and repartees are recorded as
sufficiently exasperating. Pope in the whole of that business is
to be pitied. When he speaks of his 'miserable body' let it be
recollected that he was at least aware of his deformity, as indeed
deformed persons have in general sufficient wit to be.

It is also another unhappy dispensation of Nature that deformed
persons, and more particularly those of Pope's peculiar conforma-
tion, are born with very strong passions. I believe that this is a
physical fact, the truth of which is easily ascertained. Montaigne
has in his universal speculations written a chapter upon it more
curious than decent. So that these unhappy persons have to
combat, not only against the passions which they feel, but the
repugnance they inspire. Pope was unfortunate in this respect by
being born in England; there are climates where his Hump-back
would have made his (amatory) fortune. At least I know one
notorious instance of a hunch-back who is as fortunate as the
'grand Chancelier' of the Grammont. To be sure, his climate and
the morals of his country are both of them favourable to the
material portion of that passion of which Buffon says that 'the
refined *sentiment* is alike fictitious and pernicious.'

I think that I could show if necessary that Lady Mary W^y
Montague was also greatly to blame in that ground, *not* for having
rejected, but for having encouraged him; but I would rather
decline the task, though she should have remembered her own
line '*he comes too near that comes to be denied*'.

I admire her so much, her beauty, her talents, that I should do
this reluctantly. I besides am so attached to the very name of
'*Mary*' that, as Johnson once said, 'if you called a dog *Hervey*
I should love him,' so, if you were to call a female of the same

species 'Mary', I should love it better than others (biped or quadruped) of the same sex with a different appellation. She was an extraordinary woman. She could translate *Epictetus*, and yet write a song worthy of Aristippus. The lines

> And when the long hours of the Public are past,
> And we meet with Champaigne and a Chicken at last,
> May every fond pleasure that moment endear!
> Be banished afar both discretion and fear!
> Forgetting or scorning the airs of the Crowd,
> He may cease to be formal, and I to be proud,
> Till lost in the Joy we confess that we live,
> And he may be rude, and yet I may forgive.

There, Mr Bowles, what say you to such a supper with such a woman? And her own description too? Is not her '*Champaigne and Chicken*' worth a forest or two? Is it not poetry? It appears to me that this Stanza contains the '*purée*' of the whole Philosophy of Epicurus. I mean the practical philosophy of his School, not the precepts of the Master; for I have been too long at the University not to know that the Philosopher was [*words torn off with the seal*] a moderate man. But after all, would not some of us have been as great fools as Pope? For my part I wonder that with his quick feelings, her coquetry, and his disappointment, he did no more, instead of writing some lines which are to be condemned if false and regretted if true.

411

OBSERVATIONS UPON 'OBSERVATIONS'.
A SECOND LETTER TO JOHN MURRAY, ESQ.,
ON THE REV. W. L. BOWLES'S STRICTURES
ON THE LIFE AND WRITINGS OF POPE

Ravenna, March 25th, 1821

... In the long sentence quoted from the article in 'The L[ondon] M[agazine]' there is one coarse image, the justice of whose application I shall not pretend to determine: 'The pruriency with which his [Pope's] nose is laid to the ground' is an expression which, whether founded or not, might have been omitted. But the 'anatomical minuteness' appears to me justified even by Mr B.'s own subsequent quotation. To the point: – '*Many facts* tend to prove the peculiar susceptibility of his passions; nor can we implicitly believe that the connexion between him and Martha Blount was of a nature so pure and innocent as his panegyrist Ruffhead would have us believe,' etc. – 'At *no time* could she have regarded *Pope personally* with attachment,' etc. – 'But the most extraordinary circumstance in regard to his connexion with female society, was the strange mixture of *indecent* and even *profane* levity which his conduct and language often exhibited. The cause of this particularity may be sought, perhaps, in his consciousness of physical defect, which made him affect a character uncongenial, and a language opposite to the truth.' – If this is not 'minute moral anatomy', I should be glad to know what is! It is dissection in all its branches. I shall, however, hazard a remark or two upon this quotation.

To me it appears of no very great consequence whether Martha Blount was or was not Pope's mistress, though I could have wished him better. She appears to have been a cold-hearted, un-interested, ignorant, disagreeable woman, upon whom the tenderness of Pope's heart in the desolation of his latter days was cast away, not knowing whither to turn as he drew towards his pre-mature old age, childless and lonely, – like the needle which, approaching within a certain distance of the pole, becomes help-less and useless, and, ceasing to tremble, rusts. She seems to have been so totally unworthy of tenderness, that it is an additional proof of the kindness of Pope's heart to have been able to love such a being. But we must love something. I agree with Mr B. that *she* 'could at no time have regarded *Pope personally* with attachment,' because she was incapable of attachment; but I deny that Pope could not be regarded with personal attachment by a worthier woman. It is not probable, indeed, that a woman would have fallen in love with him as he walked along the Mall, or in a box at the opera, nor from a balcony, nor in a ball-room; but in society he seems to have been as amiable as unassuming, and with the greatest disadvantages of figure, his head and face were remarkably handsome, especially his eyes. He was adored by his friends – friends of the most opposite dispositions, ages, and talents – by the old and wayward Wycherley, by the cynical Swift, the rough Atterbury, the gentle Spence, the stern attorney-bishop Warburton, the virtuous Berkeley, and the 'cankered Bolingbroke'. Bolingbroke wept over him like a child; and Spence's description of his last moments is at least as edifying as the more ostentatious account of the deathbed of Addison. The soldier Peterborough and the poet Gay, the witty Congreve and the laughing Rowe, the eccentric Cromwell and the steady Bathurst, were all his intimates. The man who could conciliate so many men of the most opposite description, not one of whom but was a remarkable or a celebrated character, might well have pretended to all the attachment which a reasonable man would desire of an amiable woman.

Pope, in fact, wherever he got it, appears to have understood the sex well. Bolingbroke, 'a judge of the subject,' says Warton, thought his 'Epistle on the Characters of Women' his 'master-piece'. And even with respect to the grosser passion, which takes occasionally the name of '*romantic*', accordingly as the degree of sentiment elevates it above the definition of love by Buffon, it may be remarked, that it does not always depend upon personal appearance, even in a woman. Madame Cottin was a plain woman, and might have been virtuous, it may be presumed, without much interruption. Virtuous she was, and the consequences of this inveterate virtue were that two different admirers (one an elderly gentleman) killed themselves in despair (see Lady Morgan's 'France'). I would not, however, recommend this rigour to plain women in general, in the hope of securing the glory of two suicides apiece. I believe that there are few men who, in the course of their observations on life, may not have perceived that it is not the greatest female beauty who forms the longest and the strongest passions . . .

But, apropos of Pope. – Voltaire tells us that the Marechal Luxembourg (who had precisely Pope's figure) was not only somewhat too amatory for a great man, but fortunate in his attachments . . .

Wilkes, with his ugliness, used to say that 'he was but a quarter of an hour behind the handsomest man in England;' and this vaunt of his is said not to have been disproved by circumstances. Swift, when neither young, nor handsome, nor rich, nor even amiable, inspired the two most extraordinary passions upon record, Vanessa's and Stella's.

> Vanessa, aged scarce a score,
> Sighs for a gown of forty-four.

He requited them bitterly; for he seems to have broken the heart of the one, and worn out that of the other; and he had his reward, for he died a solitary idiot in the hands of servants.

For my own part, I am of the opinion of Pausanias, that success in love depends upon Fortune. 'They particularly reverence Celestial Venus, into whose temple', etc., etc., etc. I remember, too, to have seen a building in Ægina in which there is a statue of Fortune, holding a horn of Amalthea; and near her there is a winged Love. The meaning of this is that the success of men in love affairs depends more on the assistance of Fortune than the charms of beauty. I am persuaded, too, with Pindar (to whose opinion I subscribe in other particulars), that Fortune is one of the Fates, and that in a certain respect she is more powerful than her sisters. . . .

Grimm has a remark of the same kind on the different destinies of the younger Crebillon and Rousseau. The former writes a licentious novel, and a young English girl of some fortune and family (a Miss Strafford) runs away, and crosses the sea to marry him; while Rousseau, the most tender and passionate of lovers, is obliged to espouse his chambermaid . . .

In regard 'to the strange mixture of indecent, and sometimes *profane* levity, which his conduct and language *often* exhibited,' and which so much shocks Mr Bowles, I object to the indefinite word '*often*'; and in the extenuation of the occasional occurrence of such language, it is to be recollected that it was less the tone of *Pope* than the tone of the *time*. With the exception of the correspondence of Pope and his friends, not many private letters of the period have come down to us; but those, such as they are – a few scattered scraps from Farquhar and others – are more indecent and coarse than anything in Pope's letters. The comedies of Congreve, Vanbrugh, Farquhar, Cibber, etc., which naturally attempted to represent the manners and conversation of private life, are decisive upon this point; as are also some of Steele's papers, and even Addison's. We all know what the conversation of Sir R. Walpole, for seventeen years the prime minister of the country, was at his own table, and his excuse for his licentious language, viz, 'that everybody understood *that*, but few could talk rationally upon less common topics'. The refinement of latter days, – which is perhaps the consequence of vice, which wishes to mask and soften itself, as much as of virtuous civilisation – had not yet made sufficient progress. Even Johnson, in his 'London', has two or three passages which cannot be read aloud, and Addison's 'Drummer' some indelicate allusions.

The expression of Mr B., 'his consciousness of physical defect', is not very clear. It may mean deformity, or debility. If it alludes to Pope's deformity, it has been attempted to be shown that this was no insuperable objection to his being beloved. If it alludes to debility, as a consequence of Pope's peculiar conformation, I believe that it is a physical and known fact that hump-backed persons are of strong and vigorous passions. Several years ago, at Mr Angelo's fencing rooms, when I was a boy and pupil of him and of Mr Jackson, who had the use of his rooms in Albany on the alternate days, I recollect a gentleman named B-ll-gh-m, remarkable for his strength, and the fineness of his figure. His skill was not inferior, for he could stand up to the great Captain Barclay himself, with the muffles on; – a task neither easy nor agreeable to a pugilistic aspirant. As the byestanders were one day admiring his athletic proportions, he remarked to us, that he had five brothers as tall and strong as himself, and that their *father and mother were both crooked, and of very small stature*; I think he said, neither of them five feet high. It would not be difficult to adduce similar instances, but I abstain, because the subject is hardly refined enough for this immaculate period, this moral millenium of expurgated editions in books, manners, and royal trials of divorce.

This laudable delicacy – this crying-out elegance of the day – reminds me of a little circumstance which occurred when I was about eighteen years of age. There was then (and there may be still) a famous French 'entremetteuse', who assisted young gentlemen in their youthful pastimes. We had been acquainted for some time, when something occurred in her line of business more than ordinary, and the refusal was offered to me (and doubtless to many others), probably because I was in cash at the moment, having taken up a decent sum from the Jews, and not having spent much above half of it. The adventure on the tapis, it seems, required some caution and circumspection. Whether my venerable friend doubted my politeness I cannot tell; but she sent me a letter couched in such English as a short residence of sixteen years in England had enabled her to acquire. After several precepts and instructions, the letter closed. But there was a postscript. It contained these words: – 'Remember, Milor, that *delicaci ensure everi succés.*' The *delicacy* of the day is exactly, in all its circumstances, like that of this respectable foreigner. 'It ensures every *succés*,' and is not a whit more moral than, and not half so honourable as, the coarser candour of our less polished ancestors ...

Mr B. is here 'peremptorily called upon to speak of a circumstance which gives him the greatest pain, – the mention of a

letter he received from the editor of *The London Magazine*.' Mr
B. seems to have embroiled himself on all sides; whether by
editing, or replying, or attributing, or quoting, – it has been an
awkward affair for him.

Poor Scott[48] is now no more. In the exercise of his vocation,
he contrived at last to make himself the subject of a coroner's
inquest. But he died like a brave man, and he lived an able one.
I knew him personally, though slightly. Although several years
my senior, we had been schoolfellows together at the 'grammar-
schule' (or, as the Aberdonians pronounce it, '*squeel*') of New
Aberdeen. He did not behave to me quite handsomely in his
capacity of editor a few years ago, but he was under no obligation
to behave otherwise. The moment was too tempting for many
friends and for all enemies. At a time when all my relations (save
one) fell from me like leaves from the tree in autumn winds, and
my few friends became still fewer, – when the whole periodical
press (I mean the daily and weekly, *not* the *literary* press) was let
loose against me in every shape of reproach, with the two strange
exceptions (from their usual opposition) of *The Courier* and *The
Examiner*, – the paper of which Scott had the direction was
neither the last nor the least vituperative. Two years ago I met
him at Venice, when he was bowed in grief by the loss of his son,
and had known, by experience, the bitterness of a domestic
privation. He was then earnest with me to return to England;
and on my telling him, with a smile, that he was once of a different
opinion, he replied to me, 'that he and others had been greatly
misled; and that some pains, and rather extraordinary means,
had been taken to excite them'. Scott is no more, but there are
more than one living who were present at this dialogue. He was a
man of very considerable talents, and of great acquirements. He
had made his way, as a literary character, with high success, and
in a few years. Poor fellow! I recollect his joy at some appoint-
ment which he had obtained, or was to obtain, through Sir Jas.
Mackintosh, and which prevented the further extension (unless
by a rapid run to Rome) of his travels in Italy. I little thought to
what it would conduct him. Peace be with him! – and may all
such other faults as are inevitable to humanity be as readily

417

forgiven him, as the little injury which he had done to one who respected his talents, and regrets his loss.

Mr G.[49] charges Mr B. with 'suggesting' that Pope 'attempted' to commit 'a rape' upon Lady M. Wortley Montague. There are two reasons why this could not be true. The first is, that like the chaste Letitia's prevention of the intended ravishment by 'Fireblood' (in *Jonathan Wild*), it might have been impeded by a timely compliance. The second is, that however this might be, Pope was probably the less robust of the two; and (if the Lines on Sappho were really intended for this lady) the asserted consequences of her acquiescence in his wishes would have been a sufficient punishment. The passage which Mr B. quotes, however, insinuates nothing of the kind; it merely charges her with encouragement, and him with wishing to profit by it, – a slight attempt at seduction, and no more. The phrase is, 'a step beyond decorum'. Any physical violence is so abhorrent to human nature, that it recoils in cold blood from the very idea. But, the seduction of a woman's mind as well as person is not, perhaps, the least heinous sin of the two in morality. Dr Johnson commends a gentleman who having seduced a girl who said, 'I am afraid we have done wrong,' replied, 'Yes, we *have* done wrong', – 'for I would not *pervert* her mind also'. Othello would not 'kill Desdemona's *soul*'. Mr B. exculpates himself from Mr G.'s cha ge; but it is by substituting another charge against Pope. 'A step beyond decorum' has a soft sound, but what does it express? ﹥ all these cases, 'ce n'est que le premier pas qui coûte'. Has not ᵗ ᵉ Scripture something upon 'the lusting after a woman' being no less criminal than the crime? 'A step beyond decorum', in short, any step beyond the instep, is a step from a precipice to the lady who permits it. For the gentleman who makes it it is also rather hazardous if he don't succeed, and still more so if he does.

Mr B. appeals to the 'Christian reader!' upon this '*Gilchristian* criticism'. Is not this play upon such words 'a step beyond decorum' in a clergyman? But I admit the temptation of a pun to be irresistible . . .

In page 14 we have a large assertion, that 'the "Eloisa" alone is sufficient to convict him of *gross licentiousness*'. Thus, out it comes at last. Mr B. *does* accuse Pope of '*gross* licentiousness', and grounds the charge upon a poem. The *licentiousness* is a 'grand peut-être', according to the turn of the times being. The grossness I deny. On the contrary, I do believe that such a subject never was, nor ever could be, treated by any poet with so much delicacy, mingled, at the same time, with such true and intense passion. Is the 'Atys' of Catullus *licentious*? No, nor even gross; and yet Catullus is often a coarse writer. The subject is nearly the same, except that Atys was the suicide of his manhood, and Abelard the victim.

The 'licentiousness' of the story was *not* Pope's – it was a fact. All that it had of gross, he has softened; – all that it had of indelicate, he has purified – all that it had of passionate, he has beautified; – all that it had of holy, he has hallowed. Mr Campbell had admirably marked this in a few words (I quote from memory), in drawing the distinction between Pope and Dryden, and pointing out where Dryden was wanting. 'I fear', says he, 'that had the subject of "Eloisa" fallen into his (Dryden's) hands, that he would have given us but a *coarse* draft of her passion'. Never was the delicacy of Pope so much shown as in this poem. With the facts and the letters of 'Eloisa' he has done what no other mind but that of the best and purest of poets could have accomplished with such materials. Ovid, Sappho (in the Ode called hers) – all that we have of ancient, all that we have of modern poetry, sinks into nothing compared with him in this production.

Let us hear no more of this trash about 'licentiousness'. Is not 'Anacreon' taught in our schools? – translated, praised, and edited? Are not his Odes the amatory praises of a boy? Is not Sappho's Ode on a girl? Is not this sublime and (according to Longinus) fierce love for one of her own sex? And is not Phillips' translation of it in the mouths of all your women? And are the English schools or the English women the more corrupt for all this? When you have thrown the ancients into the fire it will be time to denounce the moderns. 'Licentiousness'! – there is more real mischief and sapping licentiousness in a single French prose novel, in a Moravian hymn, or a German comedy, than in all the actual poetry that ever was penned or poured forth, since the rhapsodies of Orpheus. The sentimental anatomy of Rousseau and Mad^e de S[taël] are far more formidable than any quantity of verse. They are so because they sap the principles, by *reasoning* upon the *passions*; whereas poetry is in itself passion, and does not systematize. It assails, but does not argue; it may be wrong, but it does not assume pretensions to Optimism.

[. . .]

P.S. – Amongst the above-mentioned lines there occurs the following, *applied* to *Pope* –

'The assassin's vengeance, and the coward's lie.'

And Mr B. persists that he is a well-wisher to Pope!!! He has, then, edited an 'assassin' and a 'coward' wittingly, as well as lovingly. In my former letter I have remarked upon the editor's forgetfulness of Pope's benevolence. But where he mentions his faults it is 'with sorrow' – his tears drop, but they do not blot them out. The 'recording angel' differs from the recording clergyman. A fulsome editor is pardonable though tiresome, like a panegyrical son whose pious sincerity would demi-deify his father. But a detracting editor is a parricide. He sins against the nature of his office, and connection – he murders the life to come of his victim. If his author is not worthy to be remembered, do not edite at all: if he be, edite honestly, and even flatteringly. The reader will forgive the weakness in favour of mortality, and correct your adulation with a smile. But to sit down 'mingere in patrios cineres,'[50] as Mr B. has done, merits a reprobation so strong, that I am as incapable of expressing as of ceasing to feel it.

Further Addenda for insertion in the Letter to J.M. Esq., on Bowles's Pope, etc.

... In the present rank fertility of 'great poets of the age', and 'schools of poetry' – a word which, like 'schools of eloquence' and of 'philosophy', is never introduced till the decay of the art has increased with the number of its professors – in the present day, then, there have sprung up two sorts of Naturals; – the Lakers, who whine about Nature because they live in Cumberland; and their *under-sect* (which some one has maliciously called the 'Cockney School'), who are enthusiastical for the country because they live in London. It is to be observed, that the rustical founders are rather anxious to disclaim any connexion with their metropolitan followers, whom they ungraciously review, and call cockneys, atheists, foolish fellows, bad writers, and other hard names not less ungrateful than unjust. I can understand the pretensions of the aquatic gentlemen of Windermere to what Mr Braham terms '*entusymusy*', for lakes, and mountains, and daffodils, and buttercups; but I should be glad to be apprized of the foundation of the London propensities of their imitative brethren to the same 'high argument'. Southey, Wordsworth, and Coleridge have rambled over half Europe, and seen Nature in most of her varieties (although I think that they have occasionally not used her very well); but what on earth – of earth and sea, and Nature – have the others seen? Not a half, nor a tenth part so much as Pope. While they sneer at his Windsor Forest, have they ever seen any thing of Windsor except its *brick*?

The most rural of these gentlemen is my friend Leigh Hunt, who lives at Hampstead. I believe that I need not disclaim any personal or poetical hostility against that gentleman. A more amiable man in society I know not; nor (when he will allow his sense to prevail over his sectarian principles) a better writer. When he was writing his *Rimini*, I was not the last to discover its beauties, long before it was published. Even then I remonstrated against its vulgarisms; which are the more extraordinary, because the author is any thing but a vulgar man. Mr Hunt's answer was, that he wrote them upon principle; they made 'part of his *system*'!! I then said no more. When a man talks of his system, it is like a woman's talking of her *virtue*. I let them talk on ...

With the rest of his young people I have no acquaintance, except through some things of theirs (which have been sent out without my desire), and I confess that till I had read them I was not aware of the full extent of human absurdity. Like Garrick's 'Ode to Shakspeare', they '*defy criticism*'. These are of the personages who decry Pope. One of them, a Mr John Ketch, has written some lines against him, of which it were better to be the subject than the author. Mr Hunt redeems himself by occasional beauties; but the rest of these poor creatures seem so far gone that I would not 'march through Coventry with them, that's flat!' were I in Mr Hunt's place. To be sure, he has 'led his ragamuffins where they will be well peppered'; but a system-maker must receive all sorts of proselytes. When they have really seen life – when they have felt it – when they have travelled beyond the far distant boundaries of the wilds of Middlesex – when they have overpassed the Alps of Highgate, and traced to its sources the Nile of the New River – then, and not till then, can it properly be permitted to them to despise Pope; who had, if not *in Wales*, been *near* it, when he described so beautifully the '*artificial*' works of the Benefactor of Nature and mankind, the 'Man of Ross'; whose picture, still suspended in the parlour of the inn, I have so often contemplated with reverence for his memory, and admiration of the poet, without whom even his own still existing good works could hardly have preserved his honest renown.

I would also observe to my friend Hunt, that I shall be very glad to see him at *Ravenna*, not only for my sincere pleasure in his company, and the advantage which a thousand miles or so of travel might produce to a 'natural' poet, but also to point out one or two little things in 'Rimini', which he probably would not have placed in his opening to that poem, if he had ever *seen* *Ravenna*; – unless, indeed, it made 'part of his system'!! I must also crave his indulgence for having spoken of his disciples – by no means an agreeable or self-sought subject. If they had said nothing of *Pope*, they might have remained 'alone with their glory', for aught I should have said or thought about them or their nonsense. But if they interfere with the 'little Nightingale' of Twickenham, they may find others who will bear it – *I* won't. Neither time, nor distance, nor grief, nor age, can ever diminish my veneration for him, who is the great moral poet of all times, of all climes, of all feelings, and of all stages of existence. The delight of my boyhood, the study of my manhood, perhaps (if allowed to me to attain it), he may be the consolation of my age. His poetry is the Book of Life. Without canting, and yet without neglecting religion, he has assembled all that a good and

great man can gather together of moral wisdom cloathed in
consummate beauty. Sir William Temple observes, 'that of all
the numbers of mankind that live within the compass of a
thousand years, for one man that is born capable of making a
great poet, there may be a *thousand* born capable of making as
great generals and ministers of state as any in story'. Here is a
statesman's opinion of poetry: it is honourable to him, and to
the art. Such a 'poet of a thousand years' was *Pope*. A thousand
years will roll away before such another can be hoped for in our
literature. But it can want them – he himself is a literature . . .

The grand distinction of the under forms of the new school of
poets is their *vulgarity*. By this I do not mean that they are
coarse, but 'shabby-genteel', as it is termed. A man may be
coarse and yet not *vulgar*, and the reverse. Burns is often coarse,
but never *vulgar*. Chatterton is never vulgar, nor Wordsworth,
nor the higher of the Lake school, though they treat of low life in
all its branches. It is in their *finery* that the new under school are
most vulgar, and they may be known by this at once; as what we
called at Harrow 'a Sunday blood' might be easily distinguished
from a gentleman, although his cloathes might be the better
cut, and his boots the best blackened, of the two: – probably
because he made the one, or cleaned the other, with his own
hands.

In the present case, I speak of writing, not of persons. Of the
latter I know nothing; of the former, I judge as it is found. Of my
friend Hunt, I have already said, that he is any thing but vulgar
in his manners; and of his disciples, therefore, I will not judge of
their manners from their verses. They may be honourable and
gentlemanly men, for what I know; but the latter quality is
studiously excluded from their publications. They remind me of
Mr Smith and the Miss Broughtons at the Hampstead Assembly,
in *Evelina*. In these things (in private life, at least,) I pretend to
some small experience; because, in the course of my youth, I
have seen a little of all sorts of society, from the Christian prince
and the Mussulman sultan and pacha, and the higher ranks of
their countries, down to the London boxer, the '*flash and the
swell*', the Spanish muleteer, the wandering Turkish dervise, the

Scotch highlander, and the Albanian robber; – to say nothing of the curious varieties of Italian social life. Far be it from me to presume that there ever was, or can be, such a thing as an *aristocracy* of *poets*; but there *is* a nobility of thought and of style, open to all stations, and derived partly from talent, and partly from education, – which is to be found in Shakespeare, and Pope, and Burns, no less than in Dante and Alfieri, but which is nowhere to be perceived in the mock birds and bards of Mr Hunt's little chorus. If I were asked to define what this gentlemanliness is, I should say that it is only to be defined by *examples* – of those who have it, and those who have it not. In *life*, I should say that most *military* men have it, and few *naval*; – that several men of rank have it, and few lawyers; – that it is more frequent among authors than divines (when they are not pedants); that *fencing*-masters have more of it than dancing-masters, and singers than players; and that (if it be not an Irishism to say so) it is far more generally diffused among women than among men. In poetry, as well as writing in general, it will never *make* entirely a poet or a poem; but neither poet nor poem will ever be good for any thing without it. It is the *salt* of society, and the seasoning of composition. *Vulgarity* is far worse than downright *blackguardism*; for the latter comprehends wit, humour, and strong sense at times; while the former is a sad abortive attempt at all things, 'signifying nothing'. It does not depend upon low themes, or even low language, for Fielding revels in both; – but is he ever *vulgar*? No. You see the man of education, the gentleman, and the scholar, sporting with his subject, – its master, not its slave. Your vulgar writer is always most vulgar the higher his subject, as the man who showed the menagerie at Pidcock's was wont to say, – 'This, gentlemen, is the *eagle* of the sun, from Archangel, in Russia; the *otterer* it is the *igherer* he flies.' But to the proof. It is thing to be felt more than explained. Let any man take up a volume of Mr Hunt's subordinate writers, read (if possible) a couple of pages, and pronounce for himself, if they contain not the kind of writing which may be likened to 'shabby-genteel' in actual life. When he has done this, let him take up Pope; and when he has laid him down, take up the cockneys again – if he can.

Dear Moray, –

... Whether I have made out the case for Pope, I know not; but I am very sure that I have been zealous in the attempt. If it comes to the proofs, we shall beat the Blackguards. I will show more *imagery* in twenty lines of Pope than in any equal length of quotation in English poesy, and that in places where they least expect it: for instance, in his lines on *Sporus*, – now, do just *read* them over – the subject is of no consequence (whether it be Satire or Epic) – we are talking of *poetry* and *imagery* from *Nature and Art*. Now, mark the images separately and arithmetically: –

1. The thing of *Silk*.
2. *Curd* of *Ass's* milk.
3. The *Butterfly*.
4. The *Wheel*.
5. Bug with gilded wings.
6. *Painted* Child of dirt.
7. Whose *Buzz*.
8. Well-bred *Spaniels*.
9. *Shallow streams run dimpling*.
10. *Florid impotence*.
11. *Prompter. Puppet squeaks*.
12. *The Ear of Eve*.
13. *Familiar toad*.
14. *Half-froth, half-venom, spits* himself abroad.
15. *Fop* at the *toilet*.
16. *Flatterer* at the *board*.
17. *Amphibious thing*.
18. Now *trips a lady*.
19. Now *struts a Lord*.
20. A *Cherub's* face.
21. A *reptile* all the rest.
22. The *Rabbins*.
23. Pride that *licks the dust*.

> Beauty that shocks you, parts that none will trust,
> Wit that can creep, and *Pride* that *licks* the *dust*.

Now, is there a line of all the passage without the most *forcible* imagery (for his purpose)? Look at the *variety*, at the *poetry*, of the passage – at the *imagination*: there is hardly a line from which a *painting* might not be made, and *is*. But this is nothing in comparison with his higher passages in the *Essay on Man*, and many of his other poems, serious and comic. There never was such an unjust outcry in this world as that which these Scoundrels are trying against Pope ...

TO THE HON. DOUGLAS KINNAIRD   *R[avenn]a*
                                      March 23rd, 1821

My Dear Douglas, – I shall consent to nothing of the kind. Our good friends must have the goodness to 'bide a wee'. One of three events must occur: – Lady Noel will die – or Lady B. – or myself. In the first case they will be paid out of the incoming: in the second my property will be so far liberated (the offspring being a daughter) as to leave a surplus to cover more than any outstanding present debts: in the third, my executors will of course see their claims liquidated. But as to my parting at this present with a thousand guineas – I wonder if you take me for an Atheist, to make me so unchristian a proposition. It is true that I have reduced my expences in *that* line; but I have had others to encounter. On getting to dry land, I have had to buy carriages, and some new horses, and to furnish my house, for here you find only walls, *no furnished* apartments – it is not the custom. Besides, though I do not subscribe to liquidate the sum of two thousand pounds for a man of twenty thousand a year, nor write me down a contributor to the English radical societies, yet wherever I find a poor man suffering for his opinions – and there are many such in this country – I always let him have a shilling out of a guinea. You speak with some facetiousness of the *Hans* – etc. Wait till the play is played out. Whatever happens, no tyrant nor tyranny nor barbarian army shall make me change my tone or thoughts or notions, or alter anything but my temper. I say so *now*, as I said so then – now that they are at their butcher-work, as before when they were merely preparing for it.

As to Murray, I presume that you forwarded my letter. I acquiesce in what you say about the arrangement with him, but not at all in the appropriation of the fee. Let me see it in circulars, and then I will tell you whether I will pay them away or no. You must have a very bad opinion of my principles to hint at such a thing. If you pay them anything, pay them the interest, provided it is not above a hundred and fifty pounds. You persuaded me to give those bonds and now you see the consequence. It would have been better to have stood a suit out. At the worst, Rochdale will always in any case bring enough to cover the bonds, and they may seize and sell it for anything I care. I have had more trouble than profit with it. As to Lady Noel, what you say of her declining health would be very well to any one else; but the way to be immortal (I mean *not* to die at all) is to have me for your heir. I recommend you to put me in your will; and you will see that (as long as *I* live at least) you will never even catch cold.

I have written to you twice or thrice lately – and so on. I could give you some curious and interesting details on things here; but they open all letters, and I have no wish to gratify any curiosity, except that of my friends and gossips. Some day or other when we meet (if we meet) I will make your hair stand on end, and Hobhouse's wig (does he wear one still) start from its frame, and leave him under *bare poles*. There is one thing I wish particularly to propose to you patriots; and yet it can't be, without this letter went in a balloon – and, as Moleda [?] says, '*thaut's* impossible'. Let me hear from you – and as good news as you can send in that agreeable soft conciliatory style of yours.

TO RICHARD BELGRAVE HOPPNER *Ravenna, April 3, 1821*

Thanks for the translation. I have sent you some books, which I do not know whether you have read or no – you need not return them, in any case. I enclose you also a letter from Pisa. I have neither spared trouble nor expense in the care of the child; and as she was now four years old complete, and quite above the control of the servants – and as a *man* living without any woman at the head of his house cannot much attend to a nursery – I had no resource but to place her for a time (at a high pension too) in the convent of Bagna-Cavalli (twelve miles off), where the air is good, and where she will, at least, have her learning advanced, and her morals and religion inculcated. I had also another reason; – things were and are in such a state here, that I had no reason to look upon my own personal safety as particularly insurable; and I thought the infant best out of harm's way, for the present.

It is also fit that I should add that I by no means intended, nor intend, to give a *natural* child an *English* education, because with

427

the disadvantages of her birth, her after settlement would be doubly difficult. Abroad, with a fair foreign education and a portion of five or six thousand pounds, she might and may marry very respectably. In England such a dowry would be a pittance, while elsewhere it is a fortune. It is, besides, my wish that she should be a Roman Catholic, which I look upon as the best religion, as it is assuredly the oldest of the various branches of Christianity. I have now explained my notions as to the *place* where she now is – it is the best I could find for the present; but I have no prejudices in its favour.

I do not speak of politics, because it seems a hopeless subject, as long as those scoundrels are to be permitted to bully states out of their independence. Believe me,

Yours ever and truly

P.S. – There is a report here of a change in France; but with what truth is not yet known.

P.S. – My respects to Mrs H. I *have* the 'best opinion' of her countrywomen; and at my time of life, (three and thirty, 22nd January, 1821,) that is to say, after the life I have led, a *good* opinion is the only rational one which a man should entertain of the whole sex – up to *thirty*, the worst possible opinion a man can have of them in *general*, the better for himself. Afterwards, it is a matter of no importance to *them*, nor to him either, *what opinion* he entertains – his day is over, or, at least, should be.

You see how sober I am become.

TO PERCY BYSSHE SHELLEY   *Ravenna, April 26, 1821*

The child continues doing well, and the accounts are regular and favourable. It is gratifying to me that you and Mrs Shelley do not disapprove of the step which I have taken, which is merely temporary.

I am very sorry to hear what you say of Keats – is it *actually* true? I did not think criticism had been so killing. Though I differ from you essentially in your estimate of his performances, I so much abhor all unnecessary pain, that I would rather he had been seated on the highest peak of Parnassus than have perished in such a manner. Poor fellow! though with such inordinate self-love he would probably have not been very happy. I read the review of *Endymion* in the *Quarterly*. It was severe, – but surely not so severe as many reviews in that and other journals upon others.

I recollect the effect on me of the *Edinburgh* on my first poem; it was rage, and resistance, and redress – but not despondency nor despair. I grant that those are not amiable feelings; but, in this world of bustle and broil, and especially in the career of writing, a man should calculate upon his powers of *resistance* before he goes into the arena.

> Expect not life from pain nor danger free,
> Nor deem the doom of man reversed for thee.

You know my opinion of *that second-hand* school of poetry. You also know my high opinion of your own poetry, – because it is of *no* school. I read *Cenci* – but, besides that I think the *subject* essentially *un*dramatic, I am not an admirer of our old dramatists *as models*. I deny that the English have hitherto had a drama at all. Your *Cenci*, however, was a work of power, and poetry. As to *my* drama, pray revenge yourself upon it, by being as free as I have been with yours.

I have not yet got your *Prometheus*, which I long to see. I have heard nothing of mine, and do not know that it is yet published. I have published a pamphlet on the Pope controversy, which you will not like. Had I known that Keats was dead – or that he was alive and so sensitive – I should have omitted some remarks upon his poetry, to which I was provoked by his *attack* upon *Pope*, and my disapprobation of *his own* style of writing.

You want me to undertake a great poem – I have not the inclination nor the power. As I grow older, the indifference – *not* to life, for we love it by instinct – but to the stimuli of life, increases. Besides, this late failure of the Italians has latterly

disappointed me for many reasons, some public, some personal.
My respects to Mrs S.

Yours ever,

B.

P.S. – Could not you and I contrive to meet this summer? Could
not you take a run here *alone*?

TO THOMAS MOORE   *Ravenna, April 28, 1821*

You cannot have been more disappointed than myself, nor so
much deceived. I have been so at some personal risk also, which
is not yet done away with. However, no time nor circumstances
shall alter my tone nor my feelings of indignation against tyranny
triumphant. The present business has been as much a work of
treachery as of cowardice – though both may have done their
part. If ever you and I meet again, I will have a talk with you
upon the subject. At present, for obvious reasons, I can write but
little, as all letters are opened. In *mine* they shall always find *my*
sentiments, but nothing that can lead to the oppression of others.

You will please to recollect that the Neapolitans are now no-
where more execrated than in Italy, and not blame a whole
people for the vices of a province. That would be like condemn-
ing Great Britain because they plunder wrecks in Cornwall.

And now let us be literary; – a sad falling off, but it is always a
consolation. If 'Othello's occupation be gone', let us take to the
next best; and, if we cannot contribute to make mankind more
free and wise, we may amuse ourselves and those who like it.
What are you writing? I have been scribbling at intervals, and
Murray will be publishing about now.

Lady Noel has, as you say, been dangerously ill; but it may
console you to learn that she is dangerously well again.

I have written a sheet or two more of Memoranda for you; and
I kept a little Journal for about a month or two, till I had filled
the paper-book. I then left it off, as things grew busy, and, after-
wards, too gloomy to set down without a painful feeling. This I
should be glad to send you, if I had an opportunity; but a volume,

however small, don't go well by such posts as exist in this Inquisition of a country.

I have no news. As a very pretty woman said to me a few nights ago, with the tears in her eyes, as she sat at the harpsichord, 'Alas! the Italians must now return to making operas'. I fear *that* and maccaroni are their forte, and 'motley their only wear'. However, there are some high spirits among them still. Pray write.

And believe me, etc.

'MY DICTIONARY', MAY 1821, AND DETACHED THOUGHTS, 15 OCTOBER 1821–18 MAY 1822

Ravenna, May 1ˢᵗ 1821

AMONGST various journals, memoranda, diaries, etc., which I have kept in the course of my living, I began one about three months ago, and carried it on till I had filled one paper-book (thinnish), and two sheets or so of another. I then left off, partly because I thought we should have some business here, and I had furbished up my arms, and got my apparatus ready for taking a turn with the Patriots, having my drawers full of their proclamations, oaths, and resolutions, and my lower rooms of their hidden weapons of most calibres; and partly because I had filled my paper book. But the Neapolitans have betrayed themselves and all the World, and those who would have given their blood for Italy can now only give her their tears.

Some day or other, if dust holds together, I have been enough in the Secret (at least in this part of the country) to cast perhaps some little light upon the atrocious treachery which has replunged Italy into Barbarism. At present I have neither the time nor the temper. However, the *real* Italians are *not* to blame – merely the scoundrels at the *Heel of the Boot*, which the *Hun* now wears, and will trample them to ashes with for their Servility.

I have risked myself with the others *here*, and how far I may or may not be compromised is a problem at this moment: some of them like 'Craigengelt' would 'tell all and more than all to save themselves'; but, come what may, the cause was a glorious one, though it reads at present as if the Greeks had run away from Xerxes.

Happy the few who have only to reproach themselves with believing that these rascals were less *rascaille* than they proved. *Here* in Romagna the efforts were necessarily limited to preparations and good intentions, until the Germans were fairly engaged

432

in *equal* warfare, as we are upon their very frontiers without a single fort, or hill, nearer than San Marino. Whether 'Hell will be paved with' those 'good intentions', I know not; but there will probably be good store of Neapolitans to walk upon the pavement, whatever may be its composition. Slabs of lava from their mountain, with the bodies of their own damned Souls for cement, would be the fittest causeway for Satan's *Corso*.

But what shall I write? another Journal? I think not. Anything that comes uppermost – and call it 'my Dictionary'.

My Dictionary

Augustus. – I have often been puzzled with his character. Was he a great Man? Assuredly. But not one of *my* great men. I have always looked upon Sylla as the greatest Character in History, for laying down his power at the moment when it was

> too great to keep or to resign,

and thus despising them all. As to the retention of his power by Augustus, the thing was already settled. If he had given it up, the Commonwealth was gone, the republic was long past all resuscitation. Had Brutus and Cassius gained the battle of Philippi, it would not have restored the republic – its days ended with the Gracchi, the rest was a mere struggle of parties. You might as well cure a Consumption, restore a broken egg, as revive a state so long a prey to every uppermost Soldier as Rome had long been.

As for despotism, if Augustus could have been sure that all his Successors would have been like himself (I mean *not* as *Octavius*, but Augustus), or Napoleon would have insured the world that *none* of his Successors would have been like himself, the ancient or modern World might have gone on like the Empire of China – in a state of lethargic prosperity.

Suppose that there had been *no Octavius*, and Tiberius had 'jumped the life' between, and at once succeeded Julius? And yet it is difficult to say whether hereditary right, or popular choice, produce the worse Sovereigns. The Roman Consuls make a goodly show, but then they only reigned for a year, and were under a sort of personal obligation to distinguish themselves. It is still more difficult to say which form of Government is the *worst* – all are so bad. As for democracy, it is the worst of the whole; for what is (*in fact*) democracy? an Aristocracy of Blackguards. . . .

Detached Thoughts

Octr 15th 1821

I have been thinking over the other day on the various comparisons, good or evil, which I have seen published of myself in different journals English and foreign. This was suggested to me by accidentally turning over a foreign one lately; for I have made it a rule latterly never to *search* for anything of the kind, but not to avoid the perusal if presented by Chance.

To begin then – I have seen myself compared personally or poetically, in English, French, *German* (*as* interpreted to me), Italian, and Portuguese, within these nine years, to Rousseau – Göethe – Young – Aretino – Timon of Athens – 'An Alabaster Vase lighted up within' – Satan – Shakespeare – Buonaparte – Tiberius – Aeschylus – Sophocles – Euripides – Harlequin – The Clown – Sternhold and Hopkins – to the Phantasmagoria – to Henry the 8th – to Chenies – to Mirabeau – to young R. Dallas (the Schoolboy) – to Michael Angelo – to Raphael – to a *petit maître* – to Diogenes – to Childe Harold – to Lara – to the Count in Beppo – to Milton – to Pope – to Dryden – to Burns – to Savage – to Chatterton – to 'oft have I heard of thee my Lord Biron' in Shakespeare – to Churchill the poet – to Kean the Actor – to Alfieri, etc., etc., etc. The likeness to Alfieri was asserted very seriously by an Italian, who had known him in his younger days: it of course related merely to our apparent personal dispositions. He did not assert it to *me* (for we were not then good friends), but in society.

The Object of so many contradictory comparisons must probably be like something different from them all; but what *that* is, is more than *I* know, or any body else.

My Mother, before I was twenty, would have it that I was like

Rousseau, and Madame de Staël used to say so too in 1813, and the *Edin^h Review* has something of the sort in its critique on the 4th Canto of *Ch^e Ha^d*. I can't see any point of resemblance: he wrote prose, I verse: he was of the people, I of the Aristocracy: he was a philosopher, I am none: he published his first work at forty, I mine at eighteen: his first essay brought him universal applause, mine the contrary: he married his house-keeper, I could not keep house with my wife: he thought all the world in a plot against *him*, my little world seems to think *me* in a plot against it, if I may judge by their abuse in print and coterie: he liked Botany, I like flowers, and herbs, and trees, but know nothing of their pedigrees: he wrote Music, I limit my knowledge of it to what I catch by *Ear* – I never could learn any thing by *study*, not even a language, it was all by rote and ear and memory: he had a bad memory, I *had* at least an excellent one (ask Hodgson the poet, a good judge, for he has an astonishing one): he wrote with hesitation and care, I with rapidity and rarely with pains: *he* could never ride nor swim 'nor was cunning of fence', *I* am an excellent swimmer, a decent though not at all a dashing rider (having staved in a rib at eighteen in the course of scampering), and was sufficient of fence – particularly of the Highland broadsword; not a bad boxer when I could keep my temper, which was difficult, but which I strove to do ever since I knocked down Mr Purling and put his knee-pan out (with the gloves on) in Angelo's and Jackson's rooms in 1806 during the sparring; and I was besides a very fair cricketer – one of the Harrow Eleven when we play[ed] against Eton in 1805. Besides, Rousseau's way of life, his country, his manners, his whole character, were so very different, that I am at a loss to conceive how such a comparison could have arisen, as it has done three several times, and all in rather a remarkable manner. I forgot to say, that *he* was also short-sighted, and that hitherto my eyes have been the contrary to such a degree, that, in the largest theatre of Bologna, I distinguished and read some busts and inscriptions painted near the stage, from a box so distant, and so *darkly* lighted, that none of the company (composed of young and very bright-eyed people – some of them in the same box) could make out a letter, and thought it was a trick, though I had never been in that theatre before.

Altogether, I think myself justified in thinking the comparison not well founded. I don't say this out of pique, for Rousseau was a great man, and the thing if true were flattering enough; but I have no idea of being pleased with a chimera.

[. . .]

11

The Impression of Parliament upon me was that it's members are not formidable as *Speakers*, but very much so as an *audience*; because in so numerous a body there may be little Eloquence (after all there were but *two* thorough Orators in all Antiquity, and I suspect still *fewer* in modern times), but must be a leaven of thought and good sense sufficient to make them *know* what is right, though they can't express it nobly.

12

Horne Tooke and Roscoe both are said to have declared, that they left Parliament with a higher opinion of its aggregate integrity and abilities than that with which they had entered it. The general amount of both in most parliaments is probably about the same, as also the number of *Speakers* and their *talent*. I except *Orators*, of course, because *they* are things of Ages and not of Septennial or triennial reunions.

Neither house ever struck me with more awe or respect than the same number of Turks in a Divan, or of Methodists in a barn would have done. Whatever diffidence or nervousness I felt (and I felt both in a great degree) arose from the number rather than the quality of the assemblage, and the thought rather of the *public without* than the persons within – knowing (as all know) that Cicero himself, and probably the Messiah, could never have alter'd the vote of a single Lord of the Bedchamber or Bishop.

I thought *our* house dull, but the other animating enough upon great days.

[. . .]

25

A young American, named Coolidge, called on me not many months ago: he was intelligent, very handsome, and not more than twenty years old according to appearances. A little romantic, but that sits well upon youth, and mighty fond of poesy as may be suspected from his approaching me in my cavern. He brought me a message from an old Servant of my family (Joe Murray), and told me that *he* (Mr Coolidge) had obtained a copy of my bust from Thorwal[d]sen at Rome, to send to America. I confess I was more flattered by this young enthusiasm of a solitary transatlantic traveller, than if they had decreed me a Statue in the Paris Pantheon (I have seen Emperors and demagogues cast down from their pedestals even in my own time, and Grattan's name razed from the Street called after him in Dublin) I say that I was more flattered by it, because it was *single, un-political,* and was without motive or ostentation – the pure and warm feeling of a boy for the poet he admired. It must have been expensive though. *I* would not pay the price of a Thorwaldsen bust for any human head and shoulders, except Napoleon's, or my children's, or some '*absurd Womankind's*' as Monkbarns calls them, or my Sister's. If asked, *why* then I sate for my own – answer, that it was at the request particular of J.C.Hobhouse, Esqre, and for no one else. A *picture* is a different matter – every body sits for their picture; but a bust looks like putting up pretensions to permanency, and smacks something of a hankering for *public* fame rather than private remembrance.
[. . .]

29

I liked the Dandies; they were always very civil to *me*, though in general they disliked literary people, and persecuted and mystified Me de Staël, Lewis, Horace Twiss, and the like, damnably. They persuaded Me de Staël that Alvanley had a hundred thousand a year, etc., etc., till she praised him to his *face* for his *beauty*! and made a set at him for Albertine[51] (*Libertine*, as Brummell baptized her, though the poor Girl was and is as correct as maid or wife can be, and very amiable withal), and a hundred fooleries besides.

The truth is, that, though I gave up the business early, I had a tinge of Dandyism in my minority, and probably retained enough of it, to conciliate the great ones; at four and twenty I had gamed, and drank, and taken my degrees in most dissipations; and having no pedantry, and not being overbearing, we ran quietly together. I knew them all more or less, and they made me a Member of Watier's (a superb Club at that time), being, I take it, the only literary man (except *two others*, both men of the world, M. and S.) in it.

Our Masquerade was a grand one; so was the Dandy Ball, too, at the Argyle, but *that* (the latter) was given by the four Chiefs, B., M., A., and P.,[52] if I err not.

[. . .]

33

I have a notion that Gamblers are as happy as most people, being always *excited*. Women, wine, fame, the table, even Ambition, *sate* now and then; but every turn of the card, and cast of the dice, keeps the Gamester alive: besides one can Game ten times longer than one can do any thing else.

I was very fond of it when young, that is to say, of 'Hazard'; for I hate all *Card* Games, even Faro. When Macco (or whatever they spell it) was introduced, I gave up the whole thing; for I loved and missed the *rattle* and *dash* of the box and dice, and the glorious uncertainty, not only of good luck or bad luck, but of *any luck at all*, as one had sometimes to throw *often* to decide at all.

I have thrown as many as fourteen mains running, and carried off all the cash upon the table occasionally; but I had no coolness or judgement or calculation. It was the *delight* of the thing that pleased me. Upon the whole, I left off in time without being much a winner or loser. Since one and twenty years of age, I played but little, and then never above a hundred or two, or three.

34

... What a strange thing is life and man? Were I to present myself at the door of the house, where my daughter now is, the door would be shut in my face, unless (as is not impossible) I knocked down the porter; and if I had gone in that year (and perhaps now) to Drontheim (the furthest town in Norway), or into Holstein, I should have been received with open arms into the mansions of Stranger and foreigners, attached to me by no tie but that of mind and rumour.

As far as *Fame* goes, I have had my share: it has indeed been leavened by other human contingencies, and this in a greater degree than has occurred to most literary men of a *decent* rank in life; but on the whole I take it that such equipoise is the condition of humanity.

I doubt sometimes whether, after all, a quiet and unagitated life would have suited me: yet I sometimes long for it. My earliest dreams (as most boys' dreams are) were martial; but a little later they were all for *love* and retirement, till the hopeless attachment to M.C.[53] began, and continued (though sedulously concealed) *very* early in my teens; and so upwards for a time. *This* threw me out again 'alone on a wide, wide sea'.

In the year 1804, I recollect meeting my Sister at General Harcourt's in Portland Place. I was then *one* thing, and as she had always till then found me. When we met again in 1805 (she told me since), that my temper and disposition were so completely altered, that I was hardly to be recognized. I was not then sensible of the change, but I can believe it, and account for it. [. . .]

36

I have been called in as Mediator or Second at least twenty times in violent quarrels, and have always contrived to settle the business without compromising the honour of the parties, or leading them to mortal consequences; and this too sometimes in very difficult and delicate circumstances, and having to deal with very hot and haughty Spirits – Irishmen, Gamesters, Guardsmen, Captains and Cornets of horse, and the like. This was of course in my youth, when I lived in hot-headed company. I have had to carry challenges from Gentlemen to Noblemen, from Captains to Captains, from lawyers to Counsellors, and once from a Clergyman to an officer in the Lifeguards. It may seem strange, but I found the latter by far the most difficult

> ... to compose
> The bloody duel without blows.

The business being about a woman. I must add too that I never saw a *woman* behave so ill, like a cold-blooded heartless whore as she was; but very handsome for all that. A certain Susan C. was she called. I never saw her but once, and that was to induce her but to say two words (which in no degree compromised herself), and which would have had the effect of saving a priest[54] or a Lieutenant of Cavalry. She would *not* say them, and neither N. or myself (the Son of Sir E.N. and a friend of one of the parties) could prevail upon her to say them, though both of us used to deal in some sort with Womankind. At last I managed to quiet the combatants without her talisman, and, I believe, to her great disappointment. She was the d—st b—h that I ever saw, and I have seen a great many. Though my Clergyman was sure to lose either his life or his living, he was as warlike as the Bishop of Beauvais, and would hardly be pacified: but then he was in love, and that is a martial passion.
[. . .]

53

In general, I do not draw well with literary men; not that I dislike them, but I never know what to say to them after I have praised their last publication. There are several exceptions, to be sure; but then they have either been men of the world, such as Scott, and Moore, etc., or visionaries out of it, such as Shelley, etc.: but your literary every day man and I never went well in company – especially your foreigner, whom I never could abide.

Except Giordani, and – and – and – (I really can't name any other) I do not remember a man amongst them, whom I ever wished to see twice, except perhaps Mezzophanti, who is a Monster of Languages, the Briareus of parts of Speech, a walking Polyglott and more, who ought to have existed at the time of the tower of Babel as universal Interpreter. He is indeed a Marvel – unassuming also: I tried him in all the tongues of which I knew a single oath (or adjuration to the Gods against Postboys, Lawyers, Tartars, boatmen, Sailors, pilots, Gondoliers, Muleteers, Camel-drivers, Vetturini, Postmasters, post-horses, post-houses, post-everything), and Egad! he astounded me even to my English.

[. . .]

56

Of Actors, Cooke was the most natural, Kemble the most supernatural, Kean a medium between the two, but Mrs Siddons worth them all put together, of those whom I remember to have seen in England.

I have seen Sheridan weep two or three times: it may be that he was maudlin; but this only renders it more impressive, for who would see –

> From Marlborough's eyes the tears of dotage flow,
> And Swift expire a driveller and a show?

Once I saw him cry at Robin's, the Auctioneer's, after a splendid dinner full of great names and high Spirits. I had the honour of sitting next to Sheridan. The occasion of his tears was some observation or other upon the subject of the sturdiness of the Whigs in resisting Office, and keeping to their principles. Sheridan turned round – 'Sir, it is easy for my Lord G., or Earl G., or Marquis B., or Ld H., with thousands upon thousands a year – some of it either *presently* derived or *inherited* in Sinecures or acquisitions from the public money – to boast of their patriotism, and keep aloof from temptation; but they do not know from what temptations those have kept aloof, who had equal pride – at least equal talents, and not unequal passions, and nevertheless knew

441

not in the course of their lives what it was to have a shilling of their own'. And in saying this he wept.

[. . .]

60

No man would live his life over again, is an old and true saying, which all can resolve for themselves. At the same time, there are probably *moments* in most men's lives, which they would live over the rest of life to *regain*? Else, why do we live at all? Because Hope recurs to Memory, both false; but – but – but – but – and this *but* drags on till – What? I do not know, and who does? 'He that died o' Wednesday.' By the way, there is a poor devil to be shot tomorrow here (Ravenna) for murder. He hath eaten half a Turkey for his dinner, besides fruit and pudding; and he refuses to confess! Shall I go to see him exhale? No. And why? Because it is to take place at *Nine*. Now, could I *save* him, or a fly even from the same catastrophe, I would out-match years; but as I cannot, I will not get up earlier to see another man shot, than I would to run the same risk in person. Besides, I have seen more men than one die that death (and other deaths) before to-day.

It is not cruelty which áctuates mankind, but excitement, on such occasions; at least, I suppose so. It is detestable to *take* life in that way, unless it be to preserve two lives.

[. . .]

65

When I was fifteen years of age, it happened that in a Cavern in Derbyshire I had to cross in a boat (in which two people only could lie down) a stream which flows under a rock, with the rock so close upon the water, as to admit the boat only to be pushed on by a ferry-man (a sort of Charon), who wades at the stern stooping all the time. The Companion of my transit was M. A. C[haworth], with whom I had been long in love, and never told it, though *she* had discovered it without. I recollect my sensations, but cannot describe them – and it is as well.

We were a party – a Mr. W., two Miss W.'s, Mr and Mrs Cl-ke, Miss M., and *my* M.A.C. Alas! why do I say *My*? Our Union would have healed feuds, in which blood had been shed by our fathers; it would have joined lands, broad and rich; it would have joined at least *one* heart, and two persons not ill-matched in years (she is two years my elder); and – and – and – what has been the result? *She* has married a man older than herself, been wretched, and separated. I have married, and am separated: and yet *We* are *not* united.

66

One of my notions, different from those of my contemporaries, is, that the present is not a high age of English Poetry: there are *more* poets (soi-disant) than ever there were, and proportionally *less* poetry.

This *thesis* I have maintained for some years, but, strange, to say, it meeteth not with favour from my brethren of the Shell. Even Moore shakes his head, and firmly believes that it is the grand Era of British Poesy.

67

When I belonged to the D[rury] L[ane] Committee, and was one of the S. C. of Management, the number of plays upon the shelves were about *five* hundred. Conceiving that amongst these there must be *some* of merit, in person and by proxy I caused an investigation. I do not think that, of those which I saw, there was one which could be conscientiously tolerated. There never were such things as most of them.

Mathurin was very kindly recommended to me by Walter Scott, to whom I had recourse; firstly, in the hope that he would do something for us himself; and secondly, in my despair, that he would point out to us any young (or old) writer of promise . . .

I tried Coleridge, too; but he had nothing feasible in hand at the time . . .

Then the Scenes I had to go through! The authors, and the

authoresses, the Milliners, the wild Irishmen, the people from Brighton, from Blackwall, from Chatham, from Cheltenham, from Dublin, from Dundee, who came in upon me! To all of whom it was proper to give a civil answer, and a hearing, and a reading. Mrs Glover's father, an Irish dancing-Master of Sixty years, called upon me to request to play 'Archer', drest in silk stockings on a frosty morning to show his legs (which were certainly good and Irish for his age, and had been still better). Miss Emma Somebody, with a play entitled the 'Bandit of Bohemia', or some such title or production. Mr O'Higgins, then resident at Richmond, with an Irish tragedy, in which the unities could not fail to be observed, for the protagonist was chained by the leg to a pillar during the chief part of the performance. He was a wild man, of a salvage [sic] appearance; and the difficulty of not laughing at him was only to be got over by reflecting upon the probable consequences of such cachinnation.

As I am really a civil and polite person, and do hate giving pain, when it can be avoided, I sent them up to Douglas Kinnaird, who is a man of business, and sufficiently ready with a negative, and left them to settle with him. And, as at the beginning of next year, I went abroad, I have since been little aware of the progress of the theatres.

[. . .]

72

When I first went up to College, it was a new and a heavy hearted scene for me. Firstly, I so much disliked leaving Harrow, that, though it was time (I being seventeen), it broke my very rest for the last quarter with counting the days that remained. I always hated Harrow till the last year and half, but then I liked it. Secondly, I wished to go to Oxford and not to Cambridge. Thirdly, I was so completely alone in this new world, that it half broke my Spirits. My companions were not unsocial, but the contrary – lively, hospitable, of rank, and fortune, and gay far beyond my gaiety. I mingled with, and dined and supped, etc., with them; but, I know not how, it was one of the deadliest and heaviest feelings of my life to feel that I was no longer a boy.

From that moment I began to grow old in my own esteem; and in my esteem age is not estimable. I took my gradations in the vices with great promptitude, but they were not to my taste; for my early passions, though violent in the extreme, were concentrated, and hated division or spreading abroad. I could have left or lost the world with or for that which I loved; but, though my temperament was naturally burning, I could not share in the common place libertinism of the place and time without disgust. And yet this very disgust, and my heart thrown back upon itself, threw me into excesses perhaps more fatal than those from which I shrunk, as fixing upon one (at a time) the passions, which, spread amongst many, would have hurt only myself.

73

People have wondered at the Melancholy which runs through my writings. Others have wondered at my personal gaiety; but I recollect once, after an hour, in which I had been sincerely and particularly gay, and rather brilliant, in company, my wife replying to me when I said (upon her remarking my high spirits) 'and yet, Bell, I have been called the mis-called Melancholy – you must have seen how falsely, frequently'. 'No, B.,' (she answered) 'it is not so: at *heart* you are the most melancholy of mankind, and often when apparently gayest.'

74

If I could explain at length the *real* causes which have contributed to increase this perhaps *natural* temperament of mine, this Melancholy which hath made me a bye-word, nobody would wonder; but this is impossible without doing much mischief. I do not know what other men's lives have been, but I cannot conceive anything more strange than some of the earlier parts of mine. I have written my memoirs but, omitted *all* the really *consequential* and *important* parts, from deference to the dead, to the living, and to those who must be both.

75

I sometimes think that I should have written the *whole* as a *lesson*, but it might have proved a lesson to be *learnt* rather than *avoided*; for passion is a whirlpool, which is not to be viewed nearly without attraction from its Vortex.

76

I must not go on with these reflections, or I shall be letting out some secret or other to paralyze posterity.
[...]

79

My first dash into poetry was as early as 1800. It was the ebullition of a passion for my first Cousin Margaret Parker (daughter and grand-daughter of the two Admirals Parker), one of the most beautiful of evanescent beings. I have long forgotten the verses, but it would be difficult for me to forget her. Her dark eyes! her long eye-lashes! her completely Greek cast of face and figure! I was then about twelve – She rather older, perhaps a year. She died about a year or two afterwards, in consequence of a fall which injured her spine and induced consumption. Her Sister, Augusta (by some thought still more beautiful), died of the same malady; and it was indeed in attending her that Margaret met with the accident, which occasioned her own death. My sister told me that, when she went to see her shortly before her death, upon accidentally mentioning my name, Margaret coloured through the paleness of mortality to the eyes, to the great astonishment of my Sister, who (residing with her Grandmother, Lady Holderness) saw at that time but little of me for family reasons, knew nothing of our attachment, nor could conceive why my name should affect her at such a time. I knew nothing of her illness (being at Harrow and in the country), till she was gone.

Some years after, I made an attempt at an Elegy. A very dull one. I do not recollect scarcely any thing equal to the *transparent* beauty of my cousin, or to the sweetness of her temper, during the short period of our intimacy. She looked as if she had been made out of a rainbow – all beauty and peace.

My passion had its usual effects upon me: I could not sleep, could not eat; I could not rest; and although I had reason to know that she loved me, it was the torture of my life to think of the time which must elapse before we could meet again – being usually about *twelve hours* of separation! But I was a fool then, and am not much wiser now.

80

My passions were developed very early – so early, that few would believe me, if I were to state the period, and the facts which accompanied it. Perhaps this was one of the reasons which caused the anticipated melancholy of my thoughts – having anticipated life.

My earlier poems are the thoughts of one at least ten years older than the age at which they were written: I don't mean for their solidity, but their Experience. The two first Cantos of C^e H^d were completed at twenty two, and they are written as if by a man older than I shall probably ever be.
[. . .]

83

Like Sylla, I have always believed that all things depend upon Fortune, and nothing upon ourselves. I am not aware of any one thought or action worthy of being called good to myself or others, which is not to be attributed to the Good Goddess, Fortune!

84

Two or three years ago, I thought of going to one of the Americas, English or Spanish. But the accounts sent from England, in consequence of my enquiries, discouraged me. After all, I believe most countries, properly balanced, are equal to *a*

Stranger (by no means to the *native*, though). I remembered
General Ludlow's domal inscription: –

Omne solum forti patria –[55]

and sate down free in a country of Slavery for many centuries.
But there is no freedom, even for *Masters*, in the midst of slaves:
i t makes my blood boil to see the thing. I sometimes wish that
I was the Owner of Africa, to do at once, what Wilberforce will
do in time, viz. – sweep Slavery from her deserts, and look on
upon the first dance of their Freedom.

 As to *political* slavery – so general – it is man's own fault; if
they *will* be slaves, let them! Yet it is but 'a word and a blow'.
See how England formerly, France, Spain, Portugal, America,
Switzerland, freed themselves! There is no one instance of a *long*
contest, in which *men* did not triumph over Systems. If Tyranny
misses her *first* spring, she is cowardly as the tiger, and retires
to be hunted.
[. . .]

91

My School friendships were with *me passions* (for I was always
violent), but I do not know that there is one which has endured
(to be sure, some have been cut short by death) till now. That with
Lord Clare began one of the earliest and lasted longest, being only
interrupted by distance, that I know of. I never hear the word
'*Clare*' without a beating of the heart even *now*, and I write it
with the feelings of 1803–4–5 ad infinitum.
[. . .]

95

If I had to live over again, I do not know what I would change
in my life, unless it were *for not to have lived at all*. All history and
experience, and the rest, teaches us that the good and evil are
pretty equally balanced in this existence, and that what is most
to be desired is an easy passage out of it.

 What can it give us but *years*? and those have little of good but
their ending.

96

Of the Immortality of the Soul, it appears to me that there can be little doubt, if we attend for a moment to the action of Mind. It is in perpetual activity. I used to doubt of it, but reflection has taught me better. It acts also so very independent of body; in dreams for instance incoherently and madly, I grant you; but still it is *Mind*, and much more *Mind* than when we are awake. Now, that *this* should not act *separately*, as well as jointly, who can pronounce? The Stoics, Epictetus and Marcus Aurelius, call the present state 'a Soul which drags a Carcase': a heavy chain, to be sure; but all chains, being material, may be shaken off.

How far our future life will be individual, or, rather, how far it will at all resemble our *present* existence, is another question; but that the *Mind* is *eternal*, seems as probable as that the body is not so. Of course, I have ventured upon the question without recurring to Revelation, which, however, is at least as rational a solution of it as any other.

A *material* resurrection seems strange, and even absurd, except for purposes of punishment; and all punishment, which is to *revenge* rather than *correct*, must be *morally wrong*. And *when the World is at an end,* what moral or warning purpose *can* eternal tortures answer? Human passions have probably disfigured the divine doctrines here, but the whole thing is inscrutable. It is useless to tell me *not* to *reason*, but to *believe*. You might as well tell a man not to wake but *sleep*. And then to *bully* with torments! and all that; I cannot help thinking that the *menace* of Hell makes as many devils, as the severe penal codes of inhuman humanity make villains.

Man is born *passionate* of body, but with an innate though secret tendency to the love of Good in his Mainspring of Mind. But God help us all! It is at present a sad jar of atoms. [. . .]

98

I have often been inclined to Materialism in philosophy but could never bear its introduction into *Christianity*, which appears to me essentially founded upon the *Soul* . . . I own my partiality for *Spirit*.

[. . .]

102

What a strange thing is the propagation of life! A bubble of Seed which may be spilt in a whore's lap – or in the orgasm of a voluptuous dream – might (for aught we know) have formed a Caesar or a Buonaparte: there is nothing remarkable recorded of their Sires, that I know of.

103

Lord Kames has said (if I misquote not), 'that a power to call up agreeable ideas at will would be something greater for mortals than all the boons of a fairy tale'.

I have found increasing upon me (without sufficient cause at times) the depression of Spirits (with few intervals), which I have some reason to believe constitutional or inherited.

104

Plutarch says, in his life of Lysander, that Aristotle observes, 'that in general great Geniuses are of a melancholy turn, and instances Socrates, Plato, and Hercules (or Heracleitus), as examples, and Lysander, though not *while* young, yet as inclined to it when approaching towards age'. Whether I am a Genius or not, I have been called such by my friends as well as enemies, and in more countries and languages than one, and also within a no very long period of existence. Of my Genius, I can say nothing, but of my melancholy, that it is 'increasing and ought to be diminished' – but how?

[. . .]

107

I have met George Colman occasionally, and thought him extremely pleasant and convivial. Sheridan's humour, or rather wit, was always saturnine, and sometimes savage: he never laughed (at least that *I* saw, and I watched him), but Colman did. I have got very drunk with them both; but, if I had to *choose*, and could not have both at a time, I should say, 'let me begin the evening with Sheridan, and finish it with Colman'. Sheridan for dinner – Colman for Supper. Sheridan for Claret or port; but Colman for everything, from the Madeira and Champaigne at dinner – the Claret with a *layer* of *port* between the Glasses – up to the Punch of the Night, and down to the Grog or Gin and water of daybreak. All these I have threaded with both the same. Sheridan was a Grenadier Company of Life-Guards, but Colman a whole regiment – of *light Infantry*, to be sure, but still a *regiment*. [. . .]

113

Pisa, Novr 5th 1821

'There is a strange coincidence sometimes in the little things of this world, Sancho' says Sterne in a letter (if I mistake not); and so I have often found it.

Page [448], article 91, of this collection of scattered things, I had alluded to my friend Lord Clare in terms such as my feelings suggested. About a week or two afterwards, I met him on the road between Imola and Bologna, after not having met for seven or eight years. He was abroad in 1814, and came home just as I set out in 1816.

This meeting annihilated for a moment all the years between the present time and the days of *Harrow*. It was a new and inexplicable feeling, like rising from the grave, to me. Clare, too, was much agitated – *more* in appearance than even myself; for I could feel his heart beat to his fingers' ends, unless, indeed, it was the pulse of my own which made me think so. He told me that I should find a note from him, left at Bologna. I did. We were obliged to part for our different journeys – he for Rome, I for Pisa; but with the promise to meet again in Spring. We were but five minutes together, and in the public road; but I hardly recollect an hour of my existence which could be weighed against them. He had heard that I was coming on, and had left his letter for me at B., because the people with whom he was travelling could not wait longer.

Of all I have ever known, he has always been the least altered in every thing from the excellent qualities and kind affections which attached me to him so strongly at School. I should hardly have thought it possible for Society (or the World as it is called), to leave a being with so little of the leaven of bad passions. I do not speak from personal experience only, but from all I have ever heard of him from others during absence and distance. [. . .]

116

I have lately been reading Fielding over again. They talk of Radicalism, Jacobinism, etc., in England (I am told), but they should turn over the pages of 'Jonathan Wild the Great'. The inequality of conditions, and the littleness of the great, were never set forth in stronger terms; and his contempt for Conquerors and the like is such, that, had he lived *now*, he would have been denounced in 'the Courier' as the grand Mouth-piece and Factionary of the revolutionists. And yet I never recollect to have heard this turn of Fielding's mind noticed, though it is obvious in every page. [. . .]

TO THOMAS MOORE   *May 14, 1821*

. . . Well, patience is a virtue, and, I suppose, practice will make it perfect. Since last year (spring, that is) I have lost a lawsuit, of great importance, on Rochdale collieries – have occasioned a divorce – have had my poesy disparaged by Murray and the critics – my fortune refused to be placed on an advantageous settlement (in Ireland) by the trustees; – my life threatened last month (they put about a paper here to excite an attempt at my assassination, on account of politics, and a notion which the priests disseminated that I was in a league against the Germans,) – and, finally, my mother-in-law recovered last fortnight, and my play was damned last week! These are like 'the eight-and-twenty misfortunes of Harlequin'. But they must be borne. If I give in, it shall be after keeping up a spirit at least. I should not have cared so much about it, if our southern neighbours had not bungled us all out of freedom for these five hundred years to come.

Did you know John Keats? They say that he was killed by a review of him in the *Quarterly* – if he be dead, which I really don't know. I don't understand that *yielding* sensitiveness. What I feel (as at this present) is an immense rage for eight-and-forty hours, and then, as usual – unless this time it should last longer. I must get on horseback to quiet me.

Yours, etc.

TO THE HON. AUGUSTA LEIGH   *Ravenna, June 22nd, 1821*

My Dearest A., – What was I to write about? I live in a different world. You know from others that I was in tolerable plight, and all that. However write I will since you desire it. I have put my daughter in a convent for the present to begin her accomplishments by reading, to which she had a learned aversion, but the arrangement is merely temporary till I can settle some plan for her; if I return to England, it is likely that she will accompany me – if not – I sometimes think of Switzerland, and sometimes of the Italitan Conventional education; I shall hear both sides (for I have Swiss Friends – through Mr Hoppner the Consul General, he is connected by marriage with that country) and choose what seems most rational. My menagerie – (which you enquire after) has had some vacancies by the elopement of one cat, the decease of two monkies and a crow, by indigestion – but it is still a flourishing and somewhat obstreperous establishment . . .

Will you for the hundredth time apply to Lady B. about the *funds*, they are now *high*, and I could sell out to a great advantage. Don't forget this, that cursed connection crosses at every turn my fortunes, my feelings and my fame. I had no wish to nourish my detestation of her and her family, but they pursue, like an Evil Genius. I send you an Elegy upon Lady Noel's *recovery* – (made too [*here about fourteen lines of the autograph are cut off*] the parish register – I will reserve my tears for the demise of Lady

Noel, but the old — will live forever because she is so amiable and useful.

Yours ever and [illegible],

B.

P.S. – Let me know about Holmes. Oh La! – is he as great a mountebank as ever?

TO JOHN CAM HOBHOUSE   *Ravenna, July 6th, 1821*

My Dear H., – I have written by this post to Murray to omit the stanza to which you object.[56] In case he should forget, you can jog his memory. I have also agreed to a request of Madame Guiccioli's *not* to continue that poem further. She had read the French translation, and thinks it a detestable production. This will not seem strange even in Italian morality, because women all over the world always retain their freemasonry, and as that consists in the illusion of the sentiment which constitutes their sole empire (all owing to chivalry and the Goths – the Greeks knew better), all works which refer to the *comedy* of the passions, and laugh at sentimentalism, of course are proscribed by the whole *sect*. I never knew a woman who did not admire Rousseau, and hate Gil Blas, and de Grammont and the like, for the same reason. And I never met with a woman, English or foreign, who did not do as much by D[on] J[uan]. As I am docile, I yielded, and promised to confine myself to the 'highflying of Buttons', – (you remember Pope's phrase) – for the time to come. You will be very glad of this, as an earlier opponent of that poem's publication.

I only read your Canningippic in the papers, but even there it was worthy of anything since those against Anthony.

You must not give letters to me; I have taken an oath against being civil ever since – but you will see my reason in the last note to Marino Faliero.

I have sent to England a tragedy a month ago, and I am in the *fifth* act of another. Murray has not acknowledged its arrival. I must one day break with that gentleman, if he is not the civiler.

Of Burdett's affair I cannot judge, so I made an epigram on it, which I sent to Douglas K^d. By the way, now the *funds are up*, *stir him* up, and the bloody trustees. It would give me pleasure to see some of you, that I might gossip over the late revolt (or rather revolt*ing*) transactions of these parts. Things are far from quiet even now. Have you seen my 'Elegy on the recovery of Lady Noel'?

> Behold the blessings of a lucky lot!
> My play is damned – and Lady Noel *not*.

Do you know that your bust was sent to England (viâ Livorno) months ago?

Let me hear from or of you.

Yours,

B.

P.S. – Fletcher is turned money-lender, and puts out money (*here*) at 20 per cent. Query, will he get it again? *Who* knows?

TO RICHARD BELGRAVE HOPPNER   *Ravenna, July 23, 1821*

This country being in a state of proscription, and all my friends exiled or arrested – the whole family of Gamba obliged to go to Florence for the present – the father and son for politics – (and the Guiccioli, because menaced with a *convent*, as her father is *not* here,) I have determined to remove to Switzerland, and they also. Indeed, my life here is not supposed to be particularly safe – but that has been the case for this twelvemonth past, and is therefore not the primary consideration ...

You have no idea what a state of oppression this country is in – they arrested above a thousand of high and low throughout Romagna – banished some and confined others, without *trial*, *process*, or even *accusation*!! Every body says they would have done the same by me if they dared proceed openly. My motive, however, for remaining, is because *every one* of my acquaintance, to the amount of hundreds almost, have been exiled ...

455

TO JOHN MURRAY   *R^a July 30th 1821*

... Are you aware that Shelley has written an elegy on Keats,
and accuses the *Quarterly* of killing him?

> Who killed John Keats?
> I, says the Quarterly,
> So savage and Tartarly;
> 'Twas one of my feats.

> Who shot the arrow?
> The poet-priest Milman
> (So ready to kill man),
> Or Southey or Barrow.

You know very well that I did not approve of Keats's poetry,
or principles of poetry, or of his abuse of Pope; but,
as he is dead, omit *all* that is said *about him* in any MSS of mine,
or publication. His *Hyperion* is a fine monument, and will keep
his name. I do not envy the man who wrote the article: your
review people have no more right to kill than any other foot pads.
However, he who would die of an article in a review would
proably have died of something else equally trivial. The same
thing nearly happened to Kirke White, who afterwards died of
a consumption ...

TO JOHN MURRAY   *R^a August 23^d 1821*

Dear Sir, – Enclosed are the two acts corrected. With regard to
the charges about the Shipwreck, – I think that I told both you
and Mr Hobhouse, years ago, that [there] was not a *single
circumstance* of it *not* taken from *fact*; not, indeed, from any
single shipwreck, but all from *actual* facts of different wrecks.
Almost all *Don Juan* is *real* life, either my own, or from people
I knew. By the way, much of the description of the *furniture*, in
Canto 3^d, is taken from *Tully's Tripoli* (pray *note this*), and the
rest from my own observation. Remember, I never meant to
conceal this at all, and have only not stated it, because *Don Juan*
had no preface nor name to it. If you think it worth while to make

this statement, do so, in your own way. *I* laugh at such charges, convinced that no writer ever borrowed less, or made his materials more his own. Such is coincidence: for instance, Lady Morgan (in a really *excellent* book, I assure you, on Italy) calls Venice an *Ocean Rome*; I have the very same expression in *Foscari*, and yet *you* know that the play was written months ago, and sent to England. The *Italy* I received only on the 16th in[st].

Your friend, like the public, is not aware, that my dramatic simplicity is *studiously* Greek, and must continue so: *no* reform ever succeeded at first. I admire the old English dramatists; but this is quite another field, and has nothing to do with theirs. I want to make a *regular* English drama, no matter whether for the Stage or not, which is not my object, – but a *mental theatre.*

Yours ever,

B.

Is the bust arrived?

P.S. – *Can't* accept your courteous offer.
[. . .]

> But now this sheet is nearly crammed,
> So, if *you will, I* shan't be shammed,
> And if you *won't*, – *you* may be damned,
>   My Murray!

These matters must be arranged with Mr Douglas K. He is my trustee, and a man of honour. To him you can state all your mercantile reasons, which you might not like to state to me personally, such as 'heavy season' – 'flat public' – 'don't go off' – 'Lordship writes too much' – 'won't take advice' – 'declining popularity' – 'deductions for the trade' – 'make very little' – 'generally lose by him' – 'pirated edition' – 'foreign edition' – 'severe criticisms', etc., with other hints and howls for an oration, which I leave Douglas [Kinnaird], who is an orator, to answer.

You can also state them more freely to a third person, as between you and me they could only produce some smart postscripts, which would not adorn our mutual archives.

I am sorry for the Queen, and that's more than you are.

TO OCTAVIUS GILCHRIST   *Ravenna, September 5th, 1821*

Sir, – I have to acknowledge the arrival of yr three pamphlets
'from the author' whom I thank very sincerely for the attention.
The tone which Mr Bowles has taken in this controversy has
been so different with the different parties, that we are perhaps
none of us fair personal judges of the subject. Long before I had
seen Mr B's answers to myself, or the last pamphlet of the three
which you have sent to me, I had written an answer to his attack
upon yourself, which perhaps you may have seen (or at any rate
may see if you think it worth the trouble) at Mr Murray's . . . As
it was somewhat savage, on reading Mr Bowles's mild reply to me,
I suppressed its publication, recollecting also that you were
perfectly competent to your own defence, and might probably
look upon my interference as impertinent . . . I have not read
Mr Bowles's 'Sequel' to which your third pamphlet refers. Mr
Bowles has certainly not set *you* an example of forbearance in
controversy; but in *society* he really is what I have described him,
but as we are all mad upon some subject or other, and the only
reason why it does not appear in *all* is that their insane chord has
not been struck upon, our Editor seems to have been touched
upon the score of Pope, and for that reason it is a thousand pities
that he ever meddled with him. By the way, to refer to myself,
I think you might as well have omitted the mention of Don Juan
and Beppo and Little etc. as more indecent than the 'Imitation
from Horace' of Pope, for two reasons – firstly they are *not so*
indecent by any means, as for example,

> And if a tight young girl will serve the turn
> In arrant pride continues still to *churn*

> *or*

> What pushed poor Q— on the imperial whore
> T'was but to be where Charles had been before.

and in the next place, as I had been fighting Pope's battles as well
as I could, it was rather hard in an *ally* to bring in an 'odious
comparison' at the expence of his auxiliary. However this is a

trifle, and if Pope's moral reputation can be still further elevated at the expence of mine, I will yield it as freely, as I have always admired him sincerely – much more indeed than you yourself in all probability, for *I* do not think him inferior to Milton – although to state such an opinion publicly in the present day would be equivalent to saying that I do not think Shakespeare without the grossest of faults, which is another heterodox notion of my entertainment. Indeed I look upon a proper appreciation of Pope as a touchstone of taste, and the present question as not only whether Pope is or is not in the first rank of our literature, but whether *that* literature shall or shall not relapse into the Barbarism from which it has scarcely emerged for above a century and a half. I do not deny the natural powers of Mind of the courtier dramatists, but I think that their service as a *standard* is doing irreparable mischief. It is also a great error to suppose the *present* a *high* age of English poetry – it is equivalent to the age of *Statius* or *Silius Italicus* except that instead of imitating the Virgils of our language they are 'trying back' (to use a hunting phrase) upon the Ennius's and Lucilius's who had better have remained in their obscurity. Those poor idiots of the Lakes, too, are diluting our literature as much as they can. In short, all of us more or less (except Campbell and Rogers) have much to answer for, and I don't see any remedy. But I am wandering from the subject – which is to thank you for your present and to beg you to believe me your obliged and very faithl serv[t],

BYRON

TO JOHN MURRAY   *Ravenna, September 12th 1821*

Dear Sir, – By Tuesday's post, I forwarded, in three packets, the drama of '*Cain*', in three acts, of which I request the acknowledgement when arrived. To the last speech of *Eve*, in the last act (*i.e.* where she curses Cain), add these three lines to the concluding one –

> May the Grass wither from thy foot! the Woods
> Deny thee shelter! Earth a home! the Dust
> A Grave! the Sun his light! and Heaven her God!

There's as pretty a piece of Imprecation for you, when joined to the lines already sent, as you may wish to meet with in the course of your business. But don't forget the addition of the above three lines, which are clinchers to Eve's speech.

Let me know what Gifford thinks (if the play arrives in safety); for I have a good opinion of the piece, as poetry: it is in my gay metaphysical style, and in the *Manfred* line.

You must at least commend my facility and variety, when you consider what I have done within the last fifteen months, with my head, too, full of other and of mundane matters. But no doubt you will avoid saying any good of it, for fear I should raise the price upon you: that's right – stick to business! Let me know what your other ragamuffins are writing, for I suppose you don't like starting too many of your Vagabonds at once. You may give them the start, for any thing I care . . .

Why don't you publish my *Pulci*?[57] the best thing I ever wrote, with the Italian to it. I wish I was alongside of you: nothing is ever done in a man's absence; every body runs counter, because they *can*. If ever I *do* return to England, (which I shan't though,) I will write a poem to which *English Bards*, etc., shall be New Milk, in comparison. Your present literary world of mountebanks stands in need of such an Avatar; but I am not yet quite bilious enough: a season or two more, and a provocation or two, will wind me up to the point, and then, have at the whole set!

I have no patience with the sort of trash you send me out by way of books; except Scott's novels, and three or four other things, I never saw such work or works. Campbell is lecturing, Moore idling, Southey twaddling, Wordsworth driveling, Coleridge muddling, Joanna Baillie piddling, Bowles quibbling, squabbling, and sniveling. Milman will *do*, if he don't cant too much, nor imitate Southey: the fellow has poesy in him; but he is envious, and unhappy, as all the envious are. Still he is among the best of the day. Barry Cornwall will do better by and bye, I dare say, if he don't get spoilt by green tea, and the praises of Pentonville and Paradise Row. The pity of these men is, that they never lived either in *high life*, nor in *solitude*: there is no medium for the knowledge of the *busy* or the *still* world. If admitted into high life for a season, it is merely as *spectators* – they form no part of the Mechanism thereof. Now Moore and I, the one by circumstances, and the other by birth, happened to be free of the corporation, and to have entered into its pulses and passions, *quarum partes fuimus.*[58] Both of us have learnt by this much which nothing else could have taught us.

Yours,

B.

TO THOMAS MOORE   *Ravenna, September 19, 1821*

I am in all the sweat, dust, and blasphemy of an universal packing of all my things, furniture, etc., for Pisa, whither I go for the winter. The cause has been the exile of all my fellow Carbonics, and, amongst them, of the whole family of Madame G.; who, you know, was divorced from her husband last week 'on account of P.P. clerk of this parish', and who is obliged to join her father and relatives, now in exile there, to avoid being shut up in a monastery, because the Pope's decree of separation required her to reside in *casa paterna*, or else, for decorum's sake, in a convent. As I could not say with Hamlet, 'Get thee to a nunnery', I am preparing to follow them.

It is awful work, this love, and prevents all a man's projects of good or glory. I wanted to go to Greece lately (as every thing seems up here) with her brother, who is a very fine brave fellow (I have seen him put to the proof), and wild about liberty. But the tears of a woman who has left her husband for a man, and the weakness of one's own heart, are paramount to these projects, and I can hardly indulge them.

We were divided in choice between Switzerland and Tuscany, and I gave my vote for Pisa, as nearer the Mediterranean, which I love for the sake of the shores which it washes, and for my young recollections of 1809. Switzerland is a curst selfish, swinish country of brutes, placed in the most romantic region of the world. I never could bear the inhabitants, and still less their English visitors; for which reason, after writing for some information about houses, upon hearing that there was a colony of English all over the cantons of Geneva, etc., I immediately gave up the thought, and persuaded the Gambas to do the same ...

I wrote in the greatest hurry and fury, and sent it [*The Irish Avatar*] to you the day after; so, doubtless, there will be some awful constructions, and a rather lawless conscription of rhythmus.

With respect to what Anna Seward calls 'the liberty of transcript', – when complaining of Miss Matilda Muggleton, the accomplished daughter of a choral vicar of Worcester Cathedral, who had abused the said 'liberty of transcript', by inserting in the *Malvern Mercury* Miss Seward's 'Elegy on the South Pole', as her *own* production, with her *own* signature, two years after having taken a copy, by permission of the authoress – with regard, I say, to the 'liberty of transcript', I by no means oppose an occasional copy to the benevolent few, provided it does not degenerate into such licentiousness of Verb and Noun as may tend to 'disparage my parts of speech' by the carelessness of the transcribblers.

I do not think that there is much danger of the 'King's Press being abused' upon the occasion, if the publishers of journals have any regard for their remaining liberty of person. It is as pretty a piece of invective as ever put publisher in the way to 'Botany'. Therefore, if *they* meddle with it, it is at *their* peril. As for myself, I will answer any jontleman – though I by no means recognise a 'right of search' into an unpublished production and unavowed poem. The same applies to things published *sans* consent. I hope you like, at least the concluding lines of the *Pome*?

What are you doing, and where are you? in England? Nail Murray – nail him to his own counter, till he shells out the thirteens ...

TO JOHN MURRAY   *R^a Septr 20th 1821*

... The papers to which I allude, in case of survivorship, are collections of letters, etc., since I was sixteen years old, contained in the trunks in the care of Mr Hobhouse. This collection is at least doubled by those I have now here; all received since my last Ostracism. To these I should wish the Editor to have access, *not* for the purpose of *abusing confidences*, nor of *hurting* the feelings of correspondents living, or the memories of the dead; but there are things which would do neither, that I have left unnoticed or unexplained, and which (like all such things) Time only can permit to be noticed or explained, though some are to my credit. The task will, of course, require delicacy; but that will not be wanting, if Moore and Hobhouse survive me, and, I may add, yourself; and that you may all three do so, is, I assure you, my very sincere wish. I am not sure that long life is desirable for one of my temper and constitutional depression of Spirits, which of course I suppress in society; but which breaks out when alone, and in my writings, in spite of myself. It has been deepened perhaps, by some long past events (I do not allude to my marriage, etc. – on the contrary, *that* raised them by the persecution giving a fillip to my Spirits); but I call it constitutional, as I have reason to think it. You know, or you do *not* know, that my maternal Grandfather (a very clever man, and amiable, I am told) was strongly suspected of Suicide (he was found drowned in the Avon at Bath), and that another very near relative of the same branch took poison, and was merely saved by antidotes. For the first of these events there was no apparent cause, as he was rich, respected, and of considerable intellectual resources, hardly forty years of age, and not at all addicted to any unhinging vice. It was, however, but a strong suspicion, owing to the manner of his death and to his melancholy temper. The *second had* a cause, but it does not become me to touch upon it; it happened when I was far too young to be aware of it, and I never heard of it till after the death of that relative, many years afterwards. I think, then, that I may call this dejection *constitutional*. I had always been told that in *temper* I more resembled my maternal Grandfather than any of my *father's* family – that is, in the gloomier part of his temper, for he was what you call a good natured man, and I am not.

The Journal here I sent by Mawman to Moore the other day; but as it is a mere diary, only *parts* of it would ever do for publication. The other Journal, of the tour in 1816, I should think Augusta might let you have a copy of; but her nerves have been in such a state since 1815, that there is no knowing. Lady

Byron's people, and L^y Caroline Lamb's people, and a parcel of that set, got about her and frightened her with all sorts of hints and menaces, so that she has never since been able to write to *me* a *clear common letter*, and is so full of mysteries and miseries, that I can only sympathize, without always understanding her. All my loves, too, make a point of calling upon her, which puts her into a flutter (no difficult matter); and, the year before last I think, Lady F[rances] W[edderburn] W[ebster] marched in upon her, and Lady Oxford, a few years ago, spoke to her at a party; and these and such like calamities have made her afraid of her shadow. It is a very odd fancy that they all take to her: it was only six months ago, that I had some difficulty in preventing the Countess G. from invading her with an Italian letter. I should like to have seen Augusta's face, with an Etruscan Epistle, and all its Meridional style of *issimas*, and other superlatives, before her.

I am much mortified that Gifford don't take to my new dramas: to be sure, they are as opposite to the English drama as one thing can be to another; but I have a notion that, if understood, they will in time find favour (though *not* on the stage) with the reader. The Simplicity of plot is intentional, and the avoidance of *rant* also, as also the compression of the Speeches in the more severe situations. What I seek to show in *The Foscaris* is the *suppressed* passion, rather than the rant of the present day. For that matter –

> Nay, if thoul't mouth,
> I'll rant as well as thou –

would not be difficult, as I think I have shown in my younger productions – *not dramatic* ones, to be sure. But, as I said before, I am mortified that Gifford don't like them; but I see no remedy, our notions on the subject being so different. How is he? Well, I hope: let me know. I regret his demur the more that he has been always my grand patron, and I know no praise which would compensate me in my own mind for his censure. I do not mind *reviews*, as I can work them at their own weapons.

Yours ever and truly,

B.

... Hobhouse, in his preface to '*Rimini*', will probably be better able to explain my dramatic system, than I could do, as he is well acquainted with the whole thing. It is more upon the Alfieri School than the English ...

TO JOHN MURRAY   *Ravenna, September 24th, 1821*

Dear Murray, – I have been thinking over our late correspondence, and wish to propose to you the following articles for our future: –

1^{stly} That you shall write to me of yourself, of the health, wealth, and welfare of all friends; but of *me* (*quoad me*)[59] little or nothing.

2^{ndly} That you shall send me Soda powders, tooth-powder, tooth-brushes, or any such anti-odontalgic or chemical articles, as heretofore, *ad libitum*, upon being re-imbursed for the same.

3^{rdly} That you shall *not* send me any modern, or (as they are called) *new*, publications in *English whatsoever*, save and excepting any writing, prose or verse, of (or reasonably presumed to be of) Walter Scott, Crabbe, Moore, Campbell, Rogers, Gifford, Joanna Baillie, *Irving* (the American), Hogg, Wilson (*Isle of Palms* Man), or *any* especial *single* work of fancy which is thought to be of considerable merit; *Voyages* and *travels*, provided that they are *neither in Greece, Spain, Asia Minor, Albania nor Italy*, will be welcome: having travelled the countries mentioned, I know that what is said of them can convey nothing further which I desire to know about them. No other English works whatsoever.

4^{thly} That you send me *no periodical works* whatsoever – *no Edinburgh, Quarterly, Monthly*, nor any Review, Magazine, Newspaper, English or foreign, of any description.

5^{thly} That you send me *no* opinions whatsoever, either *good*, *bad*, or *indifferent* of yourself, or your friends, or others, concerning any work, or works, of mine, past, present, or to come.

6^{thly} That all negotiations in matters of business between you and me pass through the medium of the Honble Douglas Kinnaird, my friend and trustee, or Mr Hobhouse, as *Alter Ego*, and tantamount to myself during my absence, or presence.

Some of these propositions may at first seem strange, but they are founded. The quantity of trash I have received as books is incalculable, and neither amused nor instructed. Reviews and Magazines are at the best but ephemeral and superficial reading: *who thinks* of the *grand article* of *last year* in any *given review*? in the next place, if they regard *myself*, they tend to increase *Egotism*; if favourable, I do not deny that the praise *elates*, and if unfavourable, that the abuse *irritates* – the latter may conduct me to inflict a species of Satire, which would neither do good to you nor to your friends: *they* may smile *now*, and so may *you*: but if I took you all in hand, it would not be difficult to cut you up like gourds. I did as much by as powerful people at nineteen years old, and I know little as yet, in three and thirty, which should prevent me from making all your ribs Gridirons for your hearts, if such were my propensity. But it is *not*. Therefore let me hear none of your provocations. If any thing occurs so very *gross* as to require my notice, I shall hear of it from my personal friends. For the rest, I merely request to be left in ignorance.

The same applies to opinions, *good*, *bad*, or *indifferent*, of persons in conversation or correspondence: these do not *interrupt*, but they *soil* the *current* of my Mind. I am sensitive enough, but *not* till I am *touched*; and *here* I am beyond the touch of the short arms of literary England, except the few feelers of the Polypus that crawl over the Channel in the way of Extract.

All these precautions *in* England would be useless: the libeller or the flatterer would there reach me in spite of all; but in Italy we know little of literary England, and think less, except what reaches us through some garbled and brief extract in some miserable Gazette. For *two years* (excepting two or three articles cut out and sent to *you*, by the post) I never read a newspaper which was not forced upon me by some accident, and know, upon the whole, as little of England as you all do of Italy, and God knows *that* is little enough, with all your travels, etc., etc., etc. The English travellers *know Italy* as *you* know Guernsey: how much *is that*?

If any thing occurs so violently gross or personal as to require notice, Mr D^s Kinnaird will let me *know*; but of *praise* I desire to hear *nothing*.

You will say, 'to what tends all this?' I will answer THAT; – to keep my mind *free and unbiassed* by all paltry and personal irritabilities of praise or censure; – to let my Genius take its natural direction, while my feelings are like the dead, who know nothing and feel nothing of all or aught that is said or done in their regard.

If you can observe these conditions, you will spare yourself and others some pain: let me not be worked upon to rise up; for if I do, it will not be for a little: if you can *not* observe these conditions, we shall cease to be correspondents, but *not friends*; for I shall always be

Yours ever and truly,

BYRON

P.S. – I have taken these resolutions not from any irritation against *you* or *yours*, but simply upon reflection that all reading, either praise or censure, of myself has done me harm. When I was in Switzerland and Greece, I was out of the way of hearing either, and *how I wrote there*! In Italy I am out of the way of it too; but latterly, partly through my fault, and partly through your kindness in wishing to send me the *newest* and most periodical publications, I have had a crowd of reviews, etc., thrust upon me, which have bored me with their jargon, of one kind or another, and taken off my attention from greater objects. You have also sent me a parcel of trash of poetry, for no reason that I can conceive, unless to provoke me to write a new *English Bards*. Now *this* I wish to avoid; for if ever I *do*, it will be a strong production; and I desire peace, as long as the fools will keep their nonsense out of my way.

TO THE HON. AUGUSTA LEIGH   *Octr 5th, 1821*

... We have been living hitherto decently and quietly. These things here do not exclude a woman from all society as in y^r hypo-critical country. It is very odd that all my *fairs* are such romantic people; and always daggering or divorcing – or making scenes.

But this is 'positively the last time of performance' (as the playbills say), or of my getting into such scrapes for the future. Indeed – I have had my share. But this is a finisher; for you know when a woman is separated from her husband for her *Amant*, he is bound both by honour (and inclination at least I am), to live with her all his days; as long as there is no misconduct.

So you see that I have closed as papa *begun*, and *you* will probably never see me again as long as you live. Indeed you don't deserve it – for having behaved so *coldly – when I was ready to have sacrificed every thing for you – and after [you had] taken the farther* [indecipherable] *always* [indecipherable].[60]

It is nearly three years that this 'liaison' has lasted. I was dreadfully in love – and she blindly so – for she has sacrificed every thing to this headlong passion. That comes of being romantic. I can say that, without being so *furiously* in love as at first, I am more attached to her than I thought it possible to be to any woman after three years – (*except one and who was she can* YOU *guess*) and have not the least wish nor prospect of separation from her.

She herself, (and it is now a year since her separation, a year too of all kinds of vicissitudes et^c) is still more decided. Of course the *step* was a decisive one. If Lady B. would but please to die, and the Countess G.'s husband (for Catholics can't marry though divorced), we should probably have to marry – though I would rather *not* – thinking it the way to hate each other – for all people whatsoever.

However you need not calculate upon seeing me again in a hurry, if ever. How have you sent the *parcel*, and how am I to receive it at Pisa? I am anxious about the Seal – not about Hodgson's nonsense. What is the fool afraid of the *post* for? it is the *safest* – the only *safe* conveyance. They never meddle but with political packets.

Yours.

P.S. – *You* ought to be a great admirer of the *future* Lady B. for *three* reasons, 1^{stly} She is a grand patroness of the present Lady B. and always says 'that she has no doubt that' she was exceedingly ill-used by me – 2dly She is an admirer of yours; and I have had great difficulty in keeping her from writing to you eleven pages, (for she is a grand Scribe), and 3dly she having read 'Don Juan' in a *French* translation – made me promise to write *no more* of it, declaring that it was abominable etc etc that *Donna Inez* WAS meant for Lady B. and in short made me vow *not* to continue it – (this occurred lately) and since the last cantos were sent to England last year. Is this not altogether odd enough? She has a good deal of *us* too. I mean that turn for ridicule like Aunt Sophy and you and I and all the B's. Desire Georgiana to write me a letter. I suppose she can by this time.

Opened by me – and the Seal taken off – so – don't accuse the post-office without cause.

B – that's a sign – a written one where the wax was.

TO LADY BYRON⁶¹   *Pisa, November 17, 1821*

(*To the care of the Hon. Mrs Leigh, London.*)

I have to acknowledge the receipt of 'Ada's hair', which is very soft and pretty, and nearly as dark already as mine was at twelve years old, if I may judge from what I recollect of some in Augusta's possession, taken at that age. But it don't curl, – perhaps from its being let grow.

I also thank you for the inscription of the date and name, and I will tell you why; – I believe that they are the only two or three words of your hand-writing in my possession. For your letters I returned; and except the two words, or rather the one word, 'Household', written twice in an old account book, I have no other. I burnt your last note, for two reasons: – firstly, it was written in a style not very agreeable; and, secondly, I wished to take your word without documents, which are the worldly resources of suspicious people.

I suppose that this note will reach you somewhere about Ada's birthday – the 10th of December, I believe. She will then be six, so that in about twelve more I shall have some chance of meeting her; – perhaps sooner, if I am obliged to go to England by business or otherwise. Recollect, however, one thing, either in distance or nearness; – every day which keeps us asunder should, after so long a period, rather soften our mutual feelings, which must always have one rallying-point as long as our child exists, which I presume we both hope will be long after either of her parents.

The time which has elapsed since the separation has been considerably more than the whole brief period of our union, and the not much longer one of our prior acquaintance. We both made a bitter mistake; but now it is over, and irrevocably so. For, at thirty-three on my part, and a few years less on yours, though it is no very extended period of life, still it is one when the habits and thought are generally so formed as to admit of no modification; and as we could not agree when younger, we should with difficulty do so now.

I say all this, because I own to you, that, notwithstanding every thing, I considered our re-union as not impossible for more than a year after the separation; – but then I gave up the hope entirely and for ever. But this very impossibility of re-union seems to me at least a reason why, on all the few points of discussion which can arise between us, we should preserve the courtesies of life, and as much of its kindness as people who are never to meet may preserve perhaps more easily than nearer connections. For my own part, I am violent, but not malignant; for only fresh provocations can awaken my resentments. To you, who are colder and more concentrated, I would just hint, that you may sometimes mistake the depth of a cold anger for dignity, and a worse feeling for duty. I assure you that I bear you *now* (whatever I may have done) no resentment whatever. Remember, that *if you have injured me* in aught, this forgiveness is something; and that, if I have *injured you*, it is something more still, if it be true, as the moralists say, that the most offending are the least forgiving.

Whether the offence has been solely on my side, or reciprocal, or on yours chiefly, I have ceased to reflect upon any but two things, – viz, that you are the mother of my child, and that we shall never meet again. I think if you also consider the two corresponding points with reference to myself, it will be better for all three.

Yours ever,

NOEL BYRON[62]

TO JOHN MURRAY   *Pisa, December 4, 1821*

Dear Sir, – By extracts in the English papers, – in your holy Ally, Galignani's *Messenger*, – I perceive that 'the two greatest examples of human vanity in the present age' are, firstly, 'the ex-Emperor Napoleon', and secondly, 'his Lordship, etc., the noble poet', meaning your humble servant, 'poor guiltless I'.

Poor Napoleon! he little dreamed to what 'vile comparisons' the turn of the Wheel would reduce him! I cannot help thinking, however, that had our learned brother of the newspaper office seen my very moderate answer to the very scurrile epistle of my radical patron, John Hobhouse, M.P., he would have thought the thermometer of my 'Vanity' reduced to a very decent tempera-ture. By the way you do not happen to know whether Mrs Fry had commenced her reform of the prisoners at the time when Mr Hobhouse was in Newgate? there are some of his phrases, and much of his style (in that same letter), which led me to suspect that either she had not, or that he had profited less than the others by her instructions . . .

I have got here into a famous old feudal palazzo, on the Arno, large enough for a garrison, with dungeons below and cells in the walls, and so full of *Ghosts*, that the learned Fletcher (my valet) has begged leave to change his room, and then refused to occupy his *new* room, because there were more ghosts there than in the other. It is quite true that there are most extraordinary noises (as in all old buildings), which have terrified the servants so as to incommode me extremely. There is one place where people were evidently *walled up*; for there is but one possible passage, *broken* through the wall, and then meant to be closed again upon the inmate. The house belonged to the Lanfranchi family, (the same mentioned by Ugolino in his dream, as his persecutor with Sismondi,)[63] and has had a fierce owner or two in its time. The

471

staircase, etc., is said to have been built by Michel Agnolo [*sic*]. It is not yet cold enough for a fire. What a climate!

I am, however, bothered about these spectres, (as they say the last occupants were, too,) of whom I have as yet seen nothing, nor, indeed, heard (*myself*); but all the other ears have been regaled by all kinds of supernatural sounds. The first night I thought I heard an odd noise, but it has not been repeated. I have now been here more than a month.

Yours,

BYRON

TO SIR WALTER SCOTT   *Pisa, January 12, 1822*

My Dear Sir Walter, – I need not say how grateful I am for your letter, but I must own my ingratitude in not having written to you again long ago. Since I left England (and it is not for all the usual term of transportation) I have scribbled to five hundred blockheads on business, etc., without difficulty, though with no great pleasure; and yet, with the notion of addressing you a hundred times in my head, and always in my heart, I have not done what I ought to have done. I can only account for it on the same principle of tremulous anxiety with which one sometimes makes love to a beautiful woman of our own degree, with whom one is enamoured in good earnest; whereas, we attack a fresh-coloured housemaid without (I speak, of course, of earlier times) any sentimental remorse or mitigation of our virtuous purpose.

I owe to you far more than the usual obligation for the courtesies of literature and common friendship; for you went out of your way in 1817 to do me a service, when it required not merely kindness, but courage to do so: to have been recorded by you in such a manner, would have been a proud memorial at any time, but at such a time, when 'all the world and his wife', as the proverb goes, were trying to trample upon me, was something still higher to my self-esteem, – I allude to the *Quarterly Review* of the Third Canto of *Childe Harold*, which Murray told me was written by you, – and, indeed, I should have known it without his

472

information, as there could not be *two* who *could* and *would* have done this at the time. Had it been a common criticism, however eloquent or panegyrical, I should have felt pleased, undoubtedly, and grateful, but not to the extent which the extraordinary good-heartedness of the whole proceeding must induce in any mind capable of such sensations. The very *tardiness* of this acknowledgement will, at least, show that I have not forgotten the obligation; and I can assure you that my sense of it has been out at compound interest during the delay. I shall only add one word upon the subject, which is, that I think that you, and Jeffrey, and Leigh Hunt, were the only literary men, of numbers whom I know (and some of whom I had served), who dared venture even an anonymous word in my favour just then: and that, of those three, I had never seen *one* at all – of the second much less than I desired – and that the third was under no kind of obligation to me, whatever; while the other *two* had been actually attacked by me on a former occasion; *one*, indeed, with some provocation, but the other wantonly enough. So you see you have been heaping 'coals of fire', etc., in the true gospel manner, and I can assure you that they have burnt down to my very heart.

I am glad that you accepted the Inscription. I meant to have inscribed *The Foscarini* to you instead; but, first, I heard that *Cain* was thought the least bad of the two as a composition; and, 2dly, I have abused Southey like a pickpocket, in a note to *The Foscarini*, and I recollected that he is a friend of yours (though not of mine), and that it would not be the handsome thing to dedicate to one friend any thing containing such matters about another. However, I'll work the Laureate before I have done with him, as soon as I can muster Billingsgate therefor. I like a row, and always did from a boy, in the course of which propensity, I must needs say, that I have found it the most easy of all to be gratified, personally and poetically. You disclaim 'jealousies'; but I would ask, as Boswell did of Johnson, 'of *whom could* you be *jealous*?' – of none of the living certainly, and (taking all and all into consideration) of which of the dead? I don't like to bore you about the Scotch novels, (as they call them, though two of them are wholly English, and the rest half so), but nothing can or could ever persuade me, since I was the first ten minutes in your company, that you are *not* the man. To me those novels have so much of 'Auld lang syne' (I was bred a canny Scot till ten years old), that I never move without them; and when I removed from Ravenna to Pisa the other day, and sent on my library before, they were the only books that I kept by me, although I already have them by heart.

January 27, 1822

I delayed till now concluding, in the hope that I should have got *The Pirate*, who is under way for me, but has not yet hove in sight. I hear that your daughter is married, and I suppose by this time you are half a grandfather – a young one, by the way. I have heard great things of Mrs Lockhart's personal and mental charms, and much good of her lord: that you may live to see as many novel Scotts as there are Scott's novels, is the very bad pun, but sincere wish of

Yours ever most affectionately, etc.

P.S. – Why don't you take a turn in Italy? You would find yourself as well known and as welcome as in the Highlands among the natives. As for the English, you would be with them as in London; and I need not add, that I should be delighted to see you again, which is far more than I shall ever feel or say for England, or (with a few exceptions 'of kith, kin, and allies') anything that it contains. But my 'heart warms to the tartan', or to anything of Scotland, which reminds me of Aberdeen and other parts, not so far from the Highlands as that town, about Invercauld and Braemar, where I was sent to drink goat's *fey* in 1795–6, in consequence of a threatened decline after the scarlet fever. But I am gossiping, so, good night – and the gods be with your dreams!

Pray, present my respects to Lady Scott, who may, perhaps, recollect having seen me in town in 1815.

I see that one of your supporters (for, like Sir Hildebrand, I am fond of Guillim,)[64] is a *mermaid*; it is my *crest* too, and with

precisely the same curl of tail. There's concatenation for you: –
I am building a little cutter at Genoa, to go a cruising in the
summer. I know *you* like the sea too.

TO ROBERT SOUTHEY[65]   *Pisa, Fy 7th, 1822*

Sir, – My friend, the Honourable Douglas Kinnaird, will deliver
to you a message from me, to which an answer is requested.

I have the honour to be

Your very obedt. humble Servnt.

BYRON

TO THE HON. DOUGLAS KINNAIRD   [*Feb. 7th 1822*]

... P.S. – I give you a 'Carte blanche' in Southey's business. If
you agree with me that he ought to be called to account, I beg
you to convey my invitation to meet when and where he may
appoint, to settle this with him and his friend, and to let me know
in as few posts as possible, that I may join you. This will (or
ought) to prevent unnecessary delay. I wish you to observe that
if I come to England with this object, *before* my message is
delivered and the preliminaries fixed, my arrival would transpire
in the interim of the arrangement; whereas, if all is settled before
hand, we may bring the affair to a decision on the day of my land-
ing.

Better on the coast of France, as less liable to interruption or
publicity, but I presume Mr S. is too great a patriot to come off
the soil for such a purpose. The grounds are, that after the
language he has both used and preached, this is the only honour-
able way of deciding the business.

I enclose your credentials in a note to Mr Southey. I require
satisfaction for the expression in his letter in the Newspapers,
that will be the tenor of the Message, as you are well aware. Of
course you will suspend the publication of 'the Vision' [of
Judgement] till we know whether the business can be settled in
a more proper manner.

TO THOMAS MOORE   *Pisa, March 4, 1822*

. . . I am no enemy to religion, but the contrary. As a proof, I am educating my natural daughter a strict Catholic in a convent of Romagna; for I think people can never have *enough* of religion, if they are to have any. I incline, myself, very much to the Catholic doctrines; but if I am to write a drama, I must make my characters speak as I conceive them likely to argue.

As to poor Shelley, who is another bugbear to you and the world, he is, to my knowledge, the *least* selfish and the mildest of men – a man who has made more sacrifices of his fortune and feelings for others than any I ever heard of. With his speculative opinions I have nothing in common, nor desire to have.

The truth is, my dear Moore, you live near the *stove* of society, where you are unavoidably influenced by its heat and its vapours. I did so once – and too much – and enough to give a colour to my whole future existence. As my success in society was *not* inconsiderable, I am surely not a prejudiced judge upon the subject, unless in its favour; but I think it, as now constituted, *fatal* to all great original undertakings of every kind. I never courted it *then*, when I was young and high in blood, and one of its 'curled darlings'; and do you think I would do so *now*, when I am living in a clearer atmosphere? One thing *only* might lead me back to it, and that is, to try once more if I could do any good in *politics*; but *not* in the petty politics I see now preying upon our miserable country.

Do not let me be misunderstood, however. If you speak your *own* opinions, they ever had, and will have, the greatest weight with *me*. But if you merely *echo* the *monde*, (and it is difficult not to do so, being in its favour and its ferment,) I can only regret that you should ever repeat any thing to which I cannot pay attention.

But I am prosing. The gods go with you, and as much immortality of all kinds as may suit your present and all other existence.

Yours, etc.

TO JOHN MURRAY   *Pisa, April 22ᵈ 1822*

Dear Sir, You will regret to hear that I have received intelligence
of the death of my daughter Allegra of a fever in the Convent
of Bagna Cavallo, where she was placed for the last year, to
commence her education, It is a heavy blow for many reasons,
but must be borne, – with time.

It is my present intention to send her remains to England for
sepulture in Harrow Church (where I once hoped to have laid my
own), and this is my reason for troubling you with this notice. I
wish the funeral to be very private. The body is embalmed, and in
lead. It will be embarked from Leghorn. Would you have any
objection to give the proper directions on its arrival?

I am yours, etc.,

N.B.

P.S. – You are aware that protestants are not allowed holy
ground in Catholic countries.

TO PERCY BYSSHE SHELLEY   *April 23, 1822*

The blow was stunning and unexpected; for I thought the danger
over, by the long interval between her stated amelioration and
the arrival of the express. But I have borne up against it as I best
can, and so far successfully, that I can go about the usual business
of life with the same appearance of composure, and even greater.
There is nothing to prevent your coming to-morrow; but,
perhaps, to-day, and yester-evening, it was better not to have met.
I do not know that I have any thing to reproach in my conduct,
and certainly nothing in my feelings and intentions towards the
dead. But it is a moment when we are apt to think that, if this or
that had been done, such event might have been prevented, –
though every day and hour shows us that they are the most
natural and inevitable. I suppose that Time will do his usual
work – Death has done his.

Yours ever,

N.B.

TO SIR WALTER SCOTT   *Pisa, May 4, 1822*

... I have lately had some anxiety, rather than trouble, about an awkward affair here, which you may perhaps have heard of; but our minister has behaved very handsomely, and the Tuscan Government as well as it is possible for such a government to behave, which is not saying much for the latter. Some other English and Scots, and myself, had a brawl with a dragoon, who insulted one of the party, and whom we mistook for an officer, as he was medalled and well mounted, etc; but he turned out to be a serjeant-major. He called out the guard at the gates to arrest us (we being unarmed); upon which I and another (an Italian) rode through the said guard; but they succeeded in detaining others of the party. I rode to my house, and sent my secretary to give an account of the attempted and illegal arrest to the authorities, and then, without dismounting, rode back towards the gates, which are near my present mansion. Half-way I met my man vapouring away and threatening to draw upon me (who had a cane in my hand, and no other arms). I, still believing him an officer, demanded his name and address, and gave him my hand and glove thereupon. A servant of mine thrust in between us (totally without orders), but let him go on my command. He then rode off at full speed; but about forty paces further was stabbed, and very dangerously (so as to be in peril), by some *Callum Beg*[66] or other of my people (for I have some rough-handed folks about me), I need hardly say without my direction or approval. The said dragoon had been sabring our unarmed countrymen, however, at the *gate, after they were in arrest*, and held by the guards, and wounded one, Captain Hay, very severely. However, he got his paiks – having acted like an assassin, and being treated like one. *Who* wounded him, though it was done before thousands of people, they have never been able to ascertain, or prove, nor even the *weapon*; some said a *pistol*, an *air-gun*, a stiletto, a sword, a lance, a pitchfork, and what not. They have arrested and examined servants and people of all descriptions, but can make out nothing. Mr Dawkins, our minister, assures me that no suspicion is entertained of the man who wounded him having been instigated by me, or any of the party. I enclose you copies of the depositions of those with us, and Dr Crauford, a canny Scot (*not* an acquaintance), who saw the latter part of the affair. They are in Italian ...

TO JOHN MURRAY   *Montenero, May 26th, 1822, near Leghorn*

Dear Sir, – The body is embarked, in what ship I know not, neither could I enter into the details; but the Countess G. G. has had the goodness to give the necessary orders to Mr Dunn, who superintends the embarkation, and will write to you. I wish it to be buried in Harrow Church: there is a spot in the Church-*yard*, near the footpath, on the brow of the hill looking towards Windsor, and a tomb under a large tree (bearing the name of Peachie, or Peachey), where I used to sit for hours and hours when a boy: this was my favourite spot; but, as I wish to erect a tablet to her memory, the body had better be deposited in the Church. Near the door, on the left hand as you enter, there is a monument with a tablet containing these words: –

> When Sorrow weeps o'er Virtue's sacred dust,
> Our tears become us, and our Grief is just:
> Such were the tears she shed, who grateful pays
> This last sad tribute of her love and praise.

I recollect them (after seventeen years), not from any thing remarkable in them, but because from my seat in the Gallery I had generally my eyes turned towards that monument: as near it as convenient I could wish Allegra to be buried, and on the wall a marble tablet placed, with these words: –[67]

In memory of
Allegra
daughter of G. G. Lord Byron,
who died at Bagnacavallo,
in Italy, April 20th, 1822,
aged five years and three months.
'I shall go to her, but she shall not return to me.'
2d Samuel, xii. 23

The funeral I wish to be as private as is consistent with decency; and I could hope that Henry Drury will, perhaps, read the service over her. If he should decline it, it can be done by the usual Minister for the time being. I do not know that I need add more just now . . .

TO THOMAS MOORE   *Montenero, Villa Dupuy, near Leghorn, June 8, 1822*

. . . I have read the recent article of Jeffrey in a faithful transcription of the impartial Galignani. I suppose the long and short of it is, that he wishes to provoke me to reply. But I won't, for I owe him a good turn still for his kindness by-gone. Indeed, I presume that the present opportunity of attacking me again was irresistible; and I can't blame him, knowing what human nature is. I shall make but one remark: – what does he mean by elaborate? The whole volume was written with the greatest rapidity, in the midst of evolutions, and revolutions, and persecutions, and proscriptions of all who interested me in Italy. They said the same of *Lara*, which *you* know, was written amidst balls and fooleries, and after coming home from masquerades and routs, in the summer of the sovereigns. Of all I have ever written, they are perhaps the most carelessly composed; and their faults, whatever they may be, are those of negligence, and not of labour. I do not think this a merit, but it is a fact.

Yours ever and truly,

N.B.

P.S. – You see the great advantage of my new signature; – it may either stand for 'Nota Bene' or 'Noel Byron', and, as such, will save much repetition, in writing either books or letters. Since I came here, I have been invited on board of the American squadron, and treated with all possible honour and ceremony. They have asked me to sit for my picture; and, as I was going away, an American lady took a rose from me (which had been given to me by a very pretty Italian lady that very morning), because, she said, 'She was determined to send or take something

which I had about me to America'. *There* is a kind of Lalla
Rookh incident for you! However, all these American honours
arise, perhaps, not so much from their enthusiasm for my
'Poeshie', as their belief in my dislike to the English, – in which
I have the satisfaction to coincide with them. I would rather,
however, have a nod from an American, than a snuff-box from
an emperor.

TO ISAAC D'ISRAELI   *Montenero, Villa Dupuy, n^r Leghorn,*
                      June 10th 1822

(*to ye care of John Murray, Esqre*)

Dear Sir, – If you will permit me to call you so. I had some time
ago taken up my pen at Pisa to thank you for the present of your
new Edition of the *Literary Character*, which has often been to
me a consolation, and always a pleasure. I was interrupted,
however, partly by business, and partly by vexations of different
kinds, for I have not very long ago lost a child by a fever, and I
have had a good deal of petty trouble with the laws of this lawless
country, on account of the prosecution of a servant for an attack
upon a cowardly Scoundrel of a dragoon, who drew his Sword
upon some unarmed Englishmen; and whom I had done the
honour to mistake for an officer, and to treat like a Gentleman . . .

But to return to things more analogous to the *Literary Charac-
ter*. I wish to say that had I known that the book was to fall into
your hands, or that the MSS. notes you have thought worthy of
publication would have attracted your attention, I would have
made them more copious and perhaps not so careless.

I really cannot know whether I am or am not the Genius you
are pleased to call me, but I am very willing to put up with the
mistake, if it be one. It is a title dearly enough bought by most
men, to render it endurable, even when not quite clearly made
out, which it never *can* be till the Posterity, whose decisions are
merely dreams to ourselves, has sanctioned or denied it, while it
can touch us no further.

Mr Murray is in possession of an MSS. Memoir of mine (not
to be published till I am in my grave) which, strange as it may

seem, I never read over since it was written and have no desire to read over again. In it I have told what, as far as I know, is the *truth* – *not* the *whole* truth – for if I had done so I must have involved much private and some dissipated history; but, nevertheless, nothing but the truth, as far as regard for others permitted it to appear.

I do not know whether you have seen those MSS.; but as you are curious in such things as relate to the human mind, I should feel gratified if you had . . .

If there are any questions which you would like to ask me as connected with your Philosophy of the literary Mind (*if* mine be a literary mind), I will answer them fairly or give a reason for *not* – good, bad, or indifferent. At present I am paying the penalty of having helped to spoil the public taste, for, as long as I wrote in the false exaggerated style of youth and the times in which we live, they applauded me to the very echo; and within these few years, when I have endeavoured at better things, and written what I suspect to have the principle of duration in it, the Church, the Chancellor, and all men – even to my grand patron Francis Jeffrey Esqre of the *E[dinburgh] R[eview]* – have risen up against me and my later publications. Such is Truth! Men dare not look her in the face, except by degrees: they mistake her for a Gorgon, instead of knowing her to be a Minerva.

I do not mean to apply this mythological simile to my own endeavours. I have only to turn over a few pages of your volumes to find innumerable and far more illustrious instances.

It is lucky that I am of a temper not to be easily turned aside though by no means difficult to irritate. But I am making a dissertation instead of writing a letter. I write to you from the Villa Dupuy, near Leghorn, with the islands of Elba and Corsica visible from my balcony, and my old friend the Mediterranean rolling blue at my feet. As long as I retain my feeling and my passion for Nature, I can partly soften or subdue my other passions and resist or endure those of others.

I have the honour to be, truly, your obliged
and faithful Ser^t,

NOEL BYRON

TO E. J. DAWKINS   *Pisa, July 4th 1822*
[*British Minister at Florence*]

Dear Sir, – I regret to say that my anticipations were well founded.
The Gamba family received on Tuesday an order to quit the
Tuscan States in four days. Of course this is virtually my own
exile, for where they go I am no less bound by honour than by
feeling to follow. I believe we shall try to obtain leave to remain
at Lucca – if that fails, Genoa – and, failing that, possibly
America; for both Captain Chauncey of the American Squadron
(which returns in September) and Mr Bruen an American
Merchant man at Leghorn offered me a passage in the hand-
somest manner – the latter sent to me to say that he would even
send his vessel round to Genoa for us, if we chose to accept his
offer. With regard to the interpretation which will be put upon
my departure at this time, I hope that you will do me the favour
of letting the truth be known, as my own absence will deprive me
of the power of doing so for myself, and I have little doubt that
advantage will be taken of that circumstance.

This letter will be presented to you by Mr Taaffe, who is in
considerable confusion at a measure to which his own heedless-
ness has a good deal contributed. But – poor fellow – I suppose
that he meant no harm. He wanted the Countess Guiccioli to go
to Florence and fling herself at the feet of the Grand Duchess –

> a supplicant to wait
> While Ladies interpose, and Slaves debate

I can only say, that if she did anything of the kind, I would never
fling myself at *her* feet again.

Collini's office has now become a Sinecure, and I wish him joy
of it. The inconvenience and expense to me will be very con-
siderable, as I have two houses, furniture, Wines, Dinner
Services – linen, – books, my Schooner – and in short – a whole
establishment for a family – to leave at a moment's warning –
and this without knowing where the Gambas will be permitted
to rest, and of course where I can rest also.

The whole thing – the manner in which it was announced, by
the Commissary etc. was done in the most insulting manner. The

Courier treated as if he were a delinquent, and sent away with Soldiers to take charge of him and lodged in the prison of Pisa, by way of Hostel.

I trust that this just Government is now content, my countrymen have been insulted and wounded by a rascal, and my Servants treated like Criminals though guiltless while a noble and respectable family including a sick lady are ordered away like so many felons, without a shadow of justice, or even a *pretence* of *proof*.

With regard to yourself, I can only add that my obligations and feelings towards you are the same as if your exertions had been attended with Success. I certainly did at one time think, that whether they considered the person who applied in our behalf, or the persons in whose behalf the application was made, we should at least have had a *fair* trial, as I afforded every facility for the investigation. As it is, I will *not* express my sentiments – at least for the present I cannot – as no words could be at all adequate to describe my Sense of the manner in which the whole has been conducted by these people who call themselves a Government.

TO THOMAS MOORE   *Pisa, August 8, 1822*

You will have heard by this time that Shelley and another gentleman (Captain Williams) were drowned about a month ago (a *month* yesterday), in a squall off the Gulf of Spezia. There is thus another man gone, about whom the world was ill-naturedly, and ignorantly, and brutally mistaken. It will, perhaps, do him justice *now*, when he can be no better for it ...

I have written three more cantos of *Don Juan*, and am hovering on the brink of another (the ninth). The reason I want the stanzas again which I sent you is, that as these cantos contain a full detail (like the storm in Canto Second) of the siege and assault of Ismael, with much of sarcasm on those butchers in large business, your mercenary soldiery, it is a good opportunity of gracing the poem with —. With these things and these fellows, it is necessary, in the present clash of philosophy and tyranny, to throw away the scabbard. I know it is against fearful odds; but the battle must be fought; and it will eventually be for the good of mankind, whatever it may be for the individual who risks himself . . .

TO THOMAS MOORE   *Pisa, August 27, 1822*

. . . We have been burning the bodies of Shelley and Williams on the sea-shore, to render them fit for removal and regular interment. You can have no idea what an extraordinary effect such a funeral pile has, on a desolate shore, with mountains in the back-ground and the sea before, and the singular appearance the salt and frankincense gave to the flame. All of Shelley was consumed, except his *heart*, which would not take the flame, and is now preserved in spirits of wine . . .

Your old acquaintance Londonderry has quietly died at North Cray! and the virtuous De Witt was torn in pieces by the populace! What a lucky — the Irishman has been in his life and end. In him your Irish Franklin *est mort*!

Leigh Hunt is sweating articles for his new Journal; and both he and I think it somewhat shabby in *you* not to contribute. Will you become one of the *properrioters*? 'Do, and we go snacks.' I recommend you to think twice before you respond in the negative.

I have nearly (*quite three*) four new cantos of *Don Juan* ready. I obtained permission from the female Censor Morum[68] of *my* morals to continue it, provided it were immaculate; so I have been as decent as need be. There is a deal of war – a siege, and all that, in the style, graphical and technical, of the shipwreck in Canto Second, which 'took', as they say in the Row.

Yours, etc.

P.S. – That — Galignani has about ten lies in one paragraph. It was not a Bible that was found in Shelley's pocket, but John Keats's poems. However, it would not have been strange, for he was a great admirer of Scripture as a composition. *I* did not send my bust to the academy of New York; but I sat for my picture to young West, an American artist, at the request of some members of that Academy to *him* that he would take my portrait, – for the Academy, I believe.

I had, and still have, thoughts of South America, but am fluctuating between it and Greece. I should have gone, long ago, to one of them, but for my liaison with the Countess G[uiccioli]; for love, in these days, is little compatible with glory. *She* would be delighted to go too; but I do not choose to expose her to a long voyage, and a residence in an unsettled country, where I shall probably take a part of some sort.

TO MRS SHELLEY   [*Casa Saluzzo, Albaro, Genoa,*]
6ᵗʰ October, 1822

The sofa – which I regret is *not* of your furniture – it was purchased by me at Pisa since you left it.

It is convenient for my room, though of little value (about 12 pauls), and I offered to send another (now sent) in its stead. I preferred retaining the purchased furniture, but always intended that you should have as good or better in its place. I have a particular dislike to anything of Shelley's being within the same walls with Mrs Hunt's children. They are dirtier and more mischievous than Yahoos. What they can't destroy with their filth they will with their fingers. I presume you received ninety and odd crowns from the wreck of the *Don Juan*, and also the price of the boat purchased by Captain R., if not, you will have *both*. Hunt has these in hand.

With regard to any difficulties about money, I can only repeat that I will be your banker till this state of things is cleared up, and you can see what is to be done; so there is little to hinder you on that score. I was confined for four days to my bed at Lerici. Poor Hunt, with his six little blackguards, are coming slowly up; as usual he turned back once – was there ever such a *kraal* out of the Hottentot country.

N.B.

TO THE HON. AUGUSTA LEIGH   *Albaro, Genoa, Nov. 7ᵗʰ 1822*

My Dearest A., – I have yours of the 25th. My illness is quite gone, it was only at Lerici. On the fourth night I had got a little sleep, and was so wearied, that, though there were three slight shocks of an Earthquake that frightened the whole town into the streets, neither they nor the tumult awakened me.

We have had a deluge here, which has carried away half the country between this and Genoa (about two miles or less distant) but being on a hill we were only nearly knocked down by the lightning and battered by columns of rain, and our lower floor afloat, with the comfortable view of the whole landscape under water, and people screaming out of their garret windows; *two bridges* swept down, and our next door neighbours, a Cobbler, a Wigmaker, and a Ginger-bread baker, delivering up their whole stock to the elements, which marched away with a quantity of shoes, several Perukes, and Ginger-bread in all its branches. The whole came on so suddenly that there was no time to prepare. Think only, at the *top* of a hill of the road being an impassable cascade, and a child being drowned a few yards from its own door (as we heard say) in a place where Water is in general a rare commodity.

Well, after all this comes a preaching Friar and says that the day of Judgement will take place positively on the *4th* with all kinds of tempest and what not, in consequence of which the whole City (except some impious Scoffers) sent him presents to avert the wrath of Heaven by his prayers, and even the *public authorities* had warned the Captains of Ships, who, to mend the matter, almost all bought *new Cables* and anchors by way of weathering the Gale.

But the fourth turned out a very fine day. All those who had paid their money are excessively angry, and insist either upon having the day of judgement or their cash again. But the Friar's device seems to be 'no money to be returned', and he says that he merely made a mistake in the time, for the day of Judgement will certainly come for all that, either here or in some other part of Italy.

This has a little pacified the expectants. You will think this a fiction. Enquire further then. The populace actually used to kiss the fellow's feet in the streets. His Sermon, however, had small effect upon some, for they gave a ball on the 3^d, and a tradesman brought me an *over*charge on the same day, upon which I threatened him with the friar; but he said that was a reason for being paid on the 3^d as he had a sum to make up for his last account ...

TO LADY [HARDY]   *Albaro, November 10, 1822*

... You can write to me at your leisure and inclination. I have always laid it down as a maxim, and found it justified by experience, that a man and a woman make far better friendships than can exist between two of the same sex; but *these* with this condition, that they never have made, or are to make, love with each other. Lovers may, and, indeed, generally *are* enemies, but they never can be friends; because there must always be a spice of jealousy and a something of self in all their speculations.

Indeed, I rather look upon love altogether as a sort of hostile transaction, very necessary to make or to break matches, and keep the world going, but by no means a sinecure to the parties concerned.

Now, as my love perils are, I believe, pretty well over, and yours, by all accounts, are never to begin, we shall be the best friends imaginable, as far as both are concerned; and with this advantage, that we may both fall to loving right and left through all our acquaintance, without either sullenness or sorrow from that amiable passion, which are its inseparable attendants.

Believe me, etc.,

N.B.

TO JOHN MURRAY   *[Genoa, 10bre 9, 1822]*
[Fragment]

Very willing to lighten any losses ('go to'; thou art 'a fellow that hath had losses', like Dogberry, is it not so?) which you may experience from my becoming obnoxious to the Blue people.

I hope that you have a milder winter than we have here. We have had inundations worthy of the Trent or Po, and the Conductor (Franklin's) of my house was struck (or supposed to be stricken) by a thunderbolt. I was so near the window that I was dazzled and my eyes hurt for several minutes, and every body in the house felt an electric shock at the moment. Madame Guiccioli was frightened, as you may suppose.

I have thought since, that your bigots would have 'saddled me with a judgement' (as Thwackum did Square when he bit his tongue in talking Metaphysics), if any thing had happened of consequence. These fellows always forget Christ in their Christianity, and what he said when 'the tower of Siloam fell'.

To-day is the 9th, and the 10th is my surviving daughter's birthday. I have ordered, as a regale, a mutton chop and a bottle of ale. She is seven years old, I believe. Did I ever tell you that the day I came of age I dined on eggs and bacon and a bottle of ale for once in a way? They are my favourite dish and drinkable; but as neither of them agree with me, I never use them but on great jubilees – once in four or five years or so.

I see some booby represents the Hunts and Mrs Shelley as living in my house: it is a falsehood. They reside at some distance, and I do not see them twice in a month. I have not met Mr H[unt] a dozen times since I came to Genoa, or near it.

Yours ever,

N.B.

TO JOHN MURRAY   *Genoa, 10bre 25°, 1822*

... *Don Juan* will be known by and bye, for what it is intended, – a *Satire* on *abuses* of the present states of Society, and not an eulogy of vice: it may be now and then voluptuous: I can't help that. Ariosto is worse; Smollett (see Lord Strutwell in vol. 2^d of R[oderick] R[andom]) ten times worse; and Fielding no better. No Girl will ever be seduced by reading D.J.: – no, no; she will go to Little's poems and Rousseau's romans for that, or even to the immaculate De Stael: they will encourage her, and not the Don, who laughs at that, and – and – most other things. But never mind – Ça ira!

And now to a less agreeable topic, of which *pars magna es*[69] – you Murray of Albemarle St and the other Murray of Bridge Street – 'Arcades Ambo'[70] ('*Murrays both*') 'et *cant*-are pares':[71]

ye, I say, between you, are the Causes of the prosecution of John Hunt, Esqre on account of the *Vision*.[72] You, by sending him an incorrect copy, and the other, by his function. Egad, but H.'s Counsel will lay it on you with a trowel for your tergiversifying as to the MSS., etc., whereby poor H. (and, for anything I know, myself – I am willing enough) is likely to be impounded.

Now, do you see what you and your friends do by your injudicious rudeness? – actually cement a sort of connection which you strove to prevent, and which, had the H.'s *prospered*, would not in all probability have continued. As it is, I will not quit them in their adversity, though it should cost me character, fame, money, and the usual et cetera.

My original motives I already explained (in the letter which you thought proper to show): they are the *true* ones, and I abide by them, as I tell you, and I told L^h H^t when he questioned me on the subject of that letter. He was violently hurt, and never will forgive me at bottom; but I can't help that. I never meant to make a parade of it; but if he chose to question me, I could only answer the plain truth: and I confess I did not see anything in the letter to hurt him, unless I said he was 'a *bore*', which I don't remember. Had their Journal gone on well, and I could have aided to make it better for them, I should then have left them, after my safe pilotage off a lee shore, to make a prosperous voyage by themselves. As it is, I can't, and would not, if I could, leave them amidst the breakers.

As to any community of feeling, thought, or opinion, between L.H. and me, there is little or none: we meet rarely, hardly ever; but I think him a good principled and able man, and must do as I would be done by. I do not know what world he has lived in, but I have lived in three or four; and none of them like his Keats and Kangaroo *terra incognita*. Alas! poor Shelley! how he would have laughed had he lived, and how we used to laugh now and then, at various things, which are grave in the Suburbs!

You are all mistaken about Shelley. You do not know how mild, how tolerant, how good he was in Society; and as perfect a Gentleman as ever crossed a drawing-room, when he liked, and where he liked . . .

TO THOMAS MOORE   *Genoa, April 2, 1823*

I have just seen some friends of yours, who paid me a visit yesterday, which, in honour of them and of you, I returned to-day; – as I reserve my bear-skin and teeth, and paws and claws, for our enemies.

I have also seen Henry Fox, Lord Holland's son, whom I had not looked upon since I left him a pretty, mild boy, without a neck-cloth, in a jacket, and in delicate health, seven long years agone, at the period of mine eclipse – the third, I believe, as I have generally one every two or three years. I think that he has the softest and most amiable expression of countenance I ever saw, and manners correspondent. If to those he can add heredi-tary talents, he will keep the name of Fox in all its freshness for half a century more, I hope. I speak from a transient glimpse – but I love still to yield to such impressions; for I have ever found that those I liked longest and best, I took to at first sight; and I always liked that boy – perhaps, in part, from some resemblance in the less fortunate part of our destinies – I mean, to avoid mistakes, his lameness. But there is this difference, that *he* appears a halting angel, who has tripped against a star; whilst I am *Le Diable Boiteux*, – a soubriquet, which I marvel that, amongst their various *nominis umbrae*,[73] the Orthodox have not hit upon.

Your other allies whom I have found very agreeable personages, are Milor Blessington and *épouse*, travelling with a very hand-some companion, in the shape of a 'French Count'[74] (to use Farquhar's phrase in the *Beaux Stratagem*), who has all the air of a *Cupidon déchaîné*, and is one of the few specimens I have seen of our ideal of a Frenchman before the Revolution – and old friend with a new face, upon whose like I never thought that we should look again. Miladi seems highly literary, to which, and your honour's acquaintance with the family, I attribute the pleasure of having seen them. She is also very pretty even in a morning, – a species of beauty on which the sun of Italy does not shine so frequently as the chandelier. Certainly, English women wear better than their continental neighbours of the same sex. Mountjoy seems very good-natured, but is much tamed, since I recollect him in all the glory of gems and snuff-boxes, and uniforms, and theatricals, and speeches in our house – 'I mean, of peers', – (I must refer you to Pope – whom you don't read and won't appreciate – for that quotation, which you must allow to be poetical,) and sitting to Stroelling, the painter, (so you remember our visit, with Leckie, to the German?) to be dipicted as one of the heroes of Agincourt, 'with his long sword, saddle, bridle, Whack fal de', etc., etc. ...

I have been far more persecuted than you, as you may judge by my present decadence, – for I take it that I am as low in popularity and bookselling as any writer can be. At least, so my friends assure me – blessings on their benevolence! This they attribute to Hunt; but they are wrong – it must be, partly at least, owing to myself; be it so. As to Hunt, I prefer *not* having turned him to starve in the streets to any personal honour which might have accrued from some genuine philanthropy. I really act upon principle in this matter, for we have nothing much in common; and I cannot describe to you the despairing sensation of trying to do something for a man who seems incapable or unwilling to do any thing further for himself, – at least, to the purpose. It is like pulling a man out of a river who directly throws himself in again. For the last three or four years Shelley assisted, and had once actually extricated him. I have since his demise – and even before, – done what I could: but it is not in my power to make this permanent. I want Hunt to return to England, for which I would furnish him with the means in comfort; and his situation *there*, on the whole, is bettered, by the payment of a portion of his debts, etc.; and he would be on the spot to continue his Journal, or Journals, with his brother, who seems a sensible, plain, sturdy, and enduring person ...

TO THE COUNT D'ORSAY   *April 22, 1823*

My Dear Count d'Orsay (if you will permit me to address you so familiarly), – You should be content with writing in your own language, like Grammont, and succeeding in London as nobody has succeeded since the days of Charles the Second and the records of Antonio Hamilton, without deviating into our barbarous language, – which you understand and write, however, much better than it deserves.

My 'approbation', as you are pleased to term it, was very sincere, but perhaps not very impartial; for, though I love my country, I do not love my countrymen – at least, such as they now are. And, besides the seduction of talent and wit in your work, I fear that to me there was the attraction of vengeance. I have *seen* and *felt* much of what you have described so well. I have known the persons, and the re-unions so described, – (many of them, that is to say,) and the portraits are so like that I cannot but admire the painter no less than his performance.

But I am sorry for you; for if you are so well acquainted with life at your age, what will become of you when the illusion is still more dissipated? But never mind – *en avant*! live while you can; and that you may have the full enjoyment of the many advantages of youth, talent, and figure, which you possess, is the wish of an – Englishman, – I suppose, but it is no treason; for my mother was Scotch, and my name and my family are both Norman; and as for myself, I am of no country. As for my 'Works', which you are pleased to mention, let them go to the Devil, from whence (if you believe many persons) they came.

I have the honour to be your obliged, etc., etc.

TO THE COUNTESS OF BLESSINGTON *May 3, 1823*

Dear Lady Blessington, – My request would be for a copy of the miniature of Lady B. which I have seen in possession of the late Lady Noel, as I have no picture, or indeed memorial of any kind of Lady B., as all her letters were in her own possession before I left England, and we have had no correspondence since – at least on her part.

My message, with regard to the infant, is simply to this effect – that in the event of any accident occurring to the mother, and my remaining the survivor, it would be my wish to have her plans carried into effect, both with regard to the education of the child, and the person or persons under whose care Lady B. might be desirous that she should be placed. It is not my intention to interfere with her in any way on the subject during her life; and I presume that it would be some consolation to her to know (if she is in ill health, as I am given to understand,) that in *no* case would any thing be done, as far as I am concerned, but in strict conformity with Lady B.'s own wishes and intentions – left in what manner she thought proper.

Believe me, dear Lady B., your obliged, etc.

TO JOHN BOWRING   *Genoa, May 12, 1823*

Sir, – I have great pleasure in acknowledging your letter, and the honour which the Committee have done me: – I shall endeavour to deserve their confidence by every means in my power. My first wish is to go up into the Levant in person, where I might be enabled to advance, if not the cause, at least the means of obtaining information which the Committee might be desirous of acting upon; and my former residence in the country, my familiarity with the Italian language, (which is there universally spoken, or at least to the same extent as French in the more polished parts of the Continent,) and my *not* total ignorance of the Romaic, would afford me some advantages of experience. To this project the only objection is of a domestic nature, and I shall try to get over it; – if I fail in this, I must do what I can where I am; but it will be always a source of regret to me, to think that I might perhaps have done more for the cause on the spot.

Our last information of Captain Blaquiere is from Ancona, where he embarked with a fair wind for Corfu, on the 15th ult.; he is now probably at his destination. My last letter *from* him personally was dated Rome; he had been refused a passport through the Neapolitan territory, and returned to strike up through Romagna for Ancona: – little time, however, appears to have been lost by the delay.

The principal material wanted by the Greeks appears to be, first, a park of field artillery – light, and fit for mountain-service; secondly, gunpowder; thirdly, hospital or medical stores. The readiest mode of transmission is, I hear, by Idra, addressed to Mr Negri, the minister. I meant to send up a certain quantity of the two latter – no great deal – but enough for an individual to show his good wishes for the Greek success, – but am pausing, because, in case I should go myself, I can take them with me. I do not want to limit my own contribution to this merely, but more especially, if I can get to Greece myself, I should devote whatever resources I can muster of my own, to advancing the great object. I am in correspondence with Signor Nicolas Karrellas (well known to Mr Hobhouse), who is now at Pisa; but his latest advice merely stated, that the Greeks are at present employed in organising their *internal* government, and the details of its administration: this would seem to indicate *security*, but the war is however far from being terminated.

The Turks are an obstinate race, as all former wars have proved them, and will return to the charge for years to come, even if beaten, as it is to be hoped they will be. But in no case can the labours of the Committee be said to be in vain; for in the event even of the Greeks being subdued, and dispersed, the funds which could be employed in succouring and gathering together the remnant, so as to alleviate in part their distresses, and enable them to find or make a country (as so many emigrants of other nations have been compelled to do), would 'bless both those who gave and those who took', as the bounty both of justice and of mercy.

With regard to the formation of a brigade, (which Mr Hobhouse hints at in his short letter of this day's receipt, enclosing the one to which I have the honour to reply,) I would presume to suggest – but merely as an opinion, resulting rather from the melancholy experience of the brigades embarked in the Columbian service than from any experiment yet fairly tried in GREECE, – that the attention of the Committee had better perhaps be directed to the employment of *officers* of experience than the enrolment of *raw British* soldiers, which latter are apt to be unruly, and not very serviceable, in irregular warfare, by the side of foreigners. A small body of good officers, especially artillery; an engineer, with quantity (such as the Committee might deem requisite) of stores of the nature which Captain Blaquiere indicated as most wanted, would, I should conceive, be a highly useful accession. Officers, also, who had previously served in the Mediterranean would be preferable, as some knowledge of Italian is nearly indispensable.

It would also be as well that they should be aware, that they are not going 'to rough it on a beef-steak and bottle of port', – but that Greece – never, of late years, very plentifully stocked for a *mess* – is at present the country of all kinds of *privations*. This remark may seem superfluous; but I have been led to it, by observing that many *foreign* officers, Italian, French, and even, Germans (but *fewer* of the *latter*), have returned in disgust, imagining either that they were going up to make a party of pleasure, or to enjoy full pay, speedy promotion, and a very moderate degree of duty. They complain, too, of having been ill received by the Government or inhabitants; but numbers of these complainants were mere adventurers, attracted by a hope of command and plunder, and disappointed of both. Those Greeks I have seen strenuously deny the charge of inhospitality, and declare that they shared their pittance to the last crum[b] with their foreign volunteers.

I need not suggest to the Committee the very great advantage which must accrue to Great Britain from the success of the Greeks, and their probable commercial relations with England in consequence; because I feel persuaded that the first object of the Committee is their EMANCIPATION, without any interested views. But the consideration might weigh with the English people in general, in their present passion for every kind of speculation, – they need not cross the American seas for one much better worth their while, and nearer home. The resources even for an emigrant population, in the Greek islands alone, are rarely to be paralleled; and the cheapness of every kind of, not *only necessary*, but *luxury*, (that is to say, *luxury of nature*,) fruits, wine, oil, etc., in a state of peace, are far beyond those of the Cape, and Van Diemen's Land, and the other places of refuge, which the English people are searching for over the waters.

I beg that the Committee will command me in any and every way. If I am favoured with any instructions, I shall endeavour to obey them to the letter, whether conformable to my own private opinion or not. I beg leave to add, personally, my respect for the gentleman whom I have the honour of addressing.

And am, Sir, your obliged, etc.

P.S. – The best refutation of Gell will be the active exertions of the Committee; – I am too warm a controversialist; and I suspect that if Mr Hobhouse have taken him in hand, there will be little occasion for me to 'encumber him with help'. If I go up into the country, I will endeavour to transmit as accurate and impartial an account as circumstances will permit.

I shall write to Mr Karrellas. I expect intelligence from Captain Blaquiere, who has promised me some early intimation from the seat of the Provisional Government. I gave him a letter of introduction to Lord Sydney Osborne, at Corfu; but as Lord S. is in the government service, of course his reception could only be a *cautious* one.

TO THE HON. DOUGLAS KINNAIRD   *Genoa, May 21st, 1823*

My Dear Douglas, – I enclose you another corrected proof of D.J., and also a note of Mr Barry, the acting partner of Messrs Webbs, on the proposed credit in case I go up to the Levant. I do not quite know what to name as the amount – undoubtedly about 5000, in addition to what I already have in your circular notes, and in Webb's bank, would be more than sufficient for my own personal wants for *good four years*, for my habits are simple, and you are aware that I have lately reduced my other expences of every kind. But, if I do go up among the Greeks, I may have occasion to be of service to them. There may be prisoners to ransom, some cash to advance, arms to purchase, or if I was to take an angry turn some sulky morning, and raise a troop of my own (though this is unlikely), any or all of these would require a command of credit and require my resources. You will let me have what you think proper *not under* the sum above stated; but there is no *immediate* hurry, as I shall not sail till about July, if at all. It is to be understood that the *letter of credit for two thousand pounds* which I have *now untouched* is to be *returned* or left to be returned *untouched* in the hands of Messrs Webb for your house the moment I receive the more extended credit. It is also [to] be understood that, if I receive this extended credit, and from any circumstances do not go up into the Levant, then that credit is to be null and void as it would then become quite superfluous to my present occasion. I am doing all I can to get away, but I have all kinds of obstacles thrown in my way by the 'absurd womankind', who seems determined on sacrificing herself in every way, and preventing me from doing any good, and all without reason; for her relations, and her husband (who is moving the Pope and the Government here to get her to live with him again) and everybody, are earnest with her to return to Ravenna. She wants to go up to Greece too! forsooth, a precious place to go to at present! Of course the idea is ridiculous, as everything must there be sacrificed to seeing her out of harm's way. It is a case too, in which interest does not enter, and therefore hard to deal with; for I have no kind of control in that way, and if she makes a scene (and she has a turn that way) we shall have another romance, and tale of ill-usage, and abandonment, and Lady Carolining, and Lady Byroning, and Glenarvoning, all cut and dry. There never was a man who gave up so much to women, and all I have gained by it has been the character of treating them harshly. However I shall do what I can, and have hopes; for her father has been recalled from his political exile; but with this proviso, that he do not return without his daughter. If I left a woman for another woman, she might have cause to complain, but really when a man merely wishes to go on a great duty, for a good cause, this selfishness on the part of the 'feminie' is rather too much.

Ever yrs.,

N.B.

I add the enclosed letter from Mr J.M.[75] which does him credit; also another MSS for a proof from the same.

TO HENRI BEYLE   *Genoa, May 29, 1823*

Sir, – At present, that I know to whom I am indebted for a very
flattering mention in the *Rome, Naples, and Florence*, in 1817,
by Mons. Stendhal, it is fit that I should return my thanks
(however undesired or undesirable) to Mons. Beyle, with whom
I had the honour of being acquainted at Milan, in 1816. You only
did me too much honour in what you were pleased to say in that
work; but it has hardly given me less pleasure than the praise
itself, to become at length aware (which I have done by mere
accident) that I am indebted for it to one of whose good opinion
I was really ambitious. So many changes have taken place since
that period in the Milan circle, that I hardly dare recur to it; –
some dead, some banished, and some in the Austrian dungeons. –
Poor Pellico! I trust that, in his iron solitude, his Muse is consol-
ing him in part – one day to delight us again, when both she and
her Poet are restored to freedom.

Of your works I have only seen *Rome*, etc., the Lives of Haydn
and Mozart, and the *brochure* on Racine and Shakespeare. The
Histoire de la Peinture I have not yet the good fortune to possess.

There is one part of your observations in the pamphlet which
I shall venture to remark upon; – it regards Walter Scott. You
say that 'his character is little worthy of enthusiasm', at the same
time that you mention his productions in the manner they deserve.
I have known Walter Scott long and well, and in occasional
situations which call forth the *real* character – and I can assure
you that his character *is* worthy of admiration – that of all men
he is the most *open*, the most *honourable*, the most *amiable*. With
his politics I have nothing to do: they differ from mine, which
renders it difficult for me to speak of them. But he is *perfectly
sincere* in them: and Sincerity may be humble, but she cannot be
servile. I pray you, therefore, to correct or soften that passage.
You may, perhaps, attribute this officiousness of mine to a false
affectation of *candour*, as I happen to be a writer also. Attribute
it to what motive you please, but *believe* the *truth*. I say that
Walter Scott is as nearly a thorough good man as man can be,
because I *know* it by experience to be the case.

If you do me the honour of an answer, may I request a speedy one? – because it is possible (though not yet decided) that circumstances may conduct me once more to Greece. My present address is Genoa, where an answer will reach me in a short time, or be forwarded to me wherever I may be.

I beg you to believe me, with a lively recollection of our brief acquaintance, and the hope of one day renewing it,

Your ever obliged
And obedient humble servant,

NOEL BYRON

TO J. J. COULMANN   *Genoa, July 12* [?], *1823*

... I have also to return you thanks for having honoured me with your own compositions; I thought you too young and probably too amiable, to be an author. As to the Essay, etc., I am obliged to you for the present, although I had already seen it joined to the last edition of the translation. I have nothing to object to it, with regard to what concerns myself personally, though naturally there are some of the facts in it discoloured, and several errors into which the author has been led by the accounts of others. I allude to facts, and not criticisms. But the same author has cruelly calumniated my father and my grand-uncle, but more especially the former. So far from being 'brutal', he was, according to the testimony of all those who knew him, of an extremely amiable and (*enjoué*) joyous character, but care-less (*insouciant*) and dissipated. He had, consequently, the reputation of a good officer, and showed himself such in the Guards, in America. The facts themselves refute the assertion. It is not by 'brutality' that a young Officer in the Guards seduces and carries off a Marchioness, and marries two heiresses. It is true that he was a very handsome man, which goes a great way. His first wife (Lady Conyers and Marchioness of Carmarthen) did not die of grief, but of a malady which she caught by having imprudently insisted upon accompanying my father to a hunt, before she was completely recovered from the accouchement which gave birth to my sister Augusta.

His second wife, my respected mother, had, I assure you, too proud a spirit to bear the ill-usage of any man, no matter who he might be; and this she would have soon proved. I should add, that he lived a long time in Paris, and was in habits of intimacy with the old Marshal Biron, Commandant of the French Guards; who, from the similitude of names, and Norman origin of our family, supposed that there was some distant relationship between us. He died some years before the age of forty, and whatever may have been his faults, they were certainly not those of harshness and grossness (*dureté et grossièreté*). If the notice should reach England, I am certain that the passage relative to my father will give much more pain to my sister (the wife of Colonel Leigh, attached to the Court of the late Queen, *not* Caroline, but Charlotte, wife of George III.), even than to me; and this she does not deserve, for there is not a more angelic being upon earth. Augusta and I have always loved the memory of our father as much as we loved each other, and this at least forms a presumption that the stain of harshness was not applicable to it. If he dissipated his fortune, that concerns us alone, for we are his heirs; and till we reproach him with it, I know no one else who has a right to do so. As to Lord Byron, who killed Mr Chaworth in a duel, so far from retiring from the world, he made the tour of Europe, and was appointed Master of the Staghounds after that event, and did not give up society until his son had offended him by marrying in a manner contrary to his duty. So far from feeling any remorse for having killed Mr Chaworth, who was a fire-eater (*spadassin*), and celebrated for his quarrelsome disposition, he always kept the sword which he used upon that occasion in his bed-chamber, where it still was *when he died*. It is singular enough, that when very young, I formed a strong attachment for the grand-niece and heiress of Mr Chaworth, who stood in the same degree of relationship [to him] as myself to Lord Byron; and at one time it was thought that the two families would have been united in us. She was two years older than me, and we were very much together in our youth. She married a man of an ancient respectable family; but her marriage was not a happier one than my own. Her conduct, however, was irreproachable, but there was no sympathy between their characters, and a separation took place. I had not seen her for many years. When an occasion offered, I was upon the point, with her consent, of paying her a visit, when my sister, who has always had more influence over me than anyone else, persuaded me not to do it. 'For,' said she, 'if you go, you will fall in love again, and then there will be a scene; one step will lead to another, *et cela fera un éclat*', etc. I was guided by these reasons, and shortly after I married; with what success it is useless to say. Mrs C. some time after, being separated from her husband, became insane; but she has since recovered her reason, and is, I believe, reconciled to her husband. This is a long letter, and principally about my family, but it is the fault of M. Pichot, my benevolent biographer. He may say of me whatever of good or evil pleases him, but I desire that he should speak of my relations only as they deserve. If you could find an occasion of making him, as well as M. Nodier, rectify the facts relative to my father, and publish them, you would do me a great service, for I cannot bear to have him unjustly spoken of. I must conclude abruptly, for I have occupied you too long. Believe me to be very much honoured by your esteem, and always your obliged and obedient servant,

NOEL BYRON

P.S. – The tenth or twelfth of this month I shall embark for Greece. Should I return, I shall pass through Paris, and shall be much flattered in meeting you and your friends. Should I not return, give me as affectionate a place in your memory as possible.

6. THE POET AS HERO

July 1823–April 1824

INTRODUCTION

WHEN the *Hercules* put in at Leghorn, Byron heard from the exiled Greek patriot, the Metropolitan Ignatius Arta, who wrote warning him of the confusion he would find among his compatriots and warmly recommending the chieftain Marco Botzaris and his Suliotes. In this he was seconded by Constantine Mavrocordatos, who also pointed out the strategic importance of Missolonghi. The party was joined by James Hamilton Browne, recently dismissed by the British administration of the Ionian Islands for his Philhellenic activities. It was on his advice that Byron sailed to Cephalonia where the Resident, Colonel Charles James Napier, was also favourably disposed to the Greek cause. The commanding English officer of the Ionian Islands, whose headquarters were on Corfu, Sir Thomas Maitland, was for strict neutrality. On the morning of 3 August the *Hercules* anchored off the port of Argostoli, the chief town of Cephalonia. There Byron was disappointed to find that Captain Blaquière, whom he met in Genoa, and who had been sent out to Greece by the London Greek Committee to report, had, contrary to his instructions, already left for home. Byron was welcomed by the English officers of the 8th Regiment, as well as by Colonel Napier and the health officer Dr Henry Muir; but he remained on board ship, to give the appearance of maintaining neutrality, until he had news of happenings in Greece, which was slow in forthcoming. In the meanwhile a visit was made to nearby Ithaca, and it was here that Byron had the first of his convulsive fits. Byron was liberal with monetary assistance to refugees of both sides and was assiduous in trying to mitigate the most horrifying cruelties perpetrated by both Greeks and Turks.

Finally a letter arrived on 1 September from Hobhouse, requesting him to act as representative of the London Greek Committee with the Greek Government, and to dispose of such stores as arrived from England. On 2 September, possibly at the suggestion of Napier, Byron went ashore, and a few days later moved with Gamba and Dr Bruno to a small house at Metaxata, to await developments. Not encumbered with Byron's responsibilities and uncertainties the impetuous Trelawny and Browne set off on an expedition to the Morea. The executive and legislature of the Greek Government were at loggerheads; the chieftains (*klephts*), often nothing short of brigands, had little thought of Greek unity and sought Byron's money for their own purposes. The most warlike and unscrupulous of these, Kolokotrones, who held the Morea virtually at his command, wrote to Byron, as did Prince Alexander Mavrocordatos, whom Napier advised Byron to trust as being an honest patriot. The Suliotes exiled from the mainland at first aroused Byron's sympathies, but their exorbitant and ever-increasing demands on his purse, and their total lack of discipline, caused him to dismiss those whom he had taken into his service. His procrastination derived not so much from his own volatile character or indolence as from not knowing whom to trust; he had come to Greece, not to be a leader of partisans, but to try to create a genuinely representative Greek Government, and to achieve this end he was willing to dispose of large sums of his own money, while Greek deputies were sent to England to negotiate a loan. Byron was not deceived by the character of the Greeks with whom he had to deal – the results of centuries of servitude; but the cause was a grand one, and moments of temporary anger and despair were followed by more sanguine hopes.

In November two Greek deputies, who had been authorized by the Legislative Body to proceed to England to ask for a loan of £800,000, met Byron on Cephalonia and arranged with him an advance of £4,000 to allow a Greek squadron to put to sea, to relieve the Turkish blockade of Missolonghi. At this time Byron was joined by the pedantic disciple of Jeremy Bentham, the Hon. Colonel Leicester Stanhope, who was to act with him as agent of the London Greek Committee. Byron dispatched him to the Morea with a letter to the Greek leaders appealing for immediate unity, if the English loan were to be received, and war-materials purchased. Stanhope also carried a letter to Prince Mavrocordatos, on whom Byron had now pinned his hopes of finding a disinterested leader. Actual civil war had broken out between the Executive (under Kolokotrones) at Nauplia and the Legislature at Argos. In early December news reached Byron that Mavrocordatos, with the Greek squadron, was in motion, and on the 13th he heard that he had landed at Missolonghi. Byron now realized where his duty lay. Taking with him stores from the London Committee, he set out from Argostoli, and after an exciting passage, when they narrowly escaped capture by a Turkish brig, Byron and his party disembarked at Missolonghi on 5 January 1824.

The difficulties that Byron had foreseen were nothing to those with which he had to contend when he had settled in on the marshy, lagoon-bound village of Missolonghi. The valiant Marco Borzaris had been killed at the head of his troops in August, and now the remnants of his Suliotes poured into the town to join the Greeks in its defence. The effect was only to add to the confusion. All the troops, months in arrears with their pay, were undisciplined and rebellious, and Byron soon found that he was disbursing more funds from his own purse than those contributed by the Government. Much store was placed on the arrival from England of William Parry, sent by the Committee to organize an effective corps of artillery; but when he did arrive on 5 February it was found that necessary materials were lacking, and the planned attack on Lepanto, which, led by Byron, was to have given an occupation to the unruly troops and rid the town of their presence, was of necessity delayed. On 15 February, after a violent altercation with the Suliote chiefs, Byron had another seizure, with some of the symptoms of epilepsy. Next day he was bled, but the doctors had difficulty in stopping the flow of blood – as Byron wrote to Murray, making light of the event, 'They had gone too near to the temporal artery for my temporal safety . . .' Thefts, assassinations, riots, earthquakes and the refusal of the English artificers who had accompanied Parry to continue to work in such conditions – all these, with the addition of almost continual rain, which made the place a quagmire, and which prevented Byron from taking his usual daily ride, were having their effect on his nerves and physique. Fits of depression would

507

give way to gusts of passion at the incompetence of the Greeks. On the 21st there was another mutiny of the Suliotes, and Mavrocordatos had recourse to Byron for a further loan of 4,800 dollars to pay them their arrears, so that they would depart. At the end of the month George Finlay (the future historian of Greece) arrived with a letter from the *klepht* chieftain Odysseus, suggesting a meeting between him, Byron and Mavrocordatos at Salona, in an attempt to put down the dissensions between factions and to achieve a united front against the Turks. Incessant bad weather during March prevented the Salona congress, but Byron was heartened by letters he received from leading Greeks, who now looked on him as the one man whose influence could bring about unity in the common cause. Pending the completion of the London loan, Byron virtually financed what preparations were being undertaken for the spring offensive; on one day alone demands for 50,000 dollars were made on him. But by the beginning of April, Parry, who had become Byron's right-hand man, noted his mounting depression with the course of events, coupled with a deterioration in his physical condition. He feared that the proceeds from the loan would only serve factional ends. Fresh commotions had broken out among the soldiery gathered in Missolonghi. Byron surmounted each crisis with a coolness that reassured his faithful entourage. He was now looked on as the virtual commander and paymaster of the Greek insurrection, but the responsibilities and disappointments were having their toll.

On 9 April a letter from Hobhouse cheered him: 'Nothing can be more serviceable to the cause than all you have done . . . I only trust that the great sacrifices which you have made may contribute (which I have no doubt they will) to the final success of the great cause – This will indeed be something worth living for – and will make your name and character stand far above those of any contemporary.'

Caught in a heavy rainstorm on 9 April, while riding with Pietro Gamba, he complained on his return of a feverish chill. Despite this, he rode again on the following day using the saddle still wet from the previous soaking. He was gay with his visitors in the evening, but later that night he called for Dr Bruno and complained of alternating shivers and sweats, and pains in various parts of his body. His condition steadily worsened, and he refused at first to be bled. The medical facilities were inadequate and Parry was unable, because of a sirocco, to move him to Zante. Lucid periods, when he was able to give orders, conduct his correspondence and to learn the successful conclusion of the London loan, gradually gave way to bouts of delirium, followed by a comatose state. He died at six o'clock on the evening of 19 April 1824, at the age of thirty-six. His remains were conveyed home to England, where, burial in Westminster Abbey having been refused by the authorities, he was interred in the Byron family vault in Hucknall Torkard Church.

JOURNAL IN CEPHALONIA

June 19ᵗʰ 1823

The dead have been awakened – shall I sleep?
  The World's at war with tyrants – shall I crouch?
The harvest's ripe – and shall I pause to reap?
  I slumber not; the thorn is in my Couch;
Each day a trumpet soundeth in mine ear,
  Its echo in my heart –

1823

Mataxata, Cephalonia, Sepᵗ 28 [1823]

On the sixteenth (I think) of July, I sailed from Genoa in the English brig *Hercules*: Jⁿᵒ Scott, Master. On the 17th, a Gale of wind occasioning confusion and threatening damage to the horses in the hold, we bore up again for the same port, where we remained four and twenty hours longer, and then put to sea, touched at Leghorn, and pursued our voyage by the straits of Messina for Greece. Passing within sight of Elba, Corsica, the Lipari islands including Stromboli, Sicily, Italy, etc., about the 4ᵗʰ of August we anchored off Argostoli, in the chief harbour of the Island of Cephalonia.

Here I had some expectation of hearing from Capt. B[laquière], who was on a mission from the Gᵏ Committee in London to the Provisional Govᵗ of the Morea, but, rather to my surprise, learned that he was on his way home, though his latest letters to me from the peninsula, after expressing an anxious wish that I should come up without delay, stated further that he intended to remain in the country for the present. I have since received various letters from him addrest to Genoa, and forwarded to the Islands, partly explaining the cause of his unexpected return, and also (contrary to his former opinion) requesting me not to proceed to Greece *yet*, for sundry reasons, some of importance. I sent a boat to Corfu in the hopes of finding him still there, but he had already sailed for Ancona.

In the island of Cephalonia, Colonel Napier commanded in chief as Resident,[1] and Col. Duffie the 8th, a King's Regiment then forming the Garrison. We were received by both those Gentlemen, and indeed by all the officers, as well as the Civilians, with the greatest kindness and hospitality, which, if we did not deserve, I still hope that we have done nothing to forfeit, and it has continued unabated, even since the Gloss of new Acquaintance has been worn away by frequent intercourse.

We here learned, what has since been fully confirmed, that the Greeks were in a state of political dissention amongst themselves; that Mavrocordato was dismissed, or had resigned (*L'un vaut bien l'autre*) and that Colocotroni, with I know not what or whose party, was paramount in the Morea. The Turks were in force in Acarnania, etc., and the Turkish fleet blockaded the coast from Messolonghi to Chiarenza, and subsequently to Navarino. The Greek fleet, from the want of means or other causes, remained in port in Hydra, Ipsara, and Spetzas, and, for aught that is yet certainly known, may be there still. As, rather contrary to my expectations, I had no advices from Peloponnesus, and had also letters to receive from England from the Committee, I determined to remain for the interim in the Ionian Islands, especially as it was difficult to land on the opposite coast without risking the confiscation of the vessel and her contents, which Capt[n] Scott, naturally enough, declined to do, unless I would ensure to him the full amount of his possible damage . . .

Some day after our return [from a visit to Ithaca] I heard that there were letters for me at Zante; but a considerable delay took place before the Greek, to whom they were consigned, had them properly forwarded, and I was at length indebted to Col. Napier for obtaining them for me; *what* occasioned the demur or delay was never explained.

I learned, by my advices from England, the request of the Committee that I would act as their representative near the Greek Gov[t], and take charge of the proper disposition and delivery of certain stores, etc., etc., expected by a vessel which has not yet arrived up to the present date (Sept[r] 18).

Soon after my arrival, I took into my own pay a body of forty

Suliotes under their chiefs Photomara, Giavella, and Drako, and would probably have increased the number, but I found them not quite united among themselves in any thing except raising their demands on me, although I had given a dollar per man more each month than they could receive from the G^k Gov^t, and they were destitute, at the time I took them, of everything. I had acceded to their own demand, and paid them a month in advance. But, set on probably by some of the trafficking shopkeepers with whom they were in the habit of dealing on credit, they made various attempts at what I thought extortion, so that I called them together, stating my view of the case, and declining to take them on with me. But I offered them another month's pay, and the price of their passage to Acarnania, where they could now easily go, as the Turkish fleet was gone, and the blockade removed.

This part of them accepted, and they went accordingly. Some difficulty arose about restoring their arms by the Septinsular Gov^t, but these were at length obtained, and they are now with their compatriots in Etolia or Acarnania.

I also transferred to the resident in Ithaca the sum of two hundred and fifty dollars for the refugees there, and I had conveyed to Cephalonia a Moreote family who were in the greatest helplessness, and provided them with a house and decent maintenance under the protection of Messrs Corgialegno, wealthy merchants of Argostoli, to whom I had been recommended by my correspondent.

I had caused a letter to be written to Marco Borzaris, the acting commander of a body of troops in Acarnania, for whom I had letters of recommendation. His answer was probably the last he ever signed, or dictated, for he was killed in action the very day after its date, with the character of a good soldier, and an honourable man, which are not always found together nor indeed separately. I was also invited by Count Metaxa, the Governor of Messolonghi, to go over there; but it was necessary in the present state of parties, that I should have some communication with the existing Gov^t on the subject of their opinion *where* I might be, if not *most* useful, at any rate *least* obnoxious.

As I did not come here to join a faction but a nation, and to deal with honest men and not with speculators or peculators, (charges bandied about daily by the Greeks of each other) it will require much circumspection to avoid the character of a partizan, and I perceive it to be the more difficult as I have already received invitations from more than one of the contending parties, always under the pretext that *they* are the 'real Simon Pure'. After all, one should not despair, though all the foreigners that I have hitherto met with from amongst the Greeks are going or gone back disgusted.

Whoever goes into Greece at present should do it as Mrs Fry went into Newgate – not in the expectation of meeting with any especial indication of existing probity, but in the hope that time and better treatment will reclaim the present burglarious and larcenous tendencies which have followed this General Gaol delivery.

When the limbs of the Greeks are a little less stiff from the shackles of four centuries, they will not march so much 'as if they had gyves on their legs'. At present the Chains are broken indeed; but the links are still clanking, and the Saturnalia is still too recent to have converted the Slave into a sober Citizen. The worst of them is that (to use a coarse but the only expression that will not fall short of the truth) they are such damned liars; there never was such an incapacity for veracity shown since Eve lived in Paradise. One of them found fault the other day with the English language, because it had so few shades of a Negative, whereas a Greek can so modify a 'No' to a 'Yes', and *vice versa*, by the slippery qualities of his language, that prevarication may be carried to any extent and still leave a loop-hole through which perjury may slip without being perceived. This was the Gentleman's own talk, and is only to be doubted because in the words of the Syllogism 'Now Epimenides was a Cretan'. But they may be mended by and bye.

Sept. 30th

After remaining here some time in expectation of hearing from the G^k G^t I availed myself of the opportunity of Messrs B[rowne] and T[relawny] proceeding to Tripolitza, subsequently to the departure of the Turkish fleet, to write to the acting part of the Legislature. My object was not only to obtain some accurate information so as to enable me to proceed to the Spot where I might be, if not most safe, at least more serviceable, but to have an opportunity of forming a judgement on the real state of their affairs. In the meantime I hear from Mavrocordato and the Primate of Hydra, the latter inviting me to that island, the former hinting that he should like to meet me there or elsewhere.

1823

$10^{bre}\ 17^{th}$

My Journal was discontinued abruptly and has not been resumed sooner, because on the day of its former date I received a letter from my sister Augusta, that intimated the illness of my daughter, and I had not then the heart to continue it. Subsequently I had heard through the same channel that she was better, and since that she is well; if so, for me all is well.

But although I learned this early in $9^{th}\ 9^{bre}$, I know not why I have not continued my journal, though many things which would have formed a curious record have since occurred.

I know not why I resume it even now, except that, standing at the window of my apartment in this beautiful village, the calm though cool serenity of a beautiful and transparent Moonlight, showing the Islands, the Mountains, the Sea, with a distant outline of the Morea traced between the double Azure of the waves and skies, has quieted me enough to be able to write, which (however difficult it may seem for one who has written so much publicly to refrain) is, and always has been, to me a task and a painful one. I could summon testimonies, were it necessary; but my hand-writing is sufficient. It is that of one who thinks much, rapidly, perhaps deeply, but rarely with pleasure.

But – *En avant*. The Greeks are advancing in their public progress, but quarrelling amongst themselves. I shall probably, *bon grè mal grè*, be obliged to join one of the factions, which I have hitherto strenuously avoided in the hope to unite them in one common interest.

Mavrocordato has appeared at length with the Hydriote Squadron in these seas, which apparition would hardly have taken place had I not engaged to pay two hundred thousand piastres (10 piastres per dollar being the present value on the Greek continent) in aid of Messolonghi, and has commenced operations somewhat successfully but not very prudently.

Fourteen (some say seventeen) Greek ships attacked a Turkish vessel of 12 Guns, and took her. This is not quite an Ocean Thermopylae, but *n'importe*; they (*on dit*) have found on board 50,000 dollars, a sum of great service in their present exigencies, if properly applied. This prize, however, has been made within the bounds of Neutrality on the coast of Ithaca, and the Turks were (it is said) pursued on shore, and some slain. All this may involve a question of right and wrong with the not very tolerant Thomas Maitland, who is not very capable of distinguishing either. I have advanced the sum above noted to pay the said Squadron; it is not very large but is double that which Napoleon, the Emperor of Emperors, began his campaign in Italy withal – *vide Las Cases, passim*, vol. i. (*tome premier*).

The Turks have retired from before Messolonghi – nobody knows why – since they left provisions and ammunition behind them in quantities, and the Garrison made no sallies, or none to any purpose. They never invested Messolonghi this year, but bombarded Anatoliko (a sort of village which I recollect well, having passed through the whole of that country with fifty Albanians in 1809, Messolonghi included) near the Achelous. Some say Vrioni Pacha heard of an insurrection near Scutari, some one thing, some another. For my part, I have been in correspondence with the Chiefs, and their accounts are not unanimous.

The Suliotes, both there, here, and elsewhere, having taken a kind of liking *to*, or at least formed or renewed a sort of acquaintance *with*, me – (as I have aided them and their families in all that I could, according to circumstances) are apparently anxious that I should put myself forward as their Chief (if I may so say). I would rather not for the present, because there are too many divisions and Chiefs already. But if it should appear necessary why – as they are admitted to be the best and bravest of the present combatants – it might, or may, so happen that I could, would, should, or shall take to me the support of such a body of men, with whose aid I think something might be done both *in* Greece and *out* of it (for there is a good deal to put to rights in both). I could maintain them out of my own present means (always supposing my present income and means to be permanent). They are not above a thousand, and of these not six hundred *real* Suliotes; but then they are allowed to be equal (that seems a bravado though, but it is in print recently) *one* to 5 European Moslems, and ten Asiatics! Be it as it may, they are in high esteem, and my very good friends.

A soldier may be maintained on the Mainland for 25 piastres (rather *better than two* dollars a month) monthly, and find his rations out of the country, or for *five dollars*, including his paying for his rations. Therefore for between two and three thousand dollars a month (and the dollar here is to be had for 4 and 2 pence instead of 4 and 6 pence, the price in England), I could maintain between five hundred and a thousand of these warriors for as long as necessary, and I have more means than are (supposing them to last) [sufficient] to do so. For my own personal wants are very simple (except in horses as I am no great pedestrian), and my income considerable for any country but England (being equal to the President's of the United States! the English Secretaries of States or the French Ambassador's at Vienna and the greater Courts – 150,000 Francs, I believe), and I have hope to have sold a Manor besides for nearly 3,000,000 francs more. Thus I could (with what we should extract according to the usages of war also), keep on foot a respectable clan, or Sept, or tribe, or horde, for some time, and, as I have not any motive for so doing but the wellwishing to Greece, I should hope with advantage.

TO THE COUNTESS GUICCIOLI   *October 7*

Pietro has told you all the gossip of the island, – our earthquakes, our politics, and present abode in a pretty village. As his opinions and mine on the Greeks are nearly similar, I need say little on that subject. I was a fool to come here; but, being here, I must see what is to be done.

October —

We are still in Cephalonia, waiting for news of a more accurate description; for all is contradiction and division in the reports of the state of the Greeks. I shall fulfil the object of my mission from the Committee, and then return into Italy; for it does not seem likely that, as an individual, I can be of use to them; – at least no other foreigner has yet appeared to be so, nor does it seem likely that any will be at present.

Pray be as cheerful and tranquil as you can; and be assured that there is nothing here that can excite any thing but a wish to be with you again, – though we are very kindly treated by the English here of all descriptions. Of the Greeks, I can't say much good hitherto, and I do not like to speak ill of them, though they do of one another.

October 29

You may be sure that the moment I can join you again, will be as welcome to me as at any period of our recollection. There is nothing very attractive here to divide my attention; but I must attend to the Greek cause, both from honour and inclination . . . I am anxious to hear how the Spanish cause will be arranged, as I think it may have an influence on the Greek contest. I wish that both were fairly and favourably settled, that I might return to Italy, and talk over with you *our*, or rather Pietro's adventures, some of which are rather amusing, as also some of the incidents of our voyages and travels. But I reserve them, in the hope that we may laugh over them together at no very distant period.

TO THE HON. AUGUSTA LEIGH · *Cephalonia, 8bre 12th 1823*

My Dearest Augusta, – Your three letters on the subject of Ada's indisposition have made me very anxious to hear further of her amelioration. I have been subject to the same complaint, but not at so early an age, nor in so great a degree. Besides, it never affected my eyes but rather my hearing, and that only partially and slightly and for a short time. I had dreadful and almost periodical headaches till I was fourteen, and sometimes since; but abstinence and a habit of bathing my head in cold water every morning cured me, I think, at least I have been less molested since that period. Perhaps she will get quite well when she arrives at womanhood. But that is some time to look forward to, though if she is of so sanguine a habit it is probable that she may attain to that period earlier than is usual in our colder climate; — You will excuse me touching on this topic *medically* and 'en passant' because I cannot help thinking that the determination of blood to the head so early unassisted may have some connection with a similar tendency to earlier maturity. Perhaps it is a phantasy. At any rate let me know how she is. I need not say how *very* anxious I am (at this distance particularly) to hear of her welfare.

You ask why I came up amongst the Greeks? It was stated to me that my so doing might tend to their advantage in some measure in their present struggle for independence, both as an individual and as a member for the Committee now in England. How far this may be realized I cannot pretend to anticipate, but I am willing to do what I can. They have at length found leisure to quarrel among themselves, after repelling their other enemies, and it is no very easy part that I may have to play to avoid appearing partial to one or other of their factions. They have turned out Mavrocordato, who was the only *Washington* or *Kosciusko* kind of man amongst them, and they have not yet sent their deputies to London to treat for a loan, nor in short done themselves so much good as they might have done. I have written to Mr Hobhouse three several times with a budget of documents on the subject, from which he can extract all the present information for the Committee. I have written to their Gov^t at Tripolizza and Salamis, and am waiting for instructions *where* to proceed, for things are in such a state amongst them, that it is difficult to conjecture where one could be useful to them, if at all. However, I have some hopes that they will see their own interest sufficiently not to quarrel till they have received their national independence, and then they can fight it out among them in a domestic manner – and welcome. You may suppose that I have something to *think* of at least, for you can have no idea what an intriguing cunning unquiet generation they are, and as emissaries of all parties come to me at present, and I must act impartially, it makes me exclaim, as Julian did at his military exercises, 'Oh! Plato, what a task for a Philosopher!'

However, *you* won't think much of *my philosophy*; nor do I, *entre nous* . . .

I wish you would obtain from Lady B. some account of Ada's disposition, habits, studies, moral tendencies, and temper, as well as of her personal appearance, for except from the miniature drawn five years ago (and she is now double that age nearly) I have no idea of even her aspect. When I am advised on these points, I can form some notion of her character and what way her dispositions or indispositions ought to be treated. At *her* present age I have an idea that I had many feelings and notions which people would not believe if I stated them *now*, and therefore I may as well keep them to myself. Is she social or solitary, taciturn or talkative, fond of reading or otherwise? And what is her *tic*? – I mean her foible. Is she passionate? I hope that the Gods have made her anything save *poetical* – it is enough to have one such fool in a family. You can answer all this at your leisure: address to *Genoa* as usual, the letters will be forwarded better by my Correspondents, there.

Yours ever,

N.B.

TO THE GENERAL GOVERNMENT OF GREECE *Cephalonia, November 30, 1823*

The affair of the Loan, the expectations so long and vainly indulged of the arrival of the Greek fleet, and the danger to which Messolonghi is still exposed, have detained me here, and will still detain me till some of them are removed. But when the money shall be advanced for the fleet, I will start for the Morea;

not knowing, however, of what use my presence can be in the present state of things. We have heard some rumours of new dissensions, nay, of the existence of a civil war. With all my heart I pray that these reports may be false or exaggerated, for I can imagine no calamity more serious than this; and I must frankly confess that unless union and order are established, all hopes of a Loan will be vain; and all the assistance which the Greeks could expect from abroad . . . will be suspended or destroyed; and, what is worse, the great powers of Europe . . . will be persuaded that the Greeks are unable to govern themselves, and will, perhaps, themselves undertake to settle your disorders in such a way as to blast the brightest hopes of yourselves and of your friends.

Allow me to add, once for all, – *I* desire the well-being of Greece, and nothing else; *I* will do all *I* can to secure it; but I cannot consent, *I* never will consent, that the English public, or English individuals, should be deceived as to the real state of Greek affairs. The rest, Gentlemen, depends on you. You have fought gloriously; – act honourably towards your fellow-citizens and the world, and it will then no more be said, as has been repeated for two thousand years with the Roman historians, that Philopoemen was the last of the Grecians. Let no calumny itself (and it is difficult, I own, to guard against it in so arduous a struggle) compare the patriot Greek, when resting from his labours, to the Turkish pacha, whom his victories have exterminated.

I pray you accept these my sentiments as a sincere proof of my attachment to your real interests, and to believe that I am and always shall be

Yours, etc.

TO THE HON. DOUGLAS KINNAIRD 10bre *10th, 1823*

DEAR DOUGLAS, – This will be delivered by Col. Napier, whom I request you to present to the Committee. He is too well known to require me to say more than I have already said in my letter to Mr Bowring – which see.

I have had only *two* letters from you, both (I think) of August: one, however, is without date. I have often written to acknowledge both, and to sanction or approve your acceptance of the Rochdale proposition.

I have been expending monies on the Greek cause. I shall probably have to expend *more*, and therefore require *more* to *expend*. As I hope that you have gotten together the Kirkby Mallory dues – also arrears – also mine own especial fees and funds, the Rochdale produce and my income for the ensuing year (and I have still of the present year something in hand, including my Genoese credit) ought to make a pretty sufficient sort of sum to take the field withal; and I like to do so with all I can muster, in case of anything requiring the same. I shall be as saving of my purse and person as you recommend; but you know that [it] is as well to be in readiness with one or both in the event of either being required.

Yrs, ever and faithfully,

N.B.

P.S. – Col. Napier will tell you the recent events.

TO THE HON. DOUGLAS KINNAIRD   *10bre 11th, 1823*
[Postscript to a letter not preserved]

P.S. – I presume that you have also come to some agreement with Mr M[urray] about 'Werner'. The year is more than out since he published it. Although the copyright should only be worth two or three hundred pounds, I will tell you what can be done with them. For three hundred pounds I can maintain in Greece at more than *fullest pay* of the Provisional Govt., *rations* included, one hundred armed men *for three months*! It is not that I am in any pressing need of monies, especially of this kind, but it is better to have all financial matters arranged of whatever description – rents, funds, purchase-monies or printer's products. I presume that there is or will be something from 'the Island' also, and from the sale of the other writings; but I do not reckon much on anything of that kind. H. ought to have collected the

521

works by this time, as before directed, and published the whole eleven new D.J.s.

I am particular on this point only because a sum of trifling account even for a Gentleman's *personal* expences in *London* or *Paris* in Greece can arm and maintain hundreds of men. You may judge of this when I tell you that the four thousand pounds advanced by me is likely to set a fleet and an army in motion for some months.

I request you to avoid all unnecessary disbursements (excepting for the Insurances) in England. Whatever remains to be paid to lawyers and creditors (and you yourself say that it is but a sum not exceeding much my *whole*, Kirkby Mallory included, *half* year's income) can be settled after the Greek war, or the Greek Kalends; for the dogs, especially the lawyers, have already had more than ever was justly owing to them. But they shall have fair play – and I too, I hope and trust; but prithee look to these recommended affairs.

TO THE HON. DOUGLAS KINNAIRD 10bre *23rd, 1823*

... A Greek vessel has arrived from the squadron to convey me to Missolonghi, where Mavrocordato now is, and has assumed the command, so that I expect to embark immediately. Address, however, to Cephalonia (through Messrs Webb and Barry of Genoa, as usual); and get together all the means and credit of mine you can, to face the war establishment, for it is 'in for a penny, in for a pound', and I must do all that I can for the Ancients. I have advanced them four thousand pounds, which got the squadron to sea, and I made them forward the Deputies for the Loan, who ought to be soon in England, having sailed some weeks ago. I have already transmitted to you a copy of their agreement etc, – and to Hobhouse and Bowring various dispatches with copies or originals of correspondence more or less important. I am labouring to reconcile their parties, and there is some hope *now* of succeeding. Their *public* affairs go on well. The Turks have retreated from Acarnania without a battle, after a few fruitless attempts on Anatoliko [,] and Corinth is taken, and the Greeks have gained a battle in the Archipelago and the squadron here, too, has taken a Turkish corvette with some money and a cargo. In short, if they can obtain a Loan, I am of opinion that matters will assume and preserve a steady and favourable aspect for their independence.

In the mean time I stand paymaster, and what not; and lucky is that, from the nature of the warfare and of the country, the resources even of an individual can be partial and temporary service ...

Once more (as usual) recommending to you the reinforcement of my strong box and credit from all lawful sources and re-sources of mine to their practicable extent (and after all, it is better playing at nations than gaming at Almack's or Newmarket or piecing or dinnering) and also requesting Your Honour to write now and then one of those pithy epistles 'touching the needful' so agreeable to the distant traveller,

I remain ever yours,

N.B.

TO HENRY MUIR *Dragomestri, January 2, 1824*

My Dear Muir, – I wish you many returns of the season, and happiness therewithal. Gamba and the Bombard (there is a strong reason to believe) are carried into Patras by a Turkish frigate, which we saw chase them at dawn on the 31st: we had been close under the stern in the night, believing her a Greek till within pistol shot, and only escaped by a miracle of all the Saints (our captain says), and truly I am of his opinion, for we should never have got away of ourselves. They were signalising their consort with lights, and had illuminated the ship between decks, and were shouting like a mob; – but then why did they not fire? Perhaps they took us for a Greek brûlot, and were afraid of kindling us – they had no colours flying even at dawn nor after.

At daybreak my boat was on the coast, but the wind unfavour-able for *the port*; – a large vessel with the wind in her favour standing between us and the Gulf, and another in chase of the Bombard about twelve miles off, or so. Soon after they stood (*i.e.* the Bombard and frigate) apparently towards Patras, and, a Zantiote boat making signals to us from the shore to get away, away we went before the wind, and ran into a creek called Scrofes, I believe, where I landed Luke[2] and another (as Luke's life was in most danger), with some money for themselves, and a letter for Stanhope, and sent them up the country to Messolonghi, where they would be in safety, as the place where we were could be assailed by armed boats in a moment, and Gamba had all our arms except two carbines, a fowling-piece, and some pistols.

In less than an hour the vessel in chase neared us, and we dashed out again, and showing our stern (our boat sails very well), got in before night to Dragomestri, where we now are. But where is the Greek fleet? I don't know – do you? I told our master of the boat that I was inclined to think the two large vessels (there were none else in sight) Greeks. But he answered, 'They are too large – why don't they show their colours?' and his account was confirmed, be it true or false, by several boats which we met or passed, as we could not at any rate have got in with that wind without beating about for a long time; and as there was much property, and some lives to risk (the boy's especially) without any means of defence, it was necessary to let our boatmen have their own way.

I despatched yesterday another messenger to Messolonghi for an escort, but we have yet no answer. We are here (those of my boat) for the fifth day without taking our clothes off, and sleeping on deck in all weathers, but are all very well, and in good spirits. It is to be supposed that the Government will send, for their own sakes, an escort, as I have 16,000 dollars on board, the greater part for their service. I had (besides personal property to the amount of about 5000 more) 8000 dollars in specie of my own, without reckoning the Committee's stores: so that the Turks will have a good thing of it, if the prize be good.

I regret the detention of Gamba, etc., but the rest we can make up again; so tell Hancock to set my bills into cash as soon as possible, and Corgialegno to prepare the remainder of my credit with Messrs Webb to be turned into monies. I shall remain here, unless something extraordinary occurs, till Mavrocordato sends, and then go on, and act according to circumstances. My respects to the two colonels, and remembrances to all friends. Tell 'Ultima Analise'[3] that his friend [P]raidi did not make his appearance with the brig, though I think that he might as well have spoken with us *in* or *off* Zante, to give us a gentle hint of what we had to expect.

Yours ever affectionately,

N.B.

P.S. – Excuse my scrawl on account of the pen and the frosty morning at daybreak. I write in haste, a boat starting for Kalamo. I do not know whether the detention of the Bombard (if she be detained, for I cannot swear to it, and I can only judge from appearances, and what all these fellows say), be an affair of the Government, and neutrality, and, etc. – but *she was stopped at least* twelve miles distant from any port, and had all her papers regular from *Zante* for *Kalamo* and *we also*. I did not land at Zante, being anxious to lose as little time as possible; but Sir F[rederick] S[toven][4] came off to invite me, etc., and every body was as kind as could be, even in Cephalonia.

TO CHARLES HANCOCK   *Missolonghi, February 5, 1824*

... We hear that the Turks are coming down in force, and sooner than usual: and as these fellows do mind me a little, it is the opinion that I should go, – firstly, because they will sooner listen to a foreigner than one of their own people, out of native jealousies: secondly, because the Turks will sooner treat or capitulate (if such occasion should happen) with a Frank than a Greek; and, thirdly, because nobody else seems disposed to take the responsibility – Mavrocordato being very busy here, the foreign military men too young or not of authority enough to be obeyed by the natives, and the Chiefs (as aforesaid) inclined to obey any one except, or rather than, one of their own body. As for me, I am willing to do what I am bidden, and to follow my instructions. I neither seek nor shun that nor any thing else that they may wish me to attempt: as for personal safety, besides that

525

it ought not to be a consideration, I take it that a man is on the whole as safe in one place as another; and, after all, he had better end with a bullet than bark in his body. If we are not taken off with the sword, we are like to march off with an ague in this mud basket; and to conclude with a very bad pun, to the ear rather than to the eye, better *martially* than *marsh-ally*; – the situation of Messolonghi is not unknown to you. The dykes of Holland when broken down are the Deserts of Arabia for dryness, in comparison . . .

February 7, 1824

I have been interrupted by the arrival of Parry, and afterwards by the return of Hesketh, who has not brought an answer to my epistles, which rather surprises me. You will write soon, I suppose. Parry seems a fine rough subject, but will hardly be ready for the field these three weeks: he and I will (I think) be able to draw together, – at least, *I* will not interfere with or contradict him in his own department . . .

Well, it seems that I am to be Commander-in-Chief, and the post is by no means a sinecure, for we are not what Major Sturgeon calls 'a set of the most amicable officers'. Whether we shall have 'a boxing bout between Captain Sheers and the Colonel', I cannot tell; but, between Suliote chiefs, German barons, English volunteers, and adventurers of all nations, we are likely to form as goodly an allied army as ever quarrelled beneath the same banner . . .

FROM THE MANUSCRIPT BOOK
CONTAINING THE JOURNAL IN
CEPHALONIA

Febry 15th, 1824

Upon February 15th – (I write on the 17th of the same month) I had a strong shock of a convulsive description, but whether Epileptic, Paralytic, or Apoplectic, is not yet decided by the two medical men, who attend me; or whether it be of some other nature (if such there be). It was very painful, and, had it lasted a minute longer, must have extinguished my mortality – if I can judge by sensations. I was speechless with the features much distorted, but *not* foaming at the mouth, they say, and my struggles so violent that several persons – two of whom, Mr Parry the engineer, and my Servant Tita the Chasseur, are very strong men – could not hold me. It lasted about ten minutes, and came on immediately after drinking a tumbler of Cider mixed with cold water in Col. Stanhope's apartments. This is the first attack that I have had of the kind to the best of my belief. I never heard that any of my family were liable to the same, though my mother was subject to *hysterical affections*.

Yesterday (the 16th) leeches were applied to my temples. I had previously recovered a good deal, but with some feverish and variable symptoms. I bled profusely, and, as they went too near the temporal artery, there was some difficulty in stopping the blood even with the Lunar Caustic. This, however, after some hours was accomplished about eleven o'clock at night, and this day (the 17th), though weakly, I feel tolerably convalescent.

With regard to the presumed causes of this attack, as far as I know, there might be several. The state of the place and the weather permit little exercise at present. I have been violently agitated with more than one passion recently, and a good deal occupied, politically as well as privately, and amidst conflicting parties, politics, and (as far as regards public matters) circumstances. I have also been in an anxious state with regard to things which may be only interesting to my own private feelings, and, perhaps, not uniformly so temperate as I may generally affirm that I was wont to be. How far any or all of these may have acted on the mind or body of one who had already undergone many previous changes of place and passion during a life of thirty-six years, I cannot tell, nor — But I am interrupted by the arrival of a report from a party returned from reconnoitring a Turkish Brig of War, just stranded on the Coast, and which is to be attacked the moment we can get some guns to bear upon her. I shall hear what Parry says about it. Here he comes —

TO THE HON. AUGUSTA LEIGH[5]   *Missolonghi,*
[Monday] Feby 23^d 1824

My Dearest Augusta, – I received a few days ago yours and Lady B's report of Ada's health, with other letters from England for which I ought to be and am (I hope) sufficiently thankful, as they were of great comfort and I wanted some, having been recently unwell, but am now much better. So that you need not be alarmed.

You will have heard of our journeys and escapes, and so forth, perhaps with some exaggeration; but it is all very well now, and I have been for some time in Greece, which is in as good a state as could be expected considering circumstances. But I will not plague you with politics, wars, or *earthquakes*, though we had another very smart one three nights ago, which produced a scene ridiculous enough, as no damage was done except to those who stuck fast in the scuffle to get first out of the doors or windows, amongst whom some recent importations, fresh from England, who had been used to quieter elements, were rather squeezed in the press for precedence.

I have been obtaining the release of about nine and twenty Turkish prisoners – men, women, and children – and have sent them at my own expense home to their friends, but one, a pretty little girl of nine years of age named Hato or Hatagée, has expressed a strong wish to remain with me, or under my care, and I have nearly determined to adopt her. If I thought that Lady B. would let her come to England as a Companion to Ada – (they are about the same age), and we could easily provide for her; if not, I can send her to Italy for education. She is very lively and quick, and with great black oriental eyes, and Asiatic features. All her brothers were killed in the Revolution; her mother wishes to return to her husband who is at Prevesa, but says that she would rather entrust the child to me in the present state of the Country. Her extreme youth and sex have hitherto saved her life, but there is no saying what might occur in the course of the *war* (and of *such* a war), and I shall probably commit her to the charge of some English Lady in the islands for the present. The Child herself has the same wish, and seems to have a decided character for her age. You can mention this matter if you think it worth while. I merely wish her to be respectably educated and treated, and, if my years and all things be considered, I presume it would be difficult to conceive me to have any other views.

With regard to Ada's health, I am glad to hear that it is so much better. But I think it right that Lady B. should be informed, and guard against it accordingly, that her description of much of her indisposition and tendencies very nearly resemble my *own* at a similar age, except that I was much more impetuous. Her preference of *prose* (strange as it may seem) *was* and indeed *is* mine (for I hate *reading* verse, and always did), and I never invented anything but '*boats – ships*' and generally relating to the Ocean. I shewed the report to Col. Stanhope, who was struck with the resemblance of *parts* of it to the *paternal* line even *now*. But it is also fit, though unpleasant, that I should mention that my recent attack, and a very severe one, had a strong appearance of *epilepsy*. *Why* – I know not, for it is late in life – its first appearance at thirty-six – and, as far as I *know*, it is not *hereditary*, and it is that it may not *become* so, that you should tell Lady B. to take some precautions in the case of Ada. My attack has not yet returned, and I am fighting it off with abstinence and exercise, and thus far with success; if merely casual, it is all very well.

TO THE EARL OF CLARE   *Missolonghi, March 31, 1824*

My Dearest Clare, – This will be presented to you by a live Greek deputy, for whom I desiderate and solicit your countenance and goodwill. I hope that you do not forget that I always regard you as my dearest friend and love you as when we were Harrow boys together; and if I do not repeat this as often as I ought, it is that I may not tire you with what you so well know.

I refer you to Signor Zaimie, the Greek deputy, for all news, public and private. He will do better than an epistle in this respect.

I was sorry to hear that Dick had exported a married woman from Ireland, not only on account of morals but monies. I trust that the jury will be considerate. I *thought* that Richard[6] looked sentimental when I saw him at Genoa, but little expected what he was to land in. Pray who *is* the lady? The papers merely inform us by dint of asterisks that she is somebody's wife and has children, and that Dick (as usual) was the intimate friend of the confiding husband. It is to be hoped that the jury will be bachelors.

Pray take care of *yourself* Clare, my dear, for in some of your letters I had a glimpse of a similar intrigue of yours. Have a care of an *éclat*. Your Irish juries lay it on heavy; and then besides you would be fixed for life with a *second-hand épouse*, whereas I wish to see you lead a virgin heiress from Saville Row to Mount Shannon.

Let me hear from you at your best leisure, and believe me ever and most truly, my dearest Clare,

Yours,

NOEL BYRON

P.S. – The Turkish fleet are just bearing down to blockade this port; so how our deputy is to get by is a doubt, but the island boats frequently evade them.

The sight is pretty, but much finer for a limner than a lodger. It is the Squadron from the Gulf of Corinth (Hooke-Gulf of Lepanto); they (the Greeks, I mean) are all busy enough, as you may suppose, as the campaign is expected to commence next month. But as aforesaid I refer you for news to the bearer.

TO CHARLES F. BARRY[7]   *April 9th 1824*

Dear Barry, – The Account up to 11th July was 40,541, etc.,
Genoese livres in my favour: since then I have had a letter of
Credit of Messrs Webb for 60,000 Genoese livres, for which I
have drawn; but how the account stands *exactly*, you do not
state. The balance will of course be replaced by my London
Correspondent, referring more particularly to the Honble
Douglas Kinnaird, who is also my Agent and trustee, as well as
banker, and a friend besides since we were at College together –
which is favourable to business, as it gives confidence, or ought
to do so.

I had hoped that you had obtained the price of the Schooner
from Ld Blessington: you must really tell him that I must make the
affair public, and take other steps which will be agreeable to
neither, unless he speedily pays the money, so long due, and
contracted by his own headstrong wish to purchase. You *know*
how fairly I treated him in the whole affair.

Every thing except the best (*i.e.* the Green travelling Chariot)
may be disposed of, and that speedily, as it will assist to balance
our accompt. As the Greeks have gotten their loan, they may as
well repay mine, which they no longer require: and I request
you to forward a copy of the agreement to Mr Kinnaird, and
direct him from me to claim the money from the Deputies. They
were welcome to it in their difficulties, and also for good and all,
supposing that they had not got out of them; but, as it is, they
can afford repayment, and I assure you that, besides this, they
have had many 'a strong and long pull' at my purse, which has
been (and still is) disbursing pretty freely in their cause: besides,
I shall have to re-expend the same monies, having some hundred
men under orders, at my own expense, for the Gk Government
and National service.

Of all their proceedings here, health, politics, plans, acts, and
deeds, etc. – good or otherwise, Gamba or others will tell you –
truly or not truly, according to their habits.

Yours ever,

N.Bn.

NOTES

1. (p. 14) *Calamo currente* – with flowing pen.

1. THE FORMATIVE YEARS, JANUARY 1798–1811

1 (p. 39) Byron was wrong in his judgement of his servant, who was subsequently convicted of theft, and transported to Botany Bay.

2, 3, 4, 5, 6, (p. 39) Gaps caused by removal of seal.

7 (p. 45) *Paulo majora canamus*: Let us sing of slightly weightier matters. (Virgil, *Eclogues*, IV, i)

8 (p. 48) *Virum volitare per ora*: To be spoken of by men. Literally, to flit across the mouths of men. Ennius, *volito vivu per ora virum*.

9 (p. 48) *Dulce est desipere in loco*: It is pleasant to be foolish on occasion. (Horace, *Odes* IV, xii, 28)

10 (p. 49) The Earl of Carlisle.

11 (p. 49) Perhaps Dr. G. Butler, Headmaster of Harrow, with whom Byron was then on bad terms.

12 (p. 50) Known first as *English Bards*, this poem was added to and published as *English Bards and Scotch Reviewers*.

13 (p. 52) The first reference to William Fletcher, Byron's servant until his death.

14 (p. 52) Mrs Chaworth Musters.

15 (p. 55) *Alma mater* (Dear mother, i.e., Cambridge) was to me *injusta noverca* (an unjust step-mother).

16 (p. 57) *Ambra di merdo*: as written Portuguese this is nonsense, but presumably when spoken Byron made his insult plain.

17 (p. 57) *Suave mari magno*: the beginning of a line of Lucretius, of which the sense is: 'it is pleasant' for one who has escaped 'from the vast sea' to look back over dangers past.

18 (p. 60) Robert Rushton, a protégé of Byron's.

19 (p. 67) *oblitus meorum obliviscendus et illis*: forgetting my own people, and to be forgotten by them. (Horace, *Epistles* I, xi, 9)

21 (p. 68) ταπεινοτατος δουλος: very humble servant.

21 (p. 70) In *English Bards and Scotch Reviewers*:

'No muse will cheer, with renovating smile,
The paralytic puling of Carlisle.'

22 (p. 72) *Tenerezza:* tenderness.

23 (p. 73) παιδη: child (feminine, as if to indicate his effeminacy?)

24 (p. 74) ὁ μονόλοο Στράνε: (Romaic) The unique Strané (British Consul at Patras).

25 (p. 74) *Plaudite et valete:* applaud and farewell.

26 (p. 74) *Vecchio con Vecchio, Giovane con Giovane*: old men with old men, young with young.

27 (p. 75) παλικαρι: properly παλλικάρι – a young man; εὔμορφω παιδι: handsome youth.

28 (p. 75) Τί να κάμω?: what shall I do?

29 (p. 76) *'il Padre Abbate'* ... *'schuola'* ... *'Ragazzi'*: the Father Abbot ... school ... boys.

30 (p. 76) *Simplice Fanciullo:* a simple boy.

31 (p. 77) μεγαλος ... φιλος ... διὰ τὶ ἀσπάσετε?: great (meaning 'noble') ... friend ... why will you embrace?

32 (p. 77) *Morire insieme:* to die together.

33 (p. 77) *'Venite abasso'* ... *'bisogno bastonare'*: Come downstairs – it is necessary to beat.

34 (p. 77) *the 'citoyen'*: C. S. Matthews.

35 (p. 78) *'Forse'* ... *'non so, come, etc.'* ... *Buona sera a vos(tra) signoria. Bacio le mani*: perhaps ... I don't know, how ... good evening to your lordship. I kiss your hands.

36 (p. 78) *questo Giovane e vergognó*: this young man is modest.

37 (p. 79) ασπαζω: I embrace.

38 (p. 79) *nil actum reputans dum quid superesset agendum ... pl & opte*: reflecting that nothing had been done while something remained to be done ... (abbreviation for *coitum plenum et optabilem*) full and desirable intercourse.

39 (p. 79) *Et Lycam* nigris *oculis, nigroque* crine *decorum:* (properly 'Lycum'.) Horace, *Odes* I, xxxii (and sang of) Lycus, handsome with his black eyes and black hair.

40 (p. 80) Μπαίρων: Byron (in Romaic).

2. FAME AND SOCIETY, AUGUST 1811–JANUARY 1815

1 (p. 88) *One of my best friends*: Charles Skinner Matthews.

2 (p. 89) *the Cornish*: A reference to the regiment in which Hobhouse was reluctantly serving in Ireland.

NOTES

3 (p. 93) *Post mortem nihil est, ipsaque Mors nihil ... quaeris quo jaceas post obitum loco? Quo non nata jacent*: (Seneca, *Troades* – II, i.397) After death there is nothing, and Death itself is nothing ... Do you seek to know in what place you will lie after death? In that place where things not born lie.

4 (p. 93) ʽΟν ὁ θεός ἀγαπάει ἀποθνήσκει νεος. (Menander): He whom the gods love dies young.

5 (p. 96) *Felicissima Notte a Voss*, [sic] *Signoria*: A very happy night to your Lordship.

6 & 7 (pp. 96, 98) The death of John Edleston, the Cambridge chorister, in May 1811.

8 (p. 103) *Knight of Snowdon*: a musical drama by Thomas Morton.

9 (p. 104) *Propria quae maribus*: things which are suitable for males.

10 (p. 104) *the only human being*: a reference to John Edleston.

11 (p. 110) *'spolia opima'*: (literally, rich spoils) the spoils taken by the victorious general from the defeated.

12 (p. 111) *Bellua multorum capitum*: beast of many heads.

13 (p. 114) *Childe Harold*, Cantos I and II, was due to be published on 1 March 1812, but Murray held it back until the 12th.

14 (p. 115) *Basta!*: Enough!

15 (p. 116) The blank is usually taken to stand for Lady Caroline Lamb.

16 (p. 117) The events refer possibly to the disappearance of Lady Caroline Lamb from Melbourne House and the subsequent efforts to locate her.

17 (p. 119) *they*: the Bessboroughs, with Lady Caroline Lamb.

18 (p. 123) *the modern Griselda*: Miss Edgeworth's novel was published in 1804.

19 (p. 124) *Chi va piano va sano, E chi va sano va lontano*: He who goes slowly goes safely, And he who goes safely goes far.

20 (p. 126) *Cortejo*: lover.

21 (p. 128) *'Agnus'*: lamb, referring to Lady Caroline.

22 (p. 128) *palatia Circes*: the palace of Circe.

23 (p. 128) *tidings*: of the sale of Newstead Abbey.

24 (p. 131) *Fair cousin of eleven page memory:* Lady Gertrude Howard.

25 (p. 134) *the dragon of Wantley*: a reference to *The Dragon of Wantley*, a burlesque opera by Henry Carey.

26 (p. 134) *the Bow Street officer*: there was a certain Bow Street official called Townshend.

27 (p. 134) *I have been into the country*: staying with his half-sister, Mrs Augusta Leigh, at Six Mile Bottom, near Newmarket.

28 (p. 135) Annabella Milbanke had sent Lady Melbourne, with a sketch of Byron's character, her requirements for an ideal husband.

29 (p. 136) *I leave town for a few days*: on a further visit to Augusta at Six Mile Bottom.

30 (p. 143) *Marito*: husband.

31 (p. 143) *Major O'Flaherty*: a character in *The West Indian*, a play by Richard Cumberland.

32 (p. 145) *Lord Ogleby*: a character in *The Clandestine Marriage* by Colman and Garrick.

33 (p. 146) *Mrs L:— like*: possibly refers to Mrs George Lamb, Lady Caroline's sister-in-law.

34 (p. 146) Aston Hall, Rotherham, was once the property of Lady Carmarthen, who eloped with Captain John Byron, Byron's father.

35 (p. 150) *I have been endeavouring to serve him essentially*: Byron was endeavouring to negotiate a loan of £1,000 for Webster.

36 (p. 150) *Lovemore to Ly Constant:* characters from *The Way to Keep Him* by A. Murphy.

37 (p. 158) *another Turkish story: The Bride of Abydos*: published December 1813.

38 (p. 159) '*Zuleika*': The title was changed to *The Bride of Abydos;* the first Turkish tale was *The Giaour*, published in May 1813.

39 (p. 159) Pope, *Eloisa to Abelard*, l.9.

40 (p. 160) '*quaeque .... fui*': Events which I witnessed myself: And of which I was a great part. (Virgil, *Aenid,* II, 5).

41 (p. 162) εἴδωλον: an image, phantom.

42 (p. 163) *two persons*: perhaps Wedderburn Webster, to whom he lent £1,000, and Rev. Francis Hodgson, to whom he gave £1,500, to enable him to marry.

43 (p. 164) *frozen music*: 'Monday, March 23, 1829. "I have found a paper of mine among some others", said Goethe today, "in which I call architecture 'petrified music'".' *Conversations of Goethe with Eckermann.* Schelling, about the same time, spoke of architecture as 'frozen music'.

44 (p. 164) '*Orange Boven*': the rallying cry of the Dutch against the French.

45 (p. 165) *Herodes Atticus . . . Pomponius*: The first was a rich Greek, the latter a rich Roman.

46 (p. 165) *Bonneval . . . Wortley Montague*: all adventurers or men of action.

47 (p. 167) *Lord Ogleby*: a character in *The Clandestine Marriage.*

48 (p. 168) *Amant alterna Camenæ*: The Muses love alternating verses. (Virgil, *Eclogues*. iii. 59).

49 (p. 168) *Aut Caesar aut nihil*: either Caesar or nothing.

50 (p. 169) *fractus illabatur orbis*, from Horace, *Odes* III, iii, 7. The couplet runs

Si fractus illabatur orbis
Impavidum ferient ruinae.

which may be paraphrased as: Though the skies may split and fall, fearless the wreck shall smite him.

51 (p. 169) Possibly Lady Frances Webster.

52 (p. 169) *Andiamo dunque – se torniamo, bene – se non, ch'importa?*: Then let us go – if we return, well and good – if not, what's it matter?

53 (p. 171) οι πολλοι: the mob. Byron then constructed a triangle, thus:

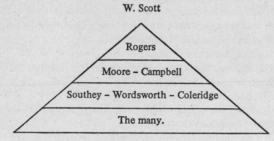

W. Scott

Rogers

Moore – Campbell

Southey – Wordsworth – Coleridge

The many.

54 (p. 171) *Valmont*: possibly the Vicomte de Valmont in *Les Liaisons dangereuses*.

55 (p. 172) Perhaps Wedderburn Webster. See p. 163.

56 (p. 172) Νωαίρων: maybe a mistake for Μπαίρων, 'Byron' in modern Greek.

57 (p. 174) *hiatus haud deflendus*: a gap not worth weeping over.

58 (p. 174) *qualis ab incepto*: such as [she was] from the beginning.

59 (p. 175) *I must go and see him again*: Leigh Hunt was in prison for a libel on the Prince Regent in *The Examiner*.

60 (p. 176) *'Oh Gioventu!'* etc.: Oh Youth! Oh Spring! youth of the year, Oh Youth! spring of life.

61 (p. 177) *the Monk: Ambrosio, or the Monk*, by M. G. 'Monk' Lewis.

62 (p. 178) *Scrub:* a character in *The Beaux' Strategem*.

63 (p. 178) *vertex sublimis*: exalted head (a reference to Horace, *Odes* I, i, 36).

64 (p. 182) *at least three weeks*: spent at Newstead, snowbound, in the company of Augusta Leigh, until 6 February 1814.

65 (p. 185) 'Privacy' is the usual reading of this word; but 'piracy' has been suggested as an alternate reading (and see following page).

66 (p. 188) *ad sudorem*: to the point of sweating.

67 (p. 188) *Out of town six days*: with Augusta Leigh at Six Mile Bottom.

68 (p. 189) *Expende – quot libras in duce summo invenies?*: Weigh him – how many pounds will you find in the greatest leader? (Juvenal, *Satires*, X, 147).

69 (p. 190) *She*: Augusta Leigh.

70 (p. 191) *Ph.*: Lady Frances Webster.

71 (p. 192) *her*: usually taken to refer to Augusta Leigh.

72 (p. 192) *I still mean to set off to-morrow*: see note 64 above.

73 (p. 194) *I found myself in . . . a scrape*: Byron's *Stanzas to a Lady Weeping*, had been published with *The Corsair*, thus revealing his authorship.

74 (p. 195) It is presumed that Augusta Leigh is referred to here.

75 (p. 196) *Divide et impera*: Divide and rule.

76 (p. 197) *quoad homo*: in so far as he is a man.

77 (p. 197) *ludite nunc alios*: now mock (mimic or ridicule) the others.

78 (p. 198) *about going*: to Seaham, Co. Durham, on an invitation by Sir Ralph Milbanke.

79 (p. 199) *'My A'*: Augusta Leigh, as opposed Lady Melbourne's 'A', Annabella Milbanke.

80 (p. 200) This almost certainly should be a comma.

81 (p. 200) Usually taken to refer to Augusta Leigh.

82 (p. 203) The name has been erased. Probably 'Augusta'.

83 (p. 203) *guessed*: 'grieved' in *Lord Byron's Correspondence*, vol. I, p. 262. 'Guessed' would seem more plausible.

84 (p. 204) *my old friend Ocean*: Byron was at Hastings with Augusta Leigh and her children from 20 July to 11 August.

85 (p. 204) Letter from Ethel Colburn Mayne, *Life & Letters of Anne Isabella Noel Lady Byron*, quoted by Marchand, pp. 471–2.

86 (p. 206) ἰατρός: doctor.

87 (p. 206) *X*: usually taken for Augusta Leigh.

3. MARRIAGE AND EXILE, JANUARY 1815–NOVEMBER 1816

1 (p. 215) *George*: the Hon. George Lamb.

2 (p. 215) *Countess and Count of the Holy Roman Empire*: Lord and Lady Cowper.

3 (p. 215) *Caro*: Lady Caroline Lamb.

4 (p. 215) *Caro George*: the Hon. Mrs George Lamb.

5 (p. 215) *William:* the Hon. William Lamb, later Lord Melbourne, the Prime Minister.

6 (p. 216) *oblitus meorum obliviscendus et illis.* See note 20 to Chapter I. p. 533. (Horace, Epistolarum, XI, 9)

7 (p. 217) *X*: The reference is to Augusta Leigh.

8 (p. 217) *an unpublished poem*: *Christabel*, first published 1816.

9 (p. 218) Byron had been appointed to the committee of Drury Lane Theatre.

10 (p. 221) *Juno Lucina*: the Goddess of birth; *fer opem*: give her aid; *opes* : wealth.

11 (p. 222) *your letter*: Sir Ralph's letter informed Byron of his wife's and her parents' wish for a separation.

12 (p. 226) *Magis pares quam similes*: equal in importance rather than similar in character.

13 (p. 229) *'Glenarvon'*: the novel by Lady Caroline Lamb, published 9 May 1816.

14 (p. 232) *I have had but one*: Claire Clairmont.

15 (p. 245) Byron at times used a similar signature in his letters to Augusta Leigh.

4. THE VENETIAN INTERLUDE, NOVEMBER 1816–DECEMBER 1819

1 (p. 256) *Aunt Sophy*: presumably Byron's, and Augusta's unmarried aunt, Sophia Maria Byron, youngest child of Admiral the Hon. John Byron.

2 (p. 256) *the Demoiselle*: Claire Clairmont. Byron's daughter by her, Clara Allegra, was born on 12 January 1817.

3 (p. 257) *nau*: Byron's word for sexual intercourse, or for those who are adulterous.

4 (p. 259) *Ganion Coheriza*: motto of Macdonald, chiefs of Clanranald – 'Gainsay who dares'.

5 (p. 260) *horrenda strage*: with dreadful carnage.

6 (p. 262) *bel' sangue*: well-born.

7 (p. 262) *Amoroso*: lover.

8 (p. 262) *estro*: itch or urge.

9 (p. 263)*your father's misfortune*: John Moore, the poet's father, had been dismised from some minor governmental post. He was thence-forth kept by his son.

10 (p. 264) *ridotto*: masquerade.

11 (p. 264) *conversazione*: a party.

12 (p. 266) Byron had heard that a bill had been filed in Chancery that would have deprived him of his paternal rights over his daughter Ada.

13 (p. 267) ταὐτόματον ἡμῶν κάλλιον βουλεύεται: perhaps best rendered by 'Fortune is juster than we'.

14 (p. 269) *Belvidera*: a character from Otway's *Venice Preserved* (1682).

15 (p. 273) *a female professor of anatomy*: perhaps Laura Bassi (1711–1778).

16 (p. 273) Byron was unaware of Lady Byron's and Mrs Villier's attempts to extract a confession from Augusta, and to 'reform' her by preventing her writing to or seeing her brother. Augusta was compelled to show all Byron's letters to Lady Byron as a price for maintaining her place in society and her position at Court, where as lady-in-waiting to Queen Charlotte she was the sole support of her large family.

17 (p. 275) *I came up to Venice from my casino*: Byron had taken a villa at La Mira on the mainland by the River Brenta.

18 (p. 276) *that he*: Although from the context it is not clear whom the 'he' refers to, it is most likely Moore, even though he is mentioned again immediately afterwards.

19 (p. 278) *the most unfortunate day of my past existence*: the date of his marriage, 2 January 1815.

20 (p. 279) *Your domestic calamity*: the death of Moore's daughter Barbara.

21 (p. 280) *Guerra di Candia*: the war of Candia. The Cretan capital taken from the Venetians by the Turks, on 29 December 1669, after a twenty-five years' siege.

22 (p. 280) Letter written by Byron, as if from his valet, William Fletcher.

23 (p. 282). Reference to *The Beaux' Stratagem*.

24 (p. 282) *Vates*: one who prophesies in verse, a seer.

25 (p. 283) *Savage*: possibly Dr Johnson's *Life of Richard Savage*, (1744).

26 (p. 284) Character in Arthur Murphy's comedy, *The Citizen*.

27 (p. 284) *Wildman*: Newstead Abbey was bought by Byron's old school-fellow, Colonel Wildman, in November 1817, for £94,500.

28 (p. 284) *Spooney*: Byron's nickname for his solicitor, John Hanson.

29 (p. 284) *the Chevalier*: the Chevalier Angelo Mengaldo.

30 (p. 287) From Fielding's *Tom Jones*.

31 (p. 289) *cum multis aliis*: with many others.

32 (p. 289) *Ladro and porco fottuto*: (literally) thief and fucked pig – so in Marchand vol. ii, p. 767, and Byron continues, 'I have had them all and thrice as many to boot since 1817'. Quennell (*Byron, a Self-Portrait*, vol. ii, p. 440) had *'Ludro and porco fottato'* and omits the next sentence. Marchand is quoting from a Murray MS.

33 (p. 294) *Countess from Ravenna*: the Countess Teresa Guiccioli.

34 (p. 293) This letter and that of 7 August 1820 are from the Marchesa Origo's *Byron, the Last Attachment* (Murray and Cape, 1949).

35 (p. 293) *Fanny*: Fanny Silvestrini, the Countess Teresa's confidante.

36 (p. 294) *Che giova a te,* etc.:

> What does it profit you, my heart, to be beloved
> What profits me to have so dear a lover.
> My harsh destiny, why do you
> Keep us apart, when love would bring us together?
> > Guarini, *Il pastor fido.*

37 (p. 295) From Sheridan's *The Rivals.*

38 (p. 295) *Shelley's agitation*: In 1816, when Byron was on Lake Geneva with the Shelleys, they spent some evenings telling ghost stories. Suddenly Shelley was seized with a panic and rushed from the room. Later he explained that looking at Mary he remembered a tale wherein a woman had eyes in place of nipples.

39 (p. 296) This letter was originally published by Lord Lovelace in *Astarte*. Certainly in a letter to John Murray on 18 May Byron refers to a letter written to Augusta the previous day and addressed to Murray's care. And see Byron's letter of 26 July 1819.

40 (p. 299) *'Martini . . . quiete'*: Martini Luigi/Begs for peace. Lucrezia Picini/Begs for eternal rest.

41 (p. 302) *Gertrude*: Geltruda Vicari.

42 (p. 303) *gelosie*: jealousies.

43 (p. 303) *One man*: perhaps Southey who spread tales of 'incest' at the Villa Diodati; or Brougham.

44 (p. 304) *Cara, tu sei troppo bella e giovane per aver' bisogno del soccorso mio*: Dear, you are too pretty and young to need my help.

45 (p. 305) *Villeggiatura*: a country holiday.

46 (p. 306) *Fornarina*: baker's wife.

47 (p. 308) *donna di governo*: housekeeper.

48 (p. 308) *'temporale'*: storm.

49 (p. 309) *disjecti membra poetae*: limbs of the dismembered poet. Horace, *Satires* I. iv. 62.

50 (p. 311) *Dougal of Bishop's Castle*: the Hon. Douglas Kinnaird, M.P. for Bishop's Castle.

51 (p. 320) *this book*: This letter, according to Moore, was written in the Countess's copy of *Corinne*.

52 (p. 321) *the idea*: of emigrating to South America.

53 (p. 323) *The Ferrara Story*: a report was circulating that Byron had abducted Countess Guiccioli.

5. CAVALIERE-SERVENTE, DECEMBER 1819–JULY 1823

1 (p. 331) *write my life*: the memoirs presented to Moore, and burnt after Byron's death.

2 (p. 331) *the good old King*: King George III died on 29 January 1820.

3 (p. 331) Hobhouse, who had been committed to Newgate for a breach of parliamentary privilege, was released at the dissolution of February 1820, and at the ensuing election was returned as a representative for Westminster.

4 (p. 332) *So Scrope is gone*: Scrope Berdmore Davies had escaped his creditors by leaving the country, first for Bruges. Subsequently he settled in Paris, and is said to have occupied his leisure by writing on his contemporaries, papers which have unfortunately been lost.

5 (p. 341) *Few Friends*: the Shelleys.

6 (p. 344) *Quarterly Review*, vol XVI, p. 172.

7 (p. 345) Dr John Polidori.

8 (p. 346) Shelley and Mary Godwin, their son, and Claire Clairmont.

9 (p. 347) perhaps Dr Johnson.

10 (p. 348) Byron had been Coleridge's benefactor, in more ways than one.

11 (p. 350) *Sicarii*: assassins.

12 (p. 351) *their separation*: the Pope's legal separation of Count Alessandro Guiccioli from his wife, Teresa.

13 (p. 352) *clamosa Fama*: noisy report.

14 (p. 352) *Ignis fatuus*: will o' the wisp.

15 (p. 352) *in quanti piedi di acqua siamo*: in how many feet of water we are.

16 (p. 354) *Shiloh*: Shelley.

17 (p. 355) *The Shiloh story is true no doubt*: Elise Foggi, a Swiss nursemaid formerly employed by the Shelleys, had spread stories, alleging that Claire Clairmont had had an affair with Shelley, and that he had consigned their child to the Foundling's Hospital in Naples. The

mystery of the child, Elena Adelaide Shelley, who was baptized in the church of S. Giuseppe a Chiaia, has never been satisfactorily solved.

18 (p. 355) *the Queen's affair*: Queen Caroline, see Index of Persons.

19 (p. 366) From *The Beaux' Strategem*.

20 (p. 368) Possibly Count Giuseppe Alborghetti, Secretary General of Lower Romagna, undoubtedly a 'trimmer', who was often Byron's informant of the government's intentions and perhaps also the recipient of his money.

21 (p. 370) *Alli*: Almost certainly Count Alborghetti.

22 (p. 371) *Love and passion*: for John Edleston.

23 (p. 372) *Constance*: Mrs Constance Spencer Smith.

24 (p. 374) *'Eheu . . . anni'*: Alas, Oh Postumus, Postumus, the fleeting years slip away . . . (Horace, *Odes* II, xiv, 1–2).

25 (p. 375) *Ancona, nearer the northern frontier*: This is puzzling, since Ancona is not nearer the northern frontier.

26 (p. 377) *'P. P. clerk of this parish'*: An allusion to Pope's 'P. P. Clerk of this Parish'.

27 (p. 377) *'Many small articles . . . oh'*: From George Colman's play, *The Review*.

28 (p. 380) 'Thus marked, with impatient strokes of the pen, by himself in the original'. Moore's *Life*.

29 (p. 381) *my drama*: Marino Faliero.

30 (p. 383) *the meeting of the Ci*: Presumably the Carbonari at Forli (or Faenza) and at Bologna.

31 (p. 383) Perhaps Count Alborghetti.

32 (p. 384) *Veglioni*: masked ball.

33 (p. 384) *Socio*: a member.

34 (p. 386) *A.*: presumably Count Alborghetti.

35 (p. 387) *'Ostasio degli Onesti'*: a character in Boccaccio's *Decameron*, Fifth Day, novel viii.

36 (p. 387) Again, it is to be presumed Count Alborghetti.

37 (p. 388) *Squire Sullen*: a character in *The Beaux' Strategem*.

38 (p. 389) *Nam . . . floribus*: For a dead life rejoices in flowers.

39 (p. 389) *deceased poet*: The reference is to Robert Burns.

40 (p. 394) The story of Bowles' sexual experience in Paris was told to Byron by Moore.

41 (p. 395) *'primum mobile'*: the first mover.

42 (p. 397) *The Shipwreck*: by William Falconer, 1762.

43 (p. 401) *'O fons Bandusiae, splendidior vitro'* O fountain of Bandusia, more transparently shining than glass. (Horace, *Odes*, III, xiii, 1).

44 (p. 403) *a tragedy*: *The Siege of Damascus* (1720).

45 (p. 403) *Fenton another*: *Marianne* (1723).

46 (p. 407) *Line trunks . . . Soho*: Pope, *Imitations of Horace*, Book II, Epistle I, 418–9.

47 (p. 409) *this couplet*:

> From furious Sappho scarce a milder fate,
> Poxed by her love, or libell'd by her hate.
>> Pope, *Imitations of Horace*, Book II, Satire I, 83–4.

48 (p. 417) *Poor Scott*: Alexander Scott.

49 (p. 418) *Mr G.*: presumably Octavius Gilchrist, who also defended Pope against Bowles's attacks.

50 (p. 420) *mingere in patrios cineres*: to piss on one's father's ashes. (Horace, *Ars Poetica*, 471)

51 (p. 437) *Albertine*: daughter of Mme de Staël, afterwards the Duchesse de Broglie.

52 (p. 438) *B., M., A., and P.*: possibly Brummell, Mildmay, Alvanley and Pierrepoint.

53 (p. 439) *M.C.*: Mary Anne Chaworth, later Mrs Chaworth Musters.

54 (p. 440) *a priest*: Rev. Francis Hodgson.

55 (p. 448) *'Omne solum forti patria'*: The full inscription ran: *Omne solum forti patria, quia Patris* – every country is a fatherland to the brave, because it is of the Father.

56 (p. 454) *the stanza to which you object*: Hobhouse to Byron, 19 June 1821: 'By the way, do not cut at poor Queeny in your Don Juan about Semiramis and her courser courier. She would feel it very much I assure you.'

57 (p. 460) *my Pulci*: Byron's translation of the first canto of Luigi Pulci's *Morgante Maggiore*, with the Italian beside it, was published in the Hunts' *The Liberal*, No. iv. pp. 193–249.

58 (p. 461) *quarum partes fuimus*: of which we were participators.

59 (p. 465) *quoad me*: as for myself.

60 (p. 468) The words in italics have been (partly) erased – by whom it is not known.

61 (p. 469) This letter was never sent, but enclosed in a letter to Lady Blessington (6 May 1823).

62 (p. 471) On the death of her mother, Lady Byron succeeded to the Wentworth estates, and, as was required by the terms of the will, Byron adopted the additional surname of Noel.

63 (p. 471) Reference to Dante, *Inferno*, xxxiii, 32.

64 (p. 474) *Guillim*: from Scott's *Rob Roy*.

65 (p. 475) Byron proposed calling out Southey, for calumnies he was alleged to have made. Hobhouse intercepted the challenge.

66 (p. 478) *Callum Beg*: from Scott's *Waverley*.

67 (p. 479) The churchwardens and parishioners of Harrow Church refused to accede to Byron's request; and Allegra was buried at the entrance to the church, without a memorial tablet.

68 (p. 485) *Censor Morum*: censor of morals, namely, the Countess Guiccioli.

69 (p. 489) *pars magna es*: you are a great part.

70 (p. 489) *Arcades ambo*: Arcadians both (i.e., rogues)

71 (p. 489) *'et cant-are pares'*: and equal in singing – with pun on 'cant'.

72 (p. 490) *the Vision*: *The Vision of Judgement*, which Byron had pre-presented to John and Leigh Hunt. The former was prosecuted for publishing it, at the instigation of a society called the Constitutional Association, for whom a lawyer, Charles Murray, acted. Hunt was convicted and fined. Byron paid both for the defence and fine.

73 (p. 491) *nominis umbrae*: shadows of a name.

74 (p. 491) *a 'French Count'*: Count Alfred d'Orsay.

75 (p. 498) *Mr J. M.*: presumably John Murray.

6. THE POET AS HERO, JULY 1823–APRIL 1824

1 (p. 511) *as Resident*: The Heptanesus, or 'Seven Islands' (The Ionian Islands), were administered by the British Government from 1815 until 1864, when the administration was ceded to the Kingdom of Greece.

2 (p. 524) *Luke*: Loukas Chalandritsanos, Byron's young Greek protégé.

3 (p. 525) *'Ultima Analise'*: in the final analysis. A favourite expression of Byron's friend on Cephalonia, Count Delladecima, and used by Byron as a nickname.

4 (p. 525) *Sir F. S.*: British Resident on Lante.

5 (p. 528) This letter was never sent, being found unfinished on Byron's desk after his death.

6 (p. 530) *Richard*: Richard Hobart Fitzgibbon, Third Earl of Clare, brother of Byron's intimate friend.

7 (p. 531) Byron's last letter. He died ten days after it was written.

INDEX OF PERSONS

Westmoreland, Lady, *née* Jane
Saunders, married 10th Earl of
Westmoreland (1800), 133

Whitbread, Samuel (1758–1815),
Whig M.P.; on Drury Lane
Committee, 202

White, Henry Kirke (1785–1806),
English minor poet, 347, 456

Wilberforce, William
(1759–1833), social reformer,
opponent of the slave trade,
283, 448

Wildman, Colonel Thomas
(1787–1859), Byron's
schoolfellow at Harrow,
bought Newstead Abbey in
1817 for £94,500, 26, 251, 284

Wilkes, John (1727–97), social
reformer especially in reform
of Parliament, 332, 414

William the Conqueror, 341

William of Orange, 169

Williams, Captain Edward, 328,
329, 484, 485

Williams, Mrs E. (Jane), 329, 330

Wilmot (Horton?), Robert
John, Byron's first cousin, 271,
274

Wilson, Harriet, Regency
courtesan, 15

Wilson, John ('Christopher
North') (1785–1854), Scottish
writer and frequent
contributor to *Blackwood's
Magazine*, 465

Windham, William (1750–1810),
M.P., 170

Wingfield, Jonathan, Harrow
school-fellow, later Lord
Powerscourt, 25, 85, 89, 90

Wollstonecraft, Mary (1759–97),
miscellaneous writer, m.
William Godwin (1796), but
died on giving birth to her
only child, a daughter, Mary,
later Mrs P. B. Shelley, 295–6,
347

Woodhouselee, Lord, Alexander
Fraser Tytler, 1st Lord,
Scottish miscellaneous writer,
42

Wordsworth, William
(1770–1850), 9, 20–21, 44–5,
171, 218–20, 276, 283, 345,
348, 399, 421, 423, 460

Wycherley, William
(1640?–1716), Restoration
dramatist, 413

Yarmouth, Lord, 243

Young, Dr Edward (1683–1765),
author of *Night Thoughts*,
reputed a brilliant talker, 43,
394, 434

Zamie, a Greek deputy in the
negotiations for the London
loan to the Greek
Government, 530

MORE ABOUT PENGUINS
AND PELICANS

For further information about books available from Penguins please write to Dept EP, Penguin Books Ltd, Harmondsworth, Middlesex UB7 0DA.

In the U.S.A.: For a complete list of books available from Penguins in the United States write to Dept CS, Penguin Books, 625 Madison Avenue, New York, New York 10022.

In Canada: For a complete list of books available from Penguins in Canada write to Penguin Books Canada Ltd, 2801 John Street, Markham, Ontario L3R 1B4.

In Australia: For a complete list of books available from Penguins in Australia write to the Marketing Department, Penguin Books Australia Ltd, P.O. Box 257, Ringwood, Victoria 3134.

In New Zealand: For a complete list of books available from Penguins in New Zealand write to the Marketing Department, Penguin Books (N.Z.) Ltd, P.O. Box 4019, Auckland 10.

The Penguin English Library

THOMAS DE QUINCEY

RECOLLECTIONS OF THE LAKES AND THE LAKE POETS

Edited by David Wright

Thomas De Quincey, best known perhaps as the author of *Confessions of an English Opium-Eater*, wrote most of the work in this volume for *Tait's Magazine* between 1834 and 1840. It is immensely readable and alive – an anecdotal, conversational, contemporaneous portrait and account of Grasmere, Wordsworth, Coleridge and Southey, and so near the bone that Wordsworth and his family would have nothing further to do with De Quincey after it appeared. Within this first-hand biographical/critical discussion of the lives and works of these poets, De Quincey's life of Wordsworth may still be the best we have.

This edition contains the most complete collection of De Quincey's Lake papers to appear in a single volume and the text used here is that of the original articles.

Also published:

CONFESSIONS OF AN ENGLISH OPIUM EATER

Edited by Alethea Hayter

The Penguin English Library

THOMAS CARLYLE

SELECTED WRITINGS

Edited by Alan Shelston

Now remembered mainly as the impressionistic historian of the French Revolution and as a forerunner of the authoritarian ideologies of the twentieth century, Carlyle enjoyed in his long lifetime an immense reputation as a prophet and preacher. For an anonymous correspondent he was 'an honoured and trusted teacher', for Charles Dickens the man who 'knows everything', for Matthew Arnold a 'moral desperado'. Certainly the voice of Thomas Carlyle is one of the most compelling of nineteenth-century England.

This selection is intended to be representative of all stages of his career, rather than a 'Best of Carlyle'. It includes the whole of *Chartism* and chapters from *Sartor Resartus*, *The French Revolution*, *Heroes and Hero-Worship*, *Past and Present* and the history of *Frederick the Great*.

The Penguin English Library

MATTHEW ARNOLD

SELECTED PROSE

Edited by P. J. Keating

Matthew Arnold is too often studied in compartments – as his father's son, as poet, educationist, literary critic, moralist, or political theorist. But Arnold was one man, and one who could fill the role of official Victorian prophet. His prose – itself shaped in a classic mould of simplicty, clarity and brevity — is almost invariably inspired by one theme: 'how to find and keep high ideals' in an age of Barbarian aristocracy, Philistine middle classes and ignorant populace. He clearly saw the future as belonging to the masses and education was therefore central to his purpose.

For this volume P. J. Keating has selected those passages which make Arnold a living force for the modern reader. In addition to prefaces, essays and letters on literary criticism, education and other topics, he has included substantial extracts from *On Translating Homer, Essays in Criticism, Culture and Anarchy,* and the entertaining but neglected *Friendship's Garland.* Arnold's religious writings are excluded.

The Penguin English Library

EDWARD JOHN TRELAWNY

RECORDS OF SHELLEY, BYRON, AND THE AUTHOR

Edited by David Wright

Edward John Trelawny was one of the most curious figures of the English Romantic Movement and his *Records* is one of its oddest and most entertaining documents. An ill-educated adventurer and incorrigible romancer, he was fascinated, almost hypnotized, by the two poets when he joined them in Italy in 1822. His account of them, which includes the death of both, is the end-product of an obsession. Its concern is less with the accuracy of detailed observation than with the creation of myth, including the myth of himself as a Romantic hero. He belongs to that fellowship of writers who 'take truth as the warp into which a weft of imagination may be woven'. But the embroidery that results often 'makes explicit or at least illuminates some inherent truth or quality that strict facts may sometimes obscure'.